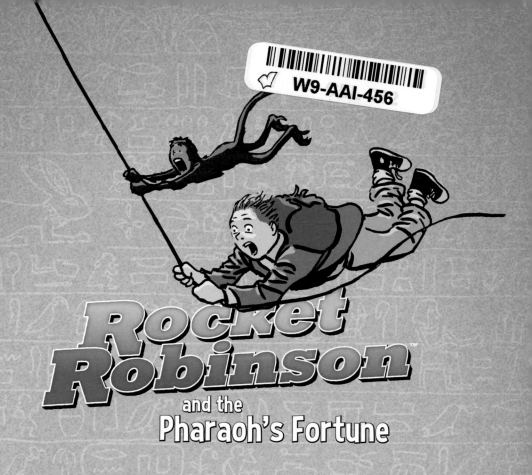

Rocket Robinson

and the
Pharaoh's Fortune

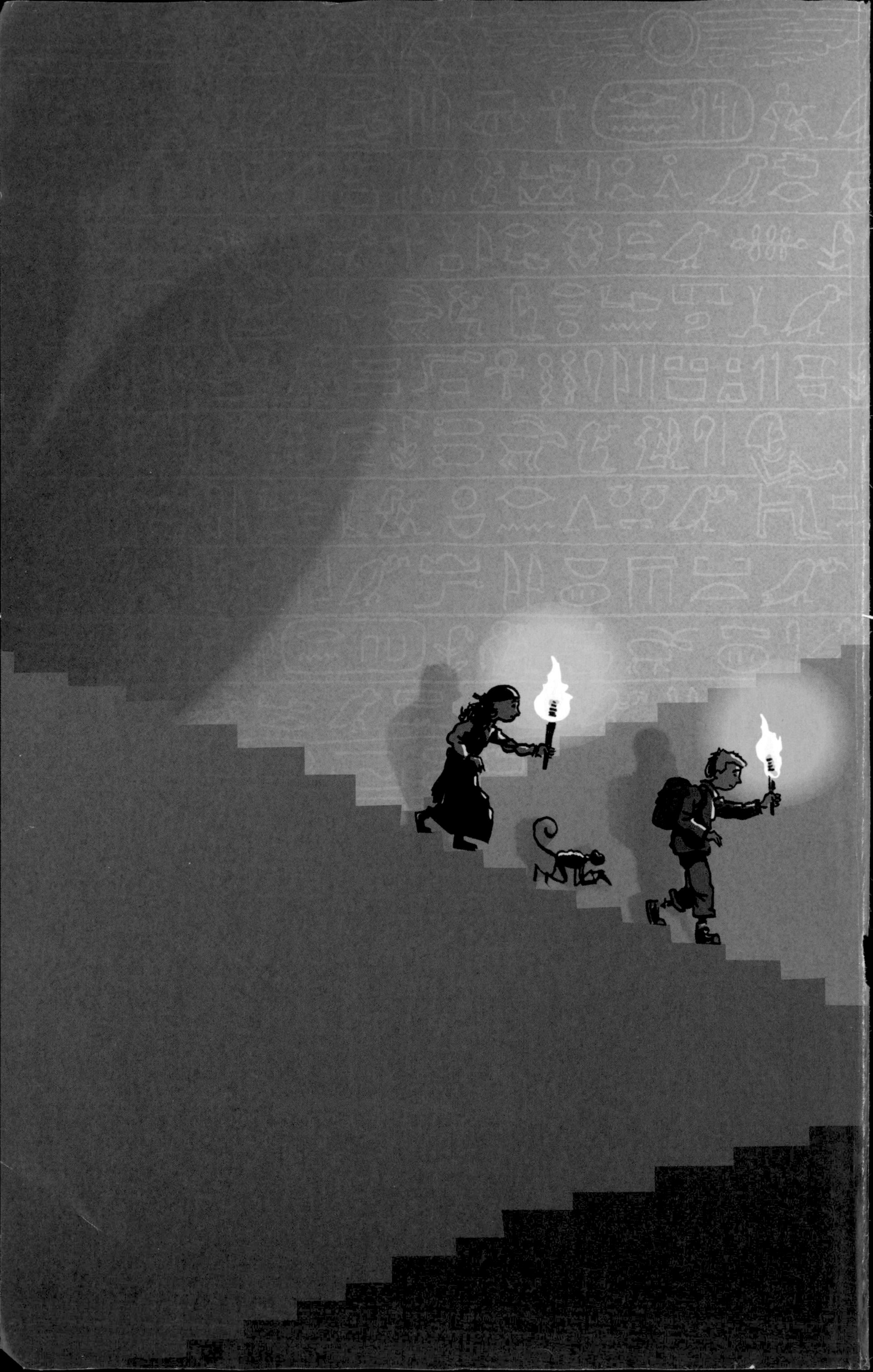

Rocket Robinson

and the
Pharaoh's Fortune

Written and illustrated by
SEAN O'NEILL

DARK HORSE BOOKS

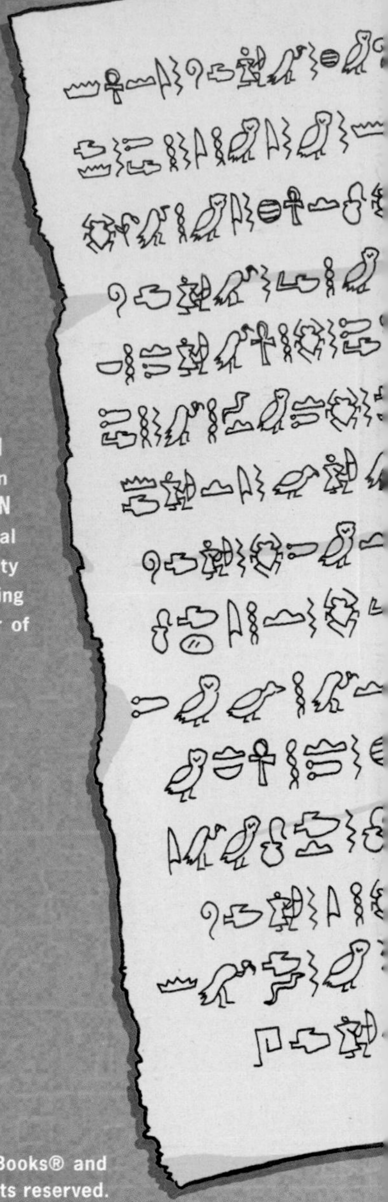

President & Publisher   **MIKE RICHARDSON**

Collection Editor   **SHANTEL LaROCQUE**

Collection Assistant Editors   **KATII O'BRIEN** and **BRETT ISRAEL**

Collection Designer   **CINDY CACEREZ-SPRAGUE**

Digital Art Technician   **CHRISTINA McKENZIE**

NEIL HANKERSON Executive Vice President **TOM WEDDLE** Chief Financial Officer **RANDY STRADLEY** Vice President of Publishing **NICK McWHORTER** Chief Business Development Officer **MATT PARKINSON** Vice President of Marketing **DALE LaFOUNTAIN** Vice President of Information Technology **CARA NIECE** Vice President of Production and Scheduling **MARK BERNARDI** Vice President of Book Trade and Digital Sales **KEN LIZZI** General Counsel **DAVE MARSHALL** Editor in Chief **DAVEY ESTRADA** Editorial Director **CHRIS WARNER** Senior Books Editor **CARY GRAZZINI** Director of Specialty Projects **LIA RIBACCHI** Art Director **VANESSA TODD-HOLMES** Director of Print Purchasing **MATT DRYER** Director of Digital Art and Prepress **MICHAEL GOMBOS** Director of International Publishing and Licensing **KARI YADRO** Director of Custom Programs

Published by Dark Horse Books
A division of Dark Horse Comics, Inc.
10956 SE Main Street
Milwaukie, OR 97222

RocketRobinson.com • DarkHorse.com
International Licensing: 503-905-2377

To find a comics shop in your area, visit ComicShopLocator.com.

First Dark Horse edition: May 2018
ISBN 978-1-50670-618-4

10 9 8 7 6 5 4 3 2 1
Printed in China

This book reprints *Rocket Robinson and the Pharaoh's Fortune* previously published by BoilerRoom Studios.

Library of Congress Cataloging-in-Publication Data

Names: O'Neill, Sean, 1968- author, illustrator.
Title: Rocket Robinson and the pharaoh's fortune / written and illustrated by Sean O'Neill.
Description: First Dark Horse edition. | Milwaukie, OR : Dark Horse Books, May 2018. | Series: Rocket Robinson ; 1 | Summary: Upon finding a note written in hieroglyphics, Rocket Robinson and his pet monkey team up with gypsy girl Nuri in 1933 Cairo to unscramble the code and locate an ancient pharaoh's fortune before thief Otto von Stcurm čan find it.
Identifiers: LCCN 2017052964 | ISBN 9781506706184
Subjects: LCSH: Graphic novels. | CYAC: Graphic novels. | Adventure and adventurers--Fiction. | Ciphers--Fiction. | Hieroglyphics--Fiction. | Cairo (Egypt)--Fiction. | Egypt--History--1919-1952--Fiction.
Classification: LCC PZ7.7.O55 Ro 2018 | DDC 741.5/973--dc23
LC record available at https://lccn.loc.gov/2017052964

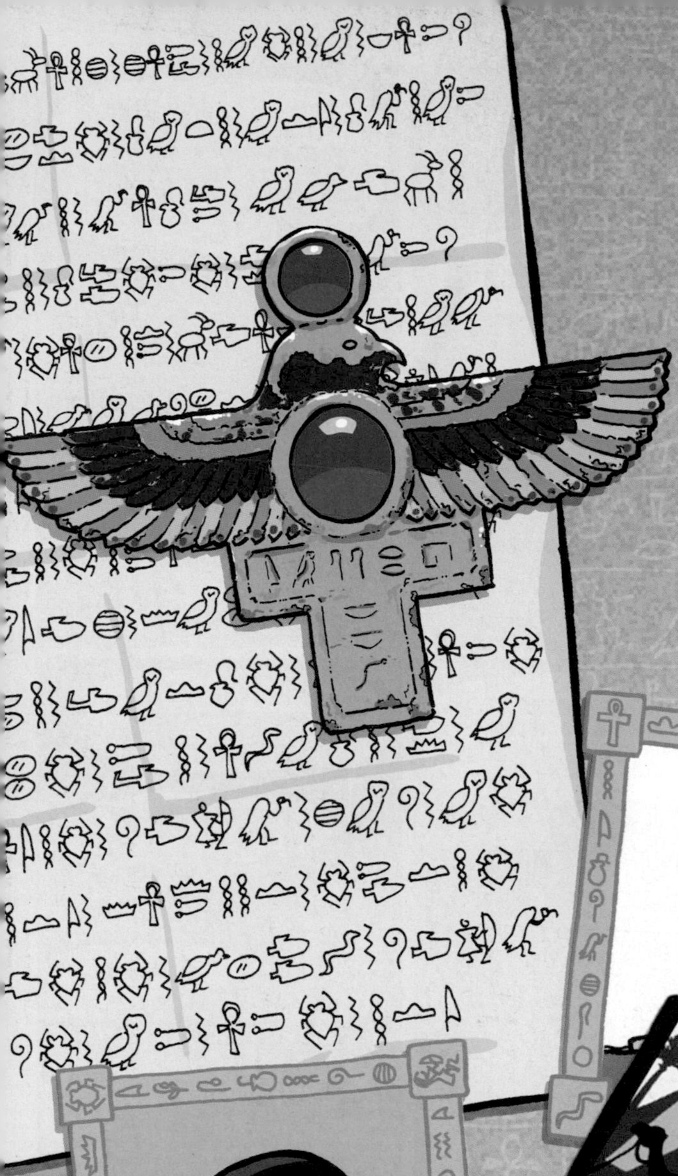

For
CHARLIE, VIOLET,
and JENNIFER

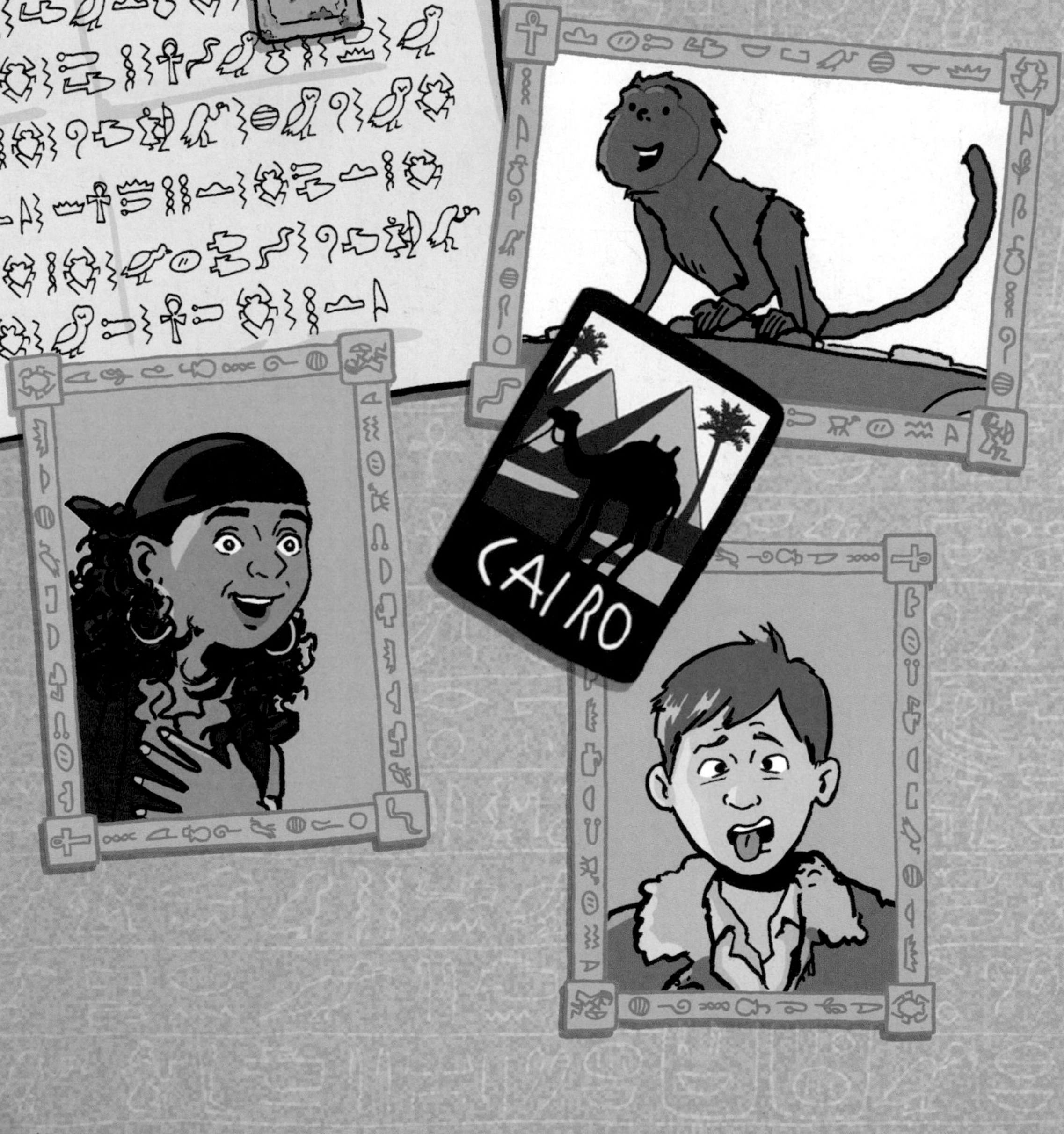
CAIRO

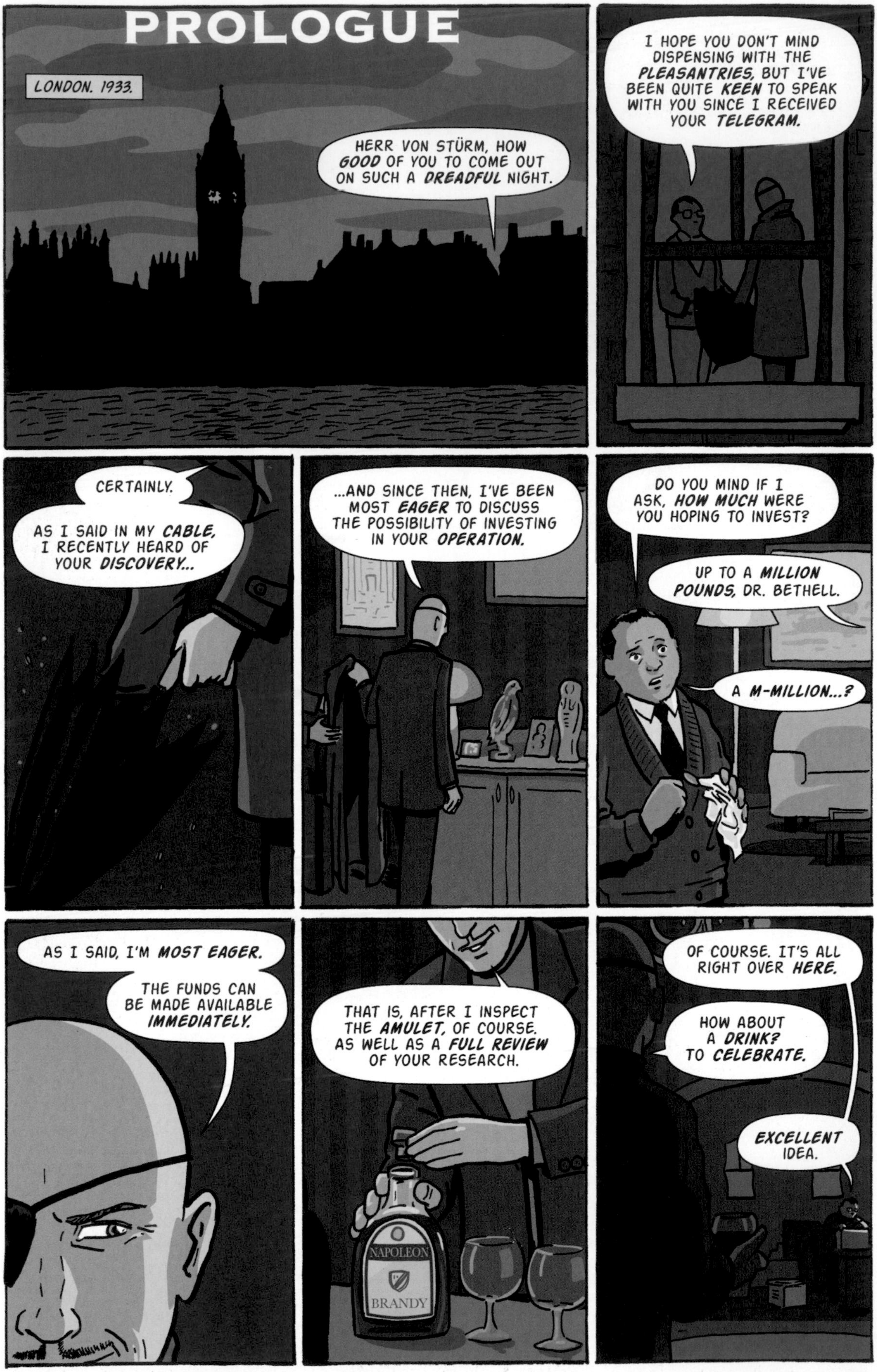
PROLOGUE
LONDON. 1933.
HERR VON STÜRM, HOW GOOD OF YOU TO COME OUT ON SUCH A DREADFUL NIGHT.
I HOPE YOU DON'T MIND DISPENSING WITH THE PLEASANTRIES, BUT I'VE BEEN QUITE KEEN TO SPEAK WITH YOU SINCE I RECEIVED YOUR TELEGRAM.
CERTAINLY.
AS I SAID IN MY CABLE, I RECENTLY HEARD OF YOUR DISCOVERY...
...AND SINCE THEN, I'VE BEEN MOST EAGER TO DISCUSS THE POSSIBILITY OF INVESTING IN YOUR OPERATION.
DO YOU MIND IF I ASK, HOW MUCH WERE YOU HOPING TO INVEST?
UP TO A MILLION POUNDS, DR. BETHELL.
A M-MILLION...?
AS I SAID, I'M MOST EAGER.
THE FUNDS CAN BE MADE AVAILABLE IMMEDIATELY.
THAT IS, AFTER I INSPECT THE AMULET, OF COURSE. AS WELL AS A FULL REVIEW OF YOUR RESEARCH.
NAPOLEON
BRANDY
OF COURSE. IT'S ALL RIGHT OVER HERE.
HOW ABOUT A DRINK? TO CELEBRATE.
EXCELLENT IDEA.

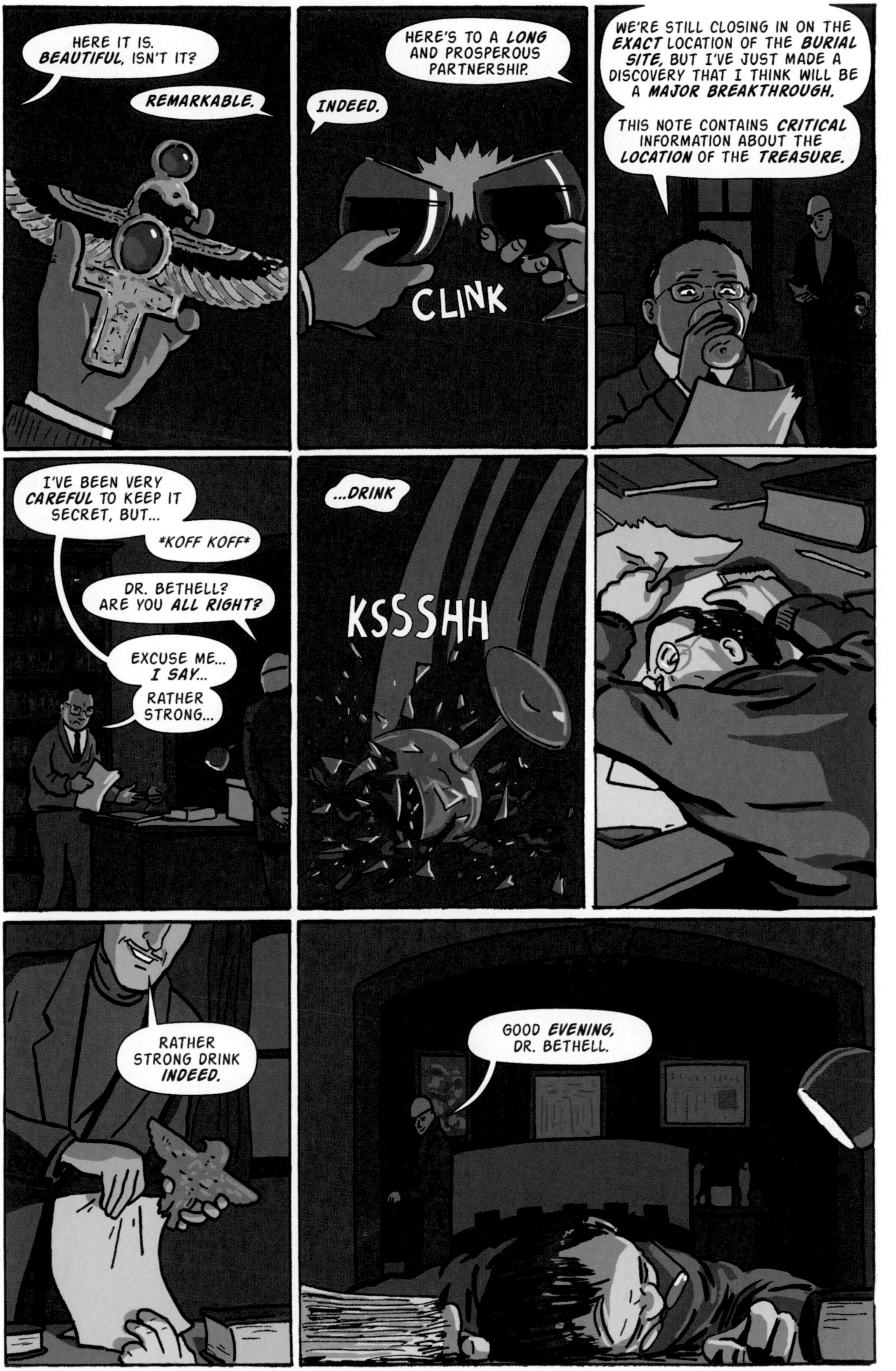
HERE IT IS. BEAUTIFUL, ISN'T IT?
REMARKABLE.
HERE'S TO A LONG AND PROSPEROUS PARTNERSHIP.
INDEED.
CLINK
WE'RE STILL CLOSING IN ON THE EXACT LOCATION OF THE BURIAL SITE, BUT I'VE JUST MADE A DISCOVERY THAT I THINK WILL BE A MAJOR BREAKTHROUGH.
THIS NOTE CONTAINS CRITICAL INFORMATION ABOUT THE LOCATION OF THE TREASURE.
I'VE BEEN VERY CAREFUL TO KEEP IT SECRET, BUT...
KOFF KOFF
DR. BETHELL? ARE YOU ALL RIGHT?
EXCUSE ME... I SAY...
RATHER STRONG...
...DRINK
KSSSHH
RATHER STRONG DRINK INDEED.
GOOD EVENING, DR. BETHELL.

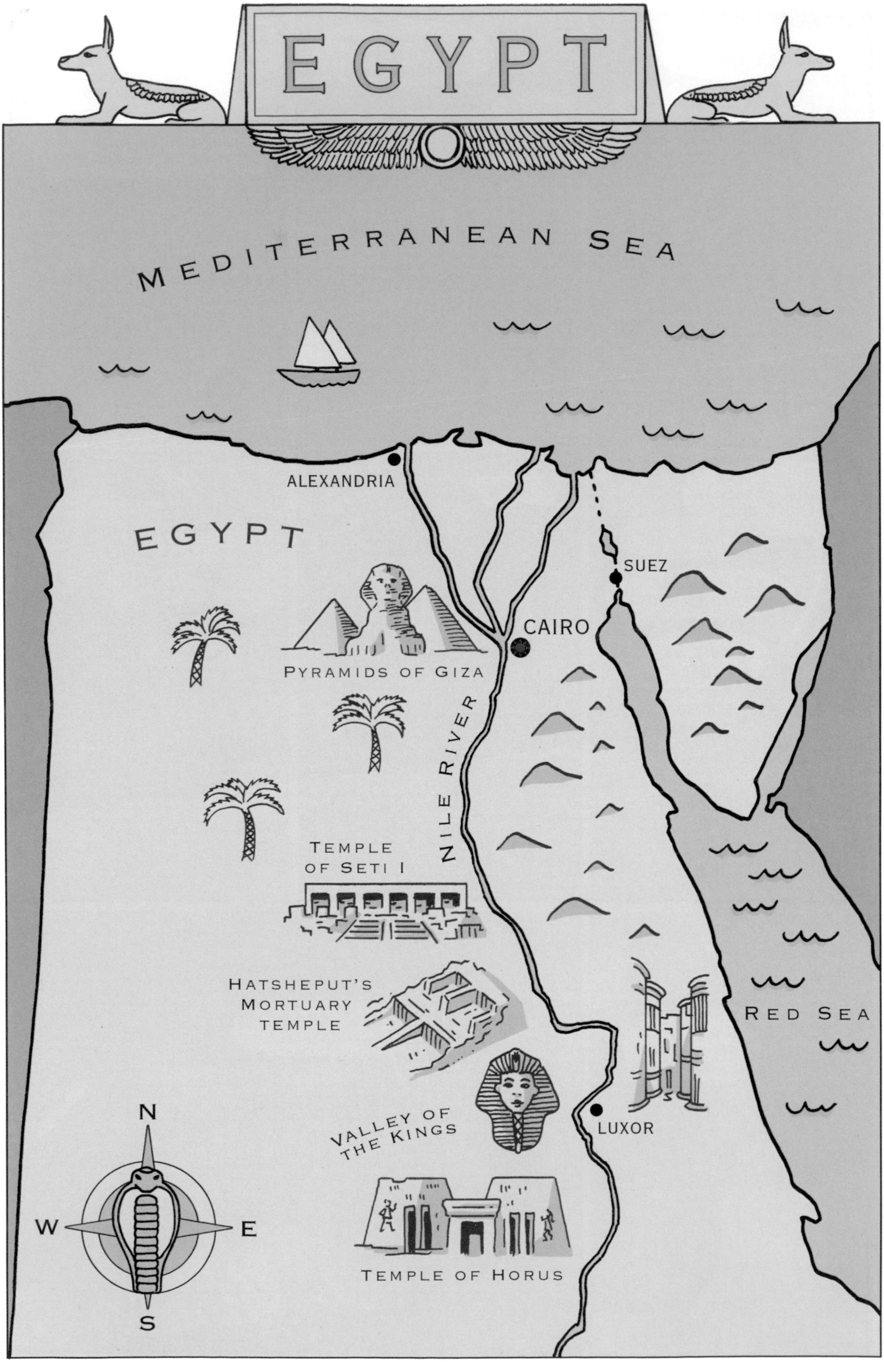
EGYPT
MEDITERRANEAN SEA
ALEXANDRIA
EGYPT
SUEZ
CAIRO
PYRAMIDS OF GIZA
NILE RIVER
TEMPLE OF SETI I
HATSHEPUT'S MORTUARY TEMPLE
RED SEA
LUXOR
VALLEY OF THE KINGS
TEMPLE OF HORUS
N
W
E
S

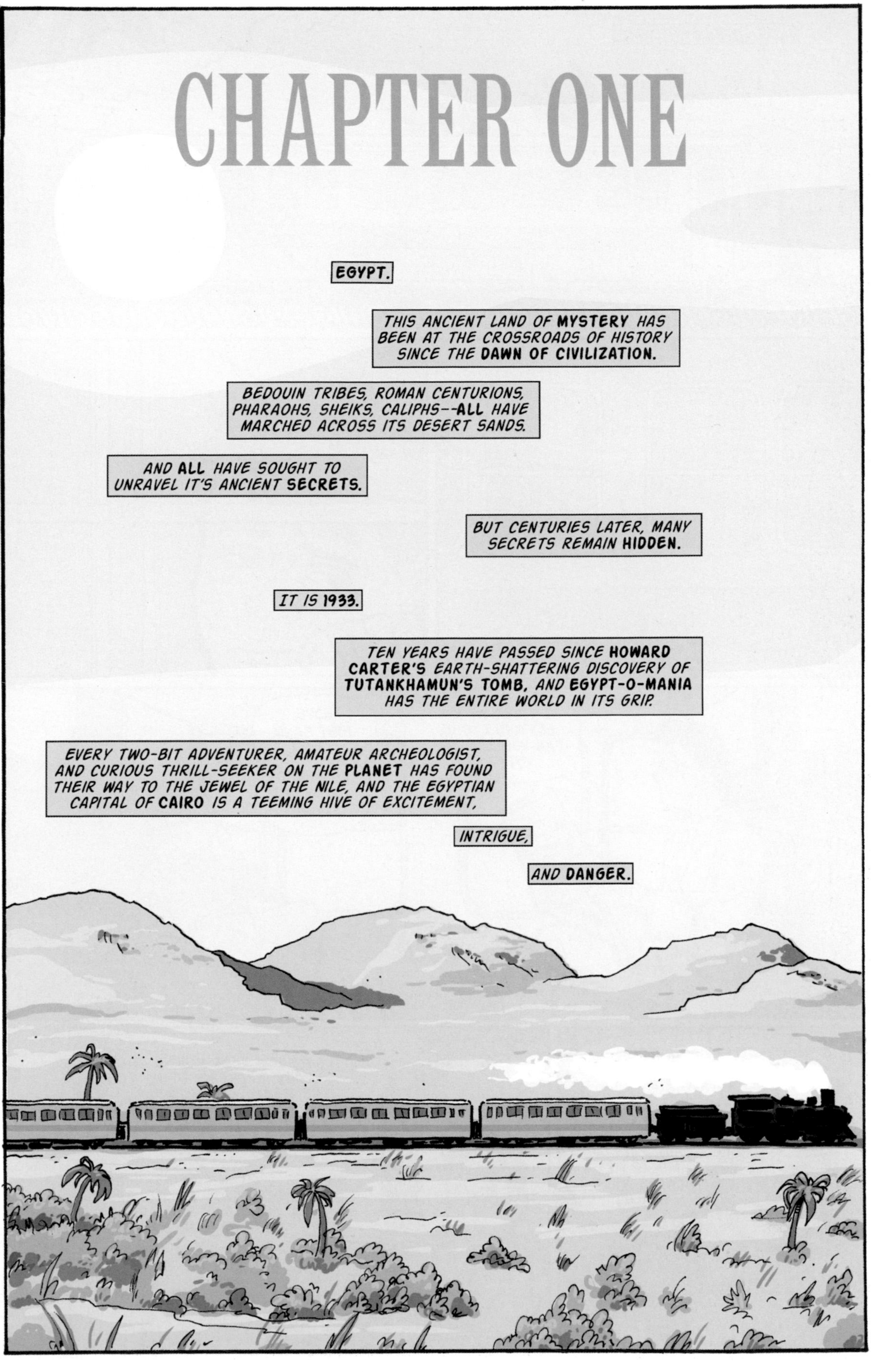
CHAPTER ONE
EGYPT.
THIS ANCIENT LAND OF MYSTERY HAS BEEN AT THE CROSSROADS OF HISTORY SINCE THE DAWN OF CIVILIZATION.
BEDOUIN TRIBES, ROMAN CENTURIONS, PHARAOHS, SHEIKS, CALIPHS--ALL HAVE MARCHED ACROSS ITS DESERT SANDS.
AND ALL HAVE SOUGHT TO UNRAVEL IT'S ANCIENT SECRETS.
BUT CENTURIES LATER, MANY SECRETS REMAIN HIDDEN.
IT IS 1933.
TEN YEARS HAVE PASSED SINCE HOWARD CARTER'S EARTH-SHATTERING DISCOVERY OF TUTANKHAMUN'S TOMB, AND EGYPT-O-MANIA HAS THE ENTIRE WORLD IN ITS GRIP.
EVERY TWO-BIT ADVENTURER, AMATEUR ARCHEOLOGIST, AND CURIOUS THRILL-SEEKER ON THE PLANET HAS FOUND THEIR WAY TO THE JEWEL OF THE NILE, AND THE EGYPTIAN CAPITAL OF CAIRO IS A TEEMING HIVE OF EXCITEMENT,
INTRIGUE,
AND DANGER.

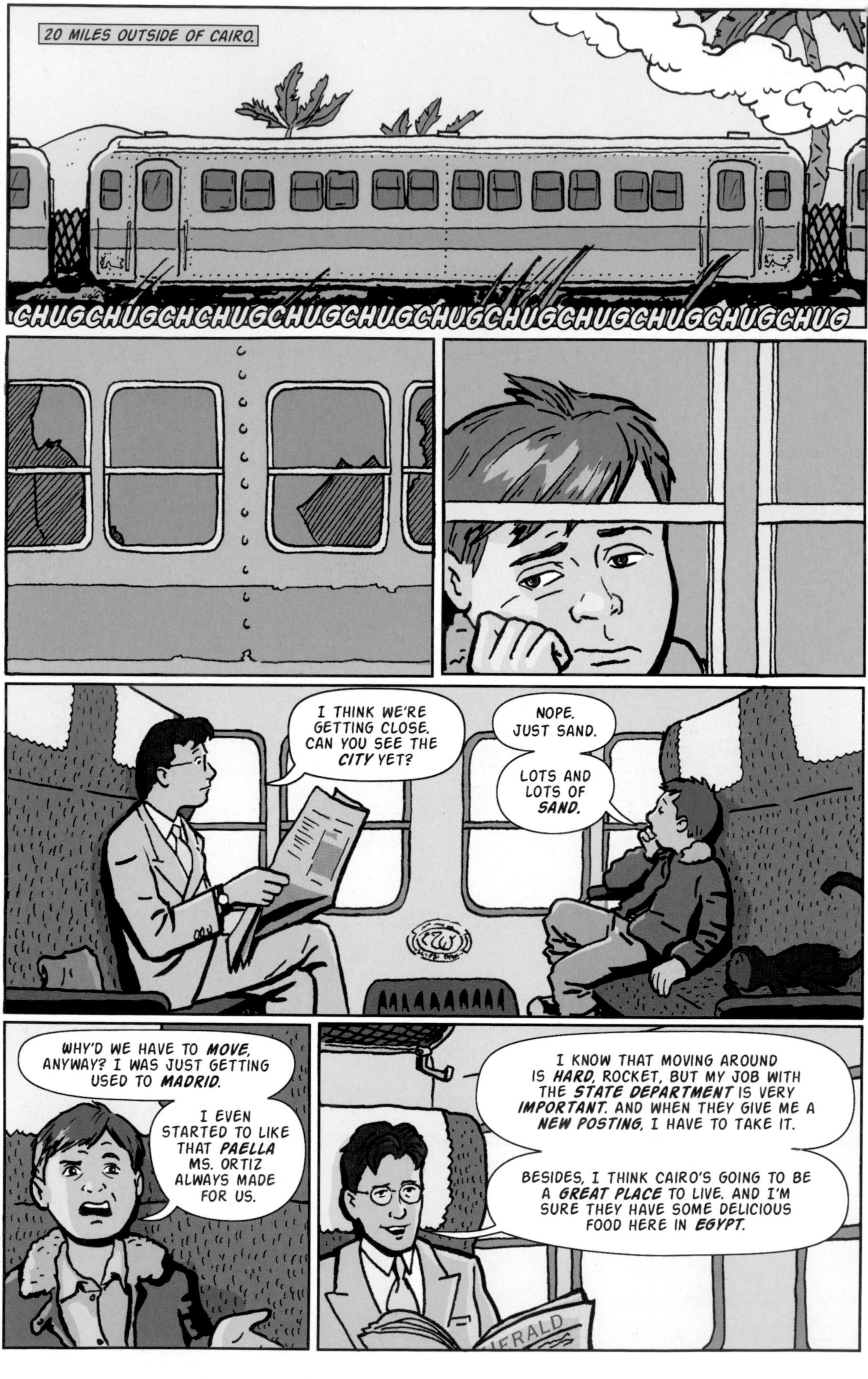
20 MILES OUTSIDE OF CAIRO.
CHUGCHUGCHUGCHUGCHUGCHUGCHUGCHUGCHUGCHUGCHUG
I THINK WE'RE GETTING CLOSE. CAN YOU SEE THE CITY YET?
NOPE. JUST SAND.
LOTS AND LOTS OF SAND.
WHY'D WE HAVE TO MOVE, ANYWAY? I WAS JUST GETTING USED TO MADRID.
I EVEN STARTED TO LIKE THAT PAELLA MS. ORTIZ ALWAYS MADE FOR US.
I KNOW THAT MOVING AROUND IS HARD, ROCKET, BUT MY JOB WITH THE STATE DEPARTMENT IS VERY IMPORTANT. AND WHEN THEY GIVE ME A NEW POSTING, I HAVE TO TAKE IT.
BESIDES, I THINK CAIRO'S GOING TO BE A GREAT PLACE TO LIVE. AND I'M SURE THEY HAVE SOME DELICIOUS FOOD HERE IN EGYPT.
HERALD

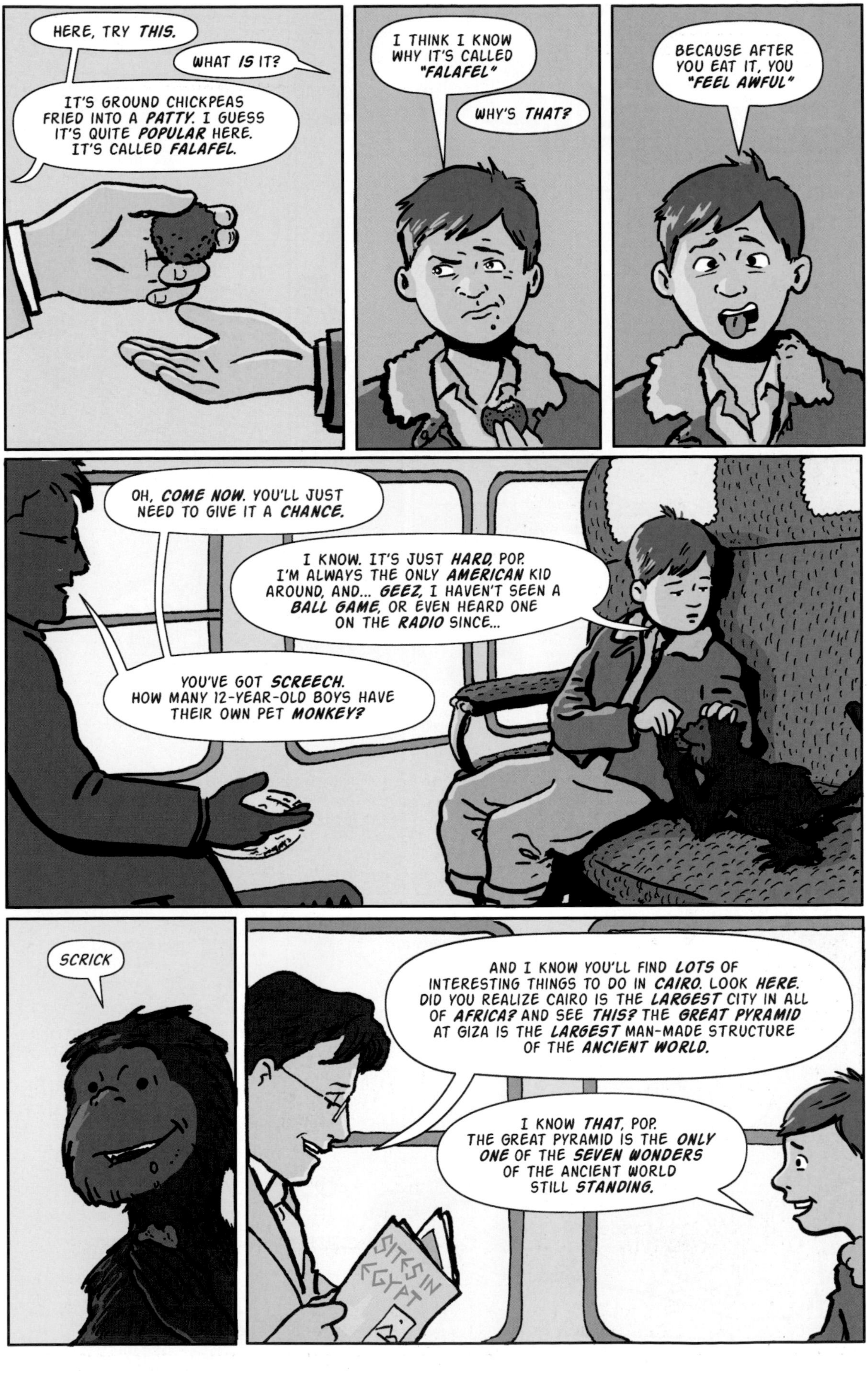
HERE, TRY THIS.
WHAT IS IT?
IT'S GROUND CHICKPEAS FRIED INTO A PATTY. I GUESS IT'S QUITE POPULAR HERE. IT'S CALLED FALAFEL.
I THINK I KNOW WHY IT'S CALLED "FALAFEL"
WHY'S THAT?
BECAUSE AFTER YOU EAT IT, YOU "FEEL AWFUL"
OH, COME NOW. YOU'LL JUST NEED TO GIVE IT A CHANCE.
I KNOW. IT'S JUST HARD, POP. I'M ALWAYS THE ONLY AMERICAN KID AROUND, AND... GEEZ, I HAVEN'T SEEN A BALL GAME, OR EVEN HEARD ONE ON THE RADIO SINCE...
YOU'VE GOT SCREECH. HOW MANY 12-YEAR-OLD BOYS HAVE THEIR OWN PET MONKEY?
SCRICK
AND I KNOW YOU'LL FIND LOTS OF INTERESTING THINGS TO DO IN CAIRO. LOOK HERE. DID YOU REALIZE CAIRO IS THE LARGEST CITY IN ALL OF AFRICA? AND SEE THIS? THE GREAT PYRAMID AT GIZA IS THE LARGEST MAN-MADE STRUCTURE OF THE ANCIENT WORLD.
SITES IN EGYPT
I KNOW THAT, POP. THE GREAT PYRAMID IS THE ONLY ONE OF THE SEVEN WONDERS OF THE ANCIENT WORLD STILL STANDING.

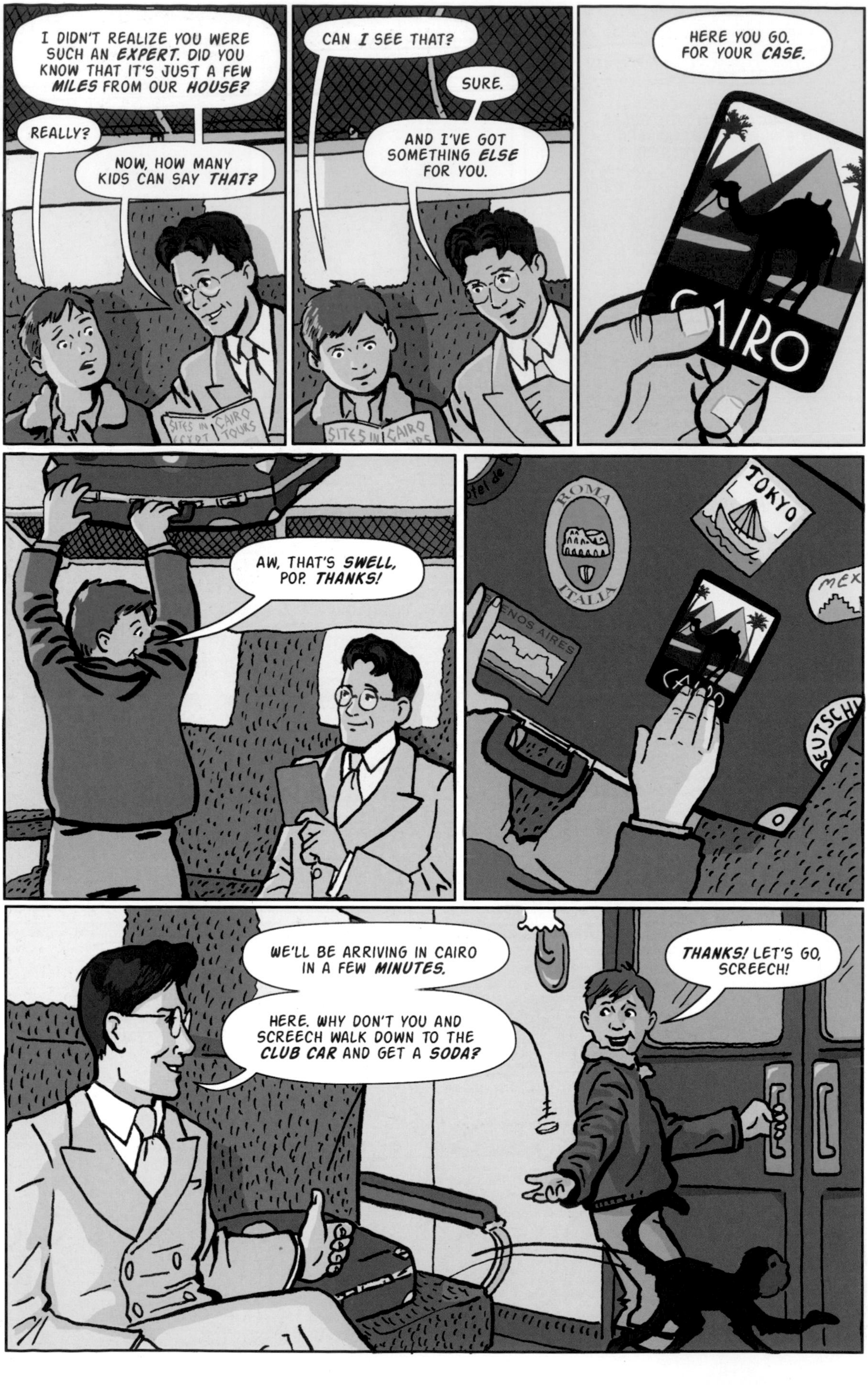
I DIDN'T REALIZE YOU WERE SUCH AN *EXPERT.* DID YOU KNOW THAT IT'S JUST A FEW *MILES* FROM OUR *HOUSE?*
REALLY?
NOW, HOW MANY KIDS CAN SAY *THAT?*
CAIRO TOURS
CAN *I* SEE THAT?
SURE.
AND I'VE GOT SOMETHING *ELSE* FOR YOU.
HERE YOU GO. FOR YOUR *CASE.*
CAIRO
AW, THAT'S *SWELL,* POP. *THANKS!*
ROMA
ITALIA
TOKYO
WE'LL BE ARRIVING IN CAIRO IN A FEW *MINUTES.*
HERE. WHY DON'T YOU AND SCREECH WALK DOWN TO THE *CLUB CAR* AND GET A *SODA?*
THANKS! LET'S GO, SCREECH!

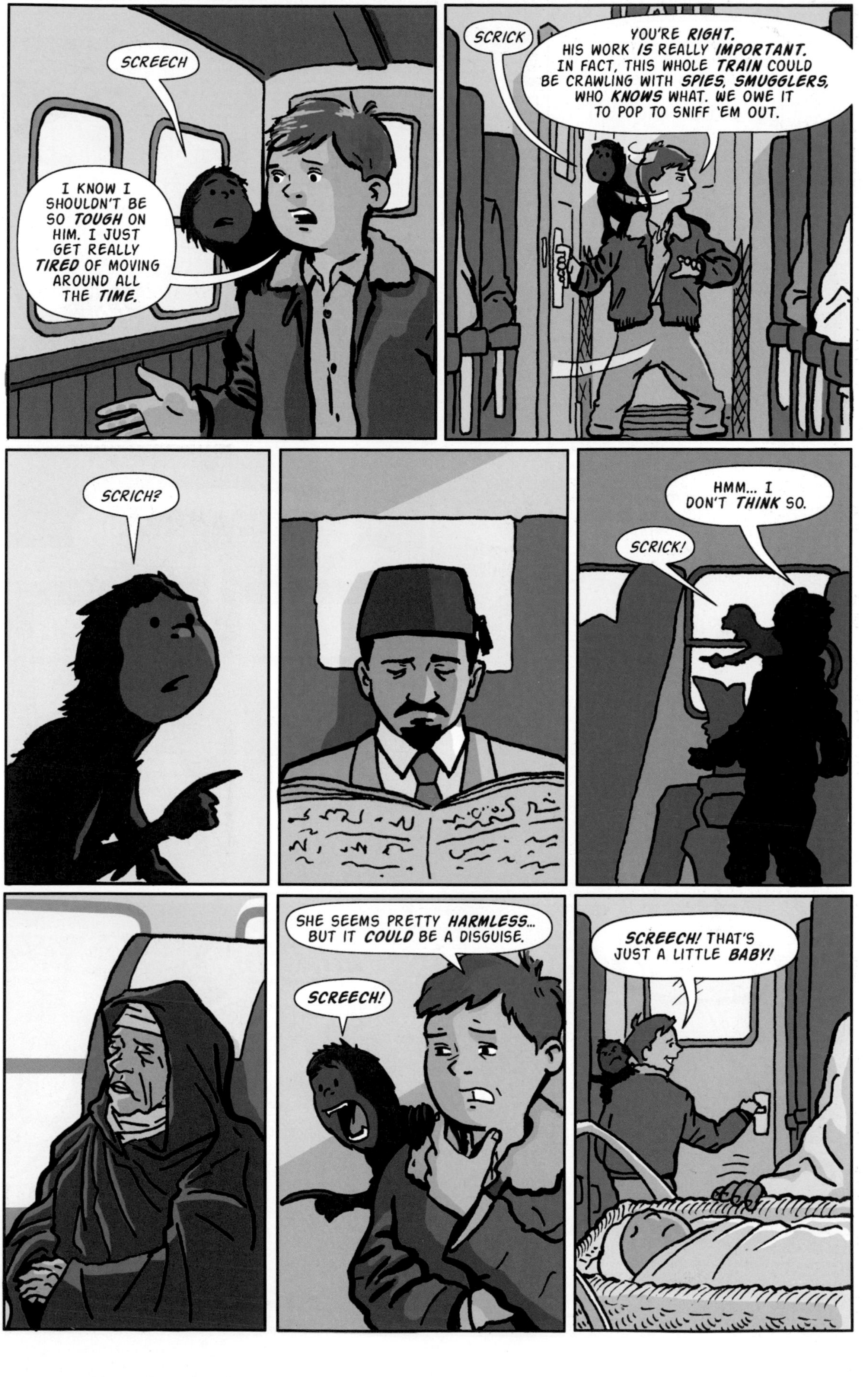
SCREECH
I KNOW I SHOULDN'T BE SO TOUGH ON HIM. I JUST GET REALLY TIRED OF MOVING AROUND ALL THE TIME.
SCRICK
YOU'RE RIGHT. HIS WORK IS REALLY IMPORTANT. IN FACT, THIS WHOLE TRAIN COULD BE CRAWLING WITH SPIES, SMUGGLERS, WHO KNOWS WHAT. WE OWE IT TO POP TO SNIFF 'EM OUT.
SCRICH?
HMM... I DON'T THINK SO.
SCRICK!
SHE SEEMS PRETTY HARMLESS... BUT IT COULD BE A DISGUISE.
SCREECH!
SCREECH! THAT'S JUST A LITTLE BABY!

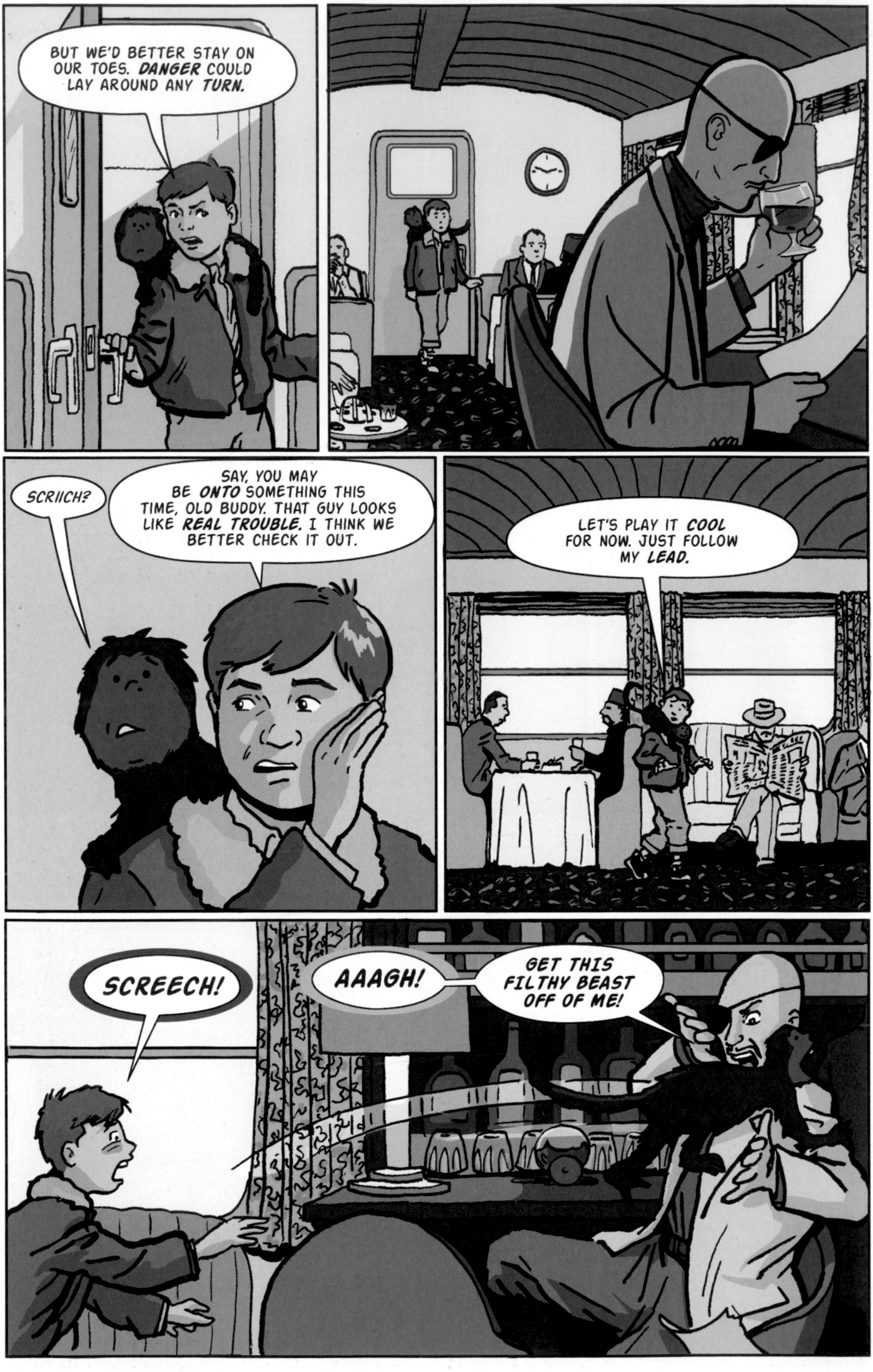

BUT WE'D BETTER STAY ON OUR TOES. DANGER COULD LAY AROUND ANY TURN.
SCRIICH?
SAY, YOU MAY BE ONTO SOMETHING THIS TIME, OLD BUDDY. THAT GUY LOOKS LIKE REAL TROUBLE. I THINK WE BETTER CHECK IT OUT.
LET'S PLAY IT COOL FOR NOW. JUST FOLLOW MY LEAD.
SCREECH!
AAAGH!
GET THIS FILTHY BEAST OFF OF ME!

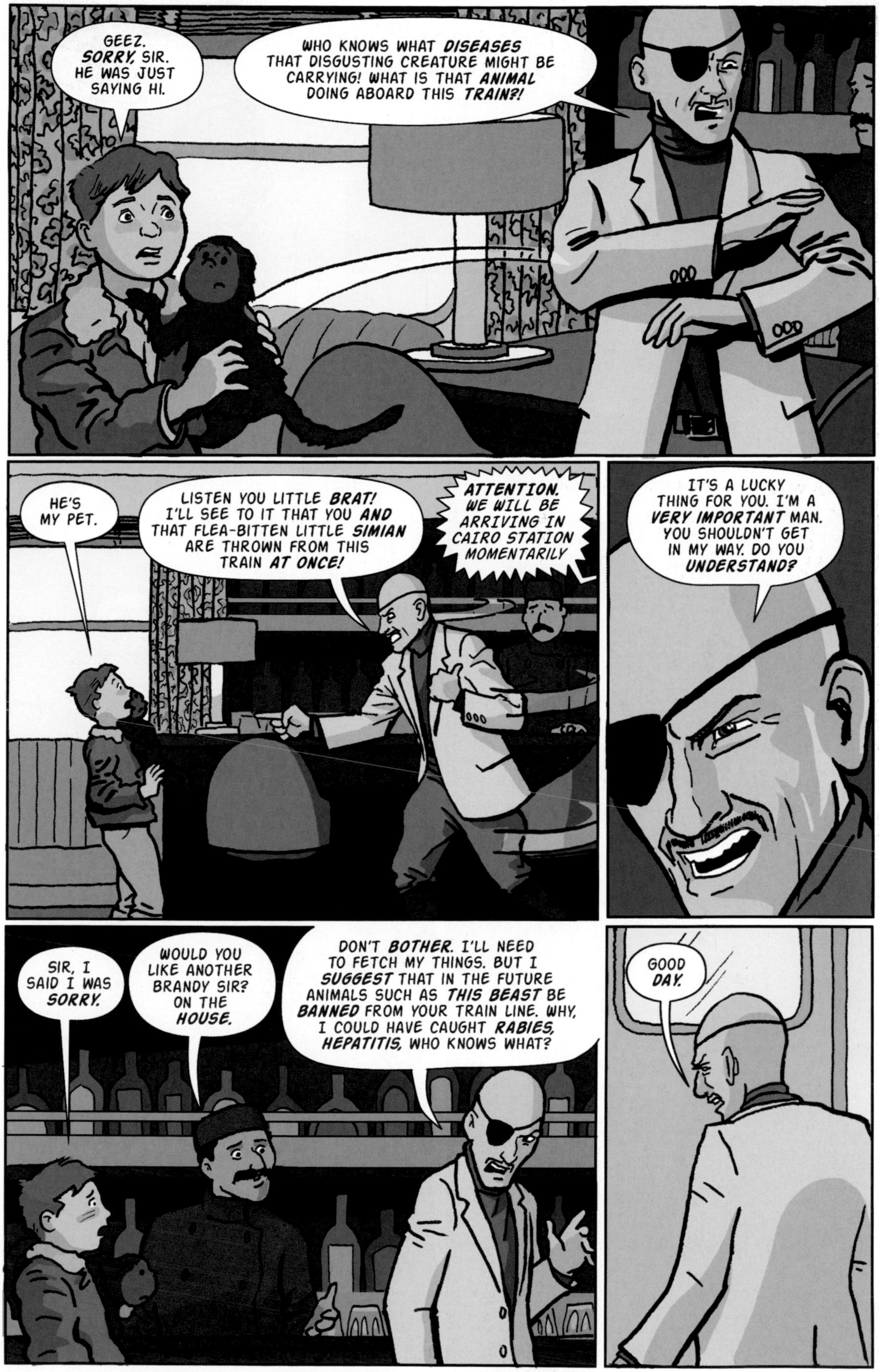
GEEZ. SORRY, SIR. HE WAS JUST SAYING HI.
WHO KNOWS WHAT DISEASES THAT DISGUSTING CREATURE MIGHT BE CARRYING! WHAT IS THAT ANIMAL DOING ABOARD THIS TRAIN?!
HE'S MY PET.
LISTEN YOU LITTLE BRAT! I'LL SEE TO IT THAT YOU AND THAT FLEA-BITTEN LITTLE SIMIAN ARE THROWN FROM THIS TRAIN AT ONCE!
ATTENTION. WE WILL BE ARRIVING IN CAIRO STATION MOMENTARILY
IT'S A LUCKY THING FOR YOU. I'M A VERY IMPORTANT MAN. YOU SHOULDN'T GET IN MY WAY. DO YOU UNDERSTAND?
SIR, I SAID I WAS SORRY.
WOULD YOU LIKE ANOTHER BRANDY SIR? ON THE HOUSE.
DON'T BOTHER. I'LL NEED TO FETCH MY THINGS. BUT I SUGGEST THAT IN THE FUTURE ANIMALS SUCH AS THIS BEAST BE BANNED FROM YOUR TRAIN LINE. WHY, I COULD HAVE CAUGHT RABIES, HEPATITIS, WHO KNOWS WHAT?
GOOD DAY.

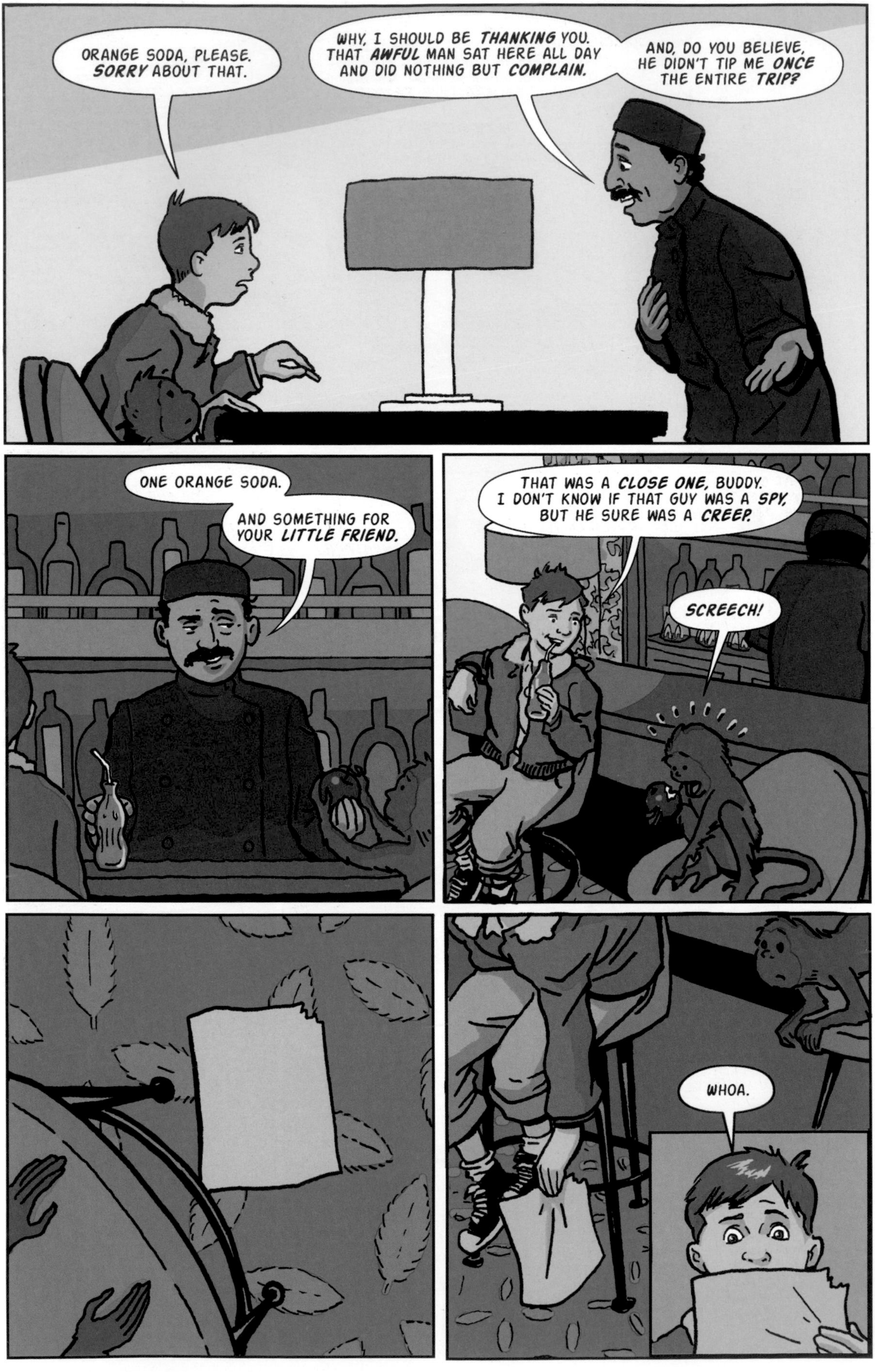

ORANGE SODA, PLEASE. SORRY ABOUT THAT.
WHY, I SHOULD BE THANKING YOU. THAT AWFUL MAN SAT HERE ALL DAY AND DID NOTHING BUT COMPLAIN.
AND, DO YOU BELIEVE, HE DIDN'T TIP ME ONCE THE ENTIRE TRIP?
ONE ORANGE SODA.
AND SOMETHING FOR YOUR LITTLE FRIEND.
THAT WAS A CLOSE ONE, BUDDY. I DON'T KNOW IF THAT GUY WAS A SPY, BUT HE SURE WAS A CREEP.
SCREECH!
WHOA.

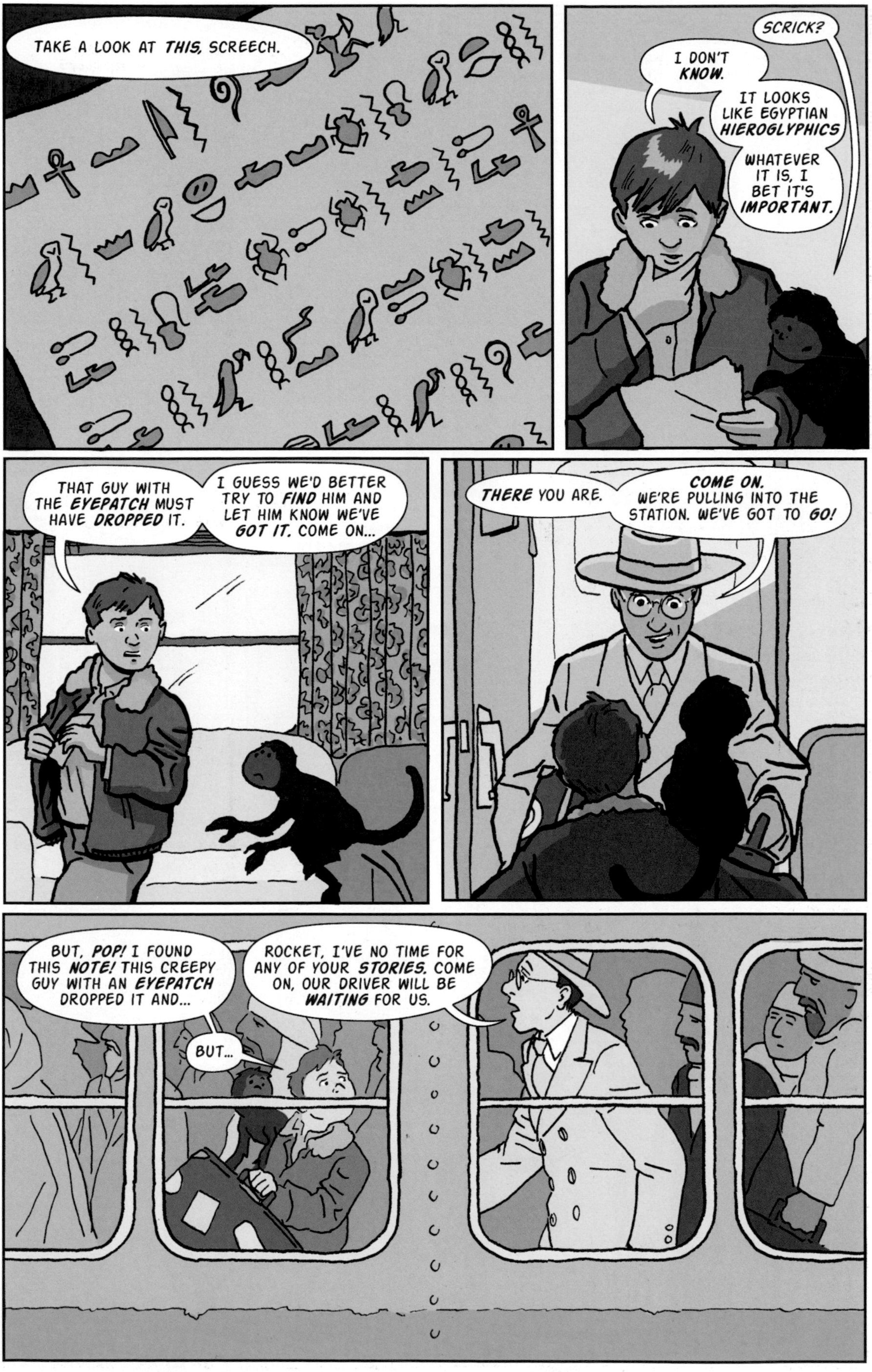
TAKE A LOOK AT THIS, SCREECH.
SCRICK?
I DON'T KNOW.
IT LOOKS LIKE EGYPTIAN HIEROGLYPHICS
WHATEVER IT IS, I BET IT'S IMPORTANT.
THAT GUY WITH THE EYEPATCH MUST HAVE DROPPED IT.
I GUESS WE'D BETTER TRY TO FIND HIM AND LET HIM KNOW WE'VE GOT IT. COME ON...
THERE YOU ARE.
COME ON. WE'RE PULLING INTO THE STATION. WE'VE GOT TO GO!
BUT, POP! I FOUND THIS NOTE! THIS CREEPY GUY WITH AN EYEPATCH DROPPED IT AND...
ROCKET, I'VE NO TIME FOR ANY OF YOUR STORIES. COME ON, OUR DRIVER WILL BE WAITING FOR US.
BUT...

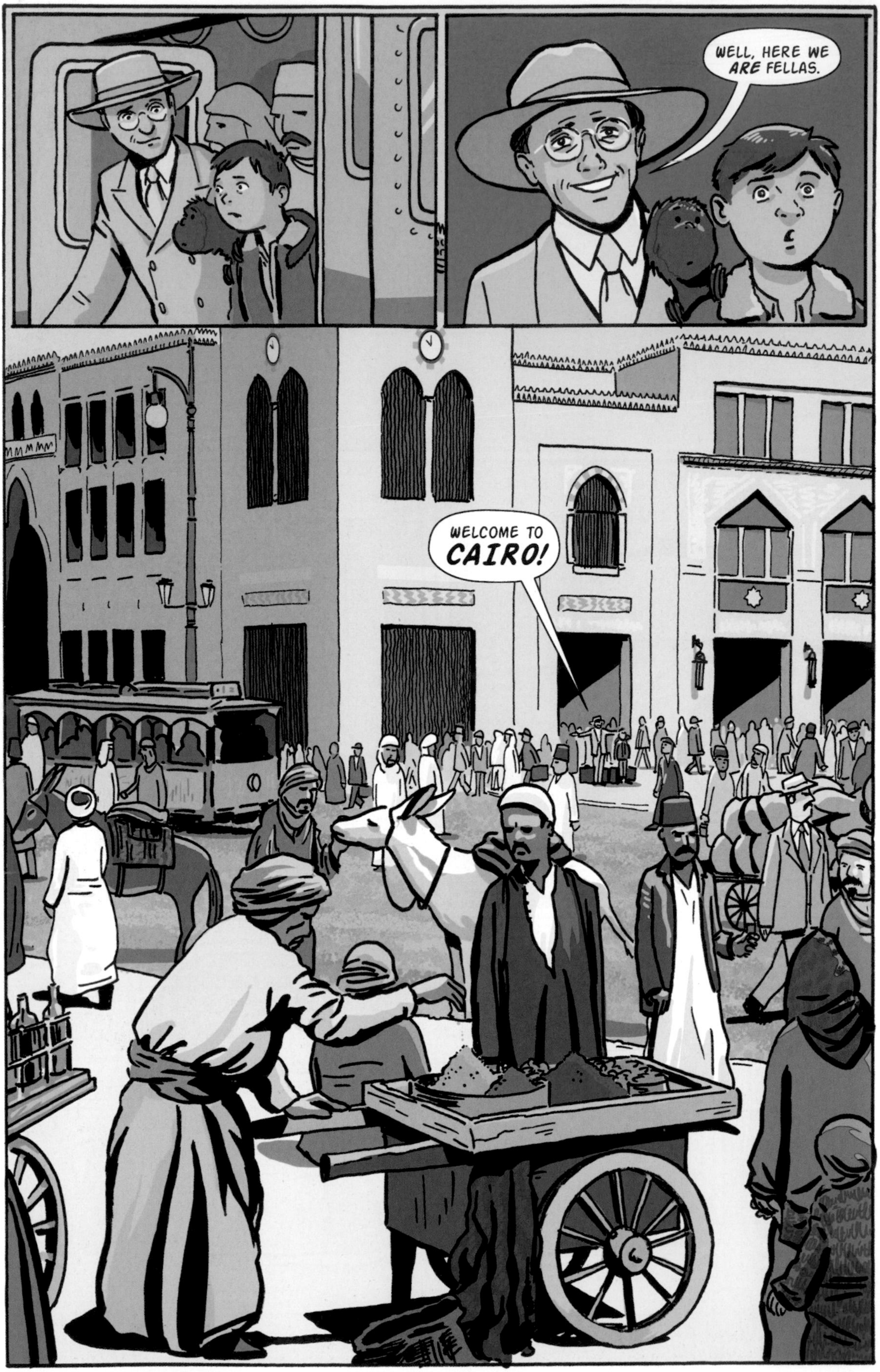
WELL, HERE WE ARE FELLAS.
WELCOME TO CAIRO!

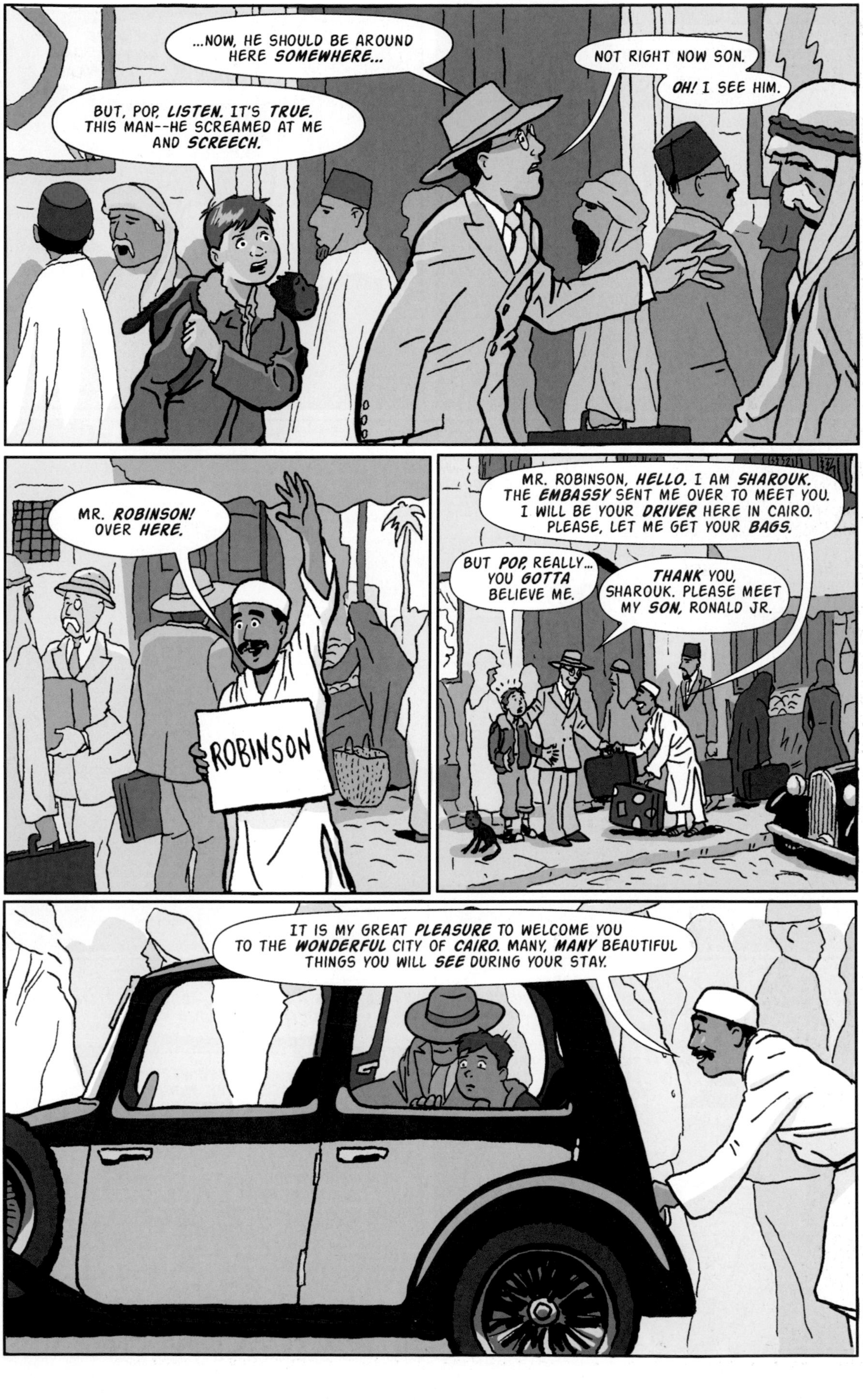
...NOW, HE SHOULD BE AROUND HERE SOMEWHERE...
BUT, POP, LISTEN. IT'S TRUE. THIS MAN--HE SCREAMED AT ME AND SCREECH.
NOT RIGHT NOW SON.
OH! I SEE HIM.
MR. ROBINSON! OVER HERE.
ROBINSON
MR. ROBINSON, HELLO. I AM SHAROUK. THE EMBASSY SENT ME OVER TO MEET YOU. I WILL BE YOUR DRIVER HERE IN CAIRO. PLEASE, LET ME GET YOUR BAGS.
BUT POP, REALLY... YOU GOTTA BELIEVE ME.
THANK YOU, SHAROUK. PLEASE MEET MY SON, RONALD JR.
IT IS MY GREAT PLEASURE TO WELCOME YOU TO THE WONDERFUL CITY OF CAIRO. MANY, MANY BEAUTIFUL THINGS YOU WILL SEE DURING YOUR STAY.

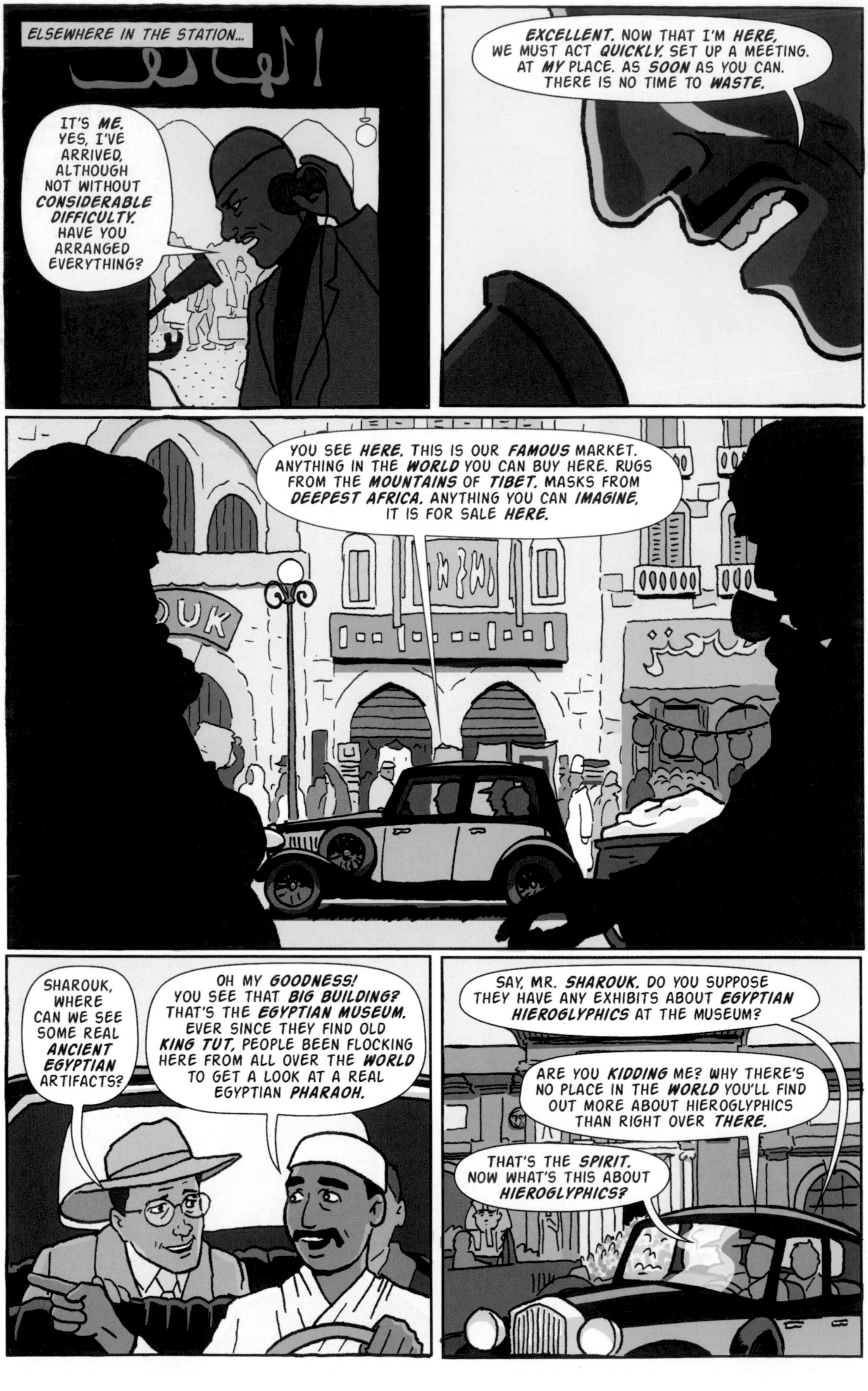
ELSEWHERE IN THE STATION...
IT'S ME. YES, I'VE ARRIVED, ALTHOUGH NOT WITHOUT CONSIDERABLE DIFFICULTY. HAVE YOU ARRANGED EVERYTHING?
EXCELLENT. NOW THAT I'M HERE, WE MUST ACT QUICKLY. SET UP A MEETING. AT MY PLACE. AS SOON AS YOU CAN. THERE IS NO TIME TO WASTE.
YOU SEE HERE. THIS IS OUR FAMOUS MARKET. ANYTHING IN THE WORLD YOU CAN BUY HERE. RUGS FROM THE MOUNTAINS OF TIBET. MASKS FROM DEEPEST AFRICA. ANYTHING YOU CAN IMAGINE, IT IS FOR SALE HERE.
OUK
SHAROUK, WHERE CAN WE SEE SOME REAL ANCIENT EGYPTIAN ARTIFACTS?
OH MY GOODNESS! YOU SEE THAT BIG BUILDING? THAT'S THE EGYPTIAN MUSEUM. EVER SINCE THEY FIND OLD KING TUT, PEOPLE BEEN FLOCKING HERE FROM ALL OVER THE WORLD TO GET A LOOK AT A REAL EGYPTIAN PHARAOH.
SAY, MR. SHAROUK. DO YOU SUPPOSE THEY HAVE ANY EXHIBITS ABOUT EGYPTIAN HIEROGLYPHICS AT THE MUSEUM?
ARE YOU KIDDING ME? WHY THERE'S NO PLACE IN THE WORLD YOU'LL FIND OUT MORE ABOUT HIEROGLYPHICS THAN RIGHT OVER THERE.
THAT'S THE SPIRIT. NOW WHAT'S THIS ABOUT HIEROGLYPHICS?

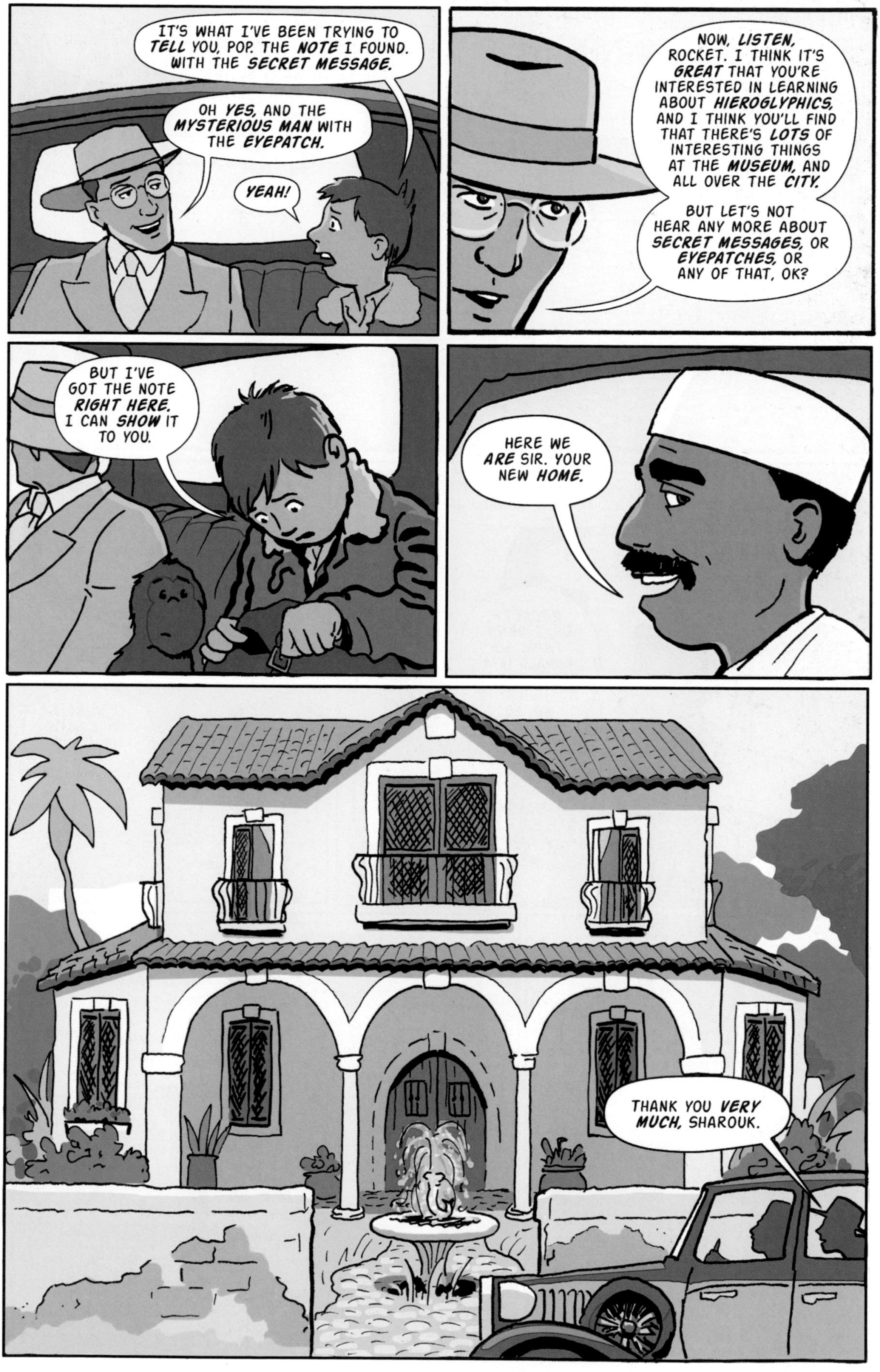
IT'S WHAT I'VE BEEN TRYING TO TELL YOU, POP. THE NOTE I FOUND. WITH THE SECRET MESSAGE.
OH YES, AND THE MYSTERIOUS MAN WITH THE EYEPATCH.
YEAH!
NOW, LISTEN, ROCKET. I THINK IT'S GREAT THAT YOU'RE INTERESTED IN LEARNING ABOUT HIEROGLYPHICS, AND I THINK YOU'LL FIND THAT THERE'S LOTS OF INTERESTING THINGS AT THE MUSEUM, AND ALL OVER THE CITY.
BUT LET'S NOT HEAR ANY MORE ABOUT SECRET MESSAGES, OR EYEPATCHES, OR ANY OF THAT, OK?
BUT I'VE GOT THE NOTE RIGHT HERE. I CAN SHOW IT TO YOU.
HERE WE ARE SIR. YOUR NEW HOME.
THANK YOU VERY MUCH, SHAROUK.

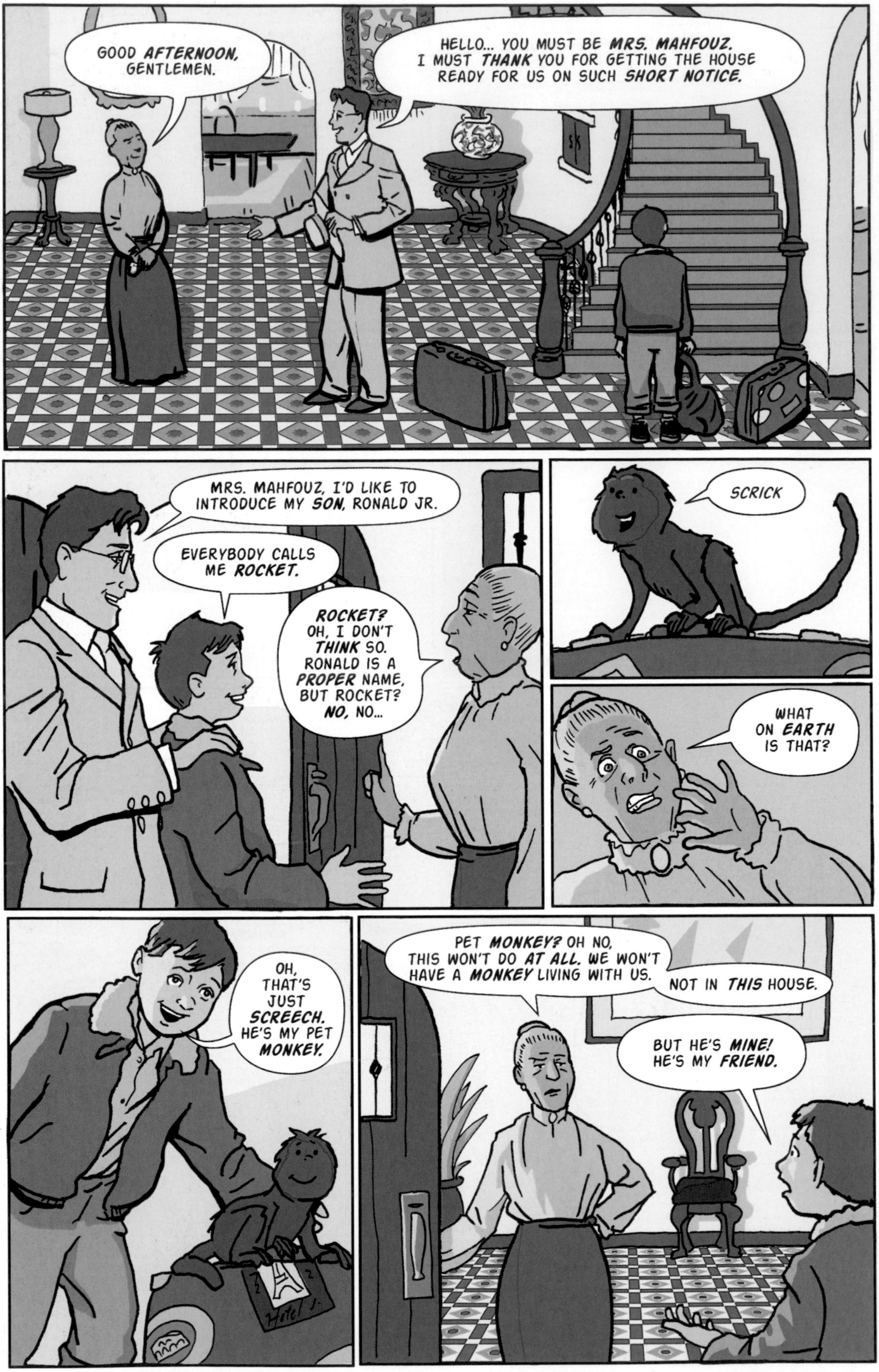
GOOD AFTERNOON, GENTLEMEN.
HELLO... YOU MUST BE MRS. MAHFOUZ. I MUST THANK YOU FOR GETTING THE HOUSE READY FOR US ON SUCH SHORT NOTICE.
MRS. MAHFOUZ, I'D LIKE TO INTRODUCE MY SON, RONALD JR.
EVERYBODY CALLS ME ROCKET.
ROCKET? OH, I DON'T THINK SO. RONALD IS A PROPER NAME, BUT ROCKET? NO, NO...
SCRICK
WHAT ON EARTH IS THAT?
OH, THAT'S JUST SCREECH. HE'S MY PET MONKEY.
PET MONKEY? OH NO, THIS WON'T DO AT ALL. WE WON'T HAVE A MONKEY LIVING WITH US.
NOT IN THIS HOUSE.
BUT HE'S MINE! HE'S MY FRIEND.

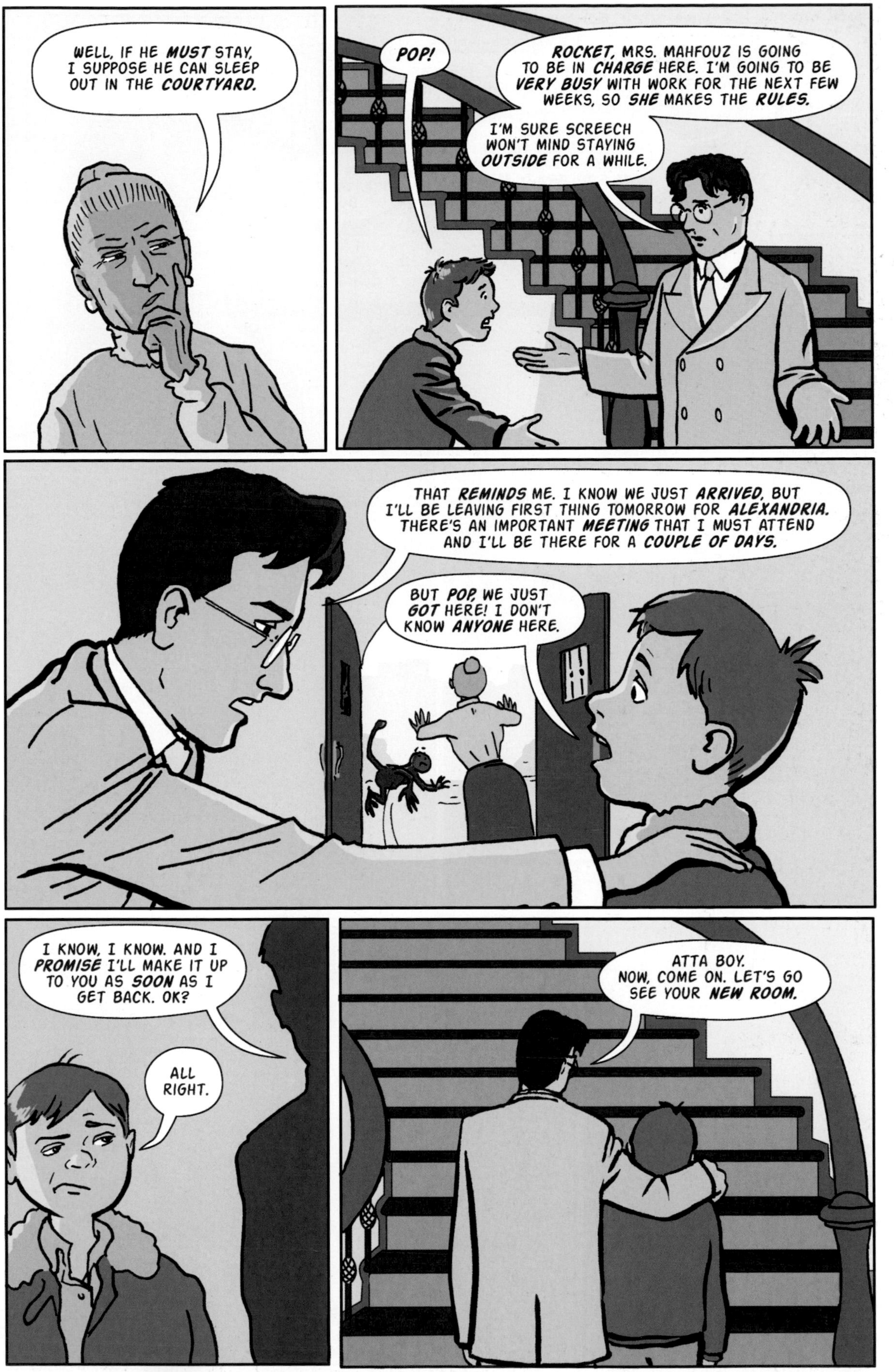
WELL, IF HE MUST STAY, I SUPPOSE HE CAN SLEEP OUT IN THE COURTYARD.
POP!
ROCKET, MRS. MAHFOUZ IS GOING TO BE IN CHARGE HERE. I'M GOING TO BE VERY BUSY WITH WORK FOR THE NEXT FEW WEEKS, SO SHE MAKES THE RULES.
I'M SURE SCREECH WON'T MIND STAYING OUTSIDE FOR A WHILE.
THAT REMINDS ME. I KNOW WE JUST ARRIVED, BUT I'LL BE LEAVING FIRST THING TOMORROW FOR ALEXANDRIA. THERE'S AN IMPORTANT MEETING THAT I MUST ATTEND AND I'LL BE THERE FOR A COUPLE OF DAYS.
BUT POP, WE JUST GOT HERE! I DON'T KNOW ANYONE HERE.
I KNOW, I KNOW. AND I PROMISE I'LL MAKE IT UP TO YOU AS SOON AS I GET BACK. OK?
ALL RIGHT.
ATTA BOY. NOW, COME ON. LET'S GO SEE YOUR NEW ROOM.

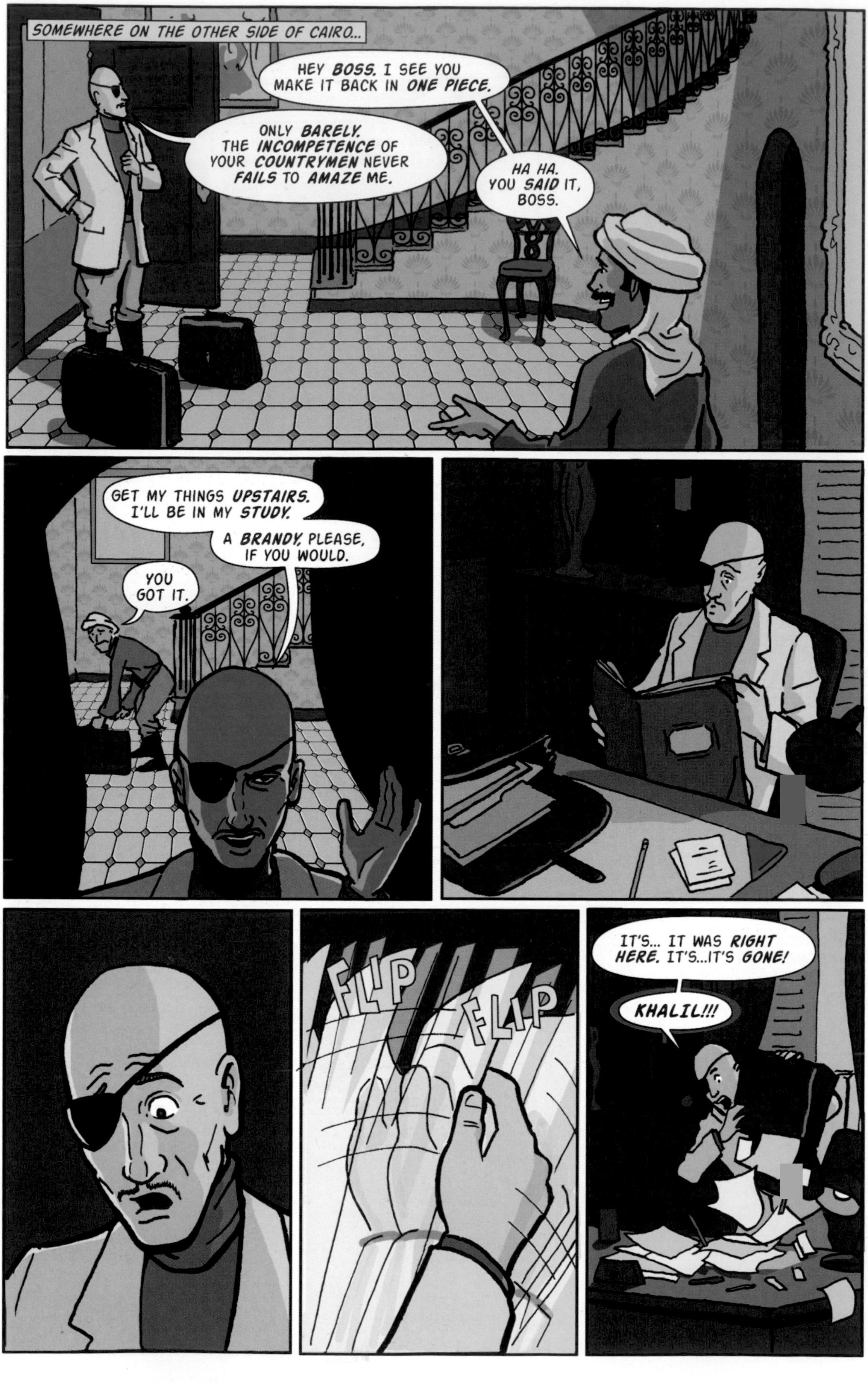
SOMEWHERE ON THE OTHER SIDE OF CAIRO...
HEY BOSS. I SEE YOU MAKE IT BACK IN ONE PIECE.
ONLY BARELY. THE INCOMPETENCE OF YOUR COUNTRYMEN NEVER FAILS TO AMAZE ME.
HA HA. YOU SAID IT, BOSS.
GET MY THINGS UPSTAIRS. I'LL BE IN MY STUDY.
A BRANDY, PLEASE, IF YOU WOULD.
YOU GOT IT.
FLIP
FLIP
IT'S... IT WAS RIGHT HERE. IT'S...IT'S GONE!
KHALIL!!!

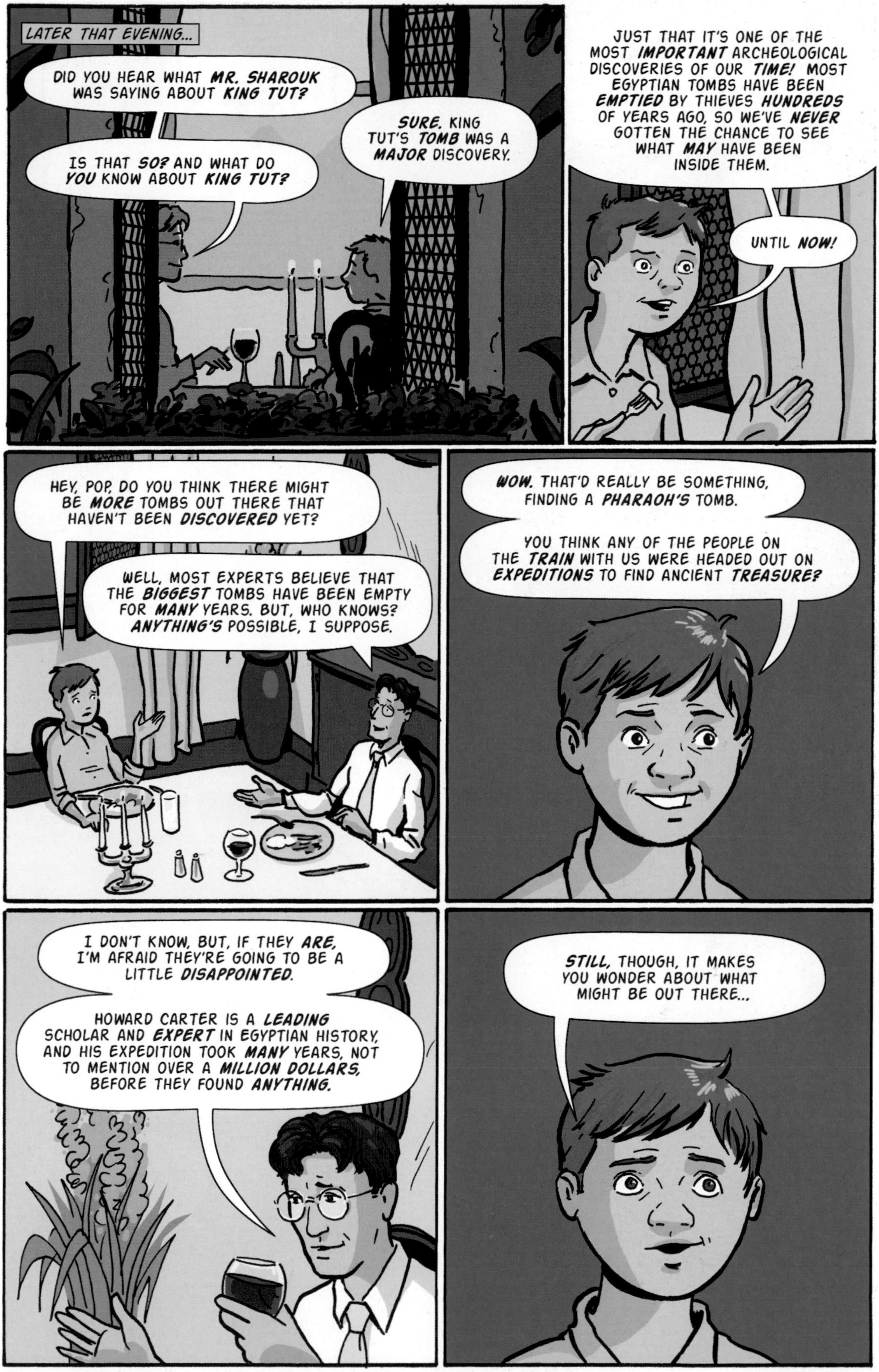

LATER THAT EVENING...
DID YOU HEAR WHAT MR. SHAROUK WAS SAYING ABOUT KING TUT?
IS THAT SO? AND WHAT DO YOU KNOW ABOUT KING TUT?
SURE. KING TUT'S TOMB WAS A MAJOR DISCOVERY.
JUST THAT IT'S ONE OF THE MOST IMPORTANT ARCHEOLOGICAL DISCOVERIES OF OUR TIME! MOST EGYPTIAN TOMBS HAVE BEEN EMPTIED BY THIEVES HUNDREDS OF YEARS AGO, SO WE'VE NEVER GOTTEN THE CHANCE TO SEE WHAT MAY HAVE BEEN INSIDE THEM.
UNTIL NOW!
HEY, POP, DO YOU THINK THERE MIGHT BE MORE TOMBS OUT THERE THAT HAVEN'T BEEN DISCOVERED YET?
WELL, MOST EXPERTS BELIEVE THAT THE BIGGEST TOMBS HAVE BEEN EMPTY FOR MANY YEARS. BUT, WHO KNOWS? ANYTHING'S POSSIBLE, I SUPPOSE.
WOW. THAT'D REALLY BE SOMETHING, FINDING A PHARAOH'S TOMB.
YOU THINK ANY OF THE PEOPLE ON THE TRAIN WITH US WERE HEADED OUT ON EXPEDITIONS TO FIND ANCIENT TREASURE?
I DON'T KNOW, BUT, IF THEY ARE, I'M AFRAID THEY'RE GOING TO BE A LITTLE DISAPPOINTED.
HOWARD CARTER IS A LEADING SCHOLAR AND EXPERT IN EGYPTIAN HISTORY, AND HIS EXPEDITION TOOK MANY YEARS, NOT TO MENTION OVER A MILLION DOLLARS, BEFORE THEY FOUND ANYTHING.
STILL, THOUGH, IT MAKES YOU WONDER ABOUT WHAT MIGHT BE OUT THERE...

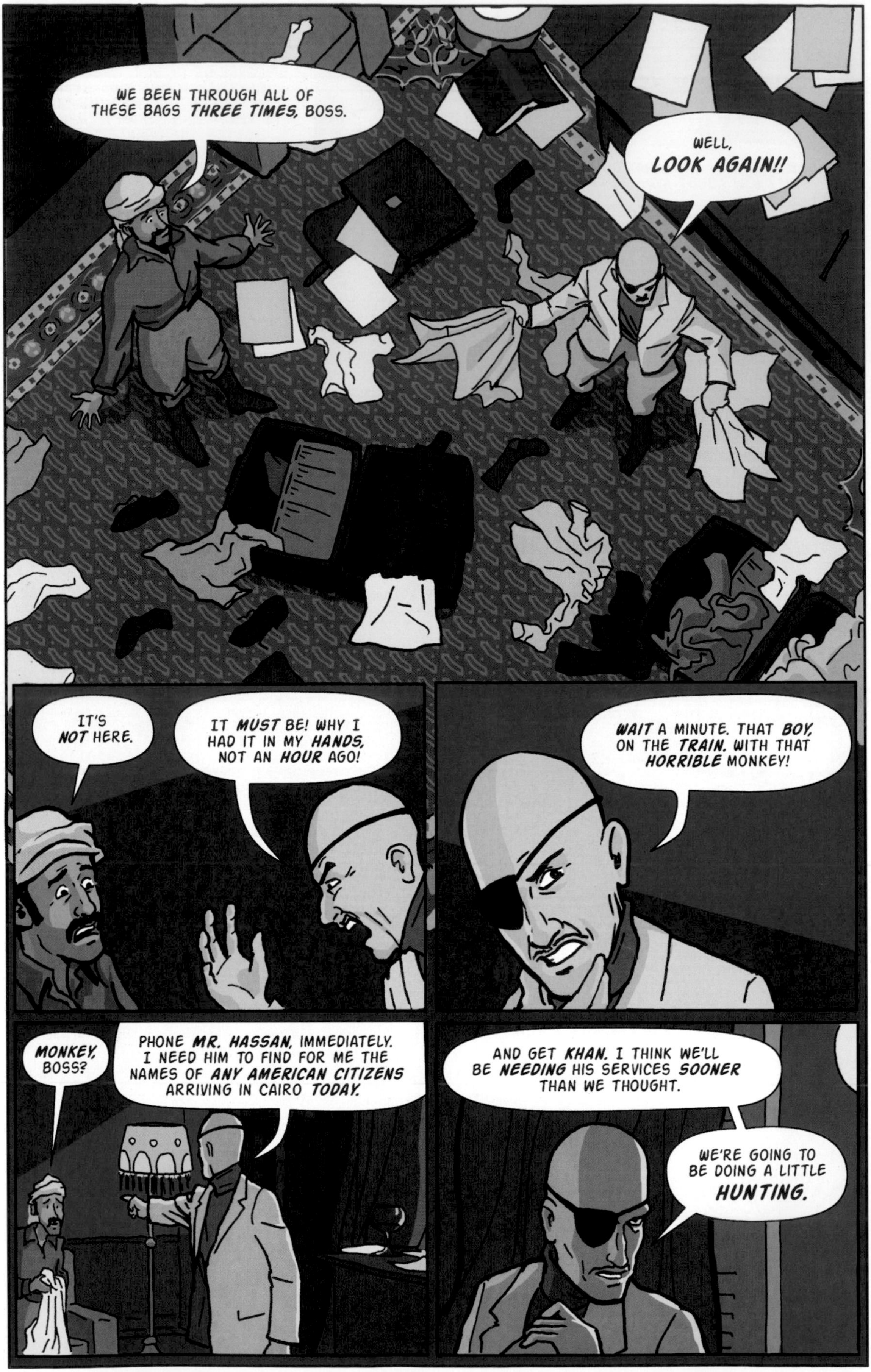
WE BEEN THROUGH ALL OF THESE BAGS THREE TIMES, BOSS.
WELL, LOOK AGAIN!!
IT'S NOT HERE.
IT MUST BE! WHY I HAD IT IN MY HANDS, NOT AN HOUR AGO!
WAIT A MINUTE. THAT BOY, ON THE TRAIN. WITH THAT HORRIBLE MONKEY!
MONKEY, BOSS?
PHONE MR. HASSAN, IMMEDIATELY. I NEED HIM TO FIND FOR ME THE NAMES OF ANY AMERICAN CITIZENS ARRIVING IN CAIRO TODAY.
AND GET KHAN. I THINK WE'LL BE NEEDING HIS SERVICES SOONER THAN WE THOUGHT.
WE'RE GOING TO BE DOING A LITTLE HUNTING.

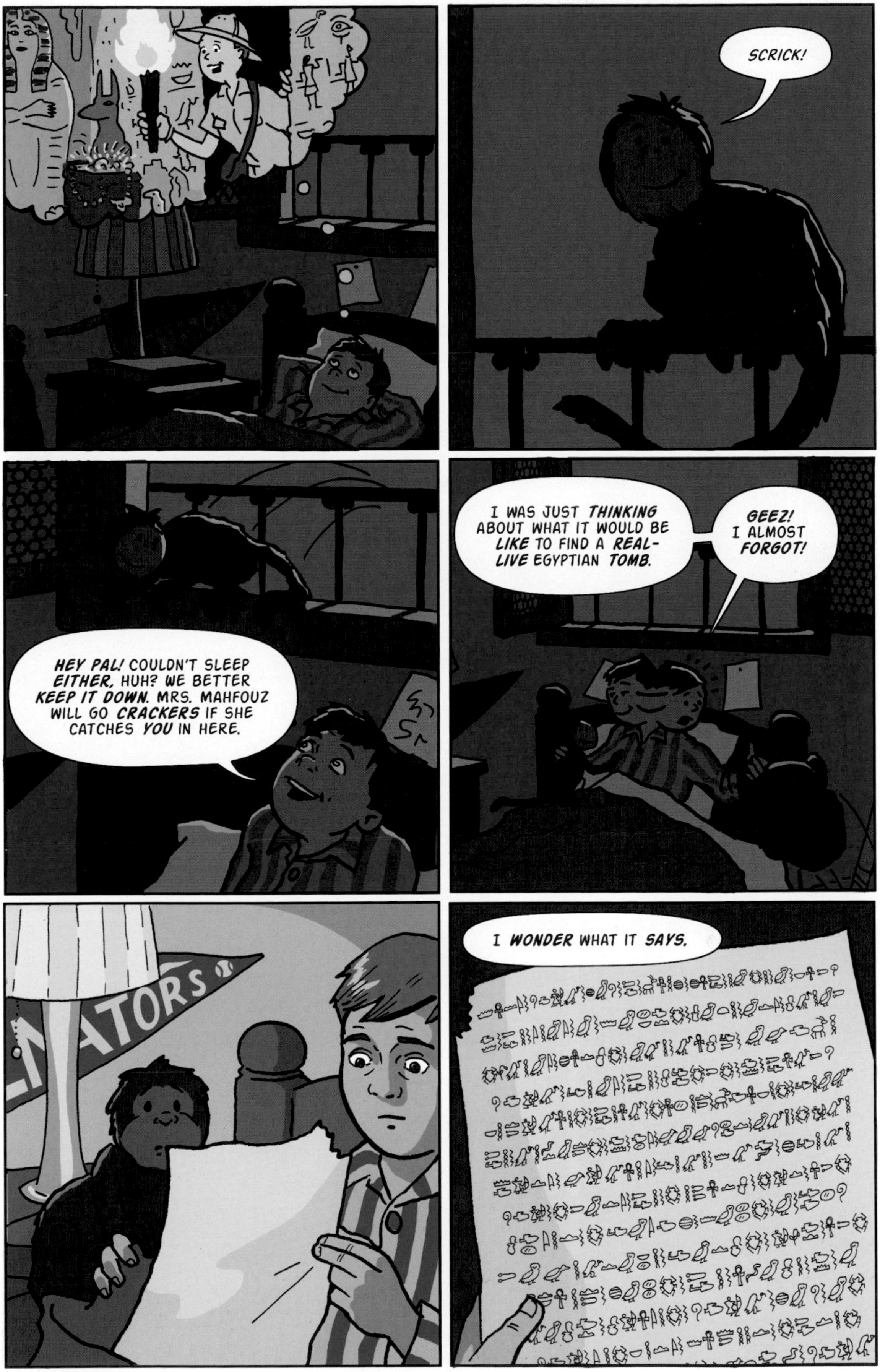
SCRICK!
HEY PAL! COULDN'T SLEEP EITHER, HUH? WE BETTER KEEP IT DOWN. MRS. MAHFOUZ WILL GO CRACKERS IF SHE CATCHES YOU IN HERE.
I WAS JUST THINKING ABOUT WHAT IT WOULD BE LIKE TO FIND A REAL-LIVE EGYPTIAN TOMB.
GEEZ! I ALMOST FORGOT!
ATORS
I WONDER WHAT IT SAYS.

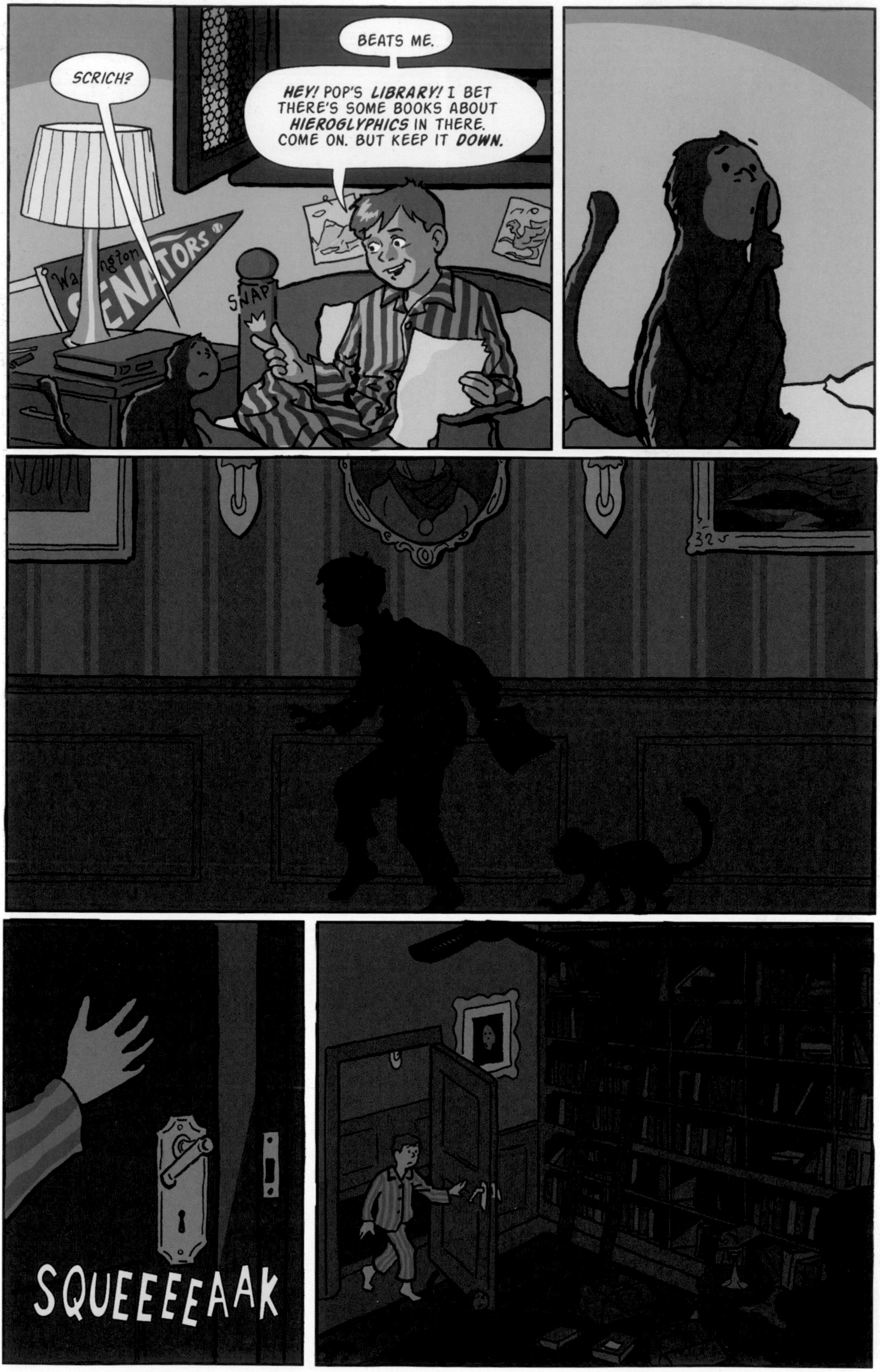
SCRICH?
BEATS ME.
HEY! POP'S LIBRARY! I BET THERE'S SOME BOOKS ABOUT HIEROGLYPHICS IN THERE. COME ON. BUT KEEP IT DOWN.
SQUEEEEAAK

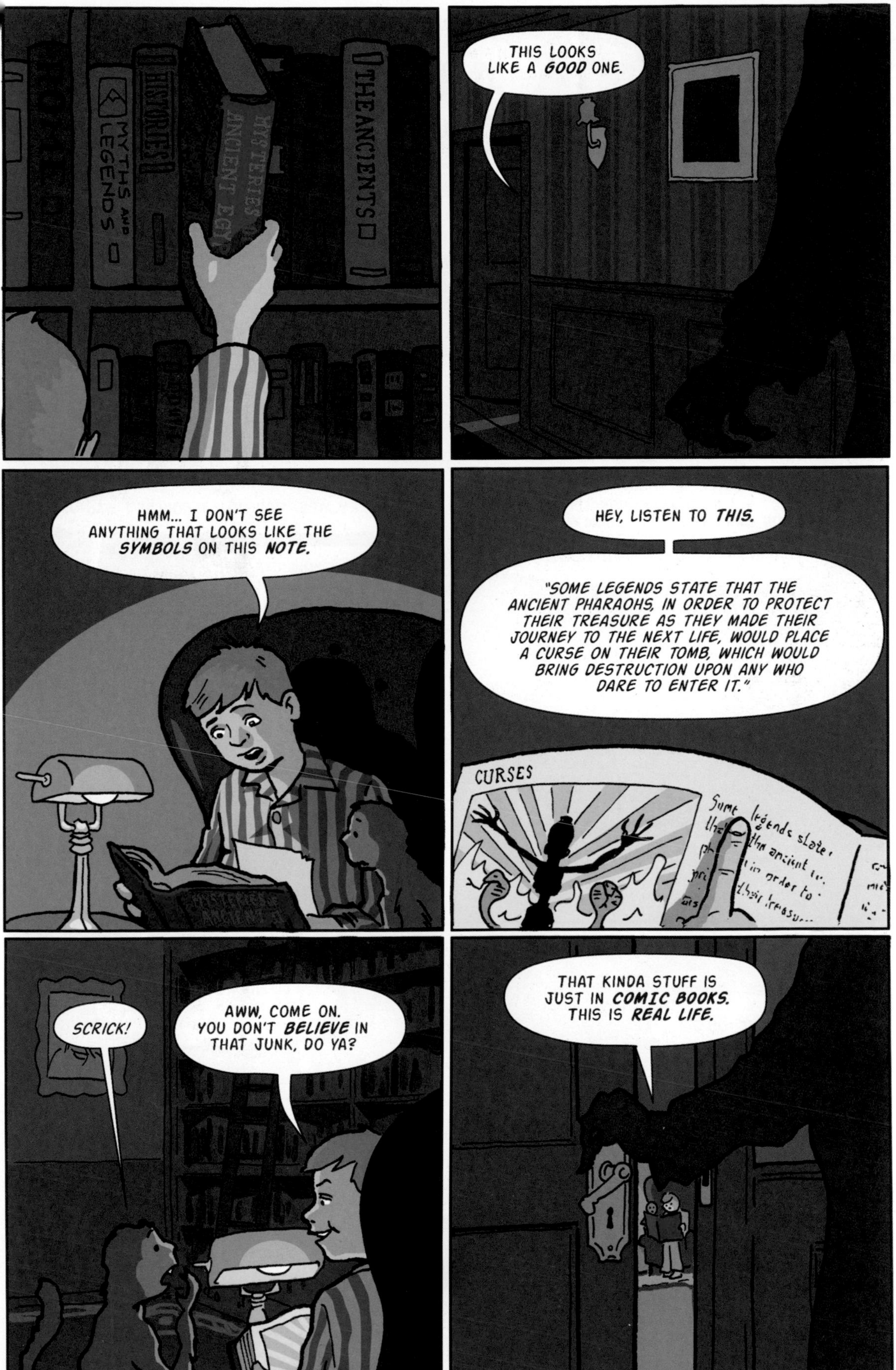
MYTHS AND LEGENDS
HISTORIES
MYSTERIES ANCIENT EGY
THE ANCIENTS
THIS LOOKS LIKE A *GOOD* ONE.
HMM... I DON'T SEE ANYTHING THAT LOOKS LIKE THE *SYMBOLS* ON THIS *NOTE.*
HEY, LISTEN TO *THIS.*
"SOME LEGENDS STATE THAT THE ANCIENT PHARAOHS, IN ORDER TO PROTECT THEIR TREASURE AS THEY MADE THEIR JOURNEY TO THE NEXT LIFE, WOULD PLACE A CURSE ON THEIR TOMB, WHICH WOULD BRING DESTRUCTION UPON ANY WHO DARE TO ENTER IT."
CURSES
SCRICK!
AWW, COME ON. YOU DON'T *BELIEVE* IN THAT JUNK, DO YA?
THAT KINDA STUFF IS JUST IN *COMIC BOOKS.* THIS IS *REAL LIFE.*

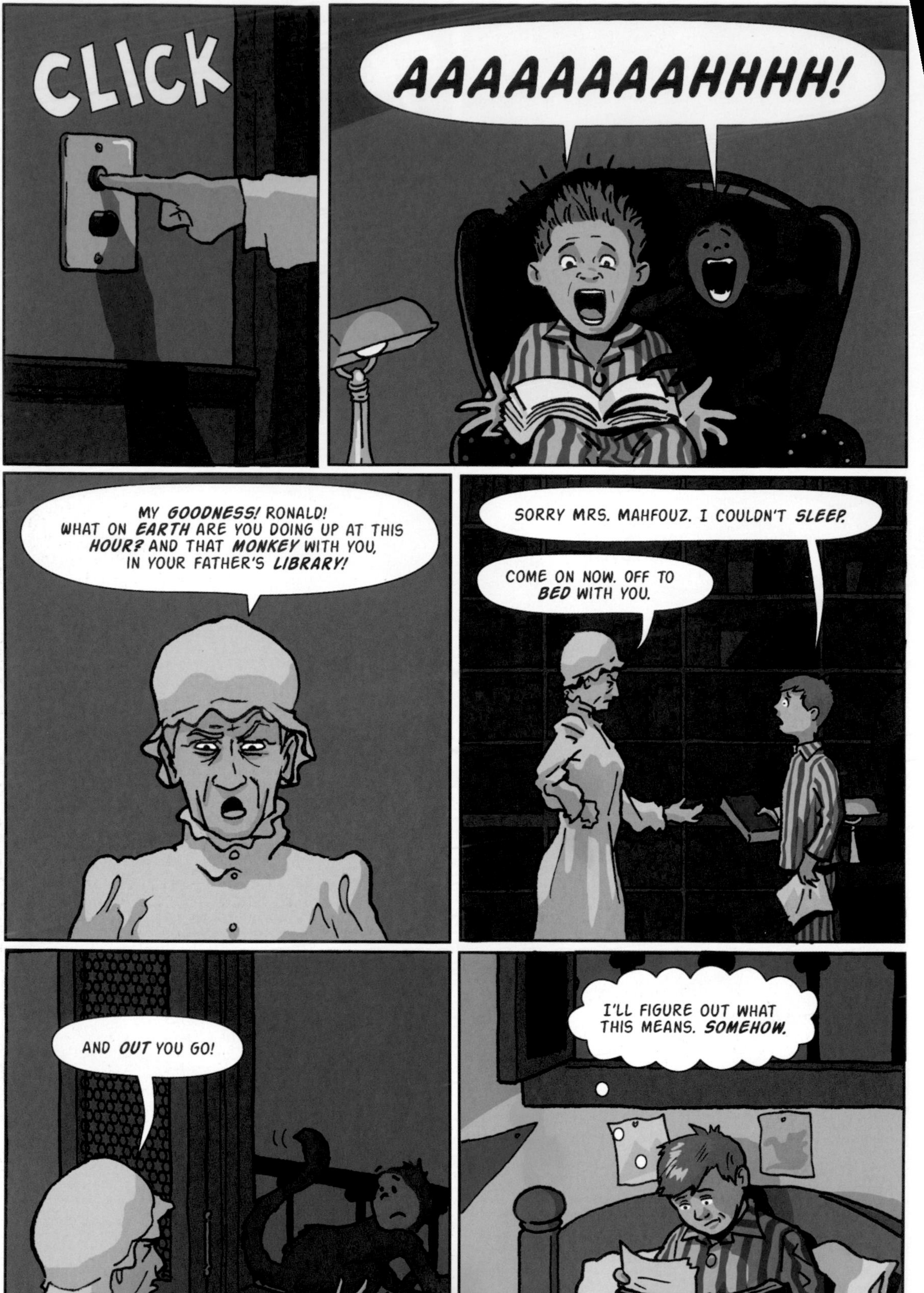
CLICK
AAAAAAAAHHHH!
MY GOODNESS! RONALD! WHAT ON EARTH ARE YOU DOING UP AT THIS HOUR? AND THAT MONKEY WITH YOU, IN YOUR FATHER'S LIBRARY!
SORRY MRS. MAHFOUZ. I COULDN'T SLEEP.
COME ON NOW. OFF TO BED WITH YOU.
AND OUT YOU GO!
I'LL FIGURE OUT WHAT THIS MEANS. SOMEHOW.
JOURNAL

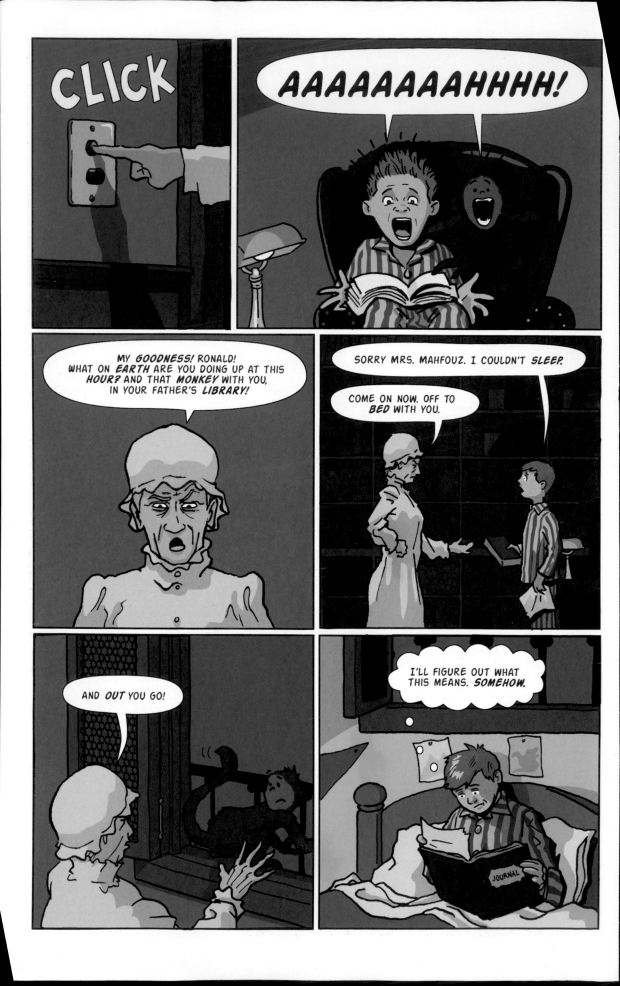

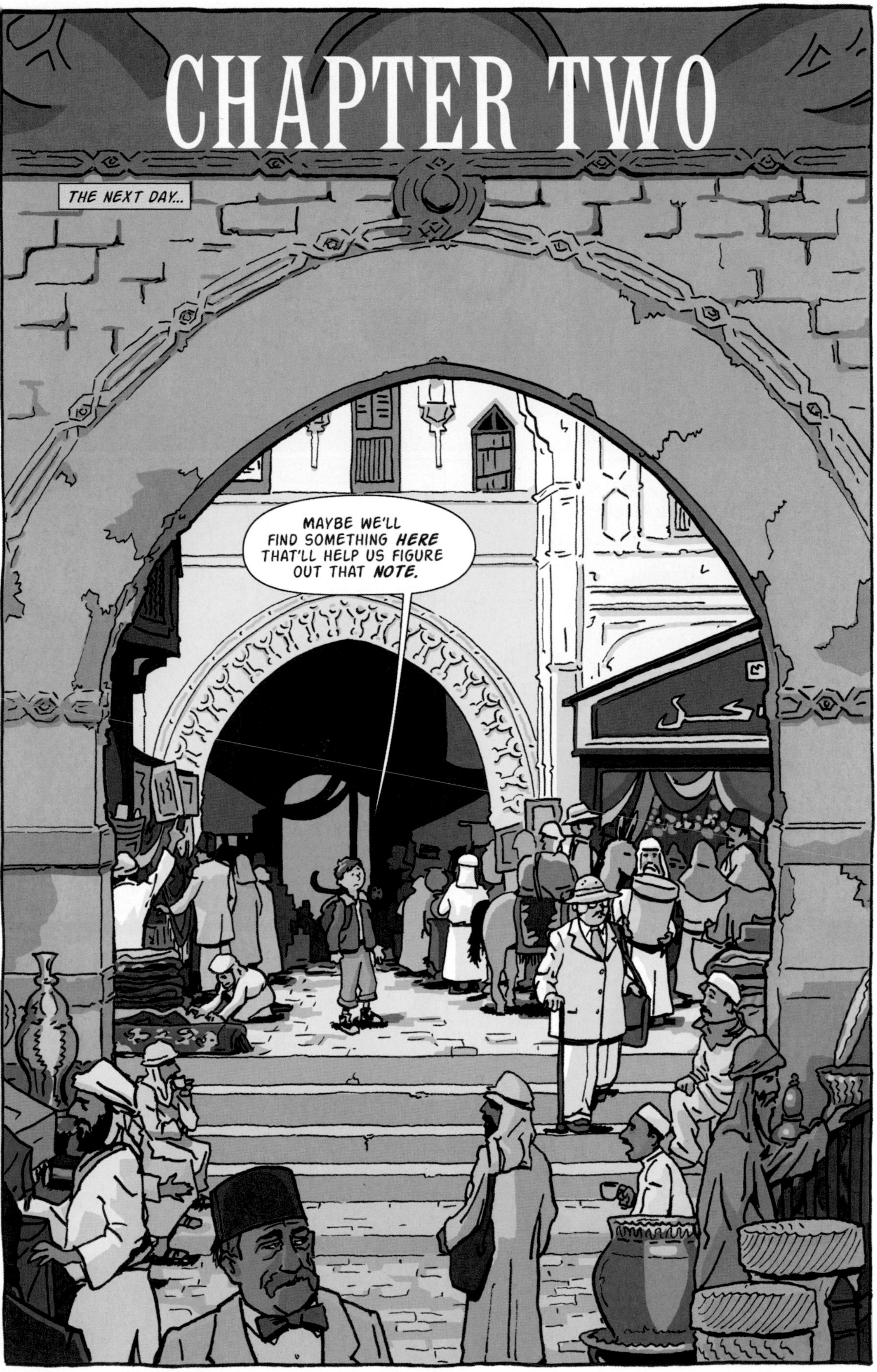
CHAPTER TWO
THE NEXT DAY...
MAYBE WE'LL FIND SOMETHING *HERE* THAT'LL HELP US FIGURE OUT THAT *NOTE*.

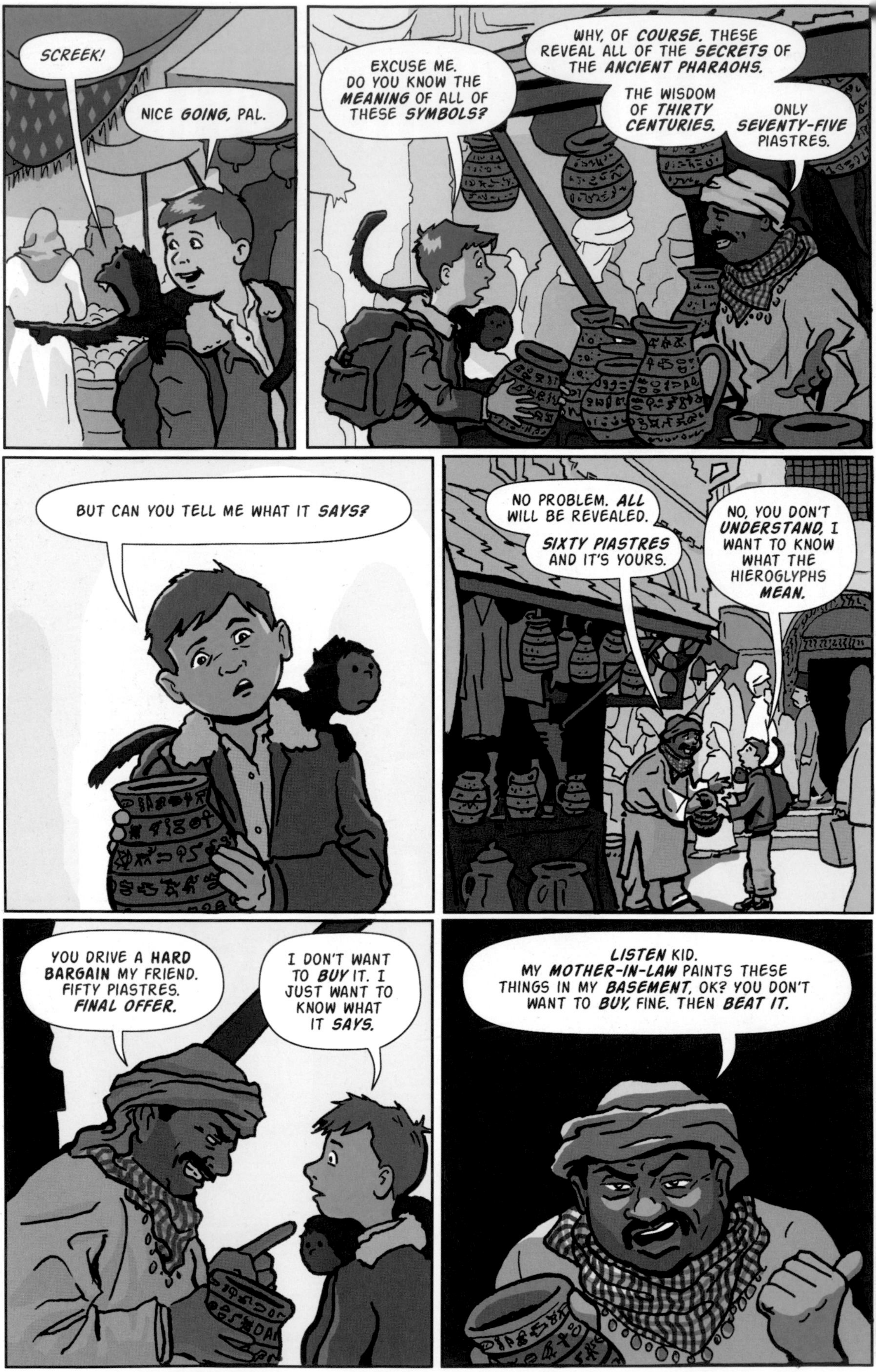

SCREEK!
NICE GOING, PAL.
EXCUSE ME. DO YOU KNOW THE MEANING OF ALL OF THESE SYMBOLS?
WHY, OF COURSE. THESE REVEAL ALL OF THE SECRETS OF THE ANCIENT PHARAOHS.
THE WISDOM OF THIRTY CENTURIES.
ONLY SEVENTY-FIVE PIASTRES.
BUT CAN YOU TELL ME WHAT IT SAYS?
NO PROBLEM. ALL WILL BE REVEALED.
SIXTY PIASTRES AND IT'S YOURS.
NO, YOU DON'T UNDERSTAND. I WANT TO KNOW WHAT THE HIEROGLYPHS MEAN.
YOU DRIVE A HARD BARGAIN MY FRIEND. FIFTY PIASTRES. FINAL OFFER.
I DON'T WANT TO BUY IT. I JUST WANT TO KNOW WHAT IT SAYS.
LISTEN KID. MY MOTHER-IN-LAW PAINTS THESE THINGS IN MY BASEMENT, OK? YOU DON'T WANT TO BUY, FINE. THEN BEAT IT.

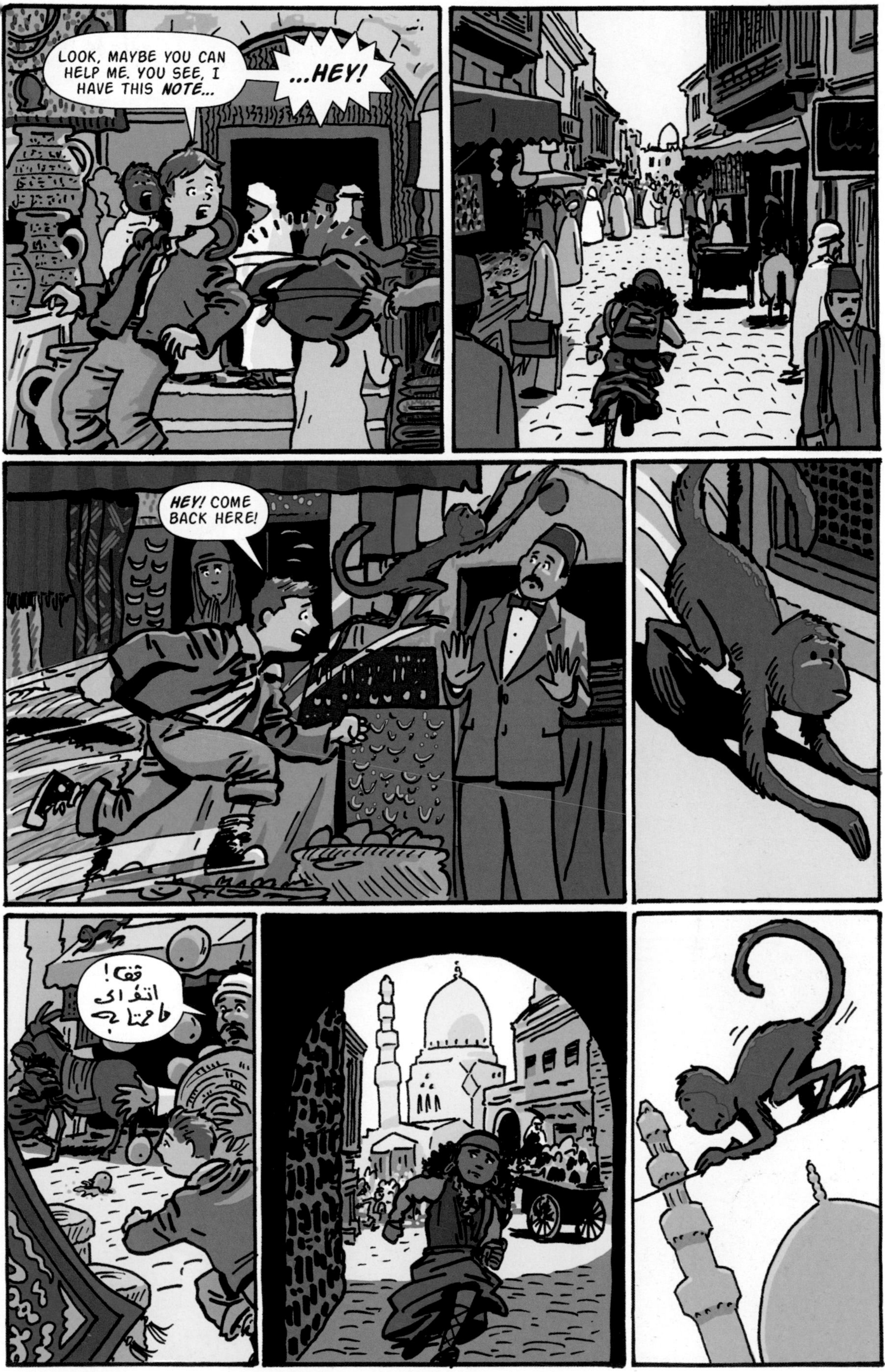
LOOK, MAYBE YOU CAN HELP ME. YOU SEE, I HAVE THIS *NOTE*...
...HEY!
HEY! COME BACK HERE!
قف!

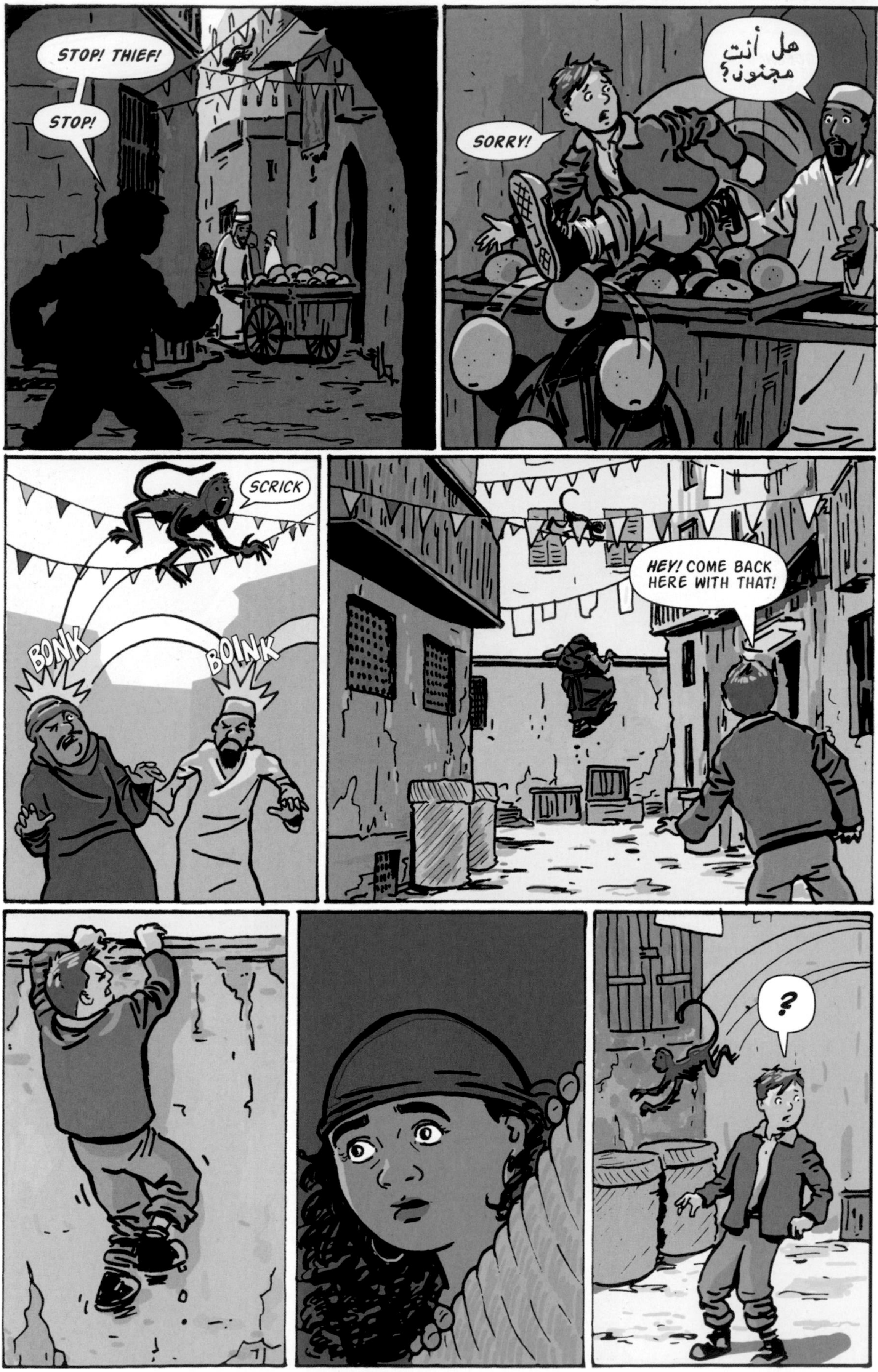
STOP! THIEF!
STOP!
هل أنت مجنون؟
SORRY!
SCRICK
BONK
BOINK
HEY! COME BACK HERE WITH THAT!
?

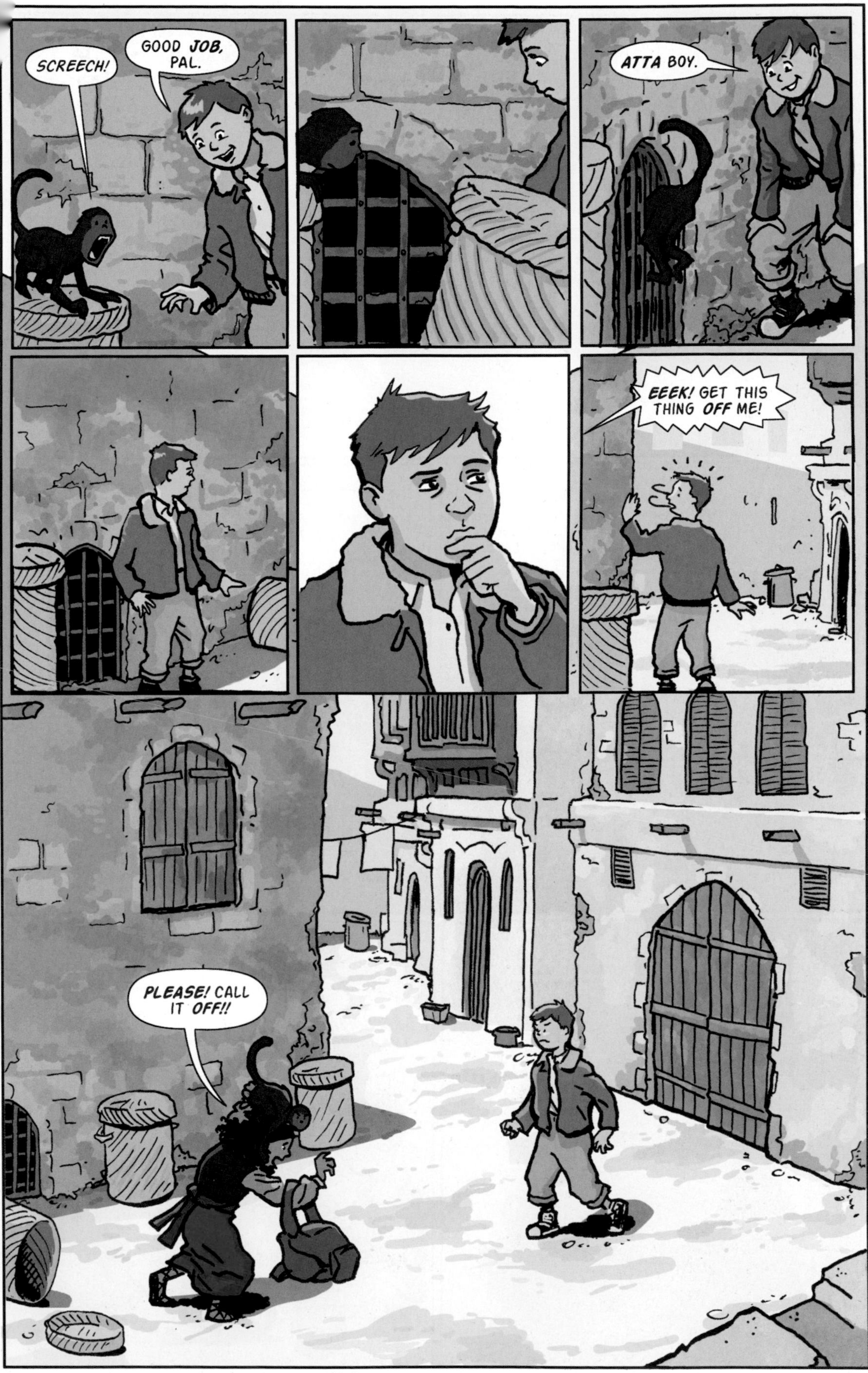
SCREECH!
GOOD JOB, PAL.
ATTA BOY.
EEEK! GET THIS THING OFF ME!
PLEASE! CALL IT OFF!!

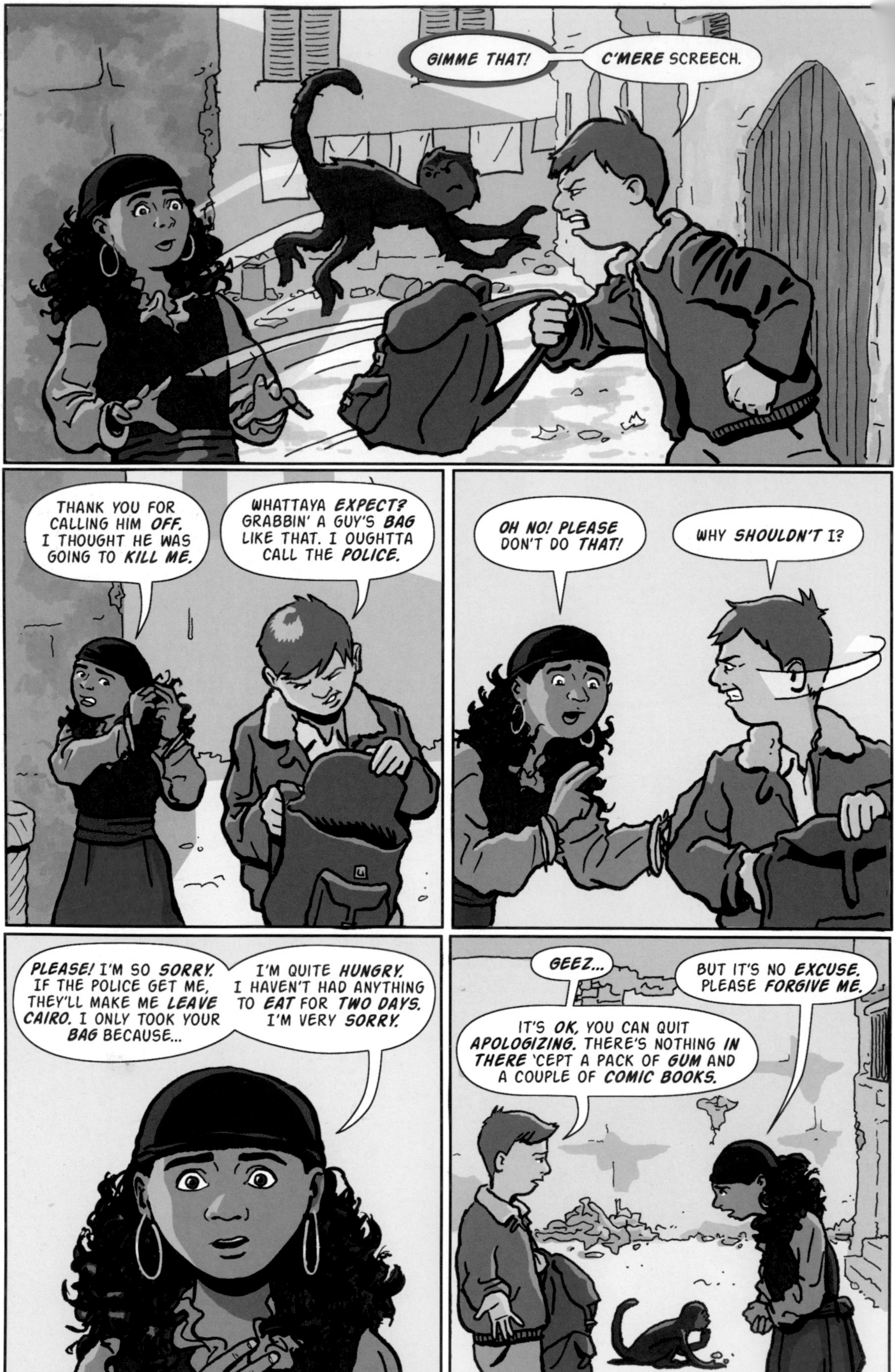
GIMME THAT!
C'MERE SCREECH.
THANK YOU FOR CALLING HIM OFF. I THOUGHT HE WAS GOING TO KILL ME.
WHATTAYA EXPECT? GRABBIN' A GUY'S BAG LIKE THAT. I OUGHTTA CALL THE POLICE.
OH NO! PLEASE DON'T DO THAT!
WHY SHOULDN'T I?
PLEASE! I'M SO SORRY. IF THE POLICE GET ME, THEY'LL MAKE ME LEAVE CAIRO. I ONLY TOOK YOUR BAG BECAUSE...
I'M QUITE HUNGRY. I HAVEN'T HAD ANYTHING TO EAT FOR TWO DAYS. I'M VERY SORRY.
GEEZ...
BUT IT'S NO EXCUSE. PLEASE FORGIVE ME.
IT'S OK, YOU CAN QUIT APOLOGIZING. THERE'S NOTHING IN THERE 'CEPT A PACK OF GUM AND A COUPLE OF COMIC BOOKS.

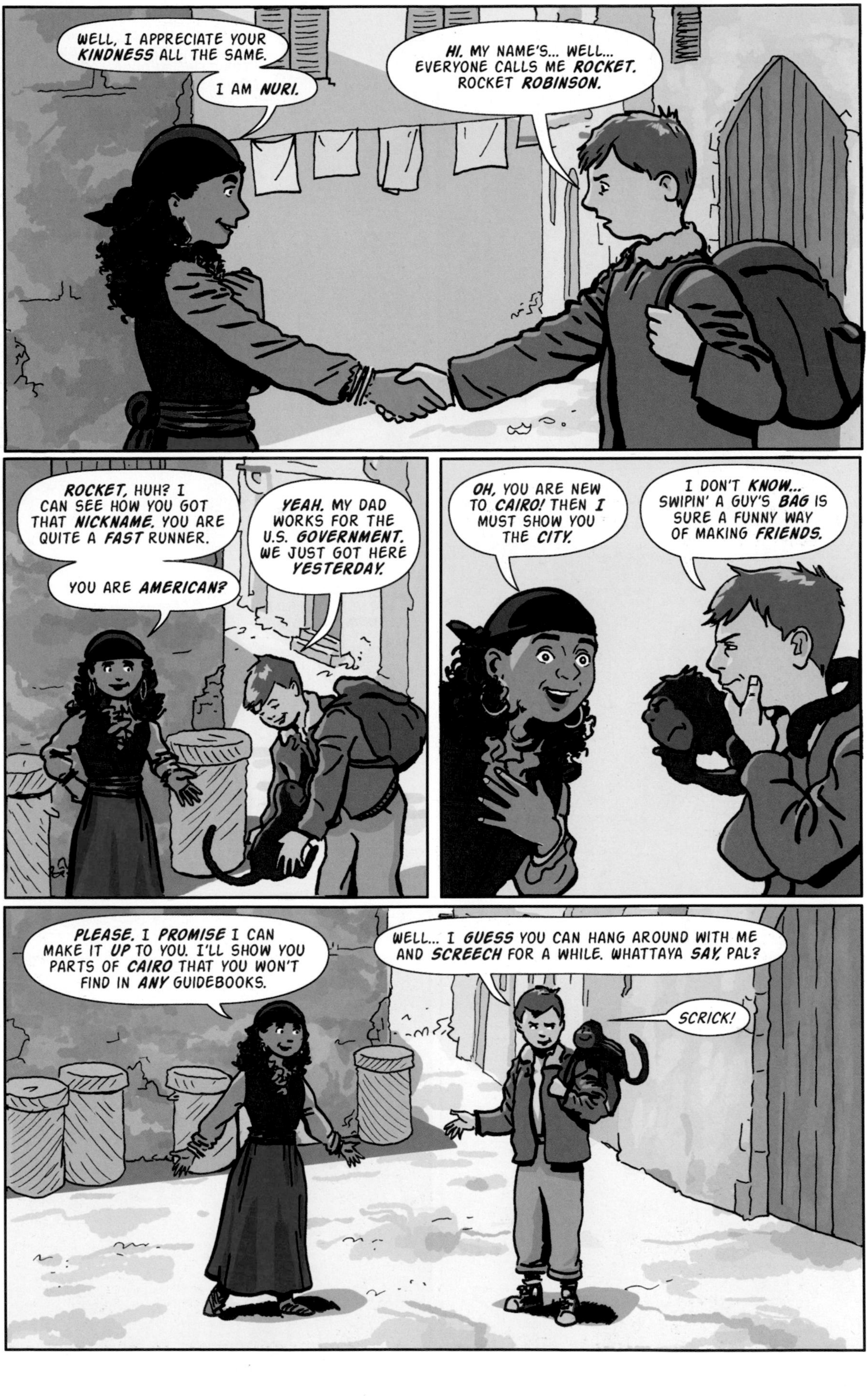
WELL, I APPRECIATE YOUR KINDNESS ALL THE SAME.
I AM NURI.
HI. MY NAME'S... WELL... EVERYONE CALLS ME ROCKET. ROCKET ROBINSON.
ROCKET, HUH? I CAN SEE HOW YOU GOT THAT NICKNAME. YOU ARE QUITE A FAST RUNNER.
YOU ARE AMERICAN?
YEAH. MY DAD WORKS FOR THE U.S. GOVERNMENT. WE JUST GOT HERE YESTERDAY.
OH, YOU ARE NEW TO CAIRO! THEN I MUST SHOW YOU THE CITY.
I DON'T KNOW... SWIPIN' A GUY'S BAG IS SURE A FUNNY WAY OF MAKING FRIENDS.
PLEASE. I PROMISE I CAN MAKE IT UP TO YOU. I'LL SHOW YOU PARTS OF CAIRO THAT YOU WON'T FIND IN ANY GUIDEBOOKS.
WELL... I GUESS YOU CAN HANG AROUND WITH ME AND SCREECH FOR A WHILE. WHATTAYA SAY, PAL?
SCRICK!

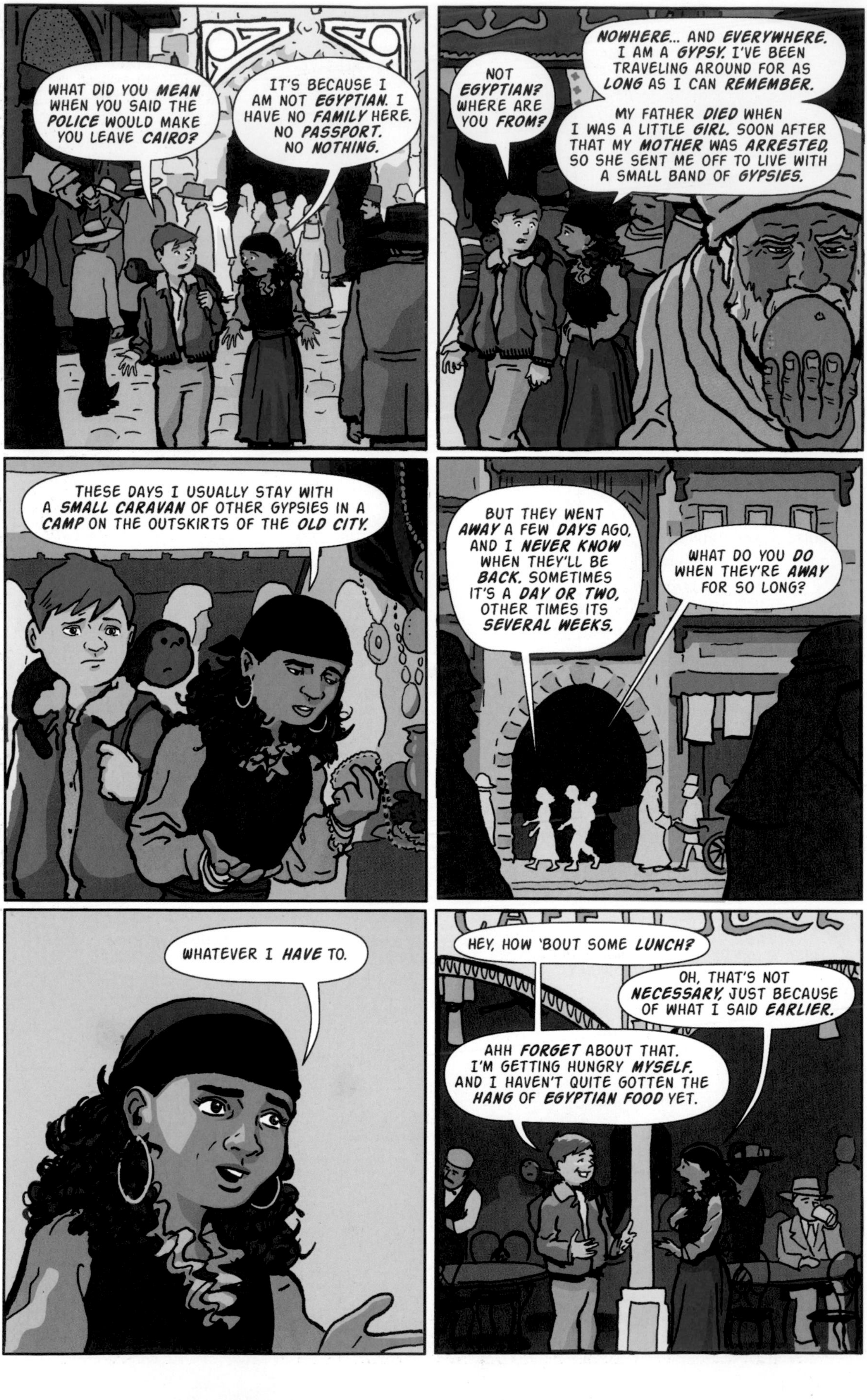
WHAT DID YOU MEAN WHEN YOU SAID THE POLICE WOULD MAKE YOU LEAVE CAIRO?
IT'S BECAUSE I AM NOT EGYPTIAN. I HAVE NO FAMILY HERE. NO PASSPORT. NO NOTHING.
NOT EGYPTIAN? WHERE ARE YOU FROM?
NOWHERE... AND EVERYWHERE. I AM A GYPSY. I'VE BEEN TRAVELING AROUND FOR AS LONG AS I CAN REMEMBER.
MY FATHER DIED WHEN I WAS A LITTLE GIRL. SOON AFTER THAT MY MOTHER WAS ARRESTED, SO SHE SENT ME OFF TO LIVE WITH A SMALL BAND OF GYPSIES.
THESE DAYS I USUALLY STAY WITH A SMALL CARAVAN OF OTHER GYPSIES IN A CAMP ON THE OUTSKIRTS OF THE OLD CITY.
BUT THEY WENT AWAY A FEW DAYS AGO, AND I NEVER KNOW WHEN THEY'LL BE BACK. SOMETIMES IT'S A DAY OR TWO, OTHER TIMES ITS SEVERAL WEEKS.
WHAT DO YOU DO WHEN THEY'RE AWAY FOR SO LONG?
WHATEVER I HAVE TO.
HEY, HOW 'BOUT SOME LUNCH?
OH, THAT'S NOT NECESSARY, JUST BECAUSE OF WHAT I SAID EARLIER.
AHH FORGET ABOUT THAT. I'M GETTING HUNGRY MYSELF. AND I HAVEN'T QUITE GOTTEN THE HANG OF EGYPTIAN FOOD YET.

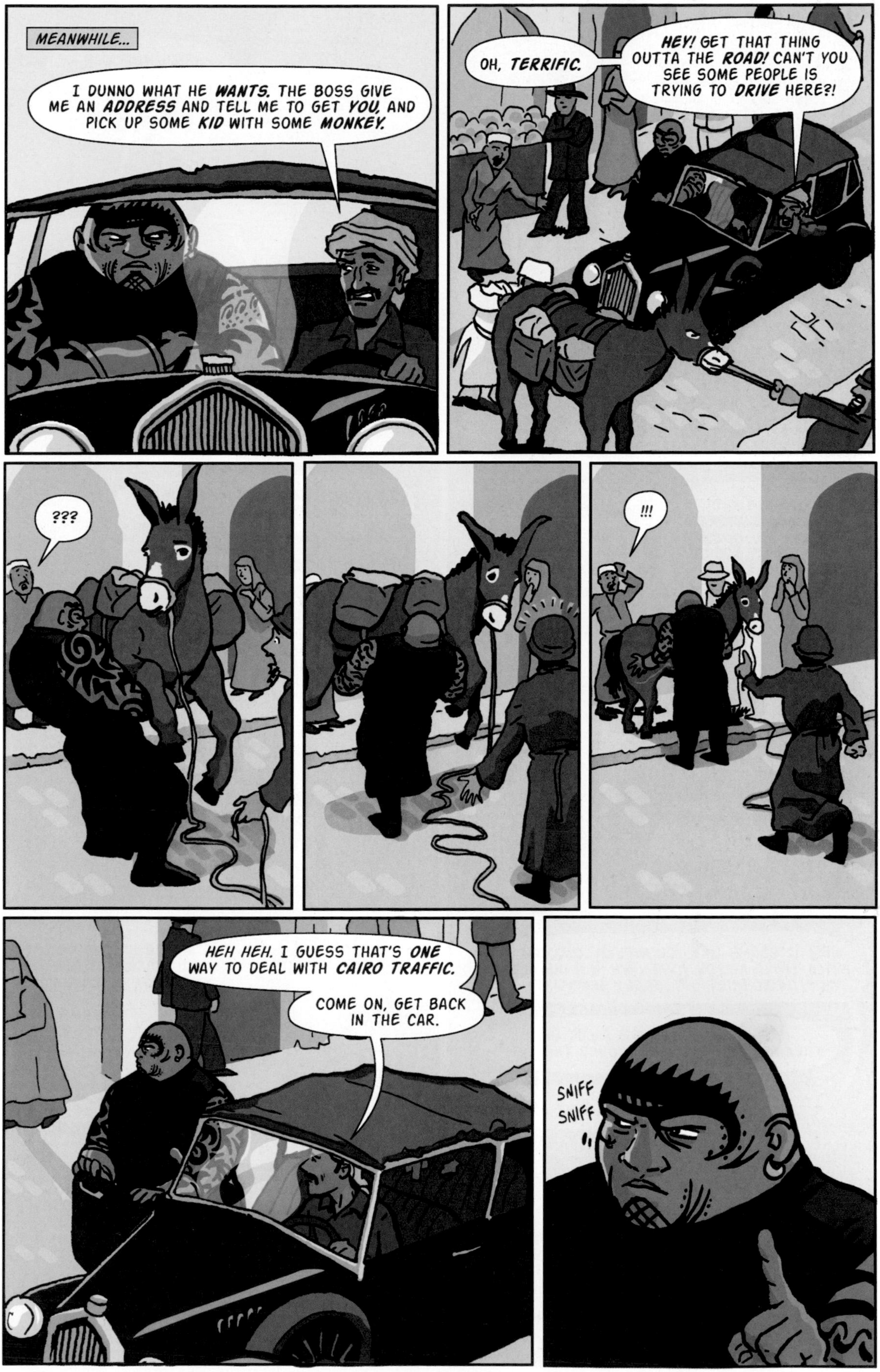
MEANWHILE...
I DUNNO WHAT HE WANTS. THE BOSS GIVE ME AN ADDRESS AND TELL ME TO GET YOU, AND PICK UP SOME KID WITH SOME MONKEY.
OH, TERRIFIC.
HEY! GET THAT THING OUTTA THE ROAD! CAN'T YOU SEE SOME PEOPLE IS TRYING TO DRIVE HERE?!
???
!!!
HEH HEH. I GUESS THAT'S ONE WAY TO DEAL WITH CAIRO TRAFFIC.
COME ON, GET BACK IN THE CAR.
SNIFF SNIFF

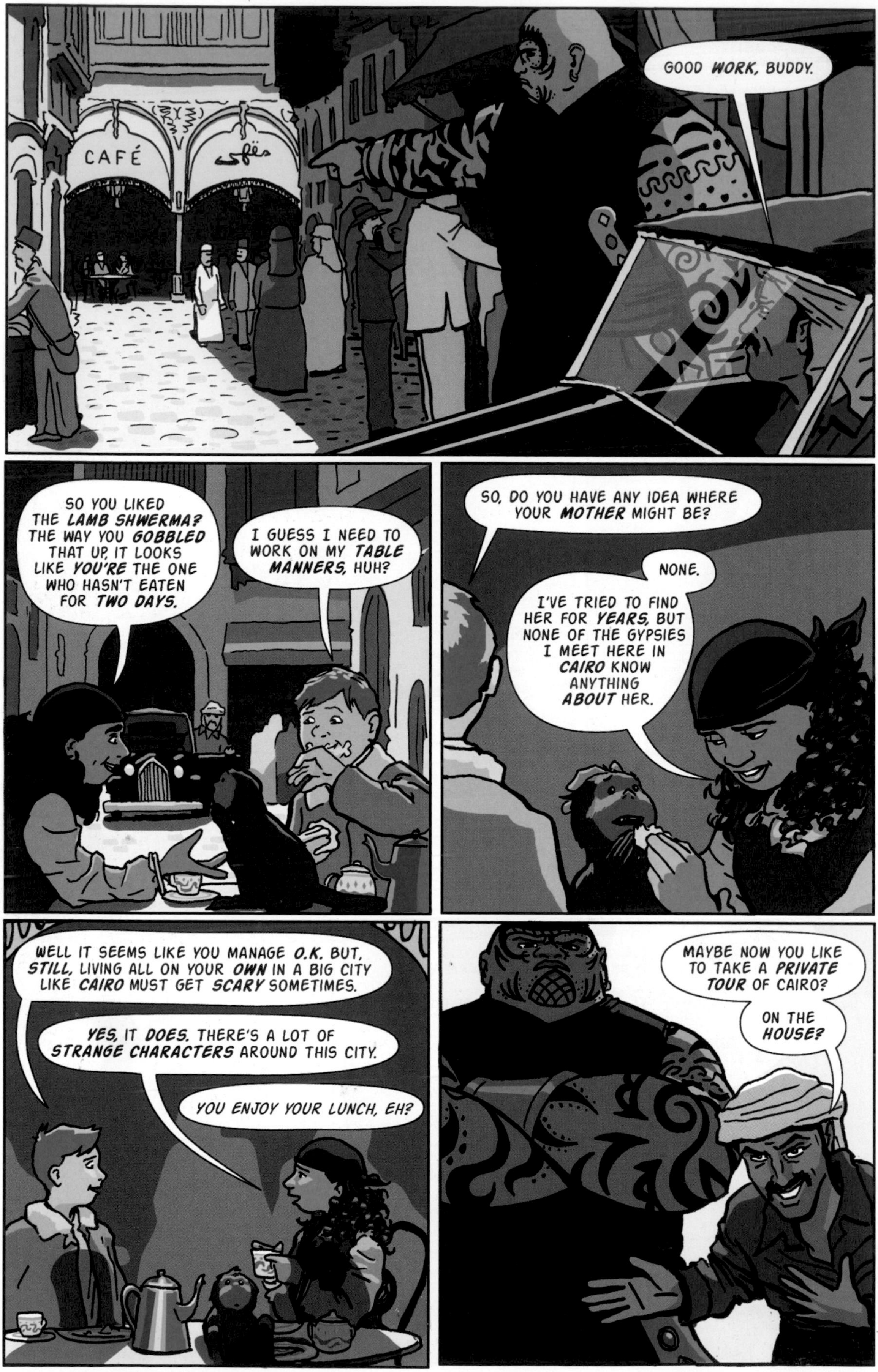
CAFÉ
GOOD WORK, BUDDY.
SO YOU LIKED THE LAMB SHWERMA? THE WAY YOU GOBBLED THAT UP, IT LOOKS LIKE YOU'RE THE ONE WHO HASN'T EATEN FOR TWO DAYS.
I GUESS I NEED TO WORK ON MY TABLE MANNERS, HUH?
SO, DO YOU HAVE ANY IDEA WHERE YOUR MOTHER MIGHT BE?
NONE.
I'VE TRIED TO FIND HER FOR YEARS, BUT NONE OF THE GYPSIES I MEET HERE IN CAIRO KNOW ANYTHING ABOUT HER.
WELL IT SEEMS LIKE YOU MANAGE O.K. BUT, STILL, LIVING ALL ON YOUR OWN IN A BIG CITY LIKE CAIRO MUST GET SCARY SOMETIMES.
YES, IT DOES. THERE'S A LOT OF STRANGE CHARACTERS AROUND THIS CITY.
YOU ENJOY YOUR LUNCH, EH?
MAYBE NOW YOU LIKE TO TAKE A PRIVATE TOUR OF CAIRO?
ON THE HOUSE?

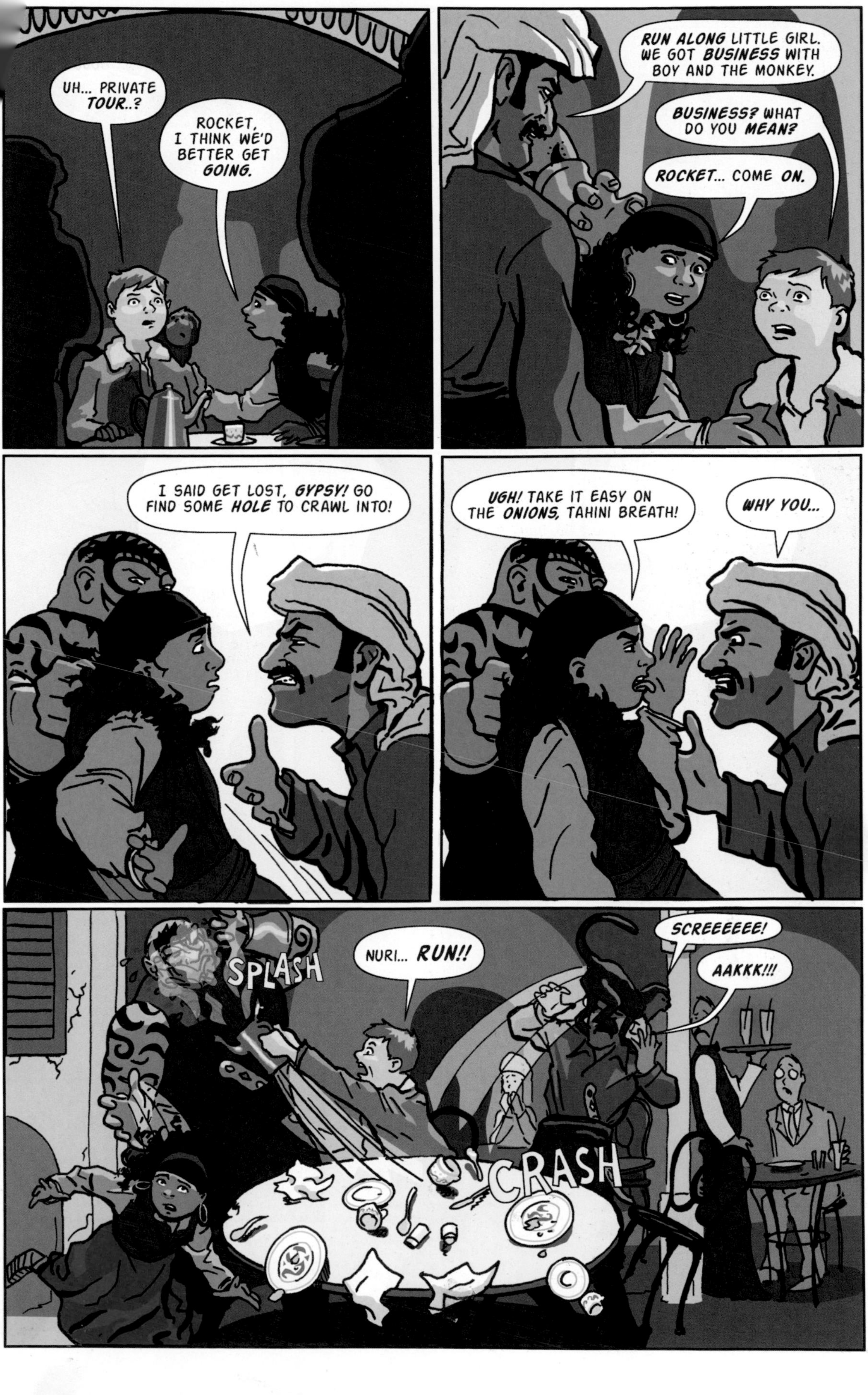

UH... PRIVATE TOUR..?
ROCKET, I THINK WE'D BETTER GET GOING.
RUN ALONG LITTLE GIRL. WE GOT BUSINESS WITH BOY AND THE MONKEY.
BUSINESS? WHAT DO YOU MEAN?
ROCKET... COME ON.
I SAID GET LOST, GYPSY! GO FIND SOME HOLE TO CRAWL INTO!
UGH! TAKE IT EASY ON THE ONIONS, TAHINI BREATH!
WHY YOU...
SPLASH
NURI... RUN!!
SCREEEEEEE!
AAKKK!!!
CRASH

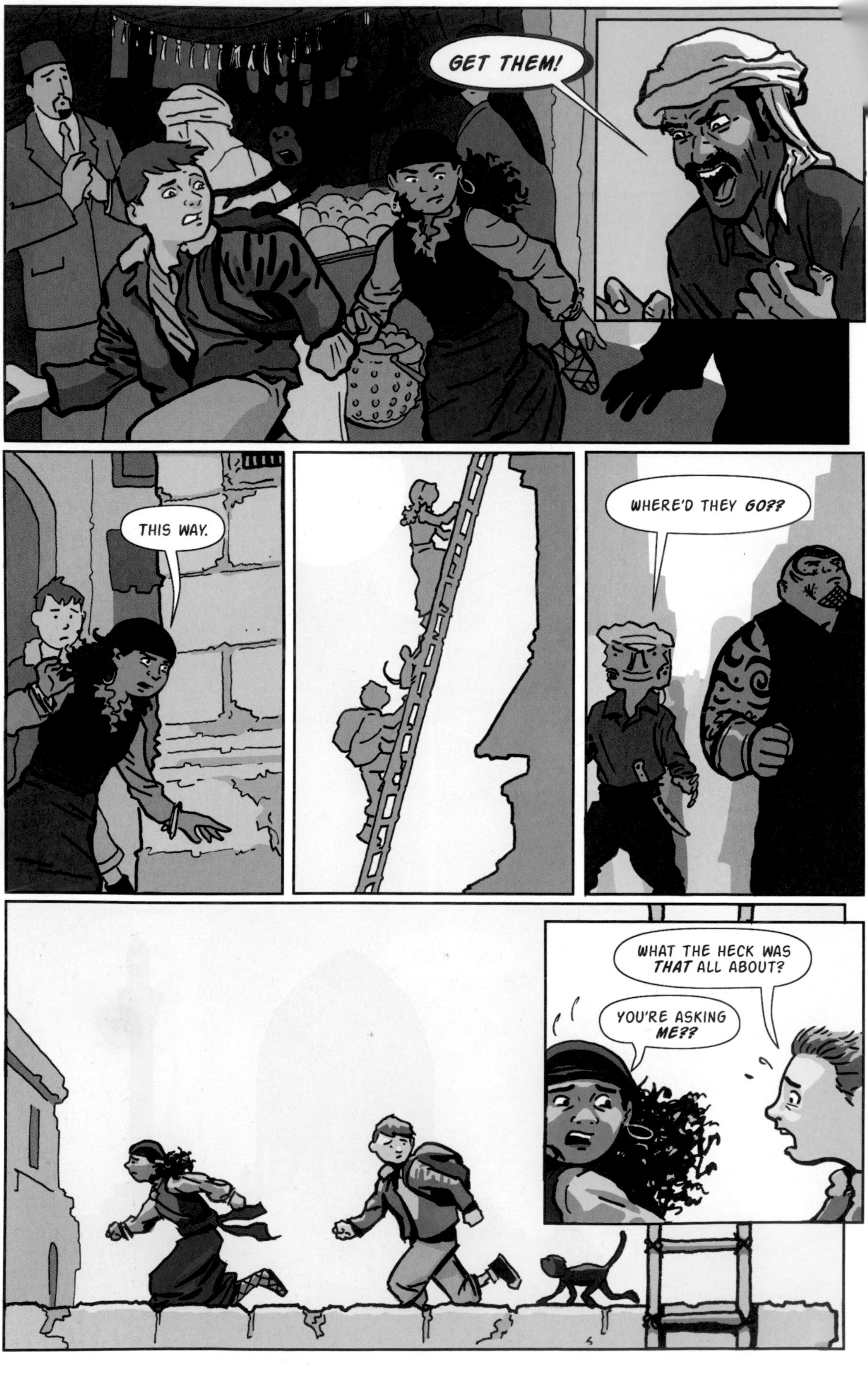
GET THEM!
THIS WAY.
WHERE'D THEY GO??
WHAT THE HECK WAS THAT ALL ABOUT?
YOU'RE ASKING ME??

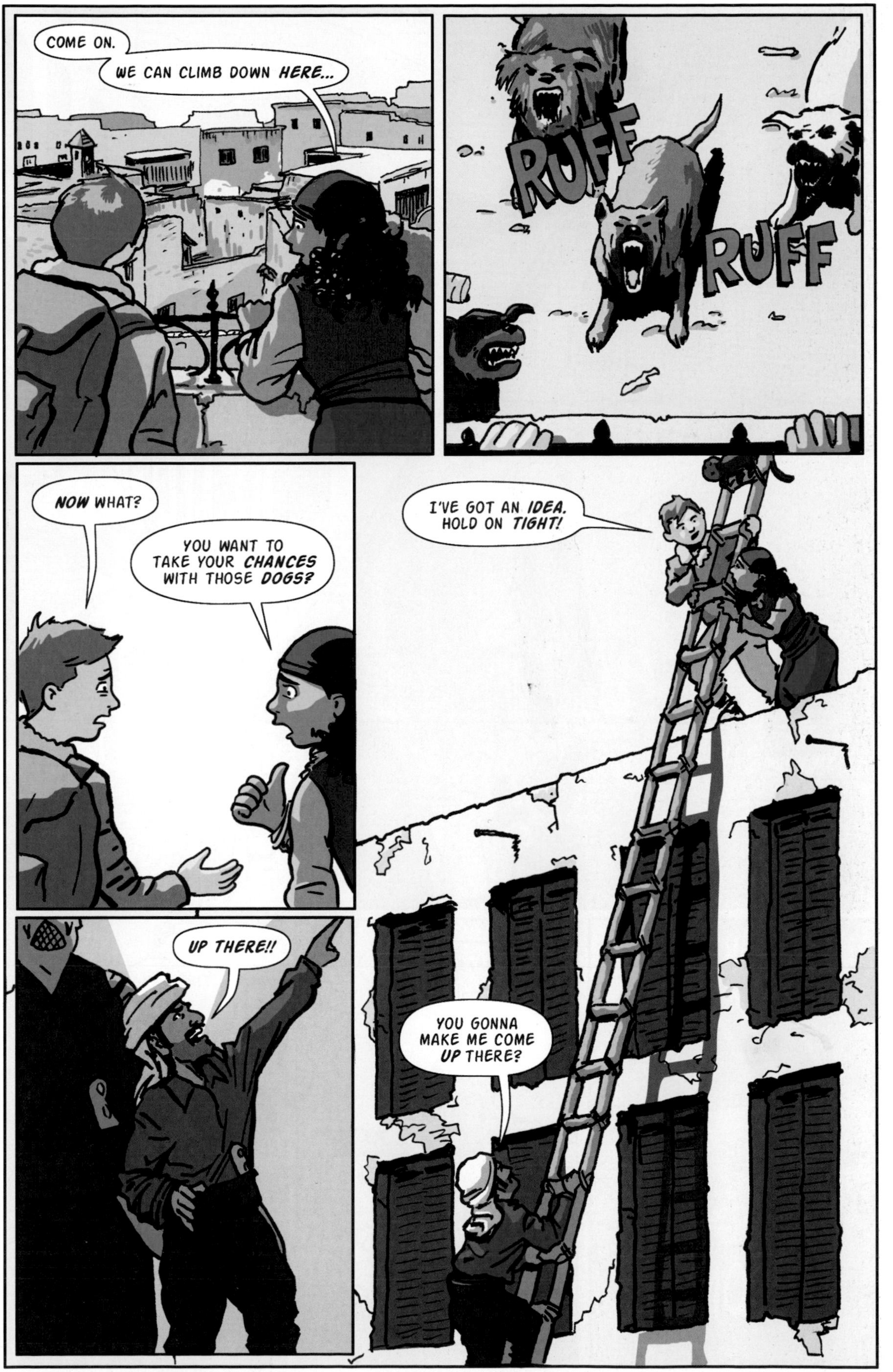
COME ON.
WE CAN CLIMB DOWN HERE...
RUFF
RUFF
NOW WHAT?
YOU WANT TO TAKE YOUR CHANCES WITH THOSE DOGS?
I'VE GOT AN IDEA. HOLD ON TIGHT!
UP THERE!!
YOU GONNA MAKE ME COME UP THERE?

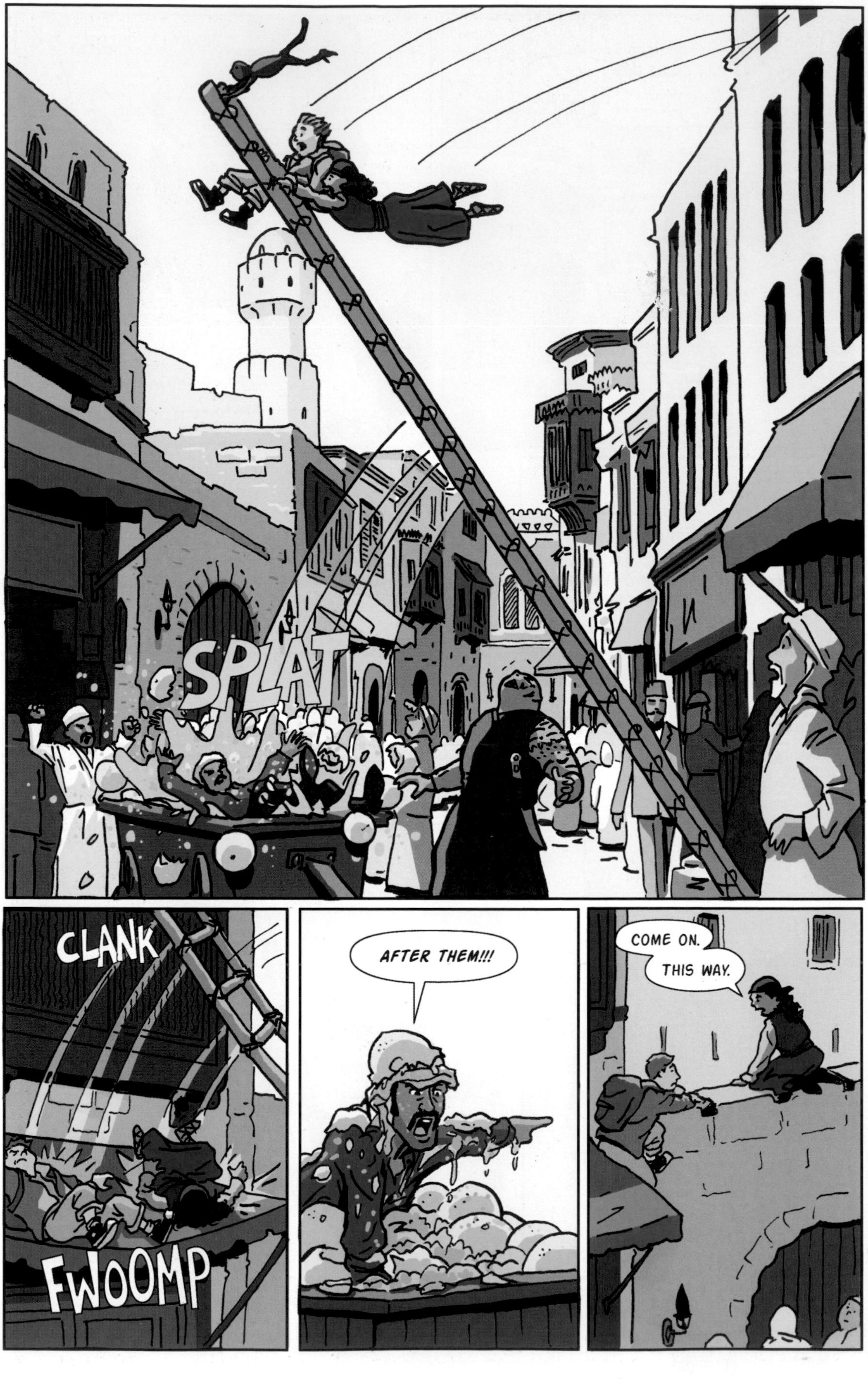
SPLAT
CLANK
FWOOMP
AFTER THEM!!!
COME ON.
THIS WAY.

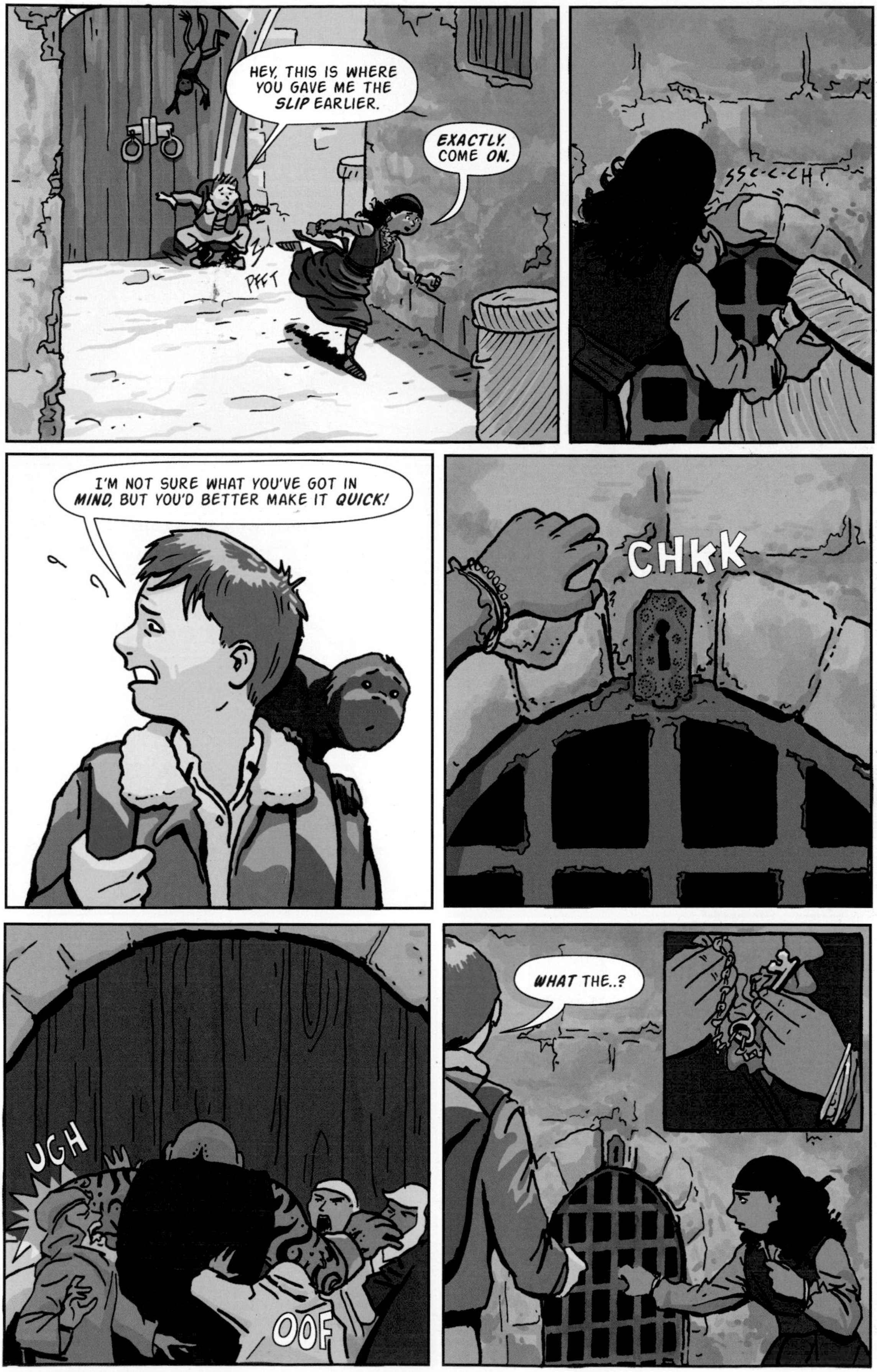
HEY, THIS IS WHERE YOU GAVE ME THE SLIP EARLIER.
EXACTLY. COME ON.
PFFT
SSC-C-CH
I'M NOT SURE WHAT YOU'VE GOT IN MIND, BUT YOU'D BETTER MAKE IT QUICK!
CHKK
UGH
OOF
WHAT THE..?

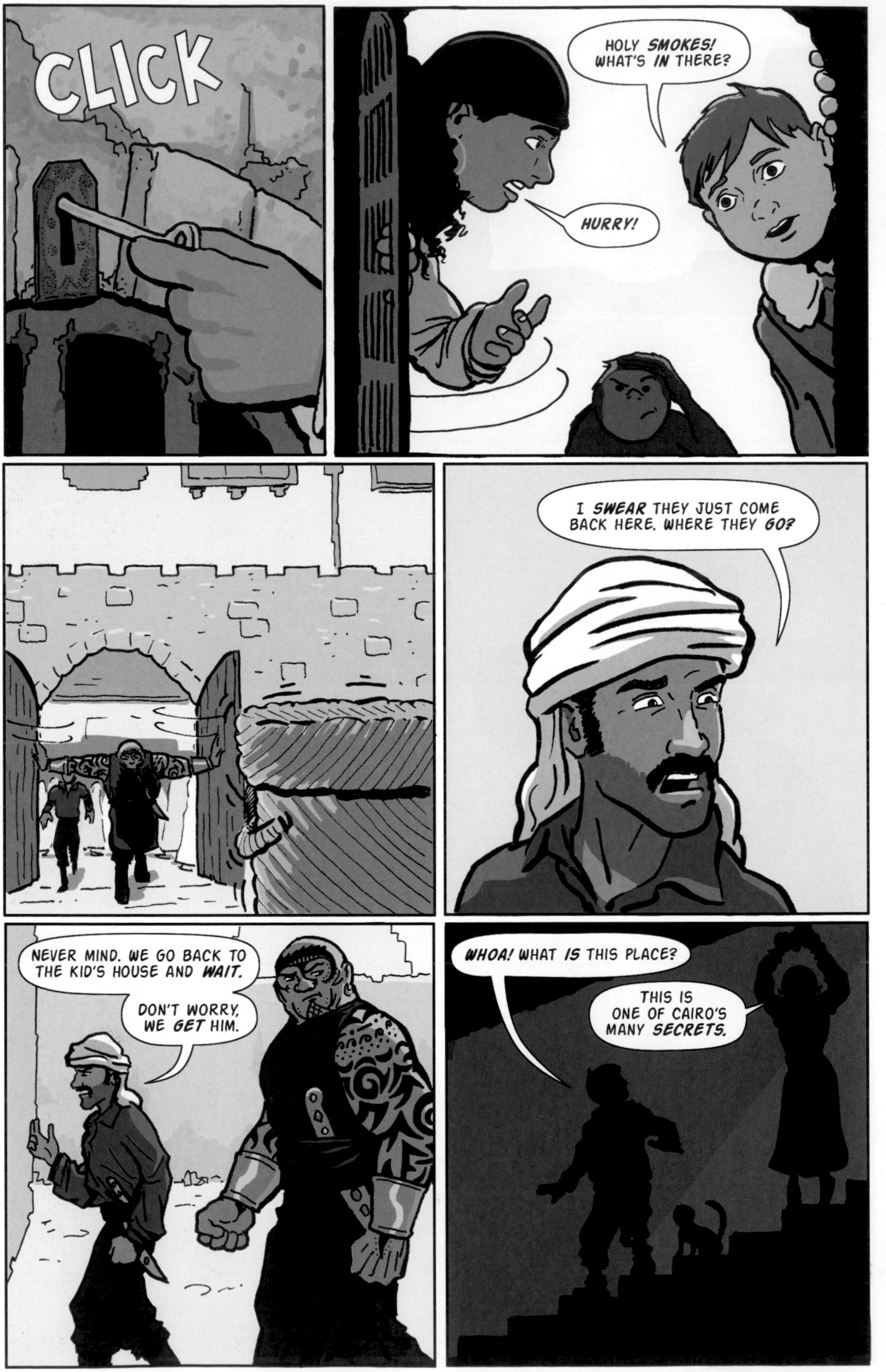
CLICK
HOLY SMOKES! WHAT'S IN THERE?
HURRY!
I SWEAR THEY JUST COME BACK HERE. WHERE THEY GO?
NEVER MIND. WE GO BACK TO THE KID'S HOUSE AND WAIT.
DON'T WORRY, WE GET HIM.
WHOA! WHAT IS THIS PLACE?
THIS IS ONE OF CAIRO'S MANY SECRETS.

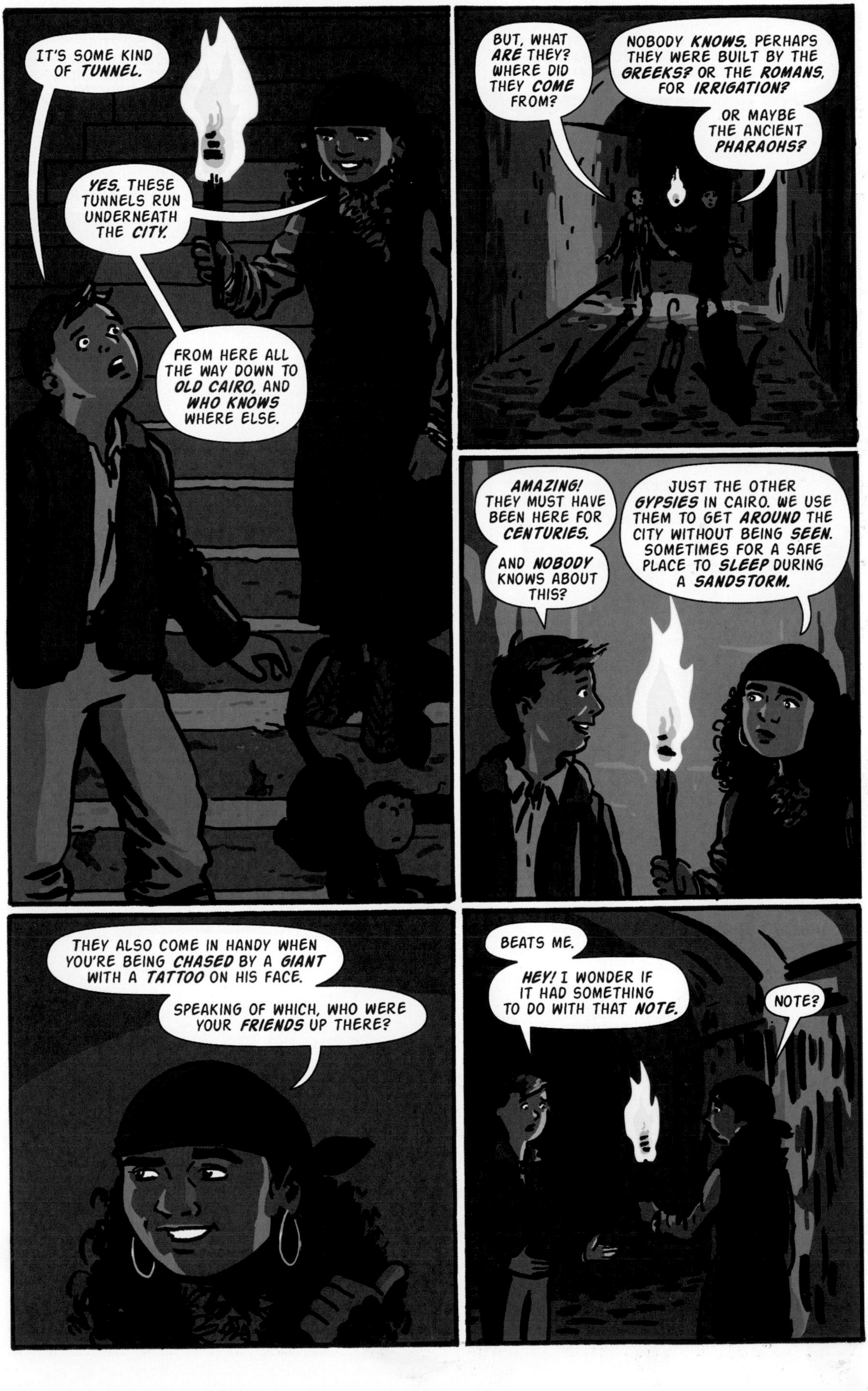
IT'S SOME KIND OF TUNNEL.
YES. THESE TUNNELS RUN UNDERNEATH THE CITY.
FROM HERE ALL THE WAY DOWN TO OLD CAIRO, AND WHO KNOWS WHERE ELSE.
BUT, WHAT ARE THEY? WHERE DID THEY COME FROM?
NOBODY KNOWS. PERHAPS THEY WERE BUILT BY THE GREEKS? OR THE ROMANS, FOR IRRIGATION?
OR MAYBE THE ANCIENT PHARAOHS?
AMAZING! THEY MUST HAVE BEEN HERE FOR CENTURIES.
AND NOBODY KNOWS ABOUT THIS?
JUST THE OTHER GYPSIES IN CAIRO. WE USE THEM TO GET AROUND THE CITY WITHOUT BEING SEEN. SOMETIMES FOR A SAFE PLACE TO SLEEP DURING A SANDSTORM.
THEY ALSO COME IN HANDY WHEN YOU'RE BEING CHASED BY A GIANT WITH A TATTOO ON HIS FACE.
SPEAKING OF WHICH, WHO WERE YOUR FRIENDS UP THERE?
BEATS ME.
HEY! I WONDER IF IT HAD SOMETHING TO DO WITH THAT NOTE.
NOTE?

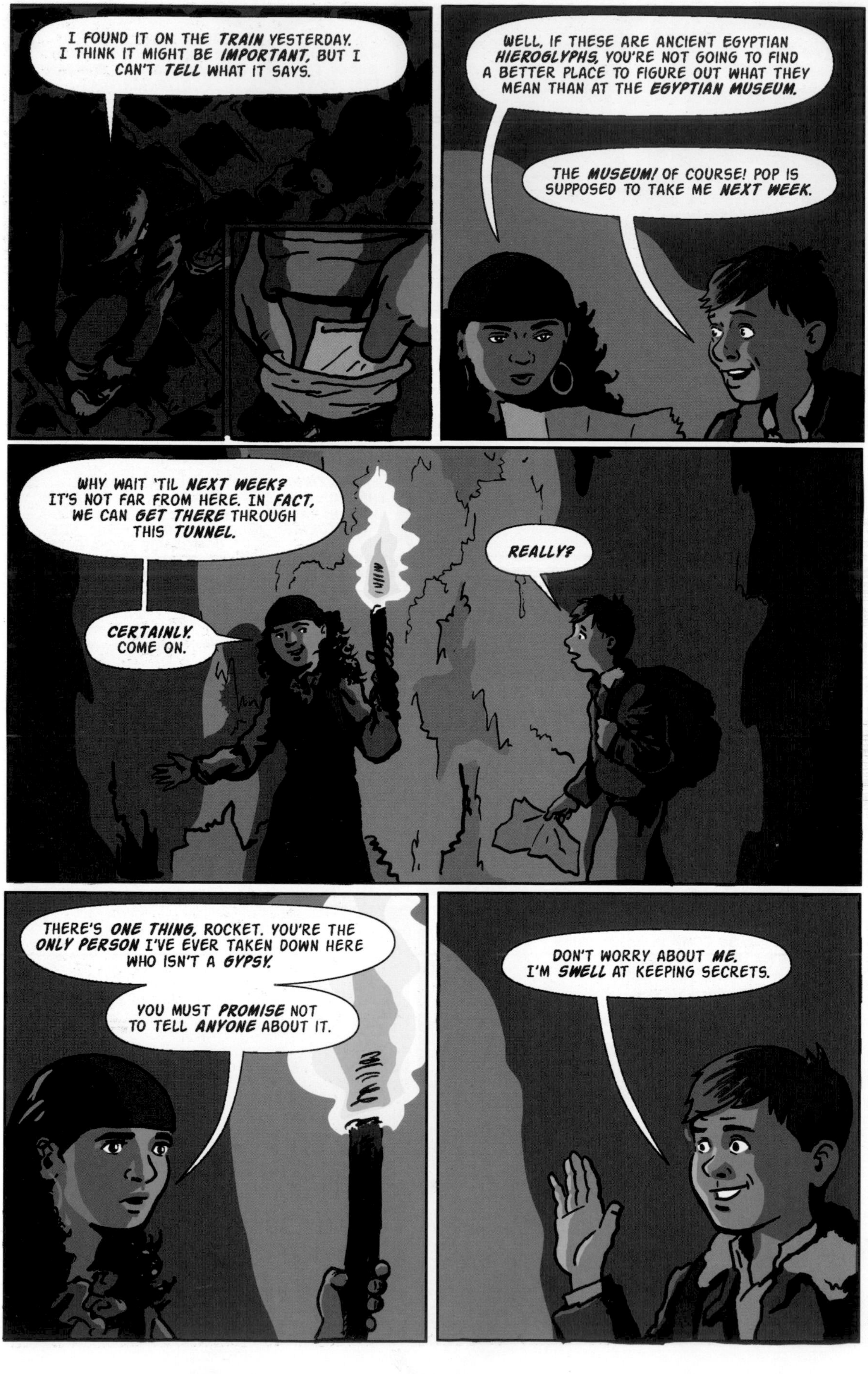
I FOUND IT ON THE TRAIN YESTERDAY. I THINK IT MIGHT BE IMPORTANT, BUT I CAN'T TELL WHAT IT SAYS.
WELL, IF THESE ARE ANCIENT EGYPTIAN HIEROGLYPHS, YOU'RE NOT GOING TO FIND A BETTER PLACE TO FIGURE OUT WHAT THEY MEAN THAN AT THE EGYPTIAN MUSEUM.
THE MUSEUM! OF COURSE! POP IS SUPPOSED TO TAKE ME NEXT WEEK.
WHY WAIT 'TIL NEXT WEEK? IT'S NOT FAR FROM HERE. IN FACT, WE CAN GET THERE THROUGH THIS TUNNEL.
REALLY?
CERTAINLY. COME ON.
THERE'S ONE THING, ROCKET. YOU'RE THE ONLY PERSON I'VE EVER TAKEN DOWN HERE WHO ISN'T A GYPSY.
YOU MUST PROMISE NOT TO TELL ANYONE ABOUT IT.
DON'T WORRY ABOUT ME. I'M SWELL AT KEEPING SECRETS.

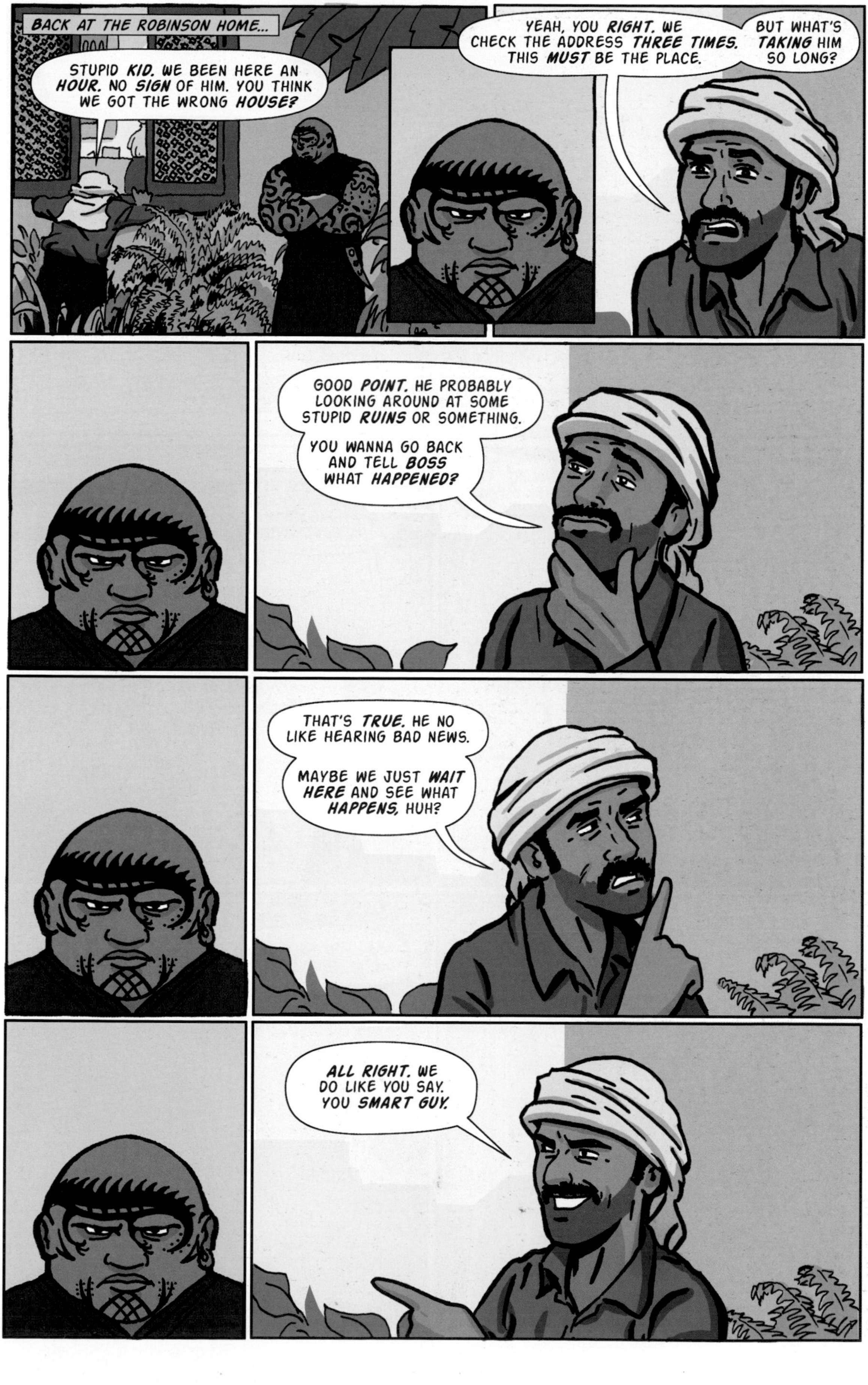
BACK AT THE ROBINSON HOME...
STUPID KID. WE BEEN HERE AN HOUR. NO SIGN OF HIM. YOU THINK WE GOT THE WRONG HOUSE?
YEAH, YOU RIGHT. WE CHECK THE ADDRESS THREE TIMES. THIS MUST BE THE PLACE.
BUT WHAT'S TAKING HIM SO LONG?
GOOD POINT. HE PROBABLY LOOKING AROUND AT SOME STUPID RUINS OR SOMETHING.
YOU WANNA GO BACK AND TELL BOSS WHAT HAPPENED?
THAT'S TRUE. HE NO LIKE HEARING BAD NEWS.
MAYBE WE JUST WAIT HERE AND SEE WHAT HAPPENS, HUH?
ALL RIGHT. WE DO LIKE YOU SAY. YOU SMART GUY.

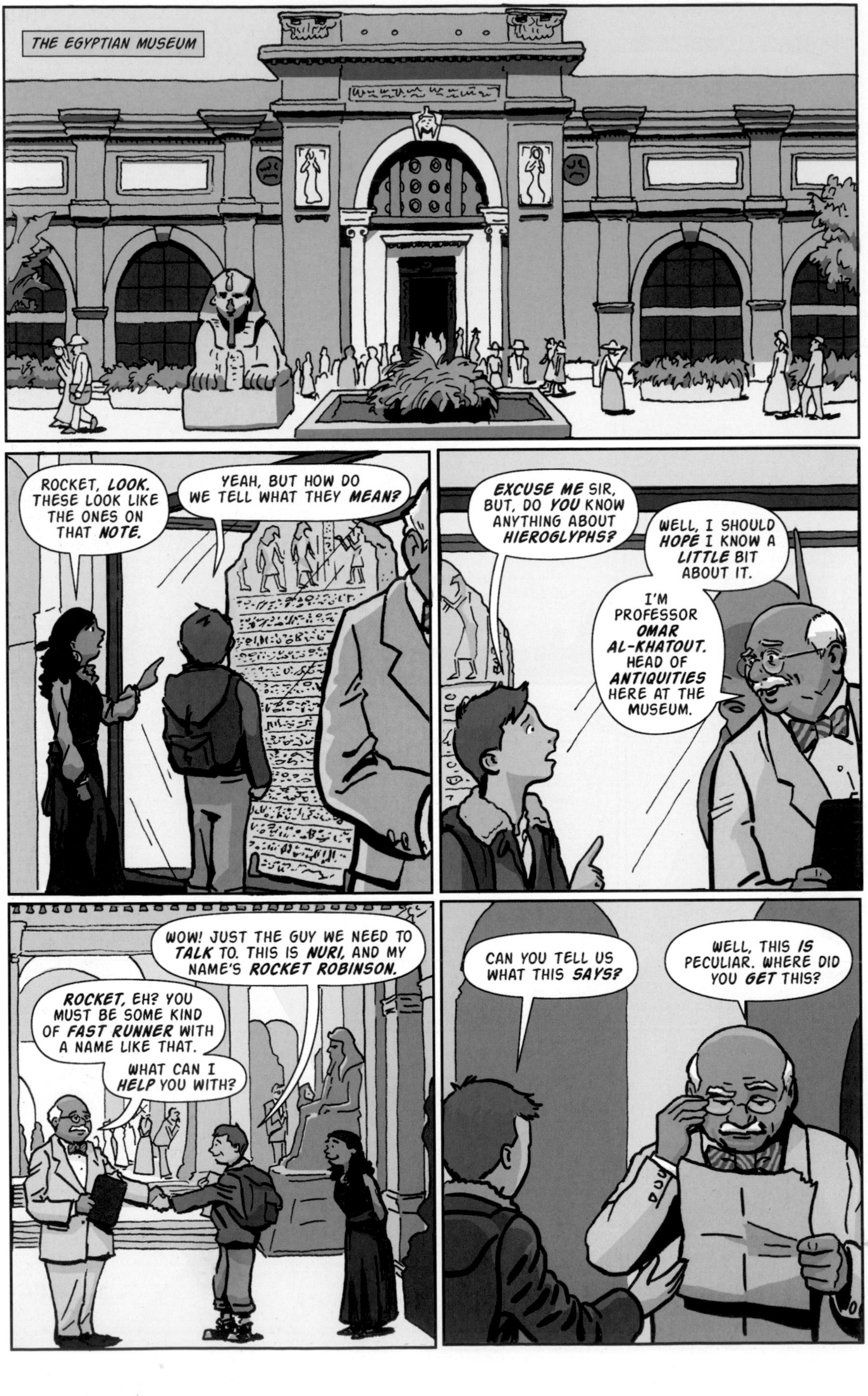
THE EGYPTIAN MUSEUM
ROCKET, LOOK. THESE LOOK LIKE THE ONES ON THAT NOTE.
YEAH, BUT HOW DO WE TELL WHAT THEY MEAN?
EXCUSE ME SIR, BUT, DO YOU KNOW ANYTHING ABOUT HIEROGLYPHS?
WELL, I SHOULD HOPE I KNOW A LITTLE BIT ABOUT IT.
I'M PROFESSOR OMAR AL-KHATOUT. HEAD OF ANTIQUITIES HERE AT THE MUSEUM.
WOW! JUST THE GUY WE NEED TO TALK TO. THIS IS NURI, AND MY NAME'S ROCKET ROBINSON.
ROCKET, EH? YOU MUST BE SOME KIND OF FAST RUNNER WITH A NAME LIKE THAT.
WHAT CAN I HELP YOU WITH?
CAN YOU TELL US WHAT THIS SAYS?
WELL, THIS IS PECULIAR. WHERE DID YOU GET THIS?

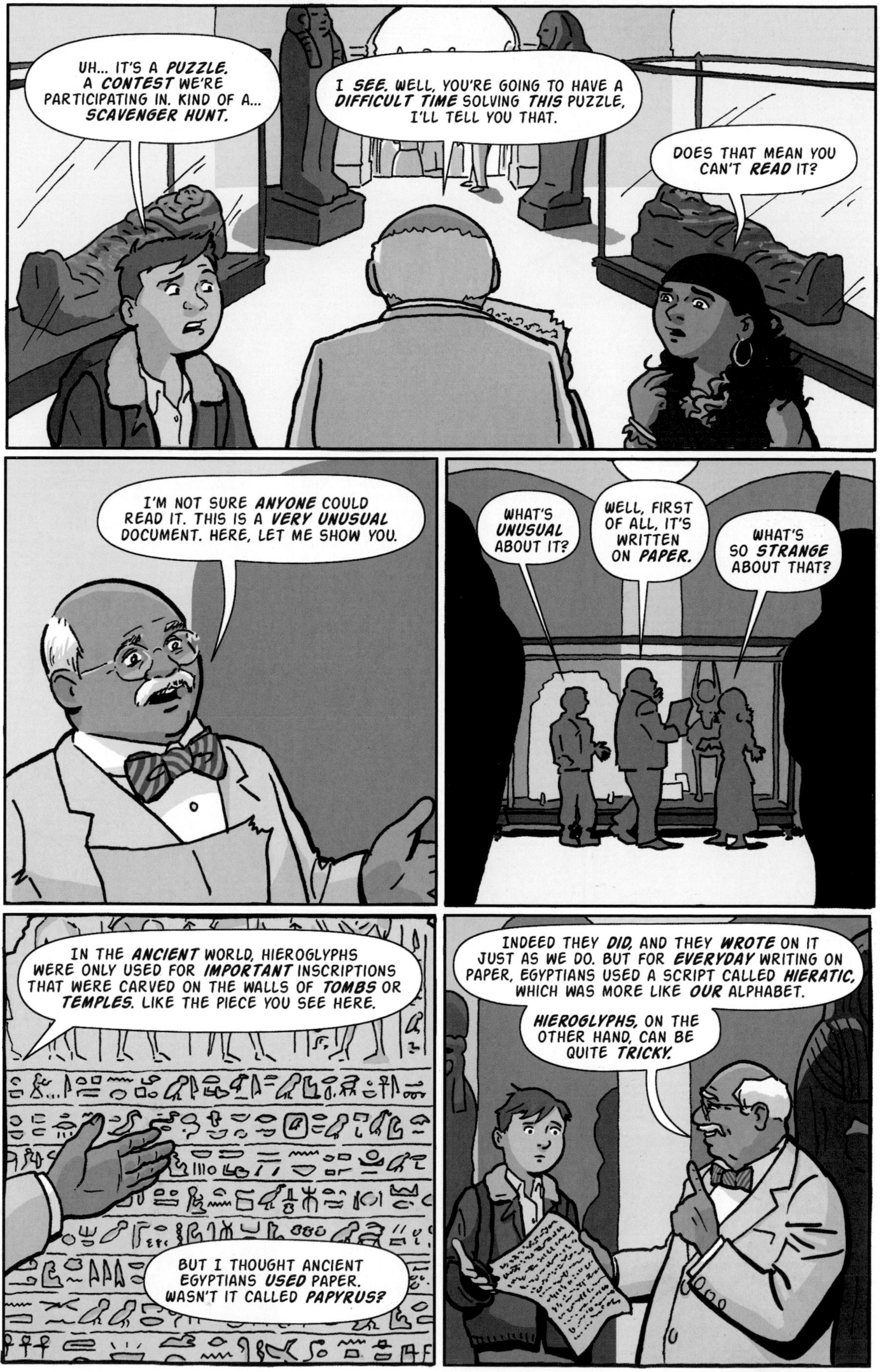
UH... IT'S A PUZZLE. A CONTEST WE'RE PARTICIPATING IN. KIND OF A... SCAVENGER HUNT.
I SEE. WELL, YOU'RE GOING TO HAVE A DIFFICULT TIME SOLVING THIS PUZZLE, I'LL TELL YOU THAT.
DOES THAT MEAN YOU CAN'T READ IT?
I'M NOT SURE ANYONE COULD READ IT. THIS IS A VERY UNUSUAL DOCUMENT. HERE, LET ME SHOW YOU.
WHAT'S UNUSUAL ABOUT IT?
WELL, FIRST OF ALL, IT'S WRITTEN ON PAPER.
WHAT'S SO STRANGE ABOUT THAT?
IN THE ANCIENT WORLD, HIEROGLYPHS WERE ONLY USED FOR IMPORTANT INSCRIPTIONS THAT WERE CARVED ON THE WALLS OF TOMBS OR TEMPLES. LIKE THE PIECE YOU SEE HERE.
BUT I THOUGHT ANCIENT EGYPTIANS USED PAPER. WASN'T IT CALLED PAPYRUS?
INDEED THEY DID, AND THEY WROTE ON IT JUST AS WE DO. BUT FOR EVERYDAY WRITING ON PAPER, EGYPTIANS USED A SCRIPT CALLED HIERATIC, WHICH WAS MORE LIKE OUR ALPHABET.
HIEROGLYPHS, ON THE OTHER HAND, CAN BE QUITE TRICKY.

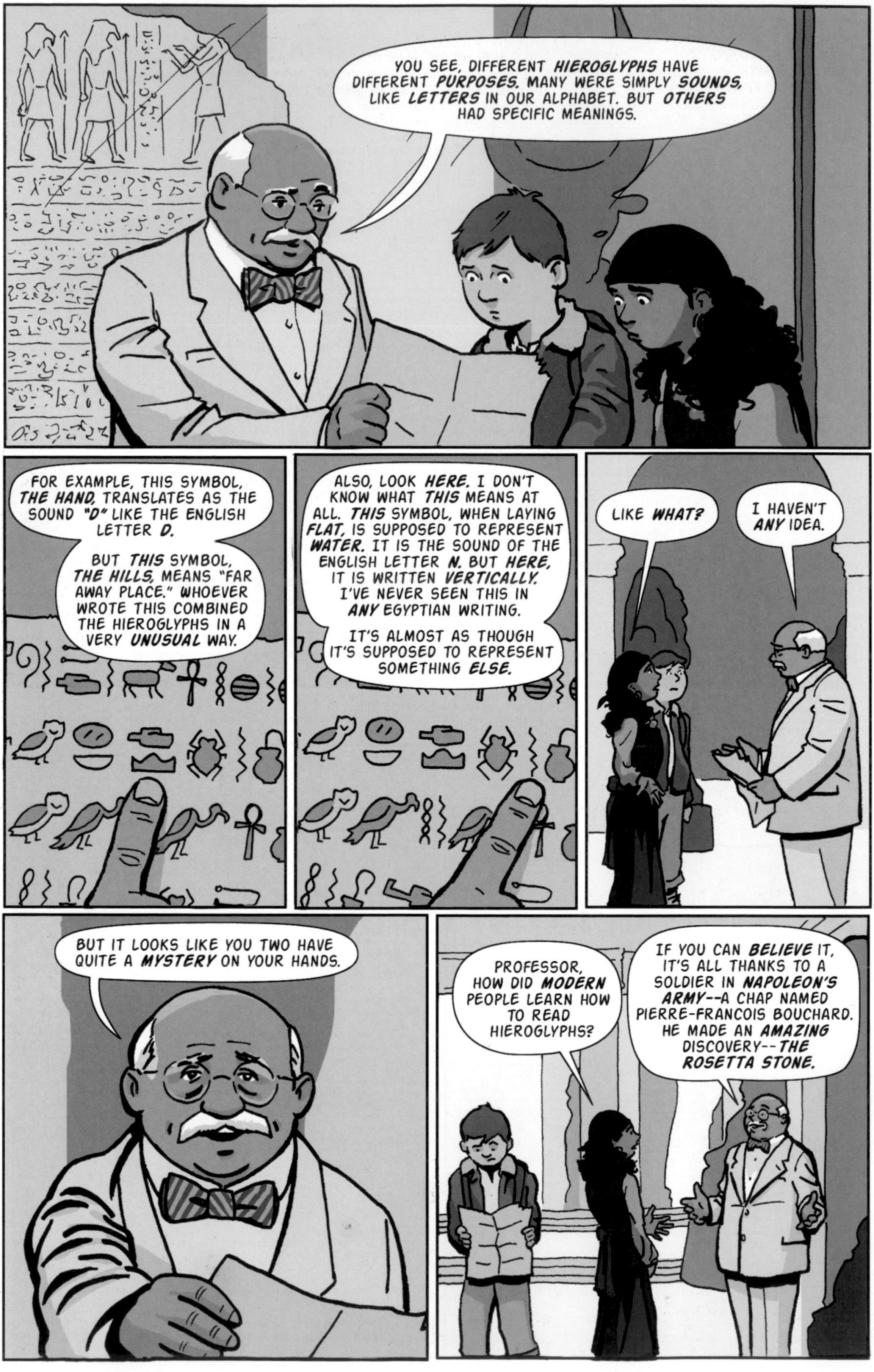
YOU SEE, DIFFERENT HIEROGLYPHS HAVE DIFFERENT PURPOSES. MANY WERE SIMPLY SOUNDS, LIKE LETTERS IN OUR ALPHABET. BUT OTHERS HAD SPECIFIC MEANINGS.
FOR EXAMPLE, THIS SYMBOL, THE HAND, TRANSLATES AS THE SOUND "D" LIKE THE ENGLISH LETTER D.
BUT THIS SYMBOL, THE HILLS, MEANS "FAR AWAY PLACE." WHOEVER WROTE THIS COMBINED THE HIEROGLYPHS IN A VERY UNUSUAL WAY.
ALSO, LOOK HERE. I DON'T KNOW WHAT THIS MEANS AT ALL. THIS SYMBOL, WHEN LAYING FLAT, IS SUPPOSED TO REPRESENT WATER. IT IS THE SOUND OF THE ENGLISH LETTER N. BUT HERE, IT IS WRITTEN VERTICALLY. I'VE NEVER SEEN THIS IN ANY EGYPTIAN WRITING.
IT'S ALMOST AS THOUGH IT'S SUPPOSED TO REPRESENT SOMETHING ELSE.
LIKE WHAT?
I HAVEN'T ANY IDEA.
BUT IT LOOKS LIKE YOU TWO HAVE QUITE A MYSTERY ON YOUR HANDS.
PROFESSOR, HOW DID MODERN PEOPLE LEARN HOW TO READ HIEROGLYPHS?
IF YOU CAN BELIEVE IT, IT'S ALL THANKS TO A SOLDIER IN NAPOLEON'S ARMY--A CHAP NAMED PIERRE-FRANCOIS BOUCHARD. HE MADE AN AMAZING DISCOVERY--THE ROSETTA STONE.

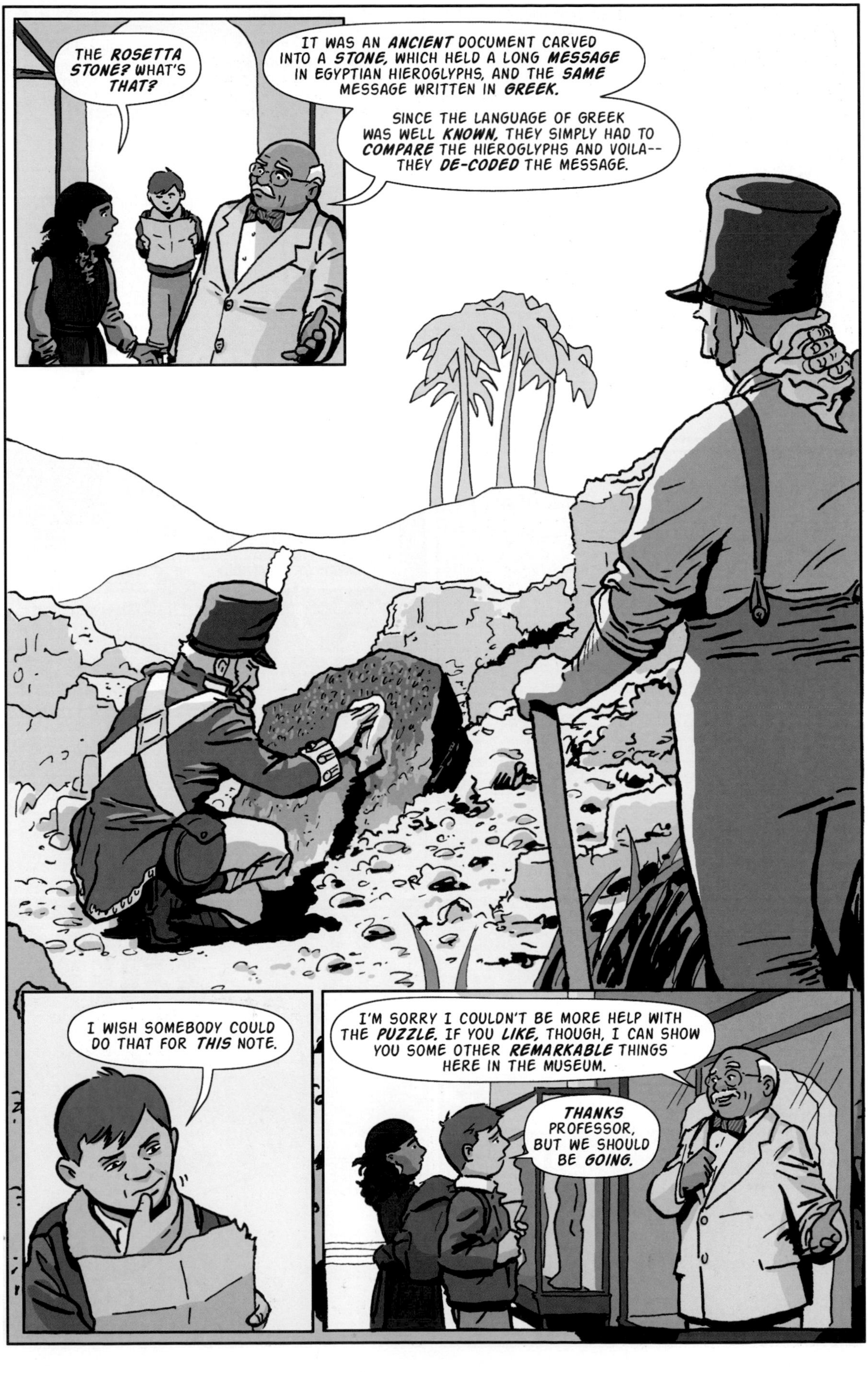
THE ROSETTA STONE? WHAT'S THAT?
IT WAS AN ANCIENT DOCUMENT CARVED INTO A STONE, WHICH HELD A LONG MESSAGE IN EGYPTIAN HIEROGLYPHS, AND THE SAME MESSAGE WRITTEN IN GREEK.
SINCE THE LANGUAGE OF GREEK WAS WELL KNOWN, THEY SIMPLY HAD TO COMPARE THE HIEROGLYPHS AND VOILA-- THEY DE-CODED THE MESSAGE.
I WISH SOMEBODY COULD DO THAT FOR THIS NOTE.
I'M SORRY I COULDN'T BE MORE HELP WITH THE PUZZLE. IF YOU LIKE, THOUGH, I CAN SHOW YOU SOME OTHER REMARKABLE THINGS HERE IN THE MUSEUM.
THANKS PROFESSOR, BUT WE SHOULD BE GOING.

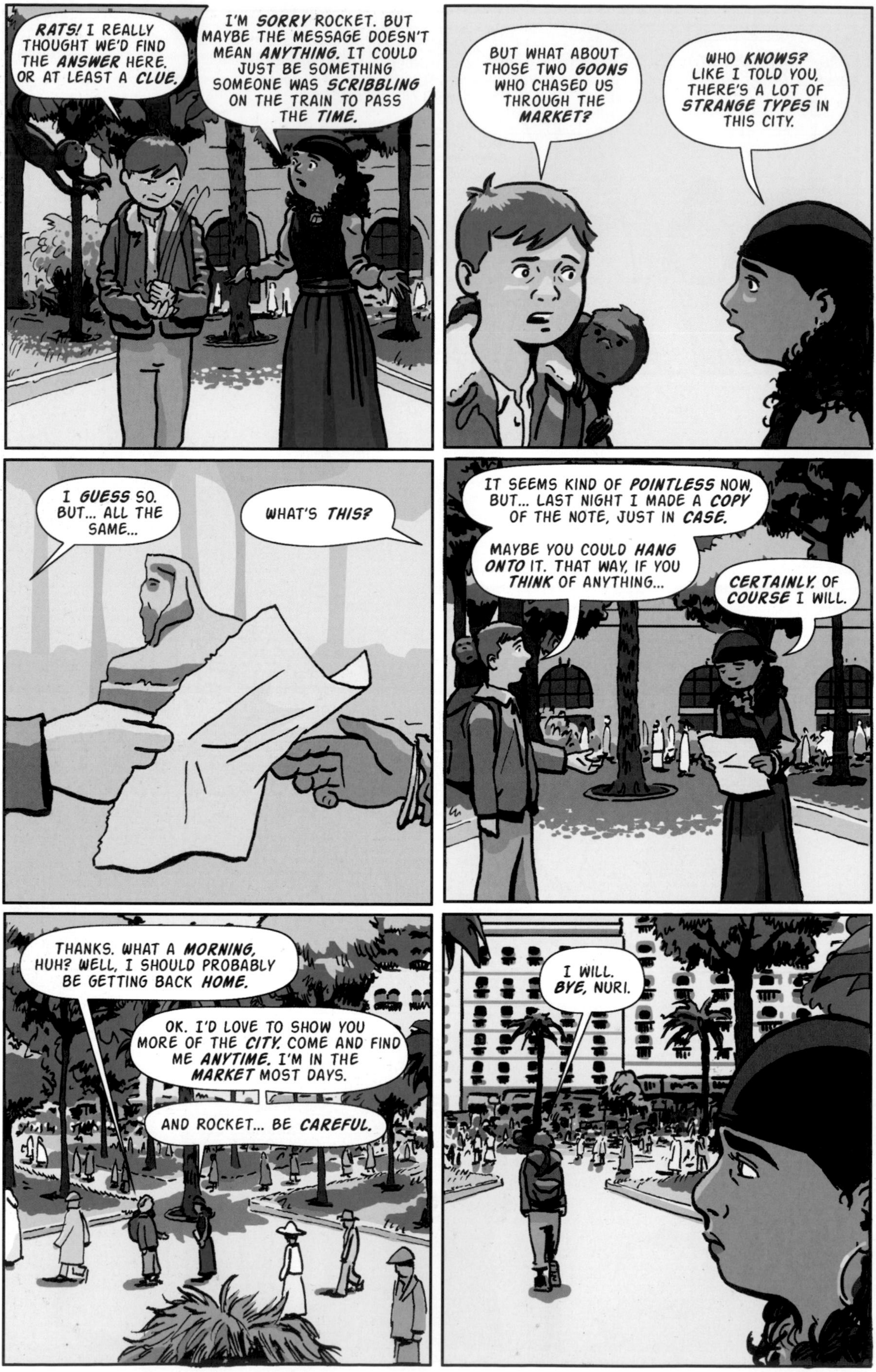
RATS! I REALLY THOUGHT WE'D FIND THE ANSWER HERE. OR AT LEAST A CLUE.
I'M SORRY ROCKET. BUT MAYBE THE MESSAGE DOESN'T MEAN ANYTHING. IT COULD JUST BE SOMETHING SOMEONE WAS SCRIBBLING ON THE TRAIN TO PASS THE TIME.
BUT WHAT ABOUT THOSE TWO GOONS WHO CHASED US THROUGH THE MARKET?
WHO KNOWS? LIKE I TOLD YOU, THERE'S A LOT OF STRANGE TYPES IN THIS CITY.
I GUESS SO. BUT... ALL THE SAME...
WHAT'S THIS?
IT SEEMS KIND OF POINTLESS NOW, BUT... LAST NIGHT I MADE A COPY OF THE NOTE, JUST IN CASE.
MAYBE YOU COULD HANG ONTO IT. THAT WAY, IF YOU THINK OF ANYTHING...
CERTAINLY. OF COURSE I WILL.
THANKS. WHAT A MORNING, HUH? WELL, I SHOULD PROBABLY BE GETTING BACK HOME.
OK. I'D LOVE TO SHOW YOU MORE OF THE CITY. COME AND FIND ME ANYTIME. I'M IN THE MARKET MOST DAYS.
AND ROCKET... BE CAREFUL.
I WILL. BYE, NURI.

CHAPTER THREE

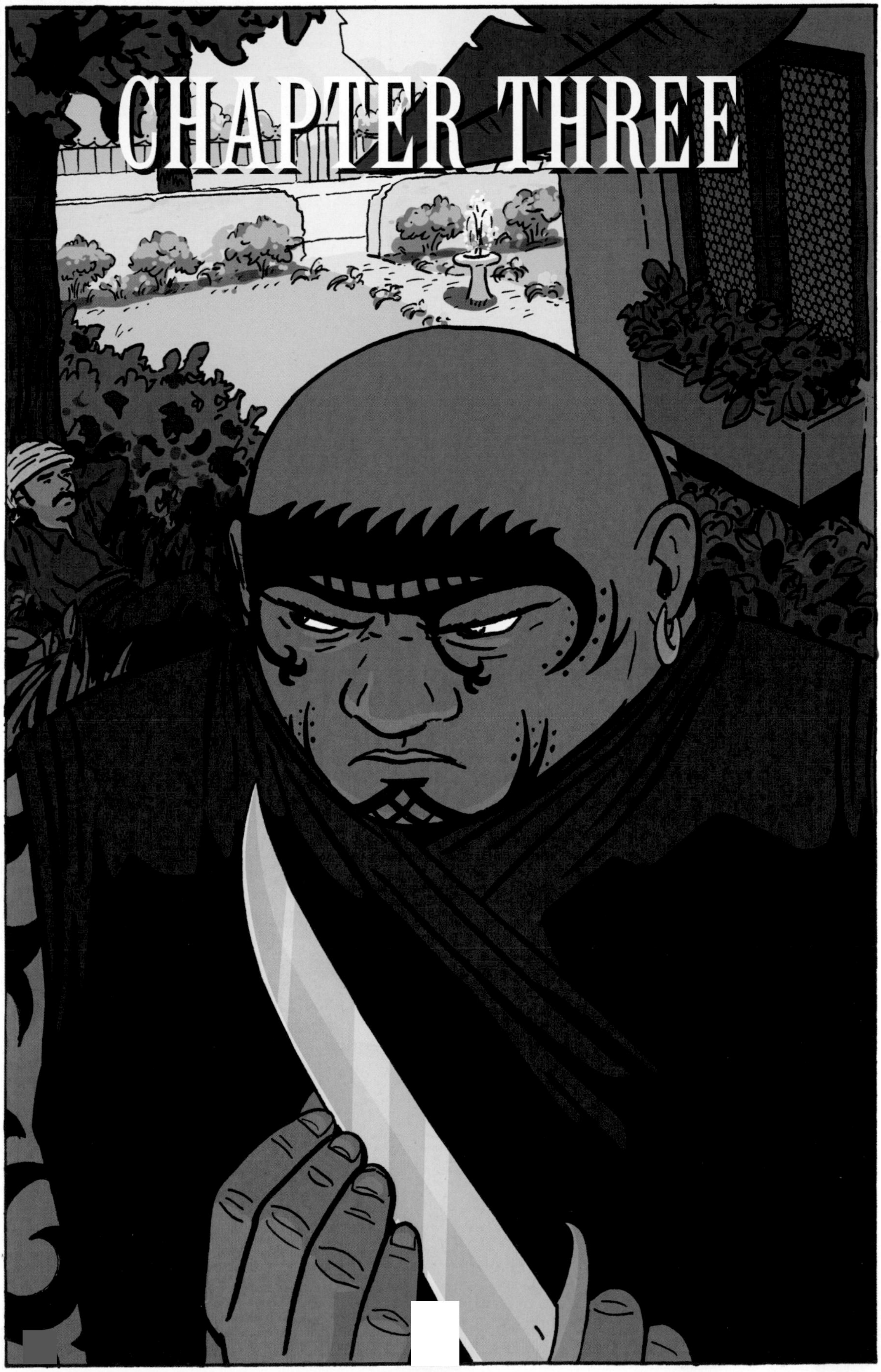

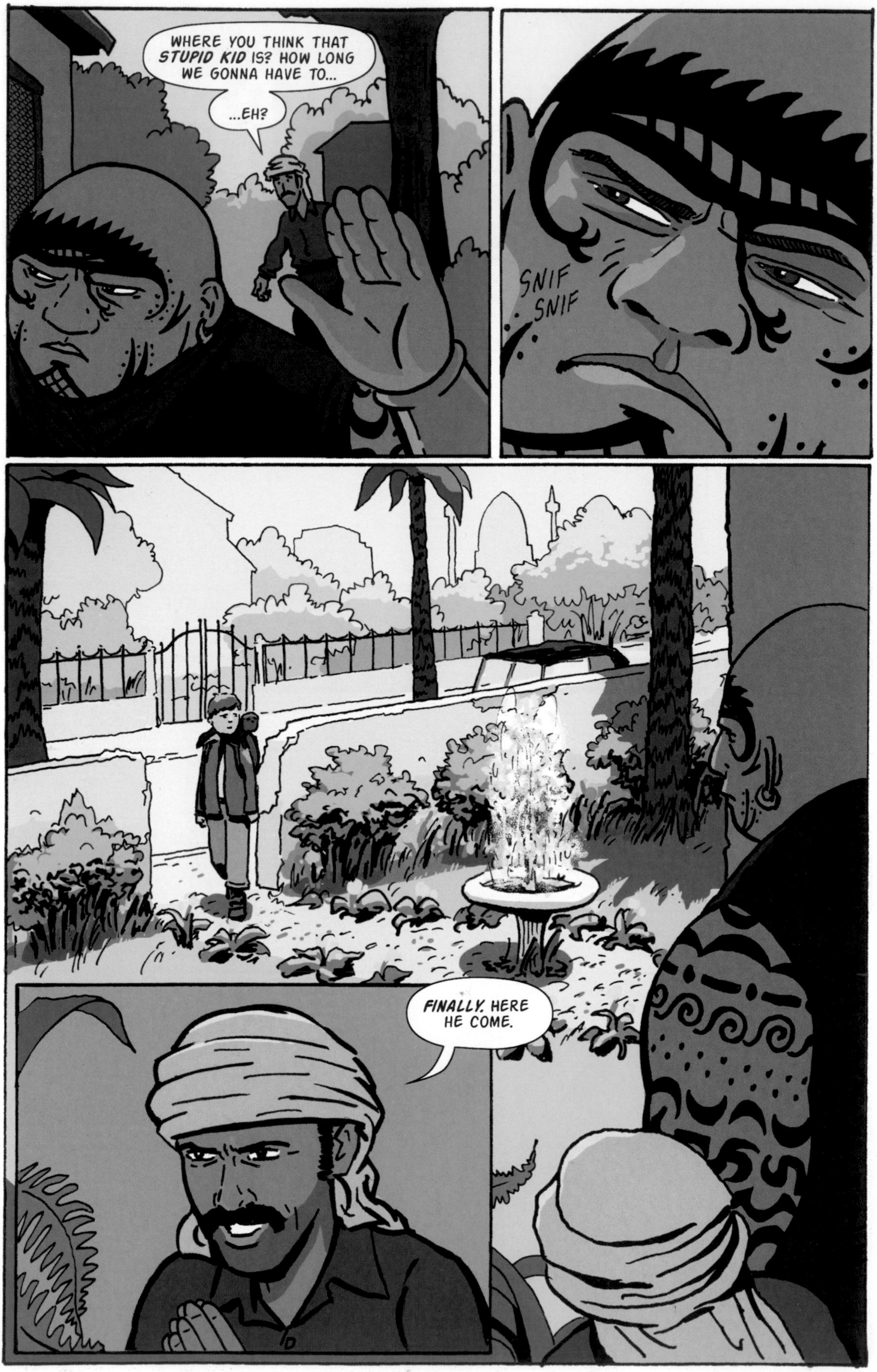
WHERE YOU THINK THAT STUPID KID IS? HOW LONG WE GONNA HAVE TO...
...EH?
SNIF SNIF
FINALLY. HERE HE COME.

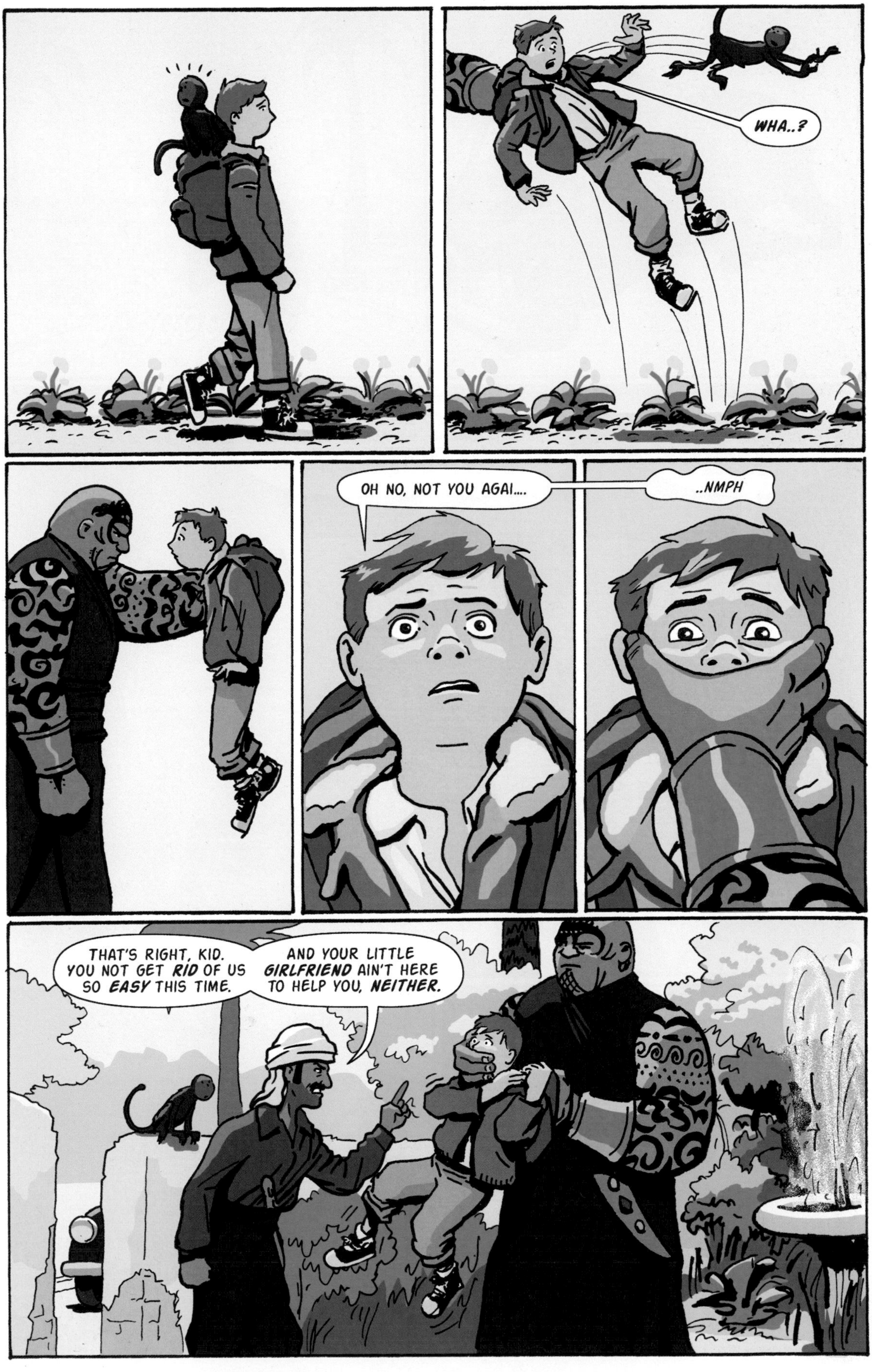
WHA..?
OH NO, NOT YOU AGAI....
..NMPH
THAT'S RIGHT, KID. YOU NOT GET *RID* OF US SO *EASY* THIS TIME.
AND YOUR LITTLE *GIRLFRIEND* AIN'T HERE TO HELP YOU, *NEITHER.*

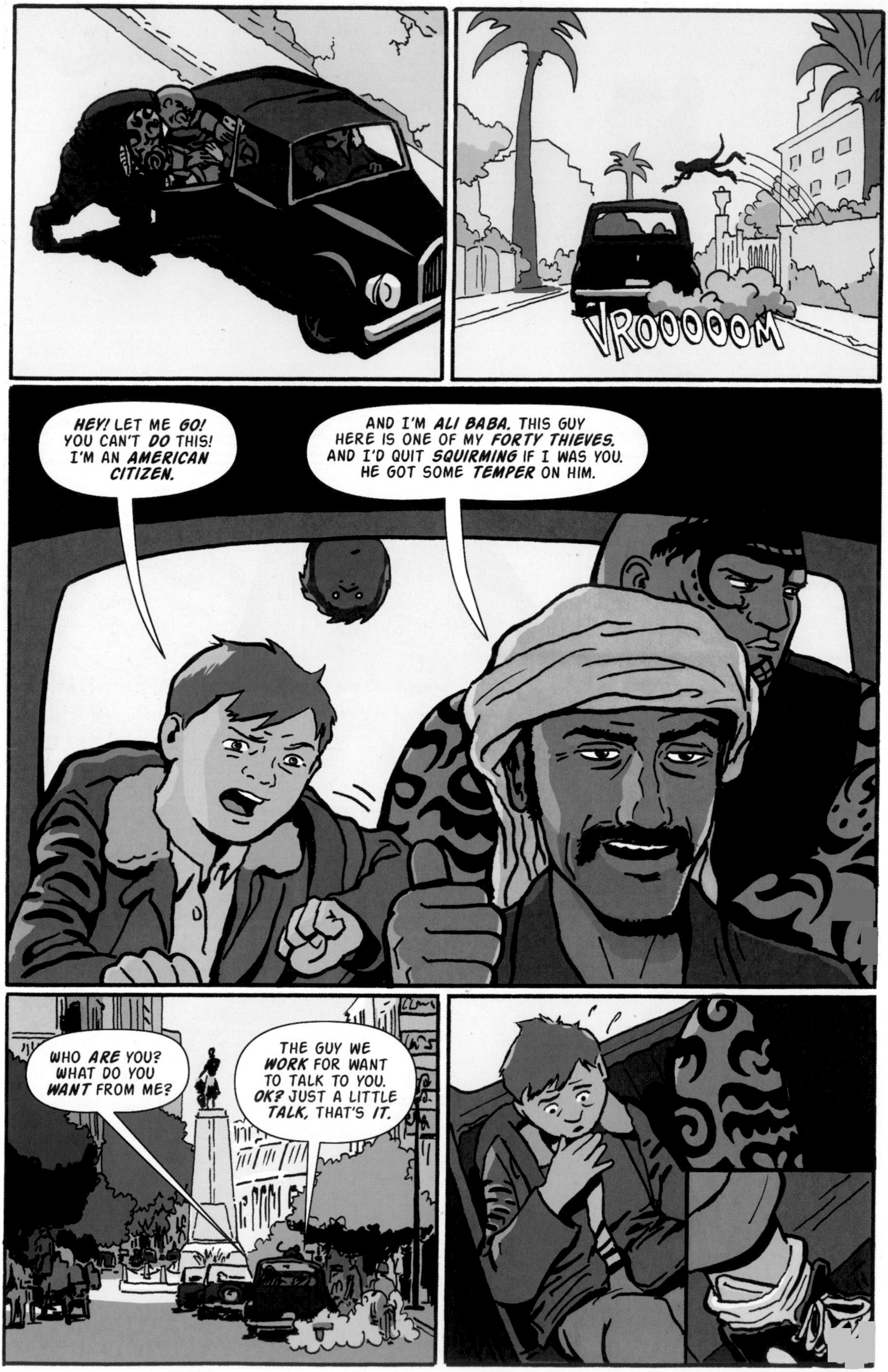
VROOOOOM
HEY! LET ME GO! YOU CAN'T DO THIS! I'M AN AMERICAN CITIZEN.
AND I'M ALI BABA. THIS GUY HERE IS ONE OF MY FORTY THIEVES. AND I'D QUIT SQUIRMING IF I WAS YOU. HE GOT SOME TEMPER ON HIM.
WHO ARE YOU? WHAT DO YOU WANT FROM ME?
THE GUY WE WORK FOR WANT TO TALK TO YOU. OK? JUST A LITTLE TALK, THAT'S IT.

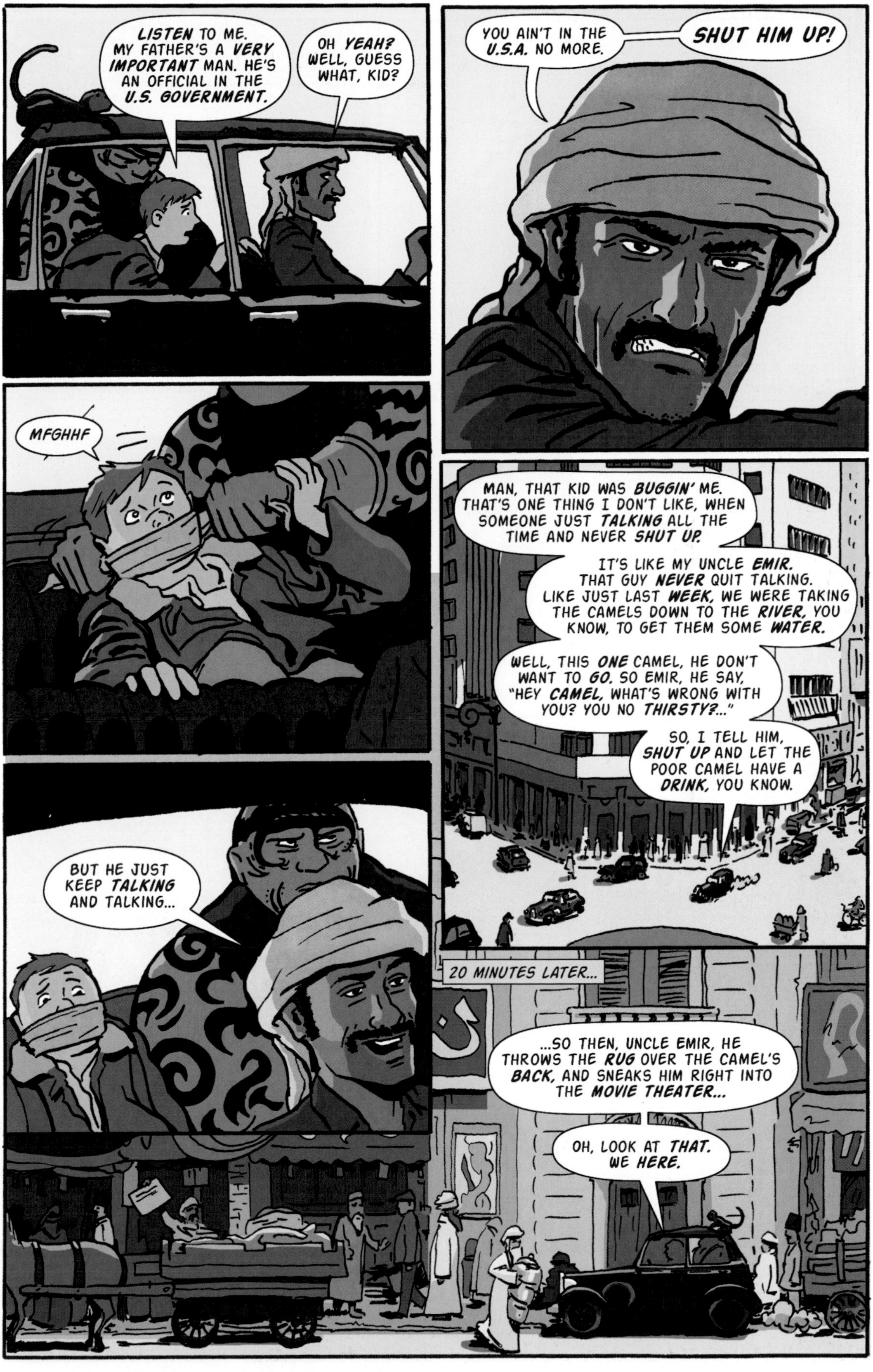

LISTEN TO ME. MY FATHER'S A VERY IMPORTANT MAN. HE'S AN OFFICIAL IN THE U.S. GOVERNMENT.
OH YEAH? WELL, GUESS WHAT, KID?
YOU AIN'T IN THE U.S.A. NO MORE.
SHUT HIM UP!
MFGHHF
MAN, THAT KID WAS BUGGIN' ME. THAT'S ONE THING I DON'T LIKE, WHEN SOMEONE JUST TALKING ALL THE TIME AND NEVER SHUT UP.
IT'S LIKE MY UNCLE EMIR. THAT GUY NEVER QUIT TALKING. LIKE JUST LAST WEEK, WE WERE TAKING THE CAMELS DOWN TO THE RIVER, YOU KNOW, TO GET THEM SOME WATER.
WELL, THIS ONE CAMEL, HE DON'T WANT TO GO. SO EMIR, HE SAY, "HEY CAMEL, WHAT'S WRONG WITH YOU? YOU NO THIRSTY?..."
SO, I TELL HIM, SHUT UP AND LET THE POOR CAMEL HAVE A DRINK, YOU KNOW.
BUT HE JUST KEEP TALKING AND TALKING...
20 MINUTES LATER...
...SO THEN, UNCLE EMIR, HE THROWS THE RUG OVER THE CAMEL'S BACK, AND SNEAKS HIM RIGHT INTO THE MOVIE THEATER...
OH, LOOK AT THAT. WE HERE.

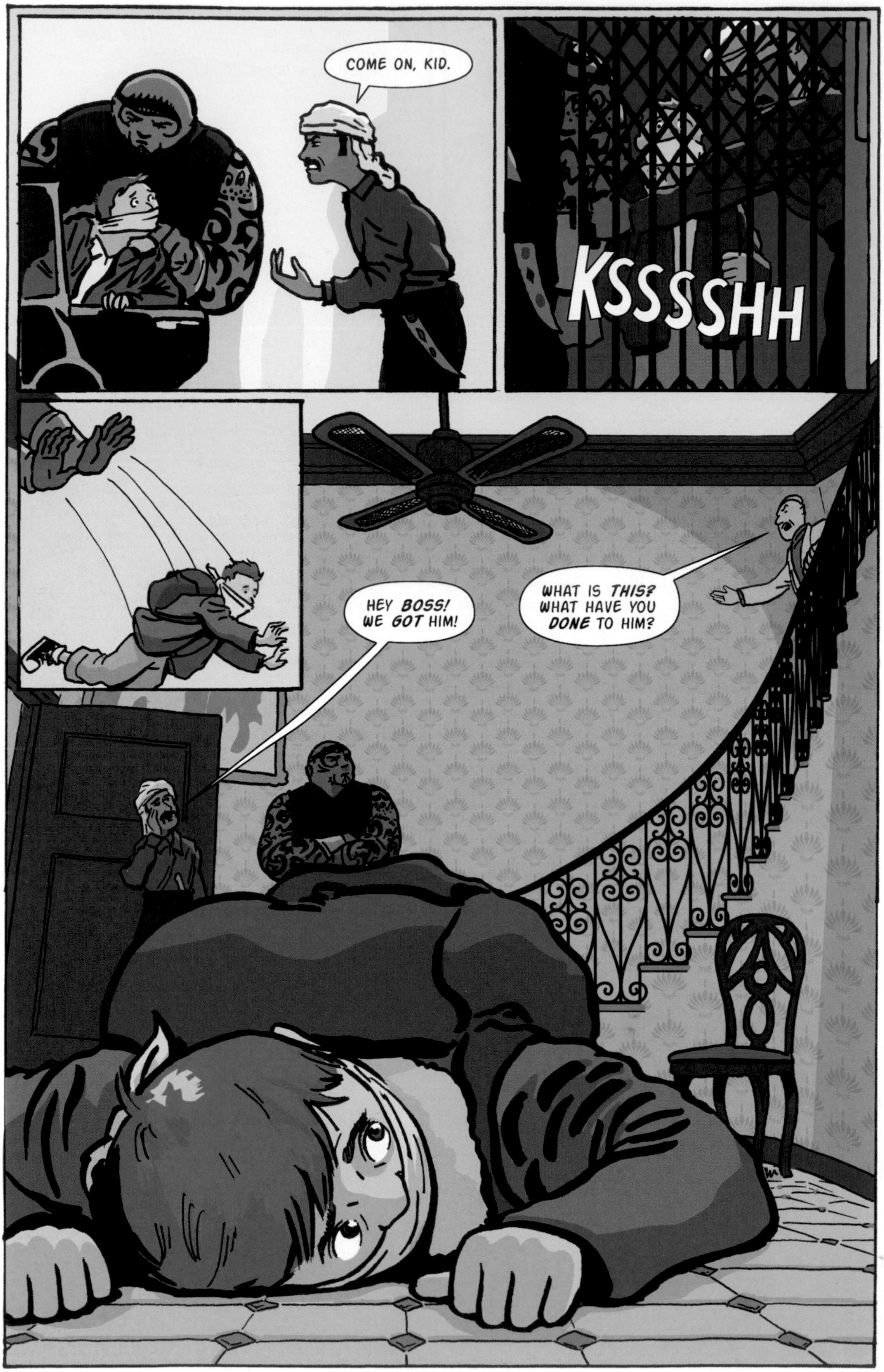
COME ON, KID.
KSSSSHH
HEY BOSS! WE GOT HIM!
WHAT IS THIS? WHAT HAVE YOU DONE TO HIM?

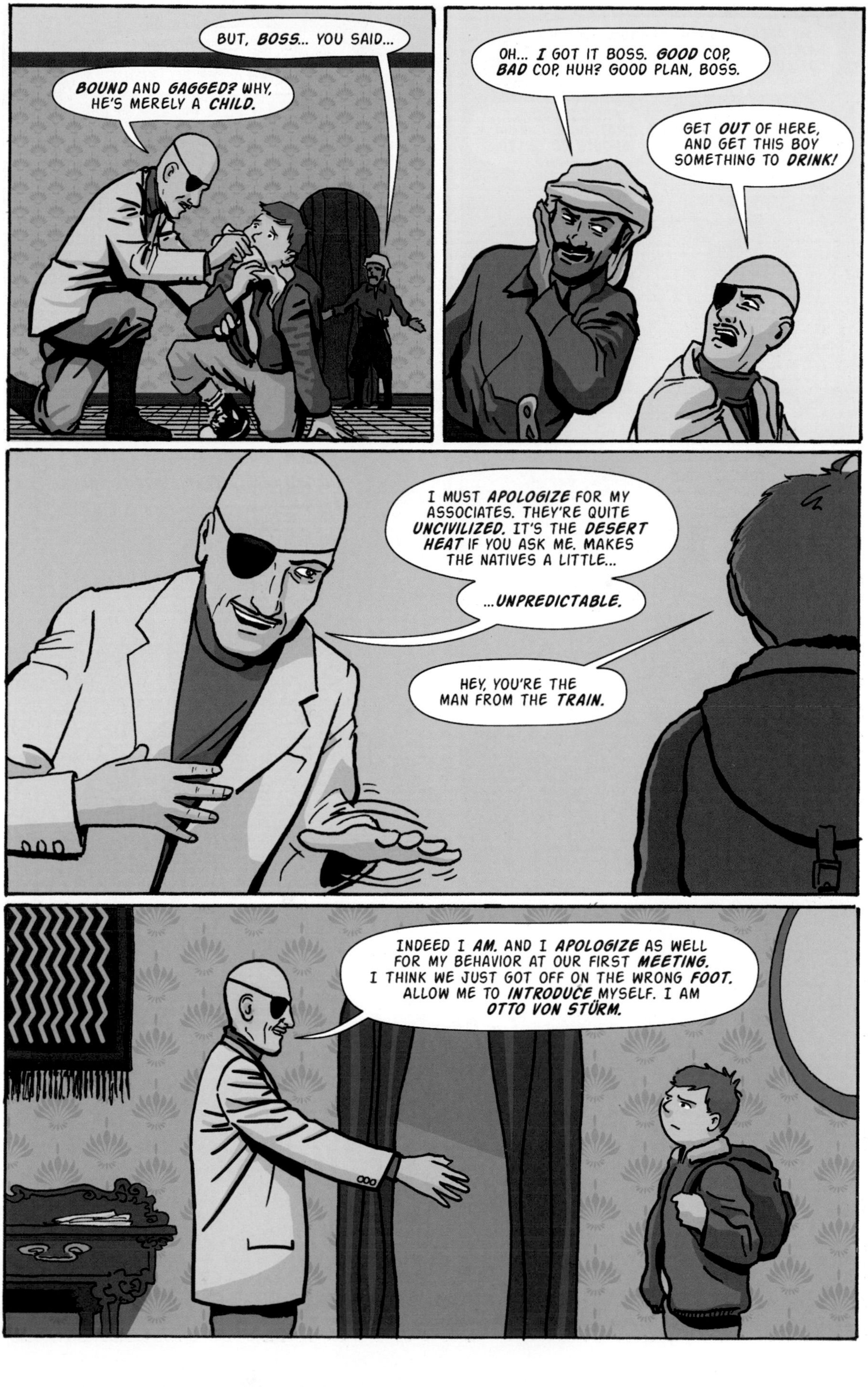
BUT, BOSS... YOU SAID...
BOUND AND GAGGED? WHY, HE'S MERELY A CHILD.
OH... I GOT IT BOSS. GOOD COP, BAD COP, HUH? GOOD PLAN, BOSS.
GET OUT OF HERE, AND GET THIS BOY SOMETHING TO DRINK!
I MUST APOLOGIZE FOR MY ASSOCIATES. THEY'RE QUITE UNCIVILIZED. IT'S THE DESERT HEAT IF YOU ASK ME. MAKES THE NATIVES A LITTLE...
...UNPREDICTABLE.
HEY, YOU'RE THE MAN FROM THE TRAIN.
INDEED I AM. AND I APOLOGIZE AS WELL FOR MY BEHAVIOR AT OUR FIRST MEETING. I THINK WE JUST GOT OFF ON THE WRONG FOOT. ALLOW ME TO INTRODUCE MYSELF. I AM OTTO VON STÜRM.

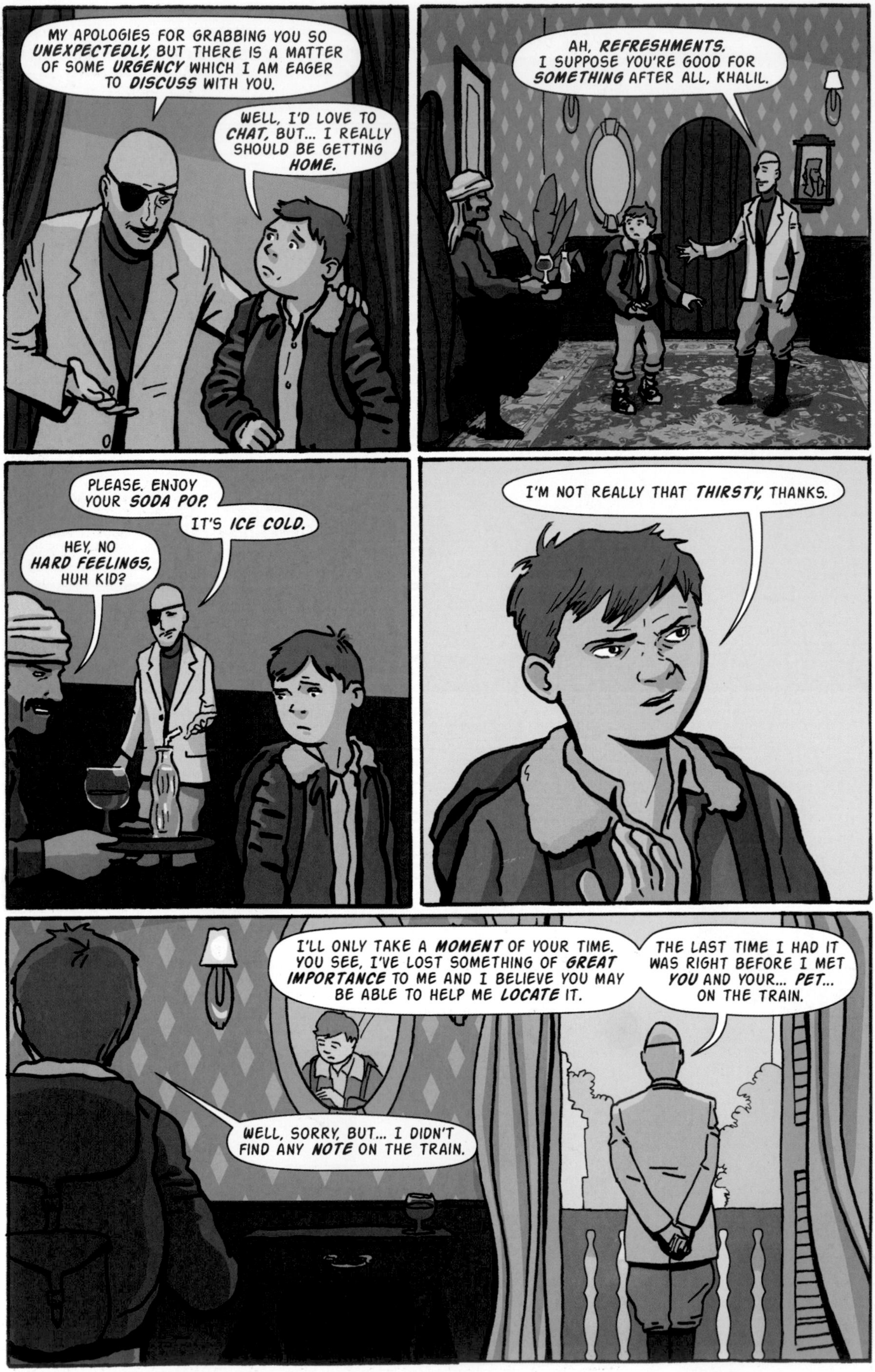
MY APOLOGIES FOR GRABBING YOU SO UNEXPECTEDLY, BUT THERE IS A MATTER OF SOME URGENCY WHICH I AM EAGER TO DISCUSS WITH YOU.
WELL, I'D LOVE TO CHAT, BUT... I REALLY SHOULD BE GETTING HOME.
AH, REFRESHMENTS. I SUPPOSE YOU'RE GOOD FOR SOMETHING AFTER ALL, KHALIL.
PLEASE. ENJOY YOUR SODA POP.
IT'S ICE COLD.
HEY, NO HARD FEELINGS, HUH KID?
I'M NOT REALLY THAT THIRSTY, THANKS.
I'LL ONLY TAKE A MOMENT OF YOUR TIME. YOU SEE, I'VE LOST SOMETHING OF GREAT IMPORTANCE TO ME AND I BELIEVE YOU MAY BE ABLE TO HELP ME LOCATE IT.
THE LAST TIME I HAD IT WAS RIGHT BEFORE I MET YOU AND YOUR... PET... ON THE TRAIN.
WELL, SORRY, BUT... I DIDN'T FIND ANY NOTE ON THE TRAIN.

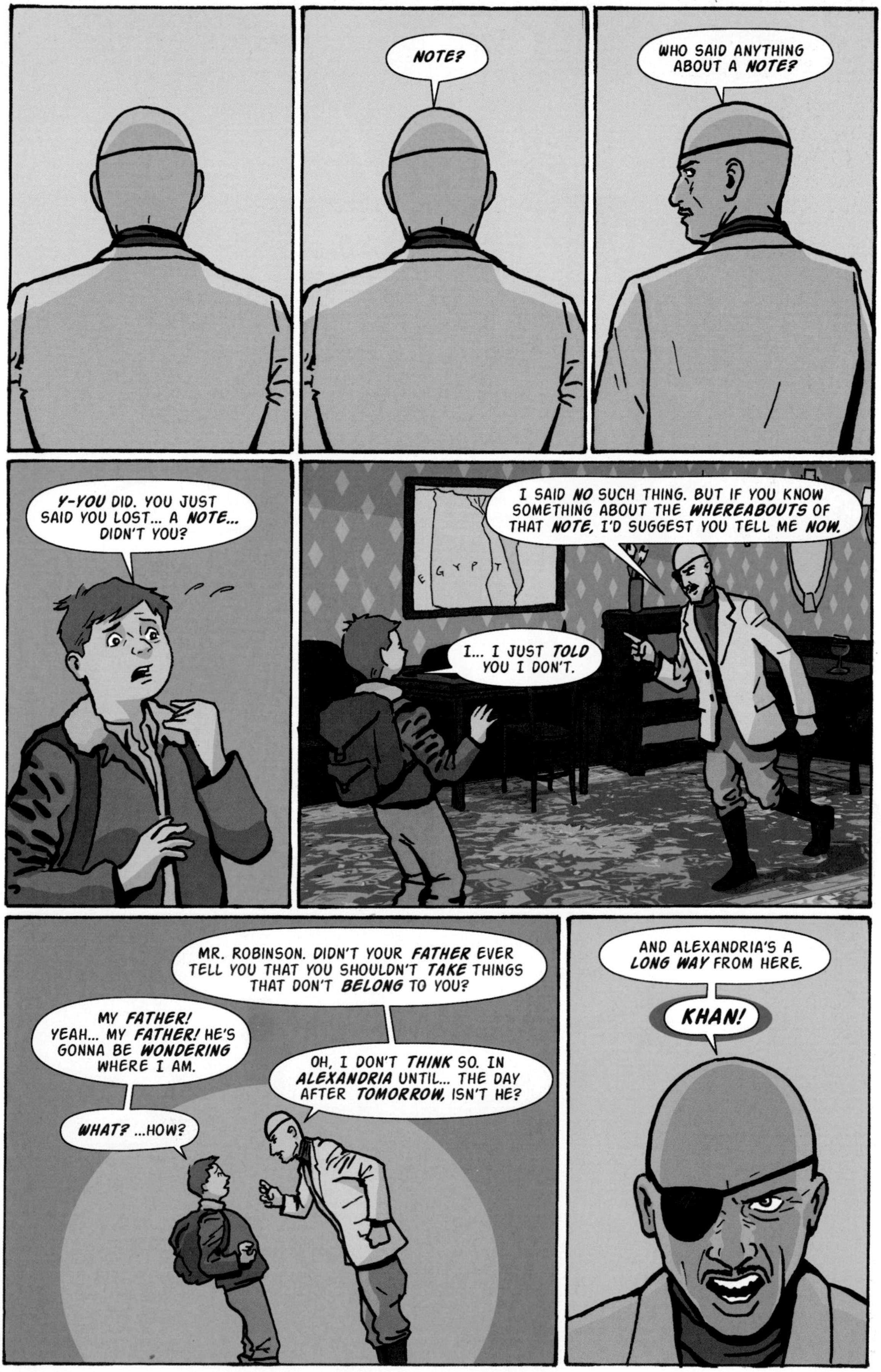
NOTE?
WHO SAID ANYTHING ABOUT A NOTE?
Y-YOU DID. YOU JUST SAID YOU LOST... A NOTE... DIDN'T YOU?
I SAID NO SUCH THING. BUT IF YOU KNOW SOMETHING ABOUT THE WHEREABOUTS OF THAT NOTE, I'D SUGGEST YOU TELL ME NOW.
EGYPT
I... I JUST TOLD YOU I DON'T.
MR. ROBINSON. DIDN'T YOUR FATHER EVER TELL YOU THAT YOU SHOULDN'T TAKE THINGS THAT DON'T BELONG TO YOU?
MY FATHER! YEAH... MY FATHER! HE'S GONNA BE WONDERING WHERE I AM.
OH, I DON'T THINK SO. IN ALEXANDRIA UNTIL... THE DAY AFTER TOMORROW, ISN'T HE?
WHAT? ...HOW?
AND ALEXANDRIA'S A LONG WAY FROM HERE.
KHAN!

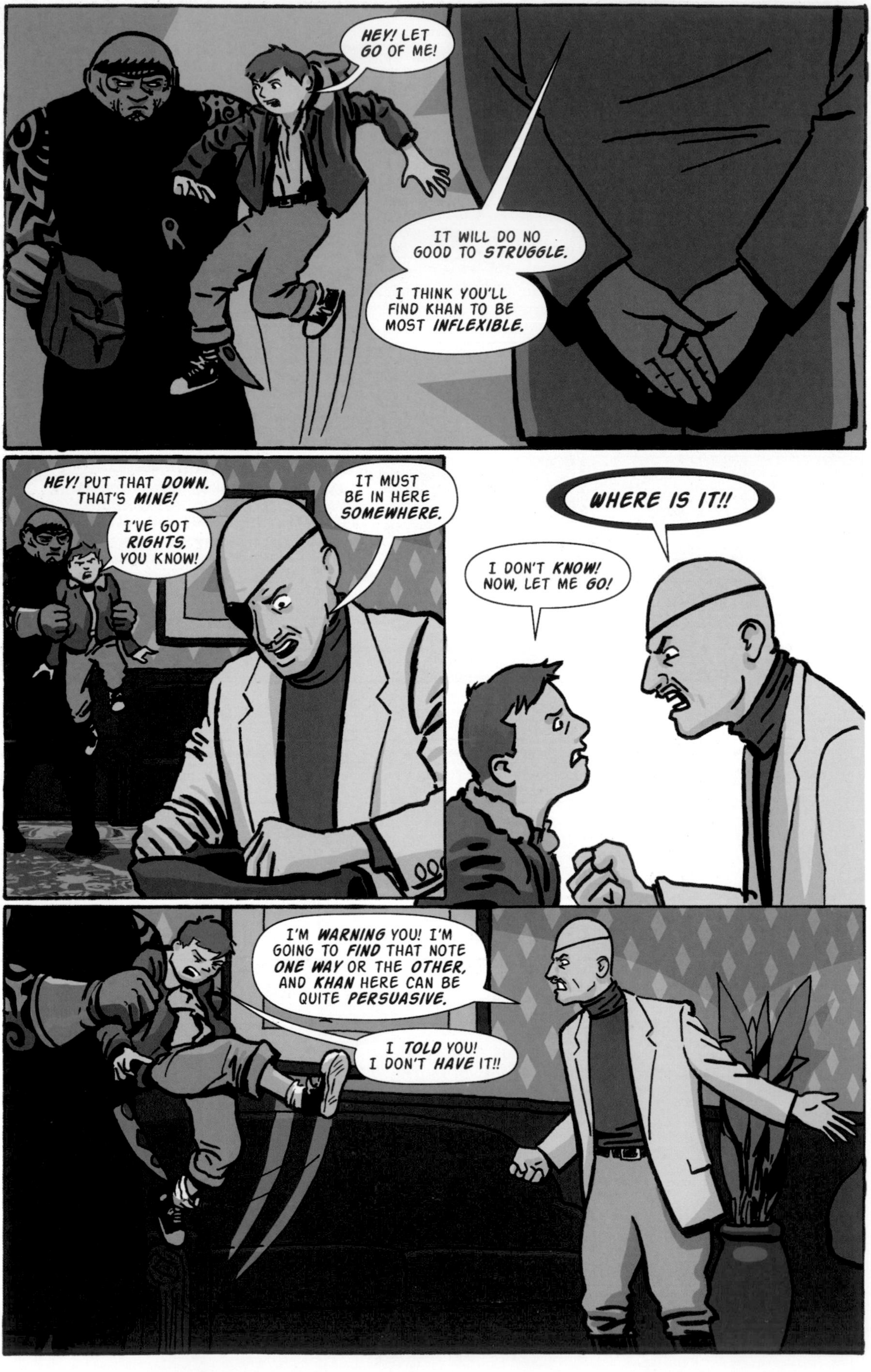
HEY! LET GO OF ME!
IT WILL DO NO GOOD TO STRUGGLE.
I THINK YOU'LL FIND KHAN TO BE MOST INFLEXIBLE.
HEY! PUT THAT DOWN. THAT'S MINE!
I'VE GOT RIGHTS, YOU KNOW!
IT MUST BE IN HERE SOMEWHERE.
WHERE IS IT!!
I DON'T KNOW! NOW, LET ME GO!
I'M WARNING YOU! I'M GOING TO FIND THAT NOTE ONE WAY OR THE OTHER, AND KHAN HERE CAN BE QUITE PERSUASIVE.
I TOLD YOU! I DON'T HAVE IT!!

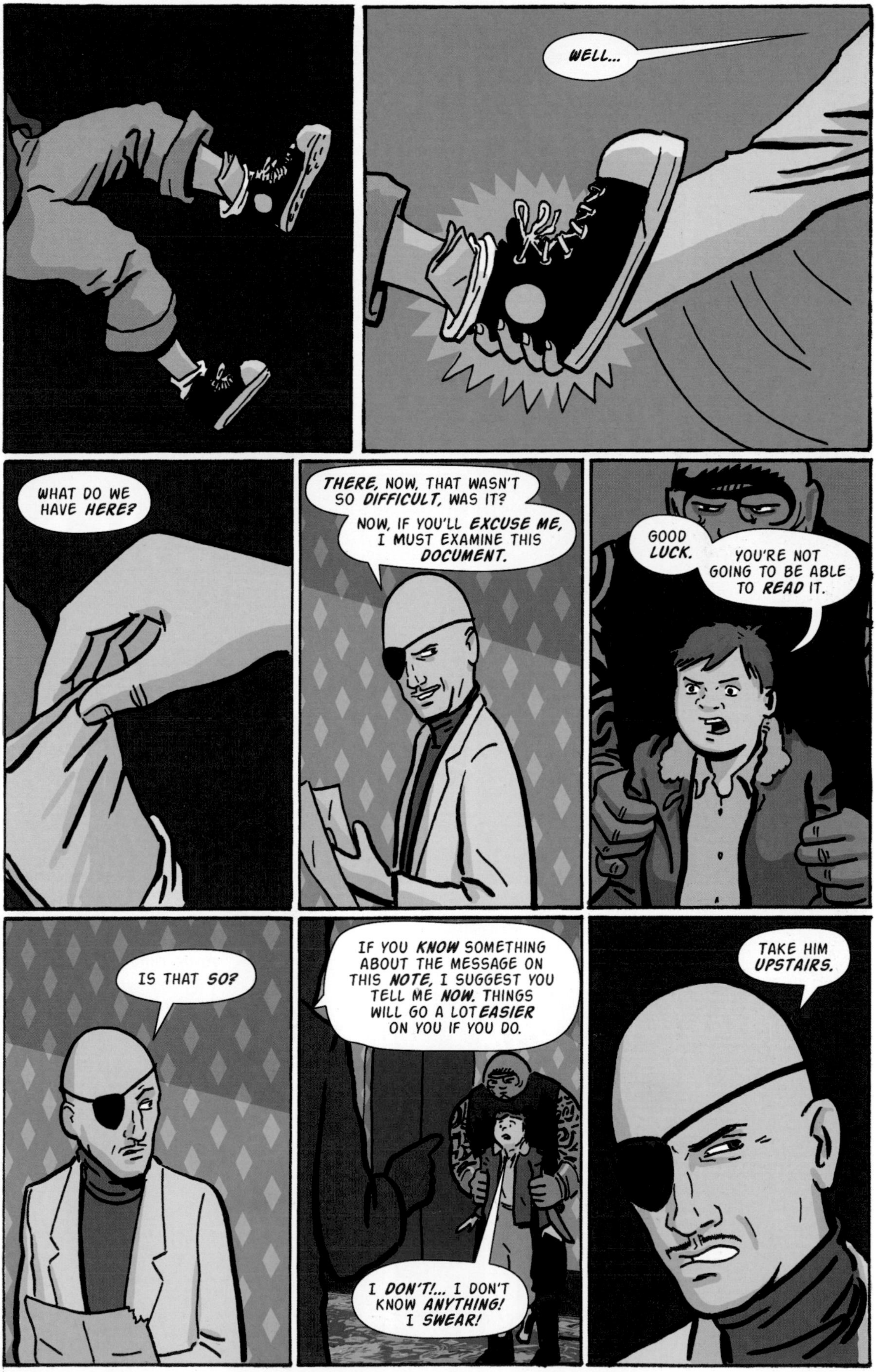
WELL...
WHAT DO WE HAVE HERE?
THERE, NOW, THAT WASN'T SO DIFFICULT, WAS IT?
NOW, IF YOU'LL EXCUSE ME, I MUST EXAMINE THIS DOCUMENT.
GOOD LUCK.
YOU'RE NOT GOING TO BE ABLE TO READ IT.
IS THAT SO?
IF YOU KNOW SOMETHING ABOUT THE MESSAGE ON THIS NOTE, I SUGGEST YOU TELL ME NOW. THINGS WILL GO A LOT EASIER ON YOU IF YOU DO.
I DON'T!... I DON'T KNOW ANYTHING! I SWEAR!
TAKE HIM UPSTAIRS.

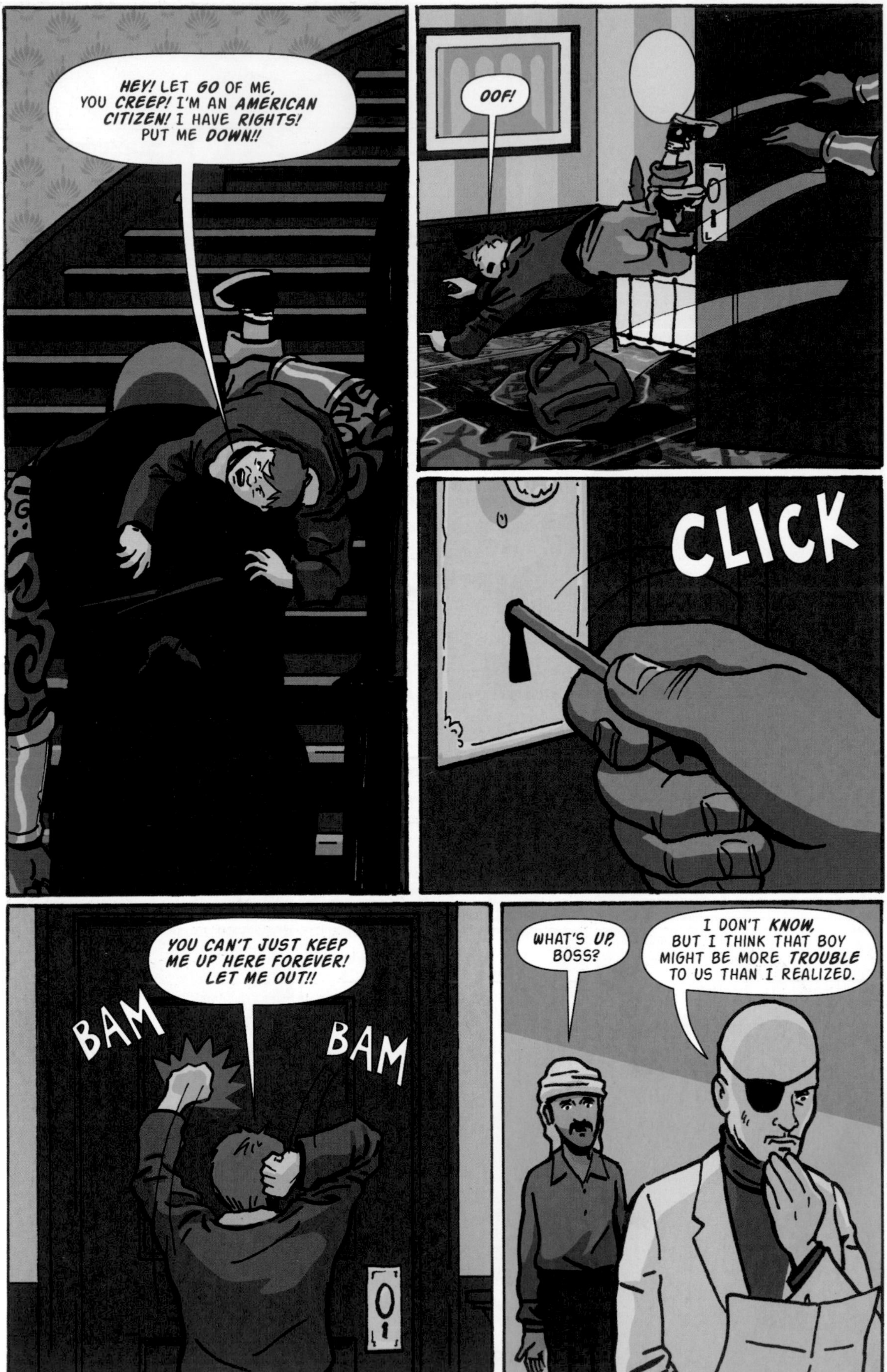
HEY! LET GO OF ME, YOU CREEP! I'M AN AMERICAN CITIZEN! I HAVE RIGHTS! PUT ME DOWN!!
OOF!
CLICK
YOU CAN'T JUST KEEP ME UP HERE FOREVER! LET ME OUT!!
BAM
BAM
WHAT'S UP, BOSS?
I DON'T KNOW, BUT I THINK THAT BOY MIGHT BE MORE TROUBLE TO US THAN I REALIZED.

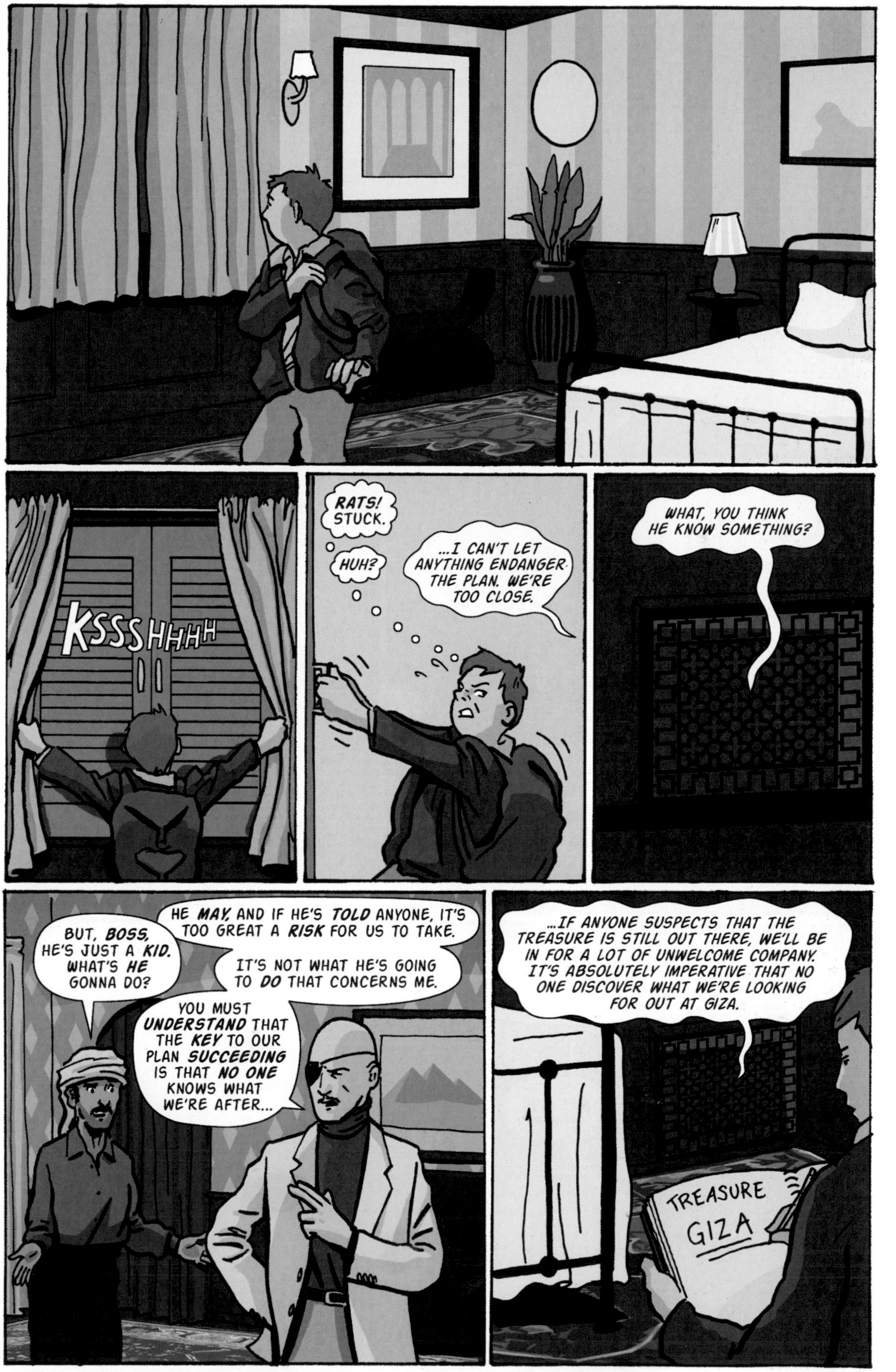
KSSSHHHH
RATS! STUCK.
HUH?
...I CAN'T LET ANYTHING ENDANGER THE PLAN. WE'RE TOO CLOSE.
WHAT, YOU THINK HE KNOW SOMETHING?
BUT, BOSS, HE'S JUST A KID. WHAT'S HE GONNA DO?
HE MAY, AND IF HE'S TOLD ANYONE, IT'S TOO GREAT A RISK FOR US TO TAKE.
IT'S NOT WHAT HE'S GOING TO DO THAT CONCERNS ME.
YOU MUST UNDERSTAND THAT THE KEY TO OUR PLAN SUCCEEDING IS THAT NO ONE KNOWS WHAT WE'RE AFTER...
...IF ANYONE SUSPECTS THAT THE TREASURE IS STILL OUT THERE, WE'LL BE IN FOR A LOT OF UNWELCOME COMPANY. IT'S ABSOLUTELY IMPERATIVE THAT NO ONE DISCOVER WHAT WE'RE LOOKING FOR OUT AT GIZA.
TREASURE
GIZA

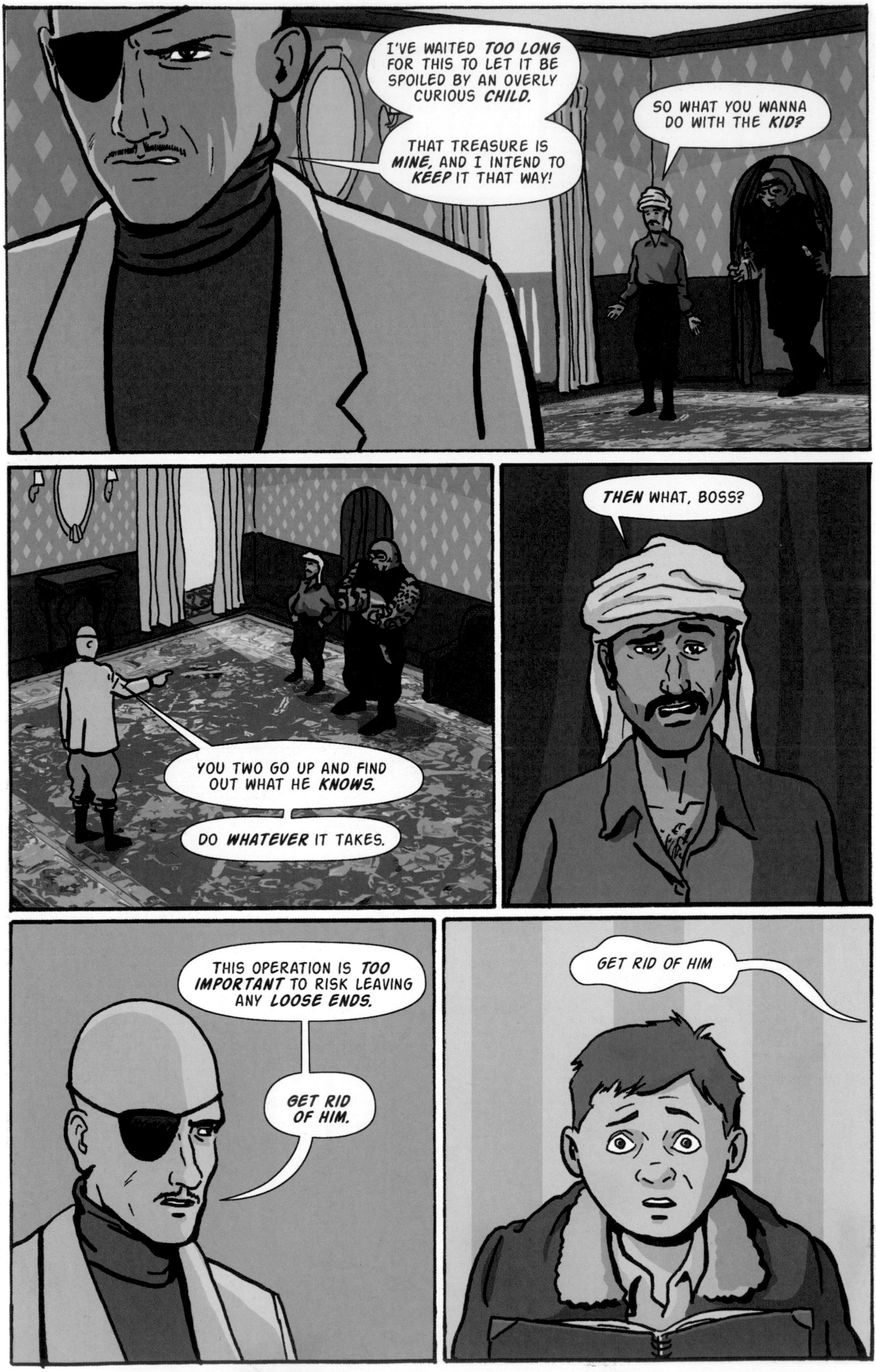
I'VE WAITED TOO LONG FOR THIS TO LET IT BE SPOILED BY AN OVERLY CURIOUS CHILD.
THAT TREASURE IS MINE, AND I INTEND TO KEEP IT THAT WAY!
SO WHAT YOU WANNA DO WITH THE KID?
YOU TWO GO UP AND FIND OUT WHAT HE KNOWS.
DO WHATEVER IT TAKES.
THEN WHAT, BOSS?
THIS OPERATION IS TOO IMPORTANT TO RISK LEAVING ANY LOOSE ENDS.
GET RID OF HIM.
GET RID OF HIM

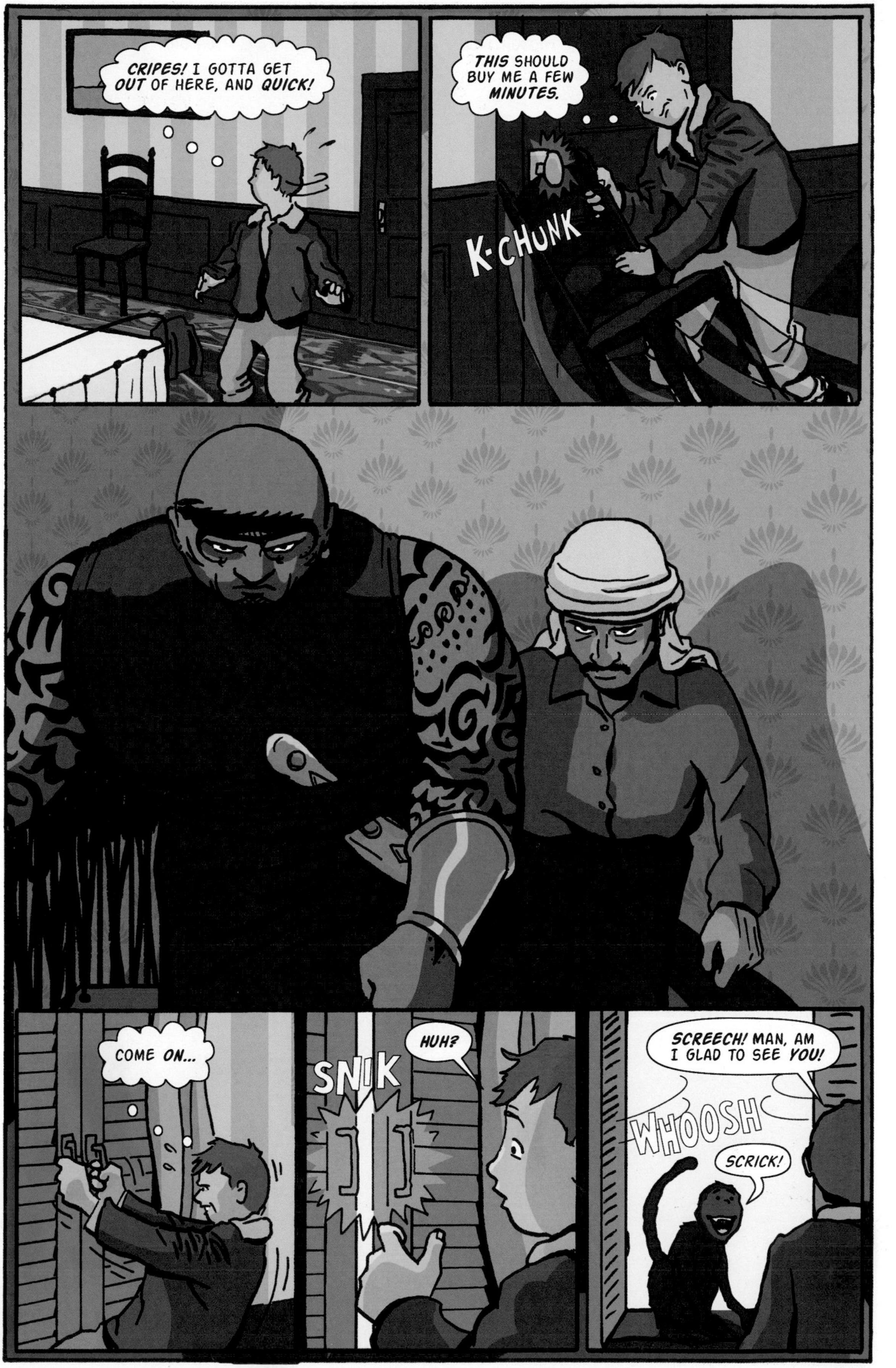
CRIPES! I GOTTA GET OUT OF HERE, AND QUICK!
THIS SHOULD BUY ME A FEW MINUTES.
K-CHUNK
COME ON...
SNIK
HUH?
SCREECH! MAN, AM I GLAD TO SEE YOU!
WHOOSH
SCRICK!

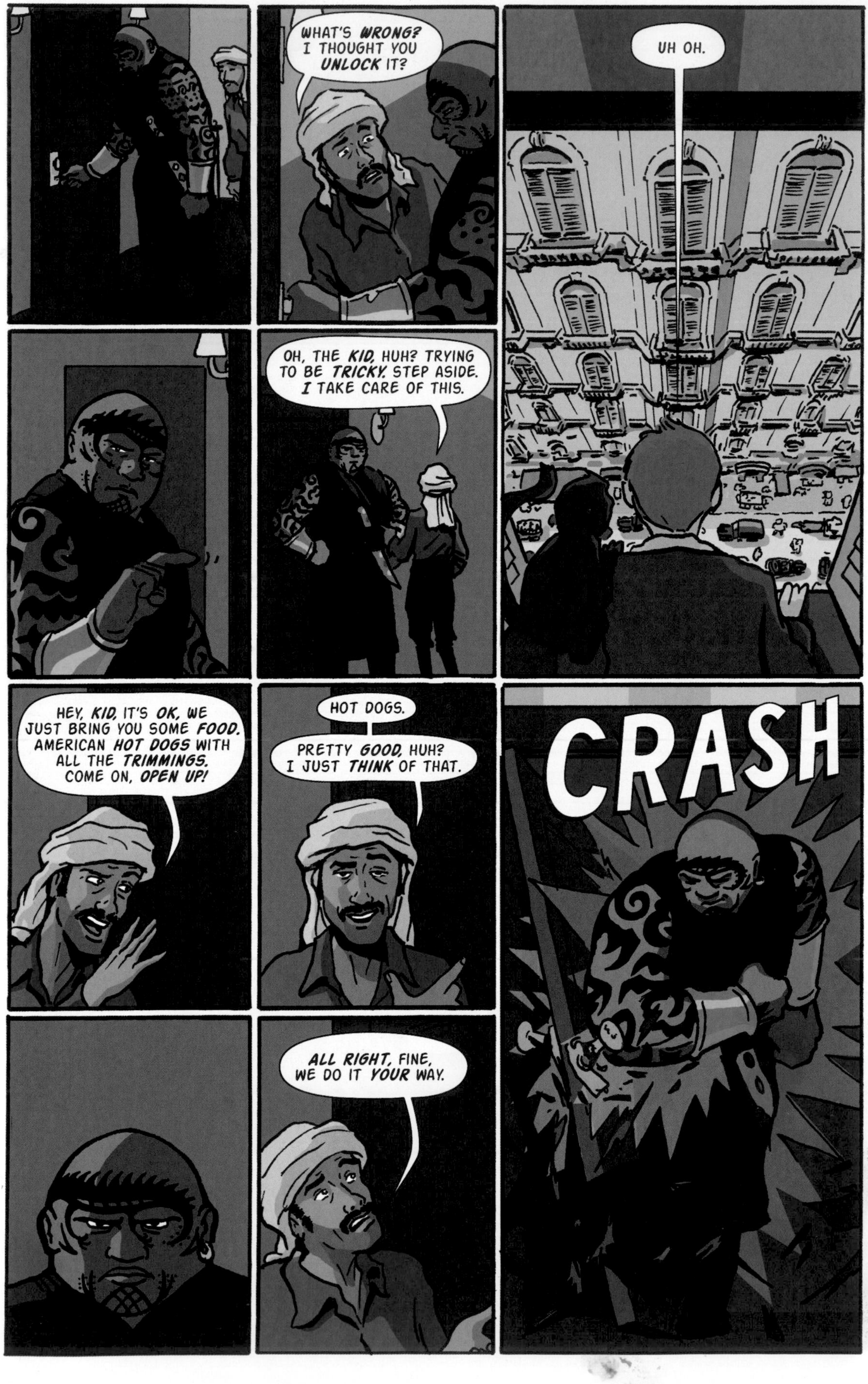
WHAT'S WRONG? I THOUGHT YOU UNLOCK IT?
UH OH.
OH, THE KID, HUH? TRYING TO BE TRICKY. STEP ASIDE. I TAKE CARE OF THIS.
HEY, KID, IT'S OK, WE JUST BRING YOU SOME FOOD. AMERICAN HOT DOGS WITH ALL THE TRIMMINGS. COME ON, OPEN UP!
HOT DOGS.
PRETTY GOOD, HUH? I JUST THINK OF THAT.
ALL RIGHT, FINE, WE DO IT YOUR WAY.
CRASH

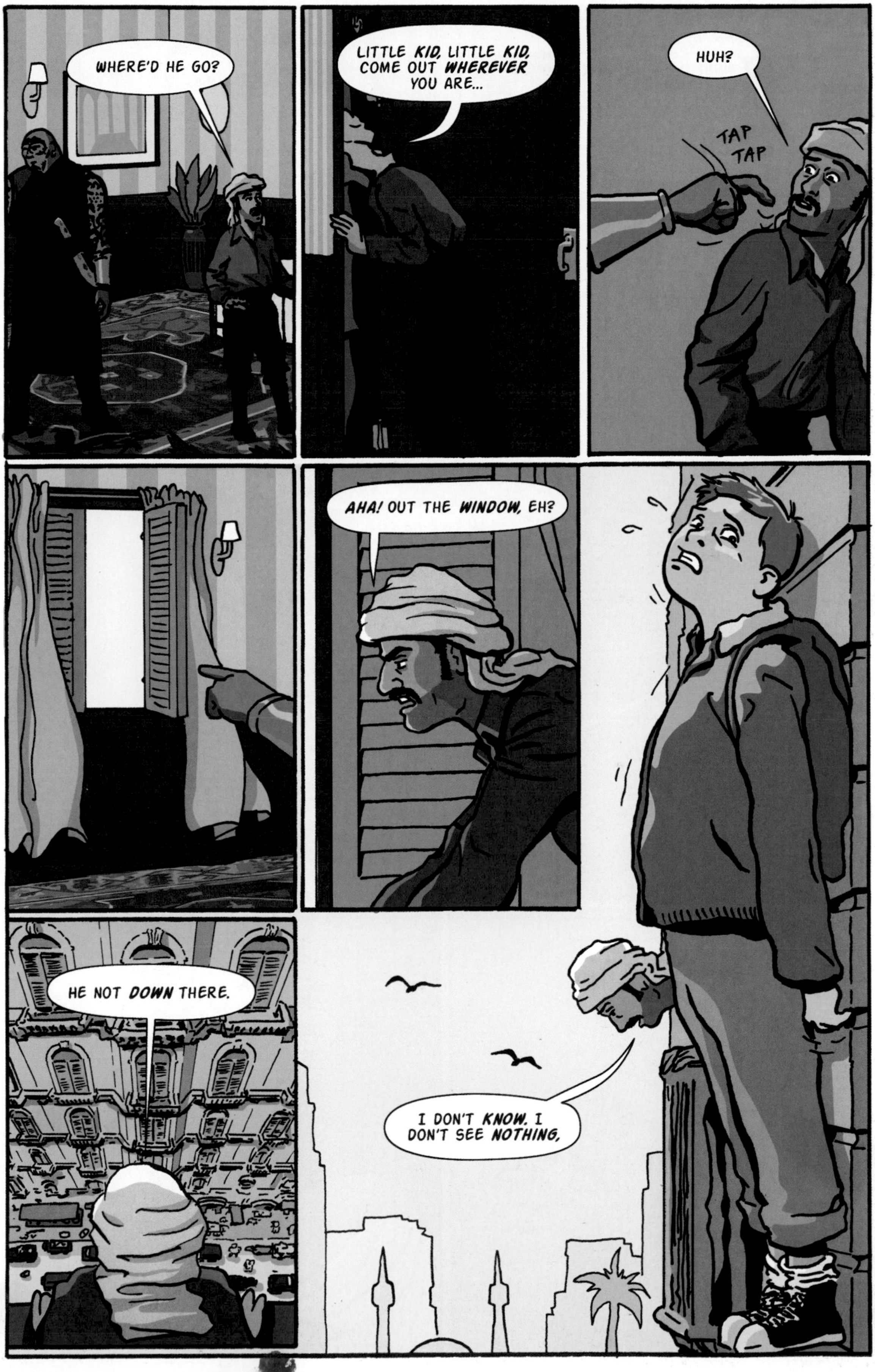
WHERE'D HE GO?
LITTLE KID, LITTLE KID, COME OUT WHEREVER YOU ARE...
HUH?
TAP TAP
AHA! OUT THE WINDOW, EH?
HE NOT DOWN THERE.
I DON'T KNOW. I DON'T SEE NOTHING.

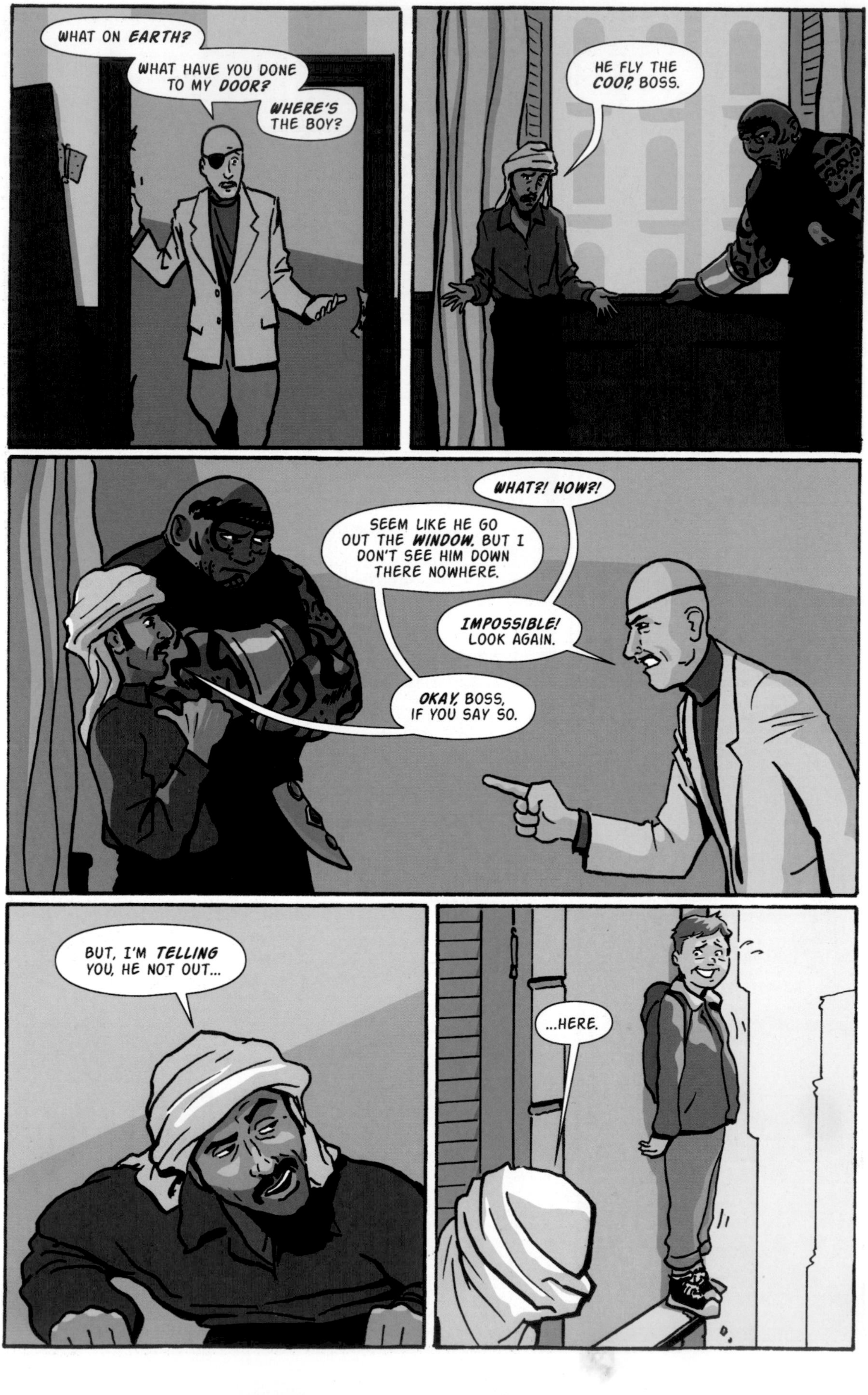
WHAT ON EARTH?
WHAT HAVE YOU DONE TO MY DOOR?
WHERE'S THE BOY?
HE FLY THE COOP, BOSS.
WHAT?! HOW?!
SEEM LIKE HE GO OUT THE WINDOW. BUT I DON'T SEE HIM DOWN THERE NOWHERE.
IMPOSSIBLE! LOOK AGAIN.
OKAY, BOSS, IF YOU SAY SO.
BUT, I'M TELLING YOU, HE NOT OUT...
...HERE.

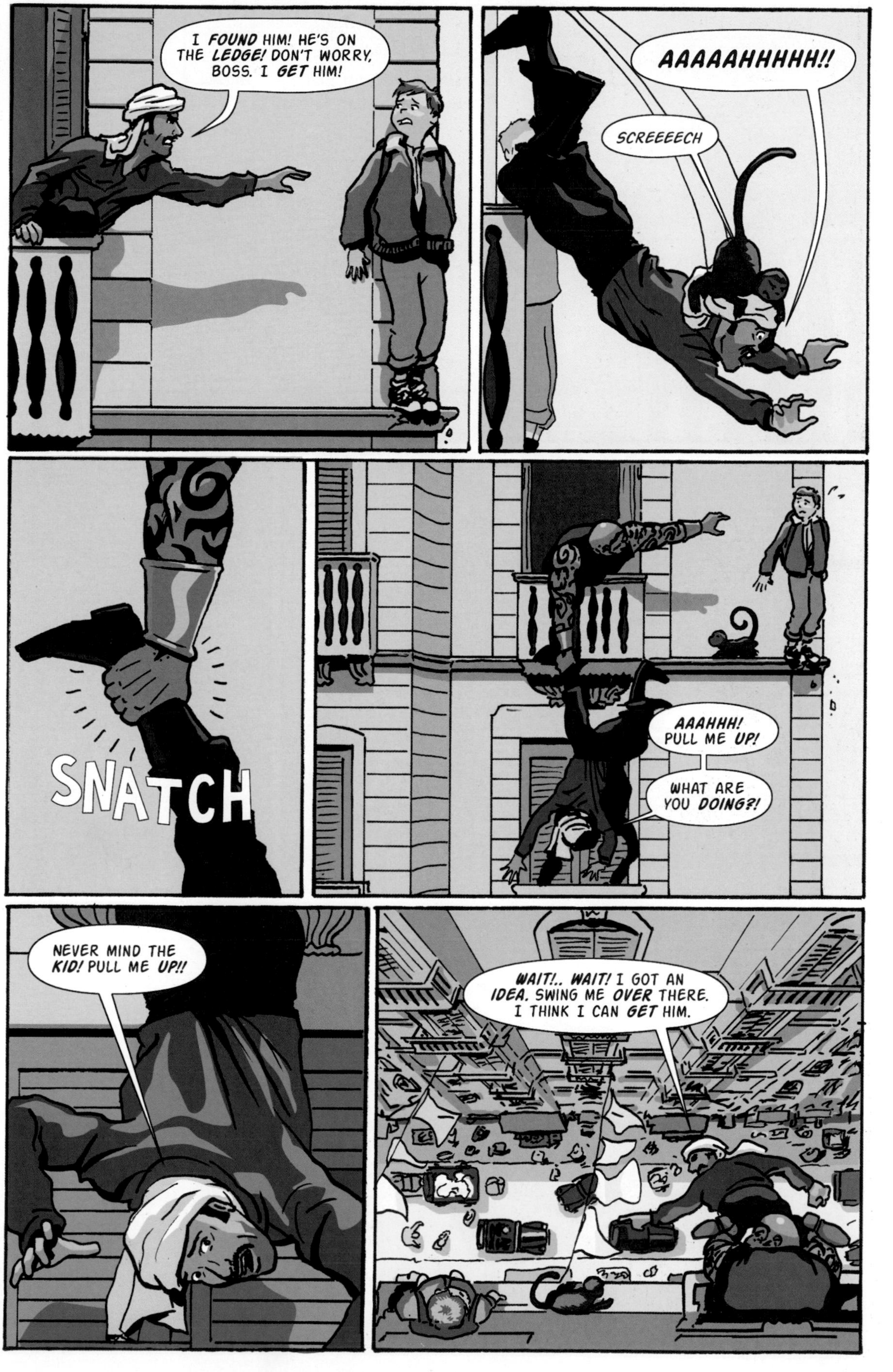
I FOUND HIM! HE'S ON THE LEDGE! DON'T WORRY, BOSS. I GET HIM!
AAAAAHHHHH!!
SCREEEECH
SNATCH
AAAHHH! PULL ME UP!
WHAT ARE YOU DOING?!
NEVER MIND THE KID! PULL ME UP!!
WAIT!.. WAIT! I GOT AN IDEA. SWING ME OVER THERE. I THINK I CAN GET HIM.

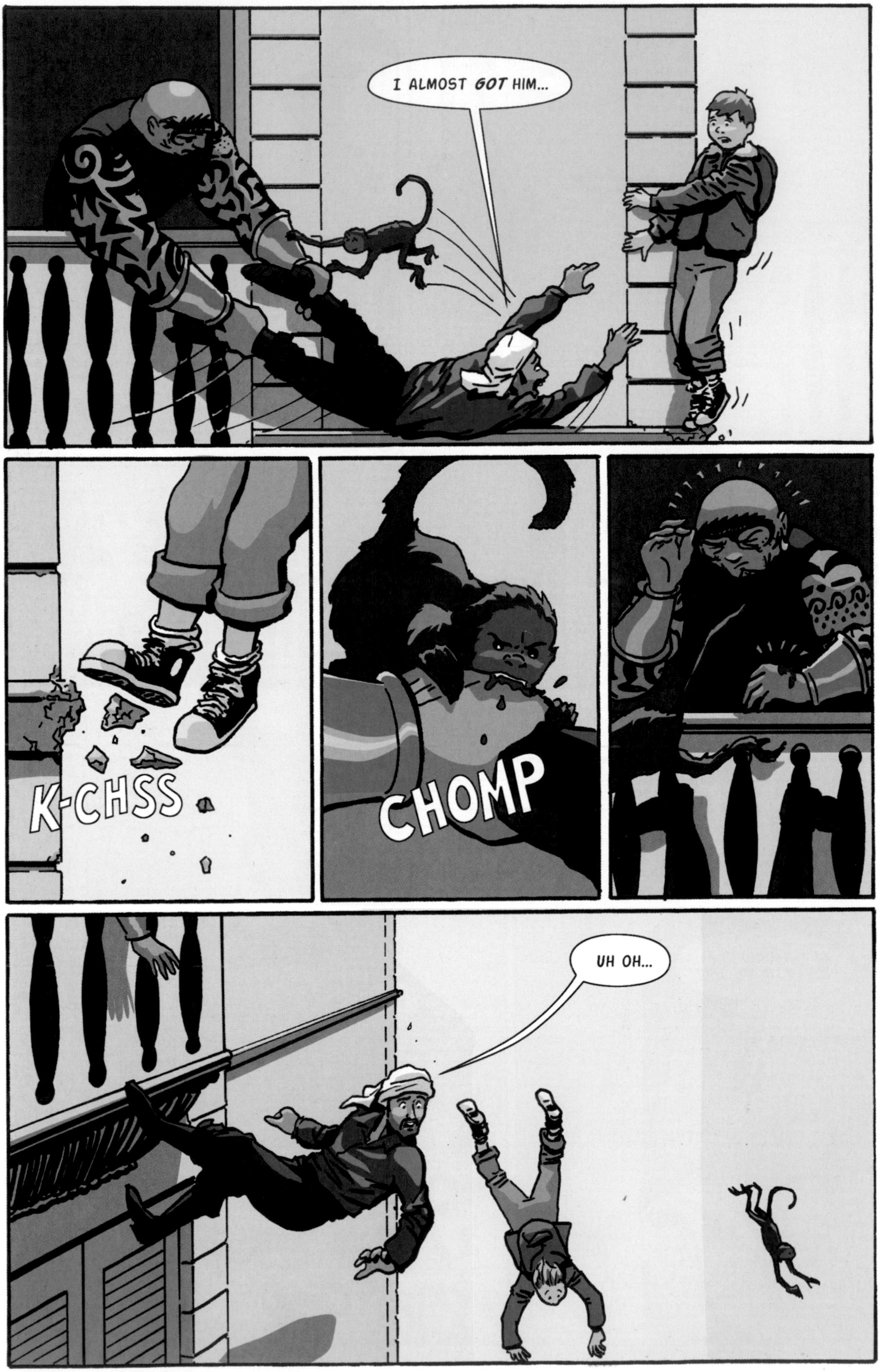
I ALMOST GOT HIM...
K-CHSS
CHOMP
UH OH...

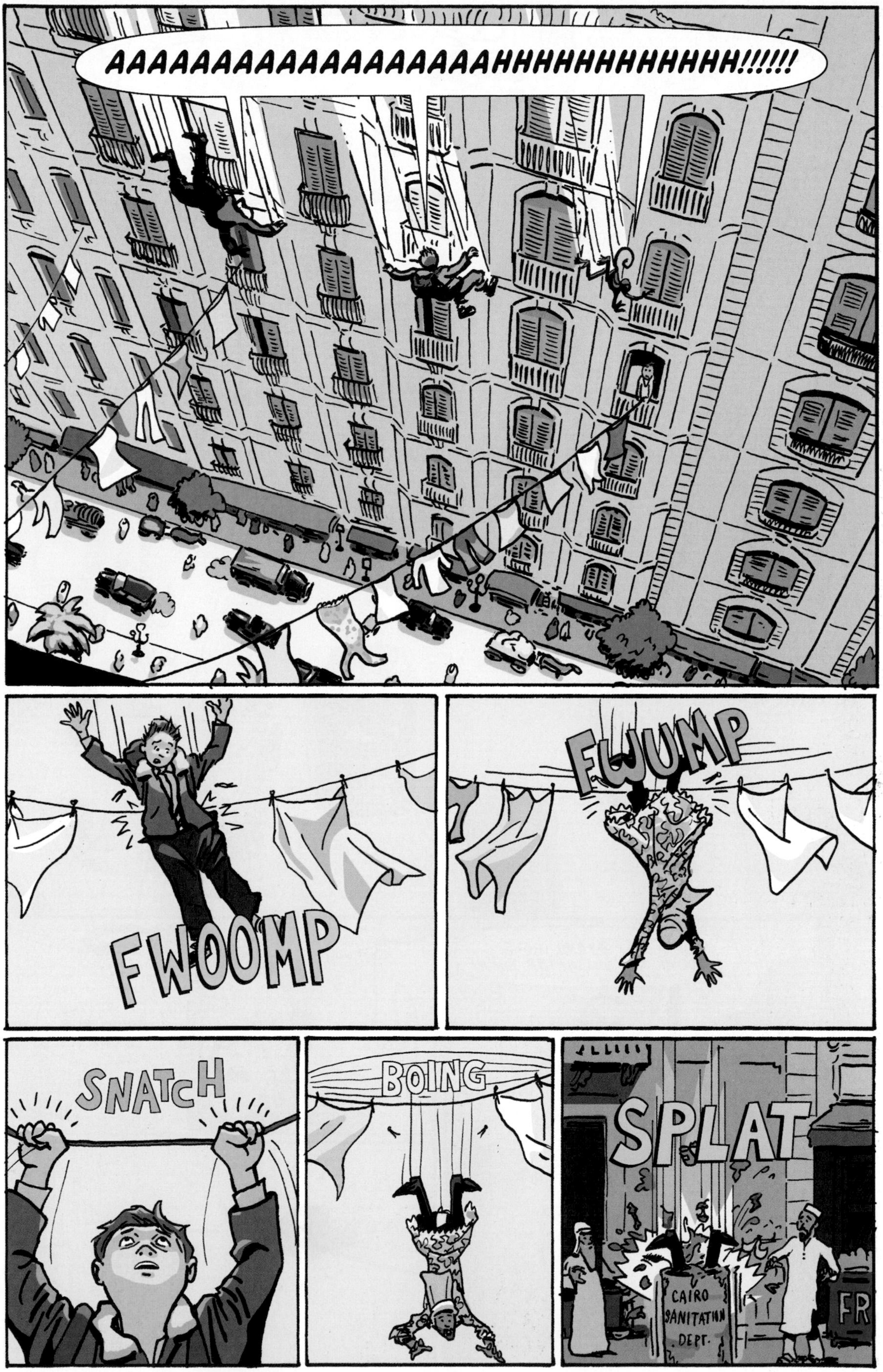
AAAAAAAAAAAAAAAAAAAAHHHHHHHHHHHHH!!!!!!
FWOOMP
FWUMP
SNATCH
BOING
SPLAT
CAIRO SANITATION DEPT.
FR

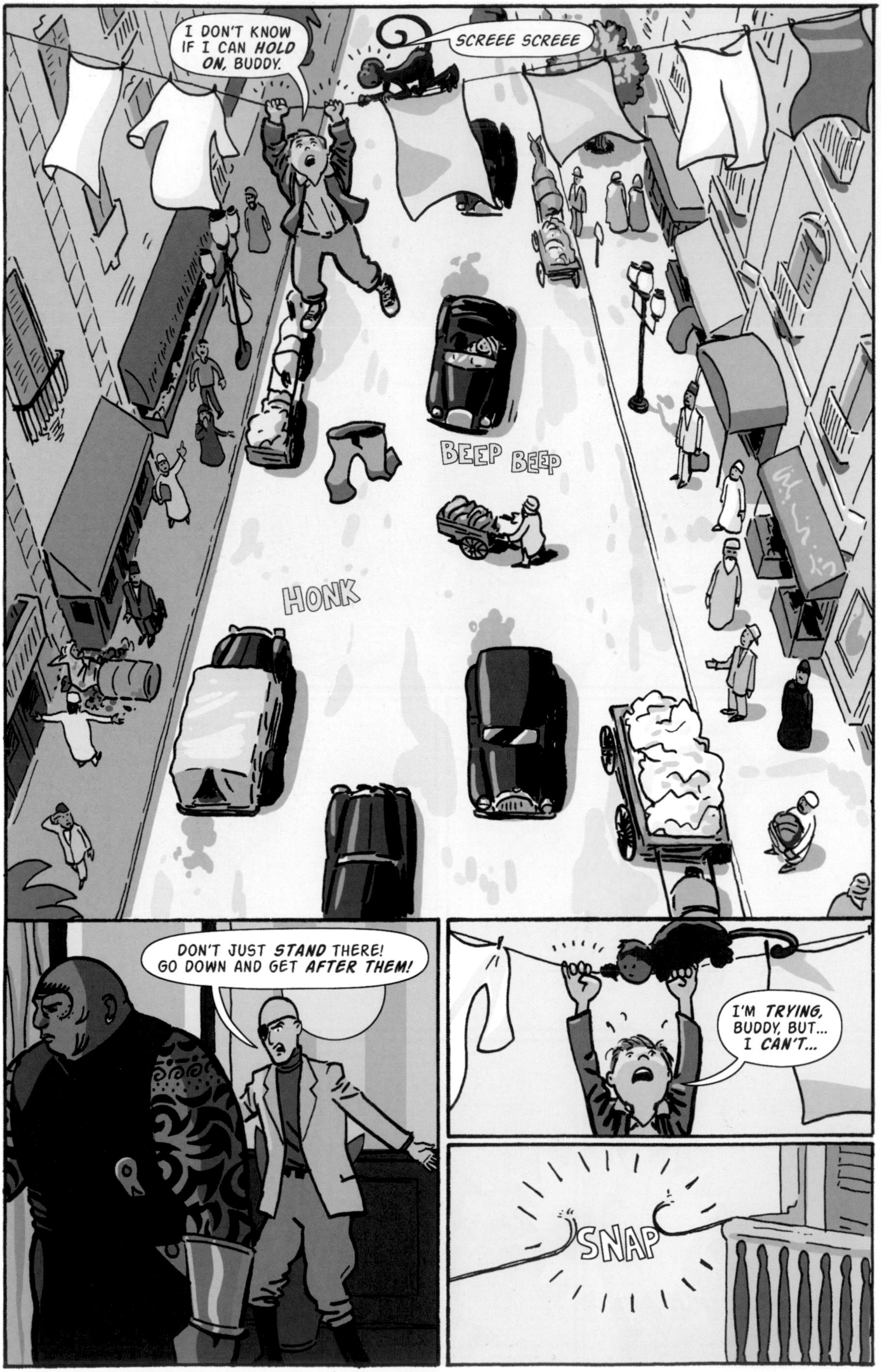
I DON'T KNOW IF I CAN HOLD ON, BUDDY.
SCREEE SCREEE
BEEP BEEP
HONK
DON'T JUST STAND THERE! GO DOWN AND GET AFTER THEM!
I'M TRYING, BUDDY, BUT... I CAN'T...
SNAP

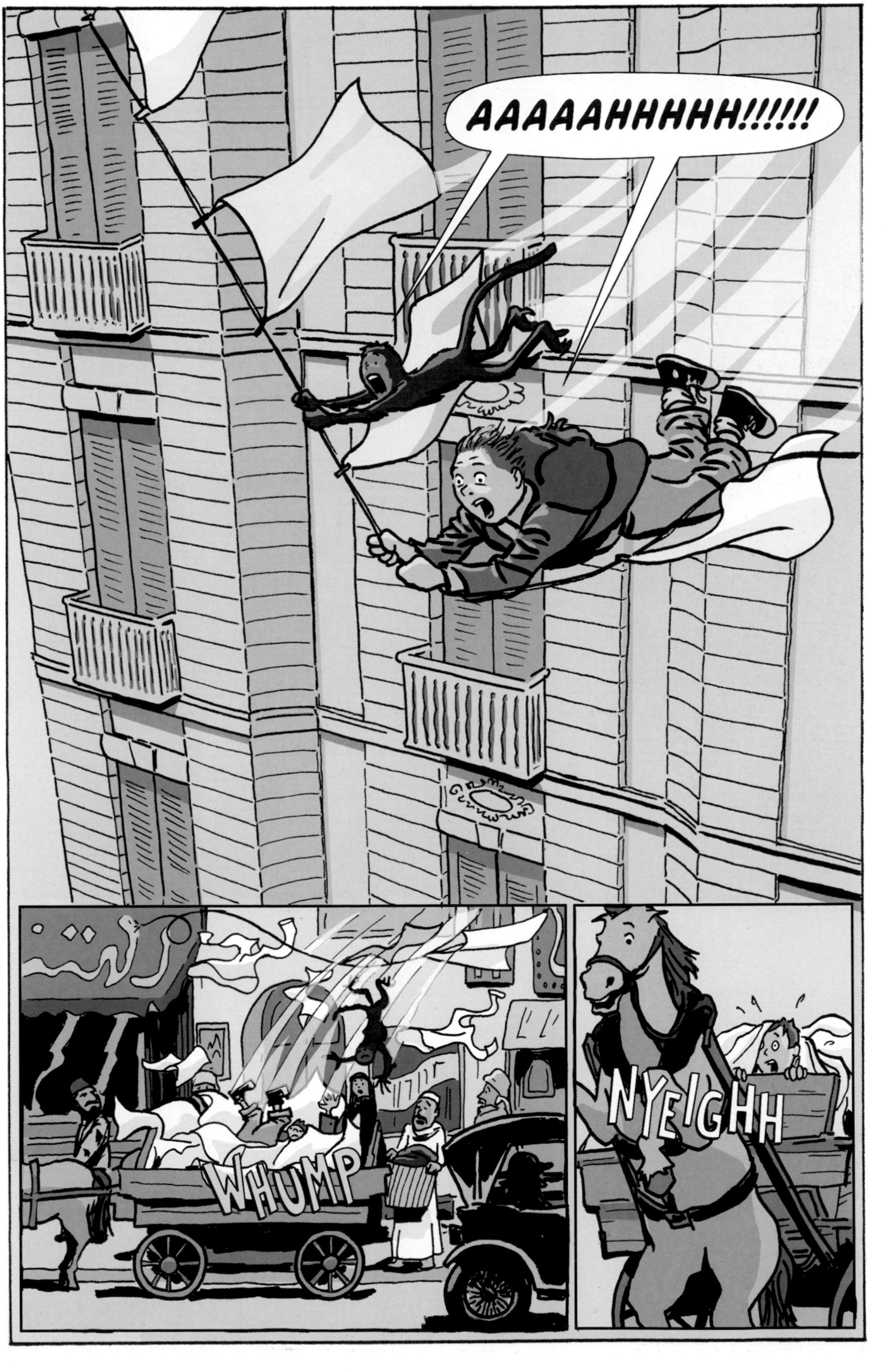
AAAAAHHHHH!!!!!!
WHUMP
NYEIGHH

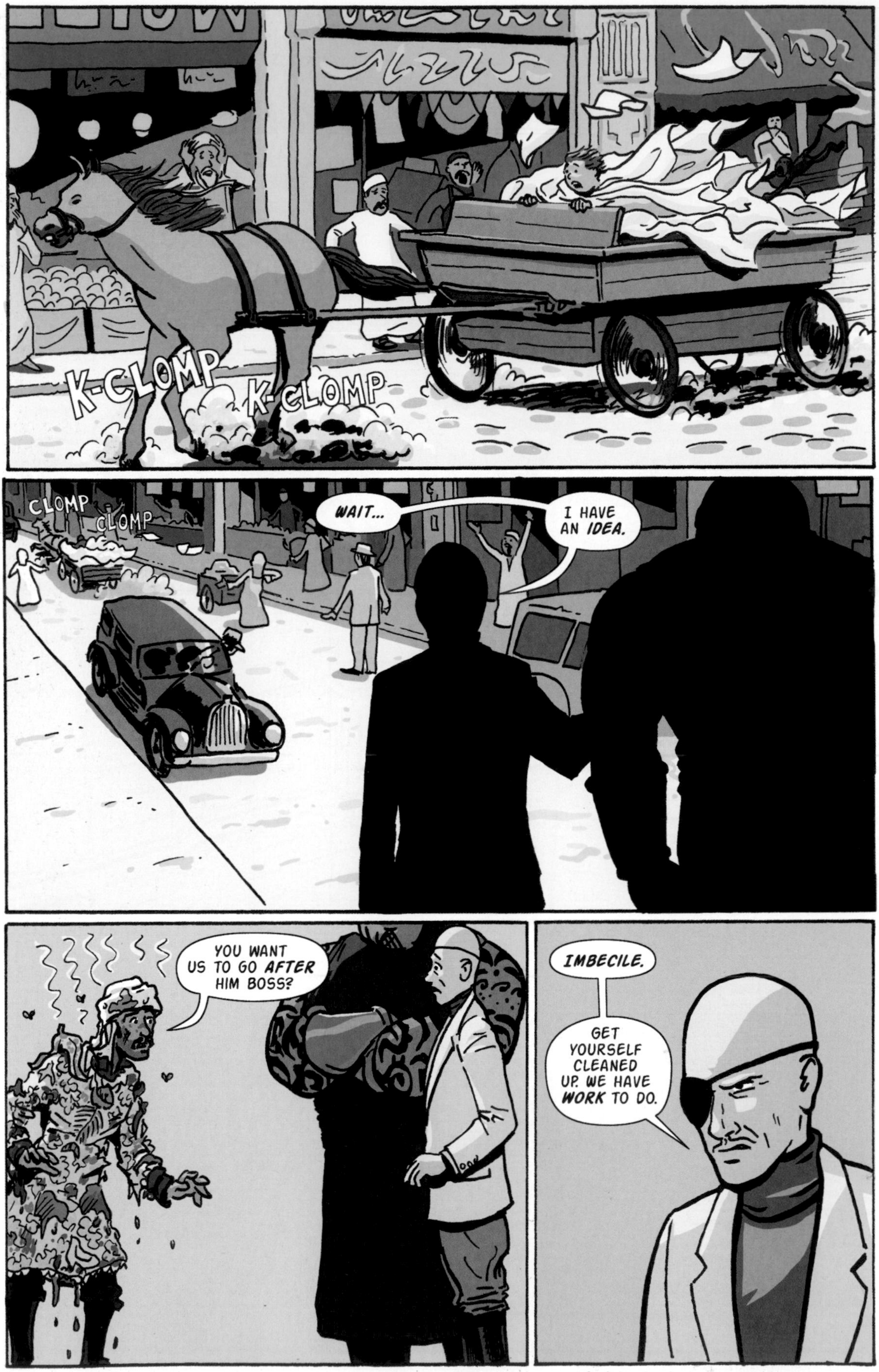
K-CLOMP
K-CLOMP
CLOMP
CLOMP
WAIT...
I HAVE AN IDEA.
YOU WANT US TO GO AFTER HIM BOSS?
IMBECILE.
GET YOURSELF CLEANED UP. WE HAVE WORK TO DO.

CHAPTER FOUR

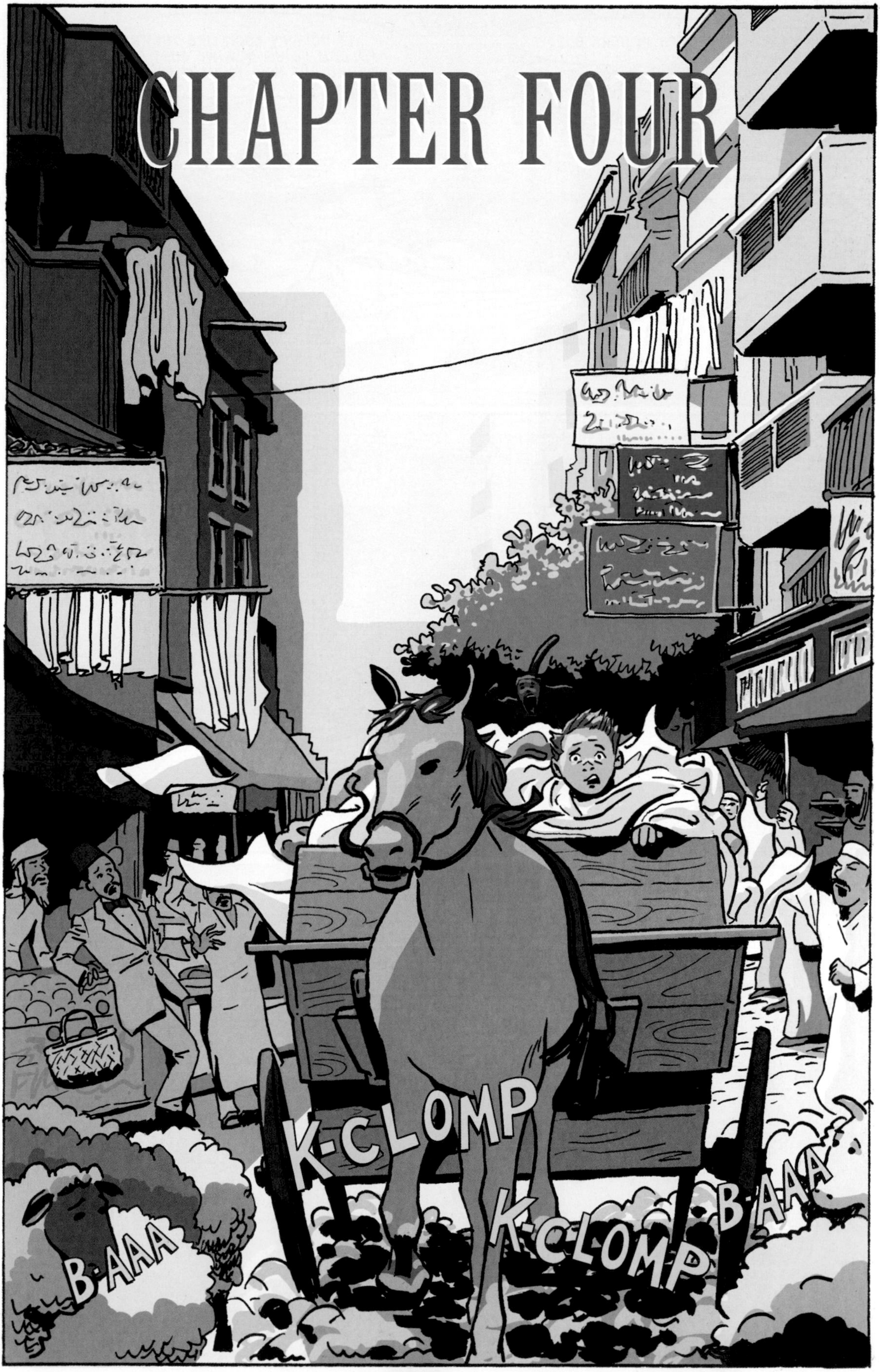
K-CLOMP
K-CLOMP
B-AAA
B-AAA

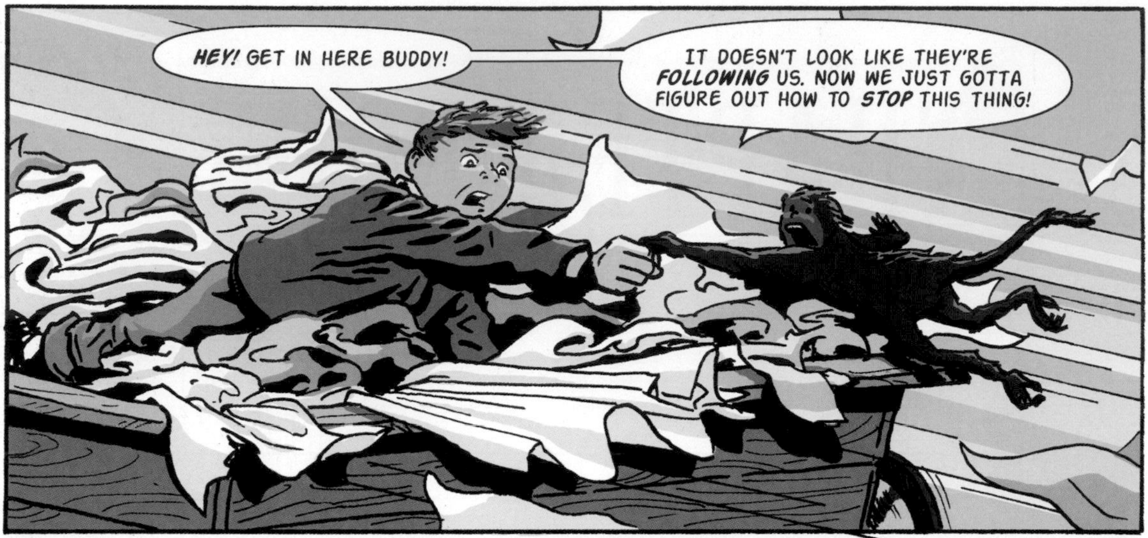
HEY! GET IN HERE BUDDY!
IT DOESN'T LOOK LIKE THEY'RE FOLLOWING US. NOW WE JUST GOTTA FIGURE OUT HOW TO STOP THIS THING!

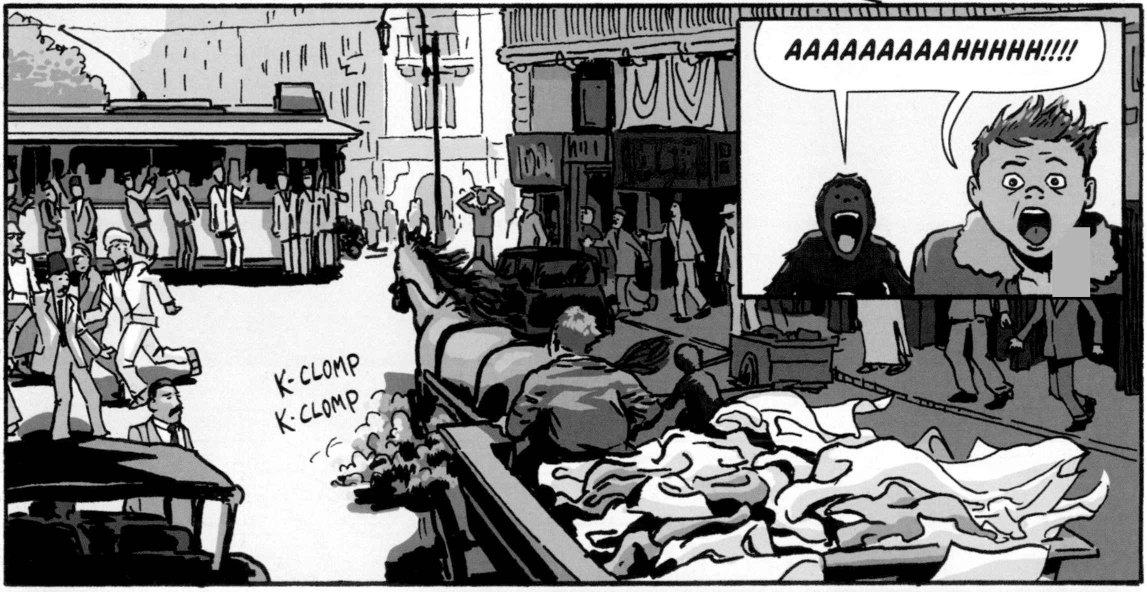
AAAAAAAAAHHHHH!!!!
K-CLOMP
K-CLOMP

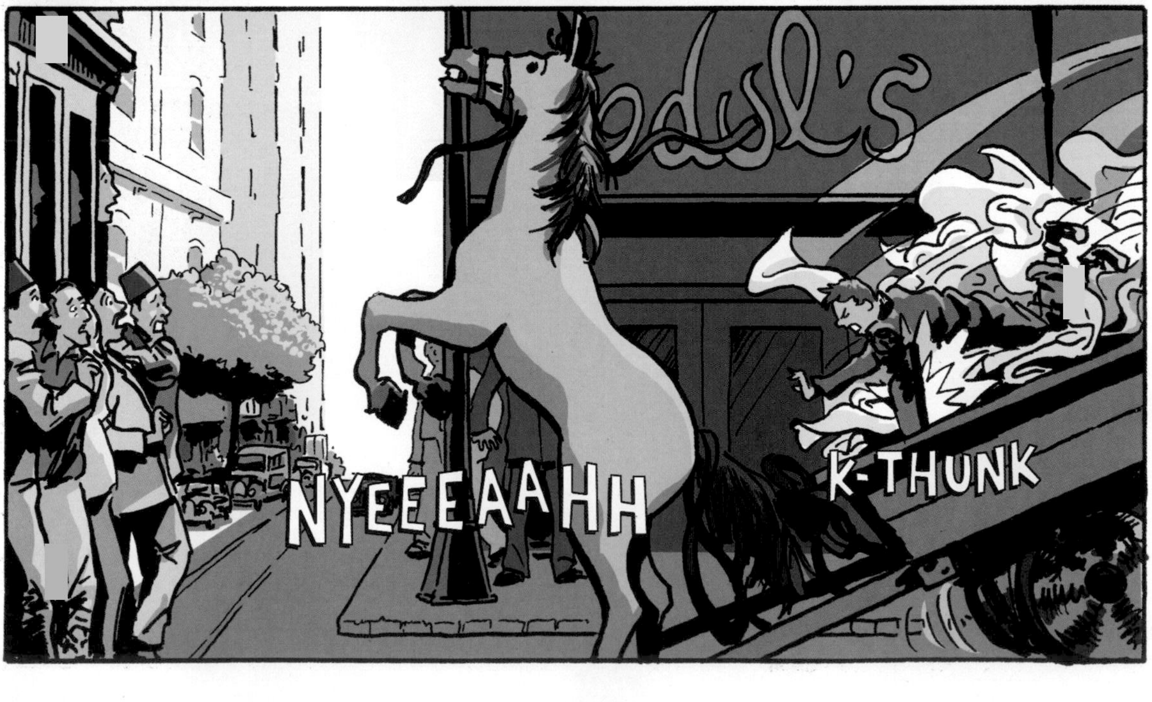
NYEEEAAHH
K-THUNK

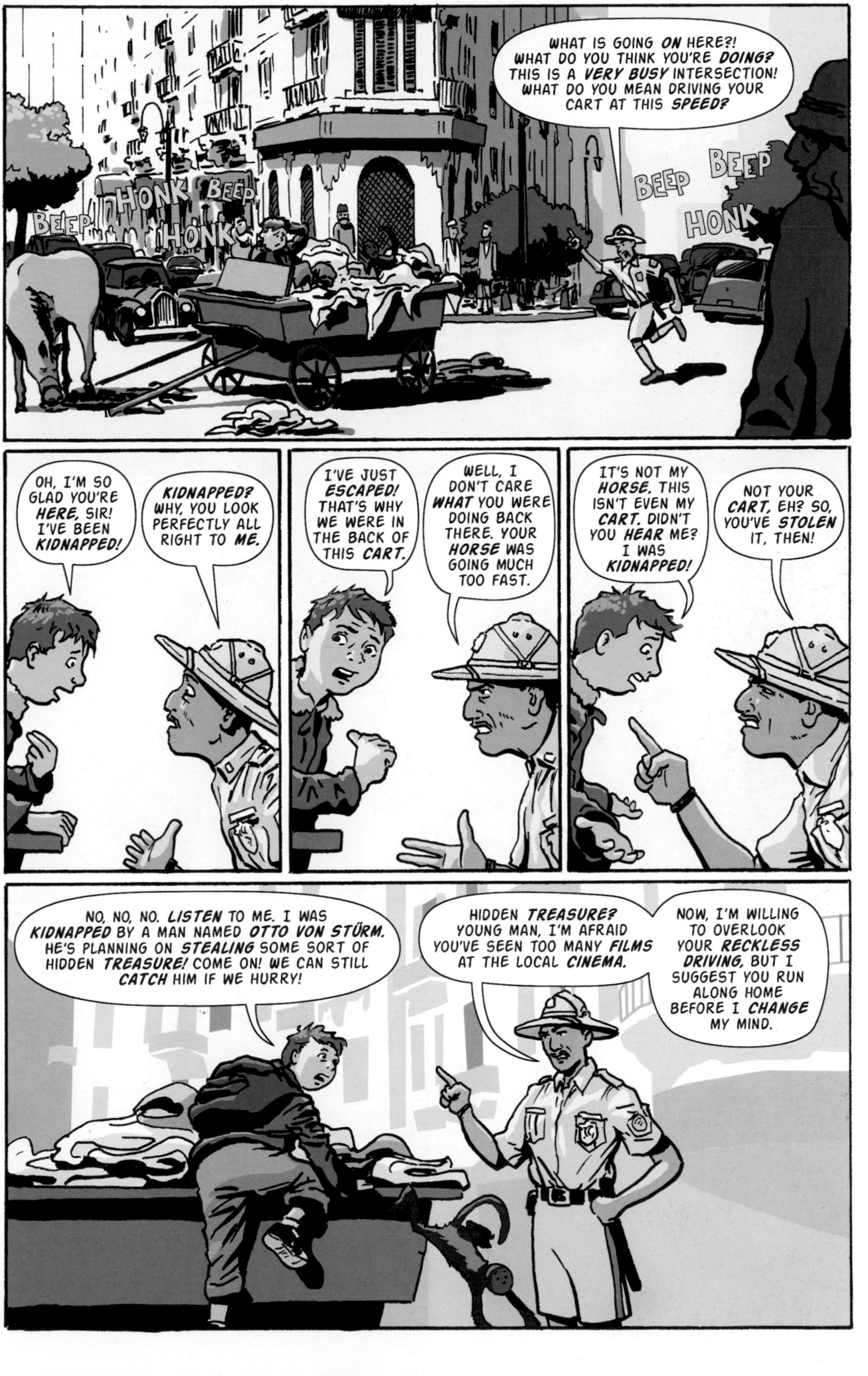
WHAT IS GOING ON HERE?! WHAT DO YOU THINK YOU'RE DOING? THIS IS A VERY BUSY INTERSECTION! WHAT DO YOU MEAN DRIVING YOUR CART AT THIS SPEED?
BEEP HONK BEEP HONK
BEEP BEEP HONK
OH, I'M SO GLAD YOU'RE HERE, SIR! I'VE BEEN KIDNAPPED!
KIDNAPPED? WHY, YOU LOOK PERFECTLY ALL RIGHT TO ME.
I'VE JUST ESCAPED! THAT'S WHY WE WERE IN THE BACK OF THIS CART.
WELL, I DON'T CARE WHAT YOU WERE DOING BACK THERE. YOUR HORSE WAS GOING MUCH TOO FAST.
IT'S NOT MY HORSE. THIS ISN'T EVEN MY CART. DIDN'T YOU HEAR ME? I WAS KIDNAPPED!
NOT YOUR CART, EH? SO, YOU'VE STOLEN IT, THEN!
NO, NO, NO. LISTEN TO ME. I WAS KIDNAPPED BY A MAN NAMED OTTO VON STÜRM. HE'S PLANNING ON STEALING SOME SORT OF HIDDEN TREASURE! COME ON! WE CAN STILL CATCH HIM IF WE HURRY!
HIDDEN TREASURE? YOUNG MAN, I'M AFRAID YOU'VE SEEN TOO MANY FILMS AT THE LOCAL CINEMA.
NOW, I'M WILLING TO OVERLOOK YOUR RECKLESS DRIVING, BUT I SUGGEST YOU RUN ALONG HOME BEFORE I CHANGE MY MIND.

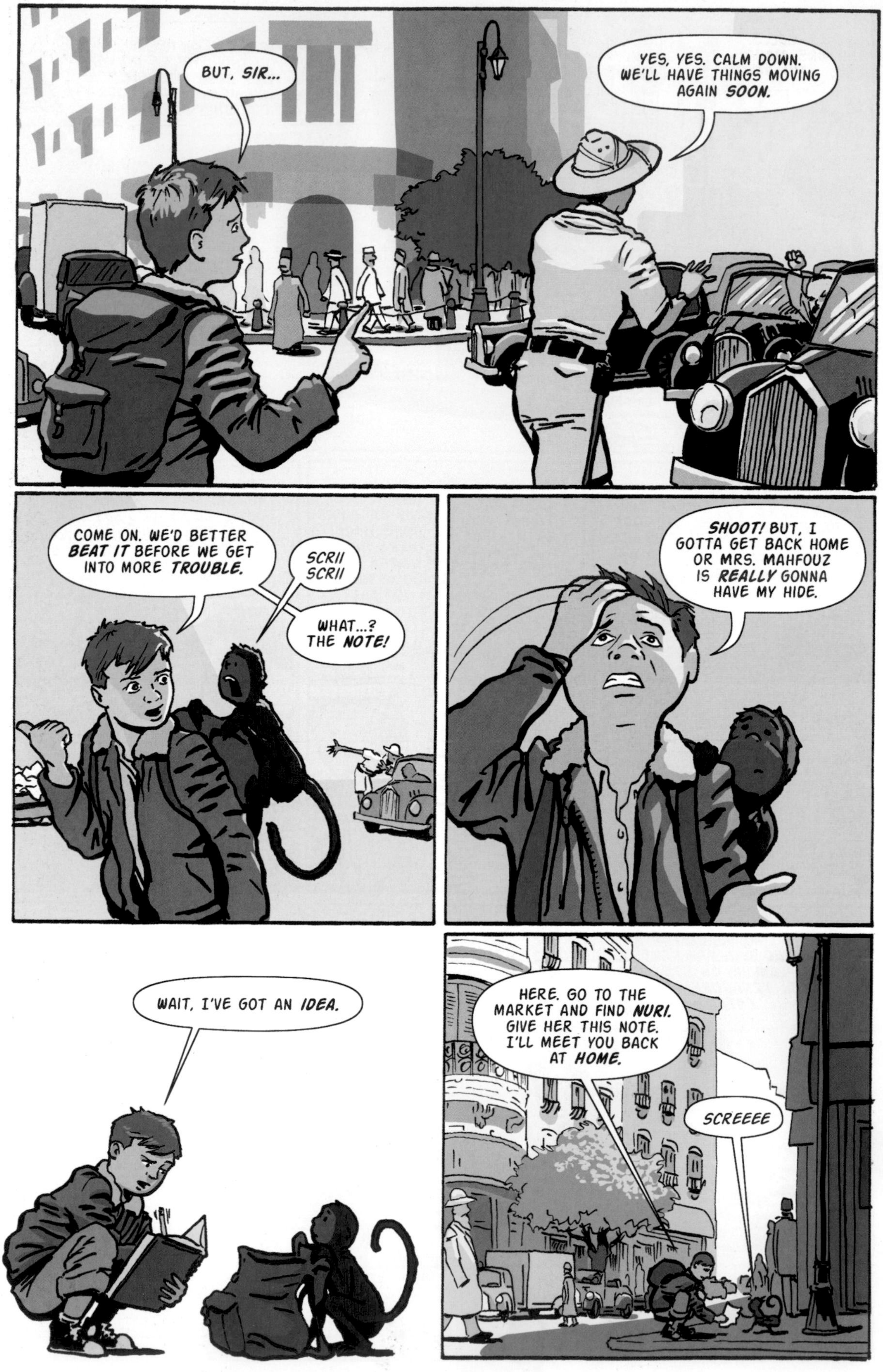
BUT, SIR...
YES, YES. CALM DOWN. WE'LL HAVE THINGS MOVING AGAIN SOON.
COME ON. WE'D BETTER BEAT IT BEFORE WE GET INTO MORE TROUBLE.
SCRII SCRII
WHAT...? THE NOTE!
SHOOT! BUT, I GOTTA GET BACK HOME OR MRS. MAHFOUZ IS REALLY GONNA HAVE MY HIDE.
WAIT, I'VE GOT AN IDEA.
HERE. GO TO THE MARKET AND FIND NURI. GIVE HER THIS NOTE. I'LL MEET YOU BACK AT HOME.
SCREEEE

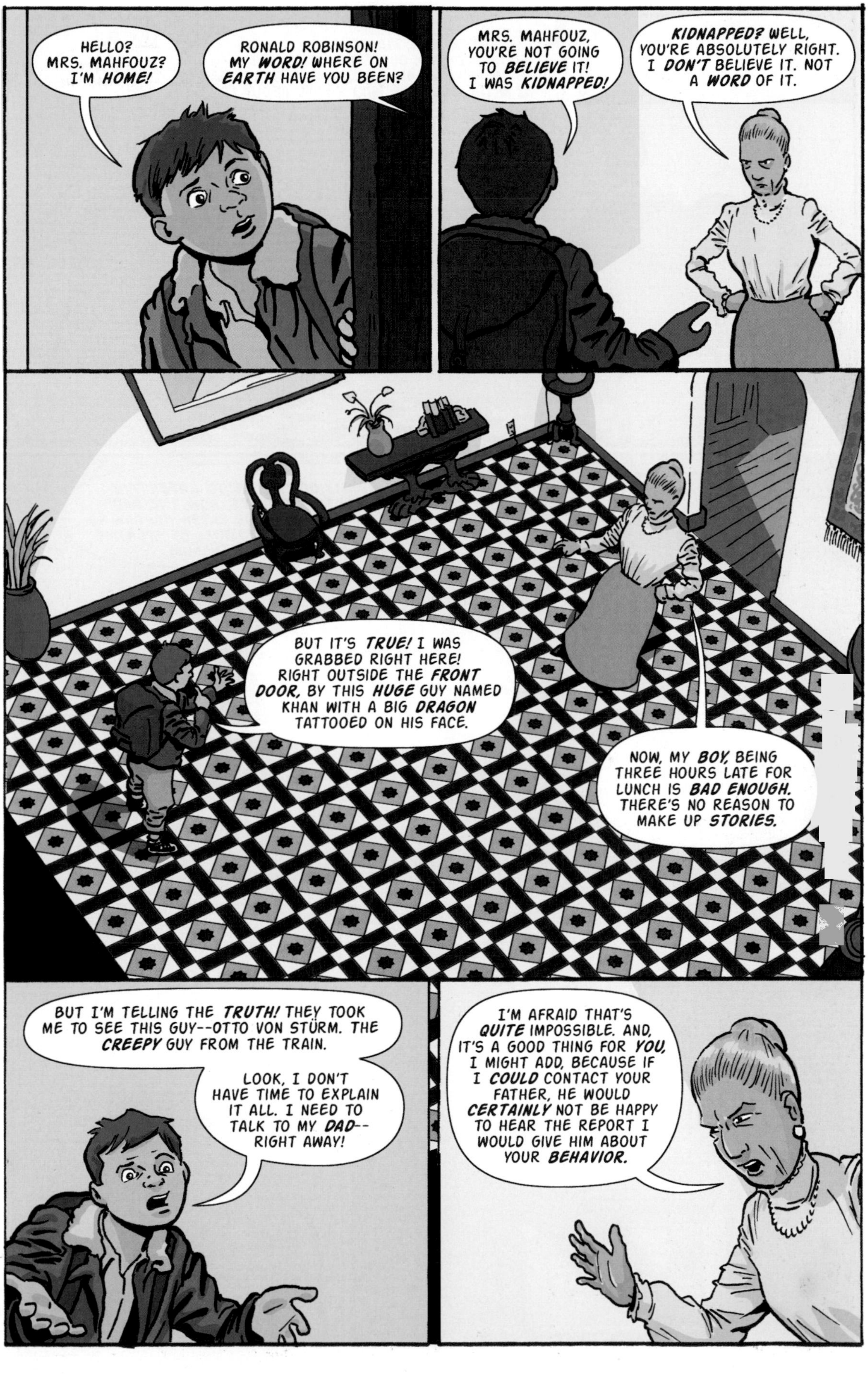
HELLO? MRS. MAHFOUZ? I'M HOME!
RONALD ROBINSON! MY WORD! WHERE ON EARTH HAVE YOU BEEN?
MRS. MAHFOUZ, YOU'RE NOT GOING TO BELIEVE IT! I WAS KIDNAPPED!
KIDNAPPED? WELL, YOU'RE ABSOLUTELY RIGHT. I DON'T BELIEVE IT. NOT A WORD OF IT.
BUT IT'S TRUE! I WAS GRABBED RIGHT HERE! RIGHT OUTSIDE THE FRONT DOOR, BY THIS HUGE GUY NAMED KHAN WITH A BIG DRAGON TATTOOED ON HIS FACE.
NOW, MY BOY, BEING THREE HOURS LATE FOR LUNCH IS BAD ENOUGH. THERE'S NO REASON TO MAKE UP STORIES.
BUT I'M TELLING THE TRUTH! THEY TOOK ME TO SEE THIS GUY--OTTO VON STÜRM. THE CREEPY GUY FROM THE TRAIN.
LOOK, I DON'T HAVE TIME TO EXPLAIN IT ALL. I NEED TO TALK TO MY DAD--RIGHT AWAY!
I'M AFRAID THAT'S QUITE IMPOSSIBLE. AND, IT'S A GOOD THING FOR YOU, I MIGHT ADD, BECAUSE IF I COULD CONTACT YOUR FATHER, HE WOULD CERTAINLY NOT BE HAPPY TO HEAR THE REPORT I WOULD GIVE HIM ABOUT YOUR BEHAVIOR.

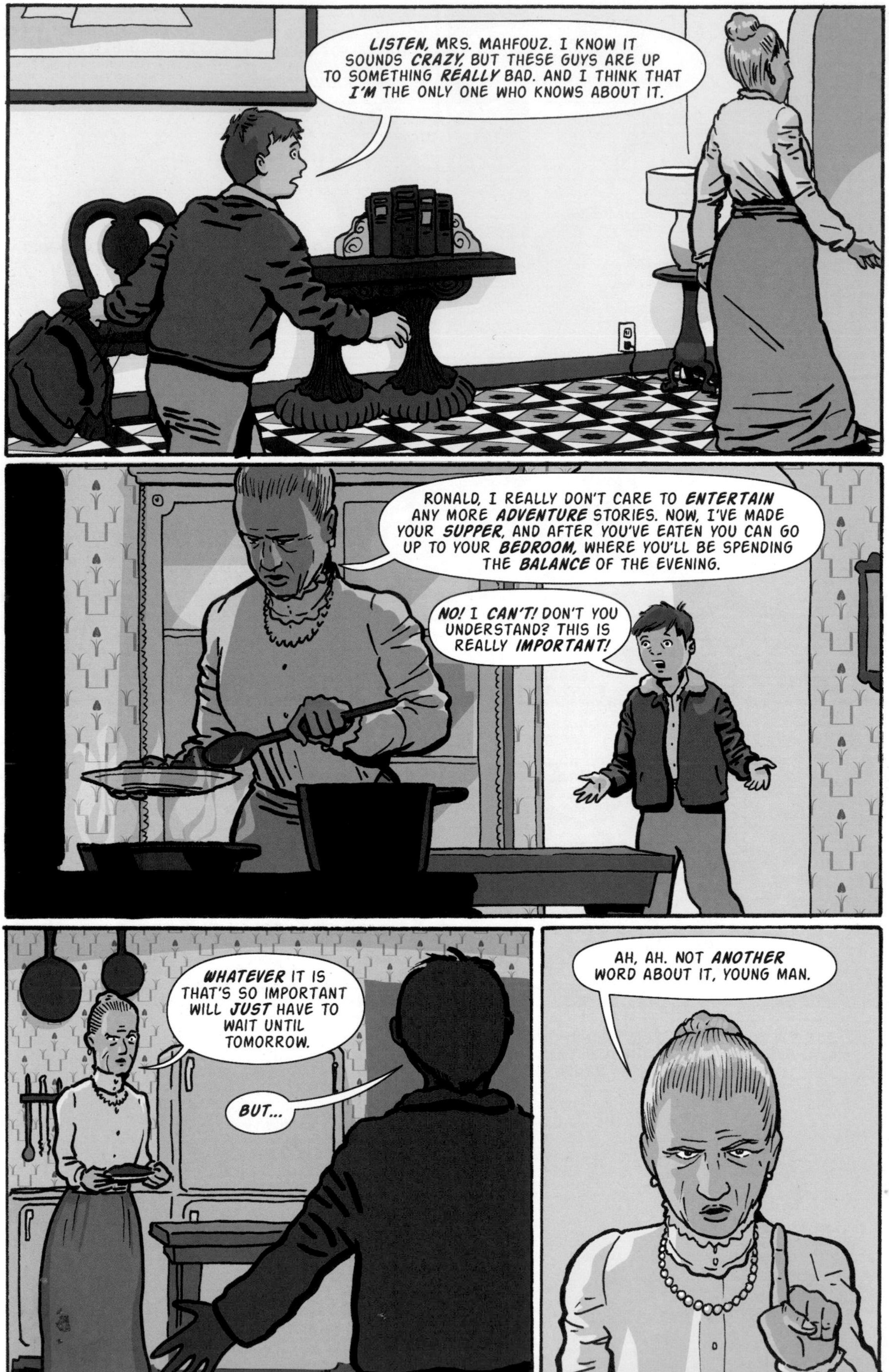
LISTEN, MRS. MAHFOUZ. I KNOW IT SOUNDS CRAZY, BUT THESE GUYS ARE UP TO SOMETHING REALLY BAD. AND I THINK THAT I'M THE ONLY ONE WHO KNOWS ABOUT IT.
RONALD, I REALLY DON'T CARE TO ENTERTAIN ANY MORE ADVENTURE STORIES. NOW, I'VE MADE YOUR SUPPER, AND AFTER YOU'VE EATEN YOU CAN GO UP TO YOUR BEDROOM, WHERE YOU'LL BE SPENDING THE BALANCE OF THE EVENING.
NO! I CAN'T! DON'T YOU UNDERSTAND? THIS IS REALLY IMPORTANT!
WHATEVER IT IS THAT'S SO IMPORTANT WILL JUST HAVE TO WAIT UNTIL TOMORROW.
BUT...
AH, AH. NOT ANOTHER WORD ABOUT IT, YOUNG MAN.

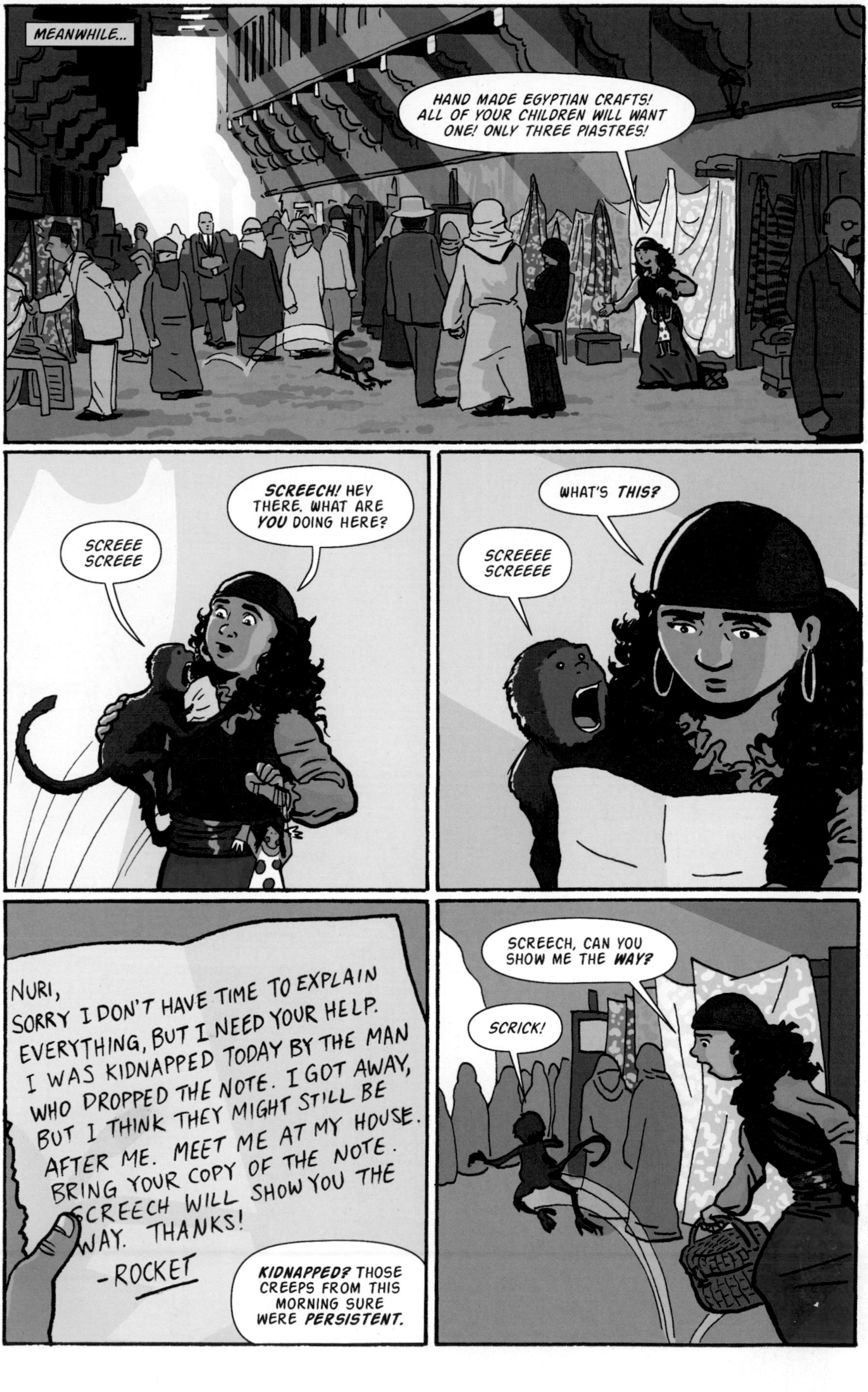
MEANWHILE...
HAND MADE EGYPTIAN CRAFTS! ALL OF YOUR CHILDREN WILL WANT ONE! ONLY THREE PIASTRES!
SCREECH! HEY THERE. WHAT ARE YOU DOING HERE?
SCREEE SCREEE
WHAT'S THIS?
SCREEEE SCREEEE
NURI, SORRY I DON'T HAVE TIME TO EXPLAIN EVERYTHING, BUT I NEED YOUR HELP. I WAS KIDNAPPED TODAY BY THE MAN WHO DROPPED THE NOTE. I GOT AWAY, BUT I THINK THEY MIGHT STILL BE AFTER ME. MEET ME AT MY HOUSE. BRING YOUR COPY OF THE NOTE. SCREECH WILL SHOW YOU THE WAY. THANKS!
-ROCKET
KIDNAPPED? THOSE CREEPS FROM THIS MORNING SURE WERE PERSISTENT.
SCREECH, CAN YOU SHOW ME THE WAY?
SCRICK!

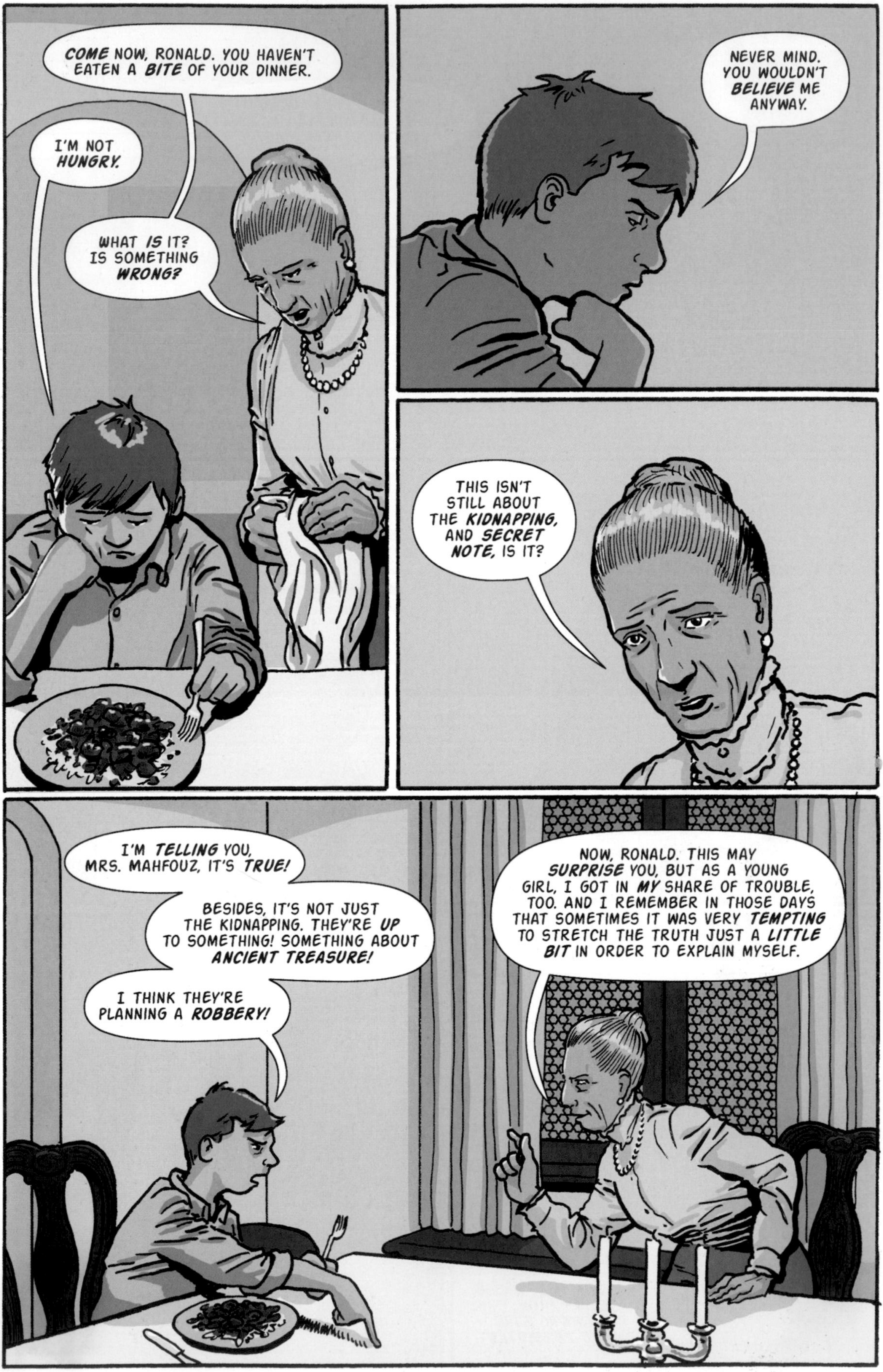
COME NOW, RONALD. YOU HAVEN'T EATEN A BITE OF YOUR DINNER.
I'M NOT HUNGRY.
WHAT IS IT? IS SOMETHING WRONG?
NEVER MIND. YOU WOULDN'T BELIEVE ME ANYWAY.
THIS ISN'T STILL ABOUT THE KIDNAPPING, AND SECRET NOTE, IS IT?
I'M TELLING YOU, MRS. MAHFOUZ, IT'S TRUE!
BESIDES, IT'S NOT JUST THE KIDNAPPING. THEY'RE UP TO SOMETHING! SOMETHING ABOUT ANCIENT TREASURE!
I THINK THEY'RE PLANNING A ROBBERY!
NOW, RONALD. THIS MAY SURPRISE YOU, BUT AS A YOUNG GIRL, I GOT IN MY SHARE OF TROUBLE, TOO. AND I REMEMBER IN THOSE DAYS THAT SOMETIMES IT WAS VERY TEMPTING TO STRETCH THE TRUTH JUST A LITTLE BIT IN ORDER TO EXPLAIN MYSELF.

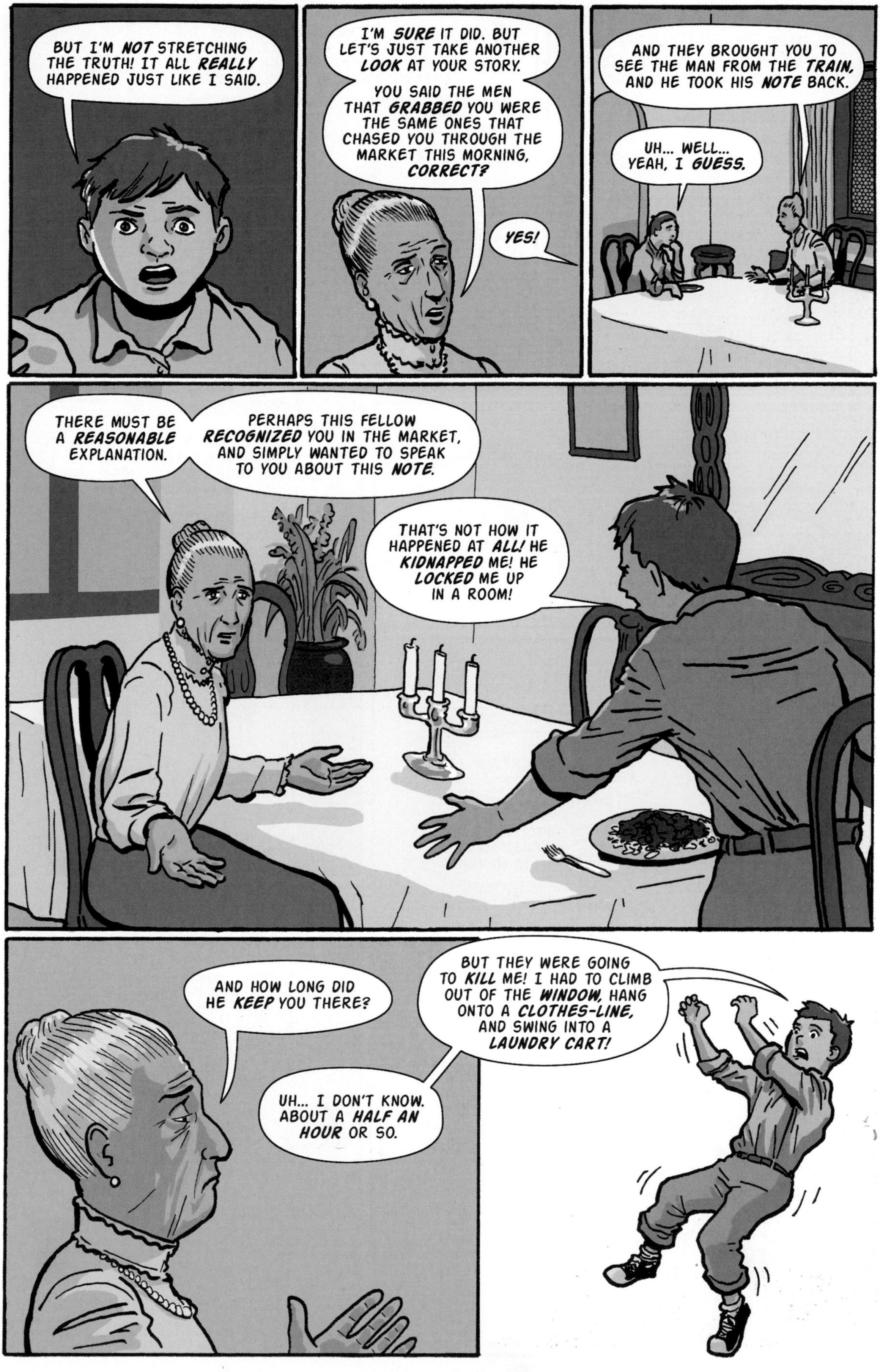
BUT I'M NOT STRETCHING THE TRUTH! IT ALL REALLY HAPPENED JUST LIKE I SAID.
I'M SURE IT DID. BUT LET'S JUST TAKE ANOTHER LOOK AT YOUR STORY.
YOU SAID THE MEN THAT GRABBED YOU WERE THE SAME ONES THAT CHASED YOU THROUGH THE MARKET THIS MORNING, CORRECT?
YES!
AND THEY BROUGHT YOU TO SEE THE MAN FROM THE TRAIN, AND HE TOOK HIS NOTE BACK.
UH... WELL... YEAH, I GUESS.
THERE MUST BE A REASONABLE EXPLANATION.
PERHAPS THIS FELLOW RECOGNIZED YOU IN THE MARKET, AND SIMPLY WANTED TO SPEAK TO YOU ABOUT THIS NOTE.
THAT'S NOT HOW IT HAPPENED AT ALL! HE KIDNAPPED ME! HE LOCKED ME UP IN A ROOM!
AND HOW LONG DID HE KEEP YOU THERE?
UH... I DON'T KNOW. ABOUT A HALF AN HOUR OR SO.
BUT THEY WERE GOING TO KILL ME! I HAD TO CLIMB OUT OF THE WINDOW, HANG ONTO A CLOTHES-LINE, AND SWING INTO A LAUNDRY CART!

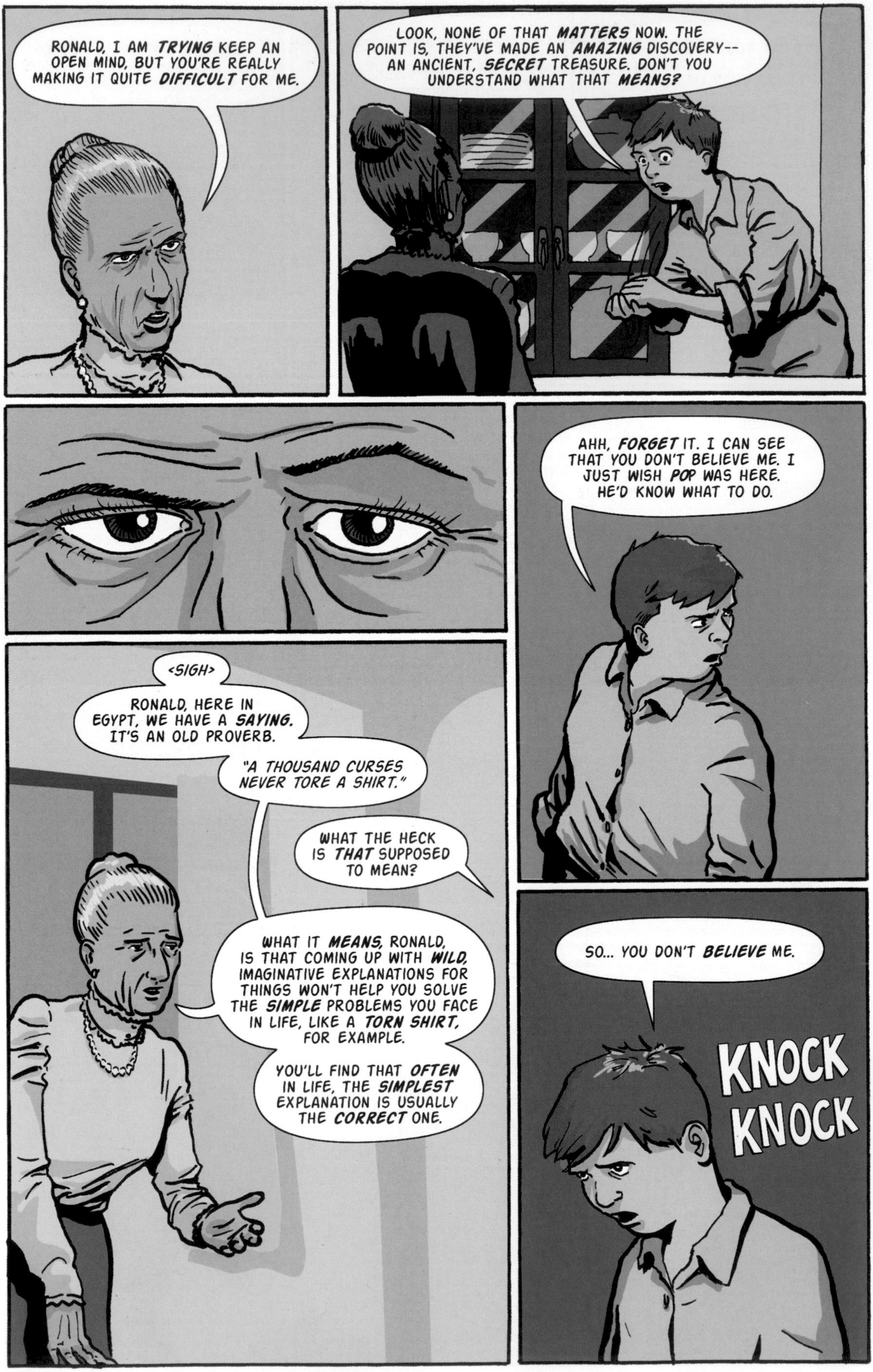
RONALD, I AM TRYING KEEP AN OPEN MIND, BUT YOU'RE REALLY MAKING IT QUITE DIFFICULT FOR ME.
LOOK, NONE OF THAT MATTERS NOW. THE POINT IS, THEY'VE MADE AN AMAZING DISCOVERY-- AN ANCIENT, SECRET TREASURE. DON'T YOU UNDERSTAND WHAT THAT MEANS?
AHH, FORGET IT. I CAN SEE THAT YOU DON'T BELIEVE ME. I JUST WISH POP WAS HERE. HE'D KNOW WHAT TO DO.
<SIGH>
RONALD, HERE IN EGYPT, WE HAVE A SAYING. IT'S AN OLD PROVERB.
"A THOUSAND CURSES NEVER TORE A SHIRT."
WHAT THE HECK IS THAT SUPPOSED TO MEAN?
WHAT IT MEANS, RONALD, IS THAT COMING UP WITH WILD, IMAGINATIVE EXPLANATIONS FOR THINGS WON'T HELP YOU SOLVE THE SIMPLE PROBLEMS YOU FACE IN LIFE, LIKE A TORN SHIRT, FOR EXAMPLE.
YOU'LL FIND THAT OFTEN IN LIFE, THE SIMPLEST EXPLANATION IS USUALLY THE CORRECT ONE.
SO... YOU DON'T BELIEVE ME.
KNOCK
KNOCK

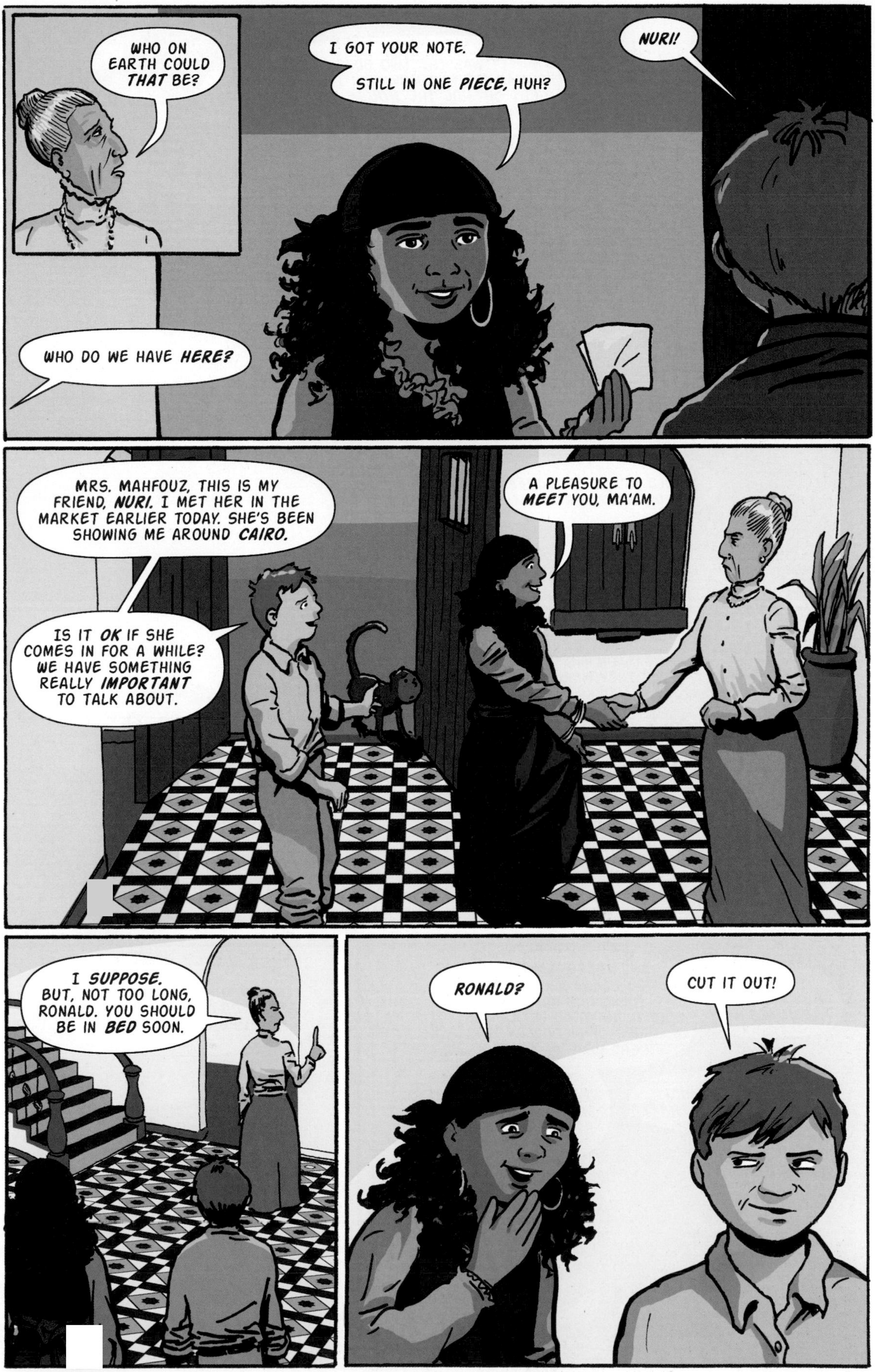
WHO ON EARTH COULD THAT BE?
I GOT YOUR NOTE.
STILL IN ONE PIECE, HUH?
NURI!
WHO DO WE HAVE HERE?
MRS. MAHFOUZ, THIS IS MY FRIEND, NURI. I MET HER IN THE MARKET EARLIER TODAY. SHE'S BEEN SHOWING ME AROUND CAIRO.
IS IT OK IF SHE COMES IN FOR A WHILE? WE HAVE SOMETHING REALLY IMPORTANT TO TALK ABOUT.
A PLEASURE TO MEET YOU, MA'AM.
I SUPPOSE. BUT, NOT TOO LONG, RONALD. YOU SHOULD BE IN BED SOON.
RONALD?
CUT IT OUT!

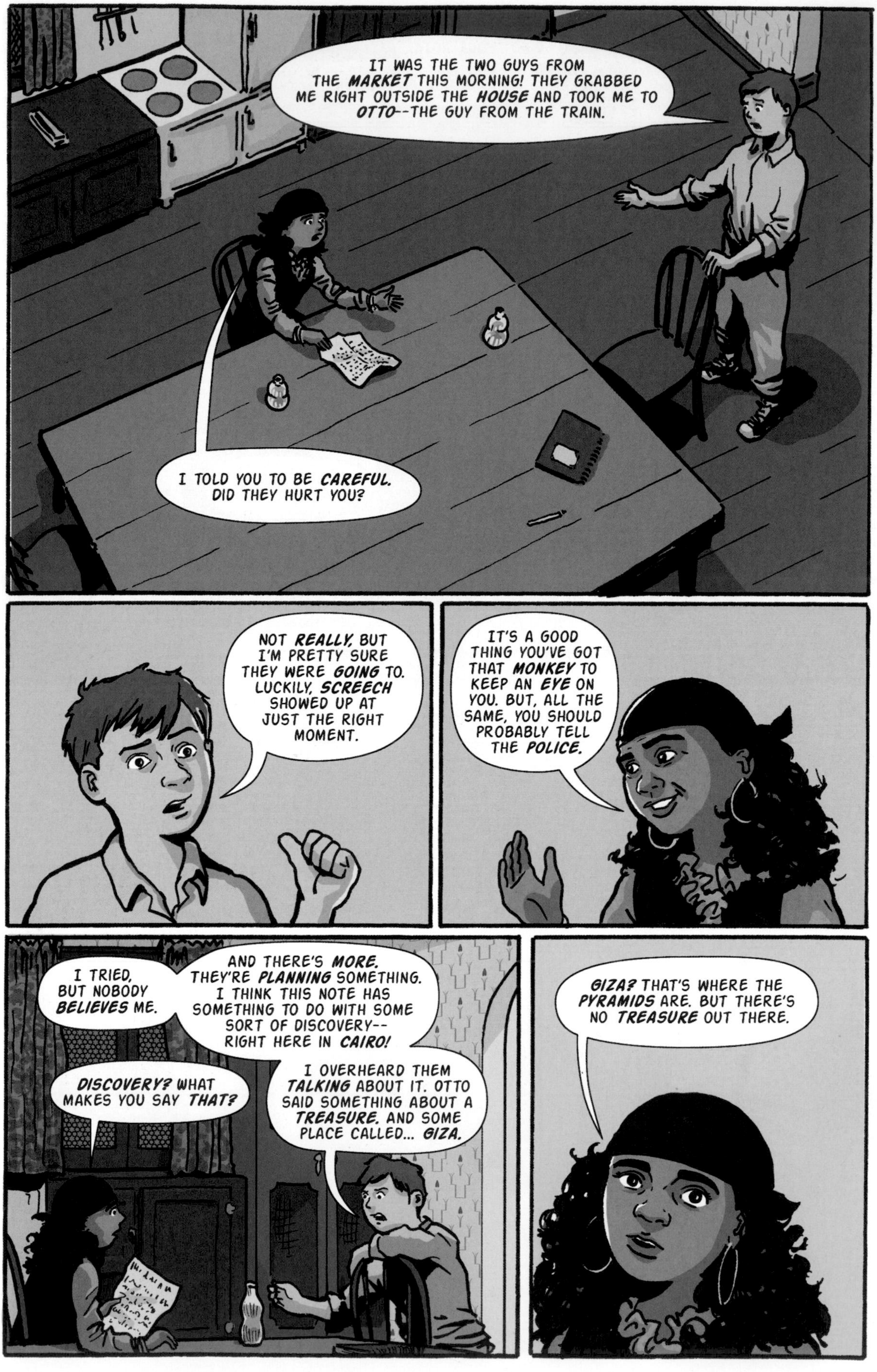
IT WAS THE TWO GUYS FROM THE MARKET THIS MORNING! THEY GRABBED ME RIGHT OUTSIDE THE HOUSE AND TOOK ME TO OTTO--THE GUY FROM THE TRAIN.
I TOLD YOU TO BE CAREFUL. DID THEY HURT YOU?
NOT REALLY, BUT I'M PRETTY SURE THEY WERE GOING TO. LUCKILY, SCREECH SHOWED UP AT JUST THE RIGHT MOMENT.
IT'S A GOOD THING YOU'VE GOT THAT MONKEY TO KEEP AN EYE ON YOU. BUT, ALL THE SAME, YOU SHOULD PROBABLY TELL THE POLICE.
I TRIED, BUT NOBODY BELIEVES ME.
AND THERE'S MORE. THEY'RE PLANNING SOMETHING. I THINK THIS NOTE HAS SOMETHING TO DO WITH SOME SORT OF DISCOVERY-- RIGHT HERE IN CAIRO!
DISCOVERY? WHAT MAKES YOU SAY THAT?
I OVERHEARD THEM TALKING ABOUT IT. OTTO SAID SOMETHING ABOUT A TREASURE. AND SOME PLACE CALLED... GIZA.
GIZA? THAT'S WHERE THE PYRAMIDS ARE. BUT THERE'S NO TREASURE OUT THERE.

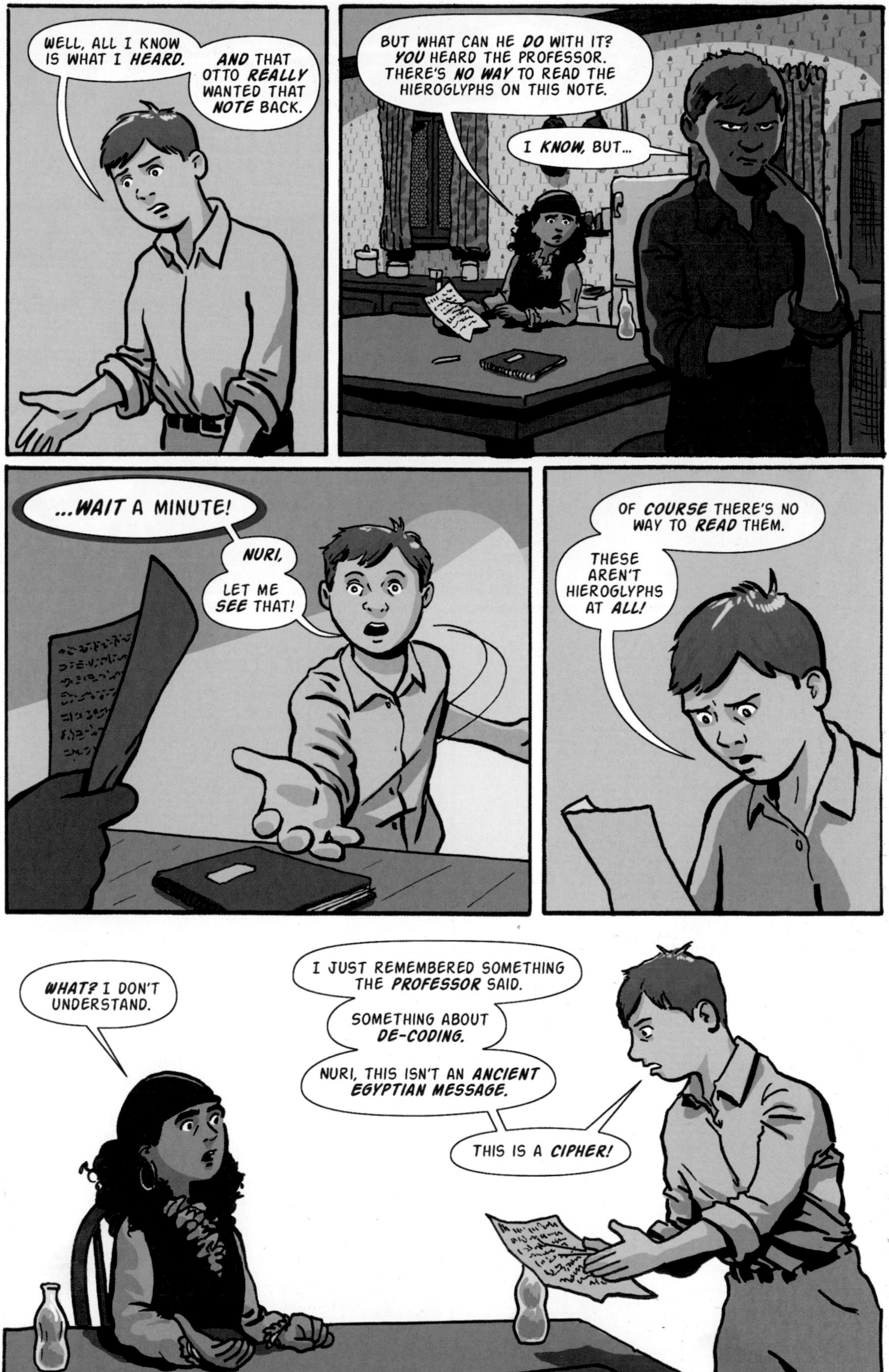
WELL, ALL I KNOW IS WHAT I *HEARD.*
AND THAT OTTO *REALLY* WANTED THAT *NOTE* BACK.
BUT WHAT CAN HE *DO* WITH IT? *YOU* HEARD THE PROFESSOR. THERE'S *NO WAY* TO READ THE HIEROGLYPHS ON THIS NOTE.
I *KNOW,* BUT...
...*WAIT* A MINUTE!
NURI,
LET ME *SEE* THAT!
OF *COURSE* THERE'S NO WAY TO *READ* THEM.
THESE AREN'T HIEROGLYPHS AT *ALL!*
WHAT? I DON'T UNDERSTAND.
I JUST REMEMBERED SOMETHING THE *PROFESSOR* SAID.
SOMETHING ABOUT *DE-CODING.*
NURI, THIS ISN'T AN *ANCIENT EGYPTIAN MESSAGE.*
THIS IS A *CIPHER!*

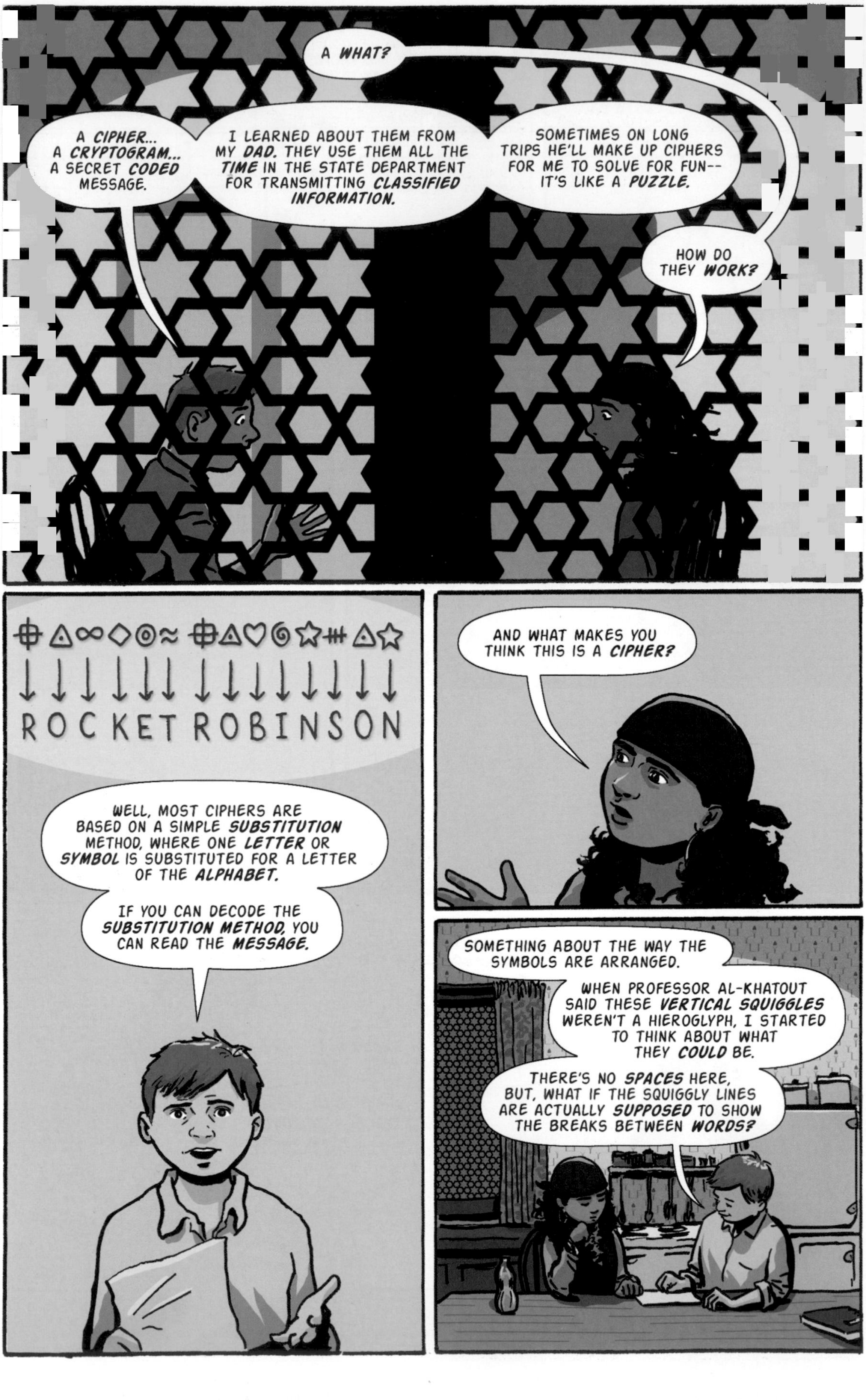
A WHAT?
A CIPHER... A CRYPTOGRAM... A SECRET CODED MESSAGE.
I LEARNED ABOUT THEM FROM MY DAD. THEY USE THEM ALL THE TIME IN THE STATE DEPARTMENT FOR TRANSMITTING CLASSIFIED INFORMATION.
SOMETIMES ON LONG TRIPS HE'LL MAKE UP CIPHERS FOR ME TO SOLVE FOR FUN-- IT'S LIKE A PUZZLE.
HOW DO THEY WORK?
ROCKET ROBINSON
WELL, MOST CIPHERS ARE BASED ON A SIMPLE SUBSTITUTION METHOD, WHERE ONE LETTER OR SYMBOL IS SUBSTITUTED FOR A LETTER OF THE ALPHABET.
IF YOU CAN DECODE THE SUBSTITUTION METHOD, YOU CAN READ THE MESSAGE.
AND WHAT MAKES YOU THINK THIS IS A CIPHER?
SOMETHING ABOUT THE WAY THE SYMBOLS ARE ARRANGED.
WHEN PROFESSOR AL-KHATOUT SAID THESE VERTICAL SQUIGGLES WEREN'T A HIEROGLYPH, I STARTED TO THINK ABOUT WHAT THEY COULD BE.
THERE'S NO SPACES HERE, BUT, WHAT IF THE SQUIGGLY LINES ARE ACTUALLY SUPPOSED TO SHOW THE BREAKS BETWEEN WORDS?

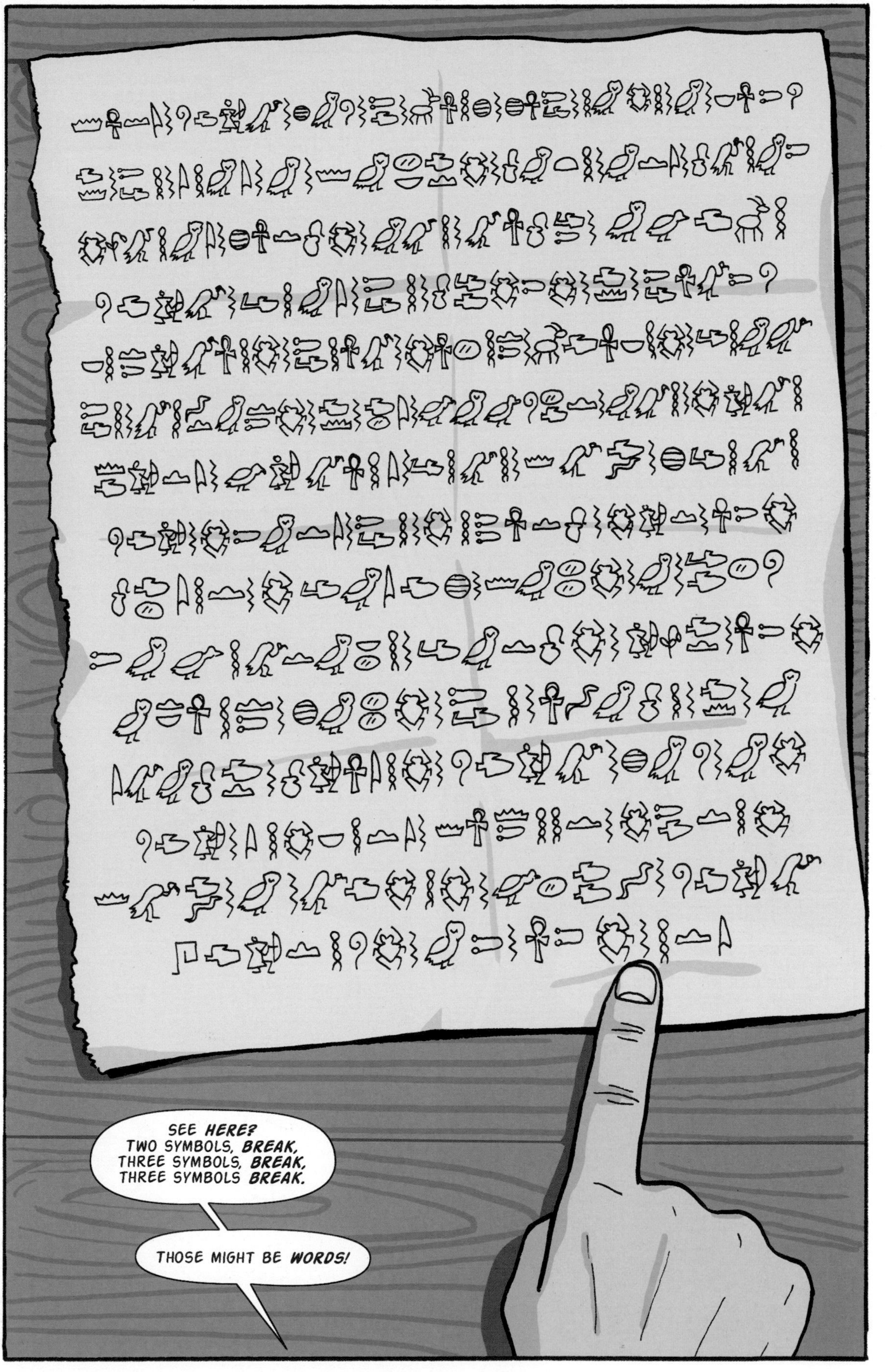
SEE HERE? TWO SYMBOLS, BREAK, THREE SYMBOLS, BREAK, THREE SYMBOLS BREAK.
THOSE MIGHT BE WORDS!

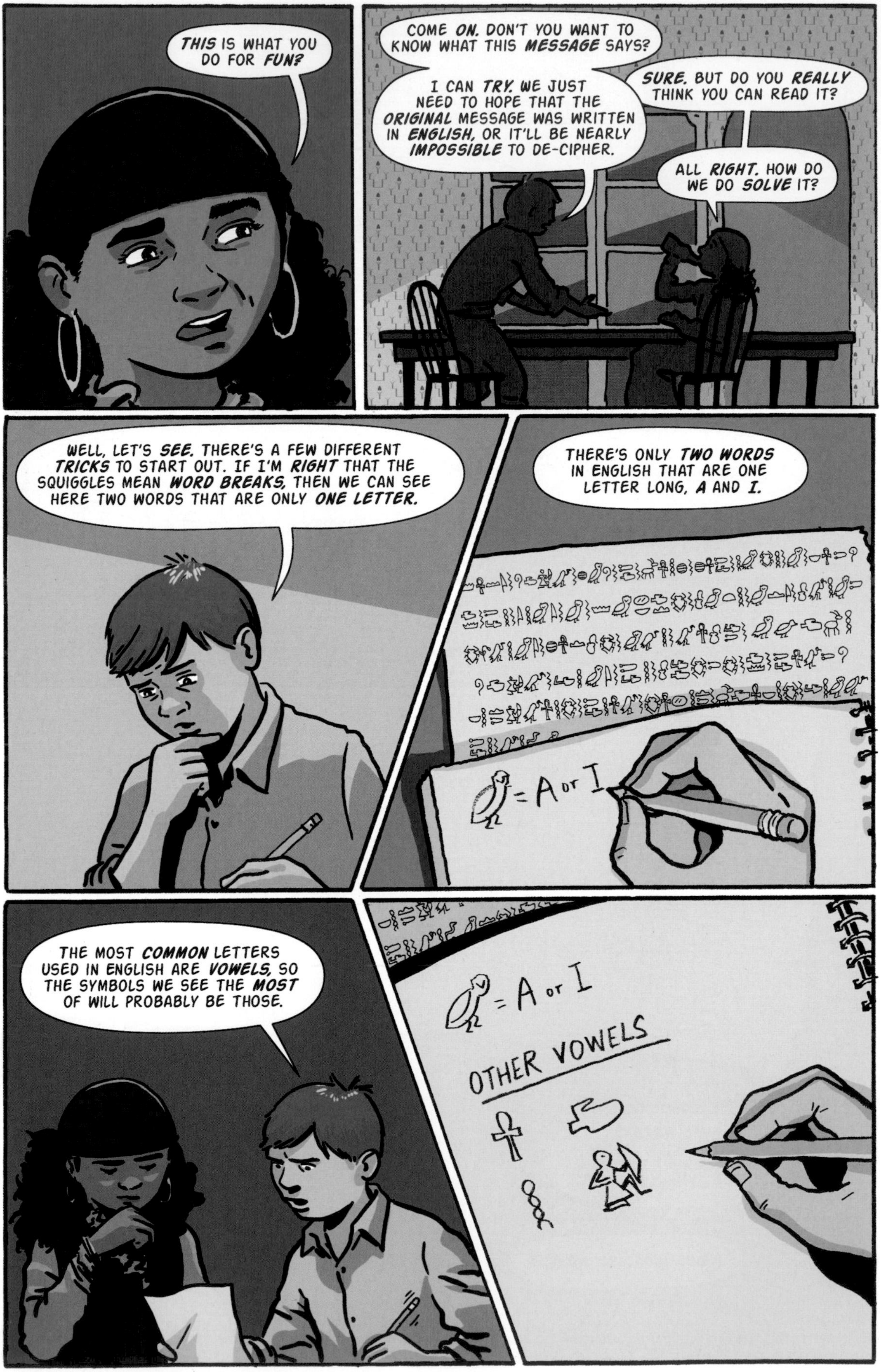

THIS IS WHAT YOU DO FOR FUN?
COME ON. DON'T YOU WANT TO KNOW WHAT THIS MESSAGE SAYS?
SURE. BUT DO YOU REALLY THINK YOU CAN READ IT?
I CAN TRY. WE JUST NEED TO HOPE THAT THE ORIGINAL MESSAGE WAS WRITTEN IN ENGLISH, OR IT'LL BE NEARLY IMPOSSIBLE TO DE-CIPHER.
ALL RIGHT. HOW DO WE DO SOLVE IT?
WELL, LET'S SEE. THERE'S A FEW DIFFERENT TRICKS TO START OUT. IF I'M RIGHT THAT THE SQUIGGLES MEAN WORD BREAKS, THEN WE CAN SEE HERE TWO WORDS THAT ARE ONLY ONE LETTER.
THERE'S ONLY TWO WORDS IN ENGLISH THAT ARE ONE LETTER LONG, A AND I.
= A or I
THE MOST COMMON LETTERS USED IN ENGLISH ARE VOWELS, SO THE SYMBOLS WE SEE THE MOST OF WILL PROBABLY BE THOSE.
= A or I
OTHER VOWELS

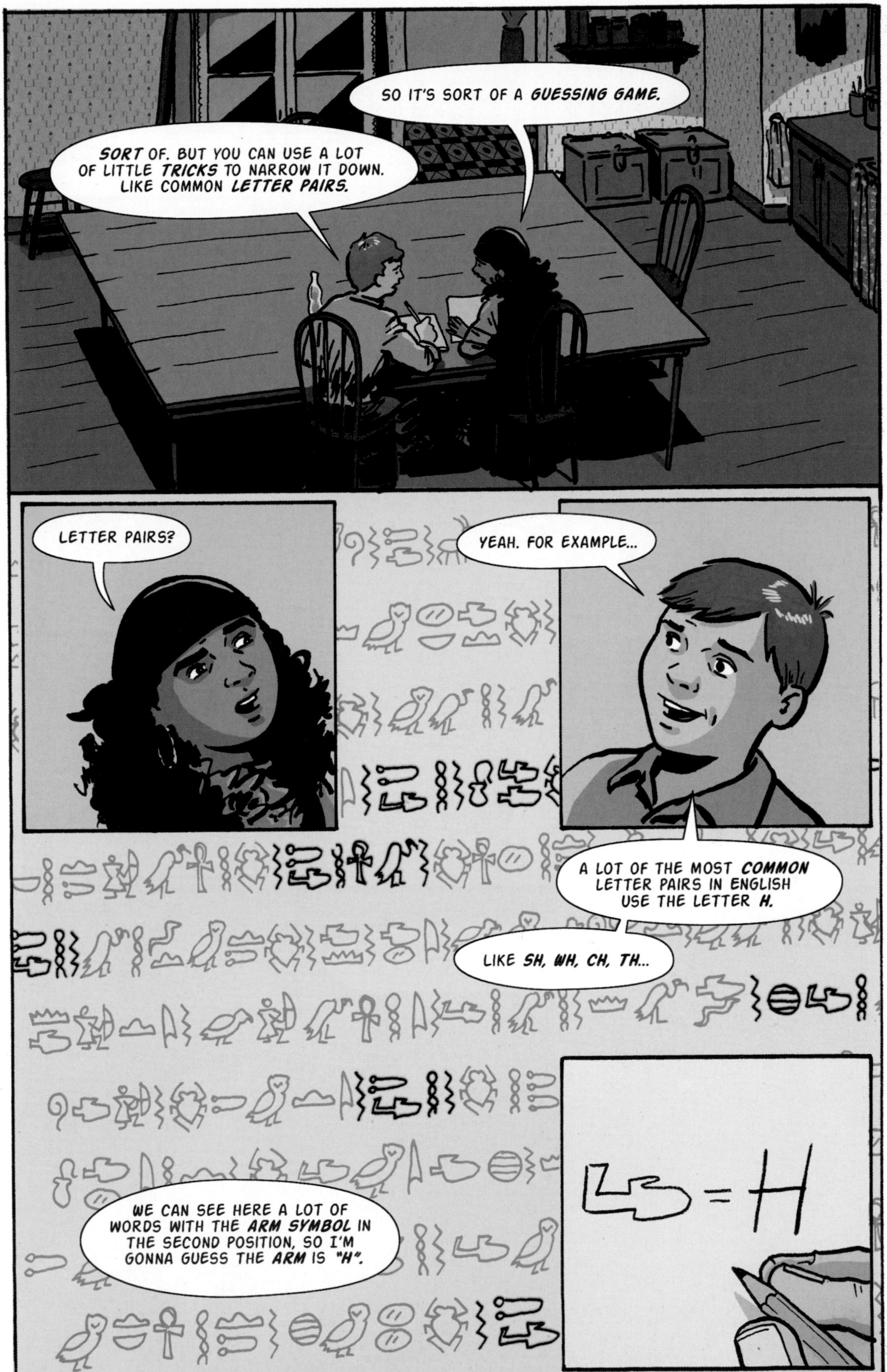
SORT OF. BUT YOU CAN USE A LOT OF LITTLE TRICKS TO NARROW IT DOWN. LIKE COMMON LETTER PAIRS.
SO IT'S SORT OF A GUESSING GAME.
LETTER PAIRS?
YEAH. FOR EXAMPLE...
A LOT OF THE MOST COMMON LETTER PAIRS IN ENGLISH USE THE LETTER H.
LIKE SH, WH, CH, TH...
WE CAN SEE HERE A LOT OF WORDS WITH THE ARM SYMBOL IN THE SECOND POSITION, SO I'M GONNA GUESS THE ARM IS "H".
= H

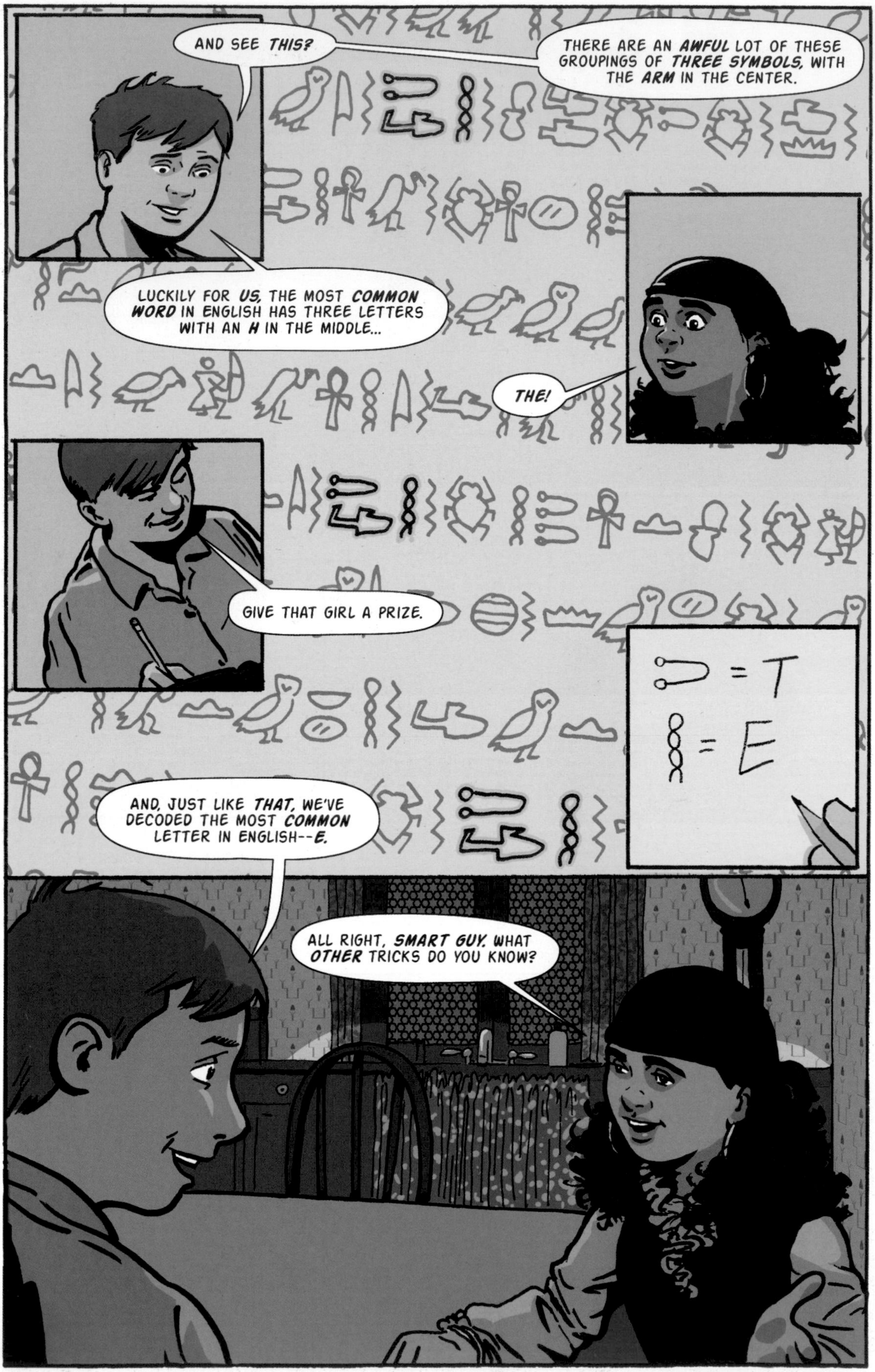
AND SEE THIS?
THERE ARE AN AWFUL LOT OF THESE GROUPINGS OF THREE SYMBOLS, WITH THE ARM IN THE CENTER.
LUCKILY FOR US, THE MOST COMMON WORD IN ENGLISH HAS THREE LETTERS WITH AN H IN THE MIDDLE...
THE!
GIVE THAT GIRL A PRIZE.
= T
= E
AND, JUST LIKE THAT, WE'VE DECODED THE MOST COMMON LETTER IN ENGLISH--E.
ALL RIGHT, SMART GUY. WHAT OTHER TRICKS DO YOU KNOW?

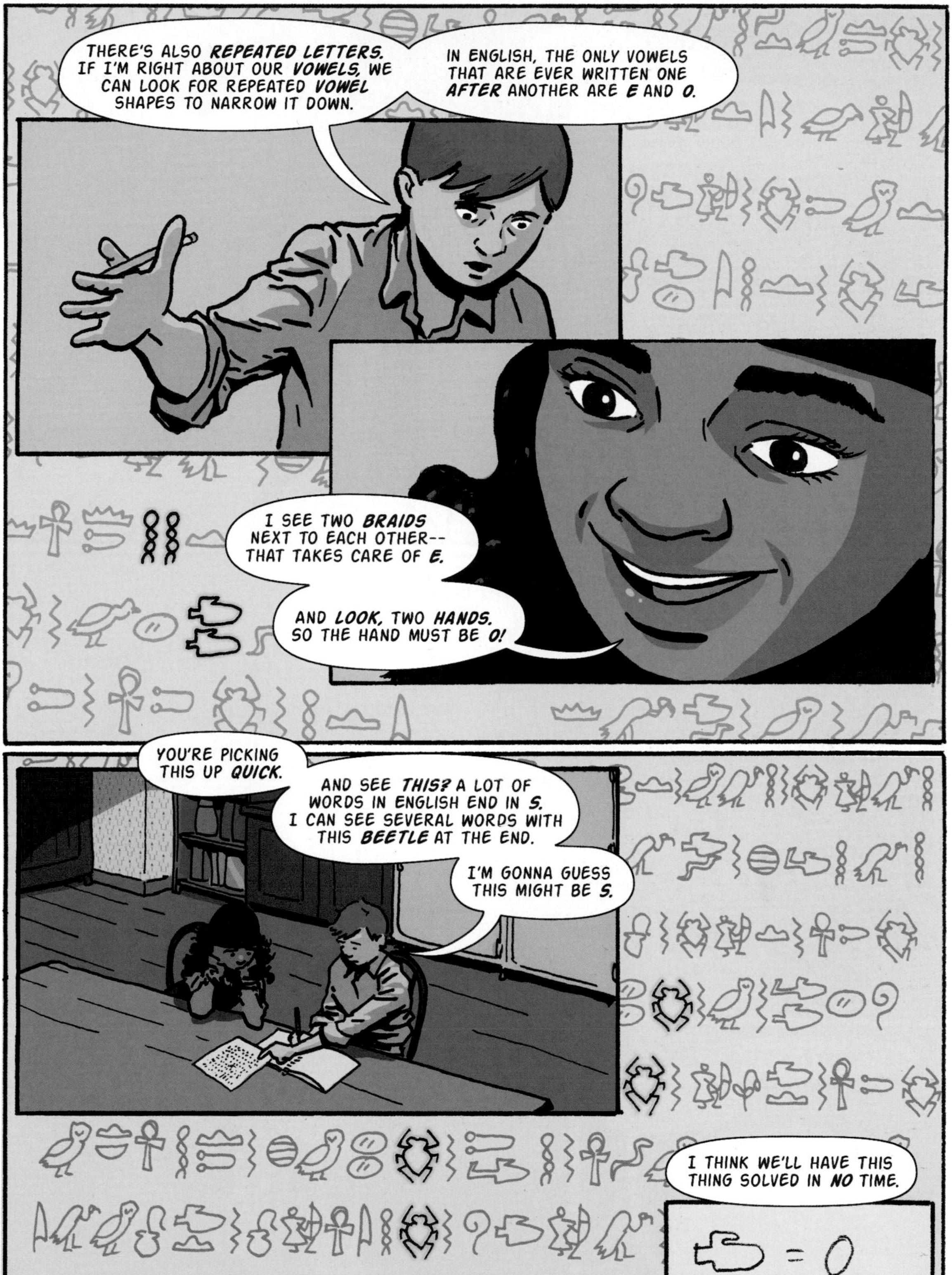

THERE'S ALSO REPEATED LETTERS. IF I'M RIGHT ABOUT OUR VOWELS, WE CAN LOOK FOR REPEATED VOWEL SHAPES TO NARROW IT DOWN.
IN ENGLISH, THE ONLY VOWELS THAT ARE EVER WRITTEN ONE AFTER ANOTHER ARE E AND O.
I SEE TWO BRAIDS NEXT TO EACH OTHER-- THAT TAKES CARE OF E.
AND LOOK, TWO HANDS. SO THE HAND MUST BE O!
YOU'RE PICKING THIS UP QUICK.
AND SEE THIS? A LOT OF WORDS IN ENGLISH END IN S. I CAN SEE SEVERAL WORDS WITH THIS BEETLE AT THE END.
I'M GONNA GUESS THIS MIGHT BE S.
I THINK WE'LL HAVE THIS THING SOLVED IN NO TIME.
= O
= S

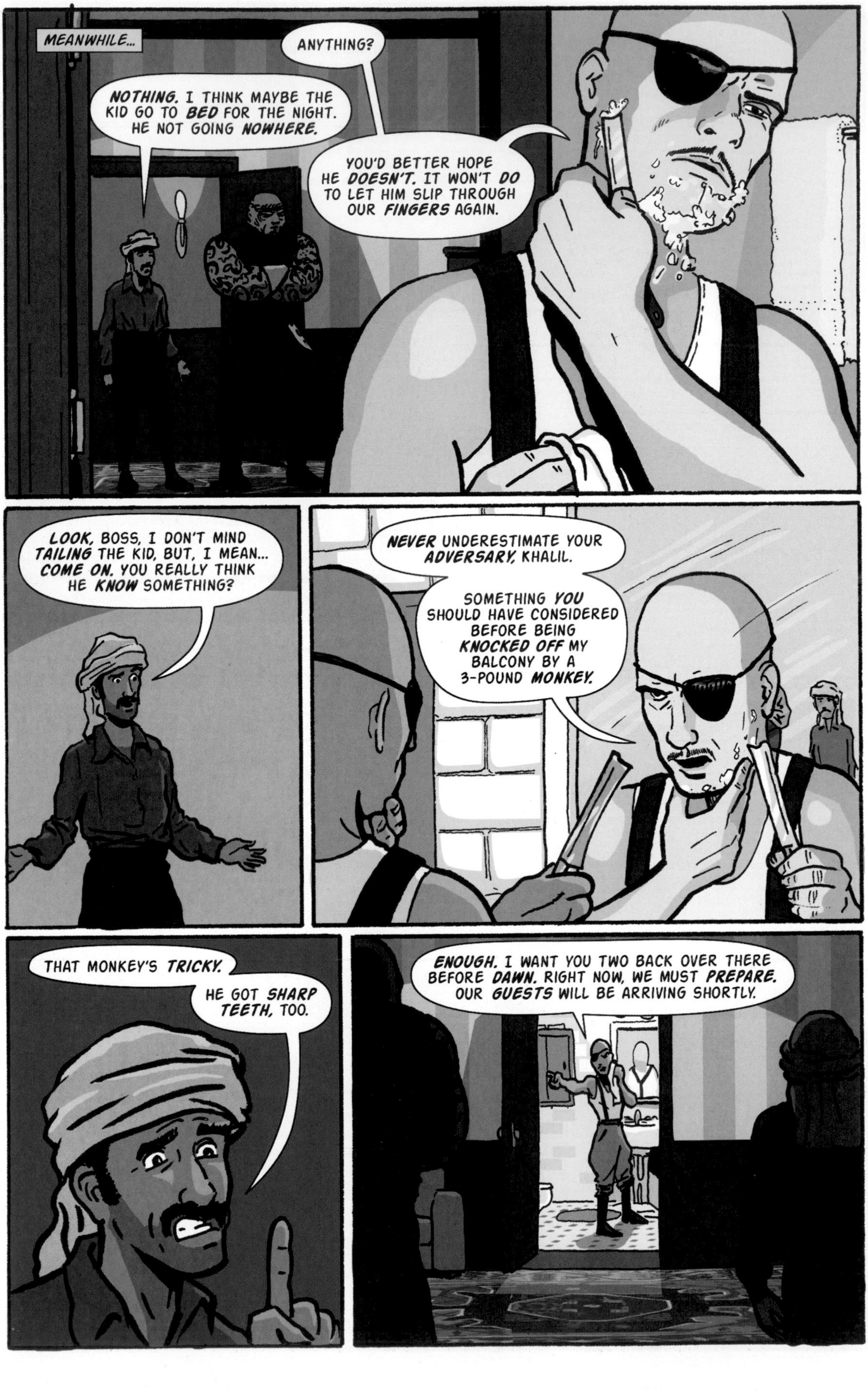
MEANWHILE...
ANYTHING?
NOTHING. I THINK MAYBE THE KID GO TO BED FOR THE NIGHT. HE NOT GOING NOWHERE.
YOU'D BETTER HOPE HE DOESN'T. IT WON'T DO TO LET HIM SLIP THROUGH OUR FINGERS AGAIN.
LOOK, BOSS, I DON'T MIND TAILING THE KID, BUT, I MEAN... COME ON. YOU REALLY THINK HE KNOW SOMETHING?
NEVER UNDERESTIMATE YOUR ADVERSARY, KHALIL.
SOMETHING YOU SHOULD HAVE CONSIDERED BEFORE BEING KNOCKED OFF MY BALCONY BY A 3-POUND MONKEY.
THAT MONKEY'S TRICKY.
HE GOT SHARP TEETH, TOO.
ENOUGH. I WANT YOU TWO BACK OVER THERE BEFORE DAWN. RIGHT NOW, WE MUST PREPARE. OUR GUESTS WILL BE ARRIVING SHORTLY.

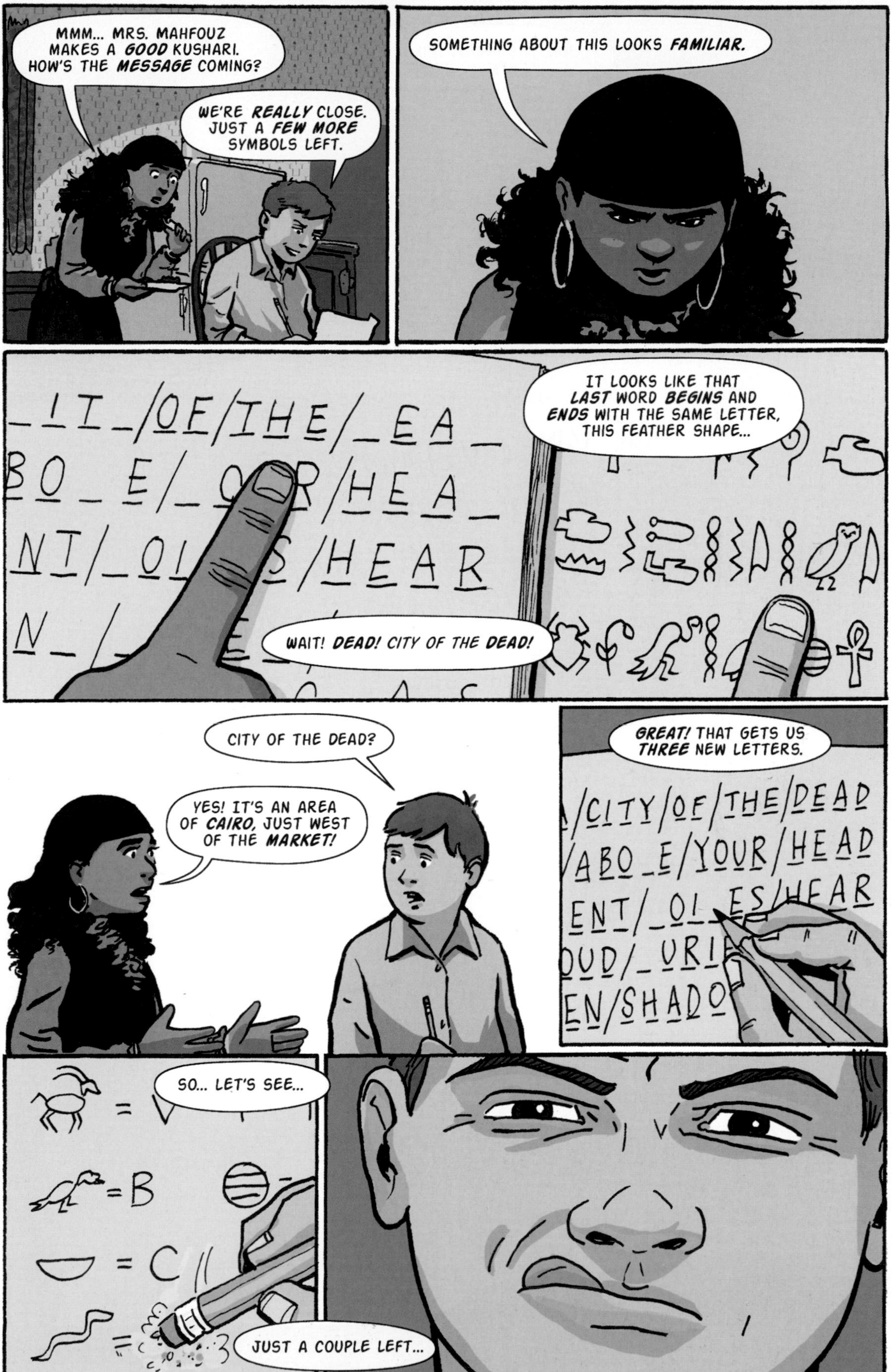
MMM... MRS. MAHFOUZ MAKES A GOOD KUSHARI. HOW'S THE MESSAGE COMING?
WE'RE REALLY CLOSE. JUST A FEW MORE SYMBOLS LEFT.
SOMETHING ABOUT THIS LOOKS FAMILIAR.
IT LOOKS LIKE THAT LAST WORD BEGINS AND ENDS WITH THE SAME LETTER, THIS FEATHER SHAPE...
WAIT! DEAD! CITY OF THE DEAD!
CITY OF THE DEAD?
YES! IT'S AN AREA OF CAIRO, JUST WEST OF THE MARKET!
GREAT! THAT GETS US THREE NEW LETTERS.
SO... LET'S SEE...
JUST A COUPLE LEFT...

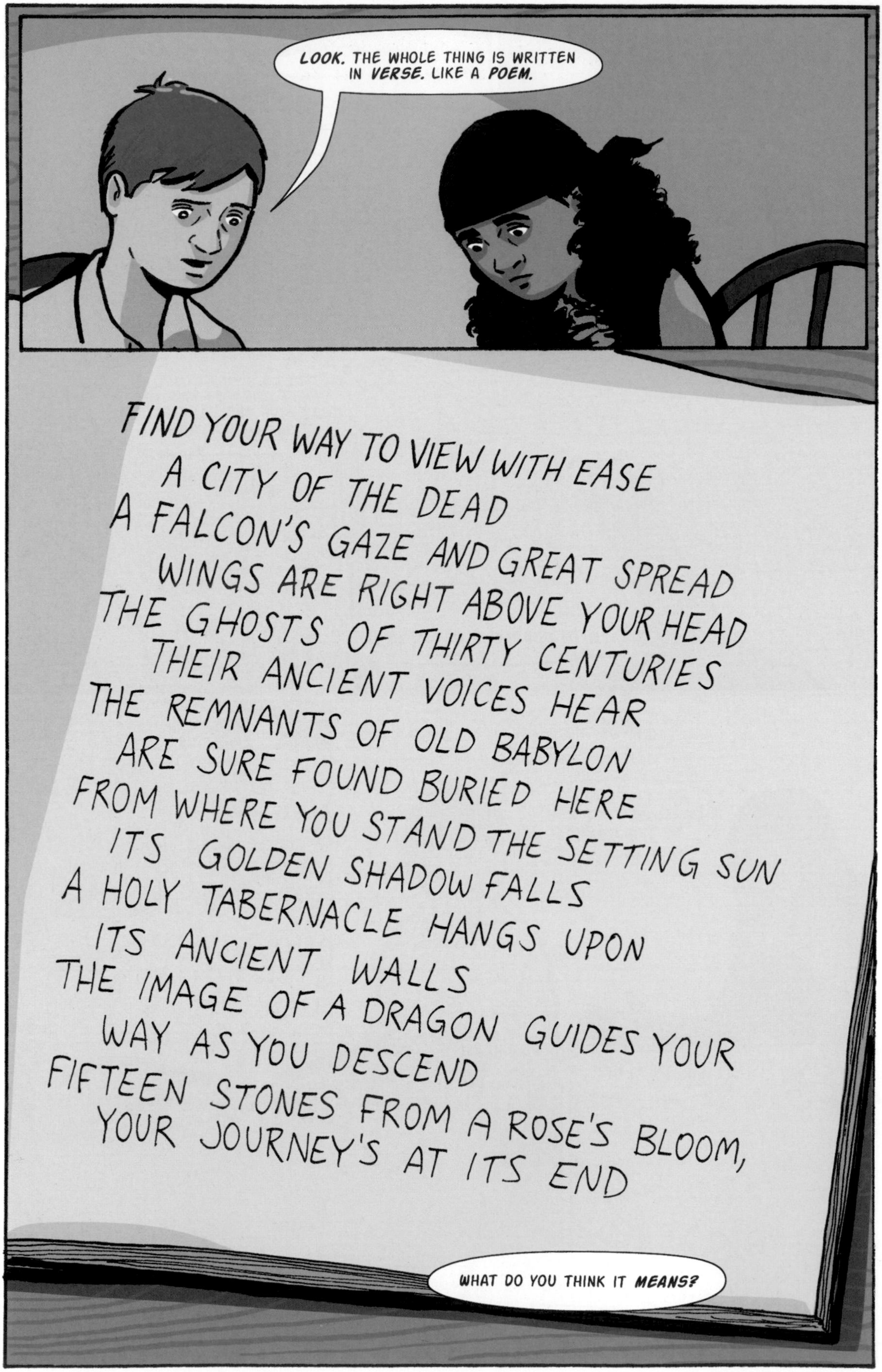
LOOK. THE WHOLE THING IS WRITTEN IN VERSE. LIKE A POEM.
FIND YOUR WAY TO VIEW WITH EASE
A CITY OF THE DEAD
A FALCON'S GAZE AND GREAT SPREAD
WINGS ARE RIGHT ABOVE YOUR HEAD
THE GHOSTS OF THIRTY CENTURIES
THEIR ANCIENT VOICES HEAR
THE REMNANTS OF OLD BABYLON
ARE SURE FOUND BURIED HERE
FROM WHERE YOU STAND THE SETTING SUN
ITS GOLDEN SHADOW FALLS
A HOLY TABERNACLE HANGS UPON
ITS ANCIENT WALLS
THE IMAGE OF A DRAGON GUIDES YOUR
WAY AS YOU DESCEND
FIFTEEN STONES FROM A ROSE'S BLOOM,
YOUR JOURNEY'S AT ITS END
WHAT DO YOU THINK IT MEANS?

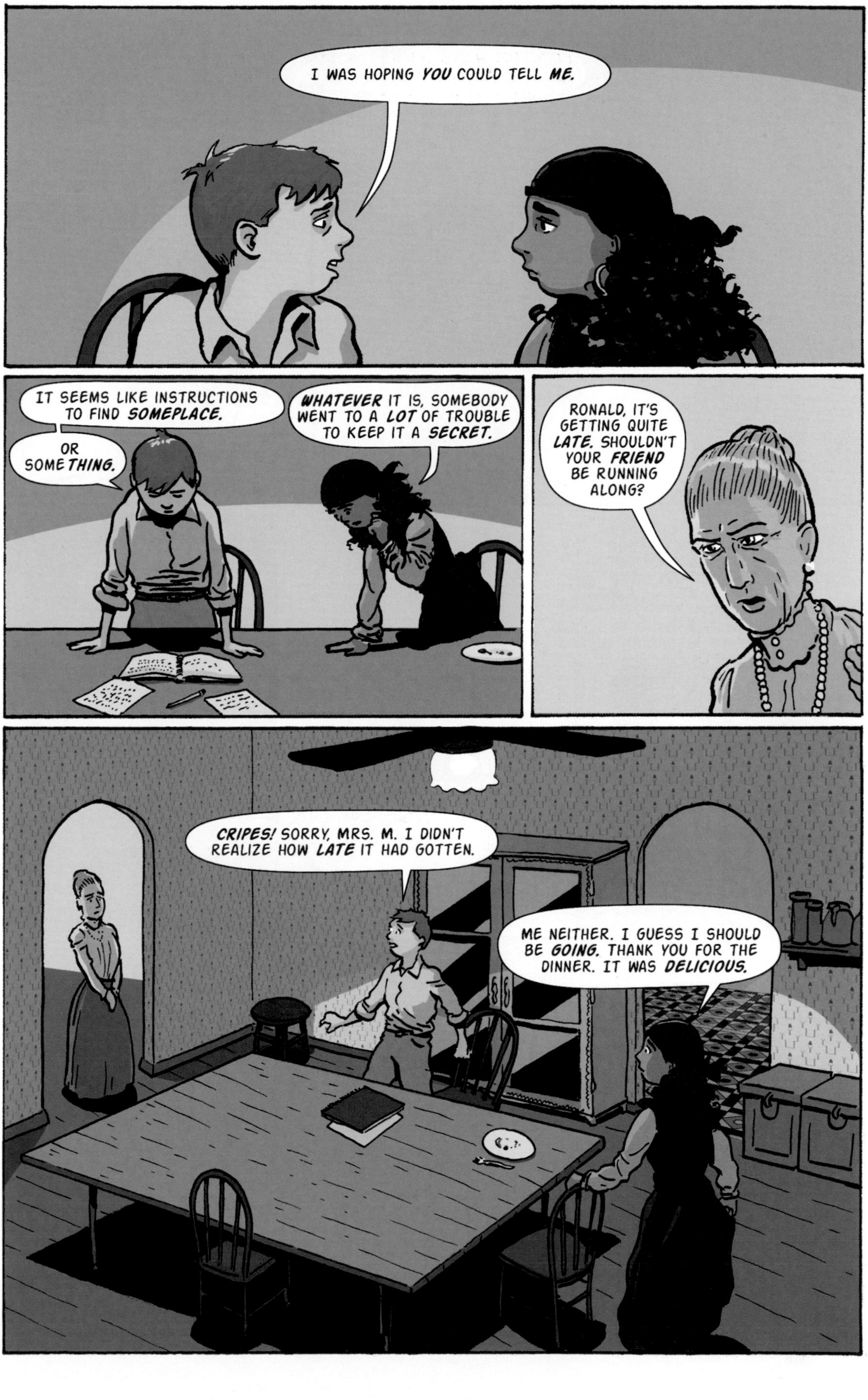
I WAS HOPING *YOU* COULD TELL *ME.*
IT SEEMS LIKE INSTRUCTIONS TO FIND *SOMEPLACE.*
OR SOME*THING.*
WHATEVER IT IS, SOMEBODY WENT TO A *LOT* OF TROUBLE TO KEEP IT A *SECRET.*
RONALD, IT'S GETTING QUITE *LATE.* SHOULDN'T YOUR *FRIEND* BE RUNNING ALONG?
CRIPES! SORRY, MRS. M. I DIDN'T REALIZE HOW *LATE* IT HAD GOTTEN.
ME NEITHER. I GUESS I SHOULD BE *GOING.* THANK YOU FOR THE DINNER. IT WAS *DELICIOUS.*

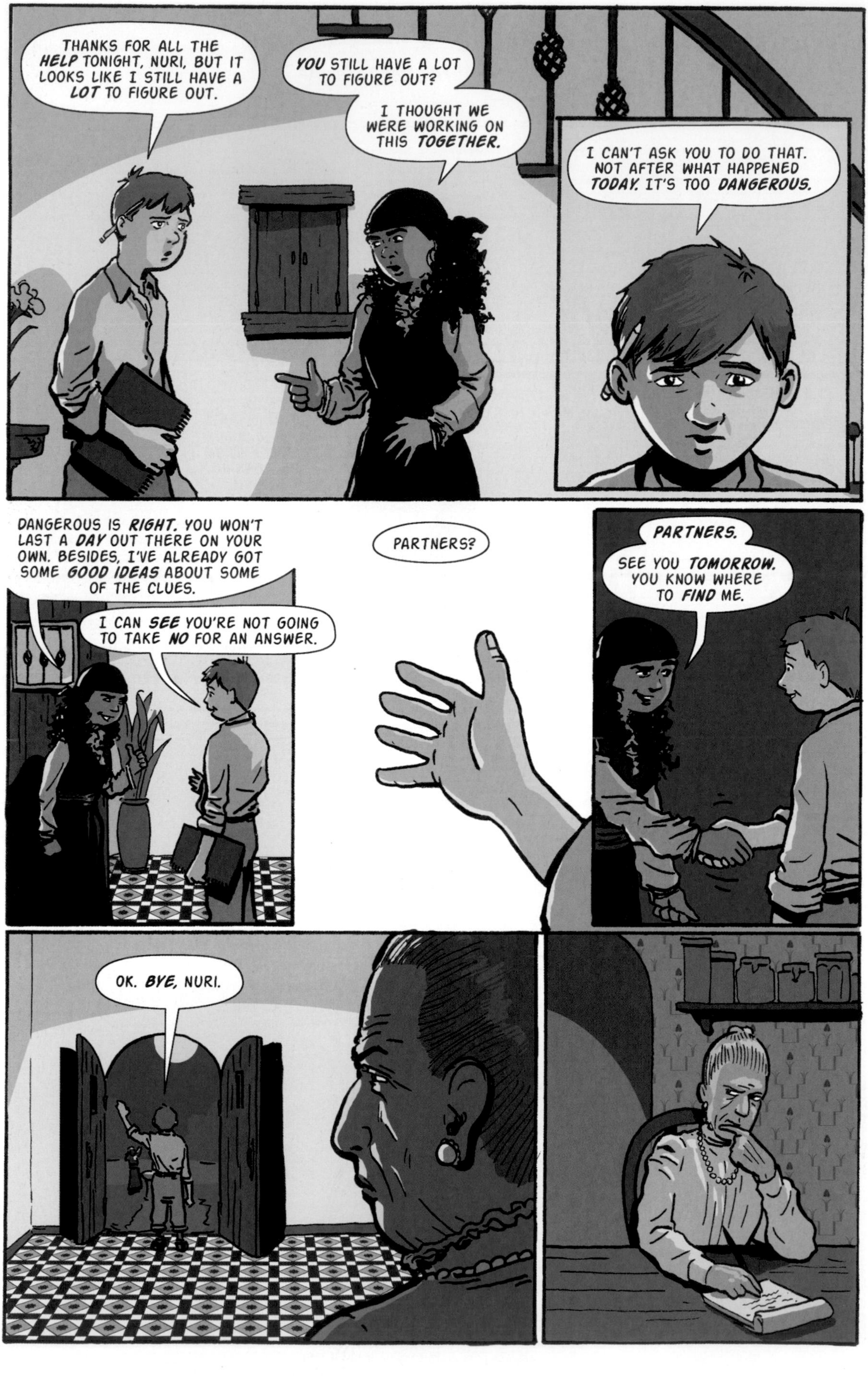
THANKS FOR ALL THE HELP TONIGHT, NURI, BUT IT LOOKS LIKE I STILL HAVE A LOT TO FIGURE OUT.
YOU STILL HAVE A LOT TO FIGURE OUT?
I THOUGHT WE WERE WORKING ON THIS TOGETHER.
I CAN'T ASK YOU TO DO THAT. NOT AFTER WHAT HAPPENED TODAY. IT'S TOO DANGEROUS.
DANGEROUS IS RIGHT. YOU WON'T LAST A DAY OUT THERE ON YOUR OWN. BESIDES, I'VE ALREADY GOT SOME GOOD IDEAS ABOUT SOME OF THE CLUES.
I CAN SEE YOU'RE NOT GOING TO TAKE NO FOR AN ANSWER.
PARTNERS?
PARTNERS.
SEE YOU TOMORROW. YOU KNOW WHERE TO FIND ME.
OK. BYE, NURI.

CHAPTER FIVE

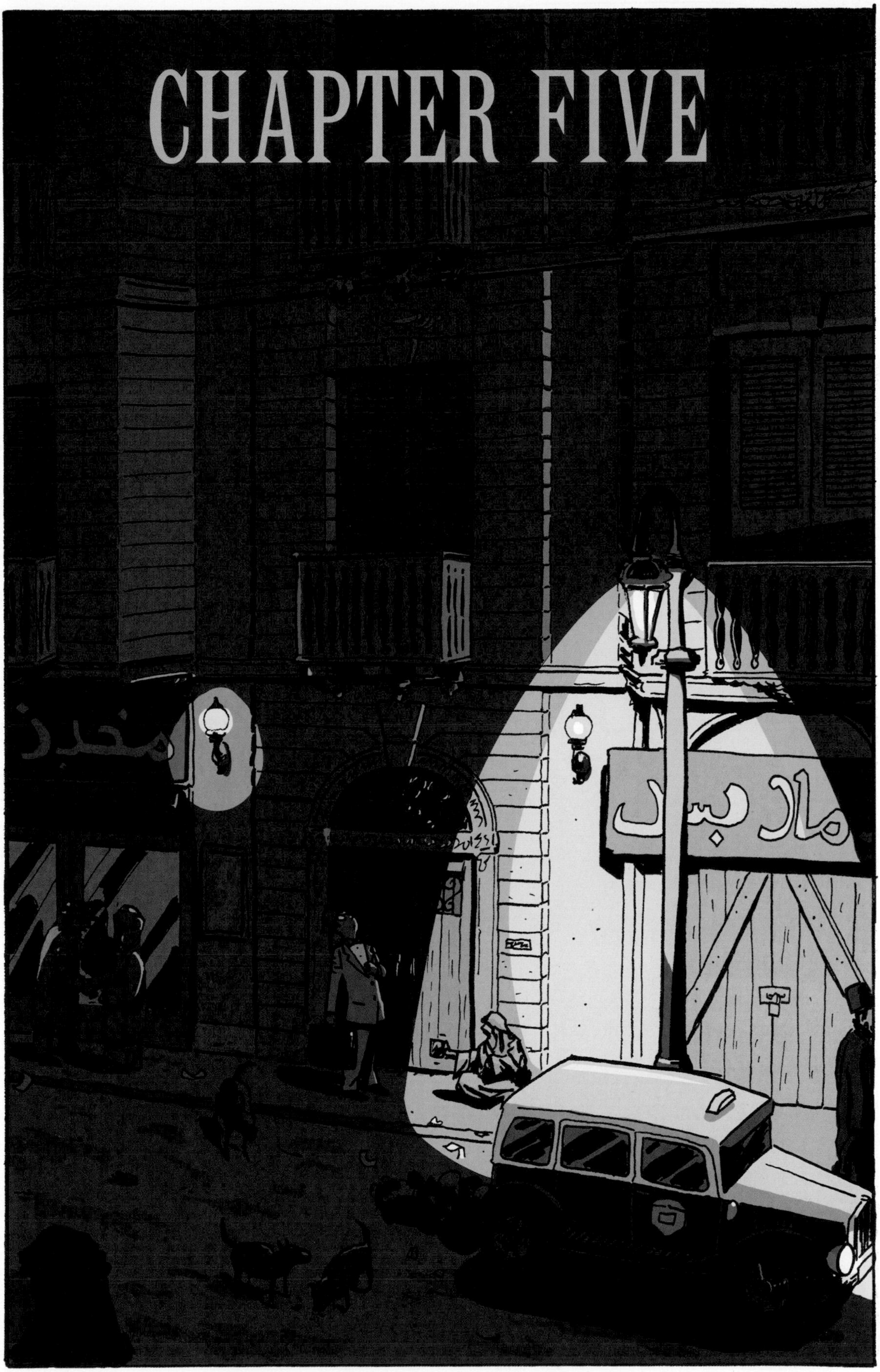

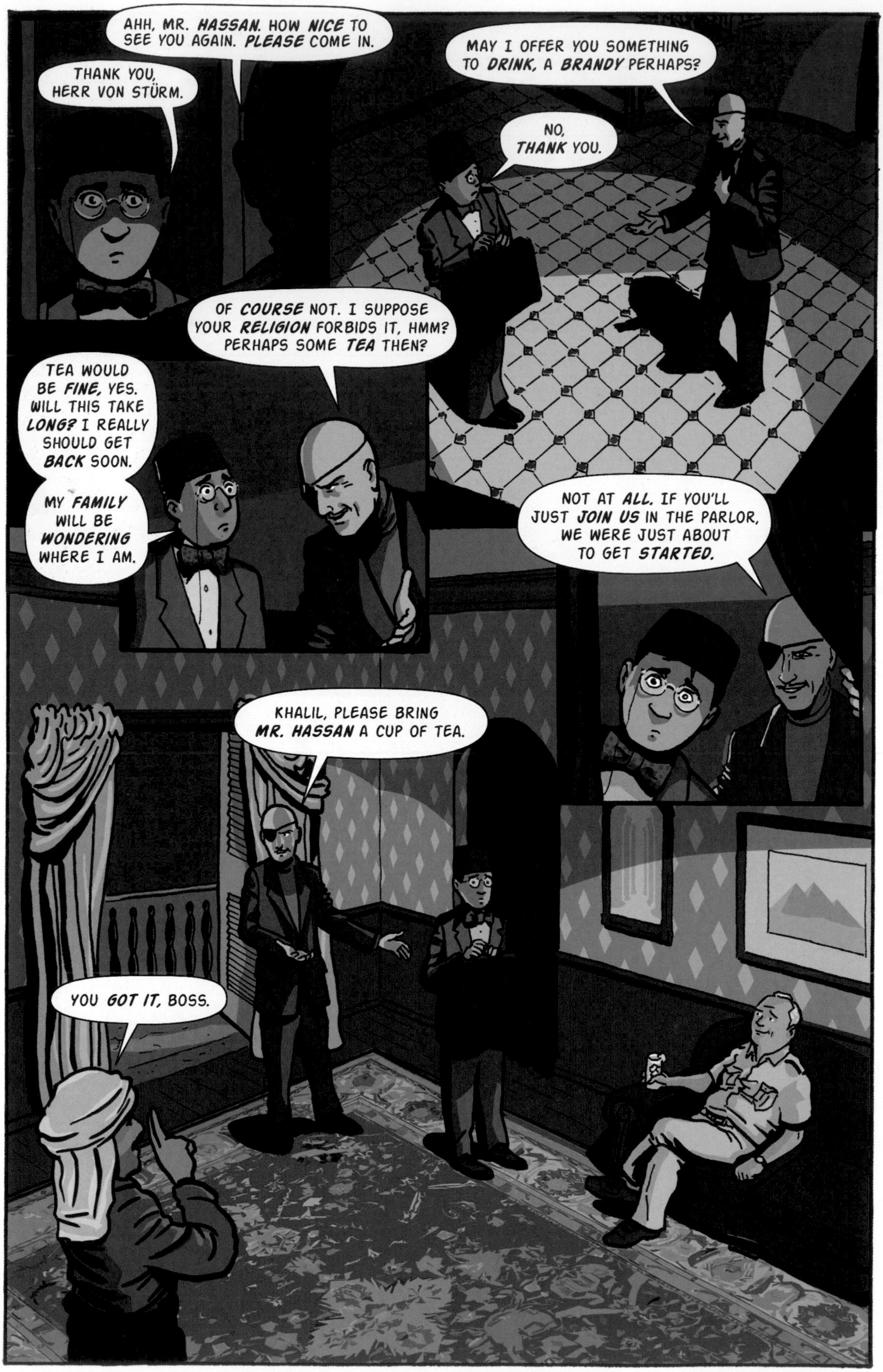
AHH, MR. HASSAN. HOW NICE TO SEE YOU AGAIN. PLEASE COME IN.
THANK YOU, HERR VON STÜRM.
MAY I OFFER YOU SOMETHING TO DRINK, A BRANDY PERHAPS?
NO, THANK YOU.
OF COURSE NOT. I SUPPOSE YOUR RELIGION FORBIDS IT, HMM? PERHAPS SOME TEA THEN?
TEA WOULD BE FINE, YES. WILL THIS TAKE LONG? I REALLY SHOULD GET BACK SOON.
MY FAMILY WILL BE WONDERING WHERE I AM.
NOT AT ALL. IF YOU'LL JUST JOIN US IN THE PARLOR, WE WERE JUST ABOUT TO GET STARTED.
KHALIL, PLEASE BRING MR. HASSAN A CUP OF TEA.
YOU GOT IT, BOSS.

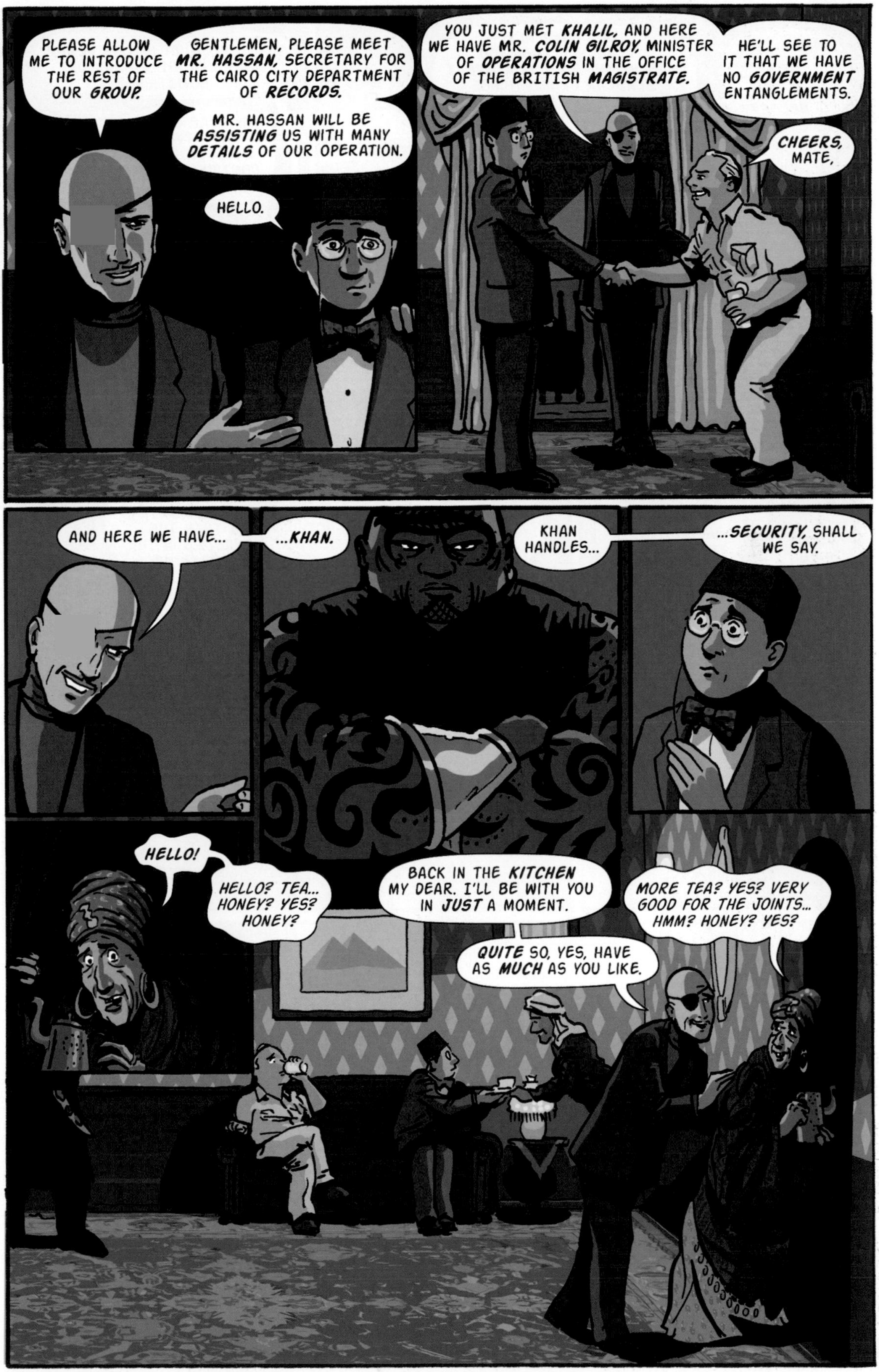
PLEASE ALLOW ME TO INTRODUCE THE REST OF OUR GROUP.
GENTLEMEN, PLEASE MEET MR. HASSAN, SECRETARY FOR THE CAIRO CITY DEPARTMENT OF RECORDS.
MR. HASSAN WILL BE ASSISTING US WITH MANY DETAILS OF OUR OPERATION.
HELLO.
YOU JUST MET KHALIL, AND HERE WE HAVE MR. COLIN GILROY, MINISTER OF OPERATIONS IN THE OFFICE OF THE BRITISH MAGISTRATE.
HE'LL SEE TO IT THAT WE HAVE NO GOVERNMENT ENTANGLEMENTS.
CHEERS, MATE,
AND HERE WE HAVE...
...KHAN.
KHAN HANDLES...
...SECURITY, SHALL WE SAY.
HELLO!
HELLO? TEA... HONEY? YES? HONEY?
BACK IN THE KITCHEN MY DEAR. I'LL BE WITH YOU IN JUST A MOMENT.
QUITE SO, YES, HAVE AS MUCH AS YOU LIKE.
MORE TEA? YES? VERY GOOD FOR THE JOINTS... HMM? HONEY? YES?

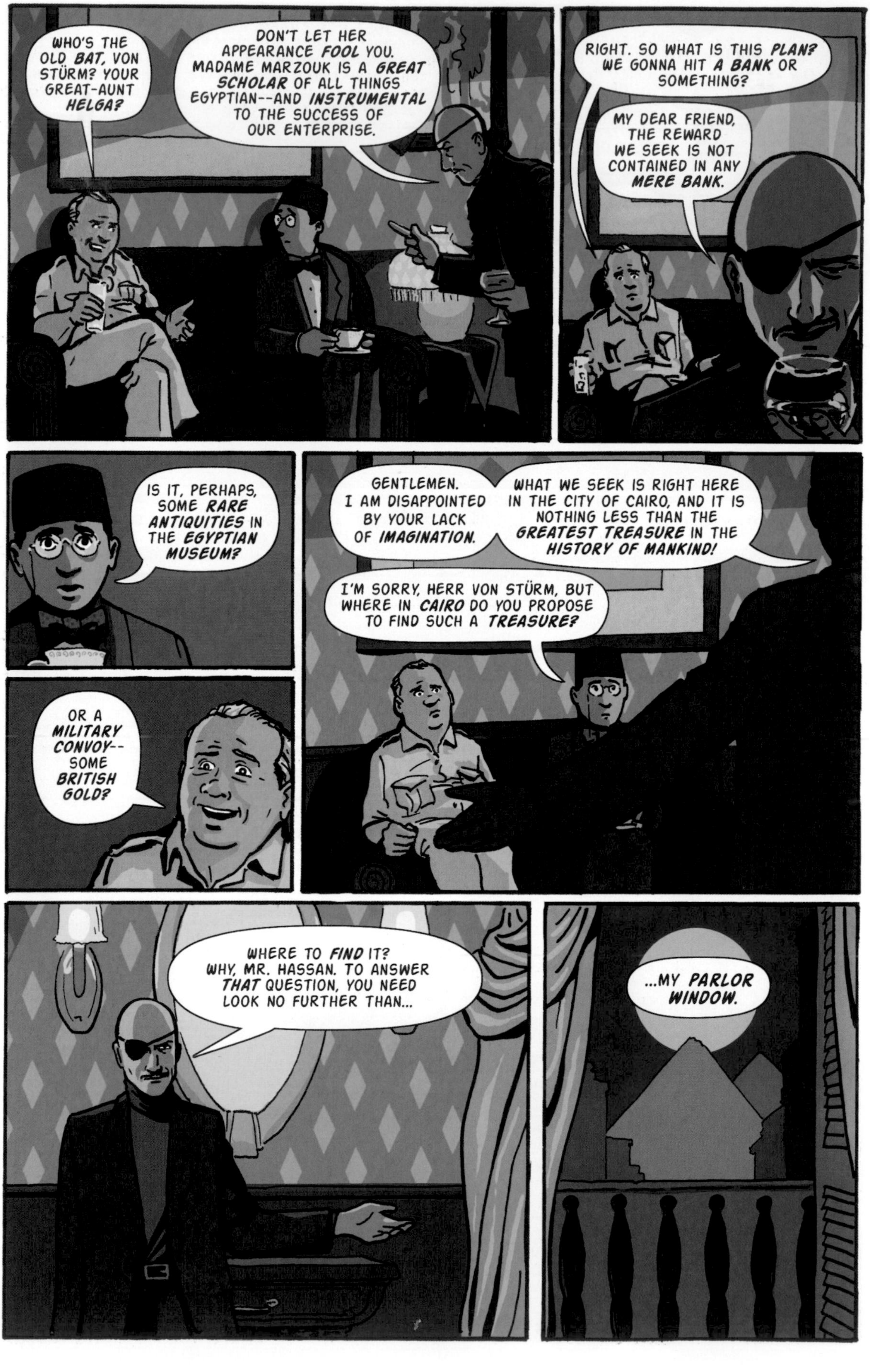
WHO'S THE OLD BAT, VON STÜRM? YOUR GREAT-AUNT HELGA?
DON'T LET HER APPEARANCE FOOL YOU. MADAME MARZOUK IS A GREAT SCHOLAR OF ALL THINGS EGYPTIAN--AND INSTRUMENTAL TO THE SUCCESS OF OUR ENTERPRISE.
RIGHT. SO WHAT IS THIS PLAN? WE GONNA HIT A BANK OR SOMETHING?
MY DEAR FRIEND, THE REWARD WE SEEK IS NOT CONTAINED IN ANY MERE BANK.
IS IT, PERHAPS, SOME RARE ANTIQUITIES IN THE EGYPTIAN MUSEUM?
OR A MILITARY CONVOY-- SOME BRITISH GOLD?
GENTLEMEN. I AM DISAPPOINTED BY YOUR LACK OF IMAGINATION.
WHAT WE SEEK IS RIGHT HERE IN THE CITY OF CAIRO, AND IT IS NOTHING LESS THAN THE GREATEST TREASURE IN THE HISTORY OF MANKIND!
I'M SORRY, HERR VON STÜRM, BUT WHERE IN CAIRO DO YOU PROPOSE TO FIND SUCH A TREASURE?
WHERE TO FIND IT? WHY, MR. HASSAN. TO ANSWER THAT QUESTION, YOU NEED LOOK NO FURTHER THAN...
...MY PARLOR WINDOW.

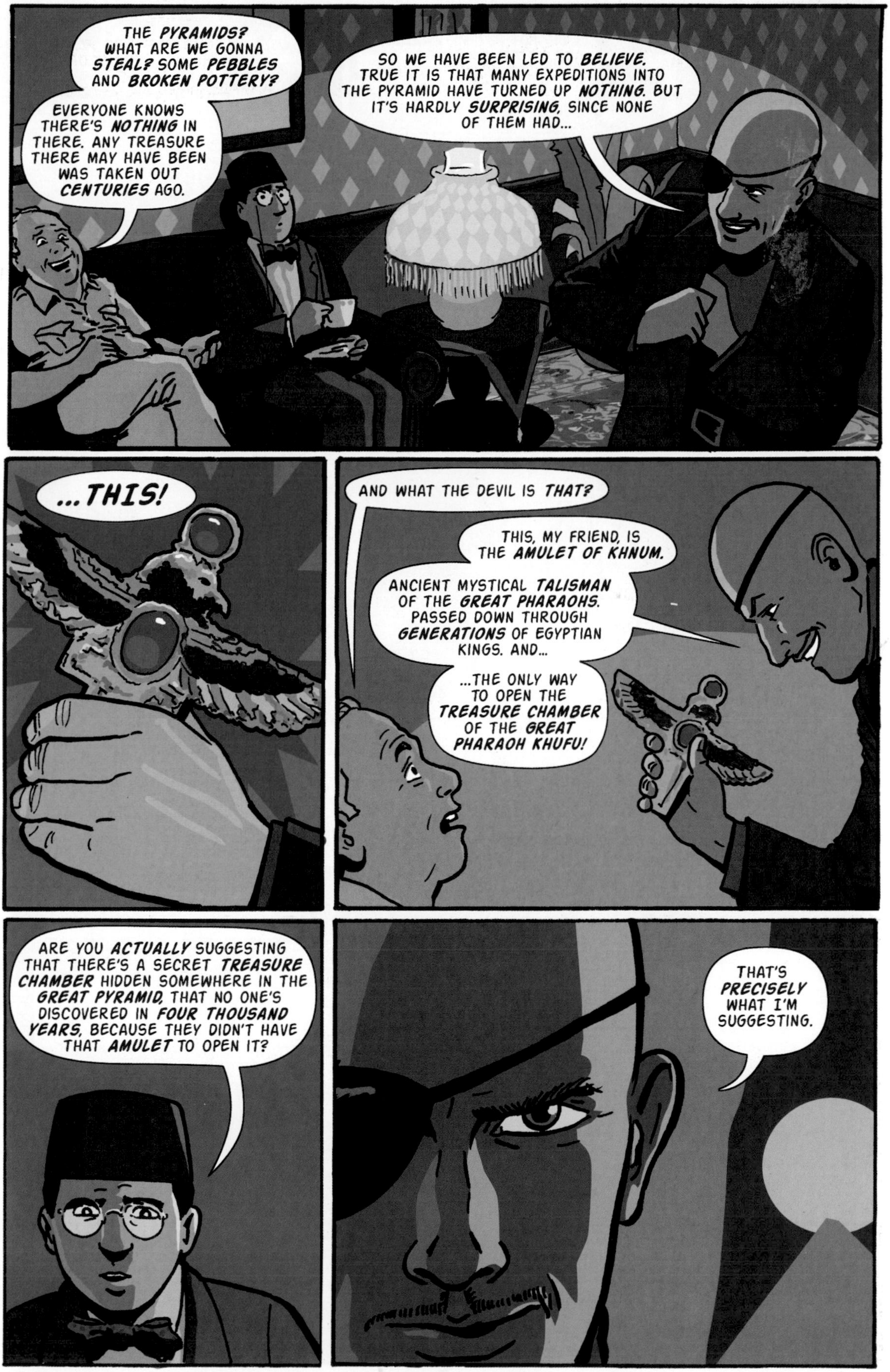
THE PYRAMIDS? WHAT ARE WE GONNA STEAL? SOME PEBBLES AND BROKEN POTTERY?
EVERYONE KNOWS THERE'S NOTHING IN THERE. ANY TREASURE THERE MAY HAVE BEEN WAS TAKEN OUT CENTURIES AGO.
SO WE HAVE BEEN LED TO BELIEVE. TRUE IT IS THAT MANY EXPEDITIONS INTO THE PYRAMID HAVE TURNED UP NOTHING. BUT IT'S HARDLY SURPRISING, SINCE NONE OF THEM HAD...
...THIS!
AND WHAT THE DEVIL IS THAT?
THIS, MY FRIEND, IS THE AMULET OF KHNUM.
ANCIENT MYSTICAL TALISMAN OF THE GREAT PHARAOHS. PASSED DOWN THROUGH GENERATIONS OF EGYPTIAN KINGS. AND...
...THE ONLY WAY TO OPEN THE TREASURE CHAMBER OF THE GREAT PHARAOH KHUFU!
ARE YOU ACTUALLY SUGGESTING THAT THERE'S A SECRET TREASURE CHAMBER HIDDEN SOMEWHERE IN THE GREAT PYRAMID, THAT NO ONE'S DISCOVERED IN FOUR THOUSAND YEARS, BECAUSE THEY DIDN'T HAVE THAT AMULET TO OPEN IT?
THAT'S PRECISELY WHAT I'M SUGGESTING.

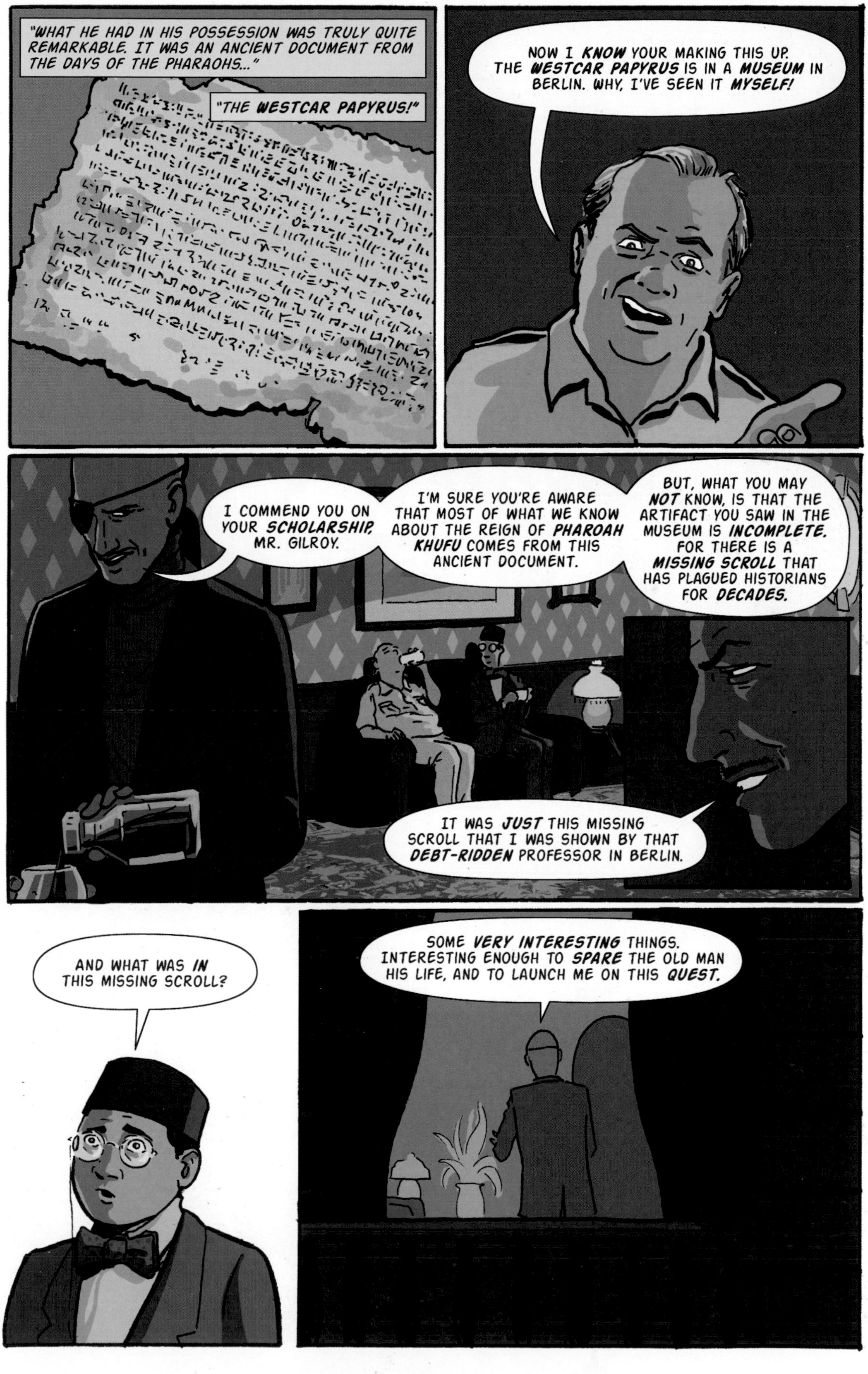
"WHAT HE HAD IN HIS POSSESSION WAS TRULY QUITE REMARKABLE. IT WAS AN ANCIENT DOCUMENT FROM THE DAYS OF THE PHARAOHS..."
"THE WESTCAR PAPYRUS!"
NOW I KNOW YOUR MAKING THIS UP. THE WESTCAR PAPYRUS IS IN A MUSEUM IN BERLIN. WHY, I'VE SEEN IT MYSELF!
I COMMEND YOU ON YOUR SCHOLARSHIP, MR. GILROY.
I'M SURE YOU'RE AWARE THAT MOST OF WHAT WE KNOW ABOUT THE REIGN OF PHAROAH KHUFU COMES FROM THIS ANCIENT DOCUMENT.
BUT, WHAT YOU MAY NOT KNOW, IS THAT THE ARTIFACT YOU SAW IN THE MUSEUM IS INCOMPLETE. FOR THERE IS A MISSING SCROLL THAT HAS PLAGUED HISTORIANS FOR DECADES.
IT WAS JUST THIS MISSING SCROLL THAT I WAS SHOWN BY THAT DEBT-RIDDEN PROFESSOR IN BERLIN.
AND WHAT WAS IN THIS MISSING SCROLL?
SOME VERY INTERESTING THINGS. INTERESTING ENOUGH TO SPARE THE OLD MAN HIS LIFE, AND TO LAUNCH ME ON THIS QUEST.

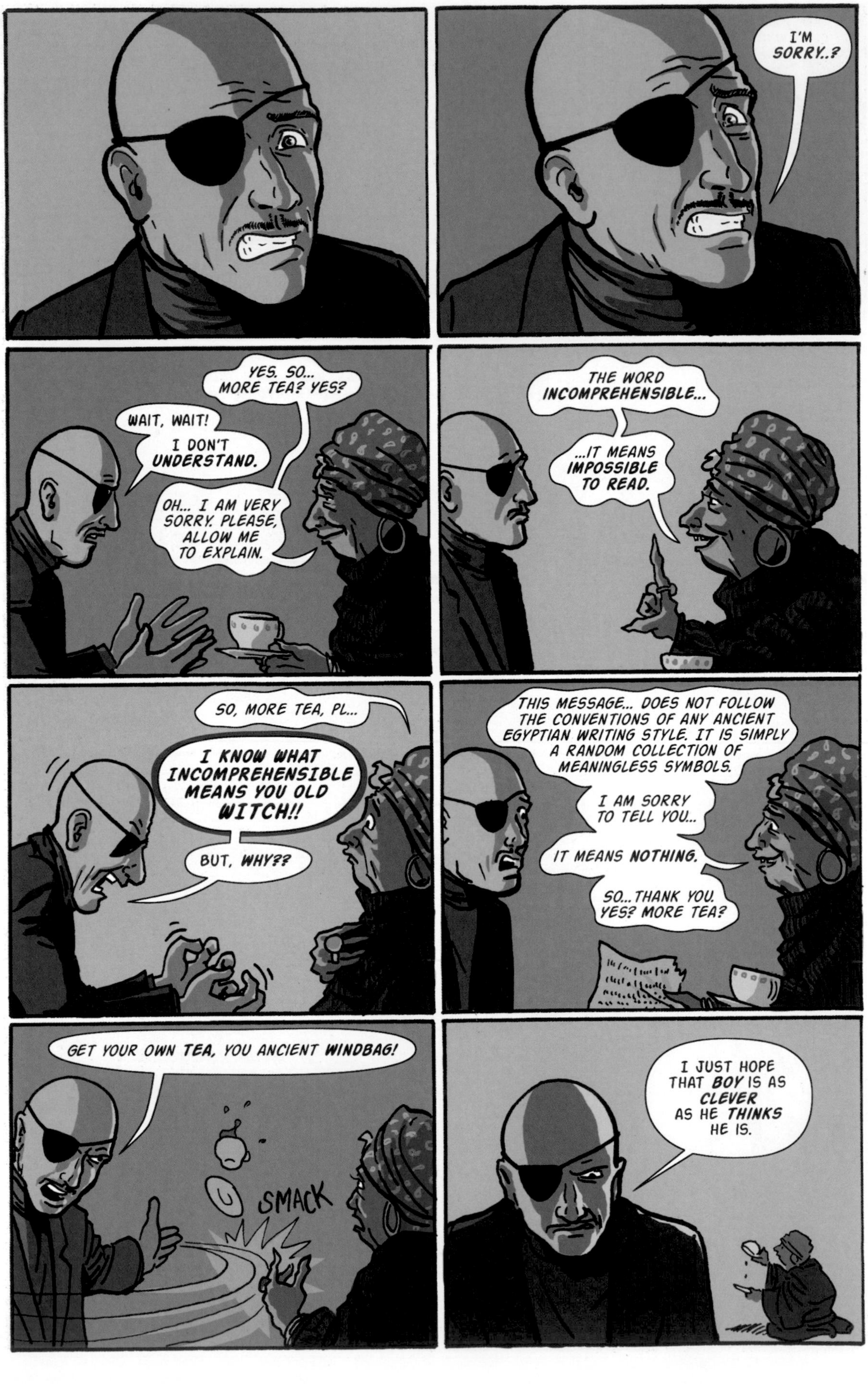

I'M SORRY..?
YES. SO... MORE TEA? YES?
WAIT, WAIT!
I DON'T UNDERSTAND.
OH... I AM VERY SORRY. PLEASE, ALLOW ME TO EXPLAIN.
THE WORD INCOMPREHENSIBLE...
...IT MEANS IMPOSSIBLE TO READ.
SO, MORE TEA, PL...
I KNOW WHAT INCOMPREHENSIBLE MEANS YOU OLD WITCH!!
BUT, WHY??
THIS MESSAGE... DOES NOT FOLLOW THE CONVENTIONS OF ANY ANCIENT EGYPTIAN WRITING STYLE. IT IS SIMPLY A RANDOM COLLECTION OF MEANINGLESS SYMBOLS.
I AM SORRY TO TELL YOU...
IT MEANS NOTHING.
SO...THANK YOU. YES? MORE TEA?
GET YOUR OWN TEA, YOU ANCIENT WINDBAG!
SMACK
I JUST HOPE THAT BOY IS AS CLEVER AS HE THINKS HE IS.

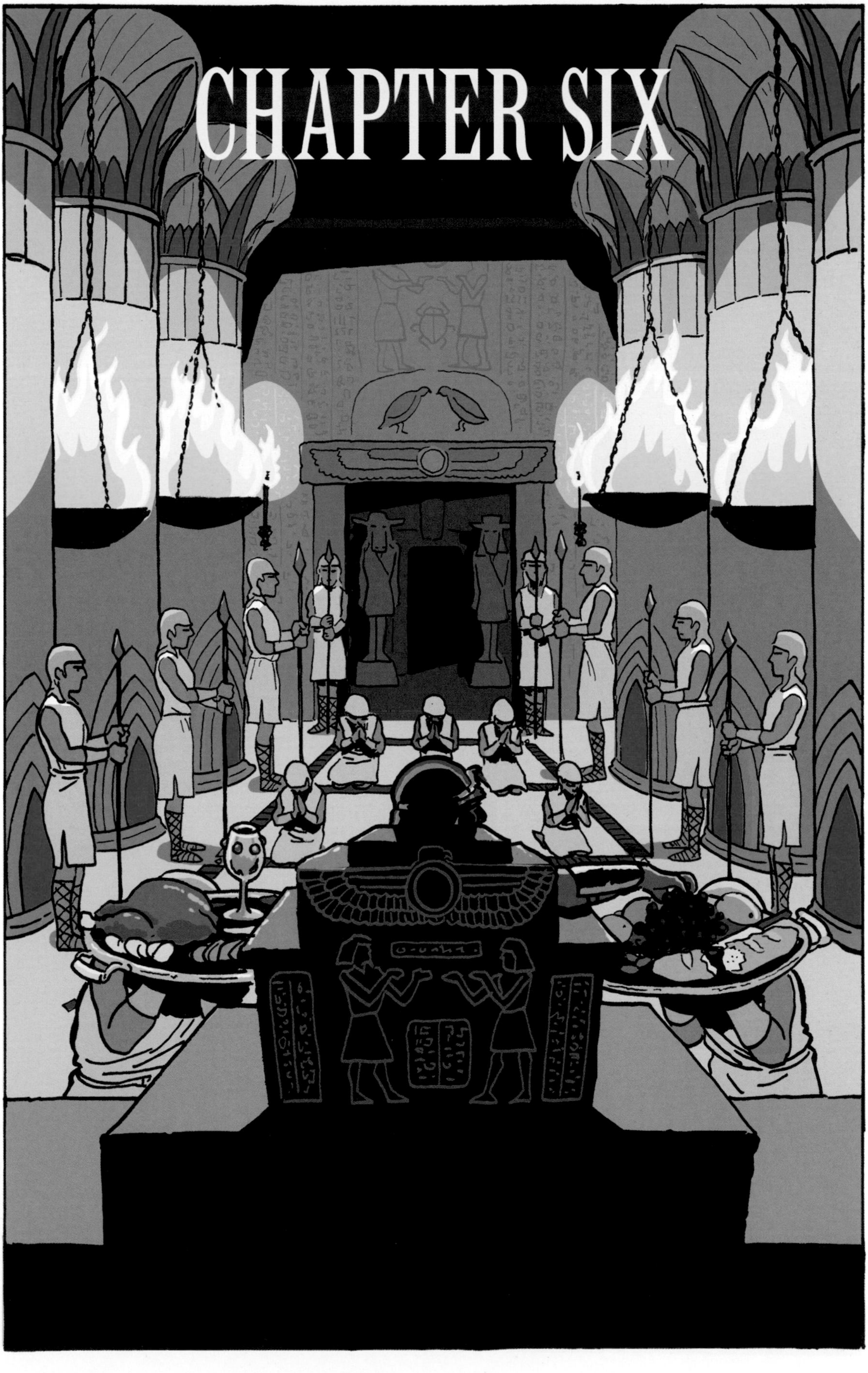
CHAPTER SIX

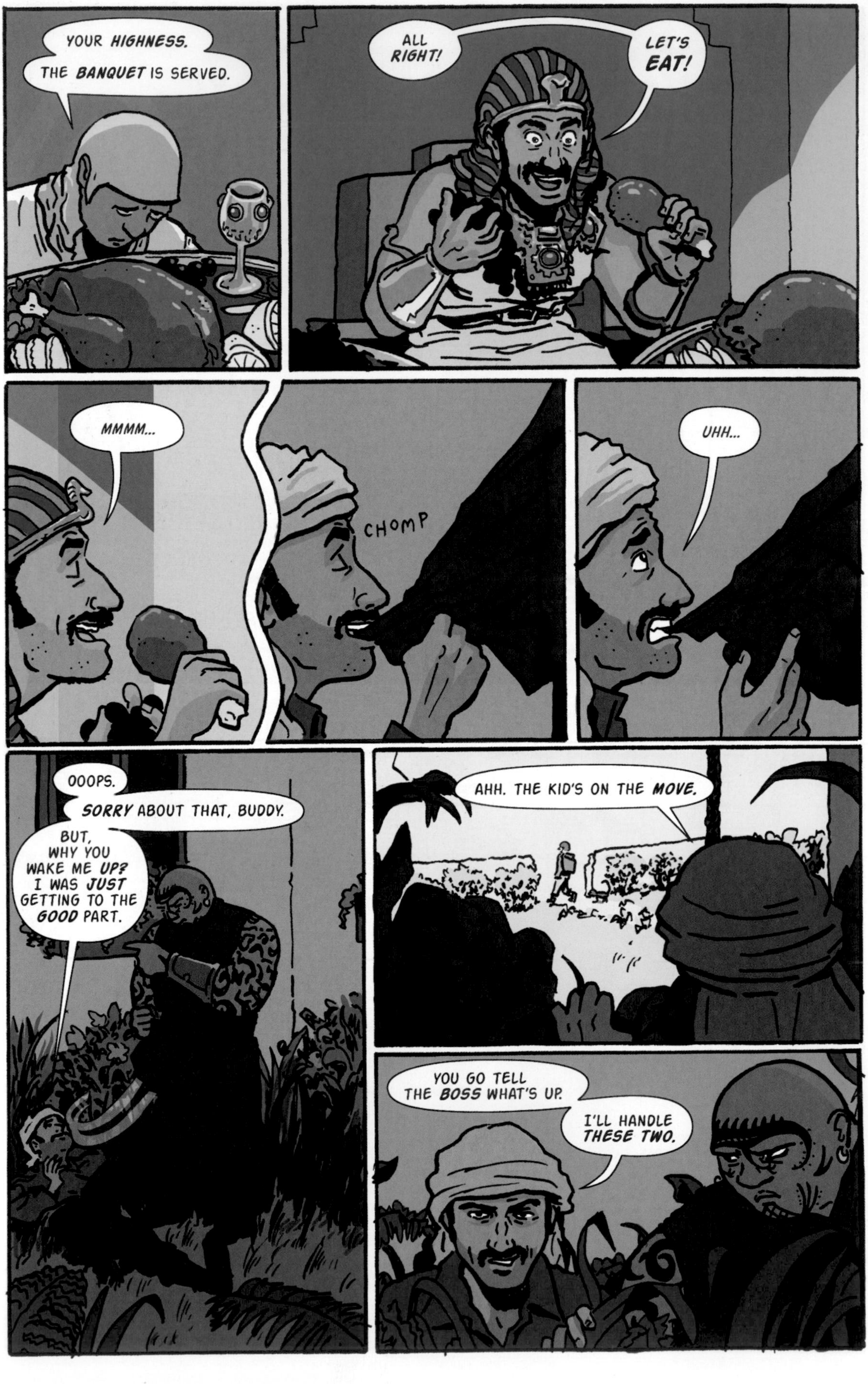
YOUR HIGHNESS.
THE BANQUET IS SERVED.
ALL RIGHT!
LET'S EAT!
MMMM...
CHOMP
UHH...
OOOPS.
SORRY ABOUT THAT, BUDDY.
BUT, WHY YOU WAKE ME UP? I WAS JUST GETTING TO THE GOOD PART.
AHH. THE KID'S ON THE MOVE.
YOU GO TELL THE BOSS WHAT'S UP.
I'LL HANDLE THESE TWO.

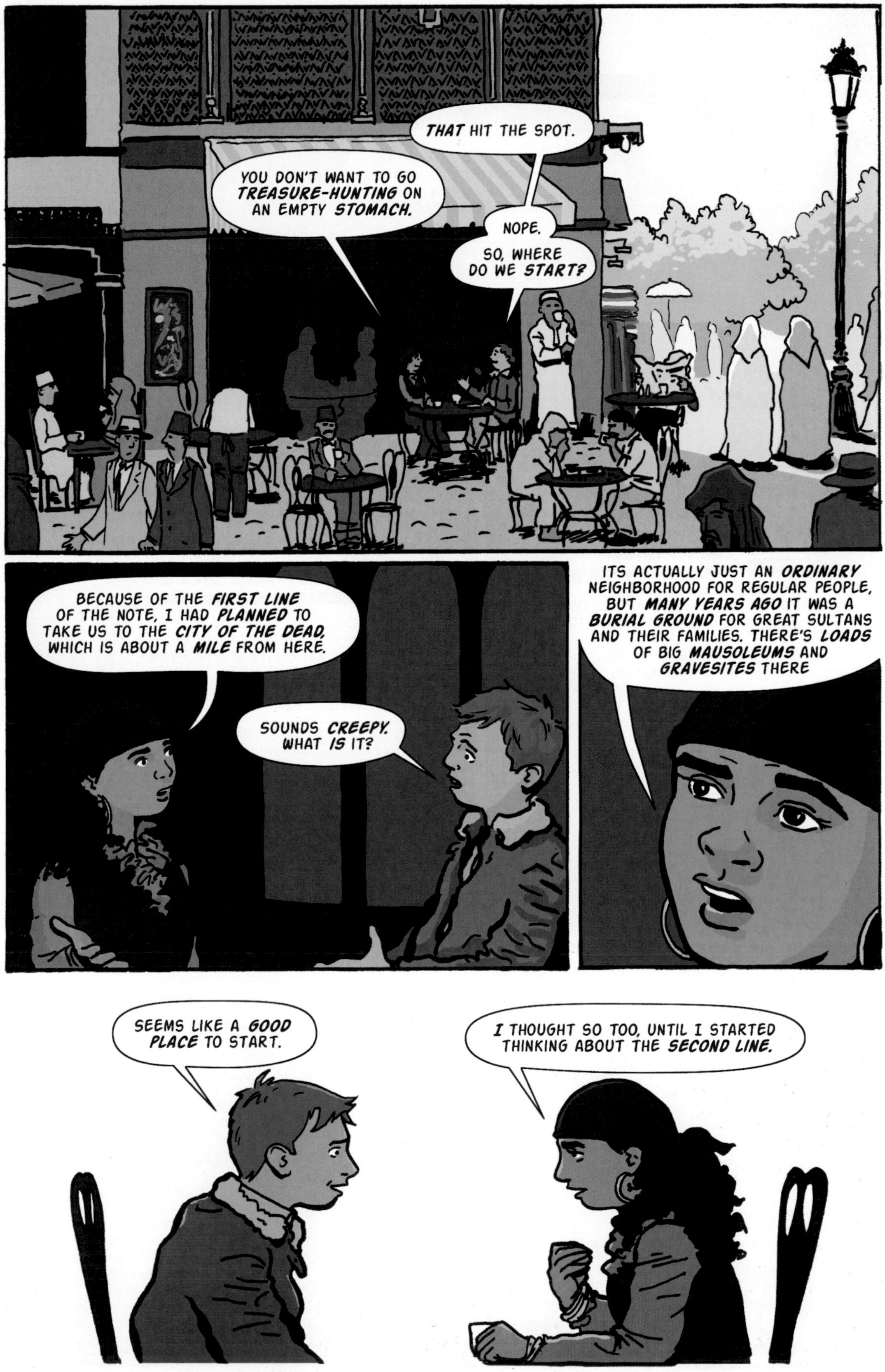
YOU DON'T WANT TO GO TREASURE-HUNTING ON AN EMPTY STOMACH.
THAT HIT THE SPOT.
NOPE.
SO, WHERE DO WE START?
BECAUSE OF THE FIRST LINE OF THE NOTE, I HAD PLANNED TO TAKE US TO THE CITY OF THE DEAD, WHICH IS ABOUT A MILE FROM HERE.
SOUNDS CREEPY. WHAT IS IT?
ITS ACTUALLY JUST AN ORDINARY NEIGHBORHOOD FOR REGULAR PEOPLE, BUT MANY YEARS AGO IT WAS A BURIAL GROUND FOR GREAT SULTANS AND THEIR FAMILIES. THERE'S LOADS OF BIG MAUSOLEUMS AND GRAVESITES THERE
SEEMS LIKE A GOOD PLACE TO START.
I THOUGHT SO TOO, UNTIL I STARTED THINKING ABOUT THE SECOND LINE.

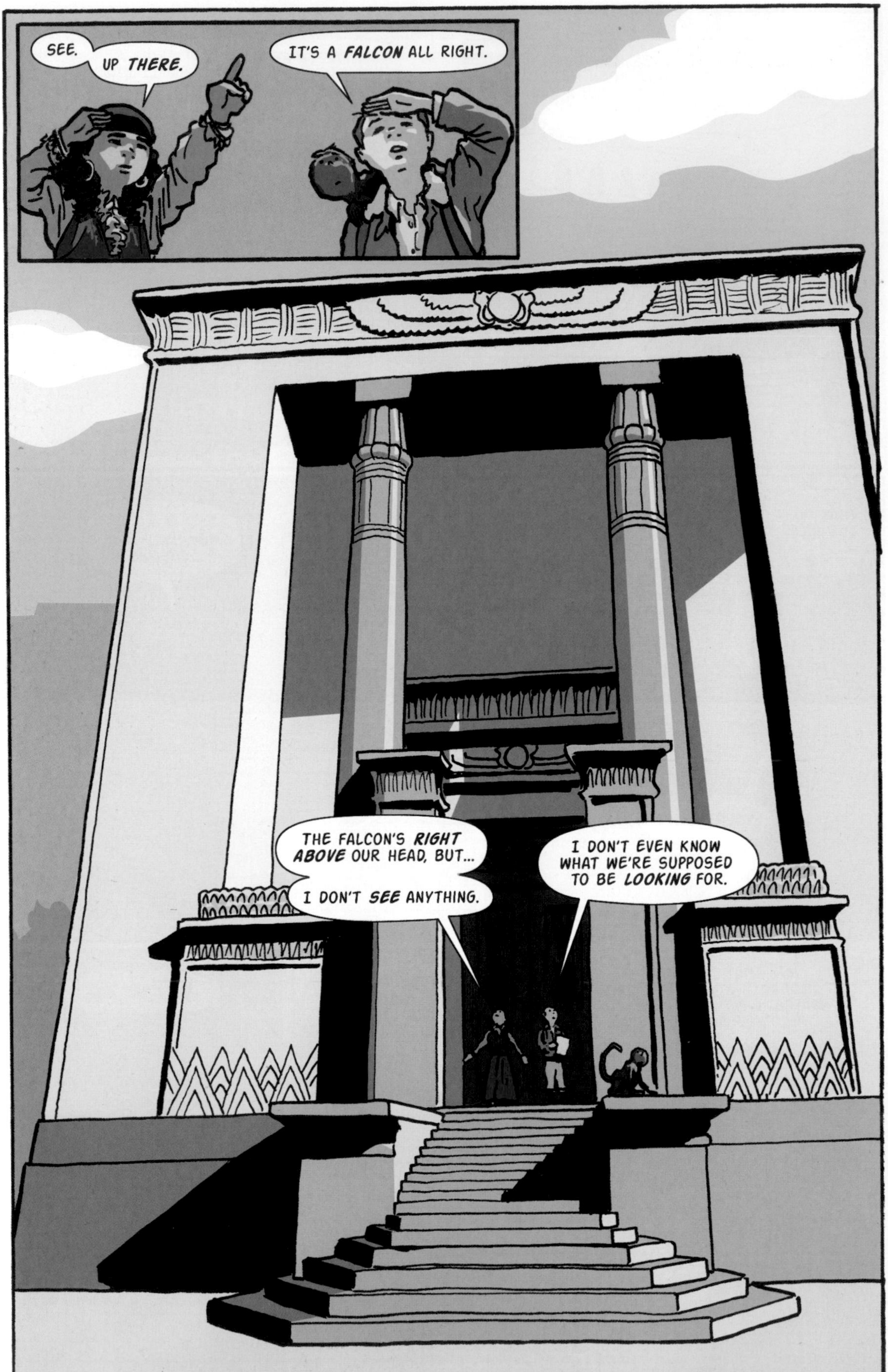
SEE.
UP THERE.
IT'S A FALCON ALL RIGHT.
THE FALCON'S RIGHT ABOVE OUR HEAD, BUT...
I DON'T SEE ANYTHING.
I DON'T EVEN KNOW WHAT WE'RE SUPPOSED TO BE LOOKING FOR.

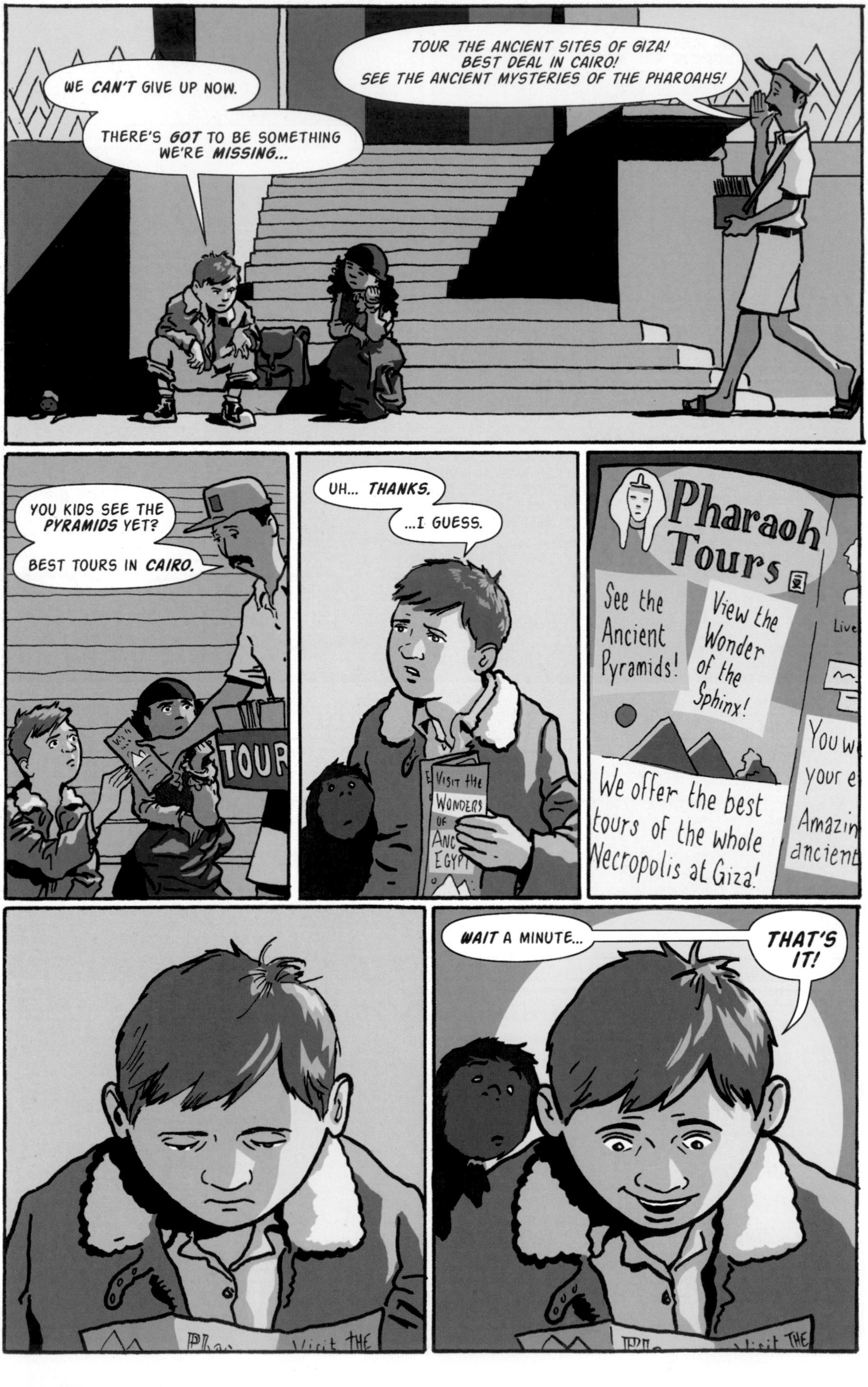
WE CAN'T GIVE UP NOW.
THERE'S GOT TO BE SOMETHING WE'RE MISSING...
TOUR THE ANCIENT SITES OF GIZA! BEST DEAL IN CAIRO! SEE THE ANCIENT MYSTERIES OF THE PHAROAHS!
YOU KIDS SEE THE PYRAMIDS YET?
BEST TOURS IN CAIRO.
TOUR
UH... THANKS.
...I GUESS.
Visit the WONDERS OF ANC EGYPT
Pharaoh Tours
See the Ancient Pyramids!
View the Wonder of the Sphinx!
We offer the best tours of the whole Necropolis at Giza!
WAIT A MINUTE...
THAT'S IT!

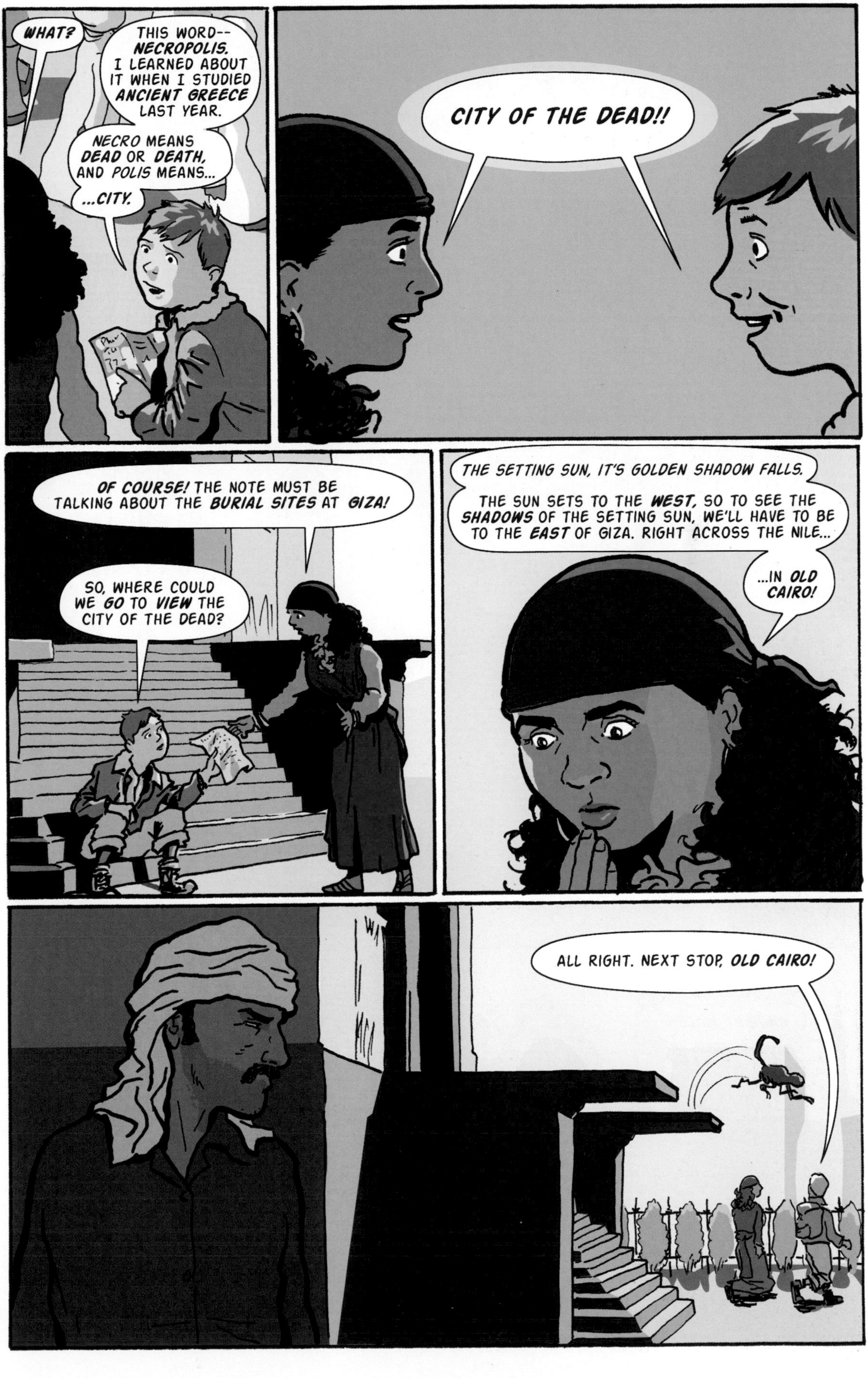
WHAT?
THIS WORD-- NECROPOLIS. I LEARNED ABOUT IT WHEN I STUDIED ANCIENT GREECE LAST YEAR.
NECRO MEANS DEAD OR DEATH, AND POLIS MEANS...
...CITY.
CITY OF THE DEAD!!
OF COURSE! THE NOTE MUST BE TALKING ABOUT THE BURIAL SITES AT GIZA!
SO, WHERE COULD WE GO TO VIEW THE CITY OF THE DEAD?
THE SETTING SUN, IT'S GOLDEN SHADOW FALLS.
THE SUN SETS TO THE WEST, SO TO SEE THE SHADOWS OF THE SETTING SUN, WE'LL HAVE TO BE TO THE EAST OF GIZA. RIGHT ACROSS THE NILE...
...IN OLD CAIRO!
ALL RIGHT. NEXT STOP, OLD CAIRO!

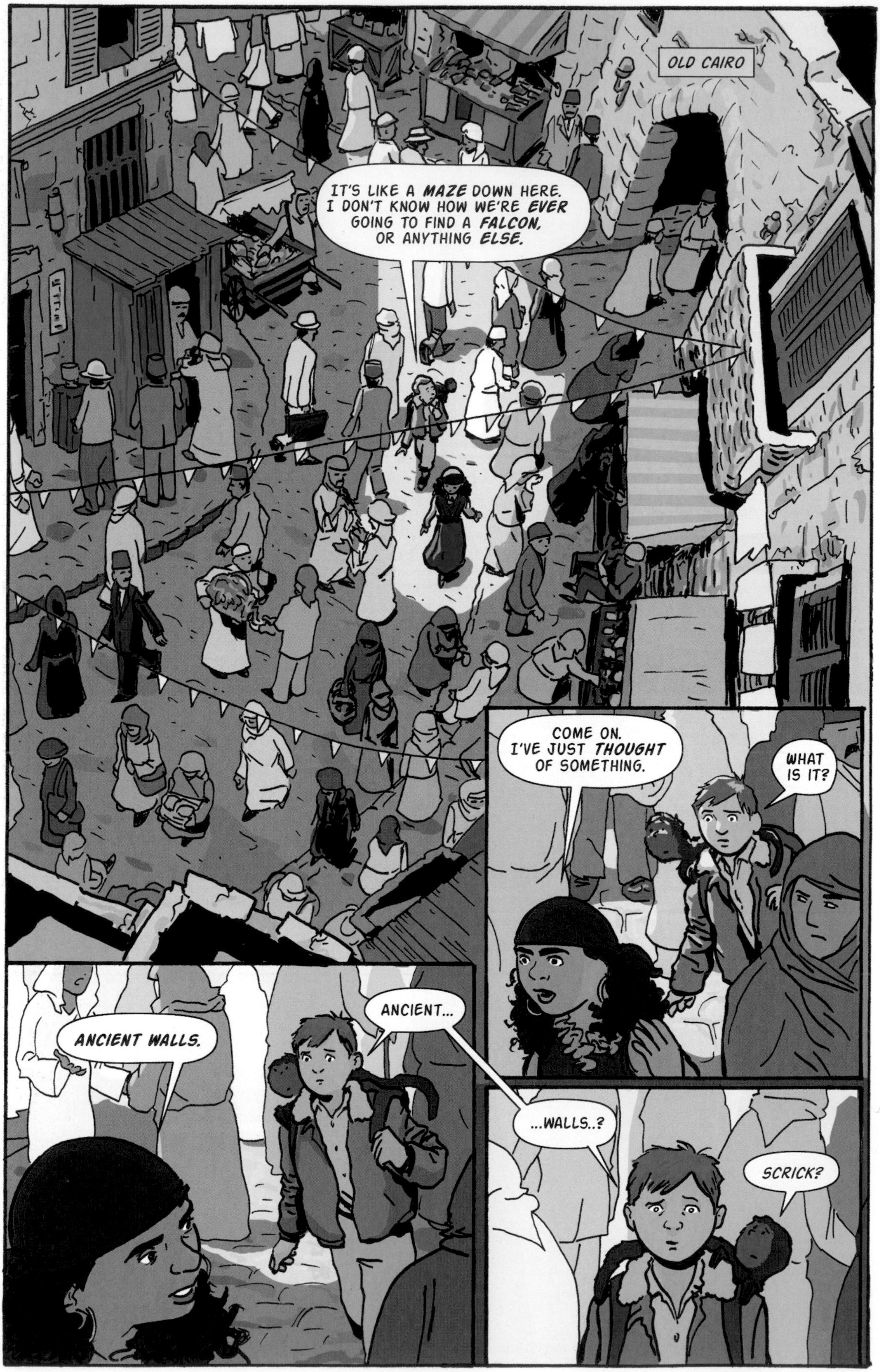
OLD CAIRO
IT'S LIKE A MAZE DOWN HERE. I DON'T KNOW HOW WE'RE EVER GOING TO FIND A FALCON, OR ANYTHING ELSE.
COME ON. I'VE JUST THOUGHT OF SOMETHING.
WHAT IS IT?
ANCIENT WALLS.
ANCIENT...
...WALLS..?
SCRICK?

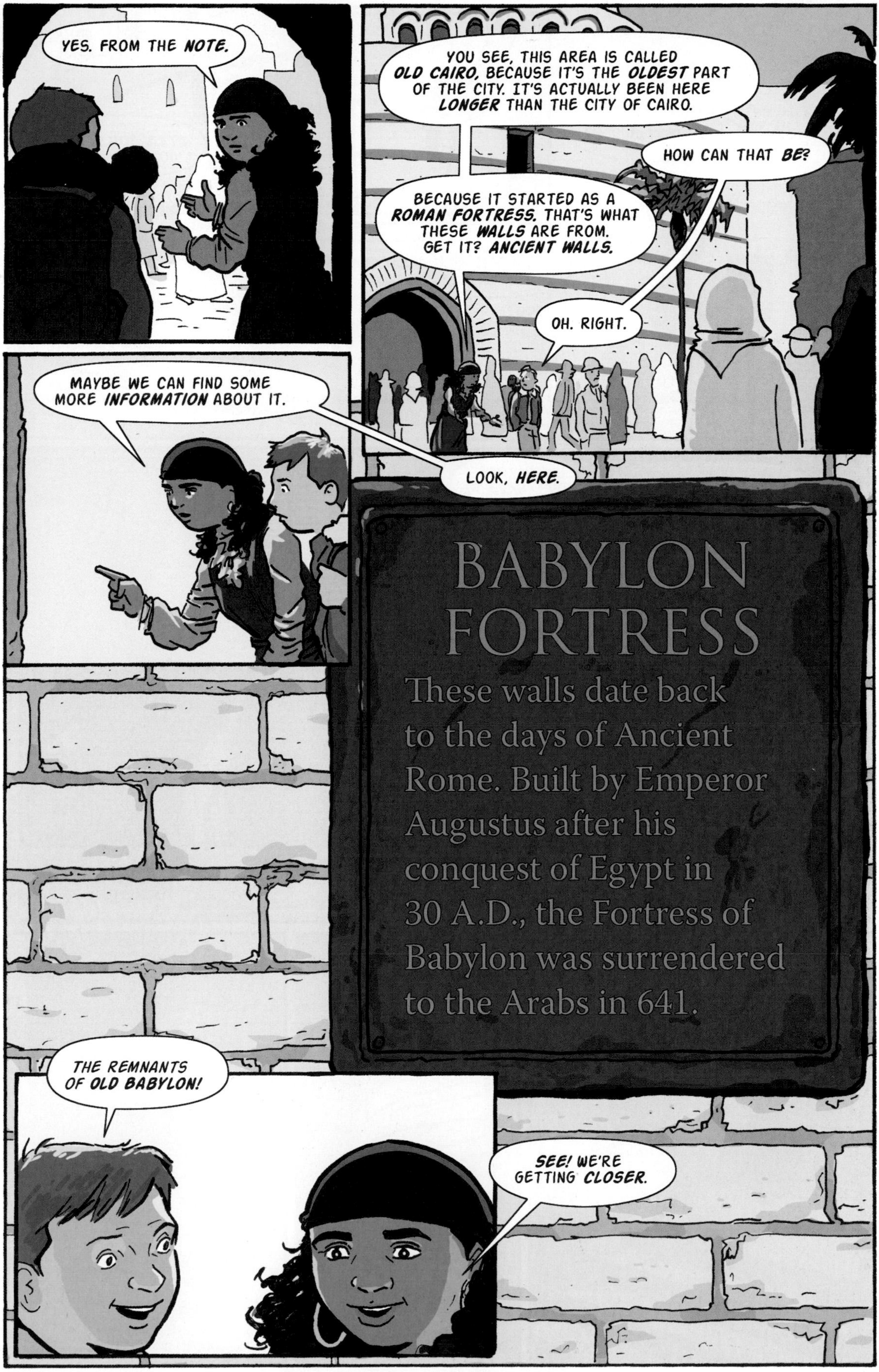

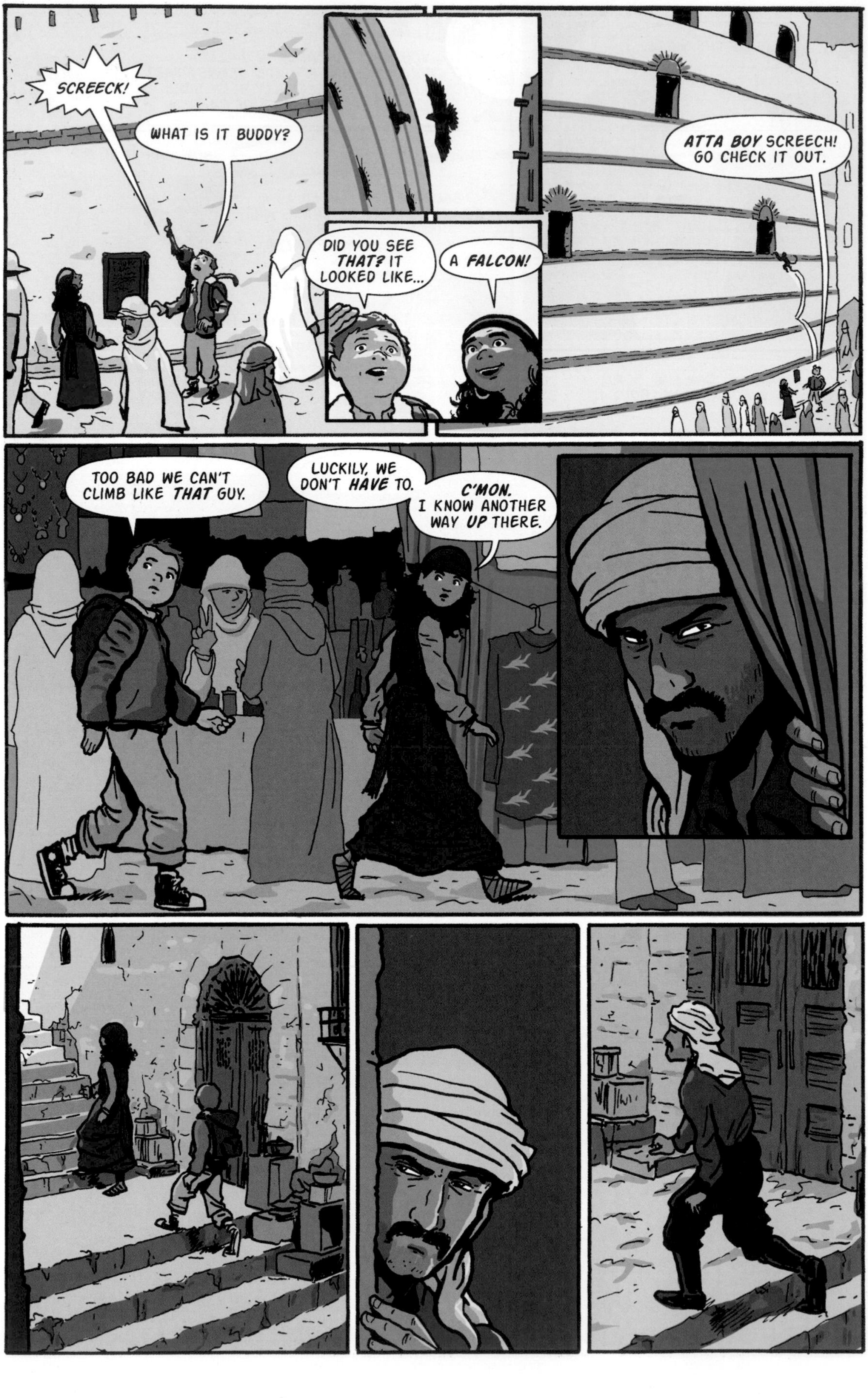
SCREECK!
WHAT IS IT BUDDY?
DID YOU SEE THAT? IT LOOKED LIKE...
A FALCON!
ATTA BOY SCREECH! GO CHECK IT OUT.
TOO BAD WE CAN'T CLIMB LIKE THAT GUY.
LUCKILY, WE DON'T HAVE TO.
C'MON. I KNOW ANOTHER WAY UP THERE.

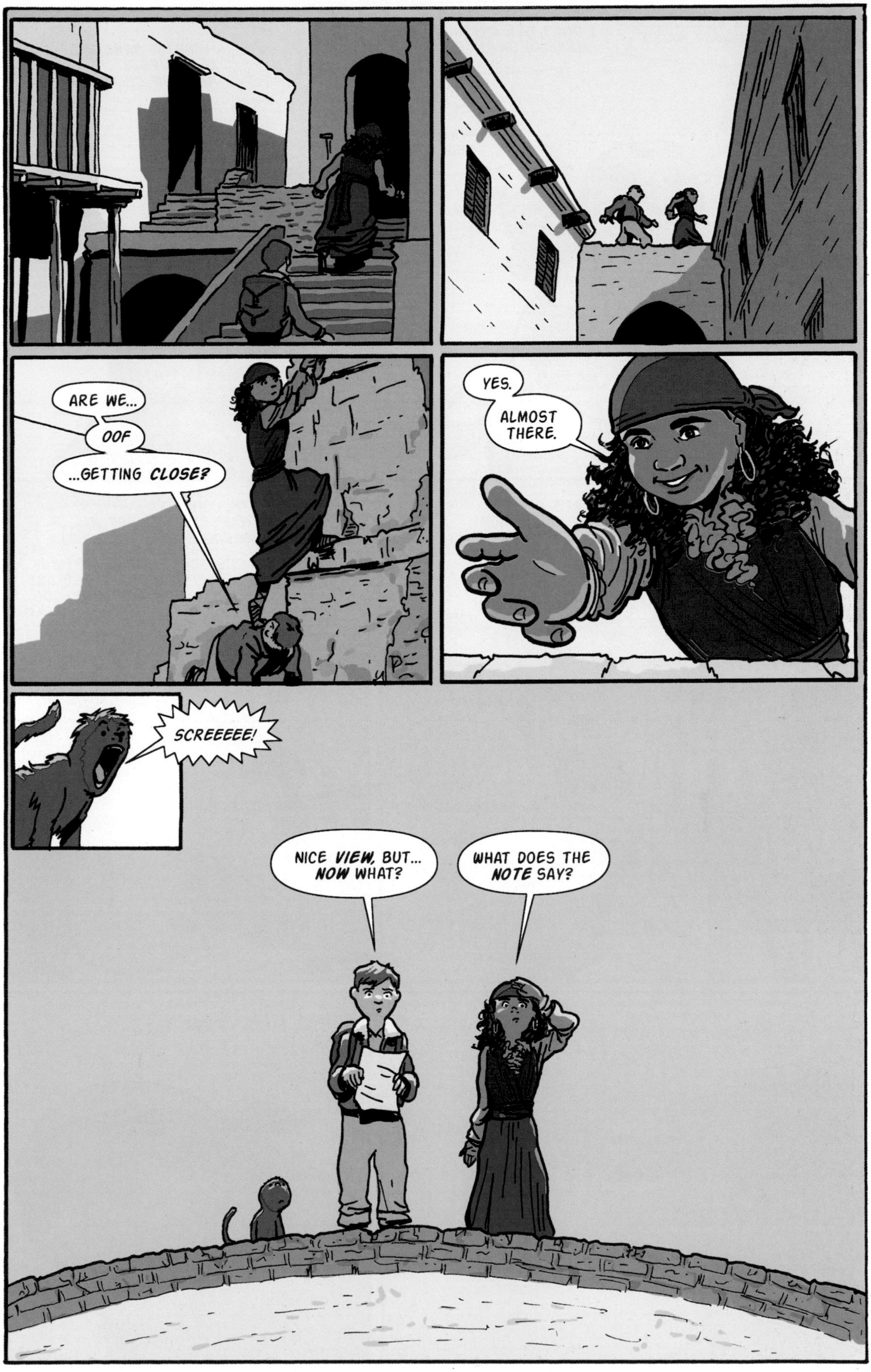
ARE WE...
OOF
...GETTING CLOSE?
YES.
ALMOST THERE.
SCREEEEE!
NICE VIEW, BUT... NOW WHAT?
WHAT DOES THE NOTE SAY?

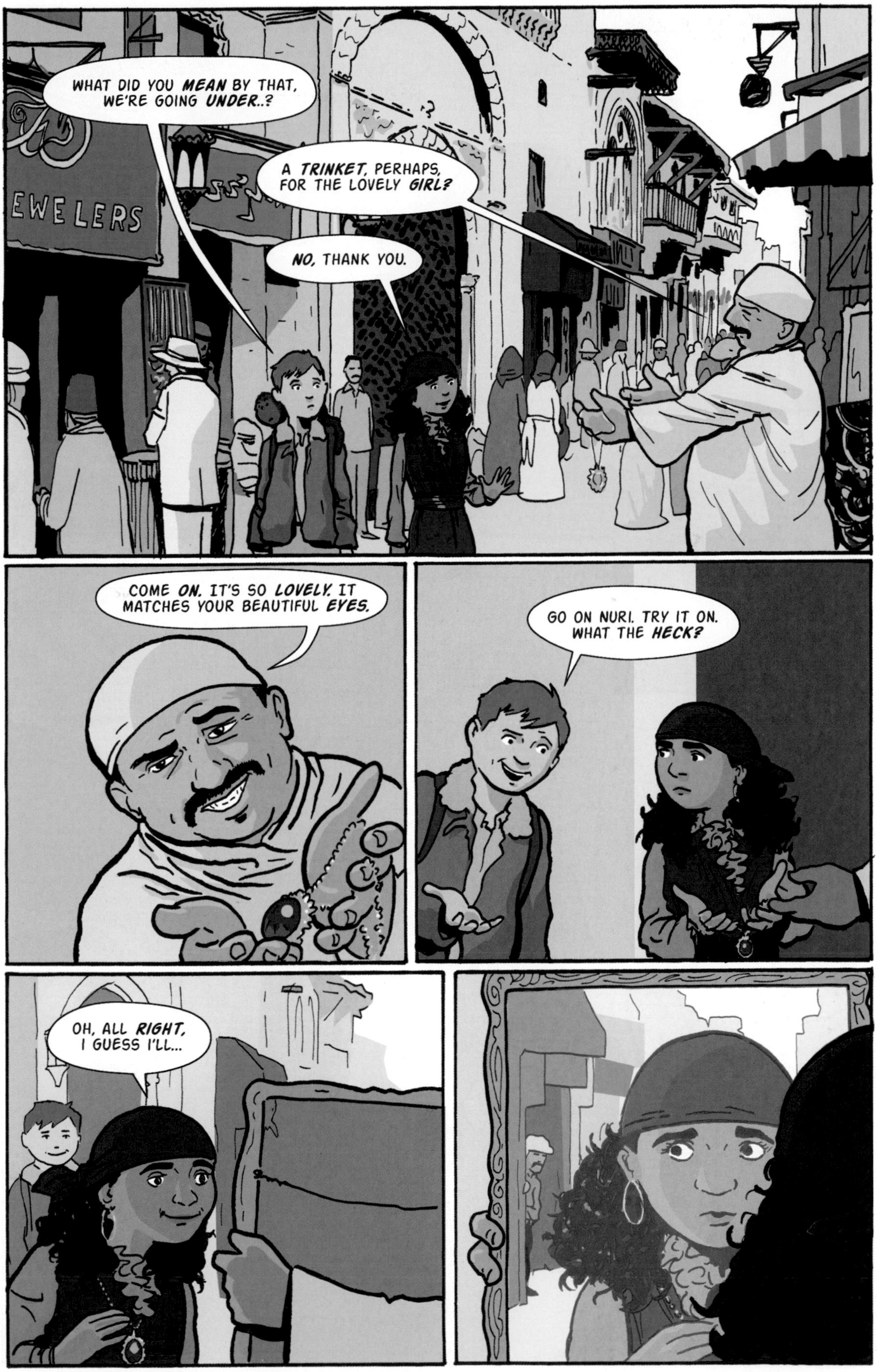
WHAT DID YOU MEAN BY THAT, WE'RE GOING UNDER..?
A TRINKET, PERHAPS, FOR THE LOVELY GIRL?
NO, THANK YOU.
EWELERS
COME ON. IT'S SO LOVELY. IT MATCHES YOUR BEAUTIFUL EYES.
GO ON NURI. TRY IT ON. WHAT THE HECK?
OH, ALL RIGHT, I GUESS I'LL...

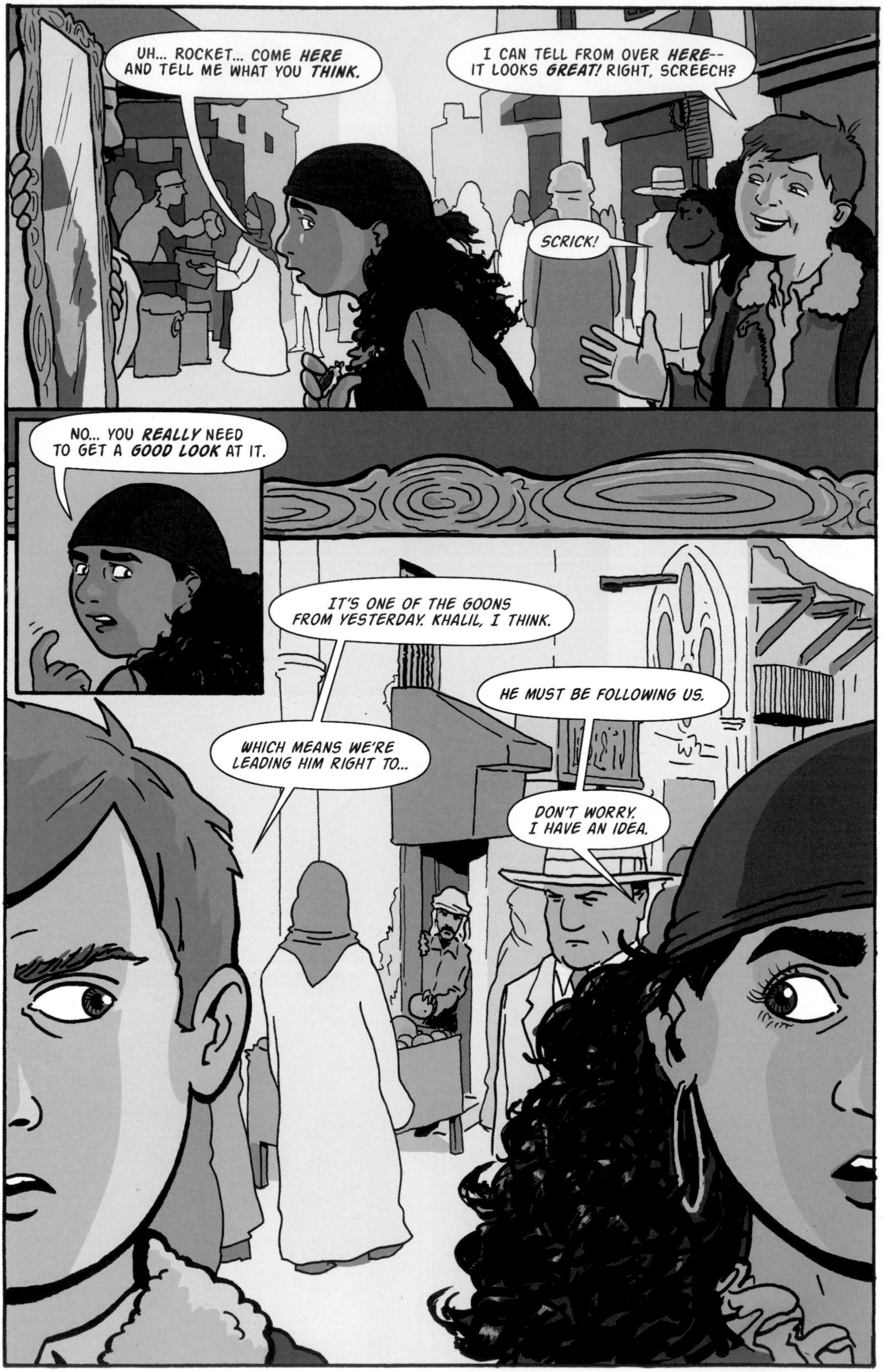
UH... ROCKET... COME HERE AND TELL ME WHAT YOU THINK.
I CAN TELL FROM OVER HERE-- IT LOOKS GREAT! RIGHT, SCREECH?
SCRICK!
NO... YOU REALLY NEED TO GET A GOOD LOOK AT IT.
IT'S ONE OF THE GOONS FROM YESTERDAY. KHALIL, I THINK.
HE MUST BE FOLLOWING US.
WHICH MEANS WE'RE LEADING HIM RIGHT TO...
DON'T WORRY. I HAVE AN IDEA.

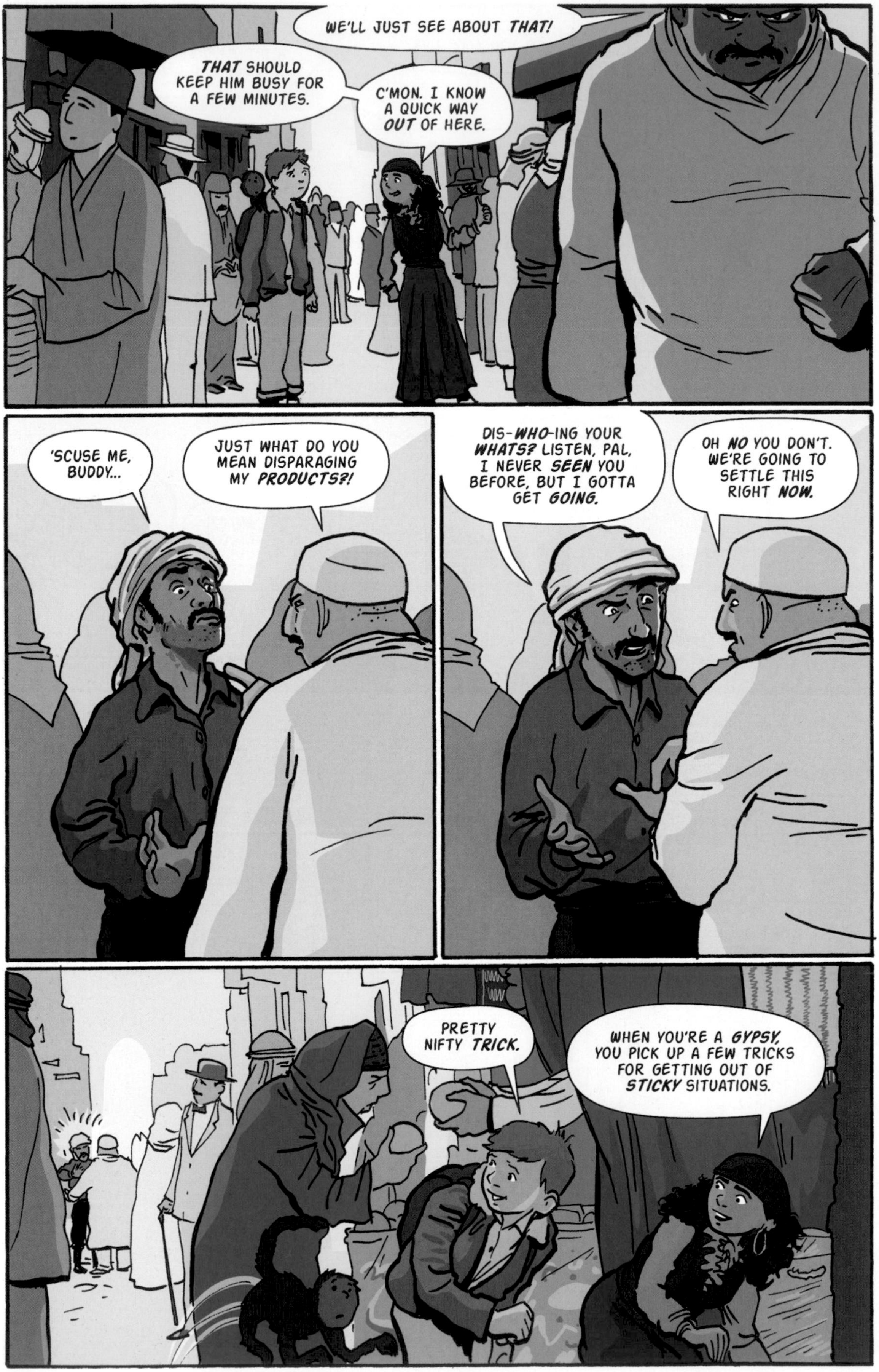

WE'LL JUST SEE ABOUT *THAT!*
THAT SHOULD KEEP HIM BUSY FOR A FEW MINUTES.
C'MON. I KNOW A QUICK WAY *OUT* OF HERE.
'SCUSE ME, BUDDY...
JUST WHAT DO YOU MEAN DISPARAGING MY *PRODUCTS?!*
DIS-*WHO*-ING YOUR *WHATS?* LISTEN, PAL, I NEVER *SEEN* YOU BEFORE, BUT I GOTTA GET *GOING.*
OH *NO* YOU DON'T. WE'RE GOING TO SETTLE THIS RIGHT *NOW.*
PRETTY NIFTY *TRICK.*
WHEN YOU'RE A *GYPSY,* YOU PICK UP A FEW TRICKS FOR GETTING OUT OF *STICKY* SITUATIONS.

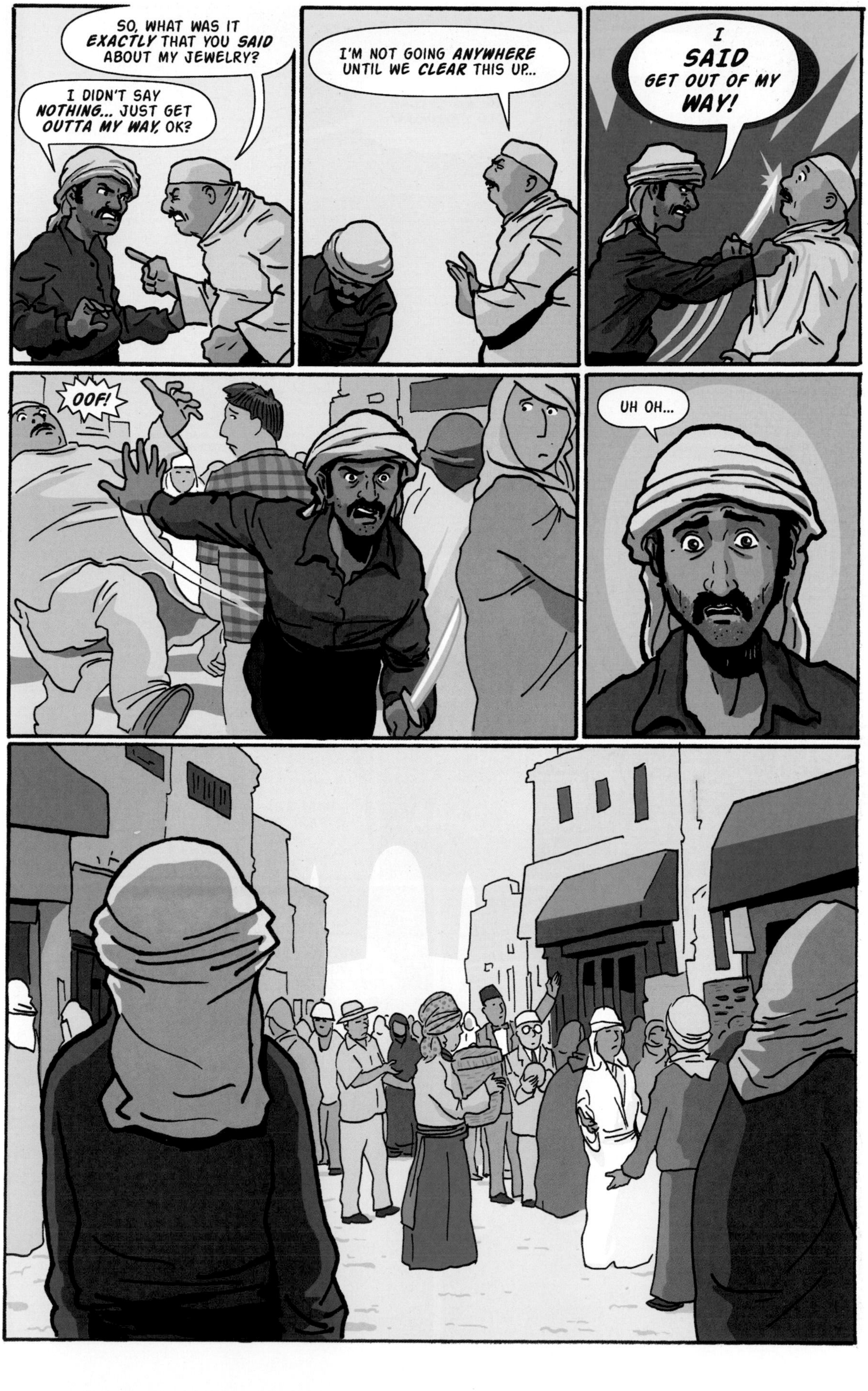
SO, WHAT WAS IT EXACTLY THAT YOU SAID ABOUT MY JEWELRY?
I DIDN'T SAY NOTHING... JUST GET OUTTA MY WAY, OK?
I'M NOT GOING ANYWHERE UNTIL WE CLEAR THIS UP...
I SAID GET OUT OF MY WAY!
OOF!
UH OH...

CHAPTER SEVEN

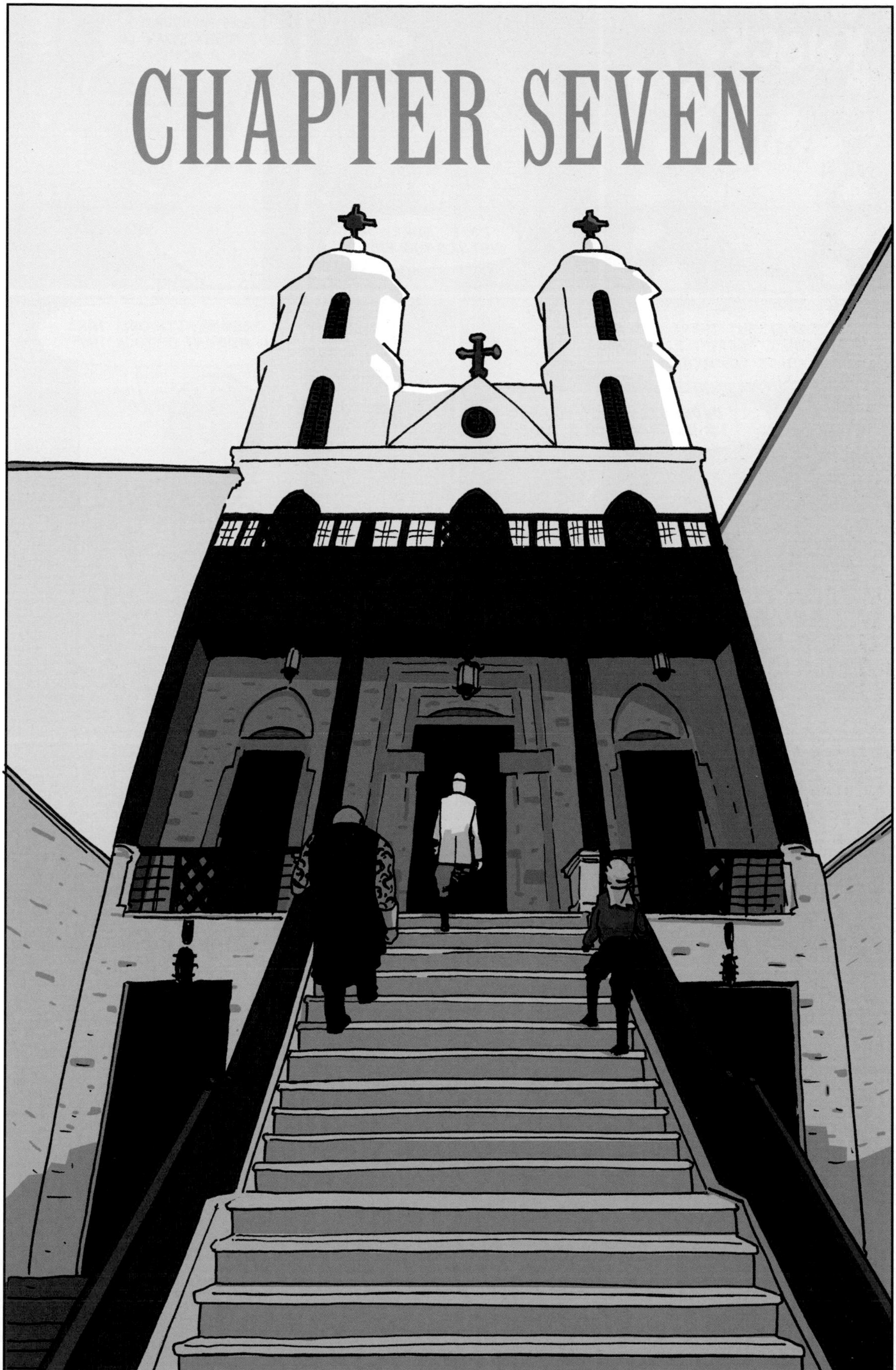

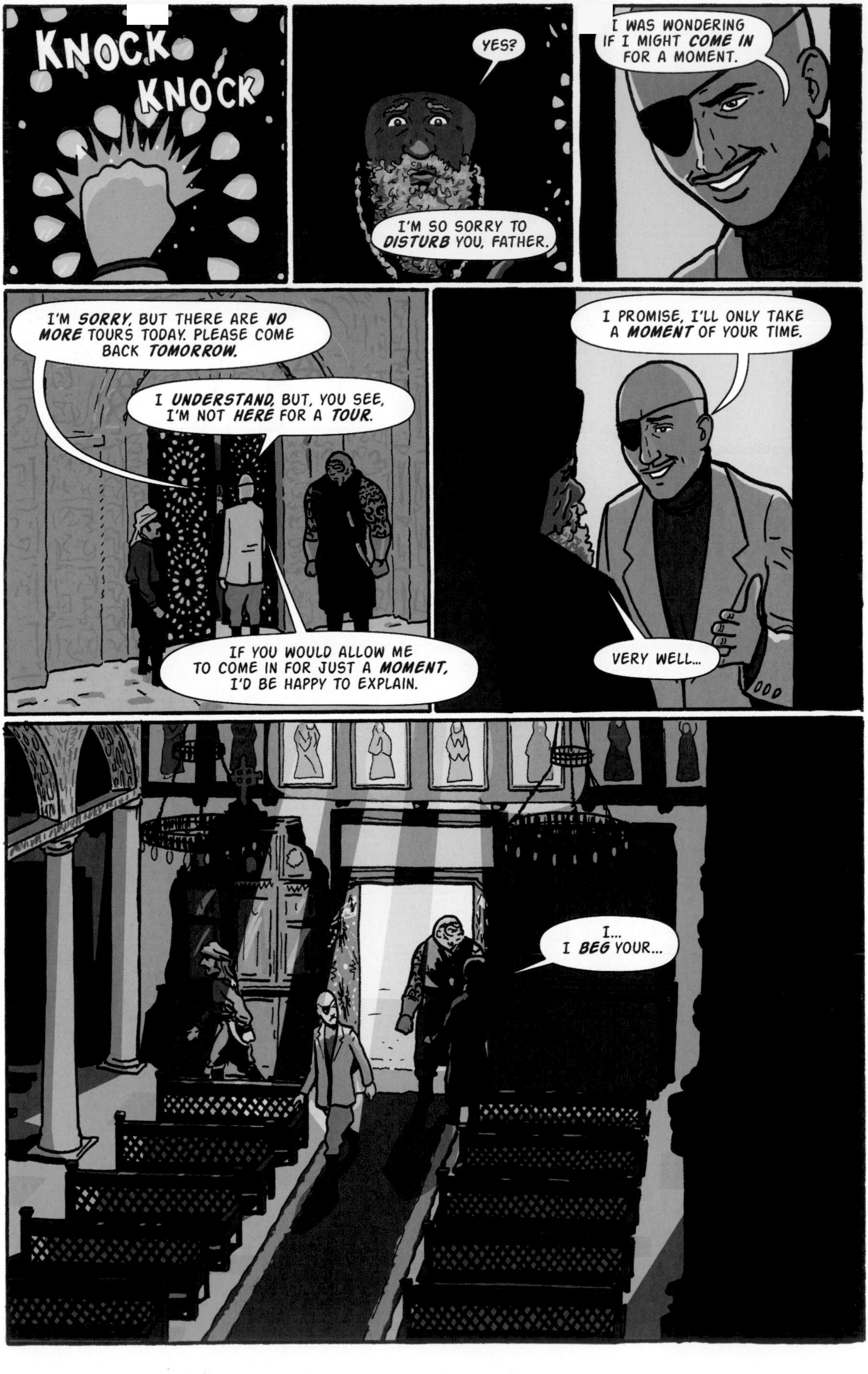
KNOCK
KNOCK
YES?
I'M SO SORRY TO *DISTURB* YOU, FATHER.
I WAS WONDERING IF I MIGHT *COME IN* FOR A MOMENT.
I'M *SORRY,* BUT THERE ARE *NO MORE* TOURS TODAY. PLEASE COME BACK *TOMORROW.*
I *UNDERSTAND,* BUT, YOU SEE, I'M NOT *HERE* FOR A *TOUR.*
IF YOU WOULD ALLOW ME TO COME IN FOR JUST A *MOMENT,* I'D BE HAPPY TO EXPLAIN.
I PROMISE, I'LL ONLY TAKE A *MOMENT* OF YOUR TIME.
VERY WELL...
I... I *BEG* YOUR...

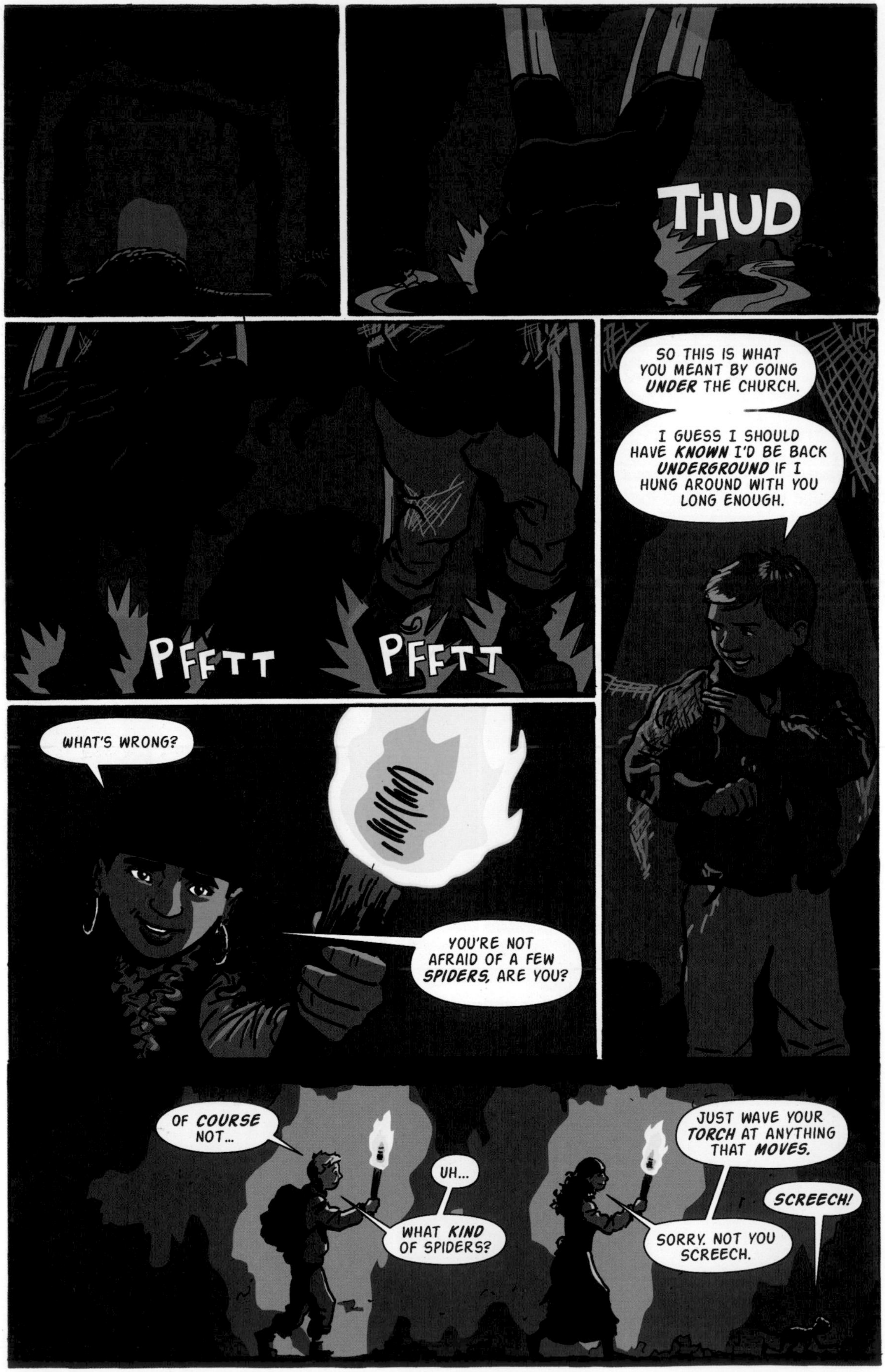
THUD
PFFTT
PFFTT
SO THIS IS WHAT YOU MEANT BY GOING UNDER THE CHURCH.
I GUESS I SHOULD HAVE KNOWN I'D BE BACK UNDERGROUND IF I HUNG AROUND WITH YOU LONG ENOUGH.
WHAT'S WRONG?
YOU'RE NOT AFRAID OF A FEW SPIDERS, ARE YOU?
OF COURSE NOT...
UH...
WHAT KIND OF SPIDERS?
JUST WAVE YOUR TORCH AT ANYTHING THAT MOVES.
SCREECH!
SORRY. NOT YOU SCREECH.

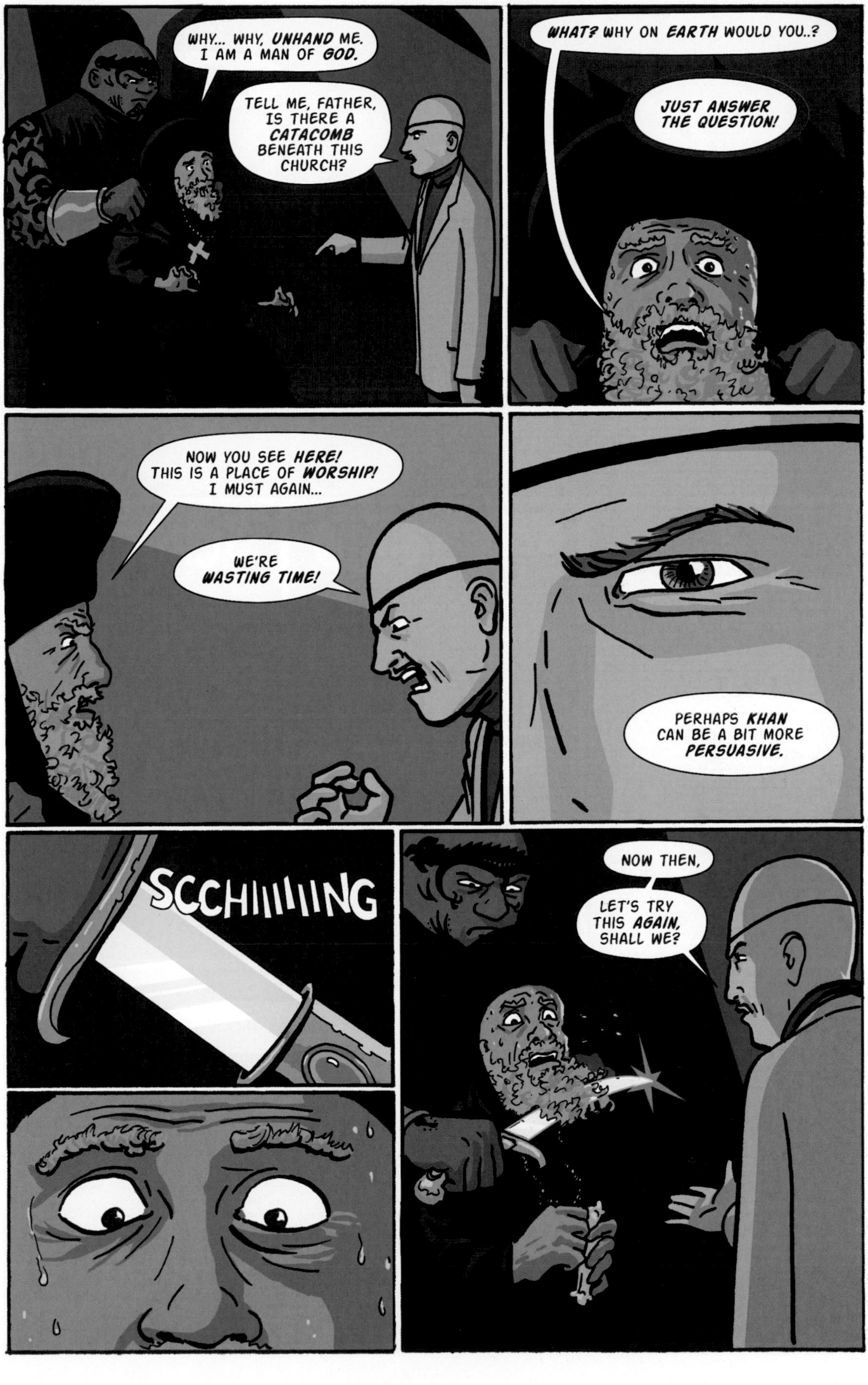
WHY... WHY, UNHAND ME. I AM A MAN OF GOD.
TELL ME, FATHER, IS THERE A CATACOMB BENEATH THIS CHURCH?
WHAT? WHY ON EARTH WOULD YOU..?
JUST ANSWER THE QUESTION!
NOW YOU SEE HERE! THIS IS A PLACE OF WORSHIP! I MUST AGAIN...
WE'RE WASTING TIME!
PERHAPS KHAN CAN BE A BIT MORE PERSUASIVE.
SCCHIIIIIING
NOW THEN,
LET'S TRY THIS AGAIN, SHALL WE?

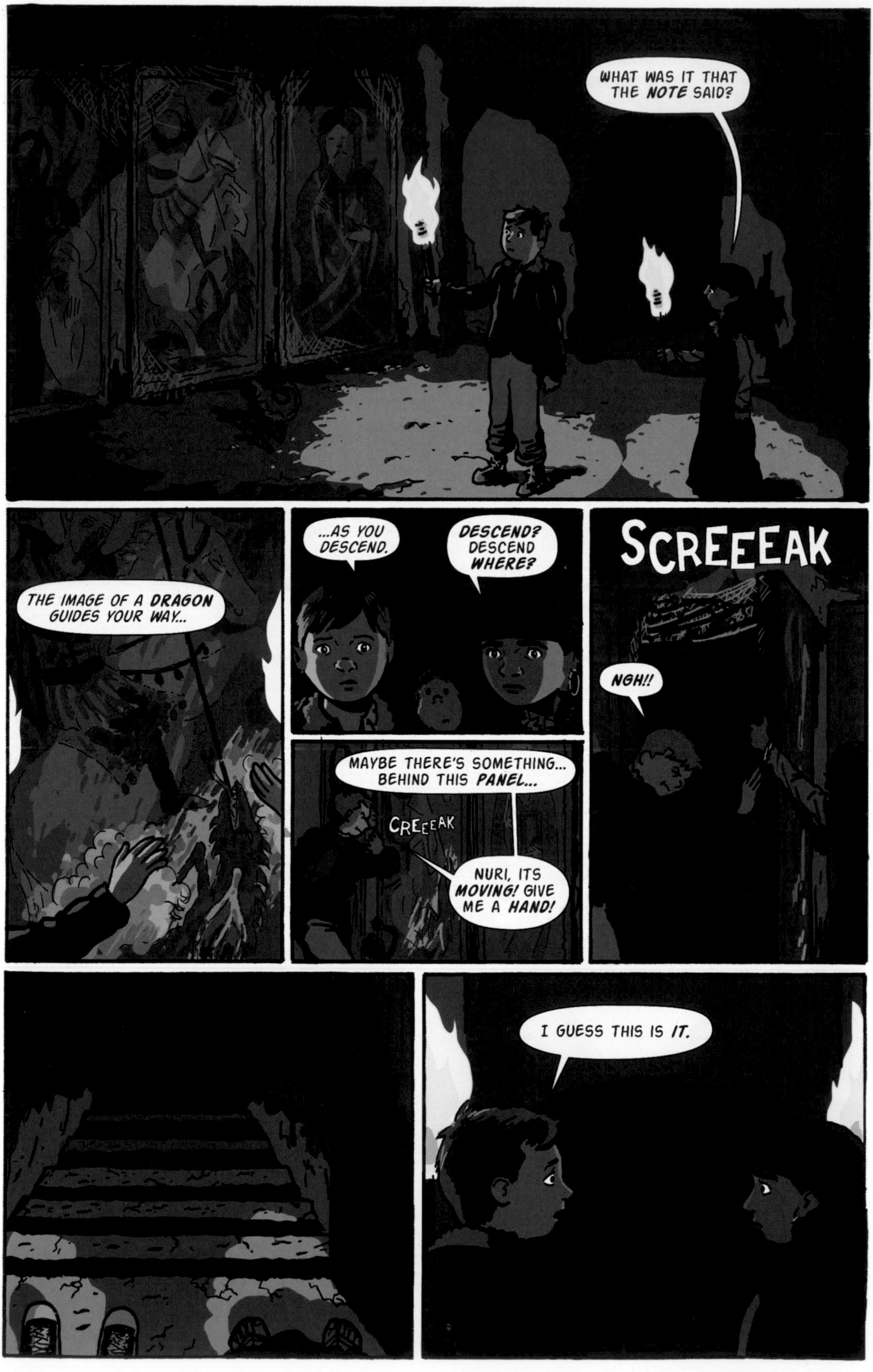
WHAT WAS IT THAT THE NOTE SAID?
THE IMAGE OF A DRAGON GUIDES YOUR WAY...
...AS YOU DESCEND.
DESCEND? DESCEND WHERE?
MAYBE THERE'S SOMETHING... BEHIND THIS PANEL...
CREEEAK
NURI, ITS MOVING! GIVE ME A HAND!
SCREEEAK
NGH!!
I GUESS THIS IS IT.

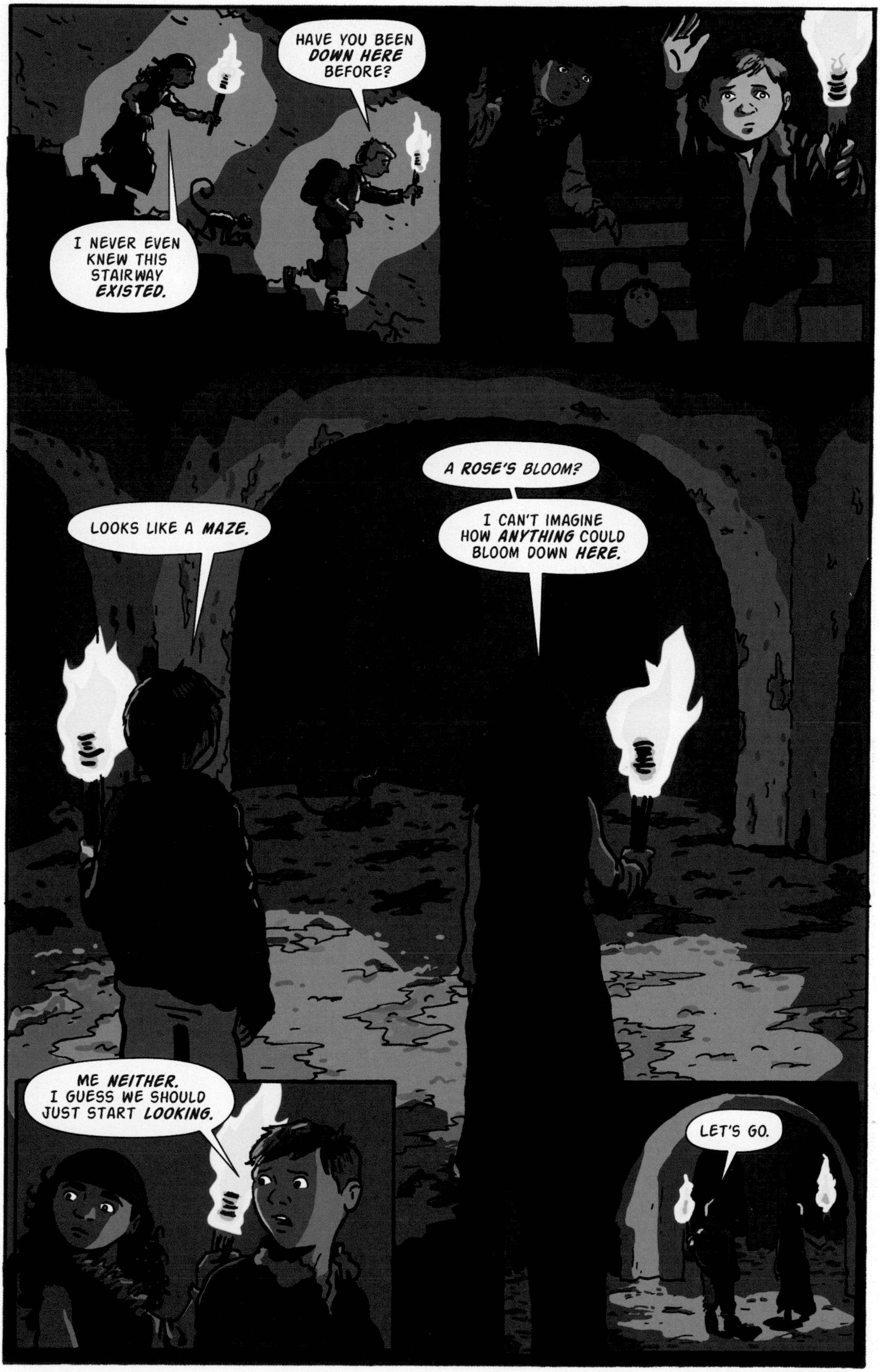
I NEVER EVEN KNEW THIS STAIRWAY EXISTED.
HAVE YOU BEEN DOWN HERE BEFORE?
LOOKS LIKE A MAZE.
A ROSE'S BLOOM?
I CAN'T IMAGINE HOW ANYTHING COULD BLOOM DOWN HERE.
ME NEITHER. I GUESS WE SHOULD JUST START LOOKING.
LET'S GO.

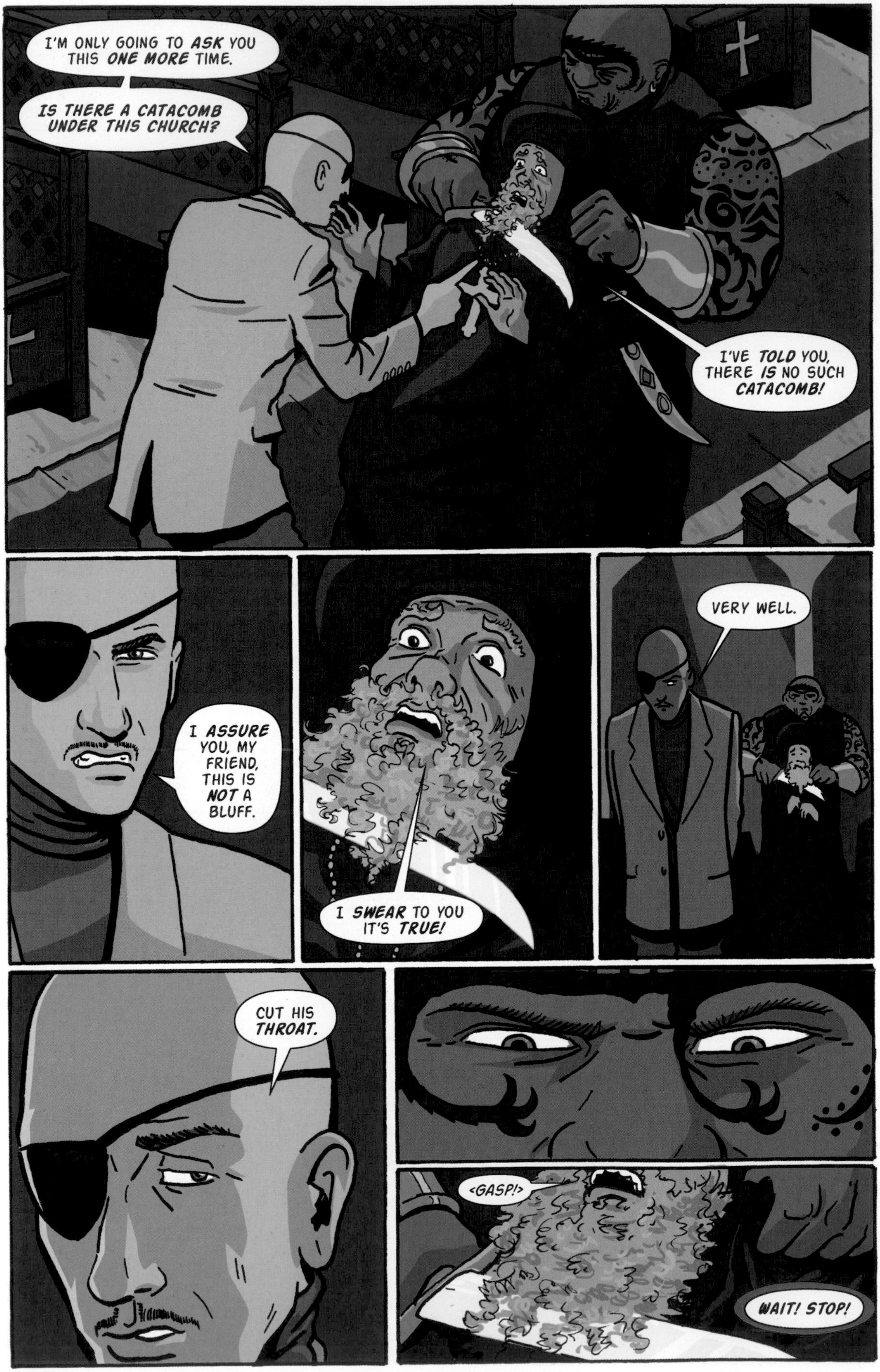
I'M ONLY GOING TO ASK YOU THIS ONE MORE TIME.
IS THERE A CATACOMB UNDER THIS CHURCH?
I'VE TOLD YOU, THERE IS NO SUCH CATACOMB!
I ASSURE YOU, MY FRIEND, THIS IS NOT A BLUFF.
I SWEAR TO YOU IT'S TRUE!
VERY WELL.
CUT HIS THROAT.
<GASP!>
WAIT! STOP!

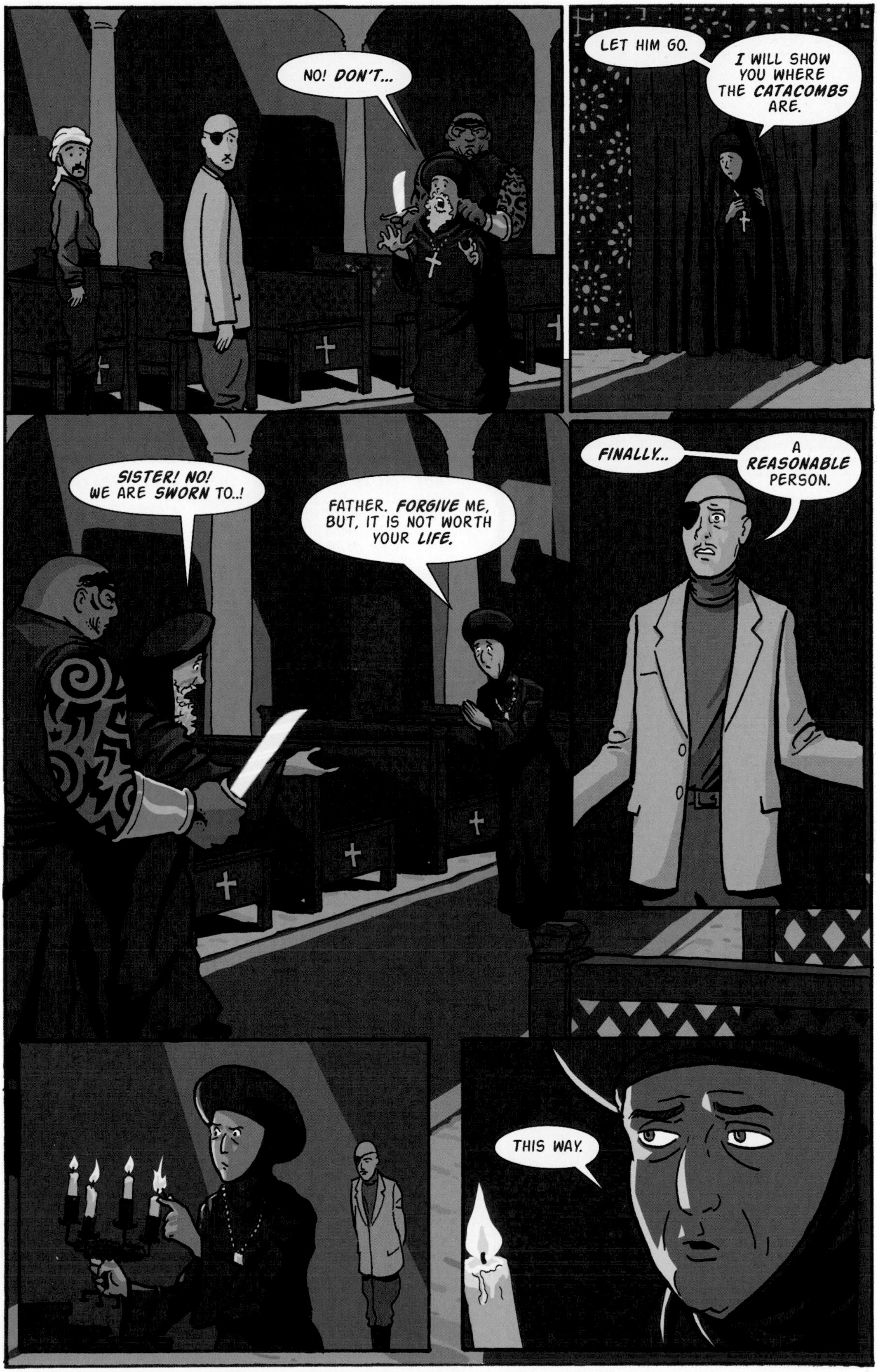
NO! DON'T...
LET HIM GO.
I WILL SHOW YOU WHERE THE CATACOMBS ARE.
SISTER! NO! WE ARE SWORN TO..!
FATHER. FORGIVE ME, BUT, IT IS NOT WORTH YOUR LIFE.
FINALLY...
A REASONABLE PERSON.
THIS WAY.

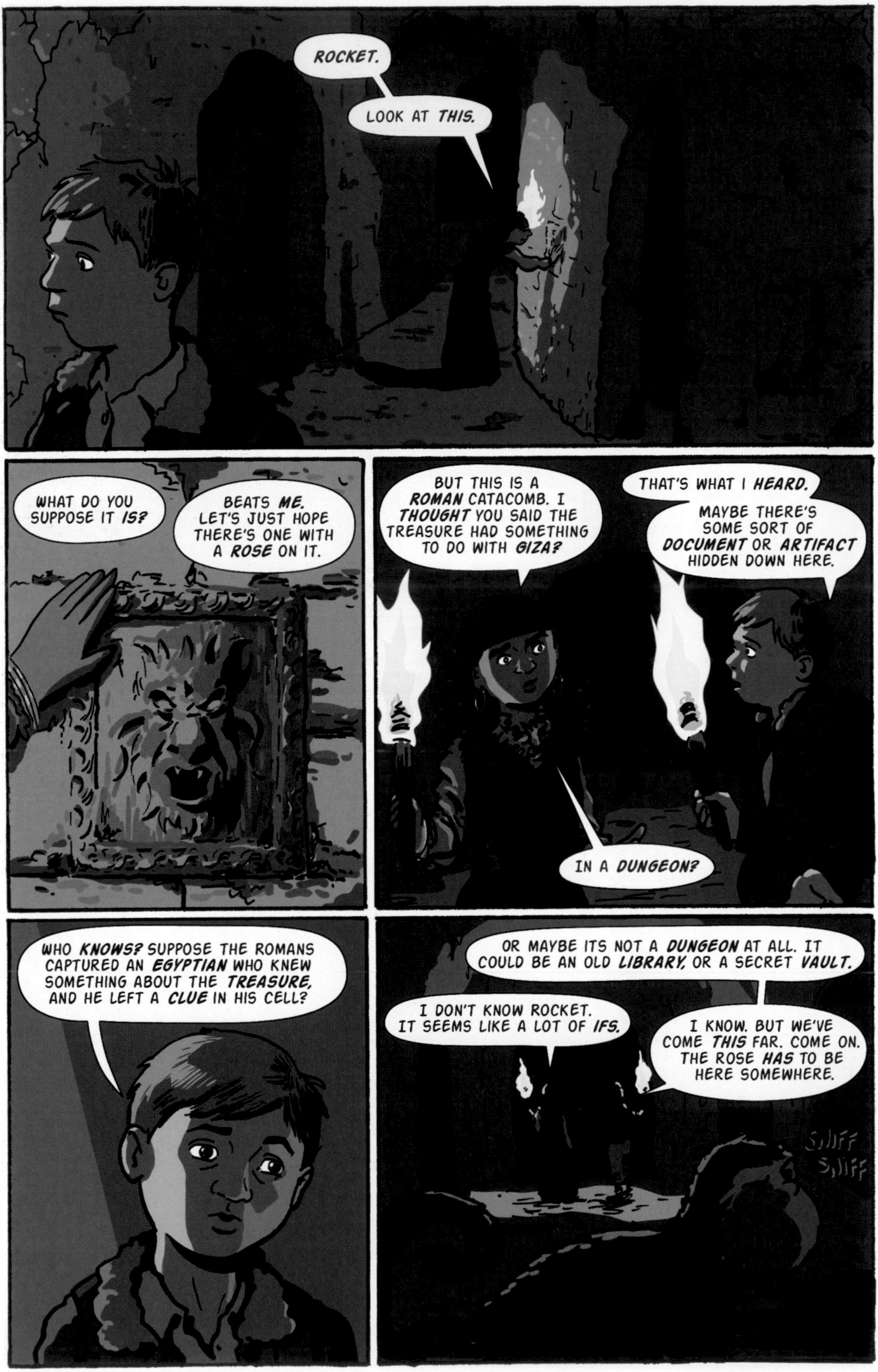
ROCKET.
LOOK AT THIS.
WHAT DO YOU SUPPOSE IT IS?
BEATS ME. LET'S JUST HOPE THERE'S ONE WITH A ROSE ON IT.
BUT THIS IS A ROMAN CATACOMB. I THOUGHT YOU SAID THE TREASURE HAD SOMETHING TO DO WITH GIZA?
THAT'S WHAT I HEARD.
MAYBE THERE'S SOME SORT OF DOCUMENT OR ARTIFACT HIDDEN DOWN HERE.
IN A DUNGEON?
WHO KNOWS? SUPPOSE THE ROMANS CAPTURED AN EGYPTIAN WHO KNEW SOMETHING ABOUT THE TREASURE, AND HE LEFT A CLUE IN HIS CELL?
OR MAYBE ITS NOT A DUNGEON AT ALL. IT COULD BE AN OLD LIBRARY, OR A SECRET VAULT.
I DON'T KNOW ROCKET. IT SEEMS LIKE A LOT OF IFS.
I KNOW. BUT WE'VE COME THIS FAR. COME ON. THE ROSE HAS TO BE HERE SOMEWHERE.
SNIFF
SNIFF

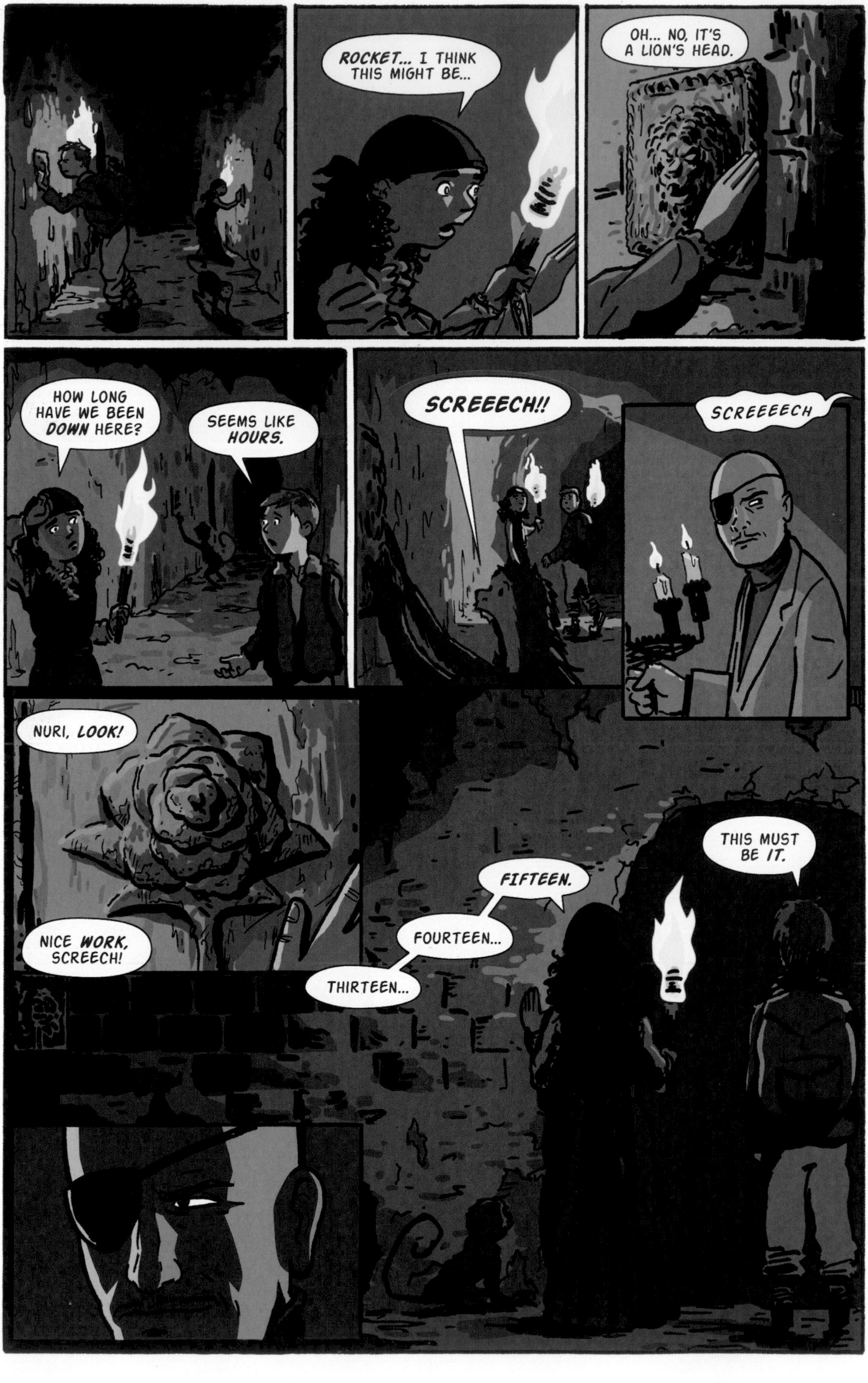
ROCKET... I THINK THIS MIGHT BE...
OH... NO, IT'S A LION'S HEAD.
HOW LONG HAVE WE BEEN DOWN HERE?
SEEMS LIKE HOURS.
SCREEECH!!
SCREEEECH
NURI, LOOK!
NICE WORK, SCREECH!
THIRTEEN...
FOURTEEN...
FIFTEEN.
THIS MUST BE IT.

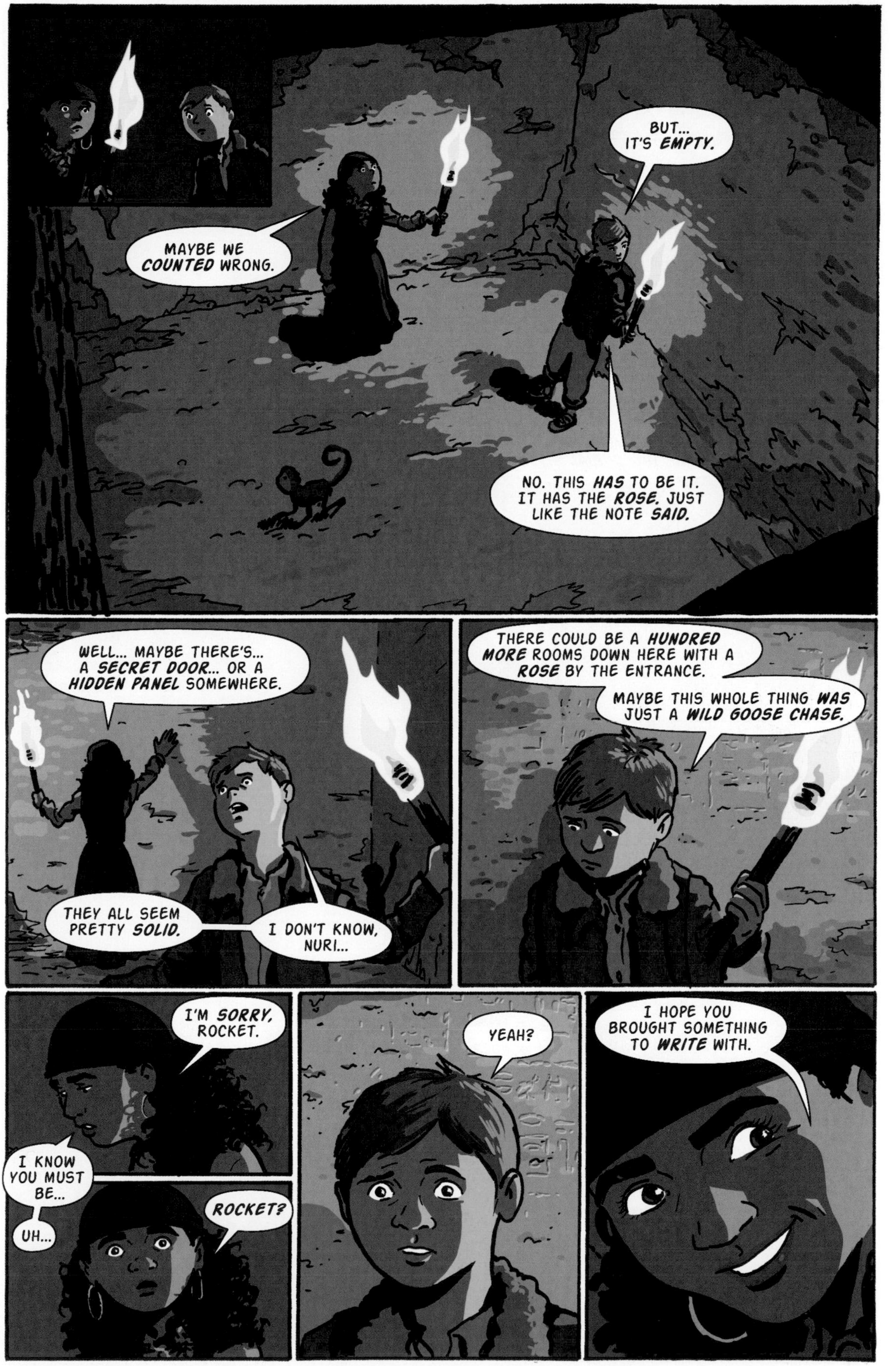
BUT... IT'S EMPTY.
MAYBE WE COUNTED WRONG.
NO. THIS HAS TO BE IT. IT HAS THE ROSE. JUST LIKE THE NOTE SAID.
WELL... MAYBE THERE'S... A SECRET DOOR... OR A HIDDEN PANEL SOMEWHERE.
I DON'T KNOW, NURI...
THEY ALL SEEM PRETTY SOLID.
THERE COULD BE A HUNDRED MORE ROOMS DOWN HERE WITH A ROSE BY THE ENTRANCE.
MAYBE THIS WHOLE THING WAS JUST A WILD GOOSE CHASE.
I'M SORRY, ROCKET.
I KNOW YOU MUST BE...
UH...
ROCKET?
YEAH?
I HOPE YOU BROUGHT SOMETHING TO WRITE WITH.

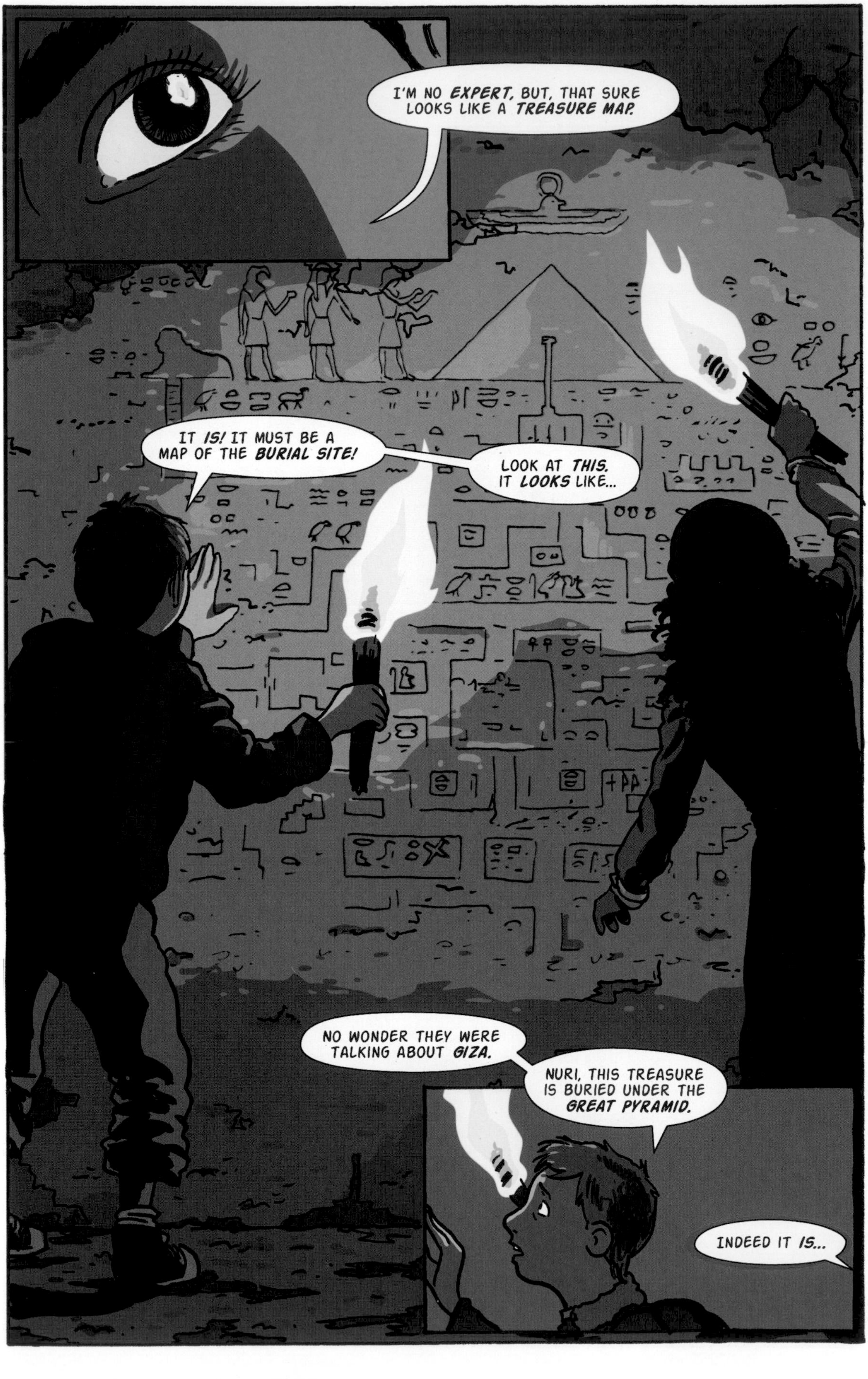
I'M NO EXPERT, BUT, THAT SURE LOOKS LIKE A TREASURE MAP.
IT IS! IT MUST BE A MAP OF THE BURIAL SITE!
LOOK AT THIS. IT LOOKS LIKE...
NO WONDER THEY WERE TALKING ABOUT GIZA.
NURI, THIS TREASURE IS BURIED UNDER THE GREAT PYRAMID.
INDEED IT IS...

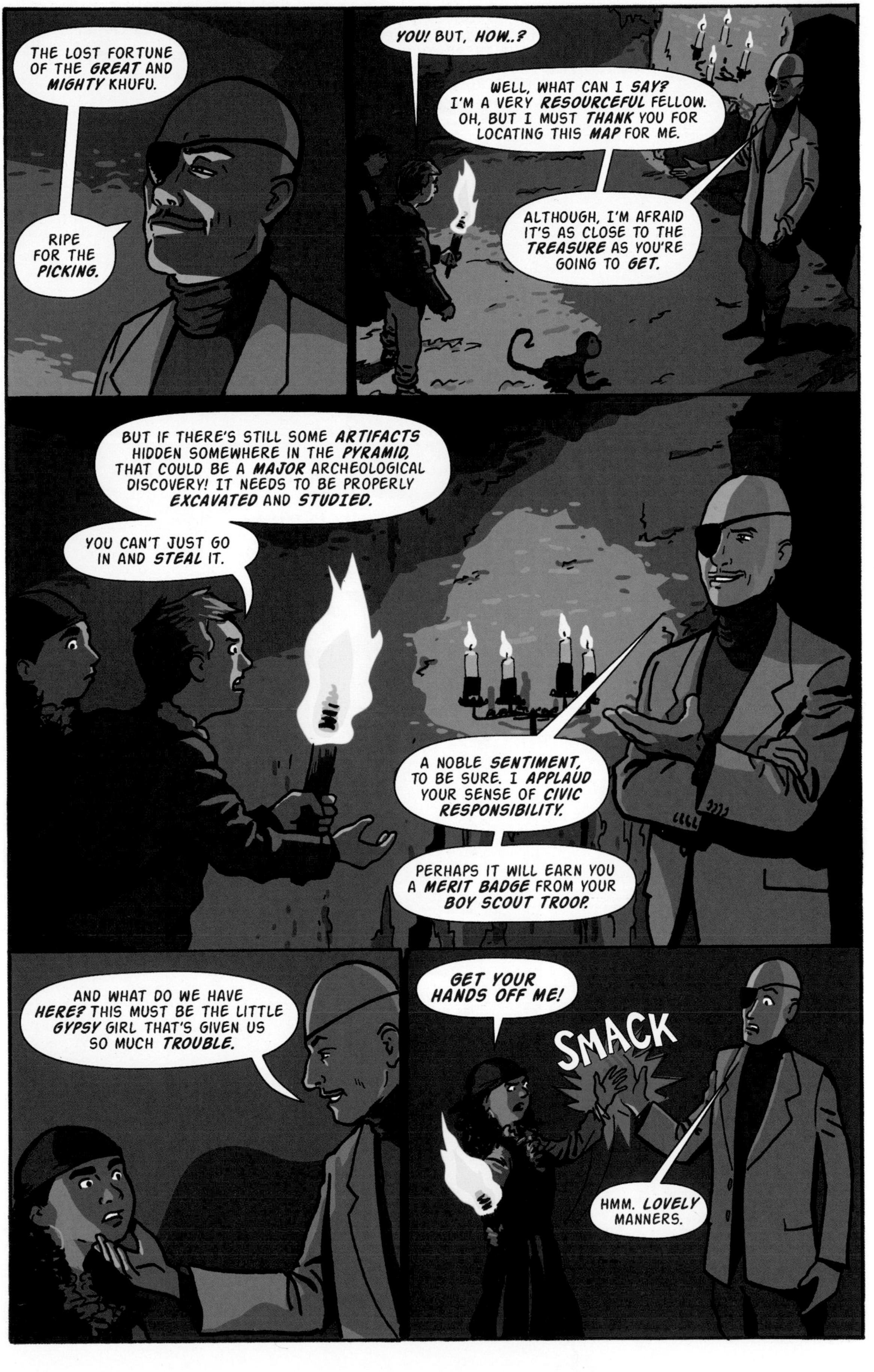
THE LOST FORTUNE OF THE GREAT AND MIGHTY KHUFU.
RIPE FOR THE PICKING.
YOU! BUT, HOW..?
WELL, WHAT CAN I SAY? I'M A VERY RESOURCEFUL FELLOW. OH, BUT I MUST THANK YOU FOR LOCATING THIS MAP FOR ME.
ALTHOUGH, I'M AFRAID IT'S AS CLOSE TO THE TREASURE AS YOU'RE GOING TO GET.
BUT IF THERE'S STILL SOME ARTIFACTS HIDDEN SOMEWHERE IN THE PYRAMID, THAT COULD BE A MAJOR ARCHEOLOGICAL DISCOVERY! IT NEEDS TO BE PROPERLY EXCAVATED AND STUDIED.
YOU CAN'T JUST GO IN AND STEAL IT.
A NOBLE SENTIMENT, TO BE SURE. I APPLAUD YOUR SENSE OF CIVIC RESPONSIBILITY.
PERHAPS IT WILL EARN YOU A MERIT BADGE FROM YOUR BOY SCOUT TROOP.
AND WHAT DO WE HAVE HERE? THIS MUST BE THE LITTLE GYPSY GIRL THAT'S GIVEN US SO MUCH TROUBLE.
GET YOUR HANDS OFF ME!
SMACK
HMM. LOVELY MANNERS.

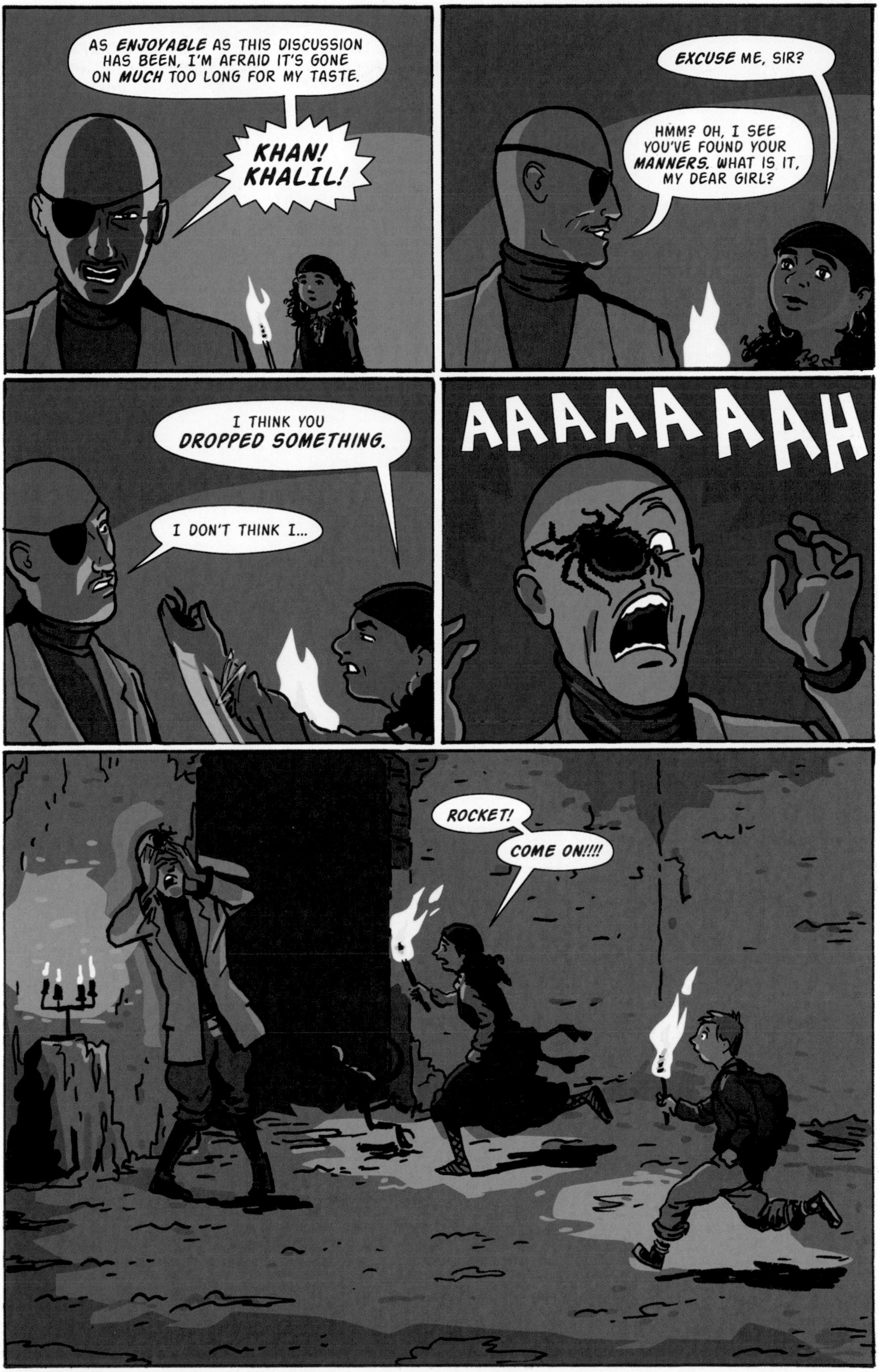
AS ENJOYABLE AS THIS DISCUSSION HAS BEEN, I'M AFRAID IT'S GONE ON MUCH TOO LONG FOR MY TASTE.
KHAN! KHALIL!
EXCUSE ME, SIR?
HMM? OH, I SEE YOU'VE FOUND YOUR MANNERS. WHAT IS IT, MY DEAR GIRL?
I THINK YOU DROPPED SOMETHING.
I DON'T THINK I...
AAAAAAAH
ROCKET!
COME ON!!!!

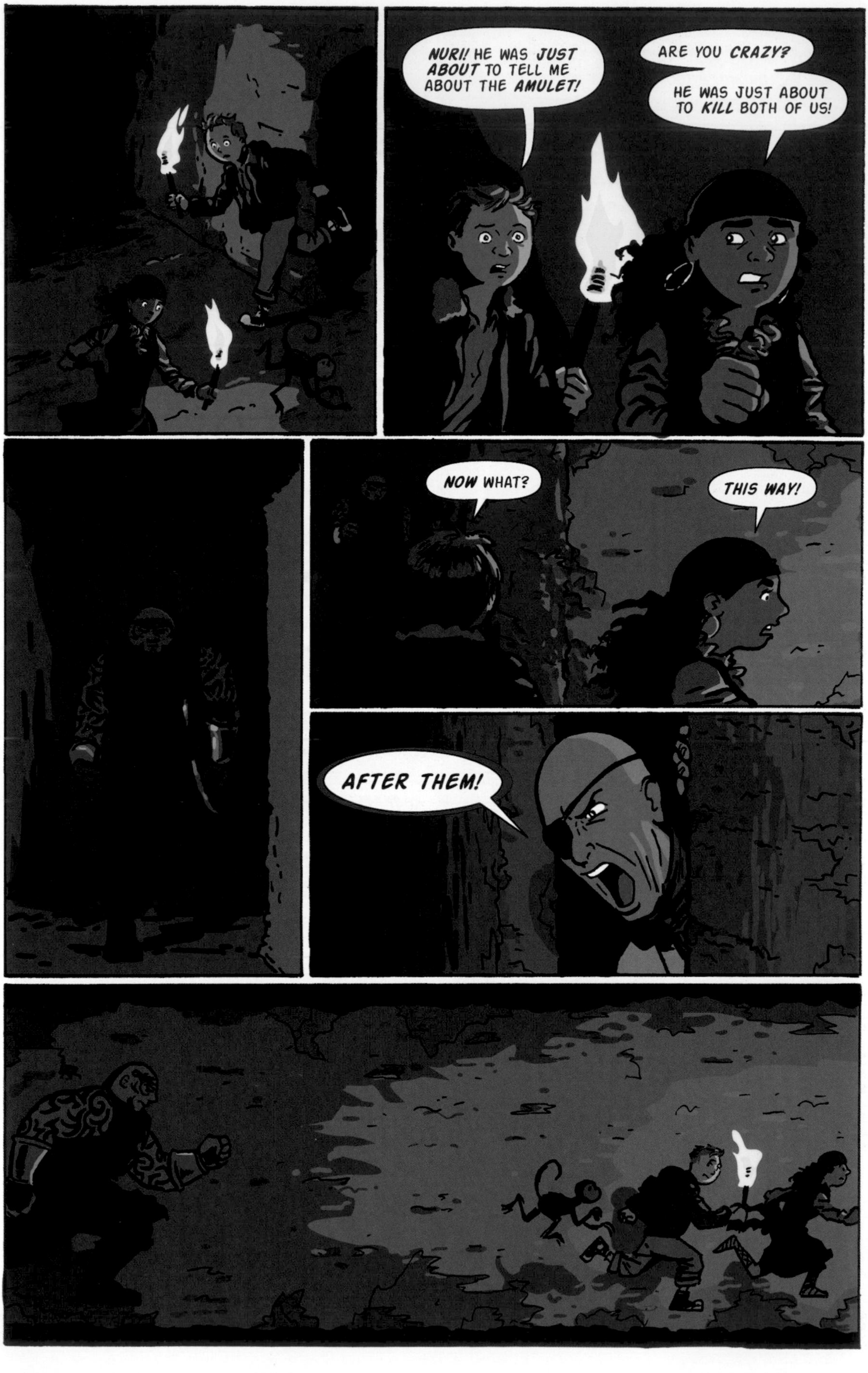
NURI! HE WAS JUST ABOUT TO TELL ME ABOUT THE AMULET!
ARE YOU CRAZY?
HE WAS JUST ABOUT TO KILL BOTH OF US!
NOW WHAT?
THIS WAY!
AFTER THEM!

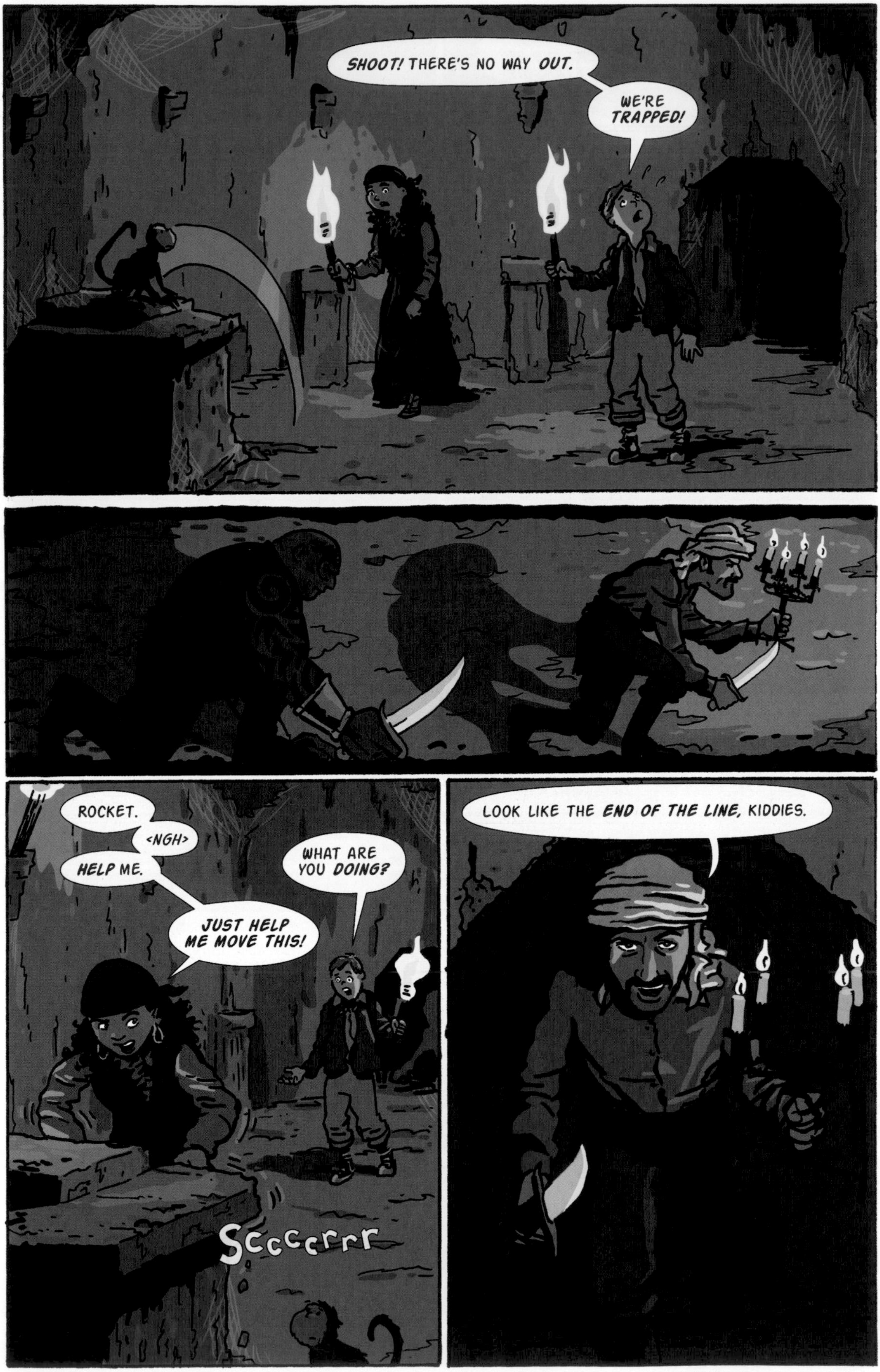
SHOOT! THERE'S NO WAY OUT.
WE'RE TRAPPED!
ROCKET.
<NGH>
HELP ME.
JUST HELP ME MOVE THIS!
WHAT ARE YOU DOING?
SCCCCRRR
LOOK LIKE THE END OF THE LINE, KIDDIES.

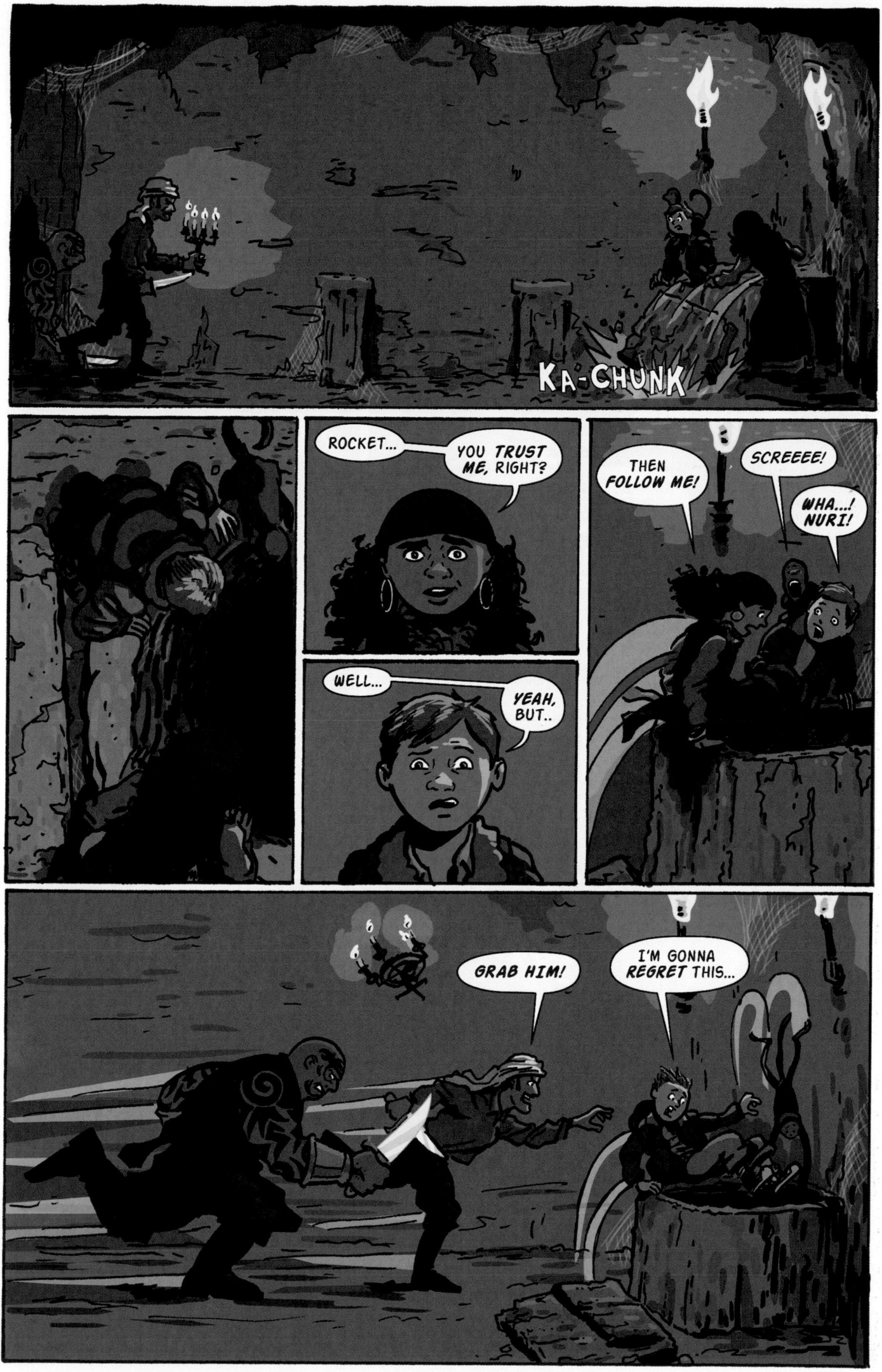
KA-CHUNK
ROCKET...
YOU *TRUST ME,* RIGHT?
WELL...
YEAH, BUT..
THEN *FOLLOW ME!*
SCREEEE!
WHA...! NURI!
GRAB HIM!
I'M GONNA *REGRET* THIS...

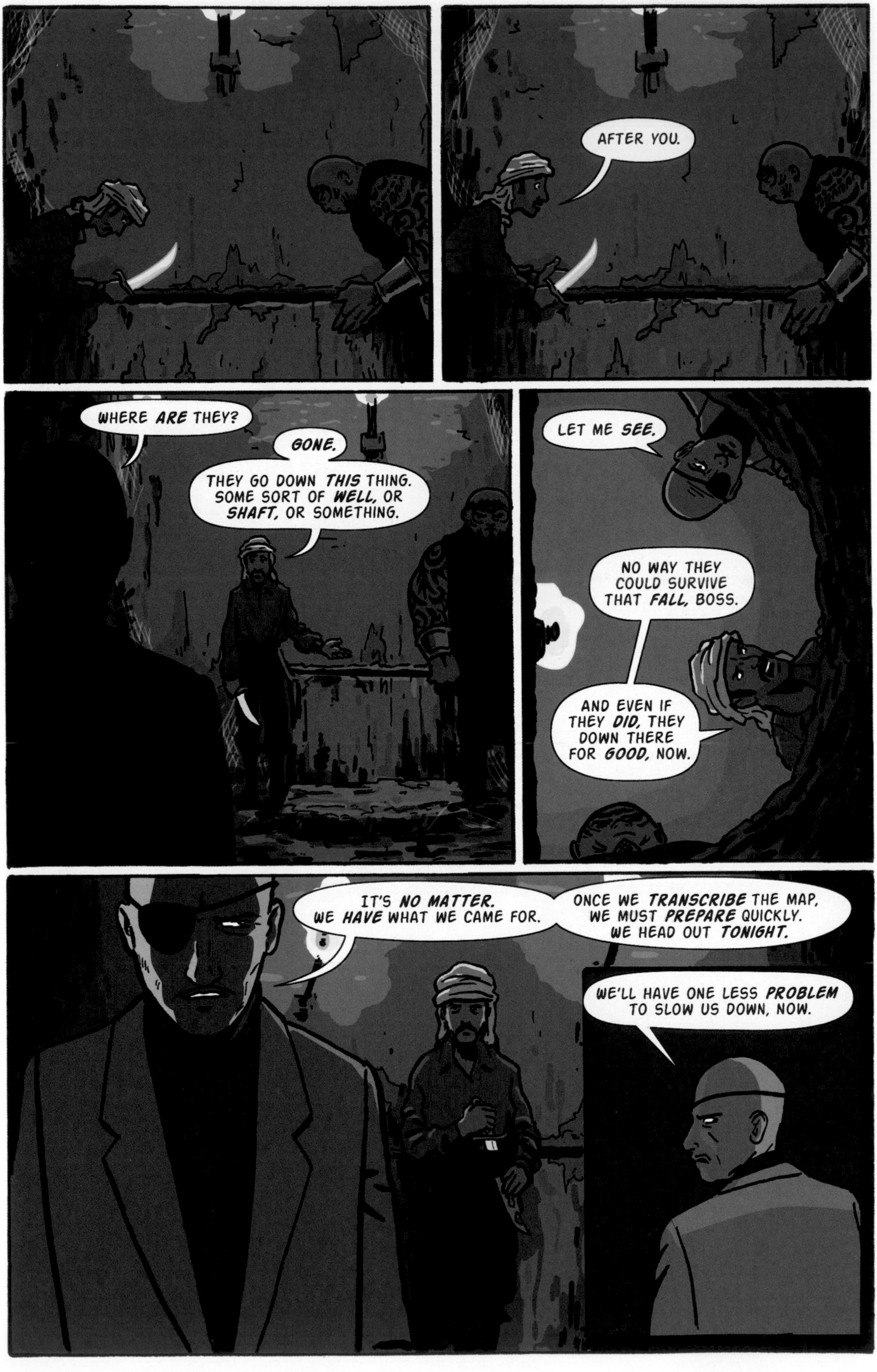
AFTER YOU.
WHERE ARE THEY?
GONE.
THEY GO DOWN THIS THING. SOME SORT OF WELL, OR SHAFT, OR SOMETHING.
LET ME SEE.
NO WAY THEY COULD SURVIVE THAT FALL, BOSS.
AND EVEN IF THEY DID, THEY DOWN THERE FOR GOOD, NOW.
IT'S NO MATTER. WE HAVE WHAT WE CAME FOR.
ONCE WE TRANSCRIBE THE MAP, WE MUST PREPARE QUICKLY. WE HEAD OUT TONIGHT.
WE'LL HAVE ONE LESS PROBLEM TO SLOW US DOWN, NOW.

CHAPTER EIGHT

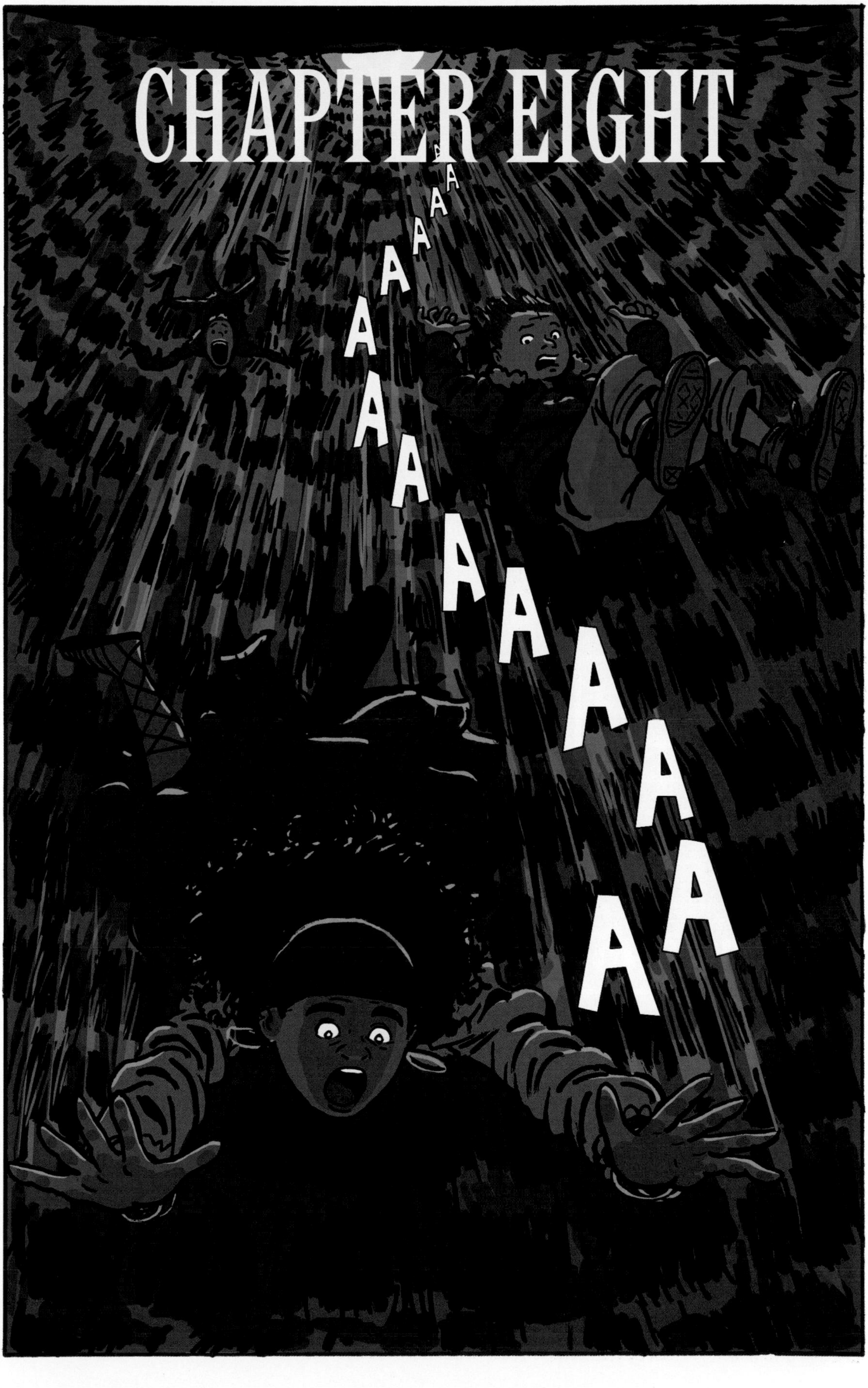
AAAAAAAAAAAAAAA

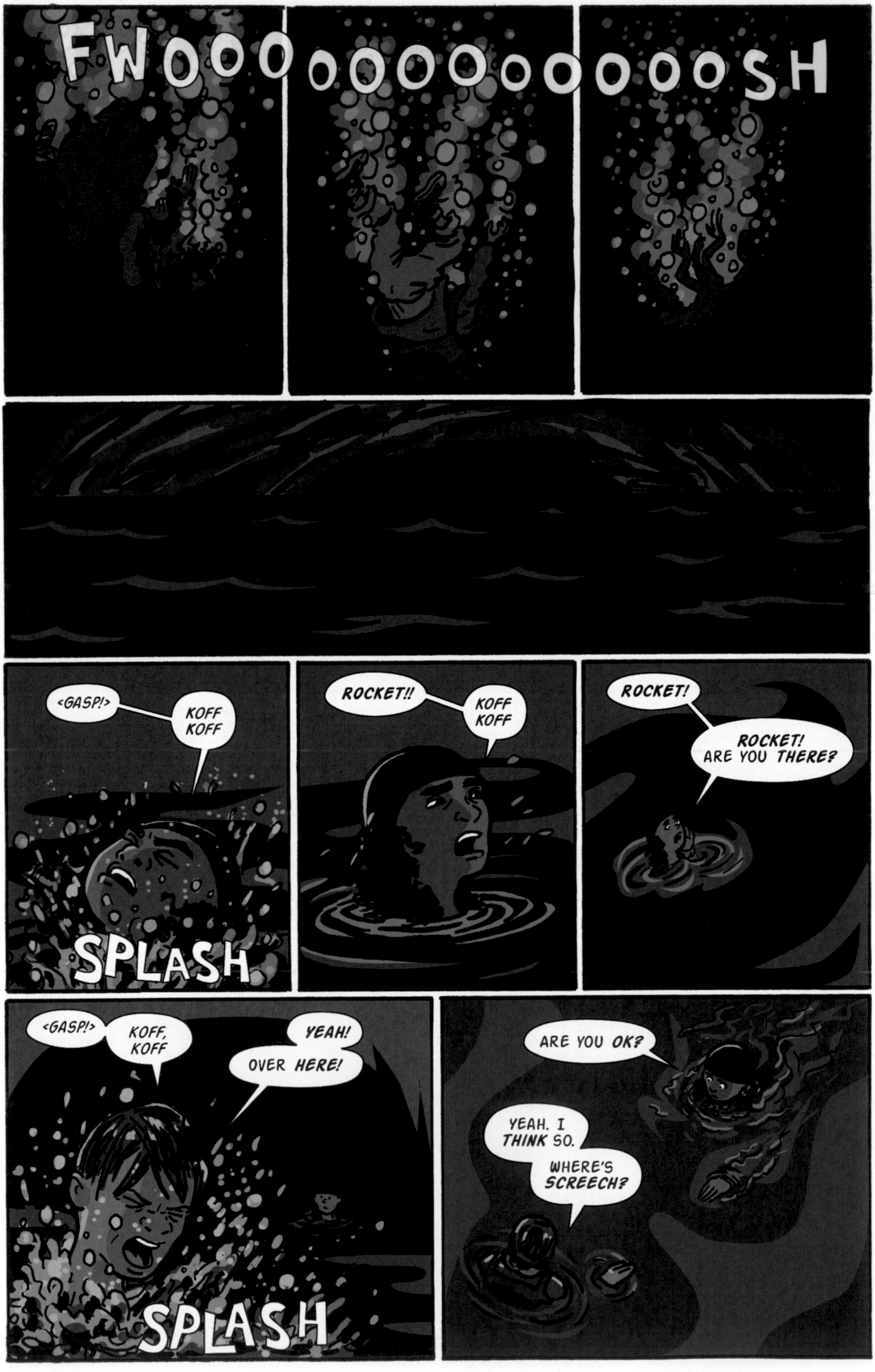
FWOOOOOOOOOOOOSH
<GASP!>
KOFF KOFF
SPLASH
ROCKET!!
KOFF KOFF
ROCKET!
ROCKET! ARE YOU THERE?
<GASP!>
KOFF, KOFF
YEAH!
OVER HERE!
SPLASH
ARE YOU OK?
YEAH. I THINK SO.
WHERE'S SCREECH?

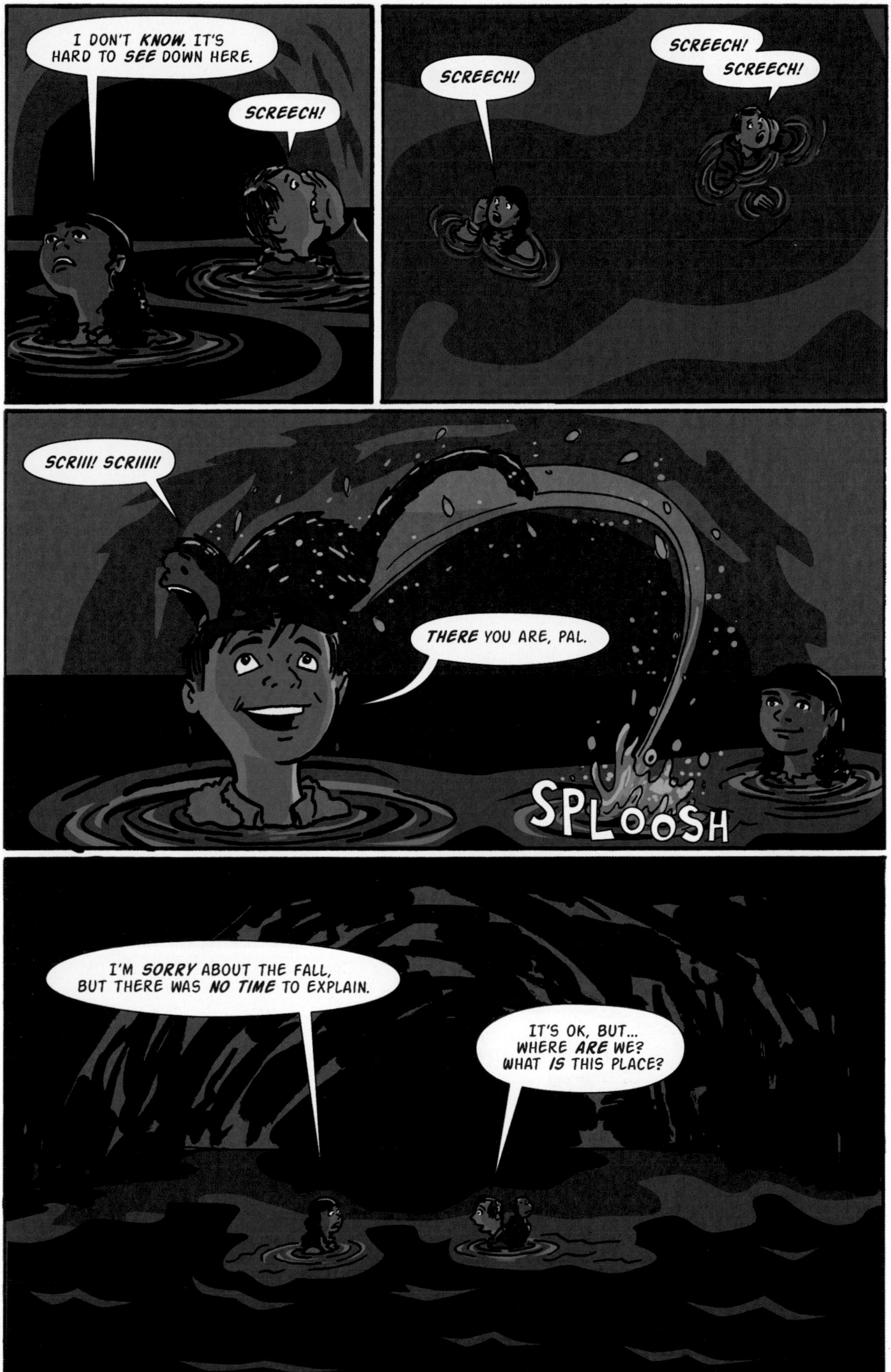
I DON'T KNOW. IT'S HARD TO SEE DOWN HERE.
SCREECH!
SCREECH!
SCREECH! SCREECH!
SCRIII! SCRIIII!
THERE YOU ARE, PAL.
SPLOOSH
I'M SORRY ABOUT THE FALL, BUT THERE WAS NO TIME TO EXPLAIN.
IT'S OK, BUT... WHERE ARE WE? WHAT IS THIS PLACE?

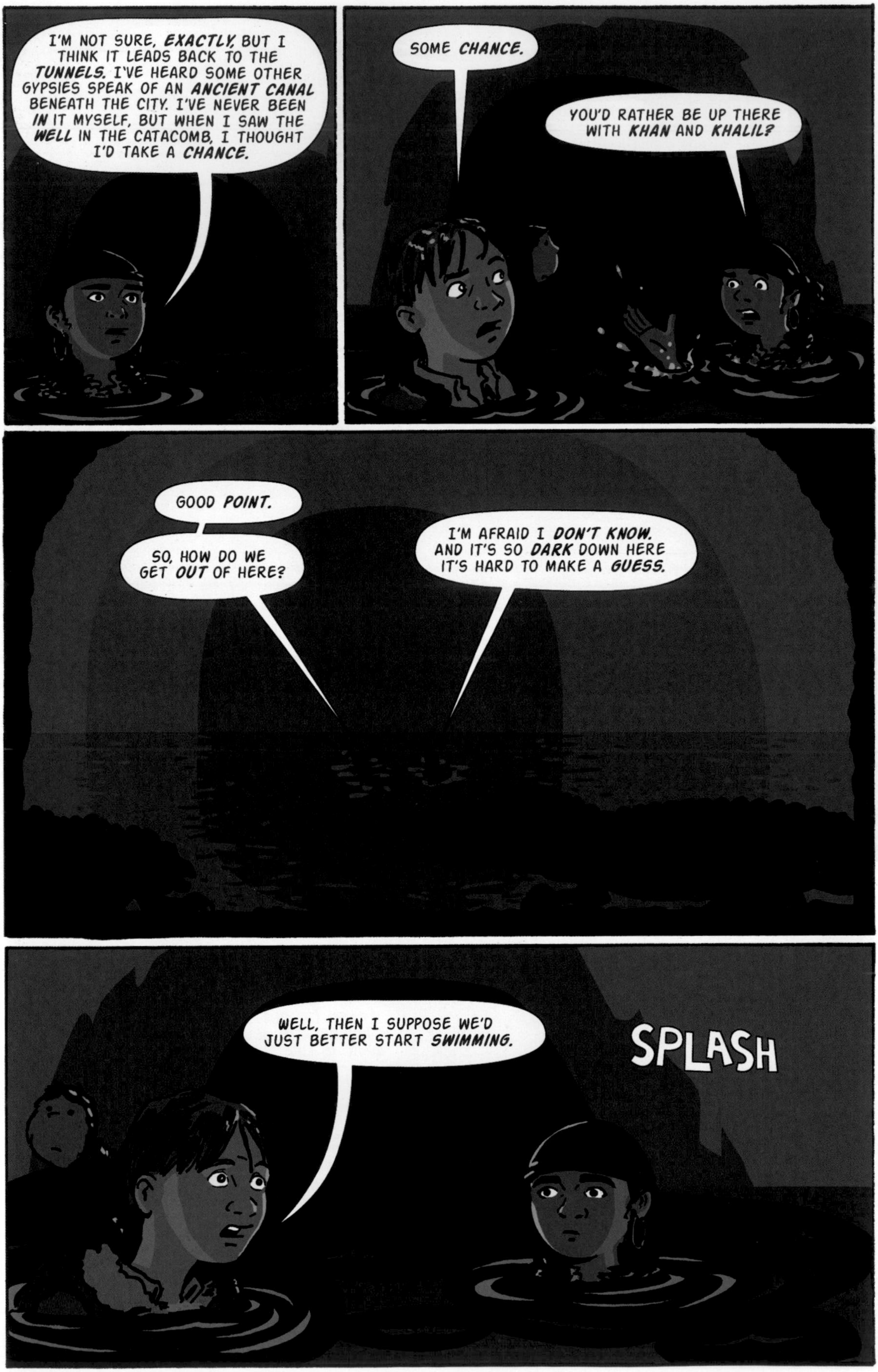
I'M NOT SURE, EXACTLY, BUT I THINK IT LEADS BACK TO THE TUNNELS. I'VE HEARD SOME OTHER GYPSIES SPEAK OF AN ANCIENT CANAL BENEATH THE CITY. I'VE NEVER BEEN IN IT MYSELF, BUT WHEN I SAW THE WELL IN THE CATACOMB, I THOUGHT I'D TAKE A CHANCE.
SOME CHANCE.
YOU'D RATHER BE UP THERE WITH KHAN AND KHALIL?
GOOD POINT.
SO, HOW DO WE GET OUT OF HERE?
I'M AFRAID I DON'T KNOW. AND IT'S SO DARK DOWN HERE IT'S HARD TO MAKE A GUESS.
WELL, THEN I SUPPOSE WE'D JUST BETTER START SWIMMING.
SPLASH

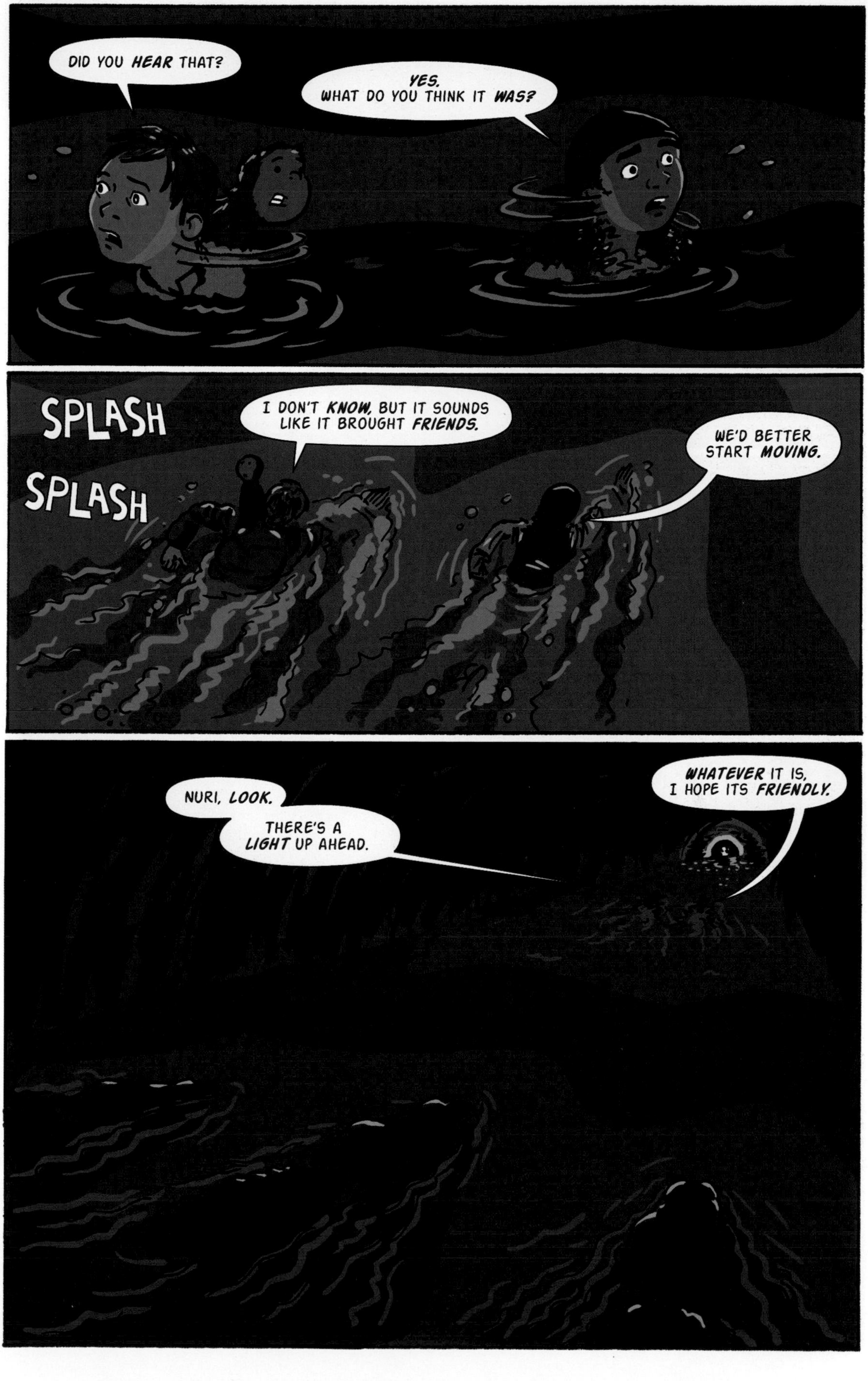
DID YOU HEAR THAT?
YES. WHAT DO YOU THINK IT WAS?
SPLASH
SPLASH
I DON'T KNOW, BUT IT SOUNDS LIKE IT BROUGHT FRIENDS.
WE'D BETTER START MOVING.
NURI, LOOK.
THERE'S A LIGHT UP AHEAD.
WHATEVER IT IS, I HOPE ITS FRIENDLY.

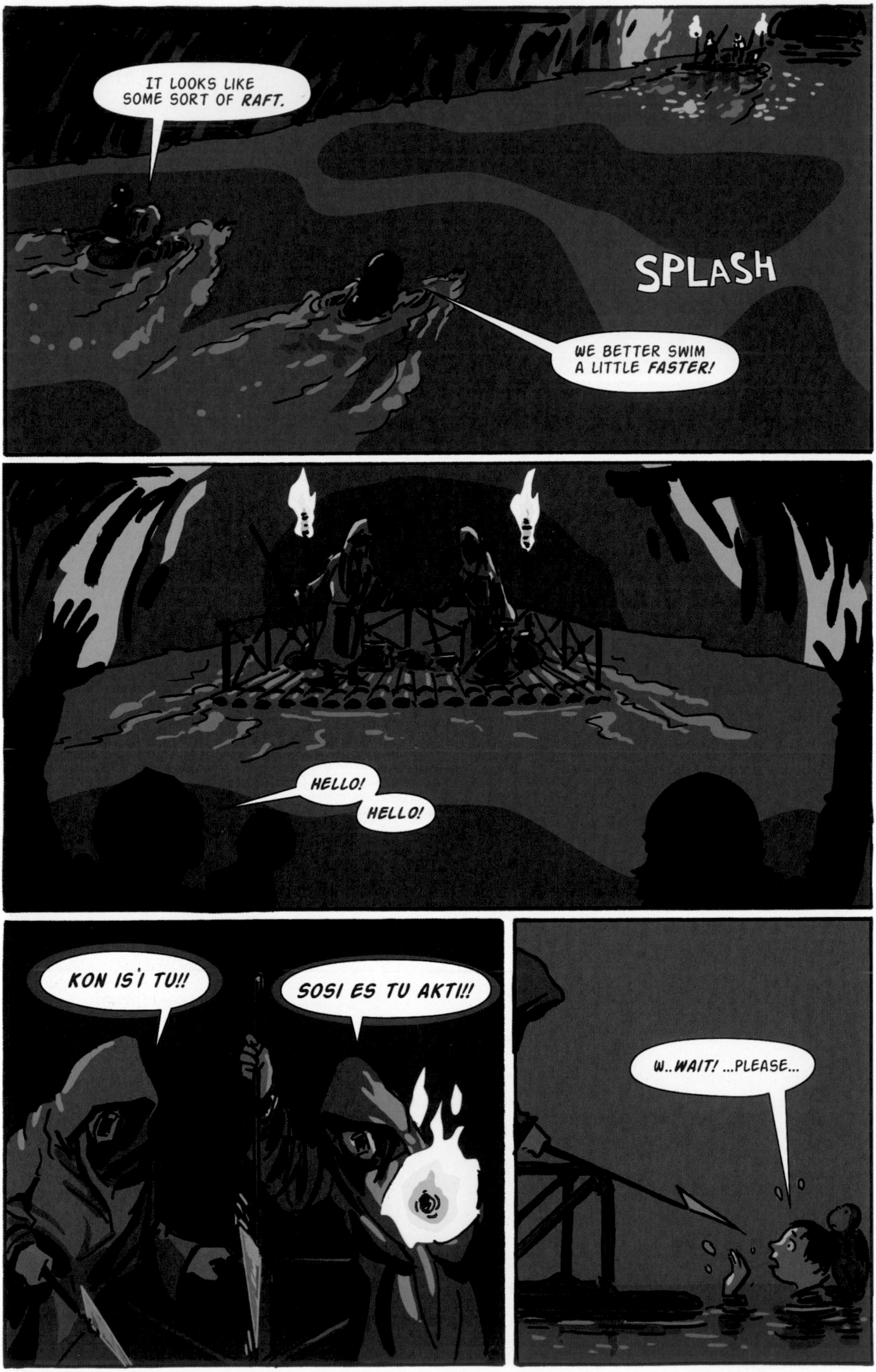
IT LOOKS LIKE SOME SORT OF RAFT.
SPLASH
WE BETTER SWIM A LITTLE FASTER!
HELLO!
HELLO!
KON IS'I TU!!
SOSI ES TU AKTI!!
W..WAIT! ...PLEASE...

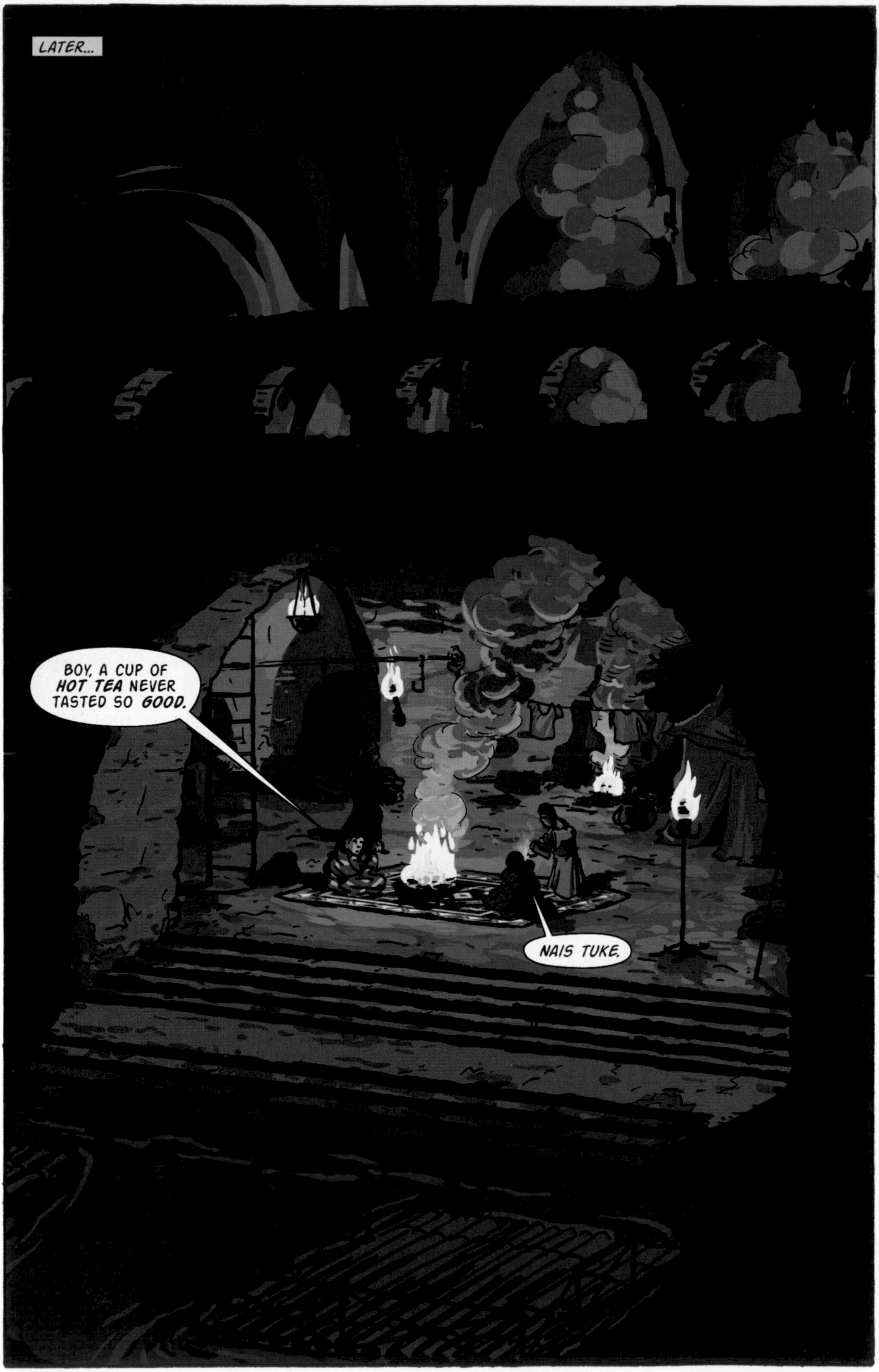
LATER...
BOY, A CUP OF HOT TEA NEVER TASTED SO GOOD.
NAIS TUKE.

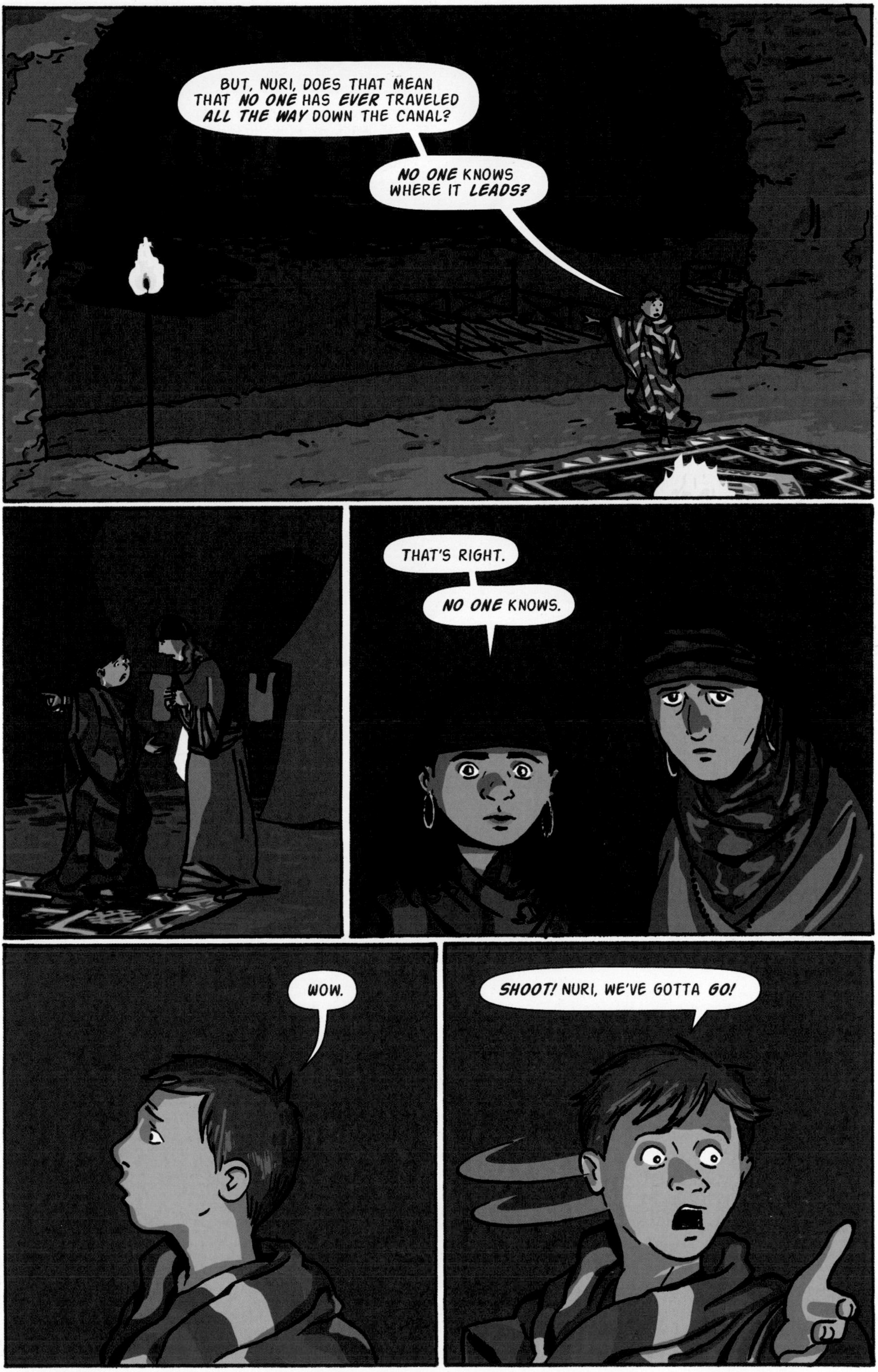
BUT, NURI, DOES THAT MEAN THAT NO ONE HAS EVER TRAVELED ALL THE WAY DOWN THE CANAL?
NO ONE KNOWS WHERE IT LEADS?
THAT'S RIGHT.
NO ONE KNOWS.
WOW.
SHOOT! NURI, WE'VE GOTTA GO!

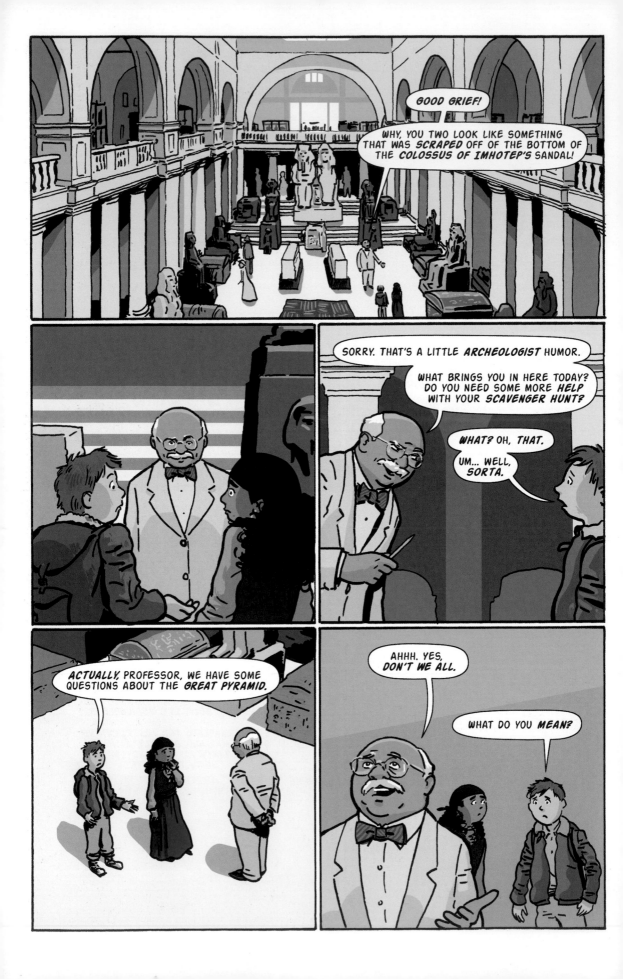

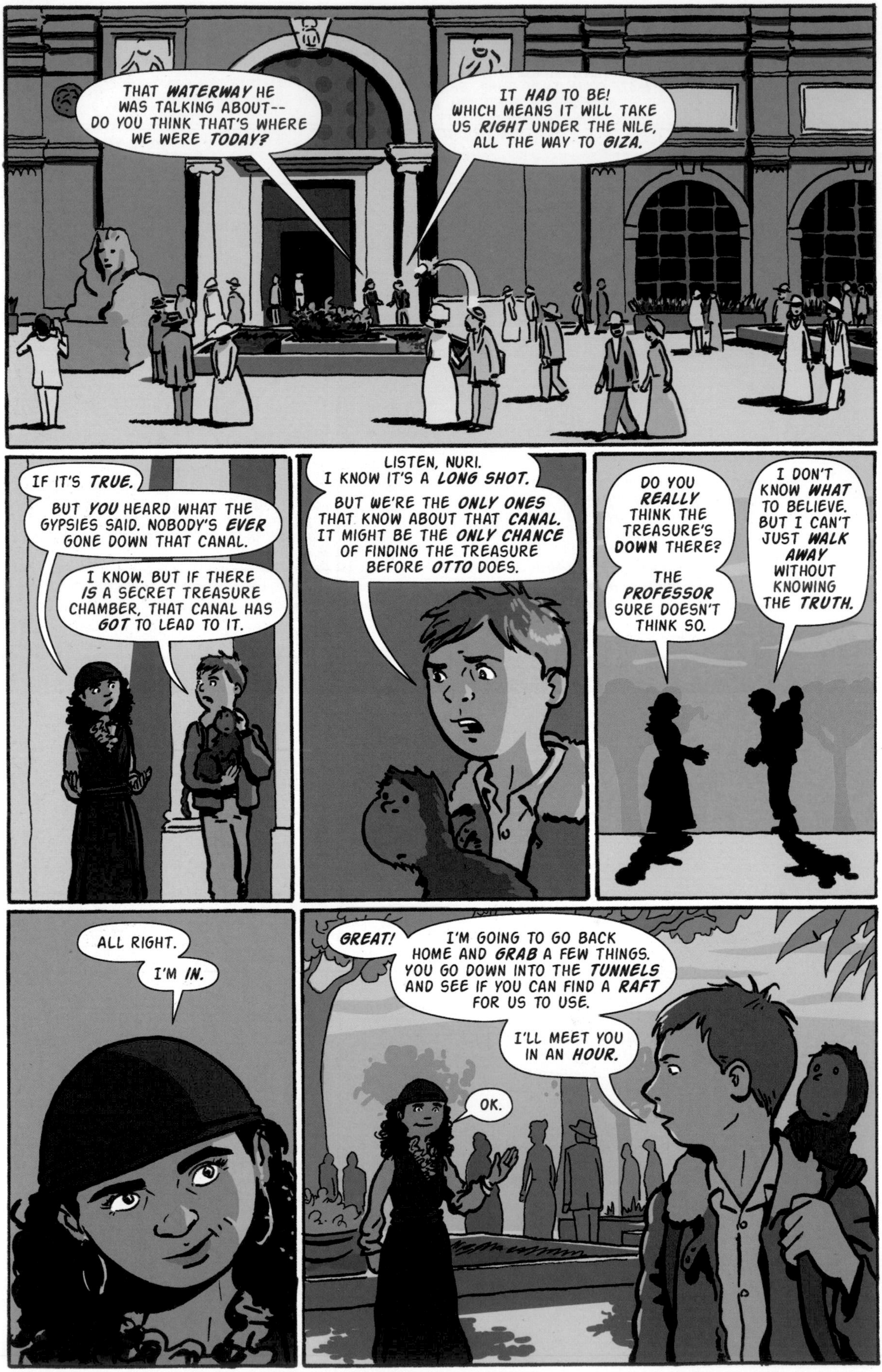
THAT *WATERWAY* HE WAS TALKING ABOUT-- DO YOU THINK THAT'S WHERE WE WERE *TODAY?*
IT *HAD* TO BE! WHICH MEANS IT WILL TAKE US *RIGHT* UNDER THE NILE, ALL THE WAY TO *GIZA.*
IF IT'S *TRUE.*
BUT *YOU* HEARD WHAT THE GYPSIES SAID. NOBODY'S *EVER* GONE DOWN THAT CANAL.
I KNOW. BUT IF THERE *IS* A SECRET TREASURE CHAMBER, THAT CANAL HAS *GOT* TO LEAD TO IT.
LISTEN, NURI. I KNOW IT'S A *LONG SHOT.*
BUT *WE'RE* THE *ONLY ONES* THAT KNOW ABOUT THAT *CANAL.* IT MIGHT BE THE *ONLY CHANCE* OF FINDING THE TREASURE BEFORE *OTTO* DOES.
DO YOU *REALLY* THINK THE TREASURE'S *DOWN* THERE?
THE *PROFESSOR* SURE DOESN'T THINK SO.
I DON'T KNOW *WHAT* TO BELIEVE. BUT I CAN'T JUST *WALK AWAY* WITHOUT KNOWING THE *TRUTH.*
ALL RIGHT.
I'M *IN.*
GREAT!
I'M GOING TO GO BACK HOME AND *GRAB* A FEW THINGS. YOU GO DOWN INTO THE *TUNNELS* AND SEE IF YOU CAN FIND A *RAFT* FOR US TO USE.
I'LL MEET YOU IN AN *HOUR.*
OK.

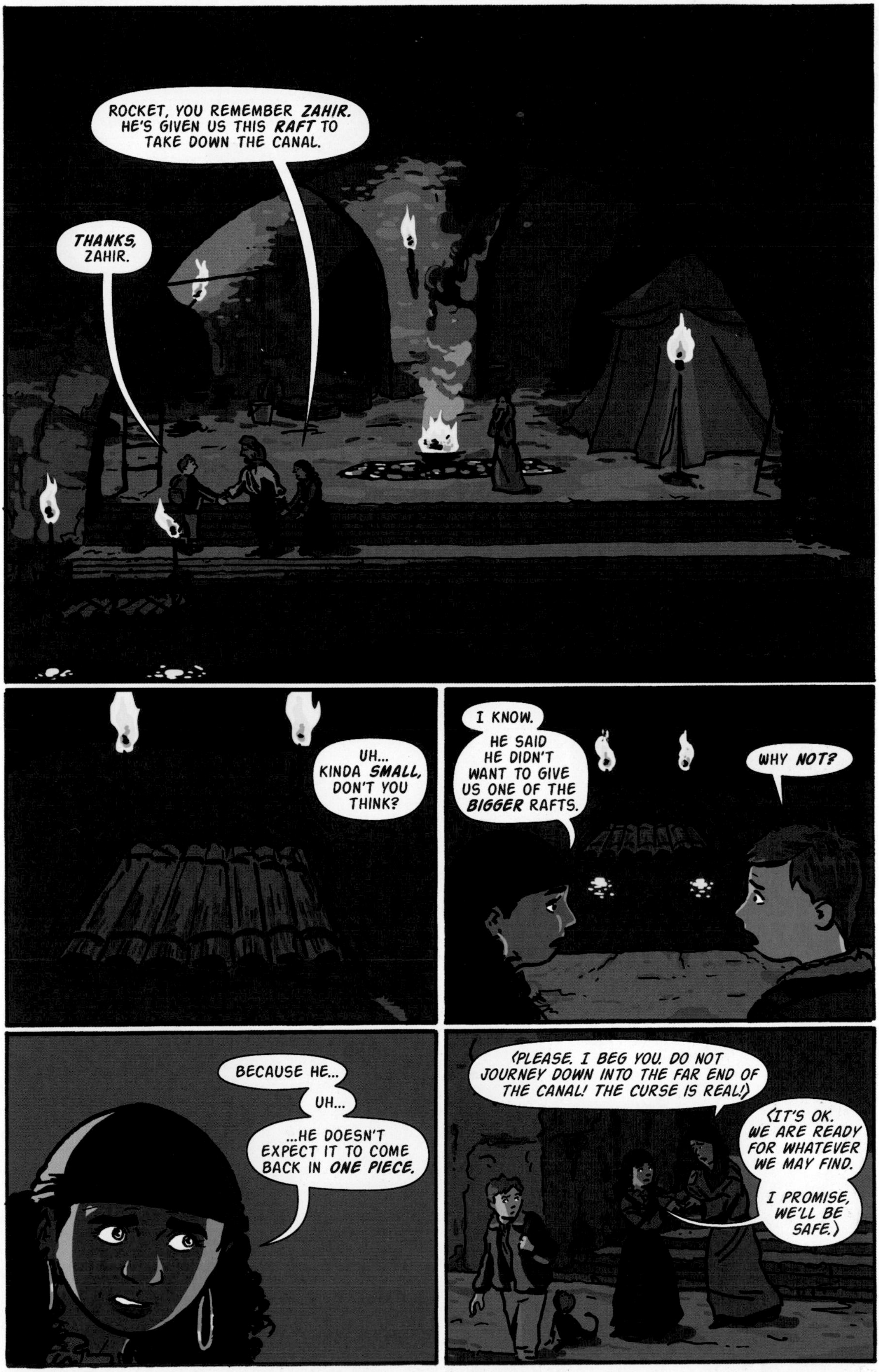
ROCKET, YOU REMEMBER ZAHIR. HE'S GIVEN US THIS RAFT TO TAKE DOWN THE CANAL.
THANKS, ZAHIR.
UH... KINDA SMALL, DON'T YOU THINK?
I KNOW.
HE SAID HE DIDN'T WANT TO GIVE US ONE OF THE BIGGER RAFTS.
WHY NOT?
BECAUSE HE...
UH...
...HE DOESN'T EXPECT IT TO COME BACK IN ONE PIECE.
〈PLEASE. I BEG YOU. DO NOT JOURNEY DOWN INTO THE FAR END OF THE CANAL! THE CURSE IS REAL!〉
〈IT'S OK. WE ARE READY FOR WHATEVER WE MAY FIND.
I PROMISE, WE'LL BE SAFE.〉

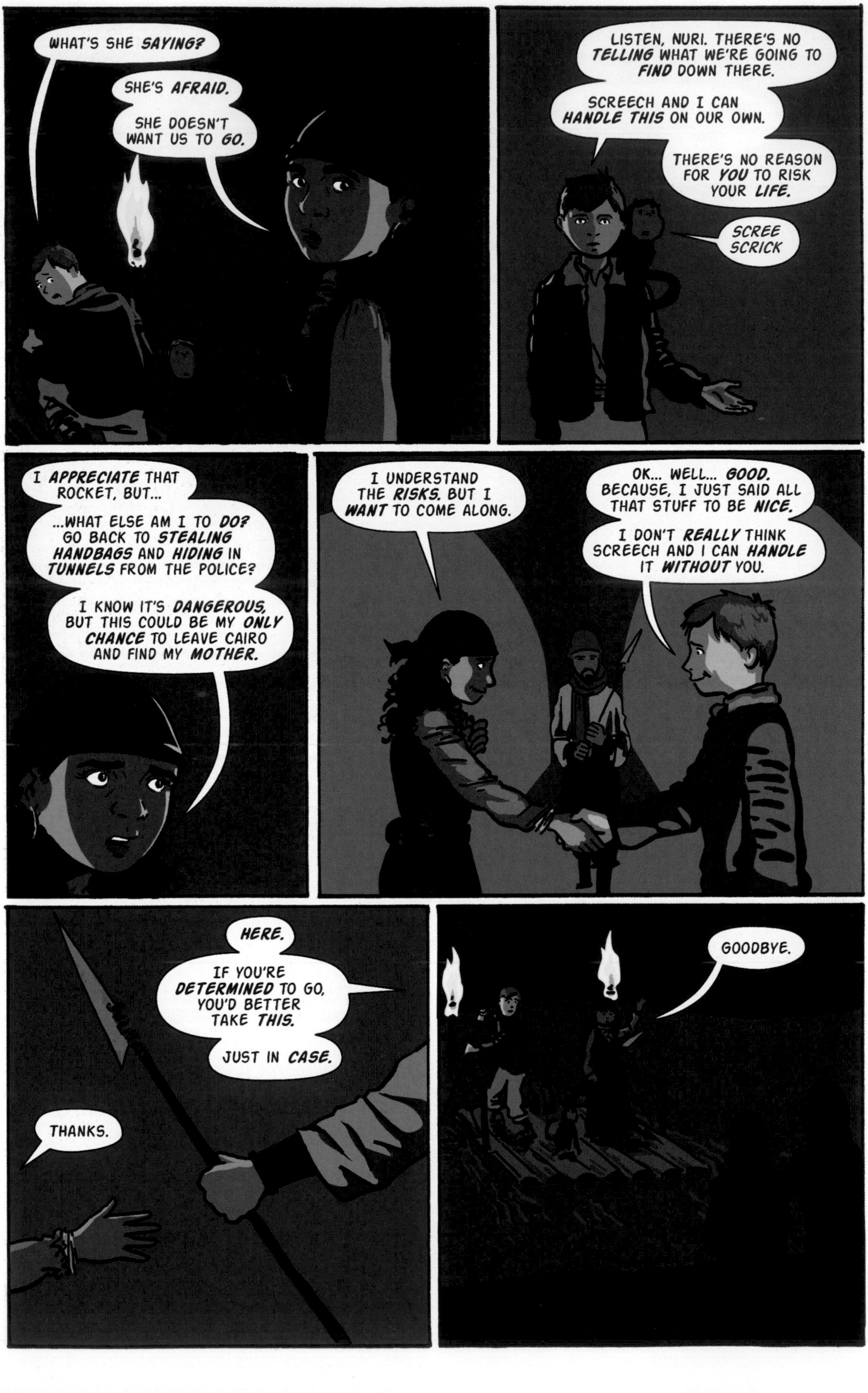
WHAT'S SHE SAYING?
SHE'S AFRAID.
SHE DOESN'T WANT US TO GO.
LISTEN, NURI. THERE'S NO TELLING WHAT WE'RE GOING TO FIND DOWN THERE.
SCREECH AND I CAN HANDLE THIS ON OUR OWN.
THERE'S NO REASON FOR YOU TO RISK YOUR LIFE.
SCREE SCRICK
I APPRECIATE THAT ROCKET, BUT...
...WHAT ELSE AM I TO DO? GO BACK TO STEALING HANDBAGS AND HIDING IN TUNNELS FROM THE POLICE?
I KNOW IT'S DANGEROUS, BUT THIS COULD BE MY ONLY CHANCE TO LEAVE CAIRO AND FIND MY MOTHER.
I UNDERSTAND THE RISKS. BUT I WANT TO COME ALONG.
OK... WELL... GOOD. BECAUSE, I JUST SAID ALL THAT STUFF TO BE NICE.
I DON'T REALLY THINK SCREECH AND I CAN HANDLE IT WITHOUT YOU.
HERE.
IF YOU'RE DETERMINED TO GO, YOU'D BETTER TAKE THIS.
JUST IN CASE.
THANKS.
GOODBYE.

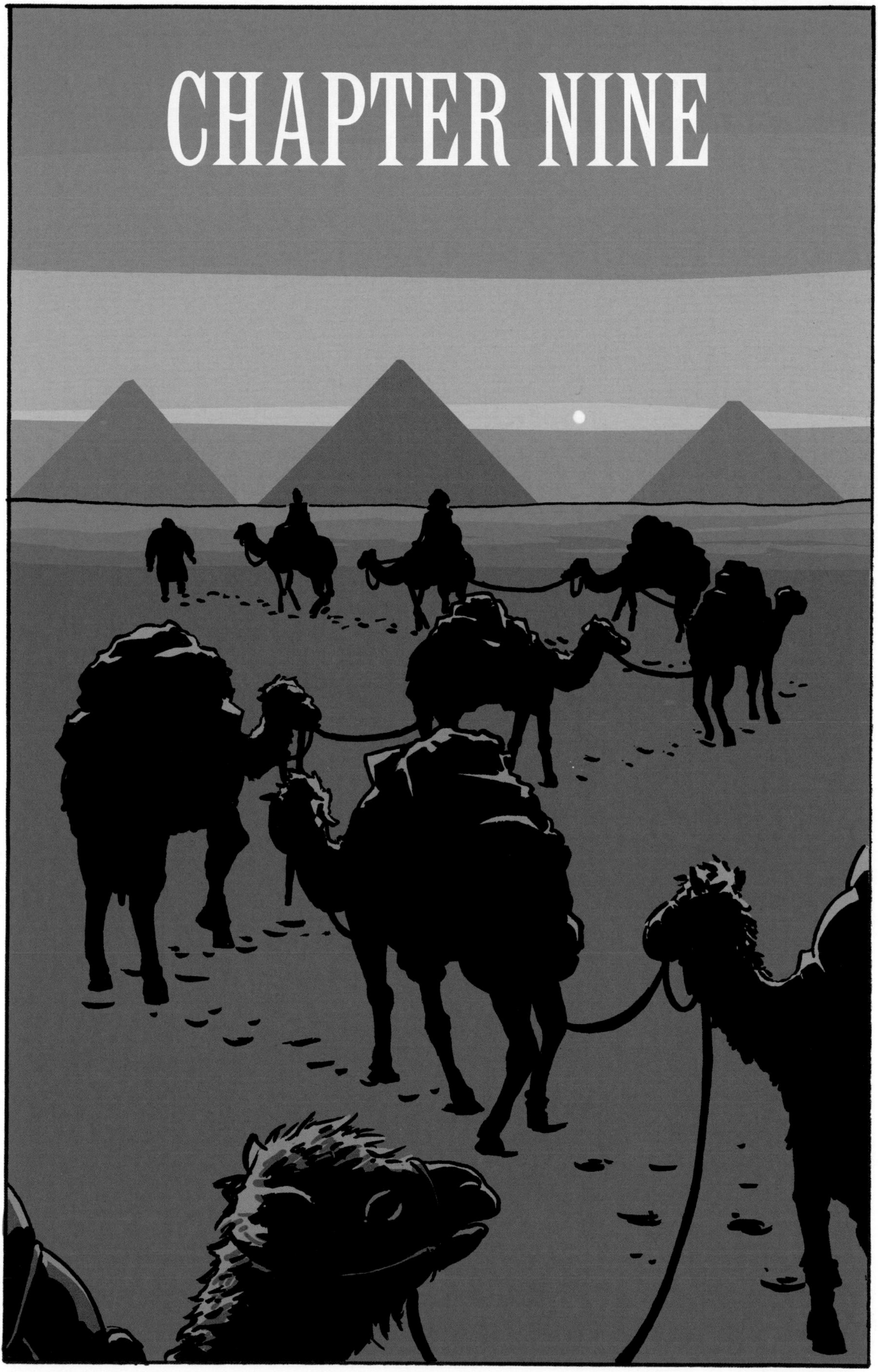
CHAPTER NINE

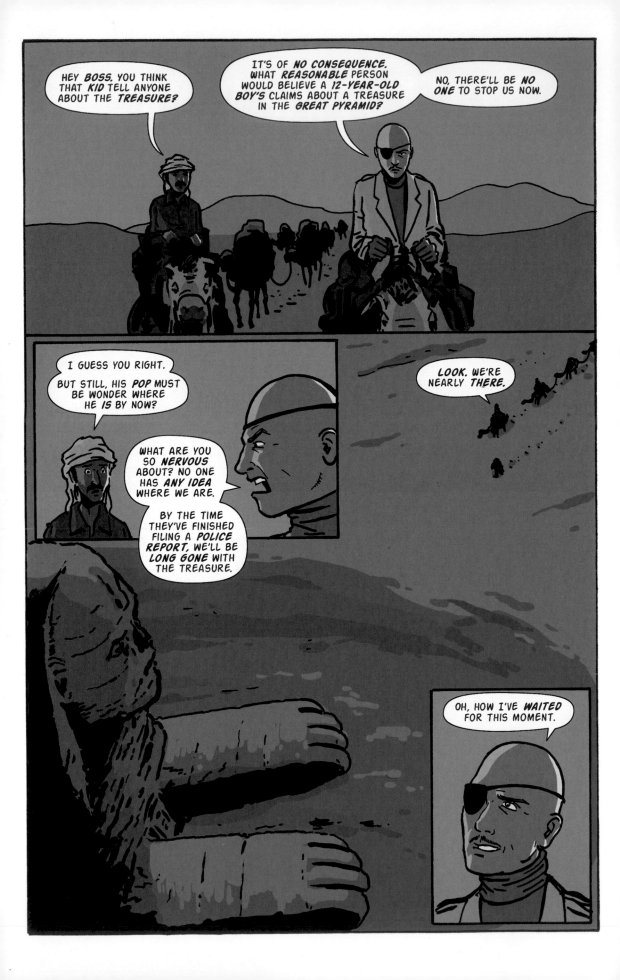

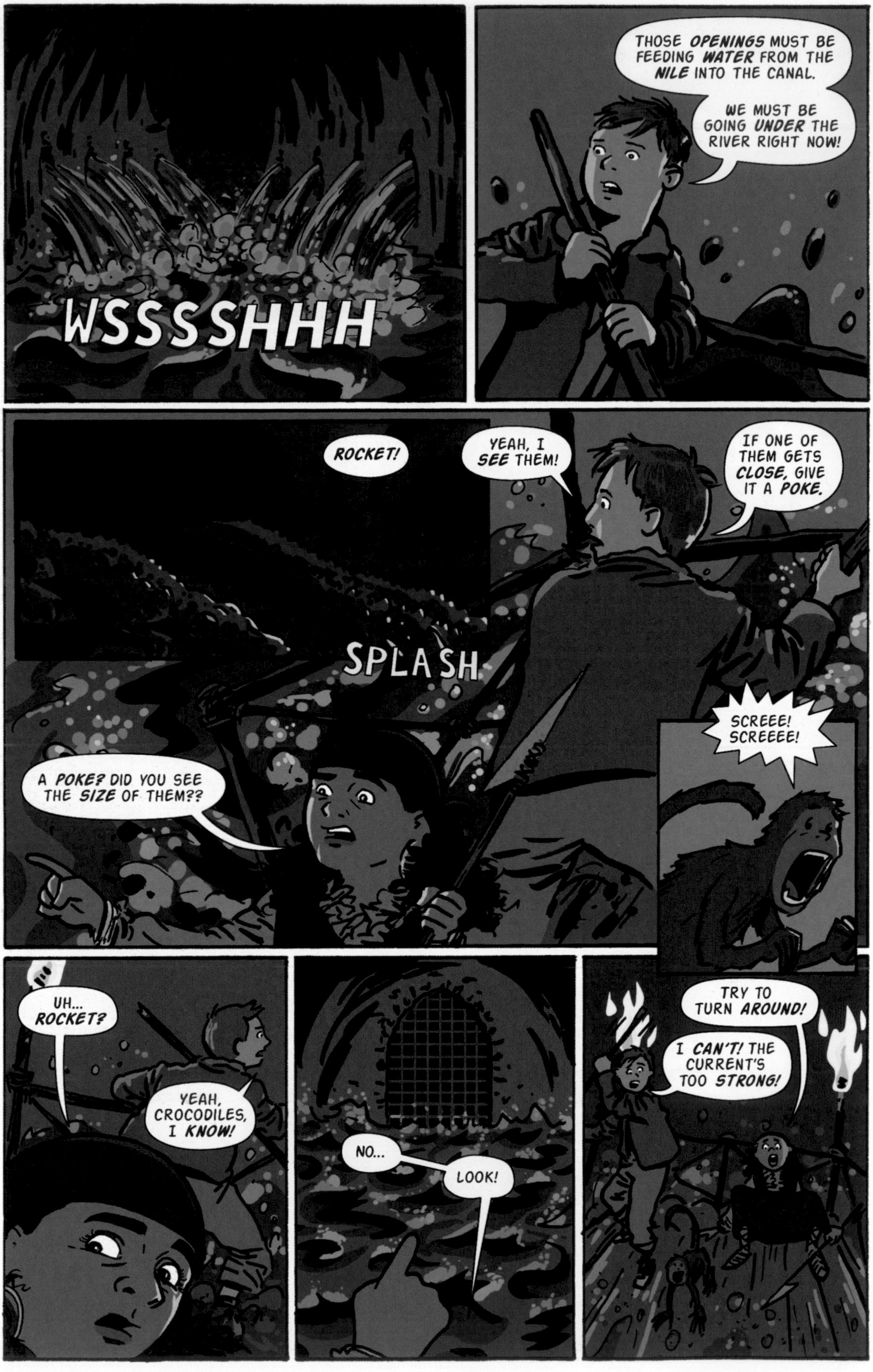
WSSSSHHH
THOSE OPENINGS MUST BE FEEDING WATER FROM THE NILE INTO THE CANAL.
WE MUST BE GOING UNDER THE RIVER RIGHT NOW!
ROCKET!
YEAH, I SEE THEM!
IF ONE OF THEM GETS CLOSE, GIVE IT A POKE.
SPLASH
A POKE? DID YOU SEE THE SIZE OF THEM??
SCREEE! SCREEEE!
UH... ROCKET?
YEAH, CROCODILES, I KNOW!
NO...
LOOK!
TRY TO TURN AROUND!
I CAN'T! THE CURRENT'S TOO STRONG!

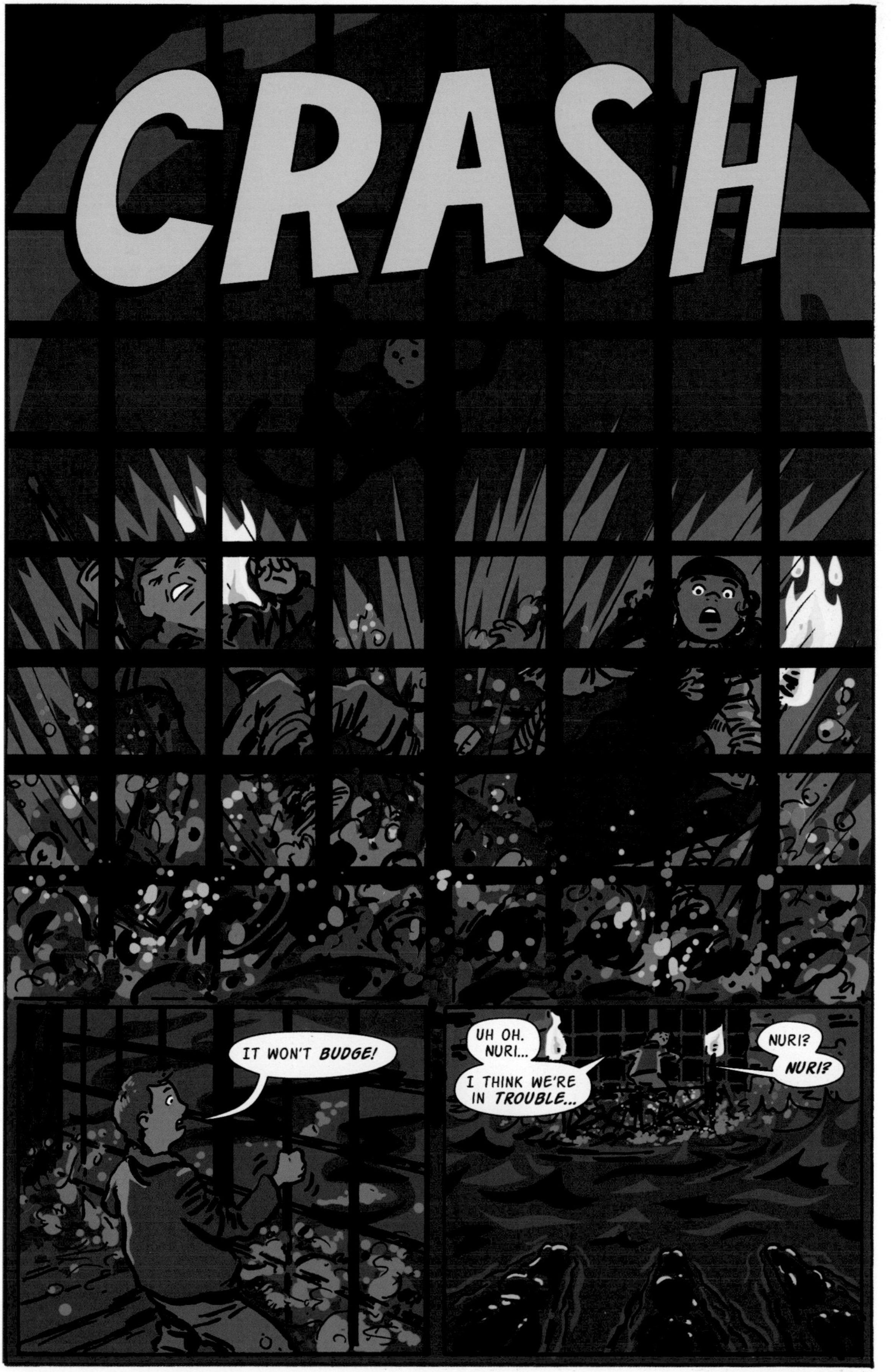
CRASH
IT WON'T *BUDGE!*
UH OH. NURI...
I THINK WE'RE IN *TROUBLE...*
NURI?
NURI?

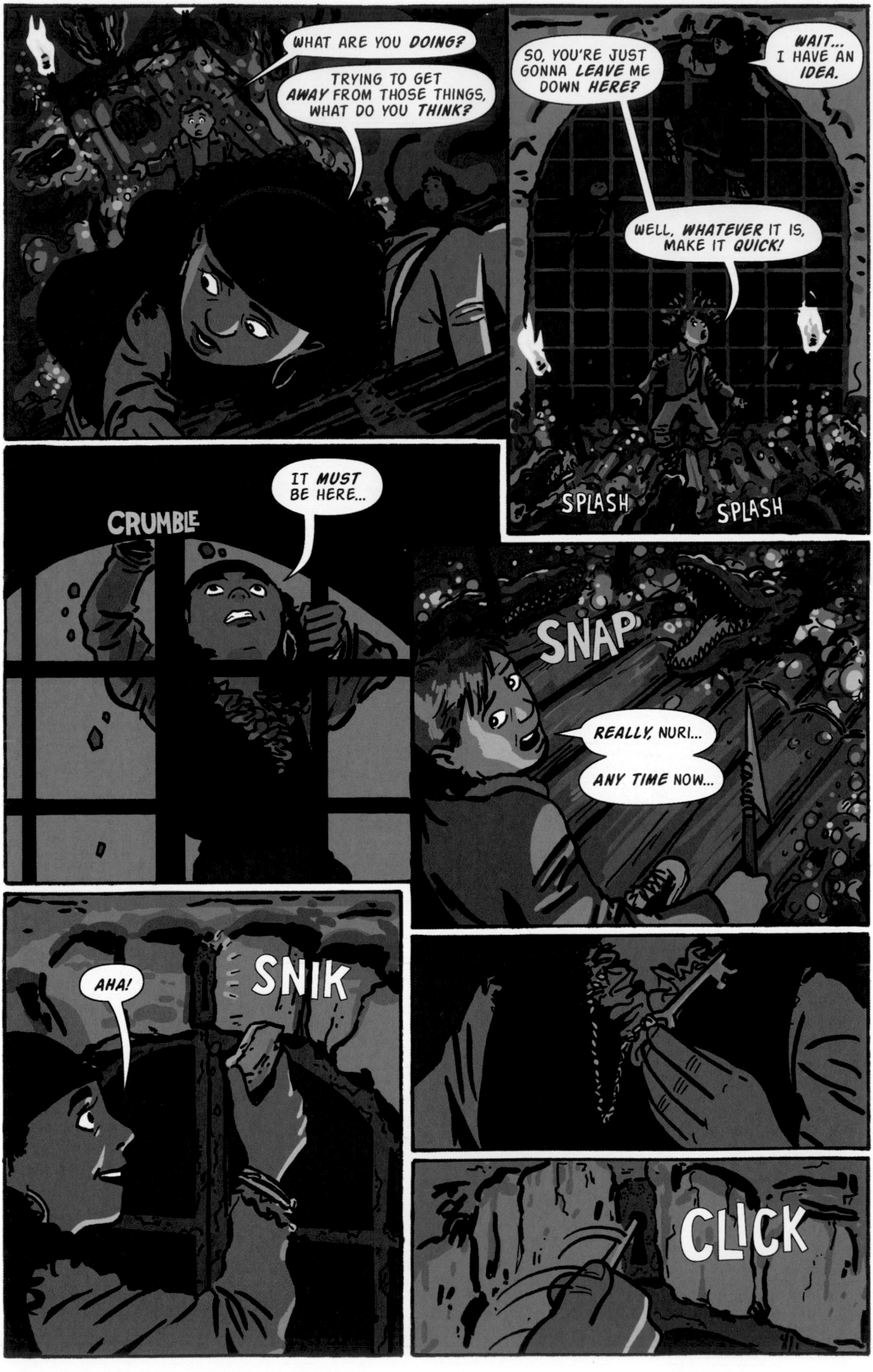
WHAT ARE YOU DOING?
TRYING TO GET AWAY FROM THOSE THINGS, WHAT DO YOU THINK?
SO, YOU'RE JUST GONNA LEAVE ME DOWN HERE?
WAIT... I HAVE AN IDEA.
WELL, WHATEVER IT IS, MAKE IT QUICK!
SPLASH
SPLASH
CRUMBLE
IT MUST BE HERE...
SNAP
REALLY, NURI...
ANY TIME NOW...
AHA!
SNIK
CLICK

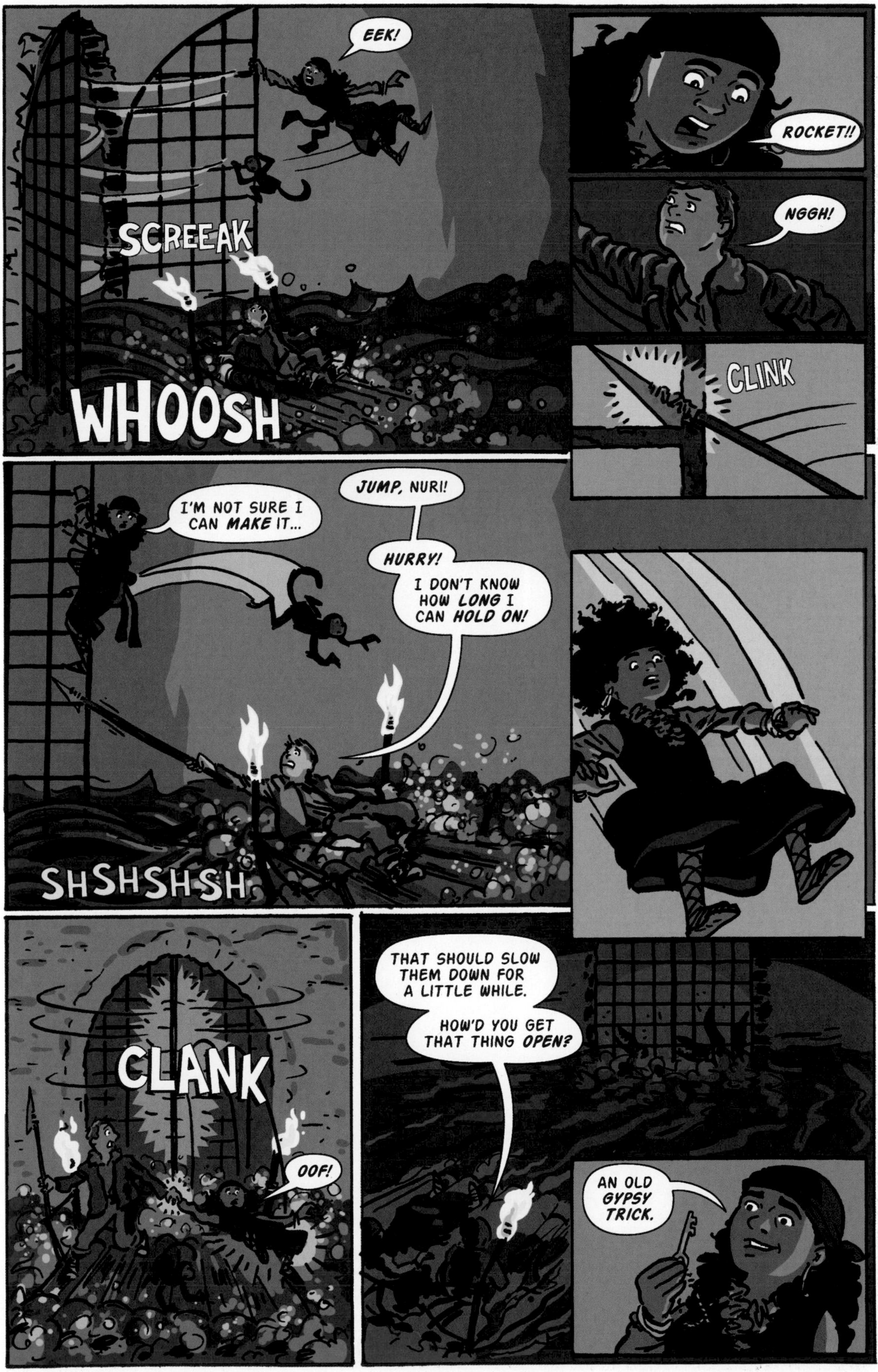
EEK!
SCREEAK
WHOOSH
ROCKET!!
NGGH!
CLINK
I'M NOT SURE I CAN MAKE IT...
JUMP, NURI!
HURRY!
I DON'T KNOW HOW LONG I CAN HOLD ON!
SHSHSHSH
CLANK
OOF!
THAT SHOULD SLOW THEM DOWN FOR A LITTLE WHILE.
HOW'D YOU GET THAT THING OPEN?
AN OLD GYPSY TRICK.

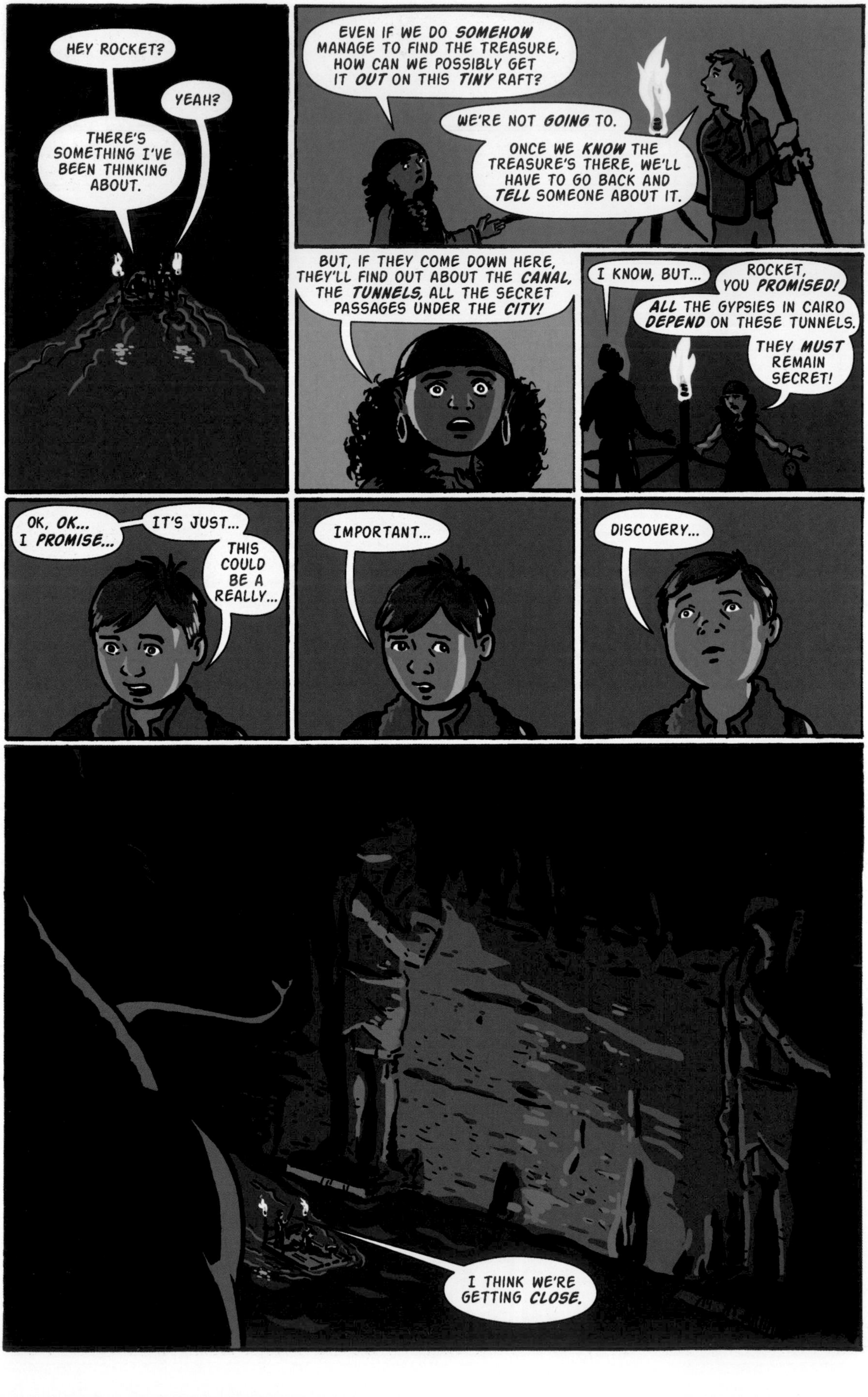
HEY ROCKET?
YEAH?
THERE'S SOMETHING I'VE BEEN THINKING ABOUT.
EVEN IF WE DO *SOMEHOW* MANAGE TO FIND THE TREASURE, HOW CAN WE POSSIBLY GET IT *OUT* ON THIS *TINY* RAFT?
WE'RE NOT *GOING* TO.
ONCE WE *KNOW* THE TREASURE'S THERE, WE'LL HAVE TO GO BACK AND *TELL* SOMEONE ABOUT IT.
BUT, IF THEY COME DOWN HERE, THEY'LL FIND OUT ABOUT THE *CANAL*, THE *TUNNELS*, ALL THE SECRET PASSAGES UNDER THE *CITY!*
I KNOW, BUT...
ROCKET, YOU *PROMISED!*
ALL THE GYPSIES IN CAIRO *DEPEND* ON THESE TUNNELS.
THEY *MUST* REMAIN SECRET!
OK, *OK...* I *PROMISE...*
IT'S JUST...
THIS COULD BE A REALLY...
IMPORTANT...
DISCOVERY...
I THINK WE'RE GETTING *CLOSE.*

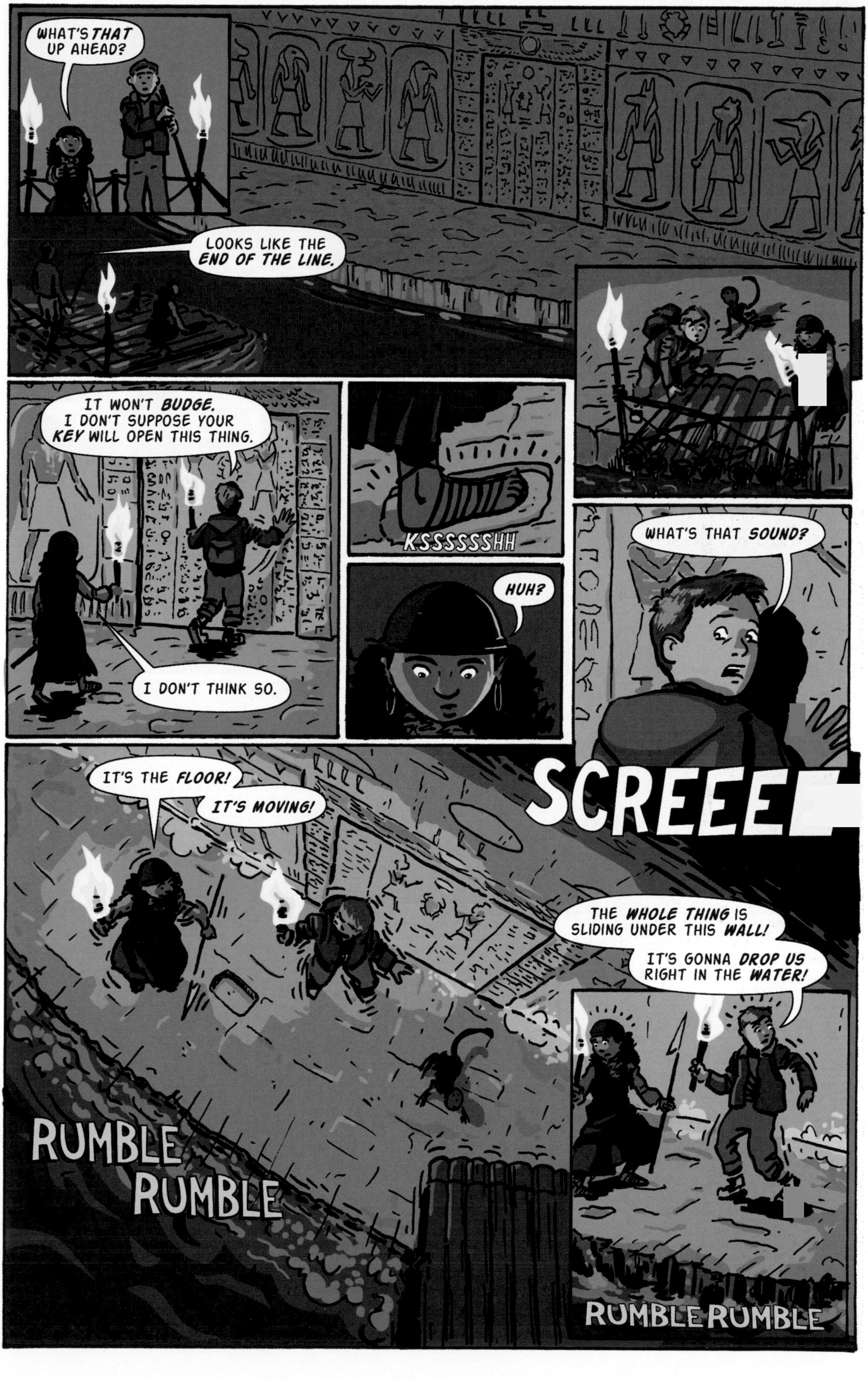

WHAT'S THAT UP AHEAD?
LOOKS LIKE THE END OF THE LINE.
IT WON'T BUDGE. I DON'T SUPPOSE YOUR KEY WILL OPEN THIS THING.
I DON'T THINK SO.
KSSSSSSHH
HUH?
WHAT'S THAT SOUND?
SCREEE
IT'S THE FLOOR!
IT'S MOVING!
THE WHOLE THING IS SLIDING UNDER THIS WALL!
IT'S GONNA DROP US RIGHT IN THE WATER!
RUMBLE RUMBLE
RUMBLE RUMBLE

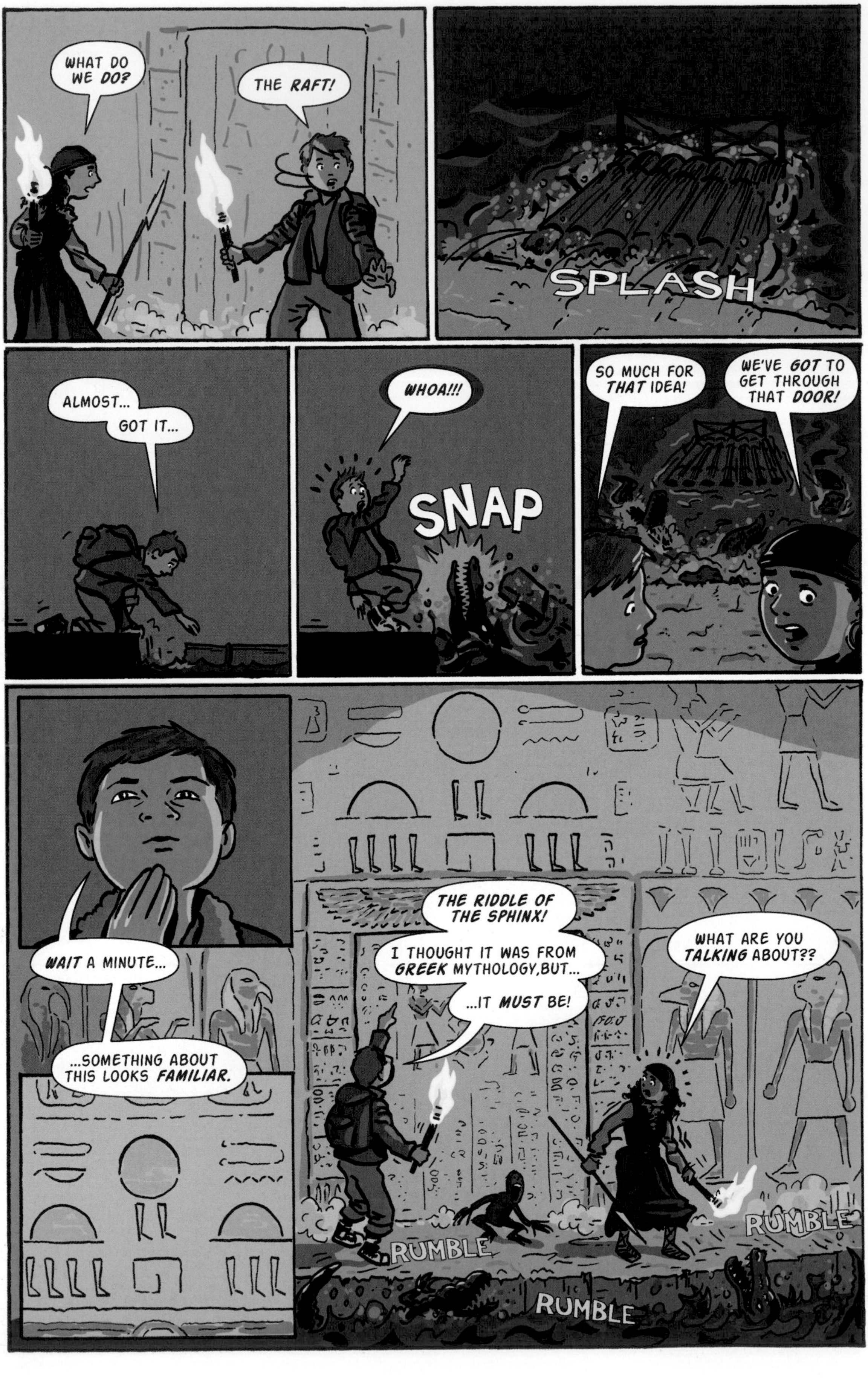
WHAT DO WE *DO?*
THE *RAFT!*
SPLASH
ALMOST... GOT IT...
WHOA!!!
SNAP
SO MUCH FOR *THAT* IDEA!
WE'VE *GOT* TO GET THROUGH THAT *DOOR!*
WAIT A MINUTE...
...SOMETHING ABOUT THIS LOOKS *FAMILIAR.*
THE RIDDLE OF THE SPHINX!
I THOUGHT IT WAS FROM *GREEK* MYTHOLOGY,BUT...
...IT *MUST* BE!
WHAT ARE YOU *TALKING* ABOUT??
RUMBLE
RUMBLE
RUMBLE

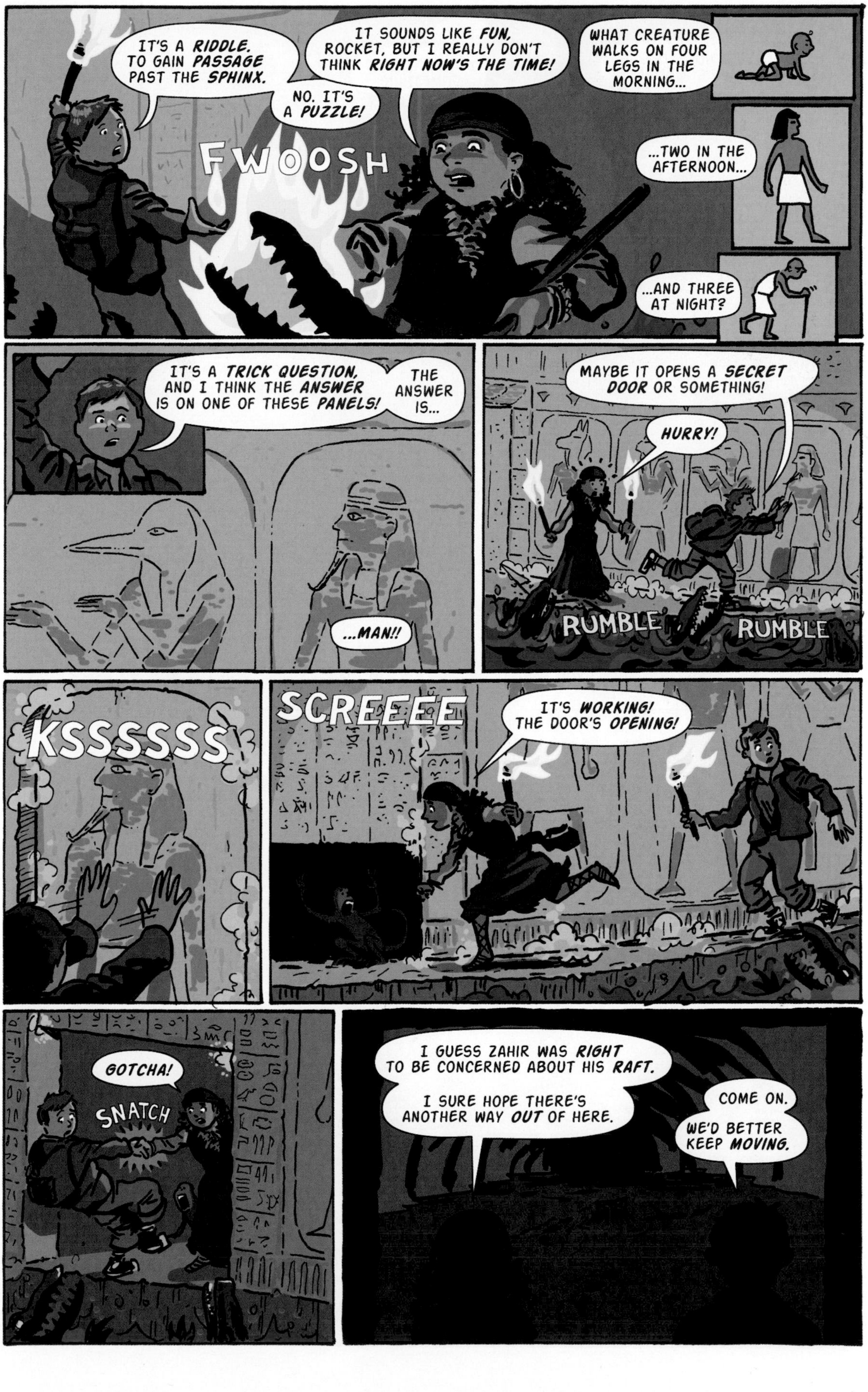
IT'S A RIDDLE. TO GAIN PASSAGE PAST THE SPHINX.
IT SOUNDS LIKE FUN, ROCKET, BUT I REALLY DON'T THINK RIGHT NOW'S THE TIME!
NO. IT'S A PUZZLE!
FWOOSH
WHAT CREATURE WALKS ON FOUR LEGS IN THE MORNING...
...TWO IN THE AFTERNOON...
...AND THREE AT NIGHT?
IT'S A TRICK QUESTION, AND I THINK THE ANSWER IS ON ONE OF THESE PANELS!
THE ANSWER IS...
...MAN!!
MAYBE IT OPENS A SECRET DOOR OR SOMETHING!
HURRY!
RUMBLE
RUMBLE
KSSSSSS
SCREEEE
IT'S WORKING! THE DOOR'S OPENING!
GOTCHA!
SNATCH
I GUESS ZAHIR WAS RIGHT TO BE CONCERNED ABOUT HIS RAFT.
I SURE HOPE THERE'S ANOTHER WAY OUT OF HERE.
COME ON.
WE'D BETTER KEEP MOVING.

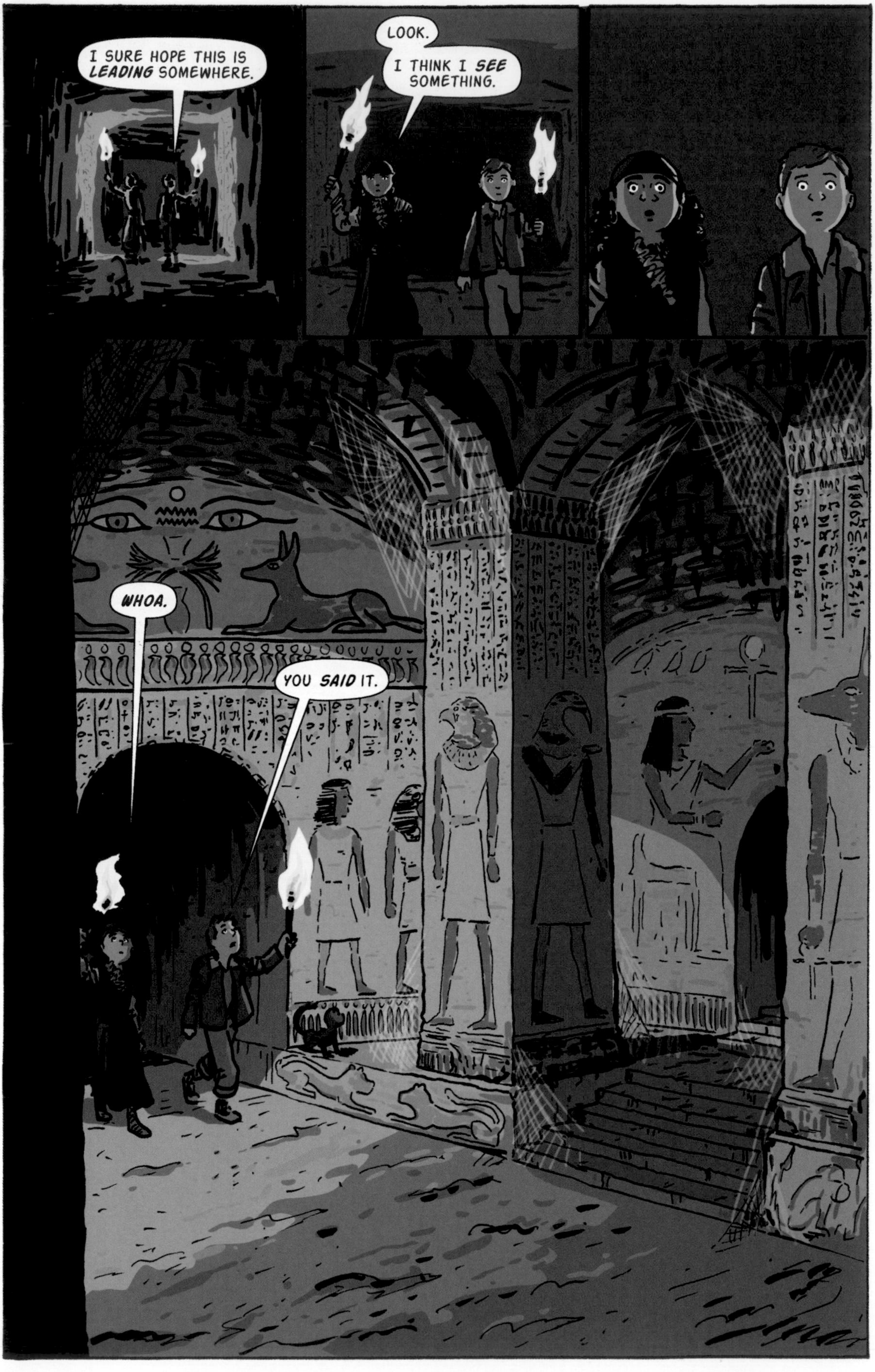
I SURE HOPE THIS IS *LEADING* SOMEWHERE.
LOOK.
I THINK I *SEE* SOMETHING.
WHOA.
YOU *SAID* IT.

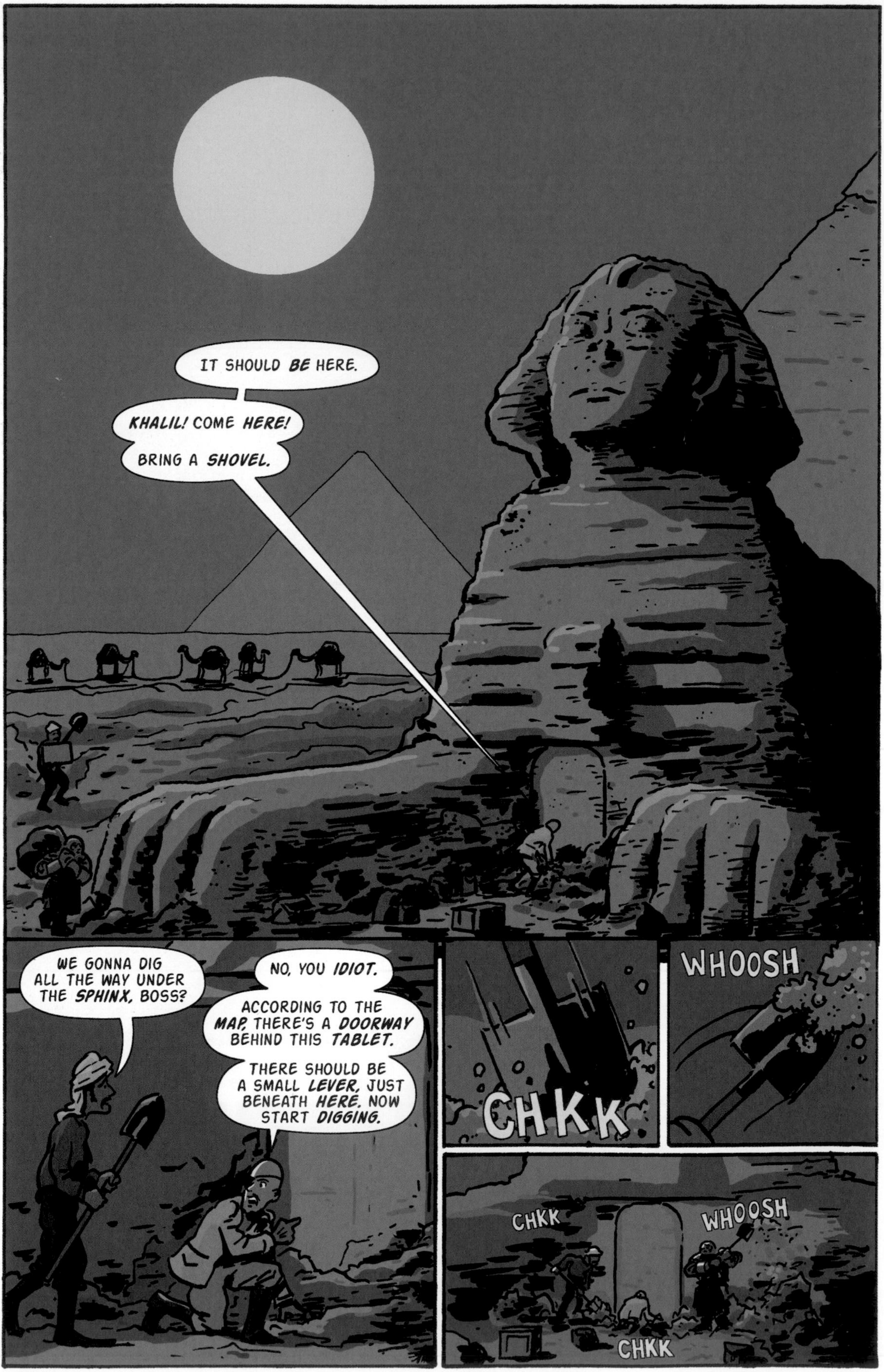

IT SHOULD *BE* HERE.
KHALIL! COME ***HERE!***
BRING A ***SHOVEL.***
WE GONNA DIG ALL THE WAY UNDER THE *SPHINX,* BOSS?
NO, YOU *IDIOT.*
ACCORDING TO THE *MAP,* THERE'S A *DOORWAY* BEHIND THIS *TABLET.*
THERE SHOULD BE A SMALL *LEVER,* JUST BENEATH *HERE.* NOW START *DIGGING.*
CHKK
WHOOSH
CHKK
WHOOSH
CHKK

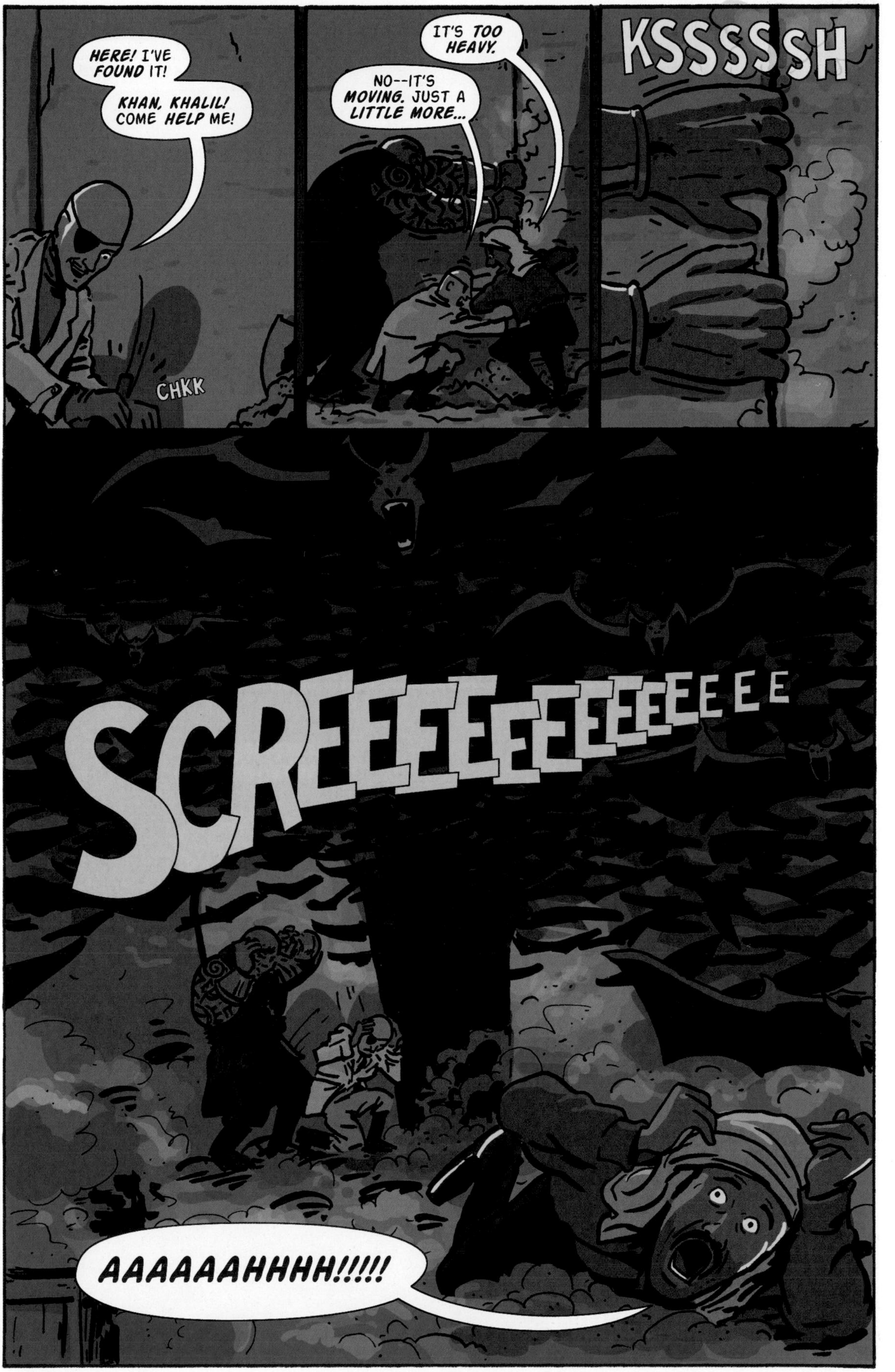
HERE! I'VE FOUND IT!
KHAN, KHALIL! COME HELP ME!
CHKK
IT'S TOO HEAVY.
NO--IT'S MOVING. JUST A LITTLE MORE...
KSSSSSH
SCREEEEEEEEEEEEE
AAAAAAHHHH!!!!!

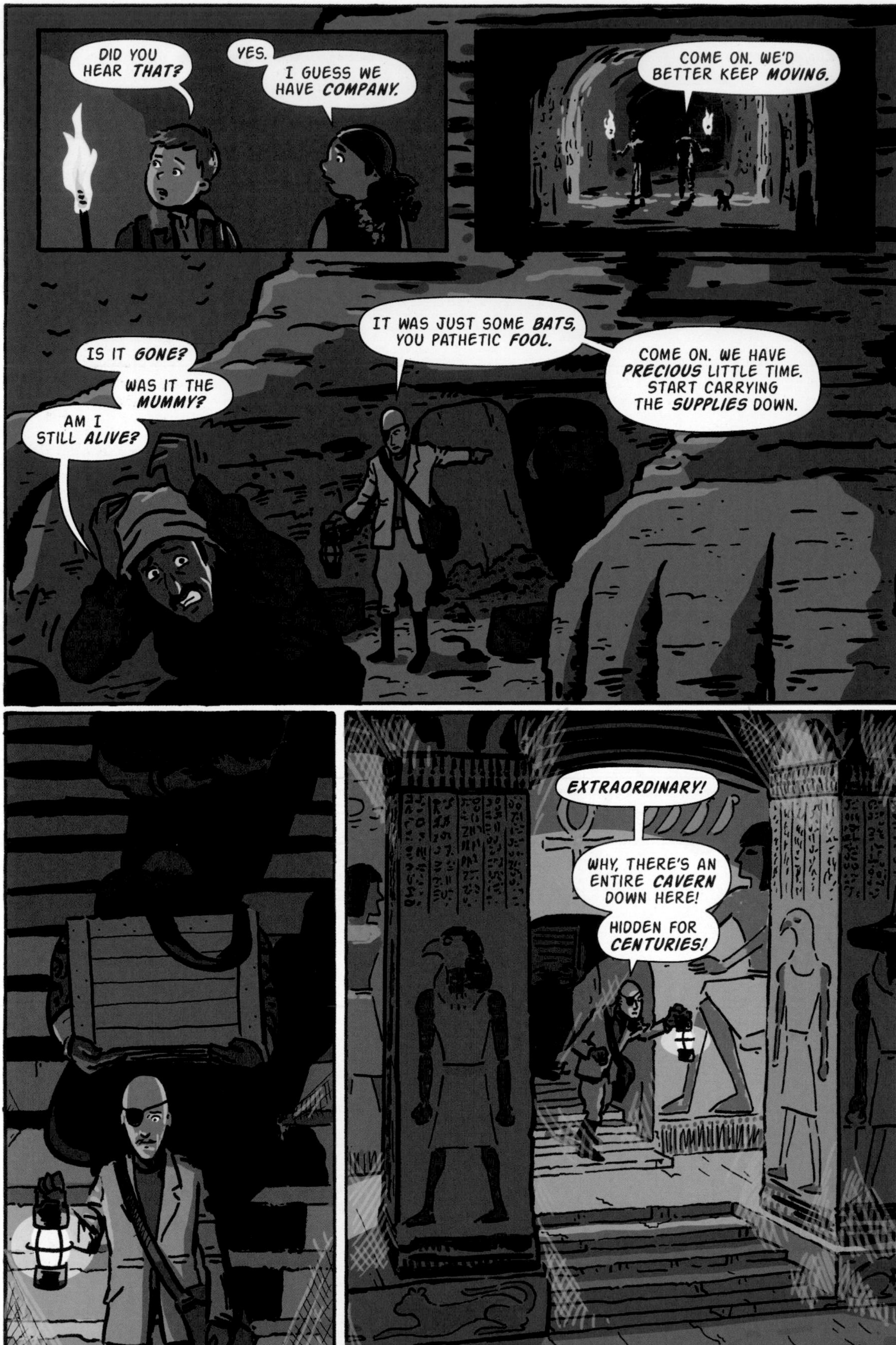
DID YOU HEAR *THAT?*
YES.
I GUESS WE HAVE *COMPANY.*
COME ON. WE'D BETTER KEEP *MOVING.*
IS IT *GONE?*
WAS IT THE *MUMMY?*
AM I STILL *ALIVE?*
IT WAS JUST SOME *BATS,* YOU PATHETIC *FOOL.*
COME ON. WE HAVE *PRECIOUS* LITTLE TIME. START CARRYING THE *SUPPLIES* DOWN.
EXTRAORDINARY!
WHY, THERE'S AN ENTIRE *CAVERN* DOWN HERE!
HIDDEN FOR *CENTURIES!*

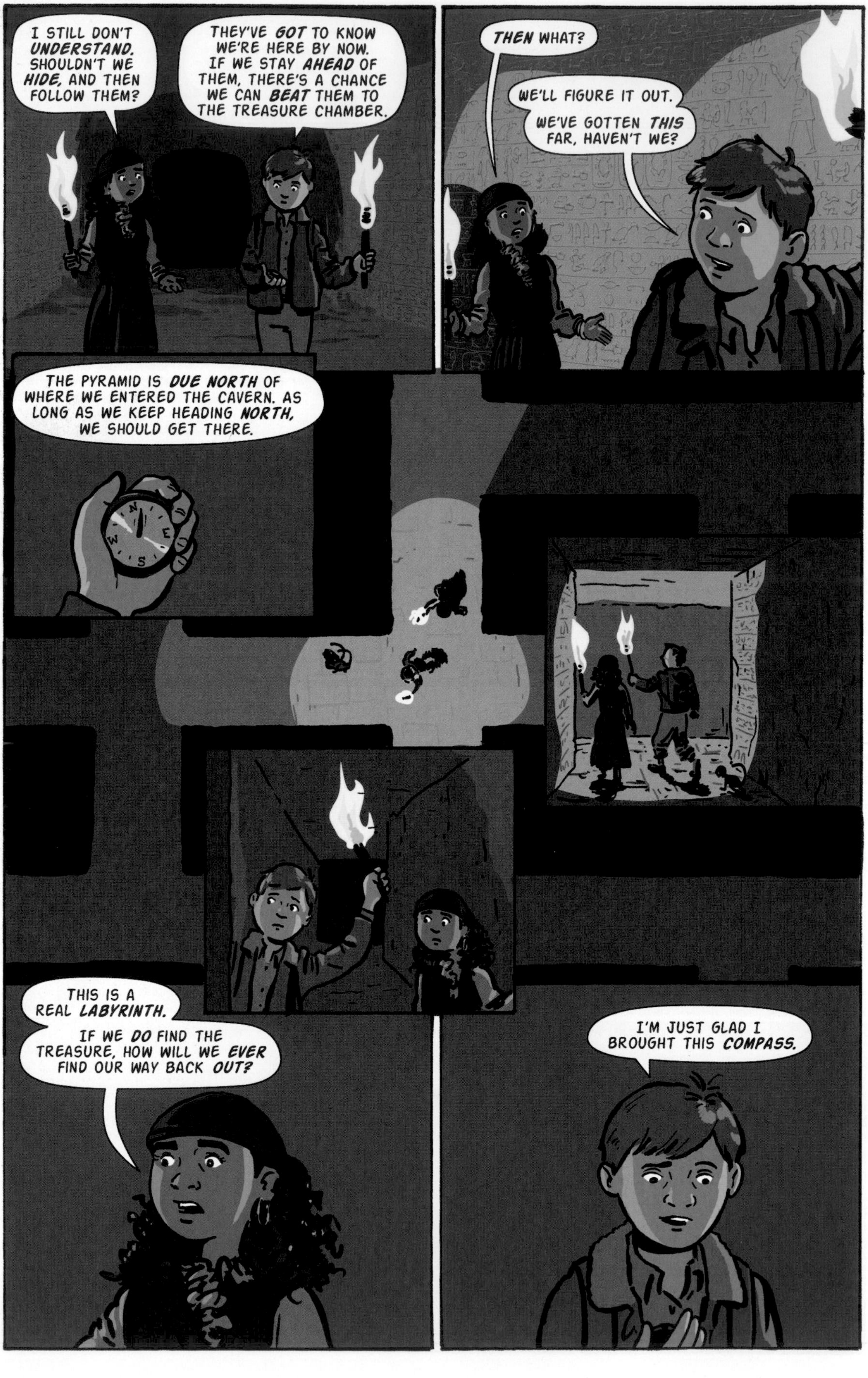
I STILL DON'T *UNDERSTAND.* SHOULDN'T WE *HIDE,* AND THEN FOLLOW THEM?
THEY'VE *GOT* TO KNOW WE'RE HERE BY NOW. IF WE STAY *AHEAD* OF THEM, THERE'S A CHANCE WE CAN *BEAT* THEM TO THE TREASURE CHAMBER.
THEN WHAT?
WE'LL FIGURE IT OUT.
WE'VE GOTTEN *THIS* FAR, HAVEN'T WE?
THE PYRAMID IS *DUE NORTH* OF WHERE WE ENTERED THE CAVERN. AS LONG AS WE KEEP HEADING *NORTH,* WE SHOULD GET THERE.
N
E
S
W
THIS IS A REAL *LABYRINTH.*
IF WE *DO* FIND THE TREASURE, HOW WILL WE *EVER* FIND OUR WAY BACK *OUT?*
I'M JUST GLAD I BROUGHT THIS *COMPASS.*

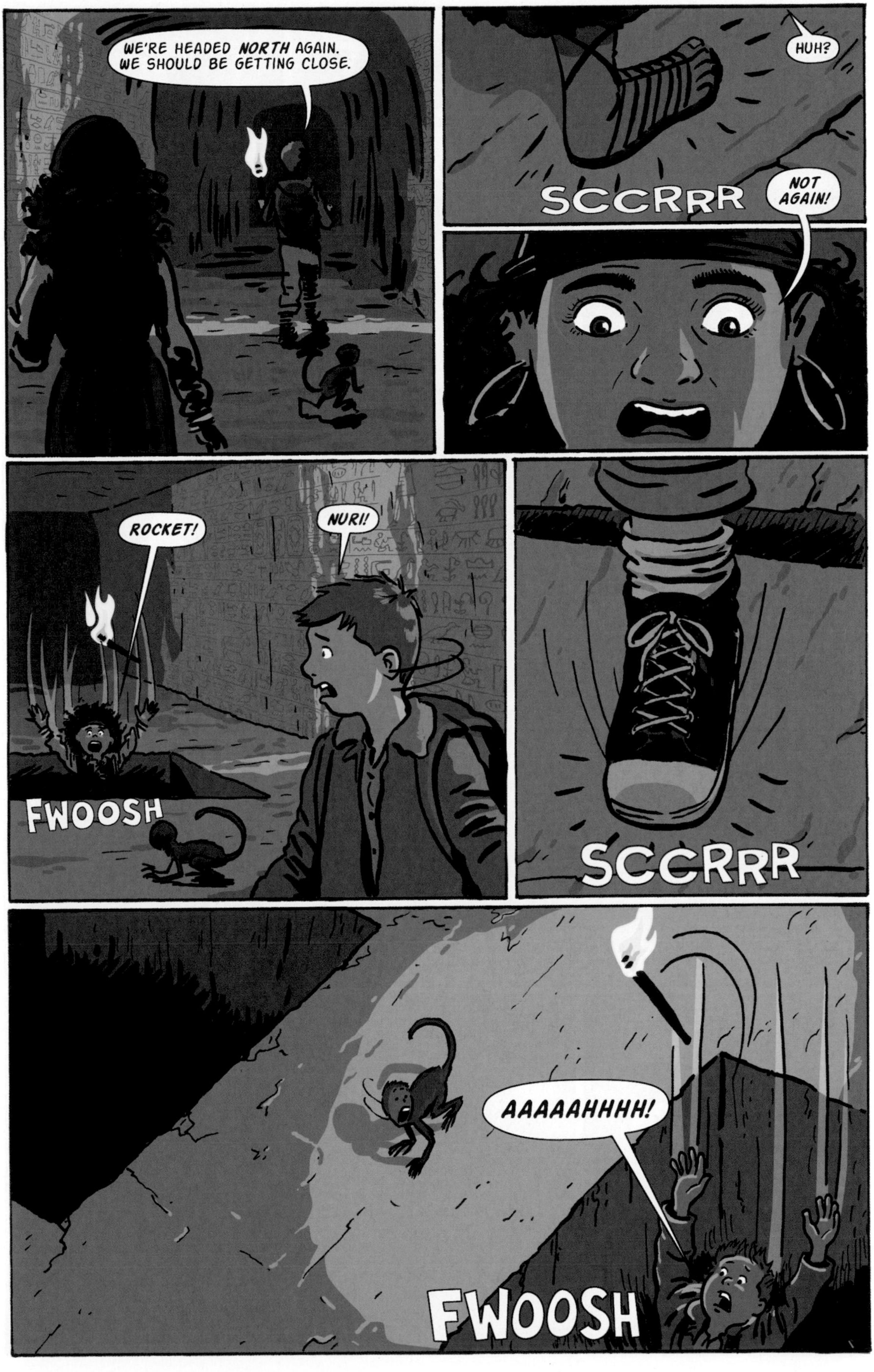

WE'RE HEADED NORTH AGAIN. WE SHOULD BE GETTING CLOSE.
HUH?
SCCRRR
NOT AGAIN!
ROCKET!
NURI!
FWOOSH
SCCRRR
AAAAAHHHH!
FWOOSH

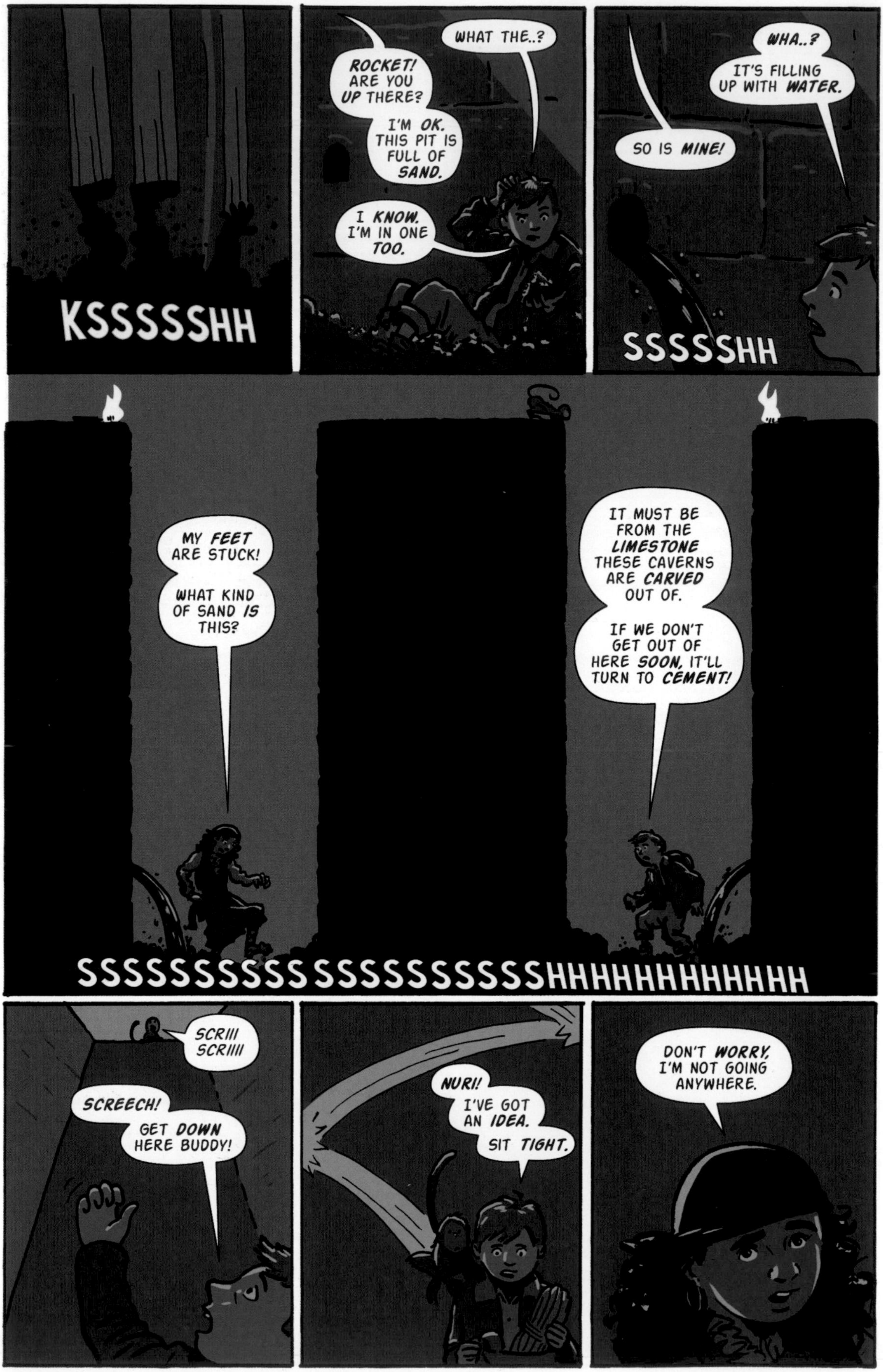

KSSSSSHH
ROCKET! ARE YOU UP THERE?
WHAT THE..?
I'M OK. THIS PIT IS FULL OF SAND.
I KNOW. I'M IN ONE TOO.
WHA..?
IT'S FILLING UP WITH WATER.
SO IS MINE!
SSSSSHH
MY FEET ARE STUCK!
WHAT KIND OF SAND IS THIS?
IT MUST BE FROM THE LIMESTONE THESE CAVERNS ARE CARVED OUT OF.
IF WE DON'T GET OUT OF HERE SOON, IT'LL TURN TO CEMENT!
SSSSSSSSSSSSSSSSSSSSSSSSHHHHHHHHHHHHHH
SCRIII SCRIIII
SCREECH!
GET DOWN HERE BUDDY!
NURI!
I'VE GOT AN IDEA.
SIT TIGHT.
DON'T WORRY, I'M NOT GOING ANYWHERE.

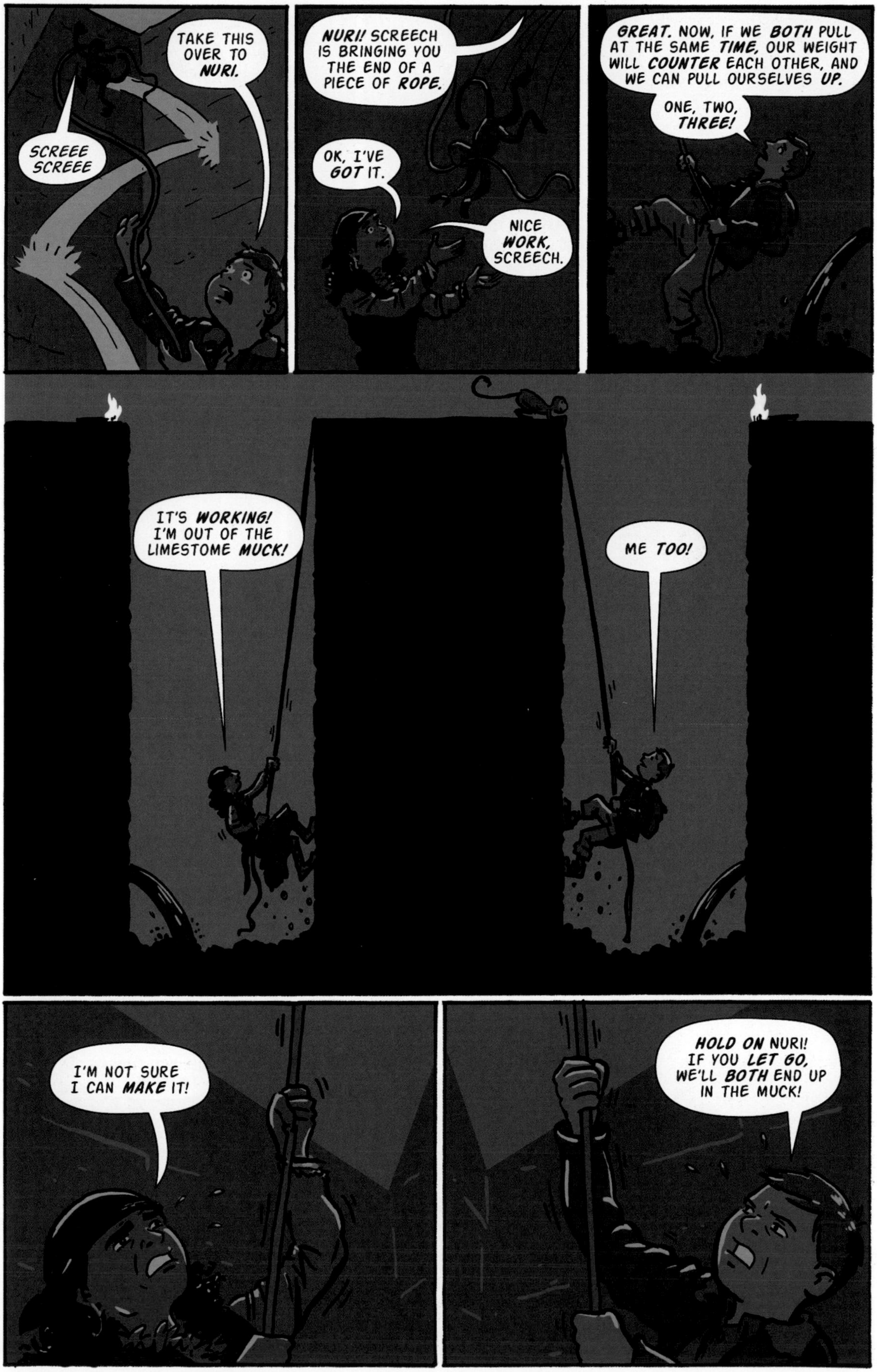
TAKE THIS OVER TO NURI.
SCREEE SCREEE
NURI! SCREECH IS BRINGING YOU THE END OF A PIECE OF ROPE.
OK, I'VE GOT IT.
NICE WORK, SCREECH.
GREAT. NOW, IF WE BOTH PULL AT THE SAME TIME, OUR WEIGHT WILL COUNTER EACH OTHER, AND WE CAN PULL OURSELVES UP.
ONE, TWO, THREE!
IT'S WORKING! I'M OUT OF THE LIMESTOME MUCK!
ME TOO!
I'M NOT SURE I CAN MAKE IT!
HOLD ON NURI! IF YOU LET GO, WE'LL BOTH END UP IN THE MUCK!

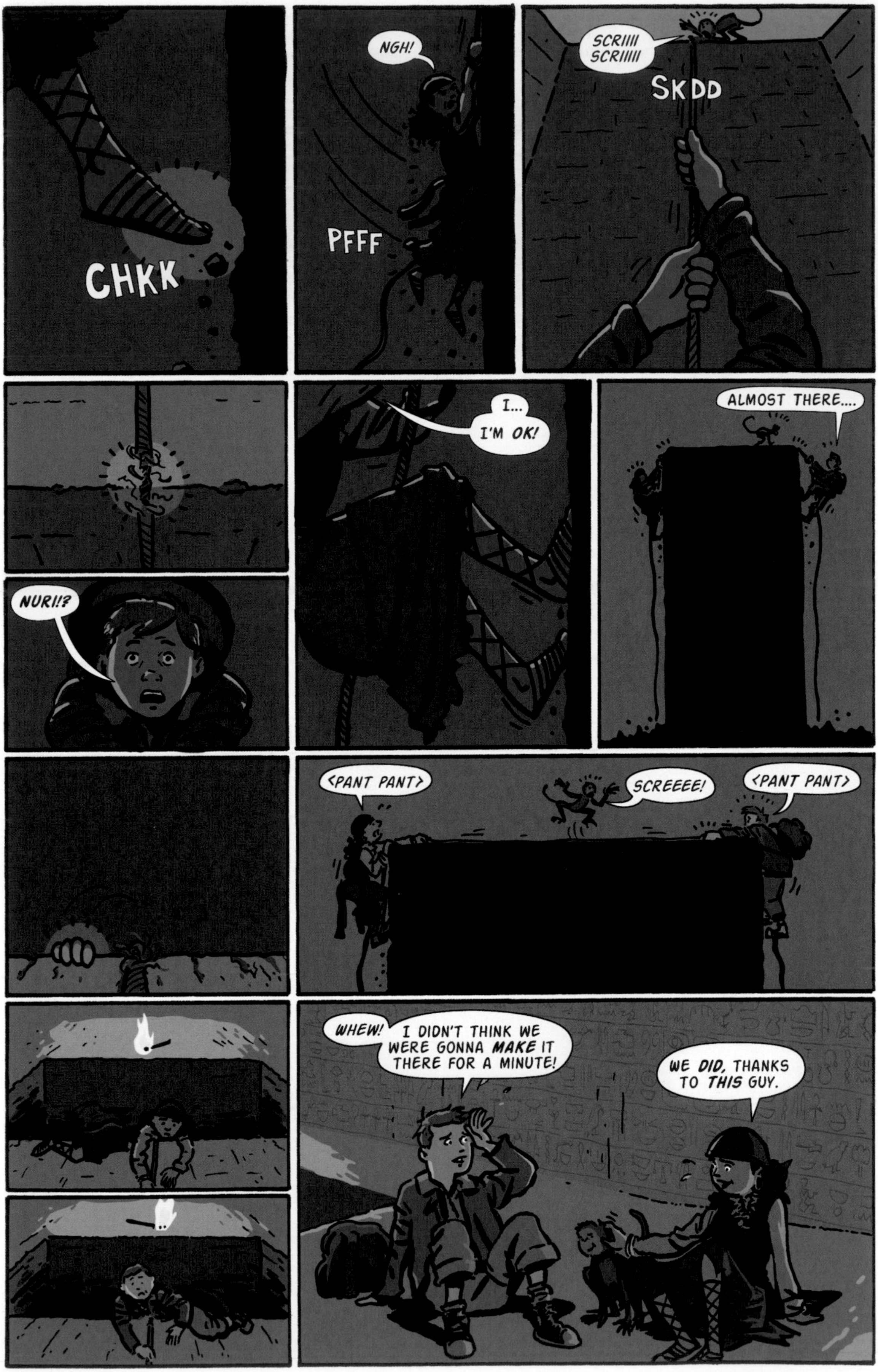
CHKK
NGH!
PFFF
SCRIIII SCRIIIII
SKDD
I... I'M OK!
NURI!?
ALMOST THERE....
<PANT PANT>
SCREEEE!
<PANT PANT>
WHEW!
I DIDN'T THINK WE WERE GONNA MAKE IT THERE FOR A MINUTE!
WE DID, THANKS TO THIS GUY.

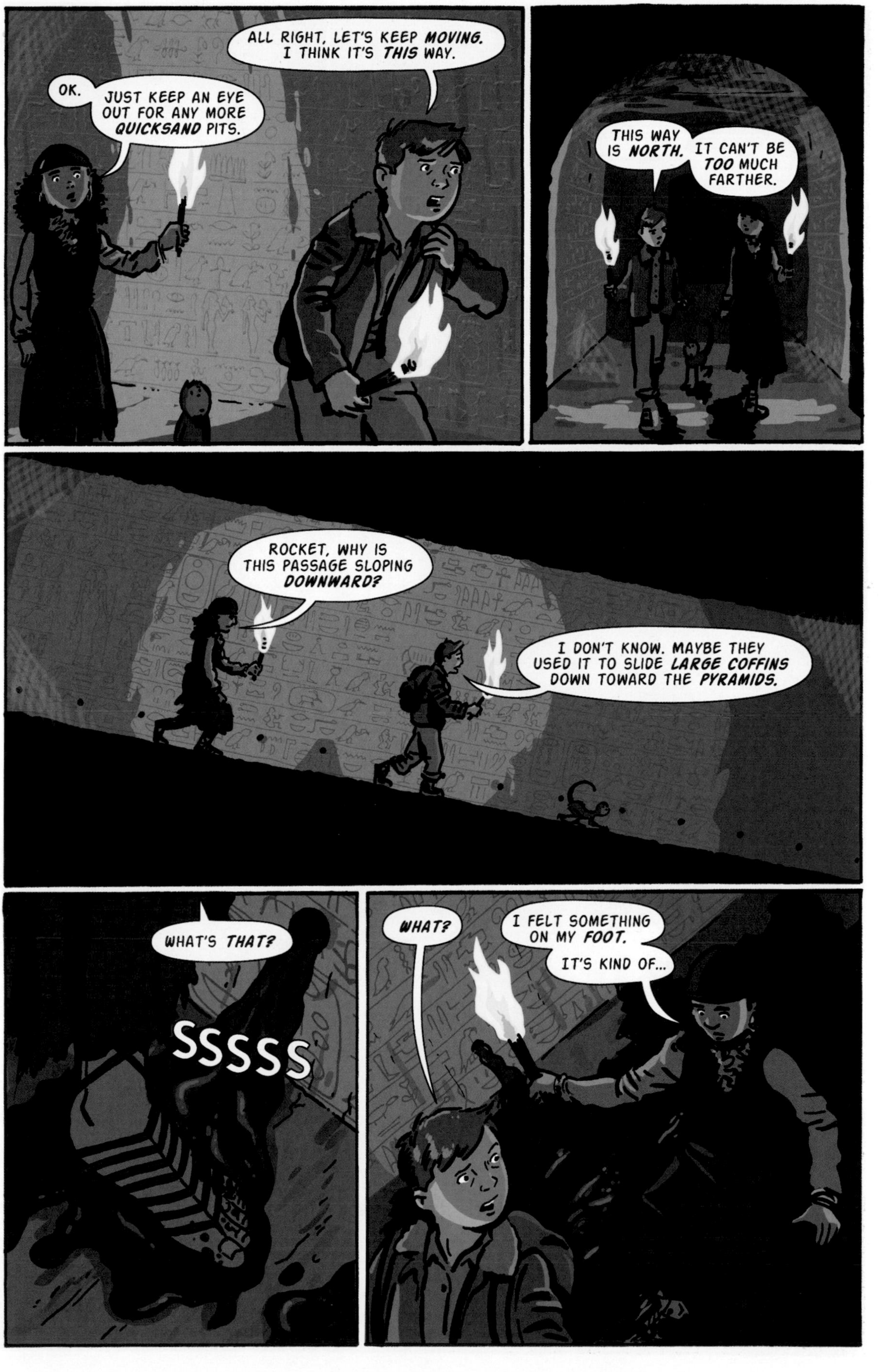
ALL RIGHT, LET'S KEEP *MOVING.* I THINK IT'S *THIS* WAY.
OK.
JUST KEEP AN EYE OUT FOR ANY MORE *QUICKSAND* PITS.
THIS WAY IS *NORTH.*
IT CAN'T BE *TOO* MUCH FARTHER.
ROCKET, WHY IS THIS PASSAGE SLOPING *DOWNWARD?*
I DON'T KNOW. MAYBE THEY USED IT TO SLIDE *LARGE COFFINS* DOWN TOWARD THE *PYRAMIDS.*
WHAT'S *THAT?*
SSSSS
WHAT?
I FELT SOMETHING ON MY *FOOT.*
IT'S KIND OF...

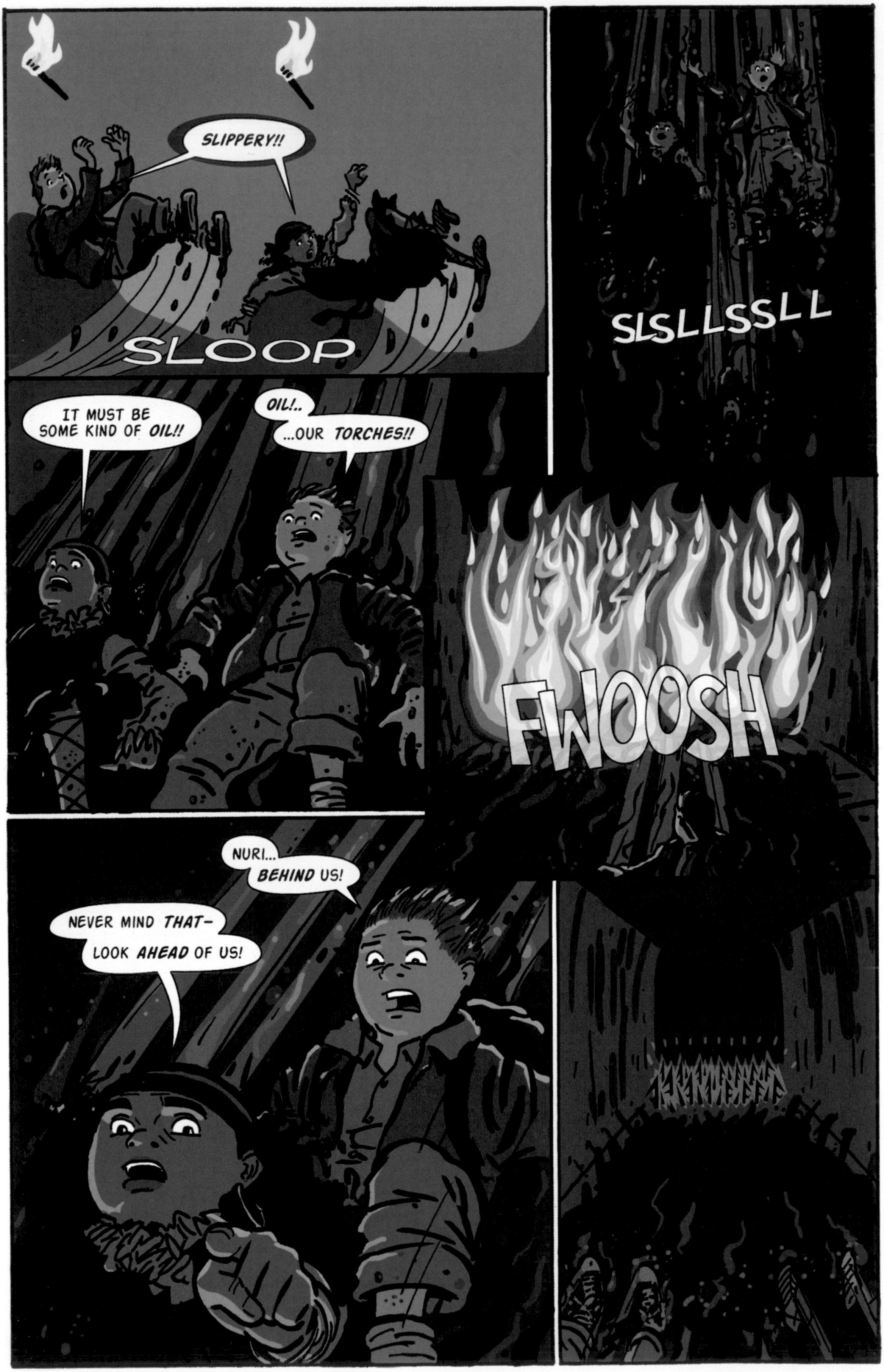

SLIPPERY!!
SLOOP
SLSLLLSSLL
IT MUST BE SOME KIND OF OIL!!
OIL!.. ...OUR TORCHES!!
FWOOSH
NURI... BEHIND US!
NEVER MIND THAT— LOOK AHEAD OF US!

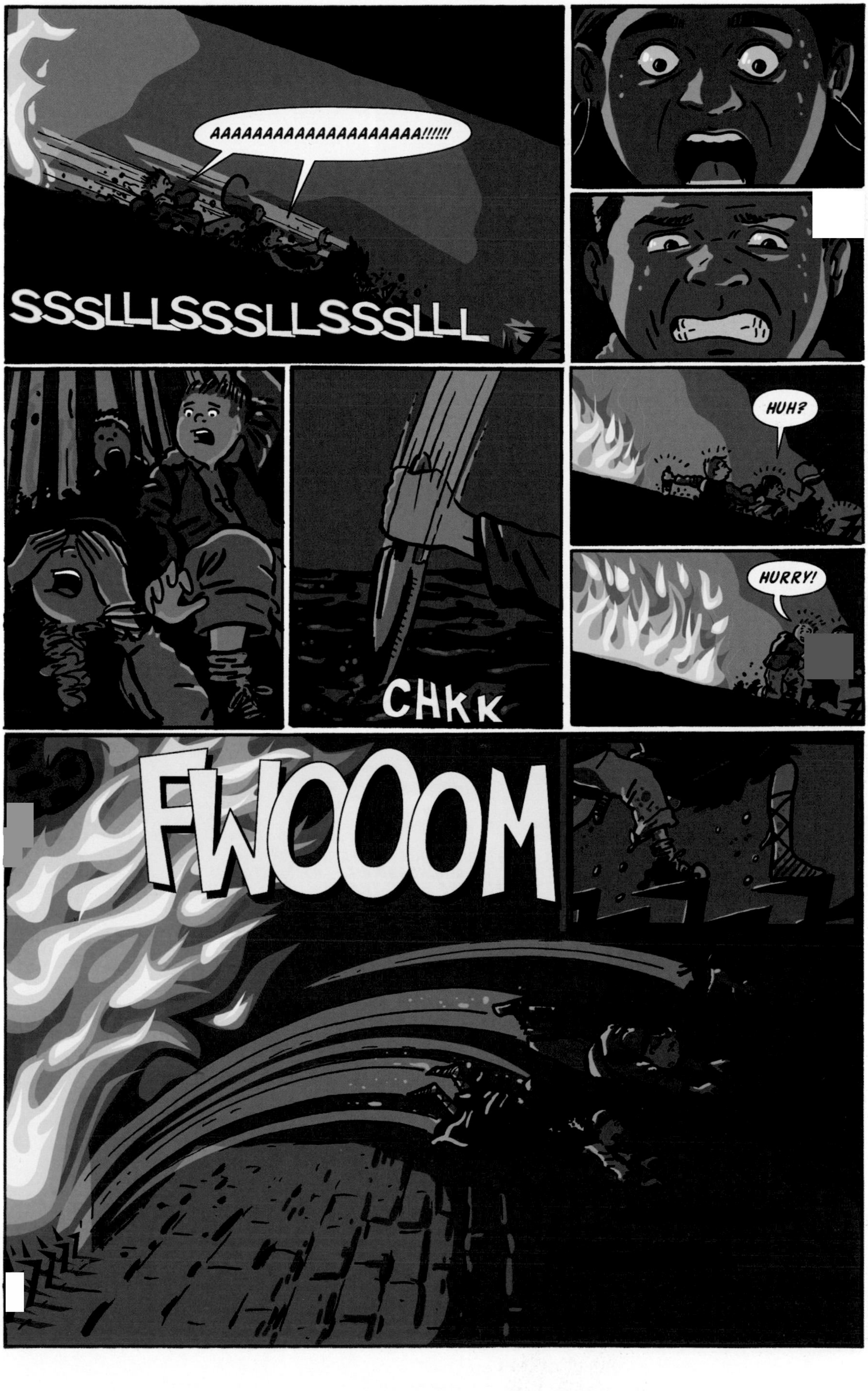
AAAAAAAAAAAAAAAAAAAA!!!!!!
SSSLLLSSSSLLSSSLLL
CHKK
HUH?
HURRY!
FWOOOM

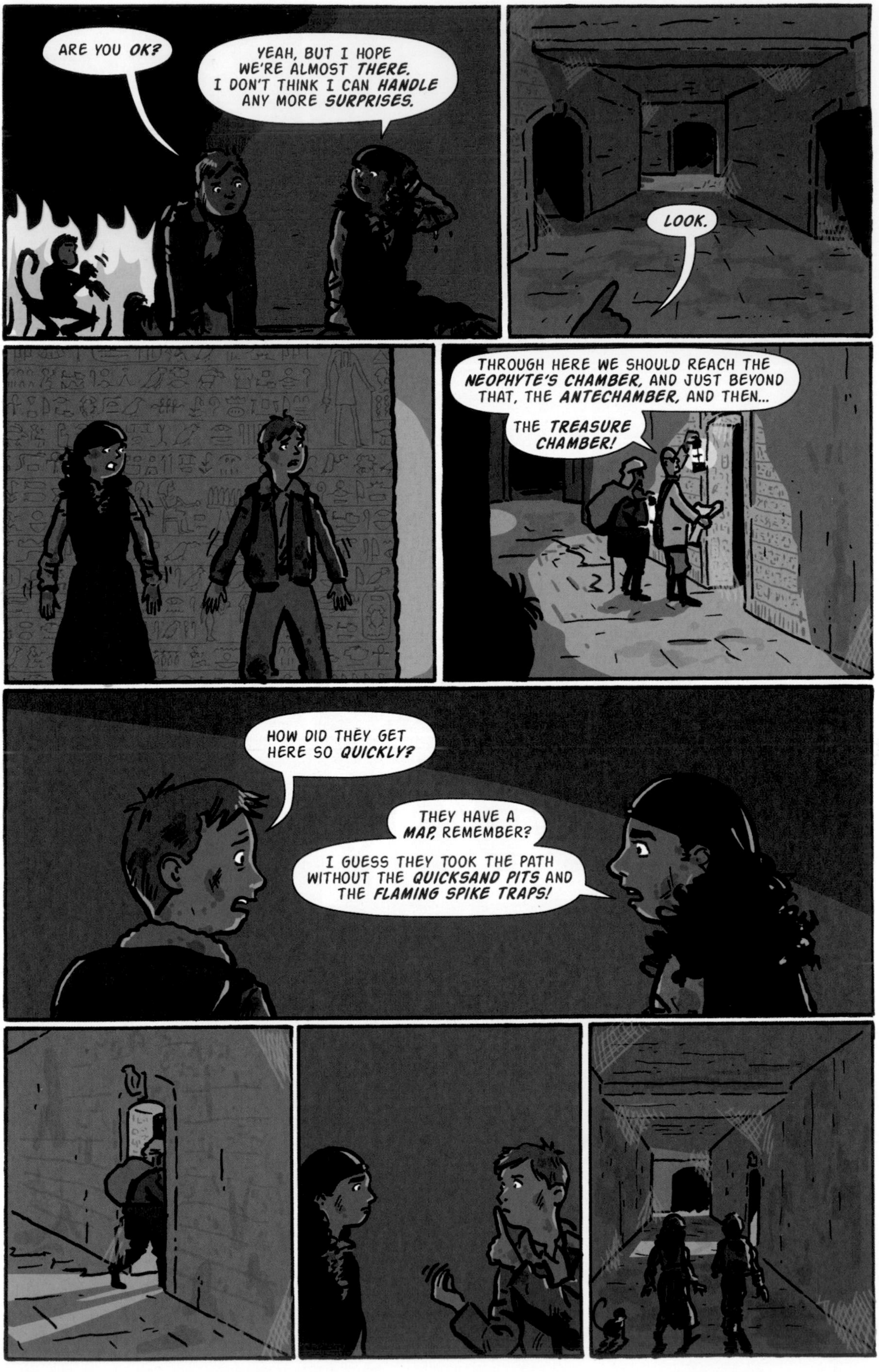

ARE YOU OK?
YEAH, BUT I HOPE WE'RE ALMOST THERE. I DON'T THINK I CAN HANDLE ANY MORE SURPRISES.
LOOK.
THROUGH HERE WE SHOULD REACH THE NEOPHYTE'S CHAMBER, AND JUST BEYOND THAT, THE ANTECHAMBER, AND THEN...
THE TREASURE CHAMBER!
HOW DID THEY GET HERE SO QUICKLY?
THEY HAVE A MAP, REMEMBER?
I GUESS THEY TOOK THE PATH WITHOUT THE QUICKSAND PITS AND THE FLAMING SPIKE TRAPS!

CHAPTER TEN

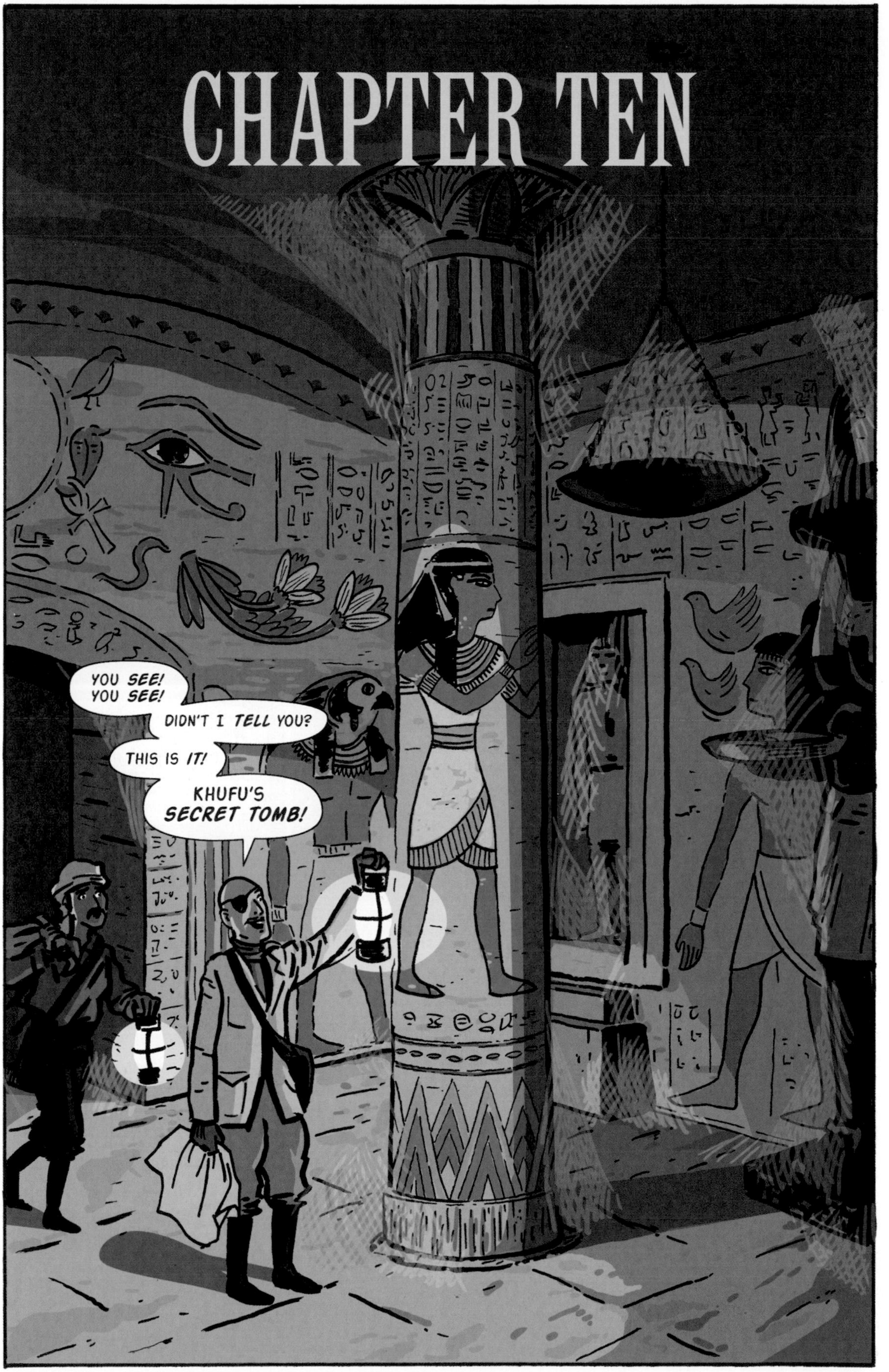
YOU SEE! YOU SEE!
DIDN'T I TELL YOU?
THIS IS IT!
KHUFU'S SECRET TOMB!

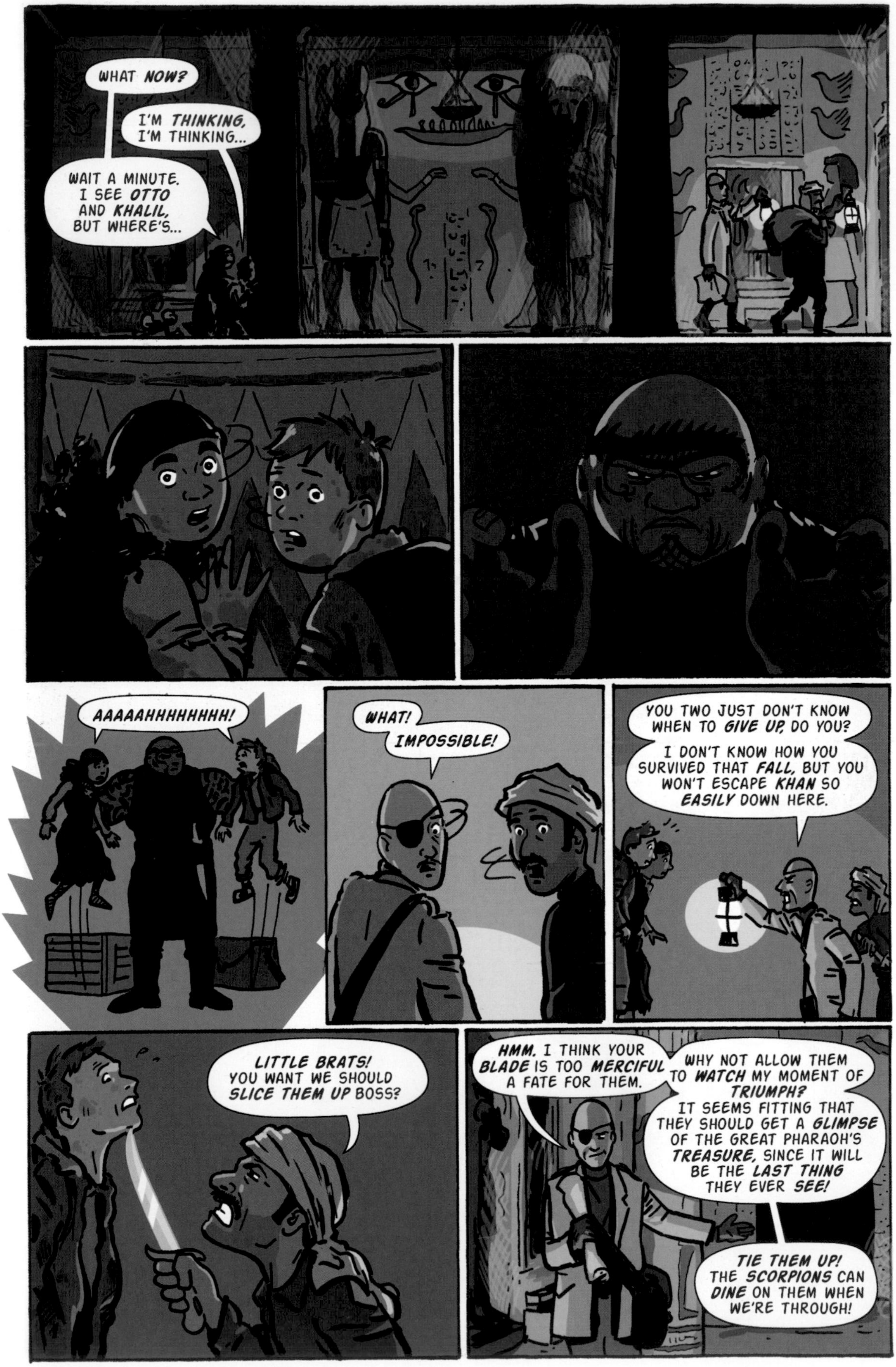

WHAT NOW?
I'M THINKING, I'M THINKING...
WAIT A MINUTE. I SEE OTTO AND KHALIL, BUT WHERE'S...
AAAAAHHHHHHHH!
WHAT! IMPOSSIBLE!
YOU TWO JUST DON'T KNOW WHEN TO GIVE UP, DO YOU?
I DON'T KNOW HOW YOU SURVIVED THAT FALL, BUT YOU WON'T ESCAPE KHAN SO EASILY DOWN HERE.
LITTLE BRATS! YOU WANT WE SHOULD SLICE THEM UP BOSS?
HMM. I THINK YOUR BLADE IS TOO MERCIFUL A FATE FOR THEM.
WHY NOT ALLOW THEM TO WATCH MY MOMENT OF TRIUMPH? IT SEEMS FITTING THAT THEY SHOULD GET A GLIMPSE OF THE GREAT PHARAOH'S TREASURE, SINCE IT WILL BE THE LAST THING THEY EVER SEE!
TIE THEM UP! THE SCORPIONS CAN DINE ON THEM WHEN WE'RE THROUGH!

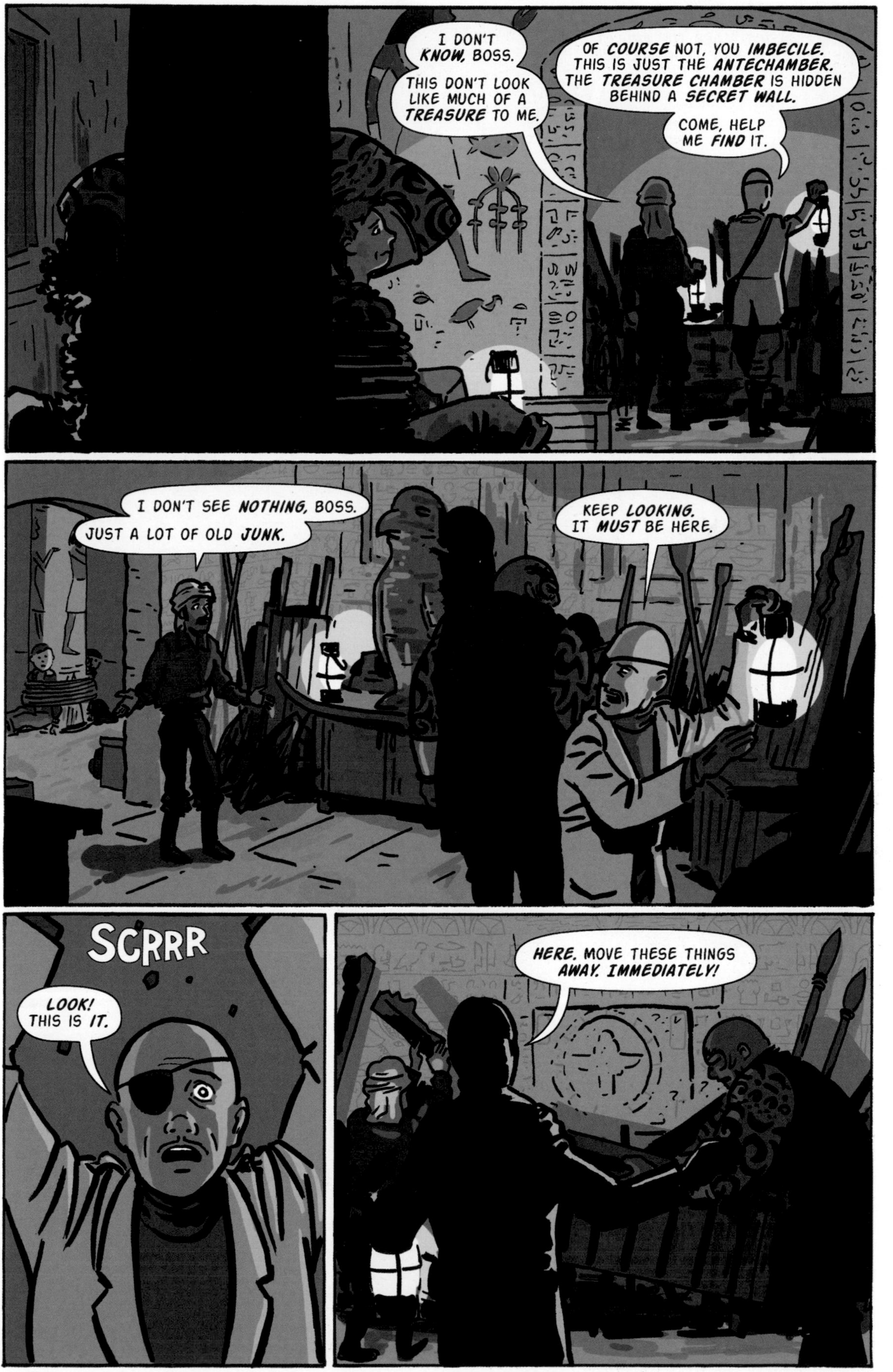
I DON'T KNOW, BOSS.
THIS DON'T LOOK LIKE MUCH OF A TREASURE TO ME.
OF COURSE NOT, YOU IMBECILE. THIS IS JUST THE ANTECHAMBER. THE TREASURE CHAMBER IS HIDDEN BEHIND A SECRET WALL.
COME, HELP ME FIND IT.
I DON'T SEE NOTHING, BOSS.
JUST A LOT OF OLD JUNK.
KEEP LOOKING. IT MUST BE HERE.
SCRRR
LOOK! THIS IS IT.
HERE. MOVE THESE THINGS AWAY. IMMEDIATELY!

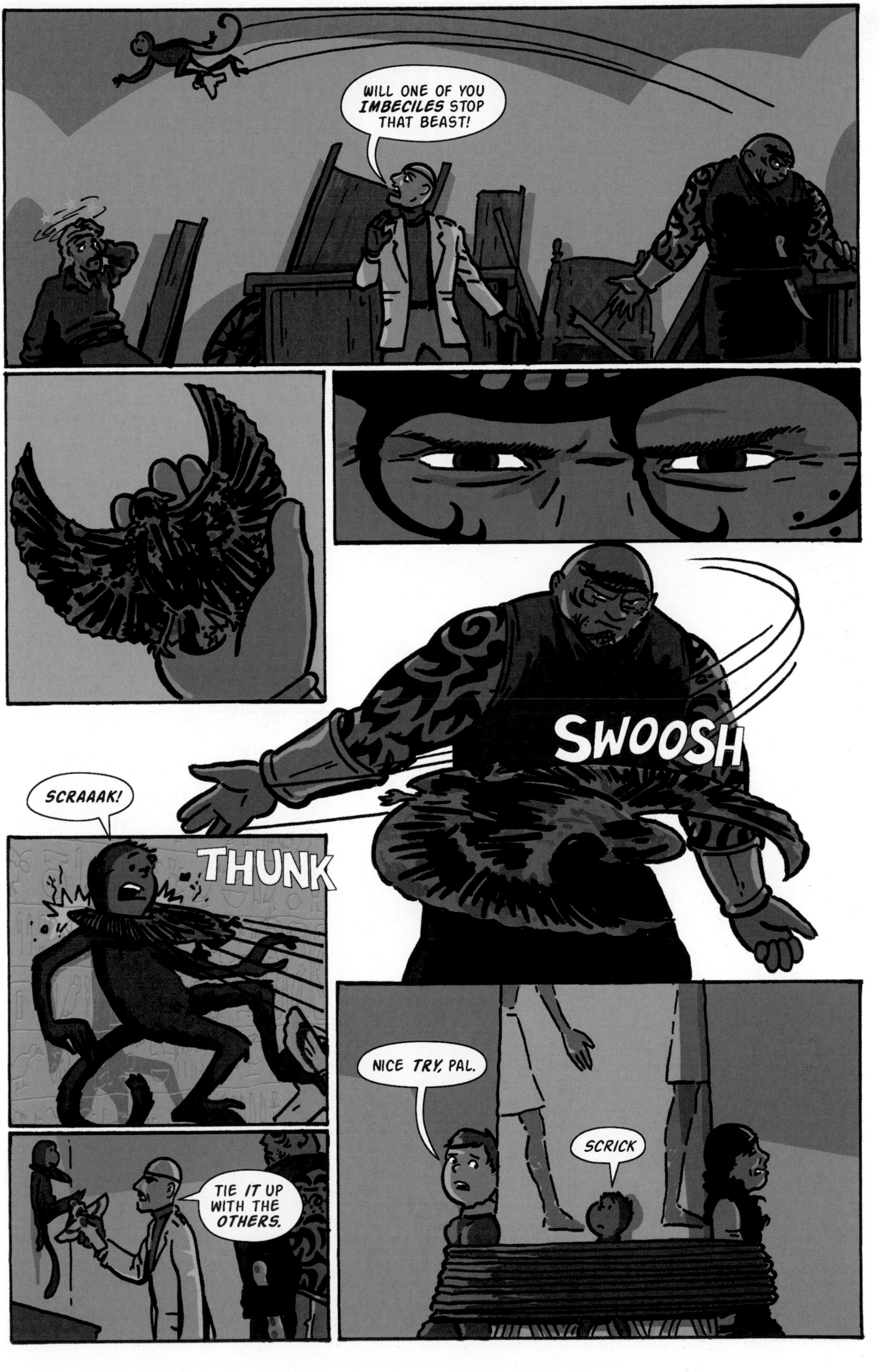

WILL ONE OF YOU *IMBECILES* STOP THAT BEAST!
SWOOSH
SCRAAAK!
THUNK
TIE *IT* UP WITH THE *OTHERS.*
NICE *TRY,* PAL.
SCRICK

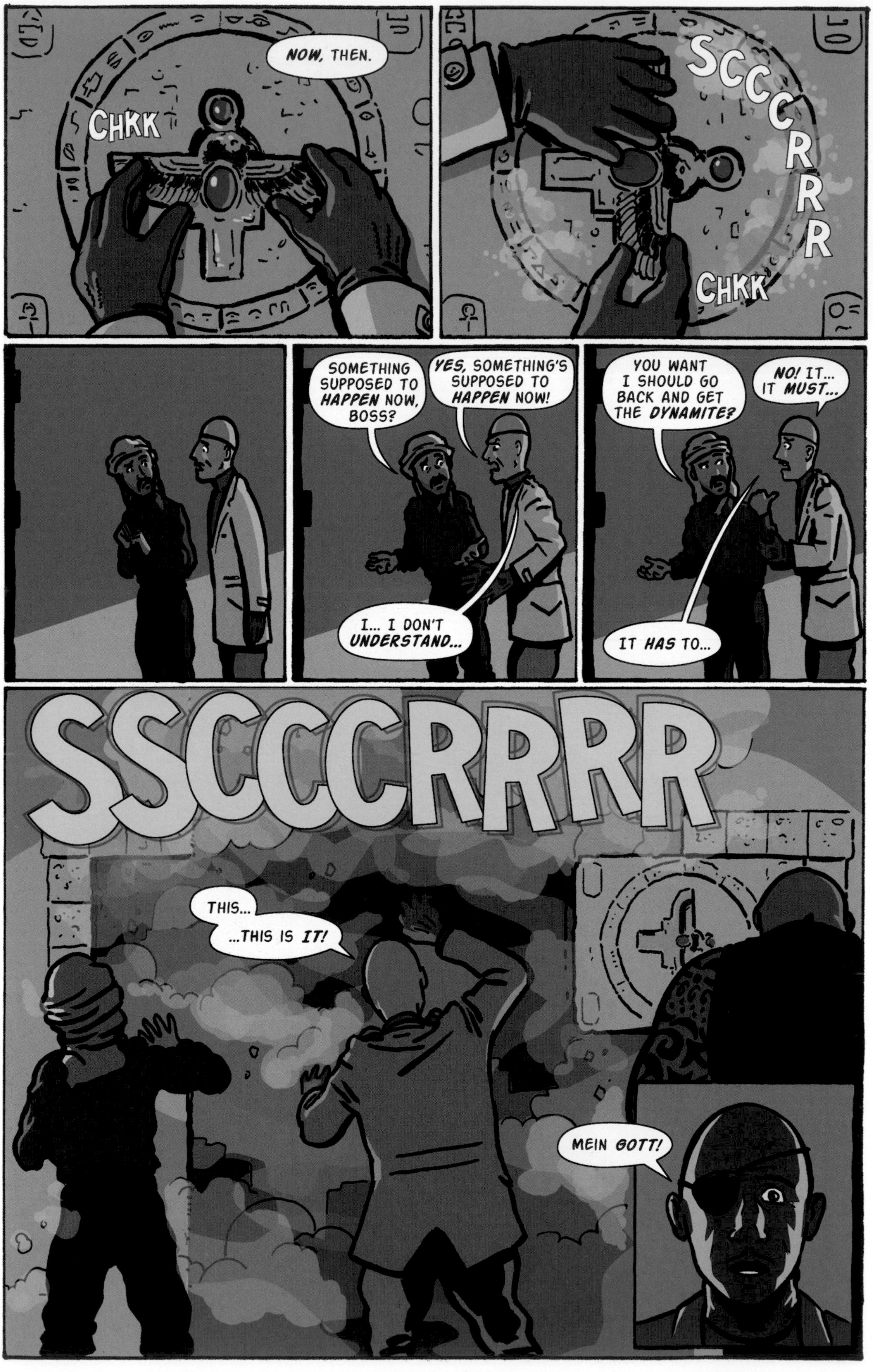
NOW, THEN.
CHKK
SCCCRRRR
CHKK
SOMETHING SUPPOSED TO HAPPEN NOW, BOSS?
YES, SOMETHING'S SUPPOSED TO HAPPEN NOW!
I... I DON'T UNDERSTAND...
YOU WANT I SHOULD GO BACK AND GET THE DYNAMITE?
NO! IT... IT MUST...
IT HAS TO...
SSCCCRRRR
THIS...
...THIS IS IT!
MEIN GOTT!

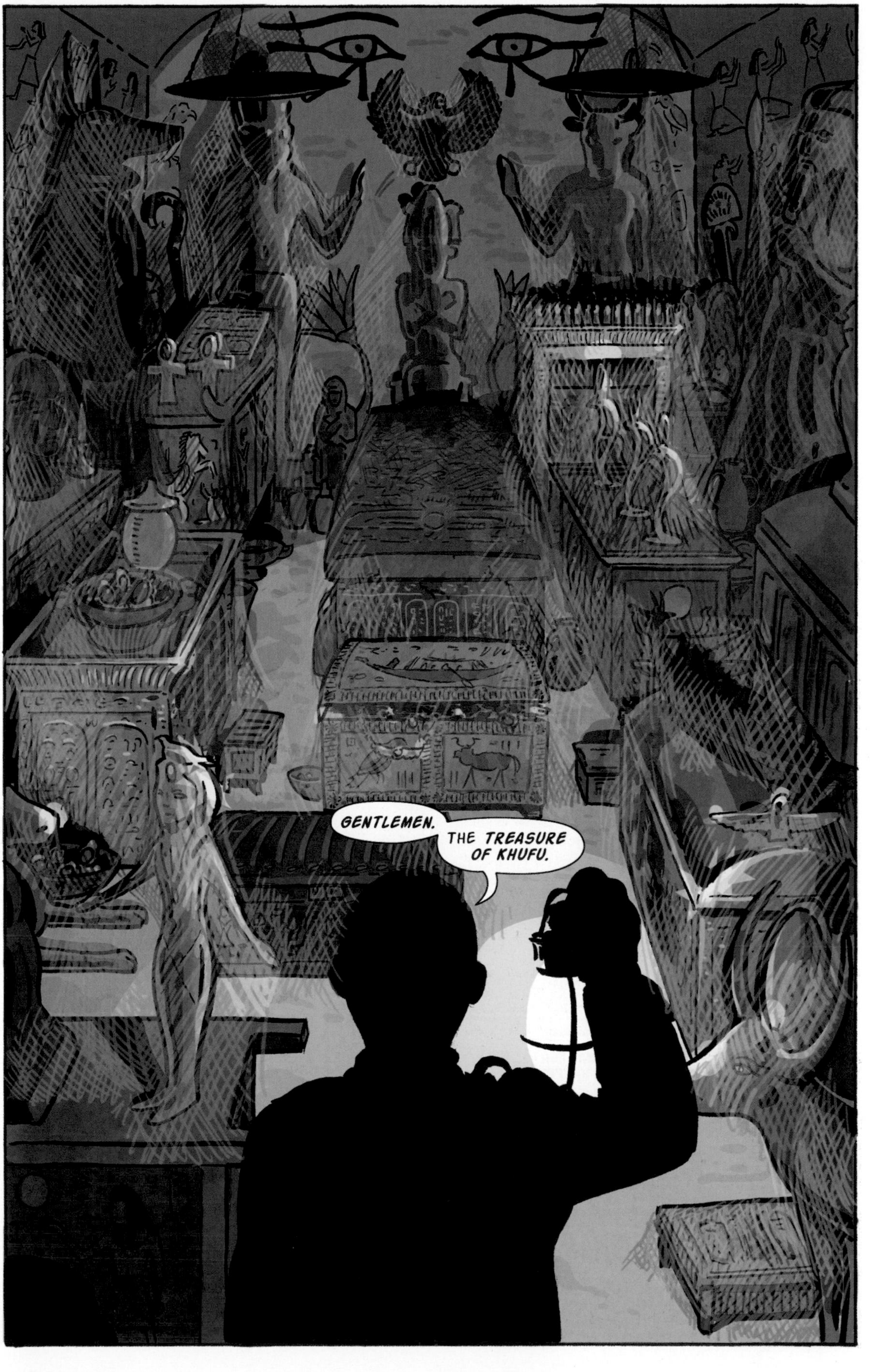
GENTLEMEN.
THE TREASURE OF KHUFU.

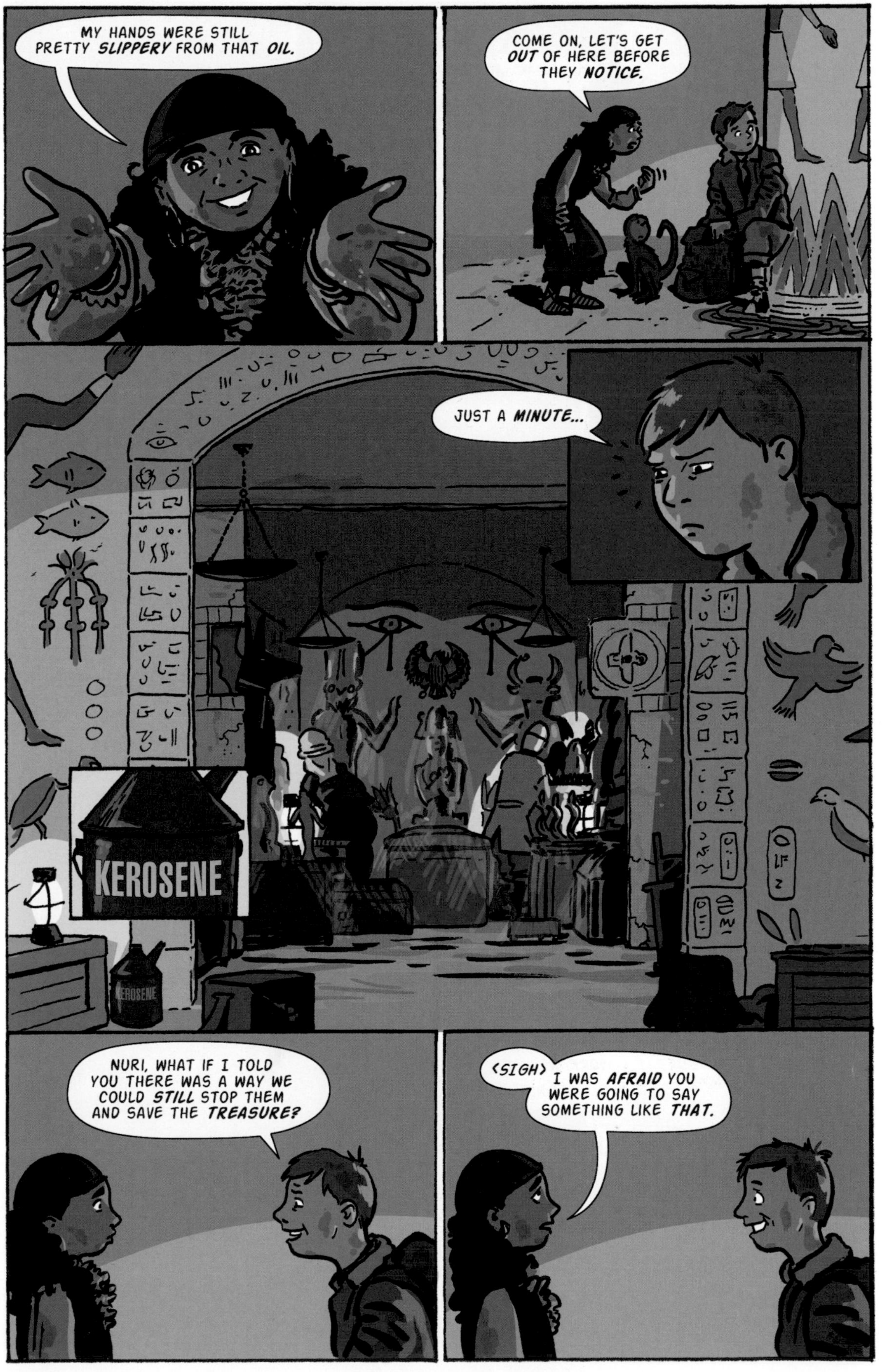
MY HANDS WERE STILL PRETTY SLIPPERY FROM THAT OIL.
COME ON, LET'S GET OUT OF HERE BEFORE THEY NOTICE.
JUST A MINUTE...
KEROSENE
KEROSENE
NURI, WHAT IF I TOLD YOU THERE WAS A WAY WE COULD STILL STOP THEM AND SAVE THE TREASURE?
<SIGH>
I WAS AFRAID YOU WERE GOING TO SAY SOMETHING LIKE THAT.

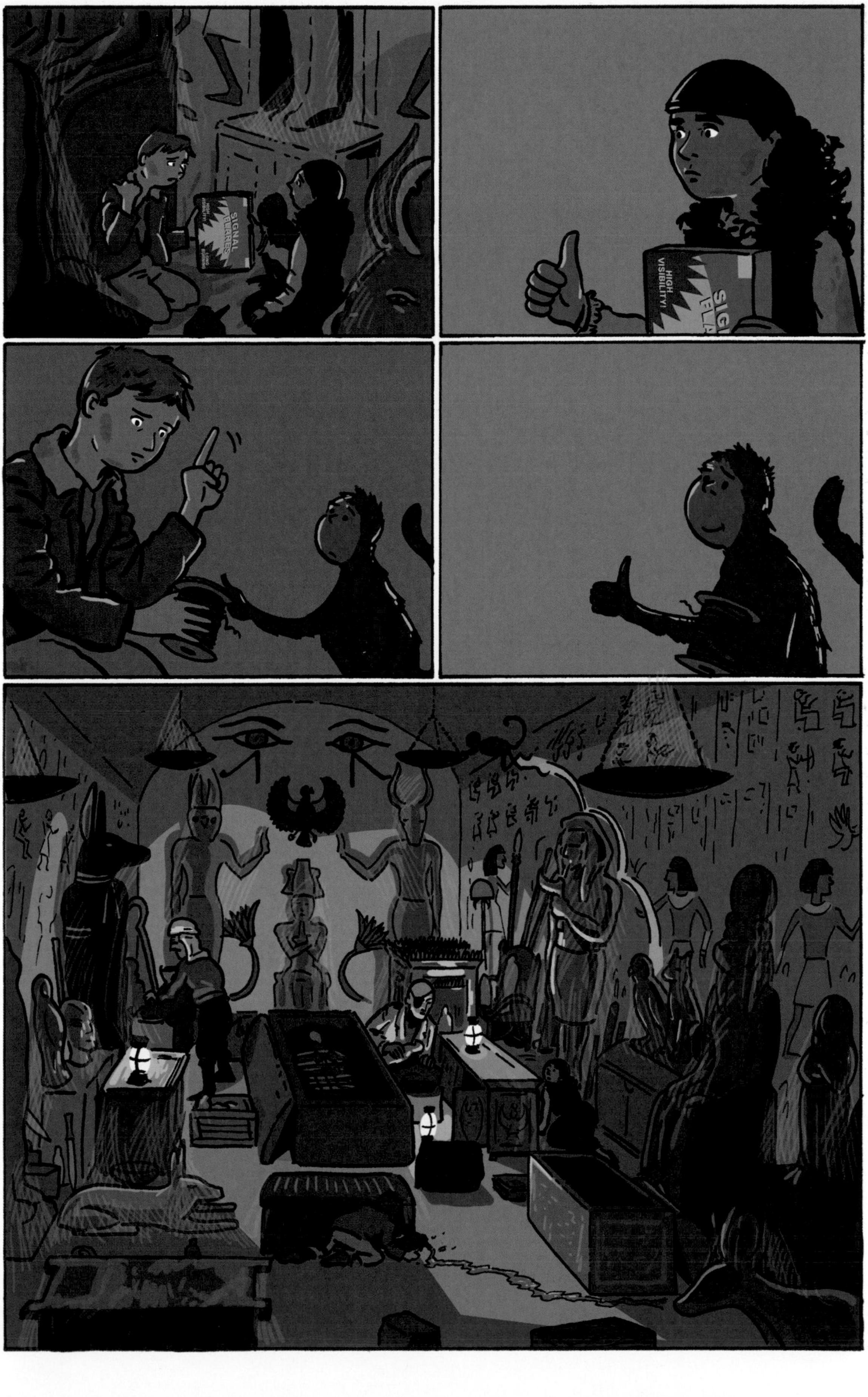
SIGNAL FLARES
HIGH VISIBILITY!

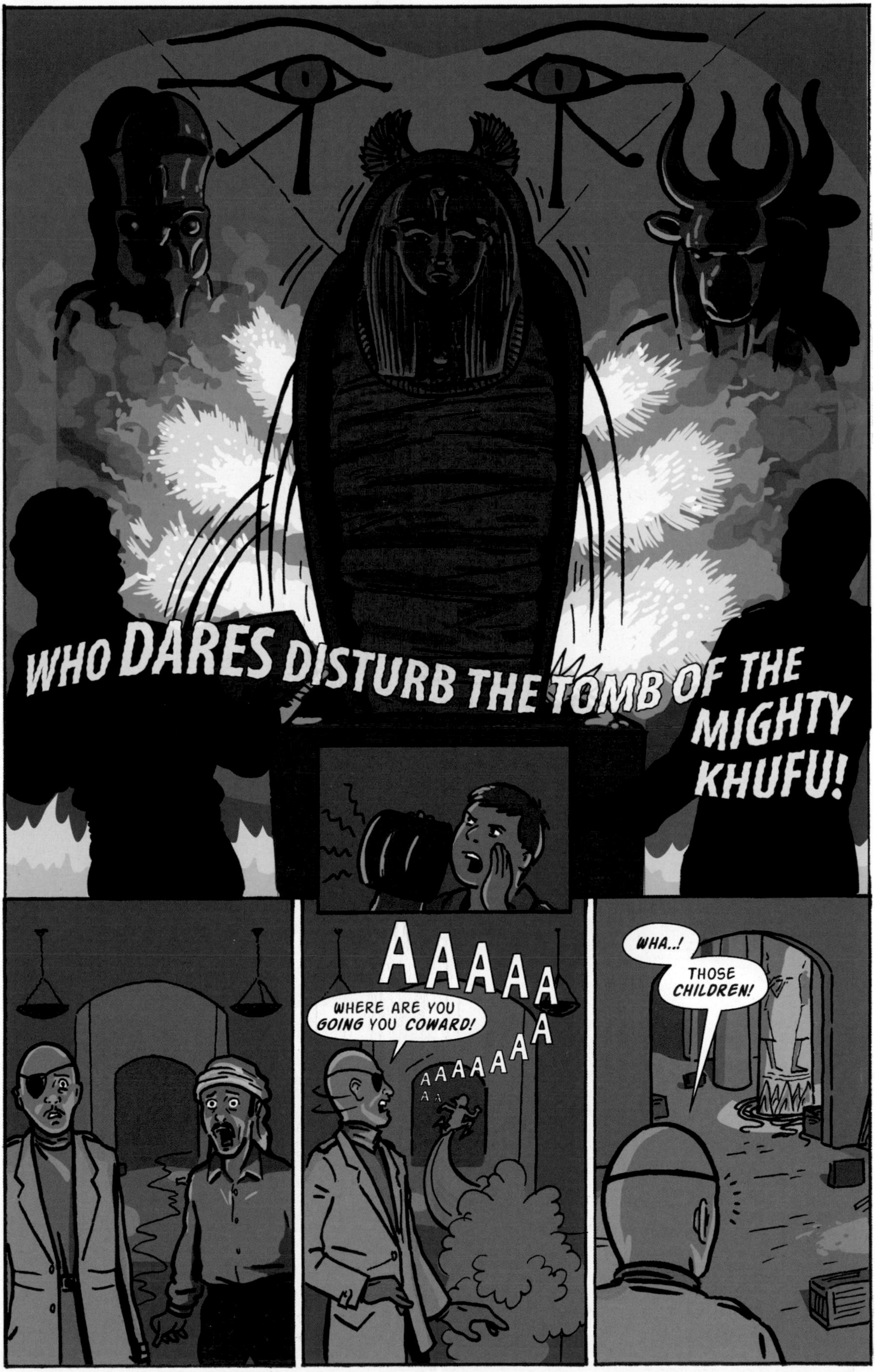
WHO DARES DISTURB THE TOMB OF THE MIGHTY KHUFU!
AAAAAA
WHERE ARE YOU GOING YOU COWARD!
AAAAAAA
AAAAA
AA
WHA..!
THOSE CHILDREN!

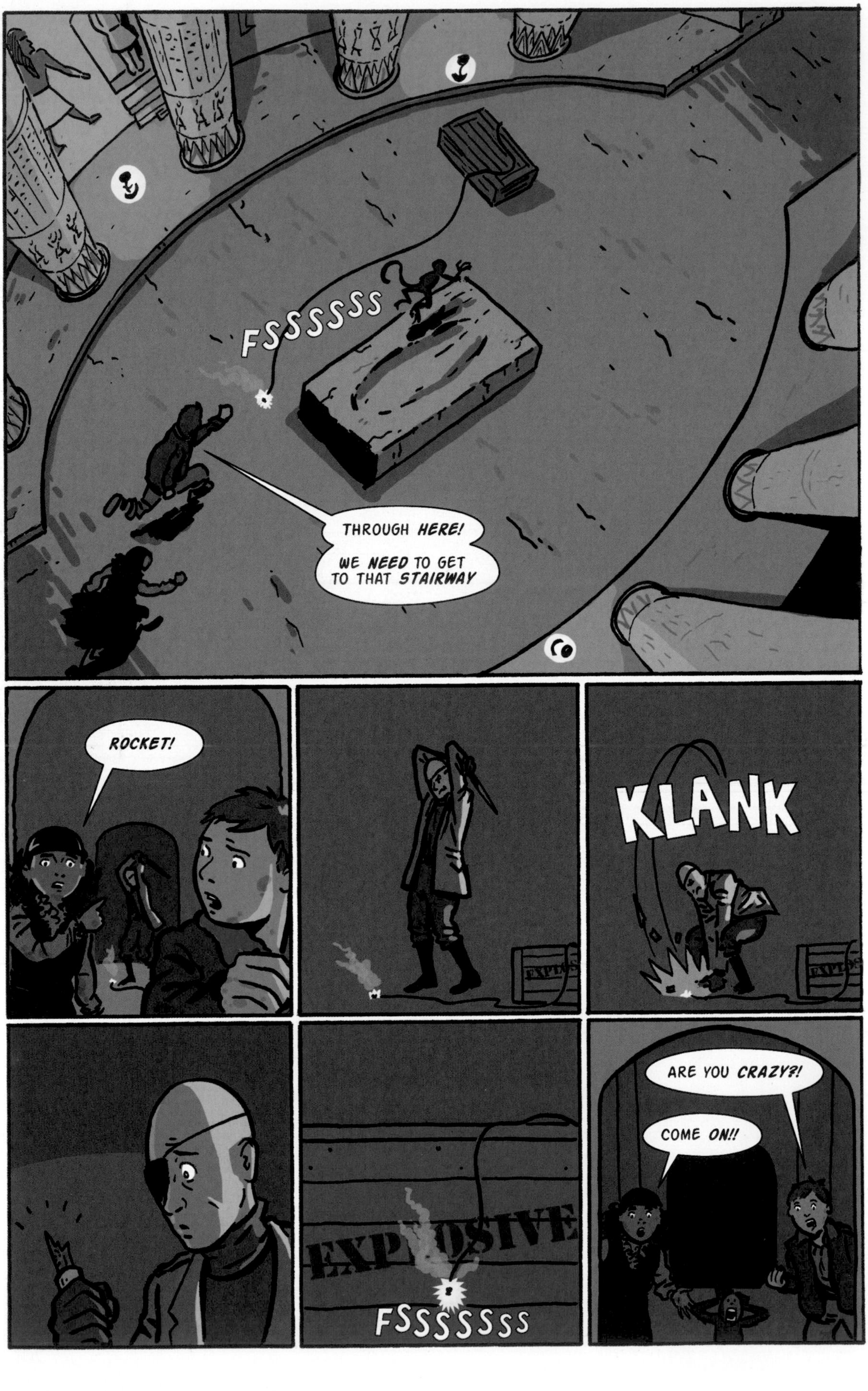
FSSSSSS
THROUGH *HERE!*
WE *NEED* TO GET TO THAT *STAIRWAY*
ROCKET!
KLANK
EXPLOSIVE
FSSSSSSS
ARE YOU *CRAZY?!*
COME *ON!!*

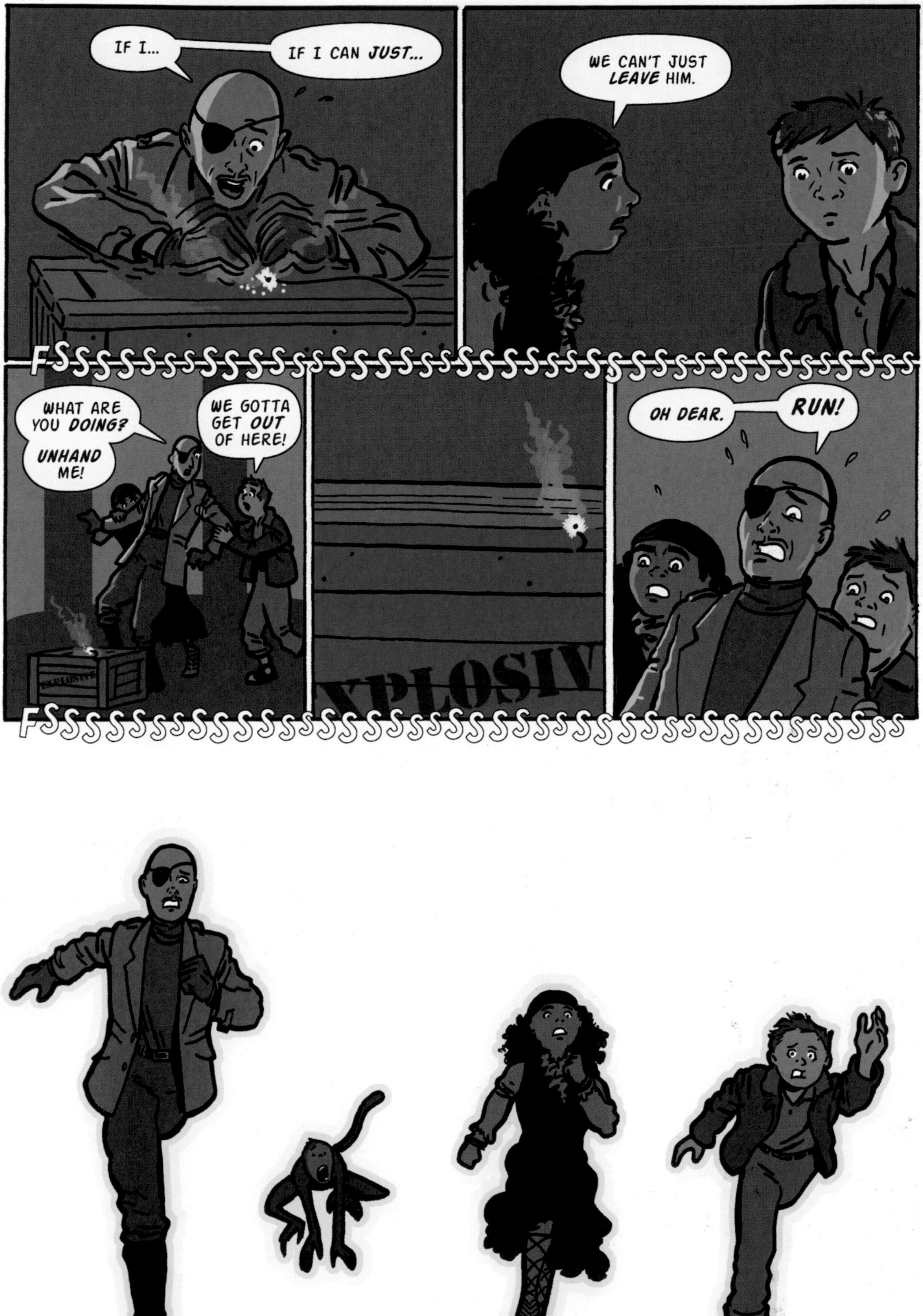
IF I...
IF I CAN JUST...
WE CAN'T JUST LEAVE HIM.
FSSSSSSSSSSSSSSSSSSSSSSSSSSSSSSSSSSSSSSSSSSSSSS
WHAT ARE YOU DOING?
UNHAND ME!
WE GOTTA GET OUT OF HERE!
EXPLOSIVE
XPLOSIV
OH DEAR.
RUN!
FSSSSSSSSSSSSSSSSSSSSSSSSSSSSSSSSSSSSSSSSSSSSSS

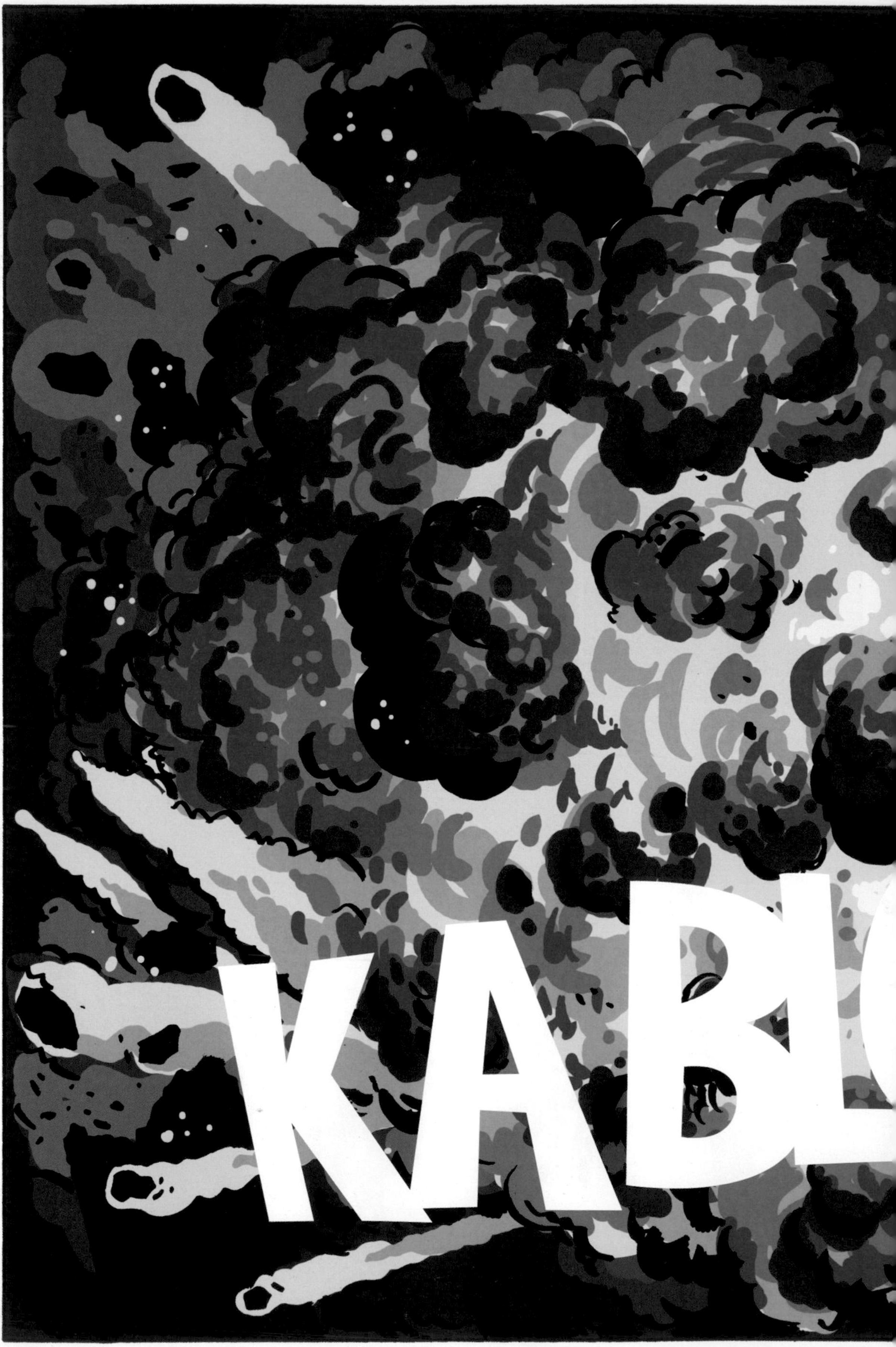
KABL

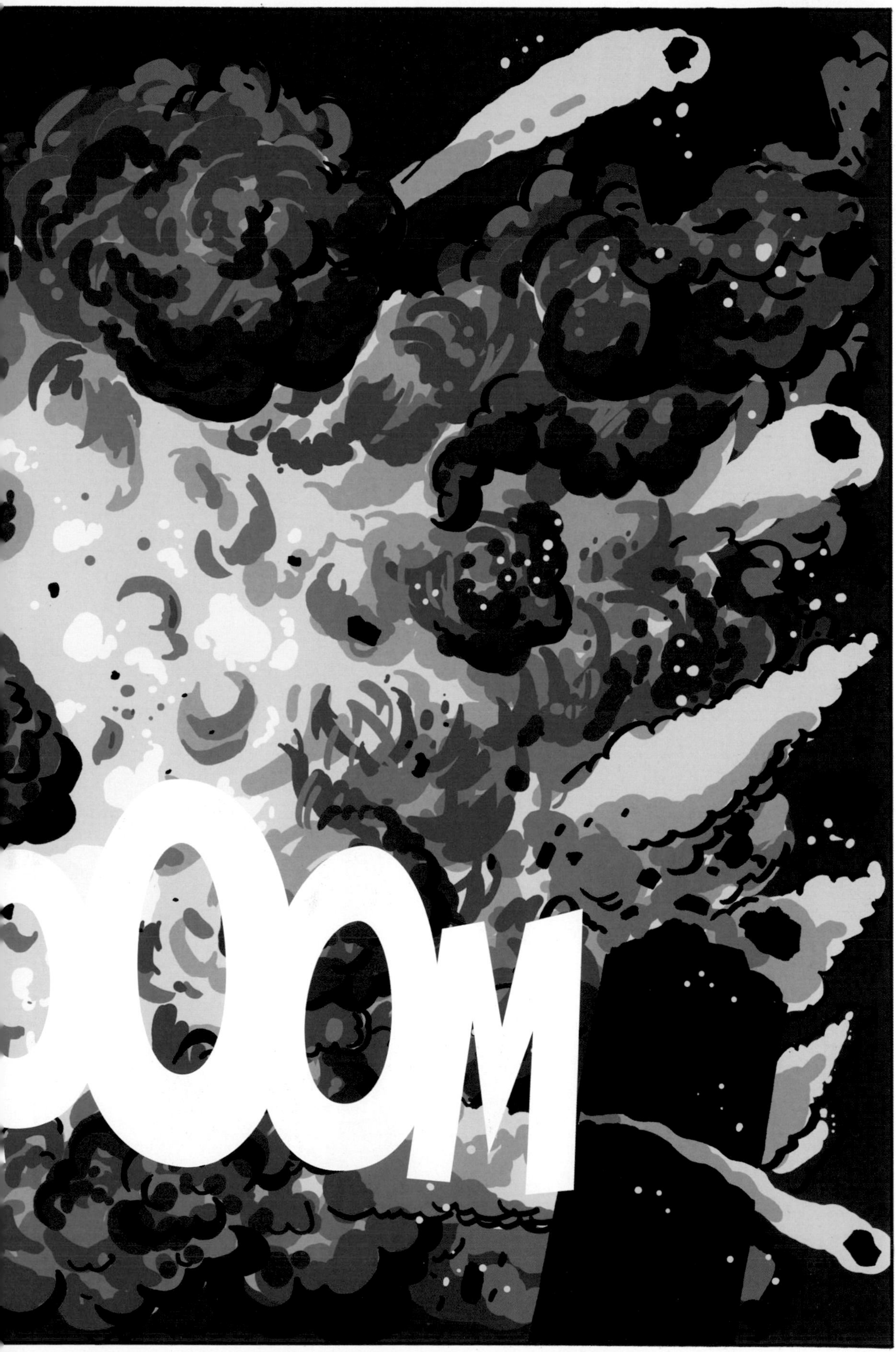
OOM

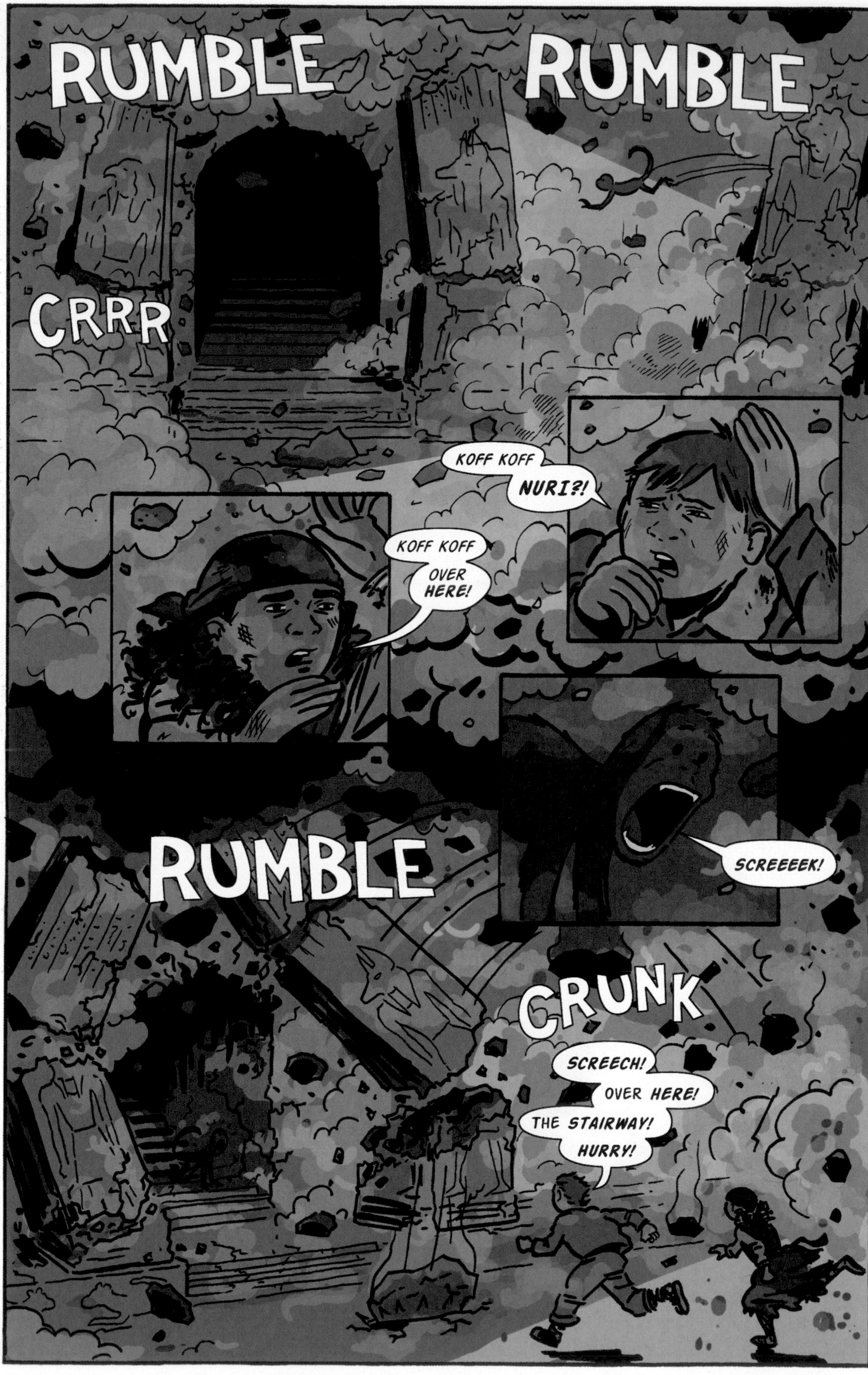
RUMBLE
RUMBLE
CRRR
KOFF KOFF
NURI?!
KOFF KOFF
OVER HERE!
RUMBLE
SCREEEEK!
CRUNK
SCREECH!
OVER HERE!
THE STAIRWAY!
HURRY!

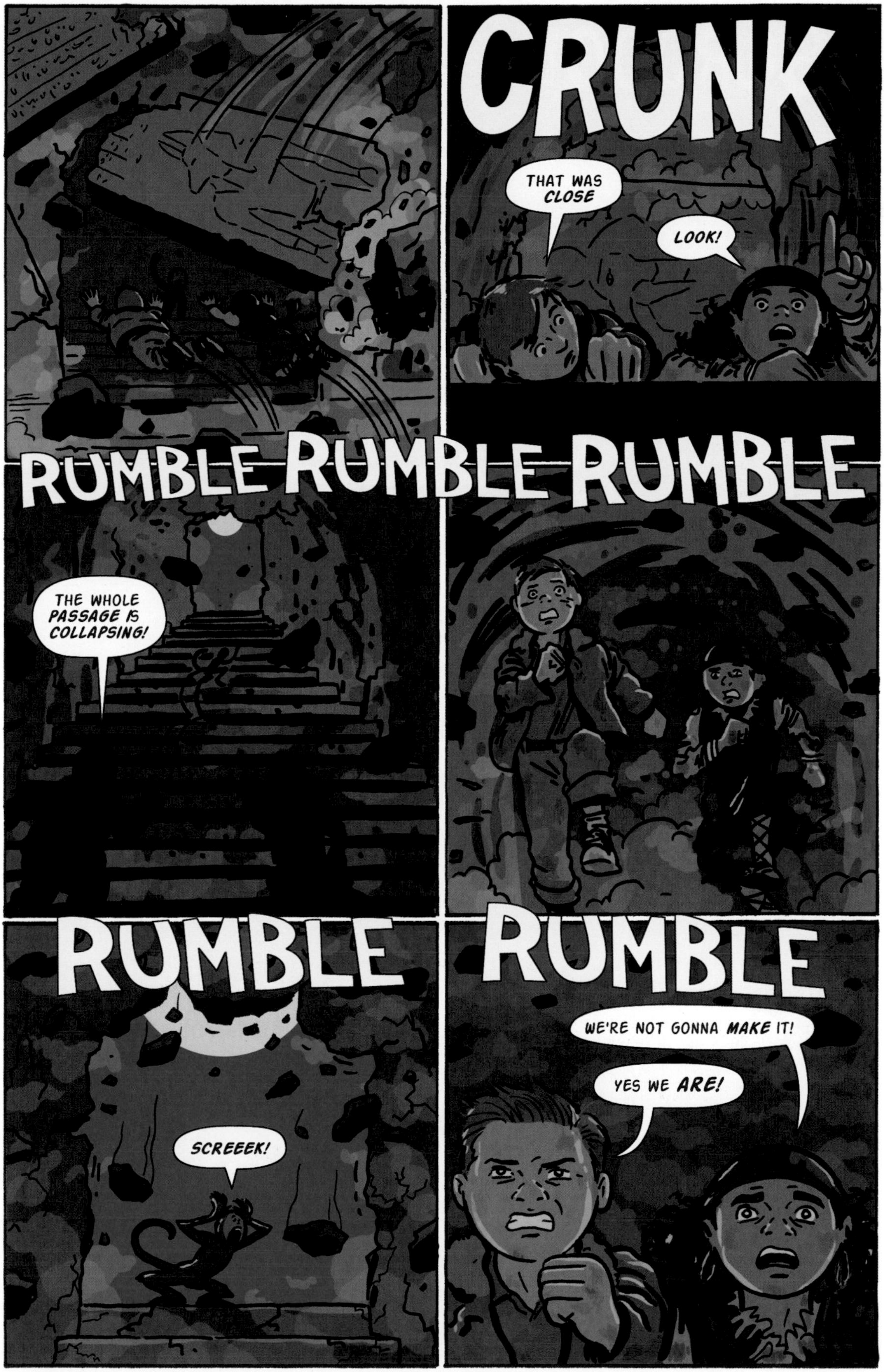
CRUNK
THAT WAS CLOSE
LOOK!
RUMBLE RUMBLE RUMBLE
THE WHOLE PASSAGE IS COLLAPSING!
RUMBLE
SCREEEK!
RUMBLE
WE'RE NOT GONNA MAKE IT!
YES WE ARE!

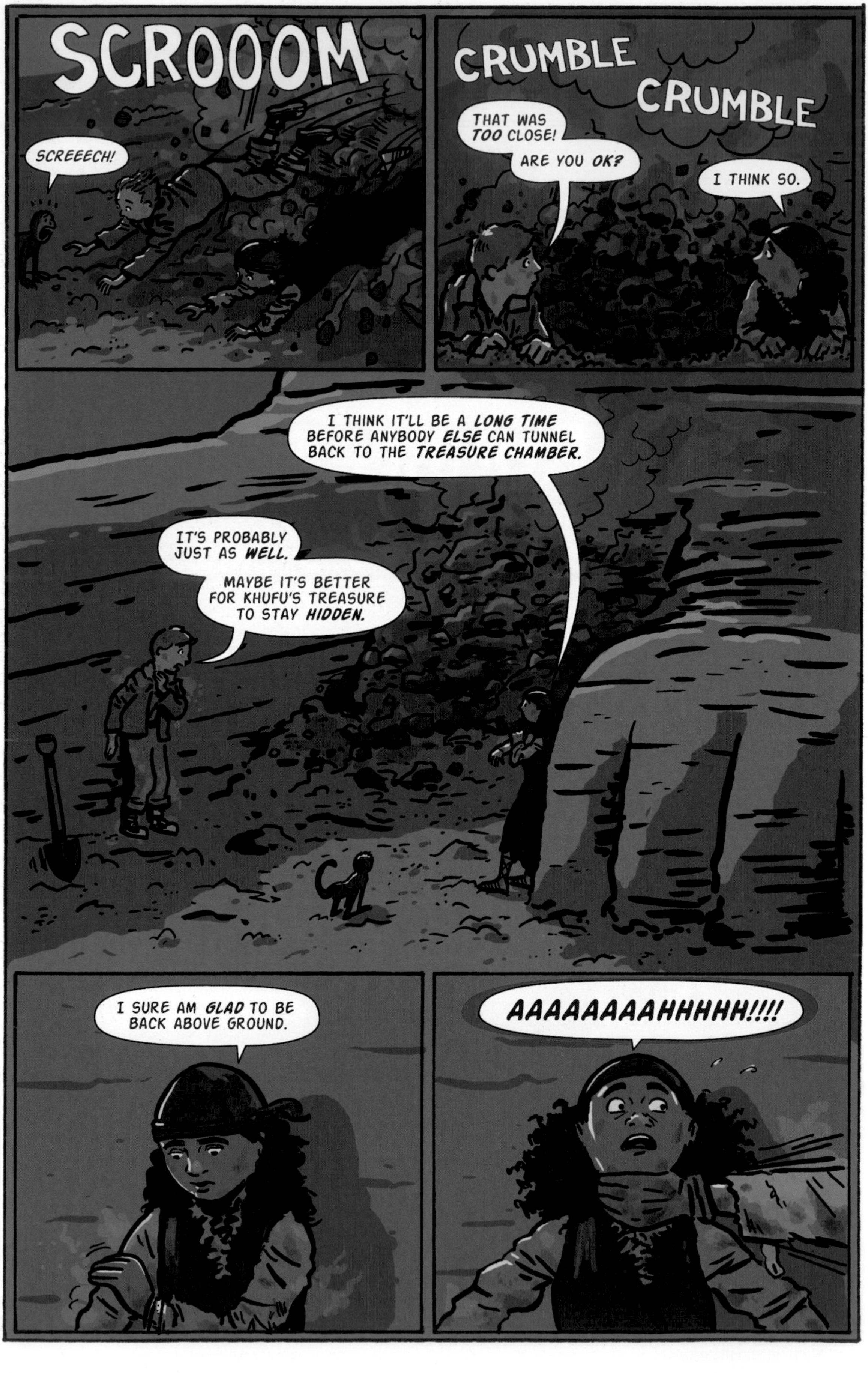
SCROOOM
SCREEECH!
CRUMBLE CRUMBLE
THAT WAS TOO CLOSE!
ARE YOU OK?
I THINK SO.
I THINK IT'LL BE A LONG TIME BEFORE ANYBODY ELSE CAN TUNNEL BACK TO THE TREASURE CHAMBER.
IT'S PROBABLY JUST AS WELL.
MAYBE IT'S BETTER FOR KHUFU'S TREASURE TO STAY HIDDEN.
I SURE AM GLAD TO BE BACK ABOVE GROUND.
AAAAAAAAHHHHH!!!!

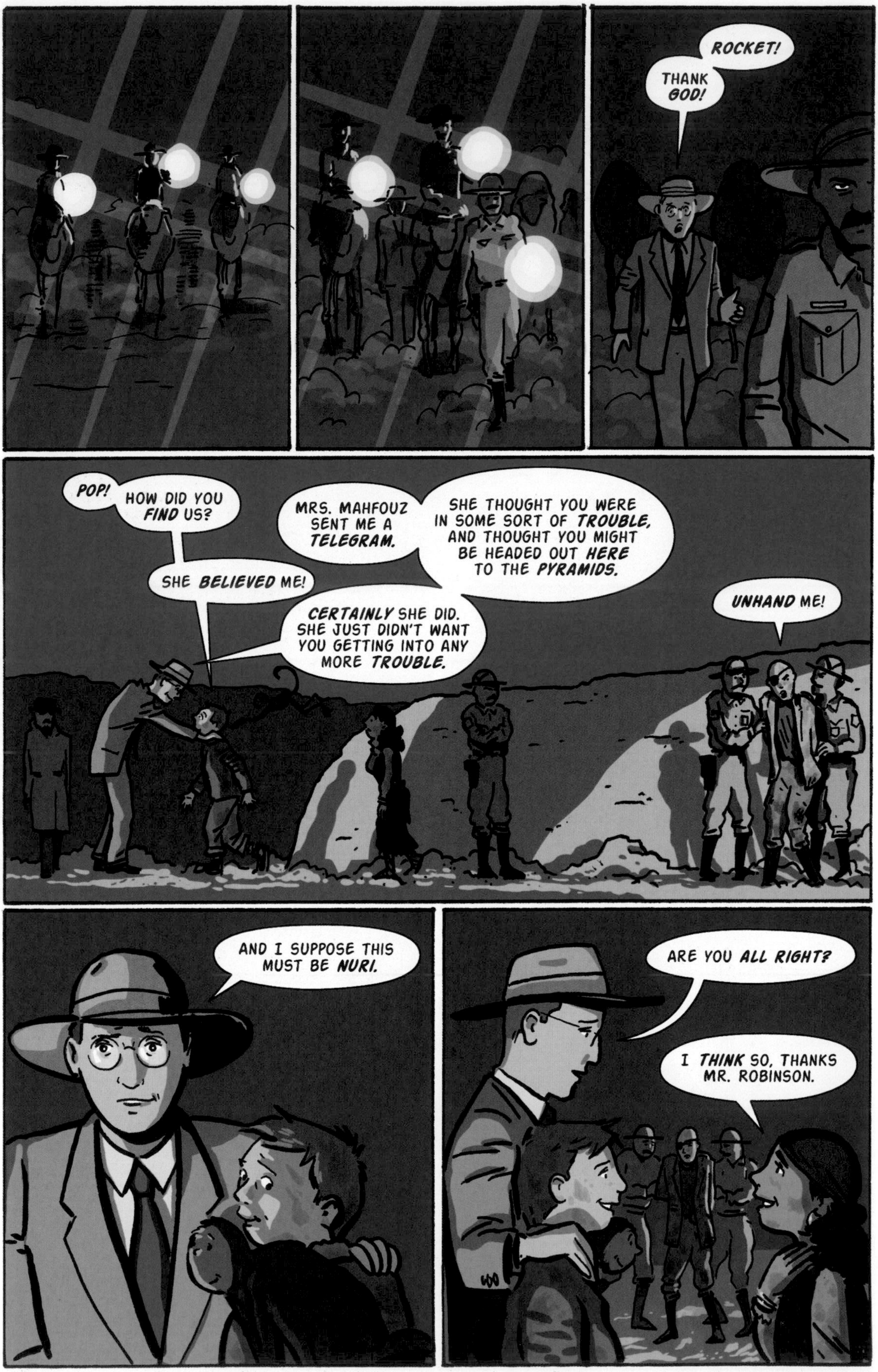
ROCKET!
THANK GOD!
POP!
HOW DID YOU FIND US?
MRS. MAHFOUZ SENT ME A TELEGRAM.
SHE THOUGHT YOU WERE IN SOME SORT OF TROUBLE, AND THOUGHT YOU MIGHT BE HEADED OUT HERE TO THE PYRAMIDS.
SHE BELIEVED ME!
CERTAINLY SHE DID. SHE JUST DIDN'T WANT YOU GETTING INTO ANY MORE TROUBLE.
UNHAND ME!
AND I SUPPOSE THIS MUST BE NURI.
ARE YOU ALL RIGHT?
I THINK SO, THANKS MR. ROBINSON.

NAME Von Stürm, Otto

HEIGHT 6' 2"   WEIGHT 180 lbs.

DISTINGUISHING MARKS Eyepatch
covering right eye

STATUS Extradited to Great Britain to
face charges of murder, assault, larceny,
wire fraud

NAME Sayed, Khalil

HEIGHT 5' 10"   WEIGHT 165 lbs.

DISTINGUISHING MARKS None

STATUS Currently in custody of Cairo
Police Dept. Awaiting trial for
larceny, kidnapping, fraud

NAME Gilroy, Colin

HEIGHT 5' 8"   WEIGHT 220 lbs.

DISTINGUISHING MARKS None

STATUS Extradited to Great Britain.
Outstanding warrants for fraud,
bribery, public intoxication

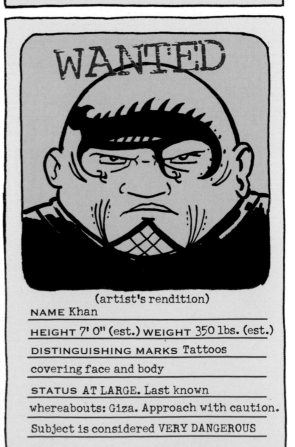

WANTED

(artist's rendition)

NAME Khan

HEIGHT 7' 0" (est.) WEIGHT 350 lbs. (est.)

DISTINGUISHING MARKS Tattoos
covering face and body

STATUS AT LARGE. Last known
whereabouts: Giza. Approach with caution.
Subject is considered VERY DANGEROUS

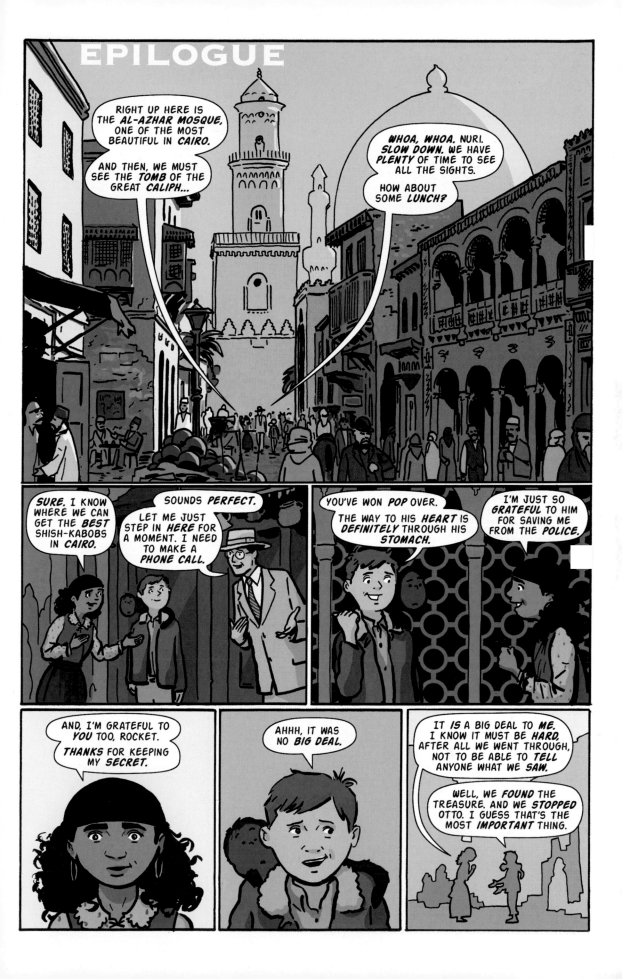

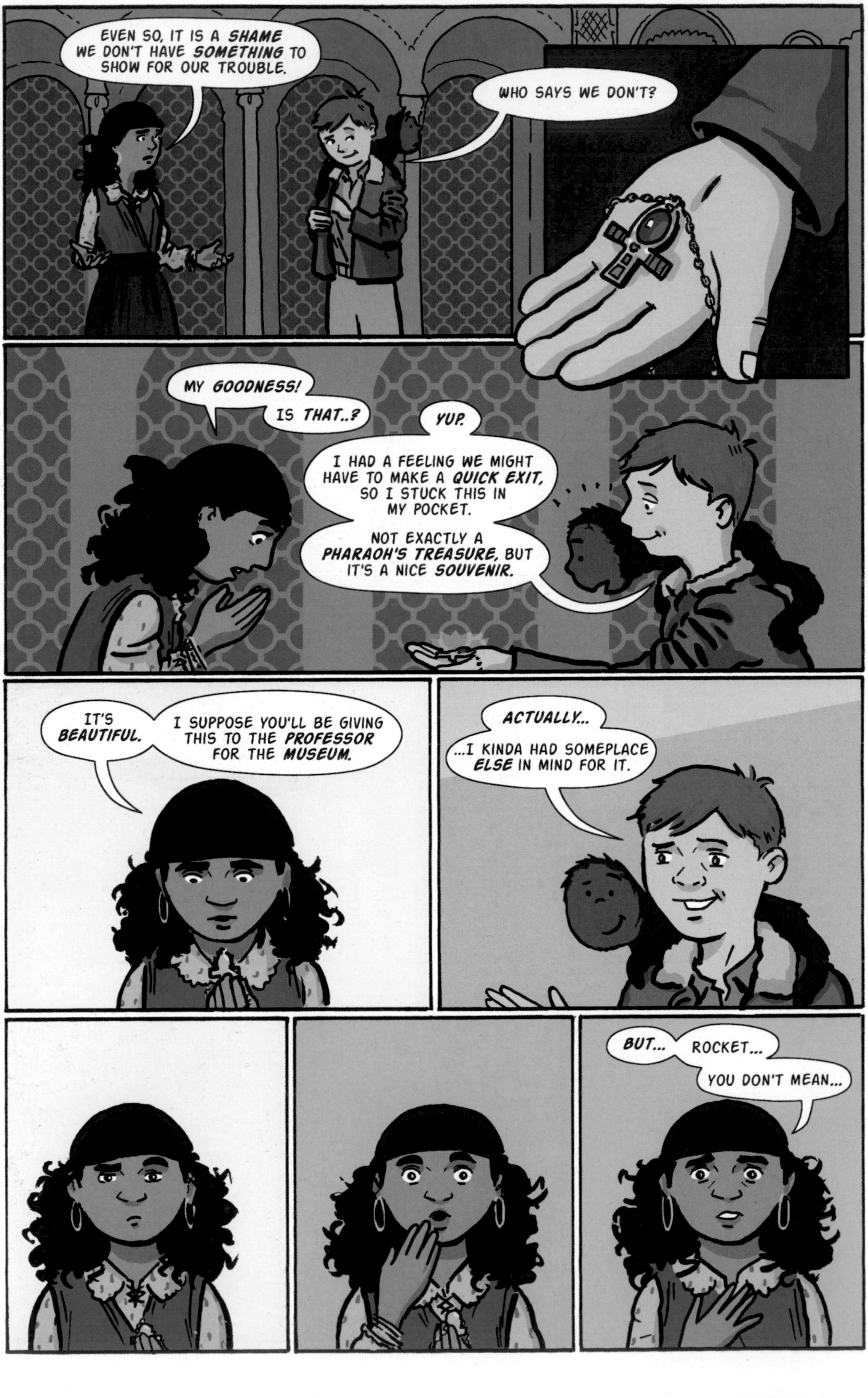
EVEN SO, IT IS A SHAME WE DON'T HAVE SOMETHING TO SHOW FOR OUR TROUBLE.
WHO SAYS WE DON'T?
MY GOODNESS!
IS THAT..?
YUP.
I HAD A FEELING WE MIGHT HAVE TO MAKE A QUICK EXIT, SO I STUCK THIS IN MY POCKET.
NOT EXACTLY A PHARAOH'S TREASURE, BUT IT'S A NICE SOUVENIR.
IT'S BEAUTIFUL.
I SUPPOSE YOU'LL BE GIVING THIS TO THE PROFESSOR FOR THE MUSEUM.
ACTUALLY...
...I KINDA HAD SOMEPLACE ELSE IN MIND FOR IT.
BUT...
ROCKET...
YOU DON'T MEAN...

THANK YOU

Many thanks to all of the following, without whose generous support completion of this book would not have been possible:

KATIE MUHTARIS and KATHY LYNCH for their invaluable editorial input and content expertise.

SCOTT HIGHT DESIGN for design and production support.

And my wonderful family, especially my amazing wife JENNIFER FARRINGTON. Thanks for making it possible.

Rocket Robinson™ and the Pharaoh's Fortune

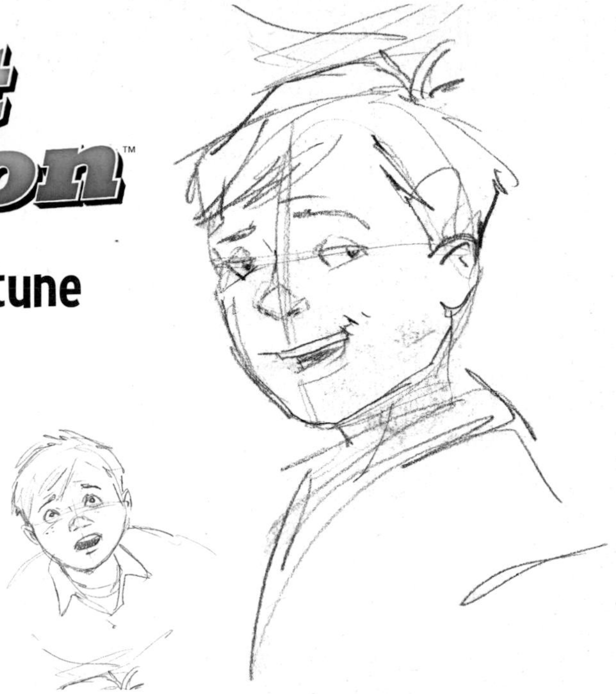

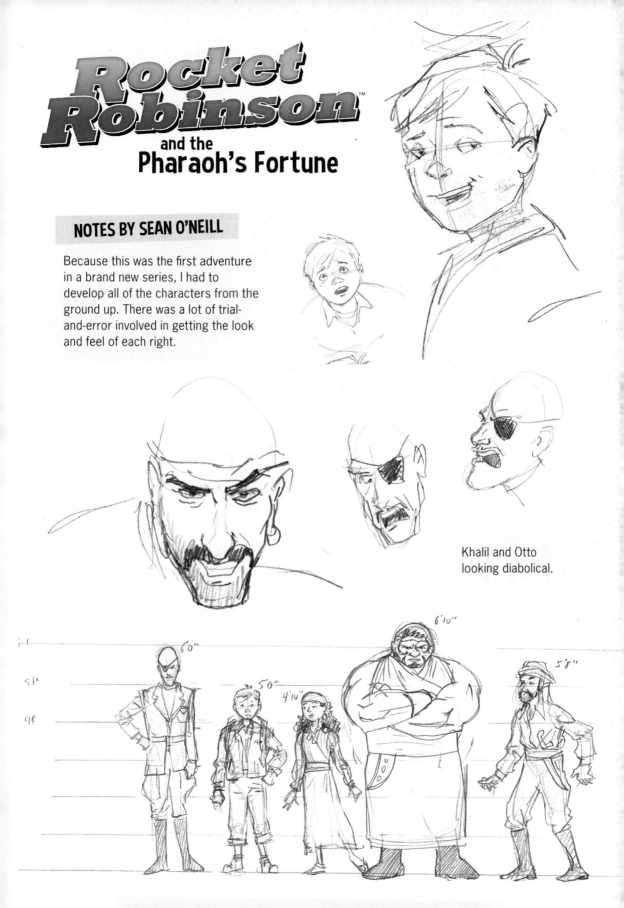

NOTES BY SEAN O'NEILL

Because this was the first adventure in a brand new series, I had to develop all of the characters from the ground up. There was a lot of trial-and-error involved in getting the look and feel of each right.

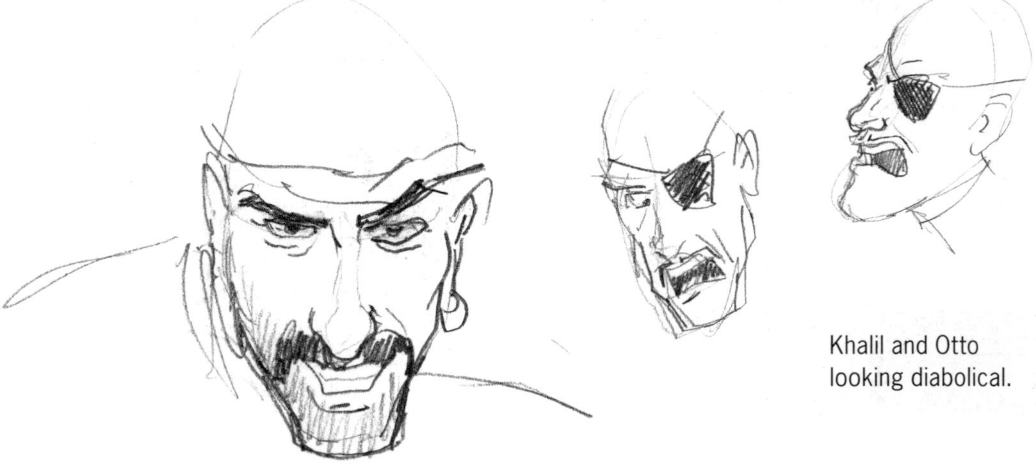

Khalil and Otto looking diabolical.

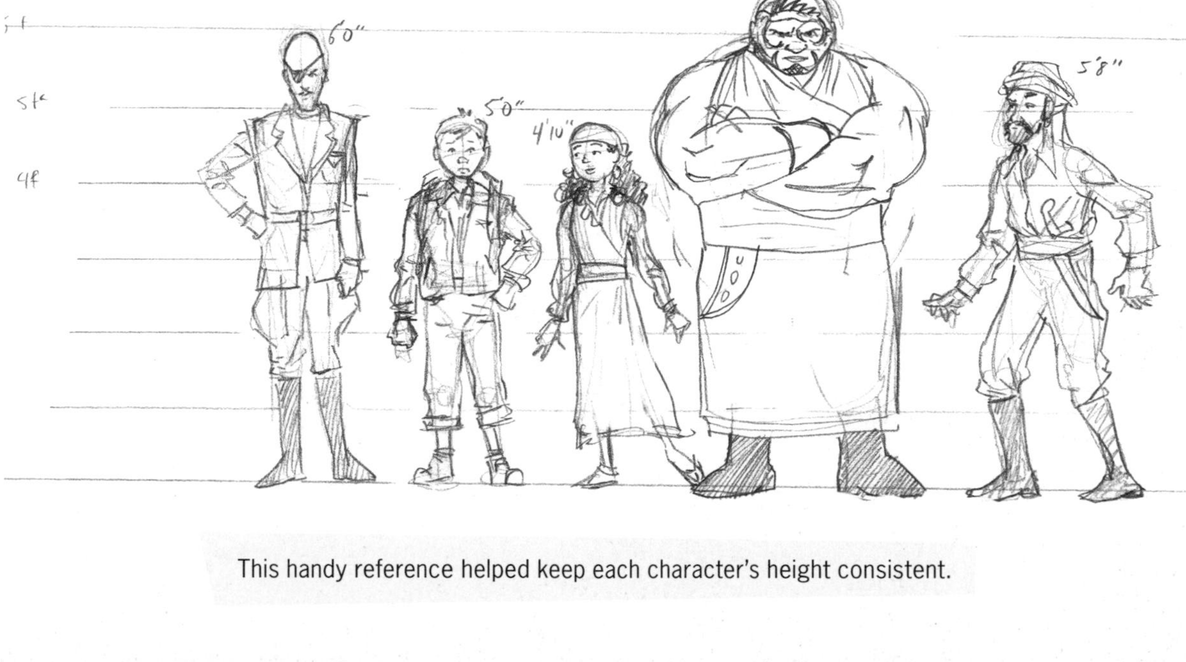
6'0"
5'0"
4'10"
6'10"
5'8"

This handy reference helped keep each character's height consistent.

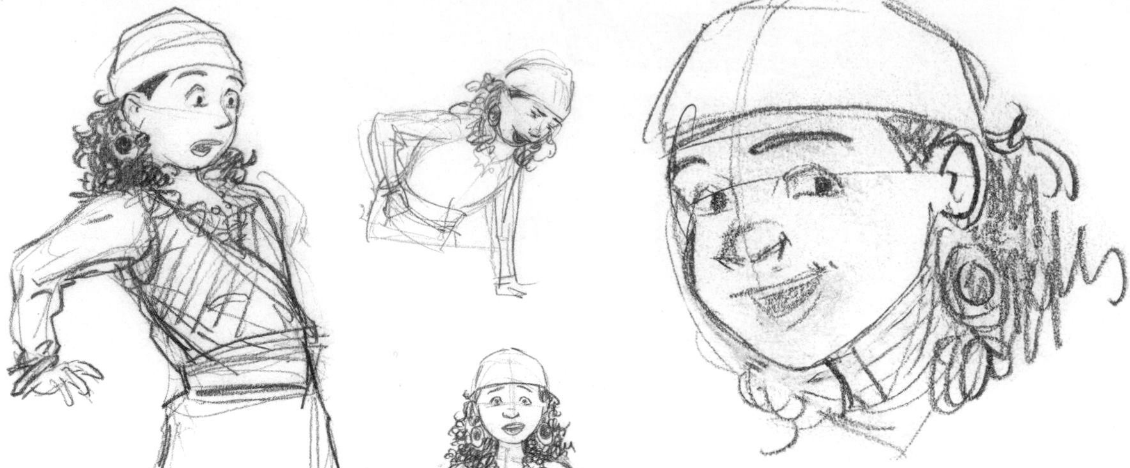

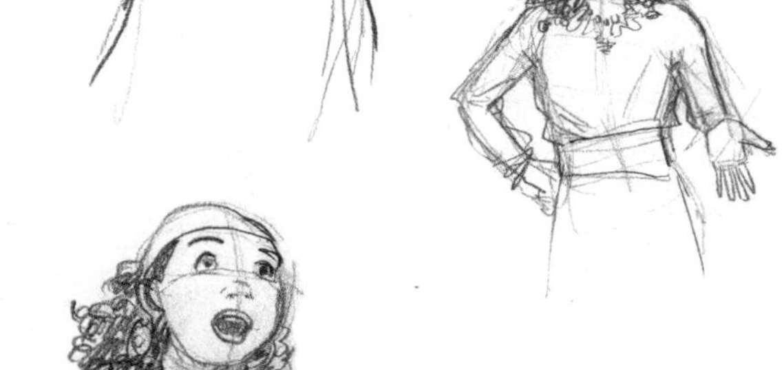

The character of Nuri changed a lot over the course of the sketching and writing process. Here's a few early takes of her with different facial expressions.

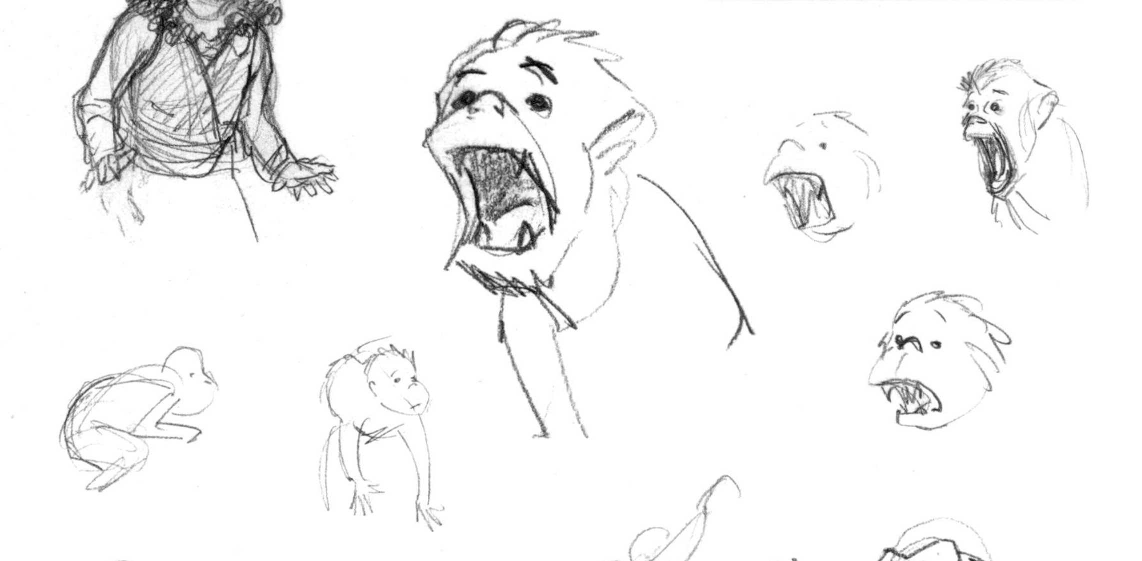

Drawing Screech was a real challenge; because he can't speak, all of his character and personality has to be expressed through body language and facial expressions.

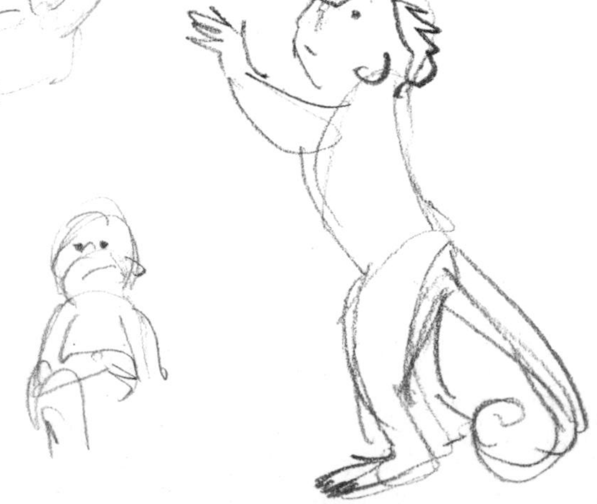

This and the following watercolor illustration were done as covers for limited-edition single-issue comics of the first two chapters.

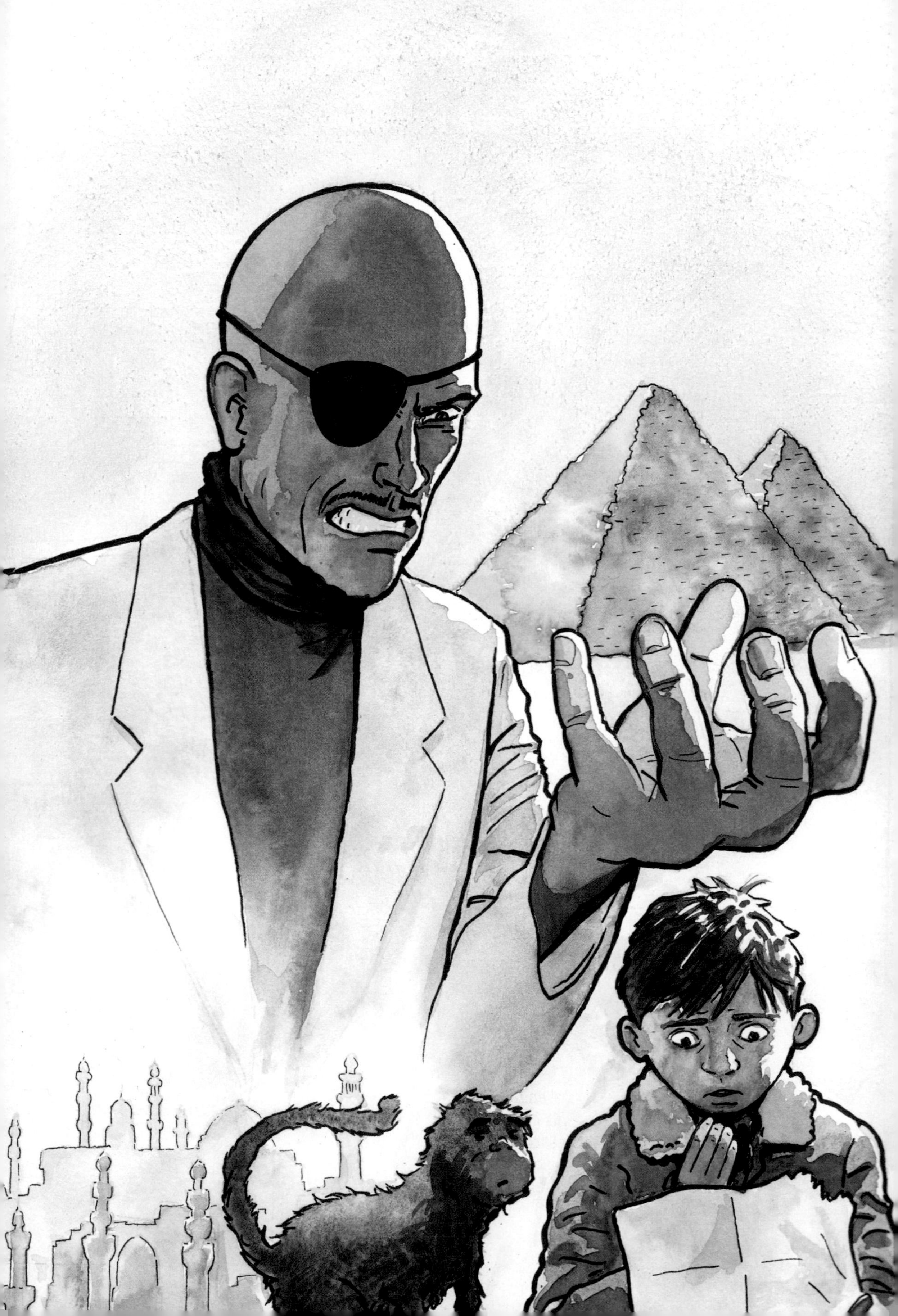

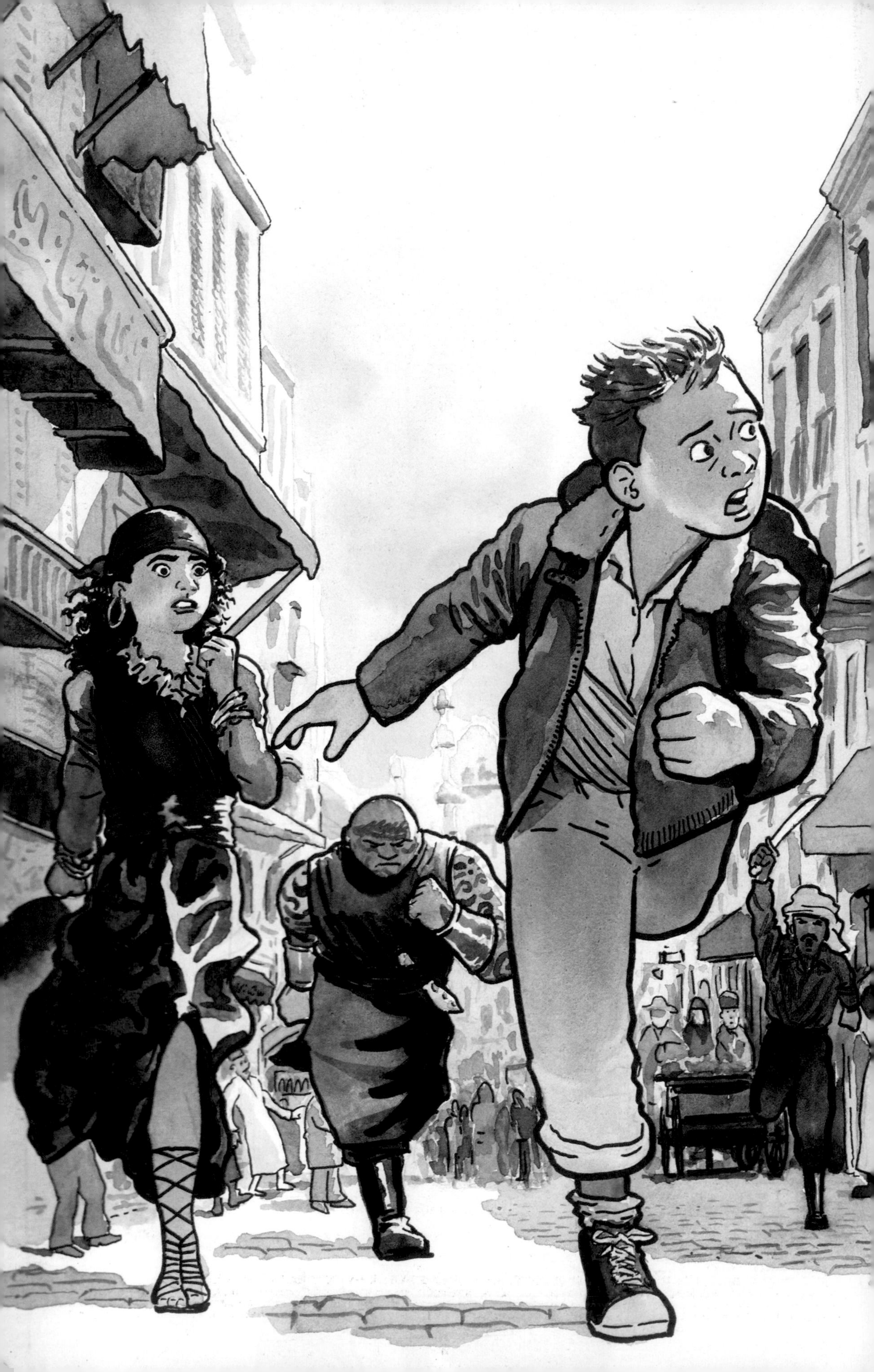

BOOKS THAT MIDDLE READERS WILL LOVE!

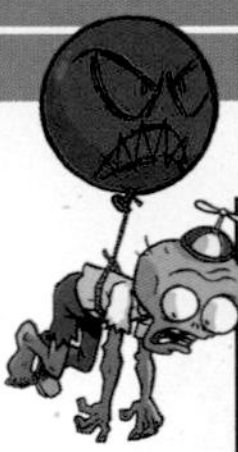

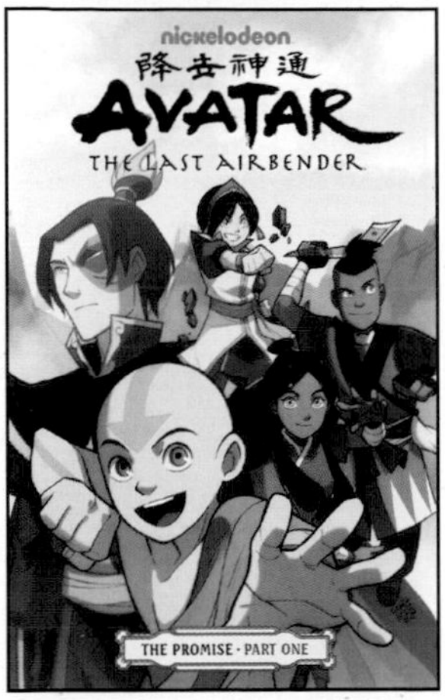
nickelodeon
降世神通
AVATAR
THE LAST AIRBENDER
THE PROMISE · PART ONE

AVATAR: THE LAST AIRBENDER

Aang and friends' adventures continue right where the TV series left off, in these beautiful oversized hardcover collections, from *Airbender* creators Michael Dante DiMartino and Bryan Konietzko and Eisner and Harvey Award winner Gene Luen Yang!

The Promise ISBN 978-1-61655-074-5
The Search ISBN 978-1-61655-226-8
The Rift ISBN 978-1-61655-550-4
Smoke and Shadow ISBN 978-1-50670-013-7
North and South ISBN 978-1-50670-195-0
(Available October 2017)
$39.99 each

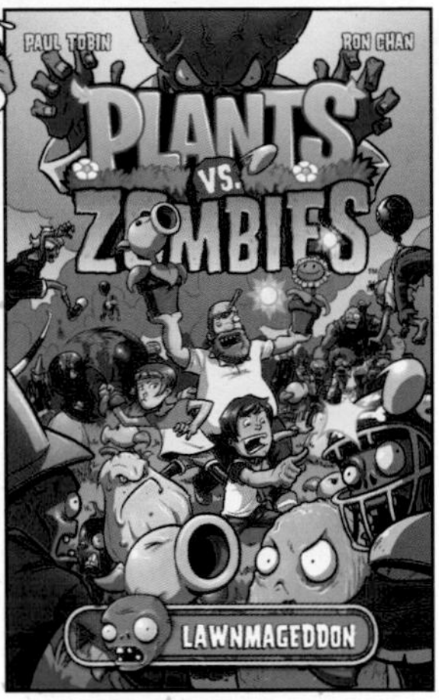
PAUL TOBIN
RON CHAN
PLANTS VS. ZOMBIES
LAWNMAGEDDON

PLANTS VS. ZOMBIES

The hit video game continues its comic book invasion! Crazy Dave—the babbling-yet-brilliant inventor and top-notch neighborhood defender—helps his niece Patrice and young adventurer Nate Timely fend off a zombie invasion! Their only hope is a brave army of chomping, squashing, and pea-shooting plants!

Boxed Set #1: Lawnmageddon, Timepocalypse, Bully for You
ISBN 978-1-50670-043-4
Boxed Set #2: Grown Sweet Home, Garden Warfare, The Art of Plants vs. Zombies
ISBN 978-1-50670-232-2
Boxed Set #3: Petal to the Metal, Boom Boom Mushroom, Battle Extravagonzo
ISBN 978-1-50670-521-7 (Available October 2017)
$29.99 each

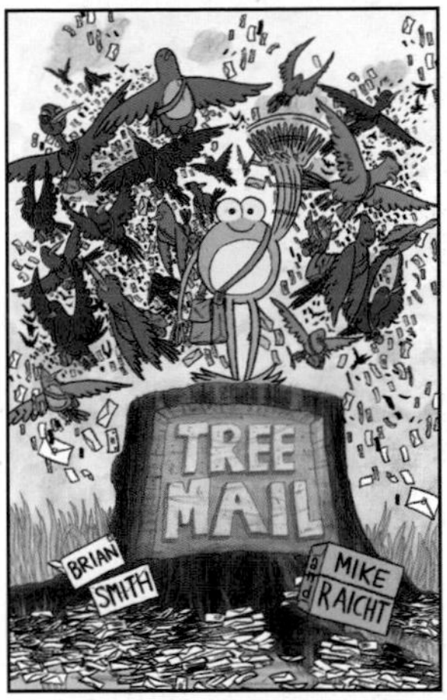
TREE MAIL
BRIAN SMITH
MIKE RAICHT

TREE MAIL

Mike Raicht, Brian Smith

Rudy—a determined frog—hopes to overcome the odds and land his dream job delivering mail to the other animals on Popomoko Island! Rudy always hops forward, no matter what obstacle seems to be in the way of his dreams!

ISBN 978-1-50670-096-0 $12.99

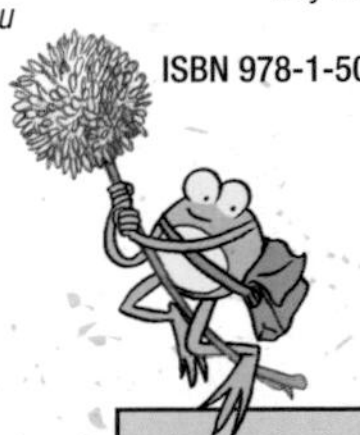

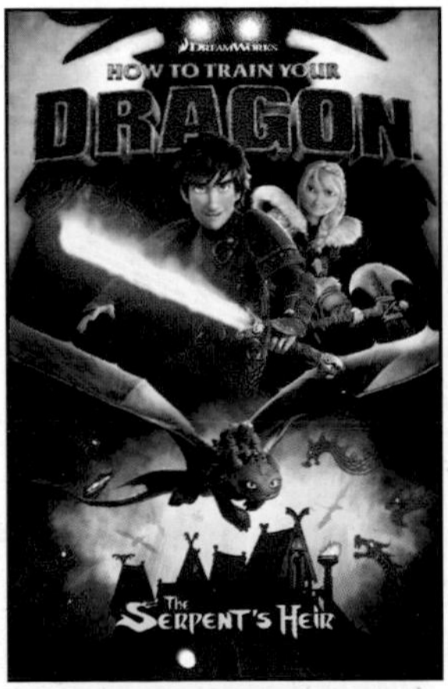
DreamWorks
HOW TO TRAIN YOUR
DRAGON
The Serpent's Heir

HOW TO TRAIN YOUR DRAGON: THE SERPENT'S HEIR

Picking up just after the events in *How to Train Your Dragon 2*, Hiccup, Astrid, and company are called upon to assist the people of an earthquake-plagued island. But their lives are imperiled by a madman and an incredible new dragon who even Toothless—the alpha dragon—may not be able to control!

ISBN 978-1-61655-931-1 $10.99

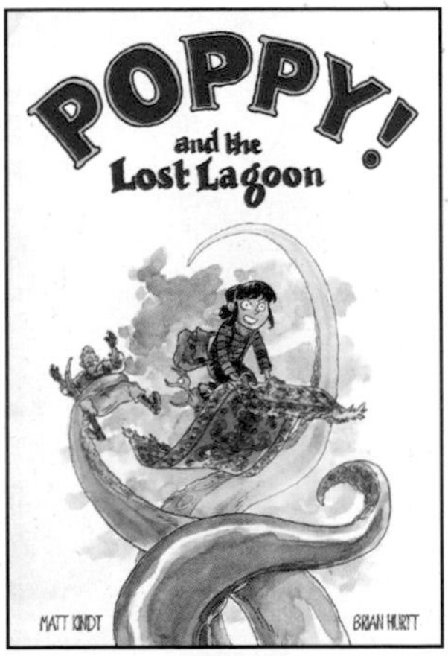
POPPY!
and the
Lost Lagoon
MATT KINDT
BRIAN HURTT

POPPY! AND THE LOST LAGOON

Matt Kindt, Brian Hurtt

At the age of ten, Poppy Pepperton is the greatest explorer since her grandfather Pappy! When a shrunken mummy head speaks, adventure calls Poppy and her sidekick/guardian, Colt Winchester, across the globe in search of an exotic fish—along the way discovering clues to what happened to Pappy all those years ago!

ISBN 978-1-61655-943-4 $14.99

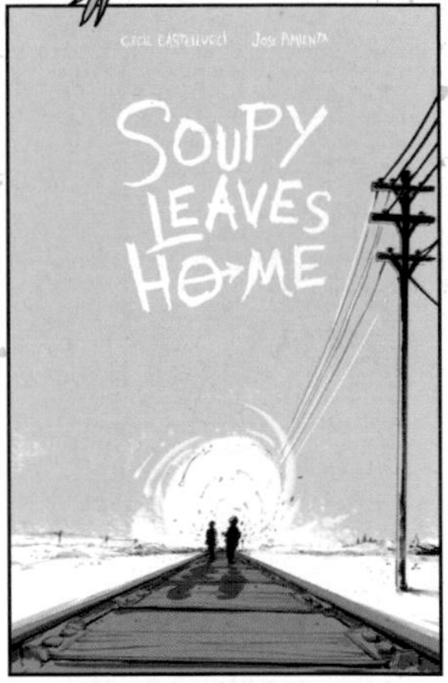
SOUPY
LEAVES
HOME

SOUPY LEAVES HOME

Cecil Castellucci, Jose Pimienta

Two misfits with no place to call home take a train-hopping journey from the cold heartbreak of their eastern homes to the sunny promise of California in this Depression-era coming-of-age tale.

ISBN 978-1-61655-431-6 $14.99

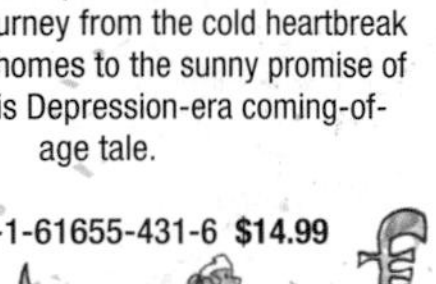

MORE TITLES FOR MIDDLE READERS!

AW YEAH COMICS!
ACTION CAT
& ADVENTURE BUG
BY ART BALTAZAR & FRANCO

AW YEAH COMICS!

Art Baltazar, Franco, and more!

It's up to Action Cat and Adventure Bug to stop the bad guys! Follow these amazing superheroes created by Art Baltazar and Franco in this comic extravaganza with bonus stories from the Aw Yeah bullpen!

Volume 1: And . . . Action!
ISBN 978-1-61655-558-0
Volume 2: Time for . . . Adventure!
ISBN 978-1-61655-689-1
Volume 3: Make Way . . . for Awesome!
ISBN 978-1-50670-045-8
Action Cat & Adventure Bug
ISBN 978-1-50670-023-6
$12.99 each

BIRD·BOY
VOLUME 1: THE SWORD OF MALI MANI
ANNE SZABLA

BIRD BOY

Anne Szabla

Bali, a ten-year-old boy, is desperate to prove his worth to his northern tribe despite his small stature. Banned from the ceremony that would make him an adult in the eyes of his people, he takes matters into his own hands. To prove that he is capable of taking care of himself, he sets out into the forbidden forest and stumbles upon a legendary weapon.

Volume 1: The Sword of Mali Mani
ISBN 978-1-61655-930-4
Volume 2: The Liminal Wood
ISBN 978-1-61655-968-7
$9.99 each

THE
COURAGEOUS
PRINCESS
BEYOND THE HUNDRED KINGDOMS
ROD ESPINOSA

THE COURAGEOUS PRINCESS

Rod Espinosa

Once upon a time, a greedy dragon kidnapped a beloved princess . . . But if you think she just waited around for some charming prince to rescue her, then you're in for a surprise! Princess Mabelrose has enough brains and bravery to fend for herself!

Volume 1: Beyond the Hundred Kingdoms
ISBN 978-1-61655-722-5
Volume 2: The Unremembered Lands
ISBN 978-1-61655-723-2
Volume 3: The Dragon Queen
ISBN 978-1-61655-724-9
$19.99 each

itty bitty
MASK
BY ART BALTAZAR & FRANCO

ITTY BITTY COMICS

Art Baltazar, Franco

Follow the adventures of your favorite Dark Horse heroes—now pintsized!

Itty Bitty Hellboy ISBN 978-1-61655-414-9 **$9.99**
Itty Bitty Hellboy: The Search for the Were-Jaguar!
ISBN 978-1-61655-801-7 **$12.99**
Itty Bitty Mask ISBN 978-1-61655-683-9 **$12.99**

andi watson
Glister

GLISTER

Andi Watson

Strange things happen around Glister Butterworth. A young girl living on her family's English estate, Glister has unusual adventures every day, like the arrival of a teapot haunted by a demanding ghost, a crop of new relatives blooming on the family tree, a stubborn house that walks off its land in a huff, and a trip to Faerieland to find her missing mother.

ISBN 978-1-50670-319-0 **$14.99**

SCARY
GODMOTHER
JILL THOMPSON

SCARY GODMOTHER

Jill Thompson

It's Halloween night and it's up to Scary Godmother to show one little girl just how much fun spooky can be! Hannah Marie with the help of Scary Godmother will stand up to her mean-spirited cousin Jimmy and her fear of monsters on her first Halloween adventure with the big kids.

ISBN 978-1-59582-589-6
Comic Book Stories ISBN 978-1-59582-723-4
$24.99 each

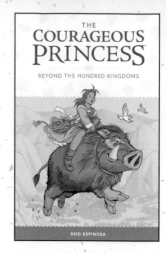